GILBERT MORRIS

APPOMATTOX SAGA

(PART 1)
1840-1861
THE ROCKLIN FAMILY AT THE DAWN
OF THE WAR BETWEEN THE STATES

THREE BOOKS IN ONE
1) A COVENANT OF LOVE
2) GATE OF HIS ENEMIES
3) WHERE HONOR DWELLS

BARBOUR
PUBLISHING

A Covenant of Love © 1992 by Gilbert Morris
Gate of His Enemies © 1992 by Gilbert Morris
Where Honor Dwells © 1993 by Gilbert Morris

ISBN 978-1-60260-178-9

Scripture quotations are taken from the King James Version of the Bible.

This book is a work of fiction. Names, characters, places, and incidents
are either products of the author's imagination or used fictitiously.
Any similarity to actual people, organizations, and/or events is purely
coincidental.

Published by Barbour Publishing, Inc., P.O. Box 719, Uhrichsville, Ohio
44683, www.barbourbooks.com

*Our mission is to publish and distribute inspirational products offering
exceptional value and biblical encouragement to the masses.*

Printed in the United States of America.

GENEALOGY OF THE ROCKLIN FAMILY

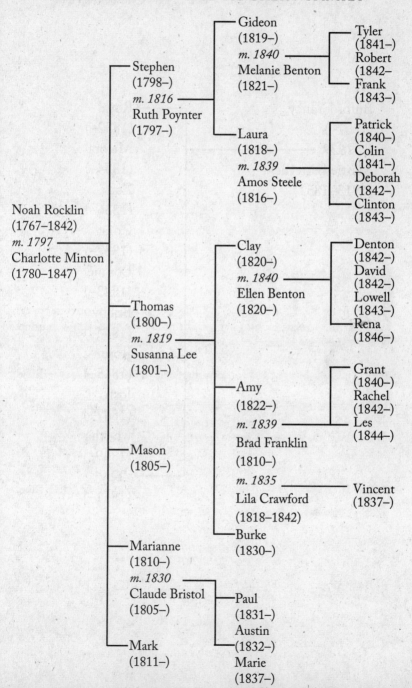

Noah Rocklin
(1767–1842)
m. 1797
Charlotte Minton
(1780–1847)

Stephen
(1798–)
m. 1816
Ruth Poynter
(1797–)

Gideon
(1819–)
m. 1840
Melanie Benton
(1821–)

Tyler
(1841–)
Robert
(1842–)
Frank
(1843–)

Laura
(1818–)
m. 1839
Amos Steele
(1816–)

Patrick
(1840–)
Colin
(1841–)
Deborah
(1842–)
Clinton
(1843–)

Thomas
(1800–)
m. 1819
Susanna Lee
(1801–)

Clay
(1820–)
m. 1840
Ellen Benton
(1820–)

Denton
(1842–)
David
(1842–)
Lowell
(1843–)
Rena
(1846–)

Amy
(1822–)
m. 1839
Brad Franklin
(1810–)

Grant
(1840–)
Rachel
(1842–)
Les
(1844–)

m. 1835
Lila Crawford
(1818–1842)

Vincent
(1837–)

Mason
(1805–)

Burke
(1830–)

Marianne
(1810–)
m. 1830
Claude Bristol
(1805–)

Paul
(1831–)
Austin
(1832–)
Marie
(1837–)

Mark
(1811–)

GENEALOGY OF THE YANCY FAMILY

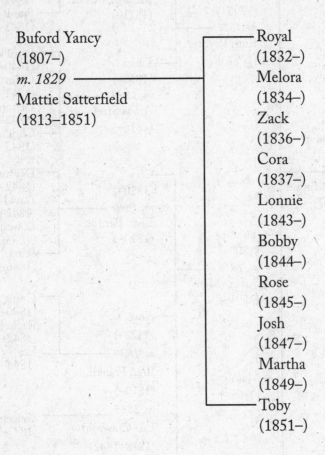

Buford Yancy
(1807–)
m. 1829
Mattie Satterfield
(1813–1851)

Royal
(1832–)
Melora
(1834–)
Zack
(1836–)
Cora
(1837–)
Lonnie
(1843–)
Bobby
(1844–)
Rose
(1845–)
Josh
(1847–)
Martha
(1849–)
Toby
(1851–)

A COVENANT
OF LOVE

To Johnnie—from her husband

We Have Saved the Best—!

Weep not because our love's first spring is past—
And hold no wake for trembling young delight,
For we have saved the best, my Love, till last!
O yes, I know the sands of time run fast—
For us these are but golden days and nights.
Weep not because our summer's love is past.
The wine we quaffed with our love's first repast
Has aged—and does more now than blur our sight,
For we have saved the best, my Love, till last!
We've sipped together from Time's silver flask;
We've heard, Sweetheart, love's golden chimes by night!
Weep not because our autumn love is past,
Swirled like aging leaves by winter's blast
Into some dreary grave far from the light,
For we have saved the best. My love, 'twill last
For us just long enough for earth's delight,
And then we'll drink forever from His cask!
Weep not because our love's first spring is past—
For we have saved, my Love, the best till last!

PART ONE
The Rivalry—1840

CHAPTER 1

A BALL AT GRACEFIELD

Clay Rocklin! You let me go this minute, you hear?"

Melanie Benton's voice was sharp, but her blue eyes were filled with laughter and her lips curved upward as she tried to pull away from the tall young man who held her easily. She showed no sign of alarm, but as he drew her closer, she glanced over her shoulder quickly, saying, "If my father sees us, he'll shoot you!"

Rocklin's grip on her waist tightened. "He can't see us," he said with a reckless grin. "This old scuppernong vine arbor is useful for something besides good wine, Mellie. From the house you can't see what's going on inside it. And I'd risk getting shot anytime for a kiss from the prettiest girl in the county!"

Melanie turned her head aside just in time to catch his kiss on one satiny cheek. "It's a wonder some jealous husband hasn't shot you before this, Clay," she said sternly. But she was pleased by his words, as she was by his appearance.

Clay Rocklin was the handsomest of all the Rocklin men. He was six feet two inches tall, lean and muscular, and as Melanie tilted her head back to look up at him, she thought, not for the first time, *He's too good-looking for his own good!* Clay was one of the "Black Rocklins," deriving his raven dark hair, black eyes, and olive skin from his father. The strain of Welsh blood that flowed through his veins showed in the strong, clean features: straight nose, wide cheekbones, deep-set eyes under black brows, and the cleft in the determined chin. He might have been charged with being too pretty save for the mouth that was too wide and the chin with the deep cleft that jutted out too aggressively.

The tendrils of the scuppernong vine overhead blocked out the warm April sun, throwing lacy patterns of shade on Melanie's face. Clay's voice grew husky as he murmured, "Mellie, you're so beautiful!" Then he kissed her, and as she stood there in his arms, Melanie tried to resist. She had always been able to handle Clay at such times, but now there was a power in his arms. Suddenly she found herself kissing him back with an ardor that she had never shown to any man. Then she realized that her hands were behind his head, and with a shock she pulled her lips away and pushed at his chest.

"I—mustn't!" she whispered. When he released her, she added, "You shouldn't do that, Clay!"

"I only did half of it, Mellie."

Though his answer angered her, she knew he was right. "Well, I shouldn't be letting you kiss me," she said. Her hands were trembling, and she turned suddenly, clasping them. "It's wrong."

He put his hands on her shoulders, turned her around, then put his hand under her chin. "What's so wrong with a kiss? Especially when you know how I feel about you."

"Clay, you've courted half the girls in Richmond," Melanie insisted. "And you've told most of them the same thing you're telling me."

A slight flush tinged Clay's cheeks, but he shook his head stubbornly. "A man's got to look around, doesn't he? Well, I've seen a few girls, but now I'm sure, Mellie. I love you, and I'll never love another woman."

Melanie was startled by the intensity in Clay's voice. She had never encouraged his attention; indeed, she had discouraged him frequently. They had grown up together, their families living only ten miles apart, bound by common interests. James and Alice Benton, Melanie's parents, ruled over the second-largest plantation in the county. But their holdings were only slightly less than Gracefield, the Rocklin estate.

Theirs was a feudal society, and it was no less rigid than the world of the Middle Ages. At the bottom of the pyramid lay the black slaves, owners of nothing, not even their own bodies. Over them, the poor whites, struggling for survival. Next were the shopkeepers and small businessmen, then the professional men—the lawyers and doctors who touched on all worlds.

At the top, at the apex of Virginia society of 1840, were the elite group of plantation owners whose estates ran into thousands of acres—and whose whims were law to the slaves and free whites who kept the cotton and rice flowing out of the rich earth. The South was ruled by this upper class, by men like Wade Hampton of South Carolina and the Lees and Hugers of Virginia.

The Rocklins and the Bentons, like most wealthy planters, liked to think of themselves as heirs to the traditions of knights and cavaliers, and they played the part stylishly. It was their code to practice chivalry toward women, kindness to inferiors, and honor among equals. They cultivated a taste for blooded horses, fine foxhounds, handmade firearms, and the Southern belles of affluent families. Many studied the arts of war, though seldom with the intention of actually using what they learned. A Mississippi planter, Jefferson Davis, stated with pride that only in the South did gentlemen who did not intend to follow the profession of arms go to a military academy.

In such a world, the marriages of sons and daughters were almost as carefully planned as those of the royal families of Europe. In the latter instance, only a young man of royal blood was considered eligible for a princess. Both the Bentons and the Rocklins would have stated promptly that the only candidates they would welcome into their family must come from the minutely small group that made up the "royalty" of Richmond.

The rigid caste system of her people was not in Melanie's thoughts as she stood facing Clay—at least, not *consciously*. But in another sense, there was never a time when knowledge of such things was not with her. She could not have put her finger on a specific time when her parents had said to her, "You must marry a man who is from your world, Mellie; who is wealthy, cultured, and Southern." And yet, as she looked up at Clay, her blood still not cooled after his embrace, she was aware (as she had been for years) that he was one of the very few men who would be welcomed without reservation by her parents.

Seeing her hesitate, Clay smiled roguishly and grasped her shoulders. "You do love me, Mellie! I know you do!" He would have kissed her again, but just at that moment the sound of a voice filtered through the arbor, startling both of them. They stepped apart quickly, and Melanie smoothed her hair nervously.

"Clay? You in here?"

Noah Rocklin's cane tapped on the stone walk that led from the house to the arbor, and his pace was so halting and slow that by the time he rounded the corner and saw his grandson and Melanie, the pair seemed calm and uninvolved. "Here we are, Grandfather," Clay said quickly, stepping forward to meet the old man. "We were making plans for the ball tomorrow. Here, sit down and help us."

"No time for that, boy." Noah Rocklin studied them, his black eyes sharp as ever despite his seventy-three years. Time may have bent his tall figure and transformed his coal-black hair to silver, but he had lost none of the astuteness that had enabled him to create an empire out of nothing. Fifty years earlier he had stepped off a boat at the dock in Richmond, a penniless lad from the coal mines of Wales. With no backing, no influence, and little education, he had shouldered his way into the cloistered world of the rich planters of Virginia. He had gotten his start by means of a bay mare that could beat any horse in the country for a quarter of a mile. Moving around from meet to meet, he had won purses, then invested in a worn-out farm that he bought for almost nothing. He had purchased one slave, Jacob, and in their first year together, the two of them had wrenched a bumper crop of cotton from the woebegone farm. Noah still had Jacob, along with 160 other slaves—and that first farm of 120 acres was now lost in an ocean of 50,000 acres, all rich, black land that sprawled over much of the county.

Only one thing held as much importance in Noah Rocklin's heart as his self-made empire, and that was his wife, Charlotte. She had brought him great joy and had blessed him with four sons—Stephen, Thomas, Mason, and Mark—and with his only daughter, Marianne. The fierce devotion Noah felt for Gracefield was nominal compared to his feelings toward his family.

Of course, Noah Rocklin's rise to power had not been unopposed—and the stories of his fits of anger were legendary.

He had fought in the War of 1812, rising to the rank of major. When that was over, he had fought three duels, winning each with contemptuous ease. Perhaps it was because he recognized too much of his own fiery temper and wild youth in his grandson Clay that he scowled now, saying, "I heard about that trouble you had with Louis Waymeyer, boy. Bad business!"

"It was a matter of honor, sir!"

"Honor!" Noah scoffed, punching his cane against the stones angrily. "It was a brawl over a silly woman between two empty-headed young men!"

His remark caused both young people to redden, but Noah went on. "You're going to get your head shot off if you keep messing around with that kind of woman, Clay."

"Grandfather, you shouldn't speak that way in front of Mellie!"

"Why not? Why, boy, she's heard the story a dozen times—and I'd guess you got some of the minute details, didn't you, missy?" A stricken look came to Melanie's face, and he laughed loudly. "Why, I heard at least six versions of it myself, and the women don't let a thing like that die!"

Clay clamped his lips shut, saying nothing, but he noticed that Melanie seemed more amused than upset. It had been a piddling affair. He had cut Louis out with Dora Seller, and Louis had called him an unpleasant name. "I had to give him satisfaction, Grandfather," he insisted.

"If some of my family has to die, I'd rather see them die over something more important than Dora Seller's petticoats." Then he laughed again. "Look at her," he said suddenly, waving toward Melanie. "You thought what the boy did was romantic, didn't you? Well, you better watch out for this one. He's too much like I was at his age!"

"I think that's a great compliment to Clay, Major Rocklin," Melanie said with a smile and patted his arm. "If I get a husband half as handsome and romantic as you, I'll be happy."

"Romantic!" Noah recoiled as if she had put a snake on his arm. "I deny it, girl!"

"You can't." Melanie giggled. "Your wife showed me some of your old letters to her!"

Noah stared at her, then muttered, "I'll beat that woman! See if I don't—and it's long overdue!" He saw that his threat didn't impress the pair and changed the subject abruptly. "Stephen and his family will be on the 1:15, Clay. You get the large buggy and bring them here."

"Yes, sir." Clay nodded. "How many will there be?"

"Why, Stephen and Ruth and the baby, of course. And Laura and that abolitionist she married."

"I'm surprised you'd let him come, Grandfather," Clay said, smiling. "You said before the wedding you'd horsewhip him if he ever stepped foot on Gracefield."

"Never mind what I said!" Noah snapped. "They'll have my great-grandson with them. He's bound to be an improvement over you young whelps I call grandsons!"

Melanie knew that the old man was fiercely proud of his grandsons, and asked, "Will Gideon be here?"

"Stephen said he would. I think he pulled some strings to get leave for him." Gideon, Stephen's son, was about to graduate from West Point, and this military career gave him a special favor with Noah Rocklin—indeed, with most of the family.

"I'll go along, Clay," Melanie said suddenly. When he gave her a sharp look, she added quickly, "To help Laura hold the baby. I'm sure she'll be worn out after that long ride from Washington."

13

Clay said stiffly, "Be pretty crowded in the carriage, Mellie."

"Oh, I don't mind," she answered with a sly smile. Clay walked off with a frown on his face, and she turned to see that Noah was studying her with his black eyes. "Why—I guess he doesn't want me to go, Major. But I am anxious to see Laura's baby."

His shrewd eyes studied her for a moment. " 'Course it's the baby you're anxious to see. Who else would it be? Certainly not that good-looking soldier grandson of mine," he said dryly.

Melanie flushed uncomfortably and glanced away. "I think I'll go anyway. Clay won't mind," she said stubbornly, then walked quickly out of the arbor. As soon as she left, the old man pulled a very old silver flask out of his hip pocket. When he had taken two large swallows, he took a deep breath, then said, "Ahhhhhh!" He sat there, the sunlight creeping through the branches causing him to narrow his eyes. He grinned suddenly, saying out loud, " 'Making plans for the ball tomorrow.' Ho! I know what you and that girl were doing, Clay Rocklin!" The thought amused him, and he lifted the flask again.

Suddenly a voice very close made him jump so abruptly that he spilled some of the liquor down the front of his shirt.

"Yas! I kotched you, din't I?" A tall, gangling Negro dressed in black pants and a white shirt had emerged from the far end of the arbor and approached to stand beside Noah. The Negro's hair was white as cotton, and despite the lines that were etched in his face, his eyes were sharp. "You gimme dat liquor now!" he insisted, holding out a pink palm. "You know Miz Charlotte and the doctuh say you kain't have no mo'!"

Noah glared at the slave, saying defiantly, "Who cares what that quack says? Get away from here, Jake!"

"I won't do it! If you don't gimme dat liquor right now,

I gonna tell Miz Charlotte!"

Noah stared at the slave, then suddenly lifted the flask and drained the last few swallows. Tossing the flask to Jacob, he laughed, "There! Now tell her whatever you like."

The tall slave shook his head in disapproval. He had been with Noah Rocklin since he was sixteen years old. The two of them had suffered together to bring Gracefield to where it was. Now that death was close, the two of them felt a special kinship that went beyond master and slave. Both knew that whichever of them went to the grave first would leave a massive gap in the heart of the other.

Carefully Jake lifted the flask and licked the last few drops of amber liquor. Then he cocked his head and asked, "Marse Clay gonna marry up with Miss Mellie?" When Noah gave him a discouraged look and merely shook his head, a curious light came into his faded eyes. "I reckon she ain't made no pick yet. You reckon she's gonna pick Marse Stephen's boy, Gideon?"

Noah stared at the black face, so familiar to his sight, and knew that no detail of his family life was safe from this one. "Don't you have enough to do without keeping up with every case of puppy love on this place?"

"No, sah, it ain't none of puppy love." Jake shook his head, thinking hard. Anything that touched Noah and Charlotte Rocklin touched him, and he saw trouble ahead. "It gonna be bad if she choose Marse Gideon, ain't it, Major?"

Noah got to his feet painfully. Leaning on his cane, he moved across the stone walk but turned as he reached the edge of the arbor. His old eyes were filled with apprehension as he said, "Jake, it's going to be bad no matter *which* of those boys she chooses!" Then he moved out of sight, leaving the tall slave staring after him, his lips drawn up in a pucker and his brow wrinkled.

"Seem lak a woman ain't nevah happy lessen she causin' men trouble!"

❧

The architect of the mansion at Gracefield had given much thought to the exterior grounds and the approach from the main road. A long, sweeping drive, lined with massive oaks and broad enough for three carriages, made a U-shape from the road to the mansion. The curve of the drive made a convenient place for carriages to wait until the balls were over.

Those arriving at the Gracefield mansion were often struck by the majestic beauty of the white frame building with white Corinthian columns across the front and down both sides. A balcony, set off by an ornate iron grill painted gleaming white, ran all the way around the house. Tall, wide windows could be seen on both floors of the house, the blue shutters breaking the gleaming white of the siding. The steeply pitched roof ran up to a center point, broken by three gables on each side, which gave light and air to the attic rooms. High-rising chimneys capped with curving covers of brick added further beauty to the building.

The house seemed to have been constructed for the purpose of formal balls; fully half of the space on the first floor was designated for that purpose. A pair of enormous oak doors opened into a spacious foyer. Upon entering, one's attention was immediately drawn to the broad stairway that divided the lower section of the house and curved to the right and left at the landing. At the left one could see the library and a large dining room; to the right, the ballroom. Behind these was a wide hallway that ran the length of the house. On the east was the very large, stately master bedroom. Most of the rest of the house was taken up by the kitchen and canning room, which were separated by a covered porch.

The second floor was composed of bedrooms, and in the largest and most ornate of these, Thomas Rocklin was helping his wife, Susanna, with the buttons on the back of her dress. "There," he said finally, then stepped back and took a careful look at her. "You'll be the belle of the ball," he pronounced. "You're as beautiful as ever."

Susanna gave him a smile. She was a handsome woman of thirty-nine, only one year younger than her husband. Her auburn hair gleamed in the lamplight, and the green silk dress she wore set off her blue-green eyes. Patting Thomas's arm lightly, she said, "Thank you, dear. And you'll be the finest-looking man." She gave him a quick glance of inspection, pulled his tie into line, and thought that he might just *be* the handsomest man at the ball. He had the blackest possible hair, with the dark eyes and complexion to match. His bad habits had not yet put signs of dissipation on his face. For one instant, Susanna felt a wave of sadness, and the thought came to her, as it had many times before, *I wish your ways were as handsome as your looks!*

But she allowed none of that to show on her face. Instead she said, "It's good to have Stephen and his family for a visit. I wish we could see more of them."

"Not much chance of that." Thomas shrugged. "I'm surprised my hardworking brother let himself be pulled away from that factory of his. Must be the first vacation he's had in two or three years." He glanced at the lower walnut table close to the massive bed, then moved toward it and poured himself a drink from the cut-crystal bottle. "Stephen's changed a lot. He's become a Yankee peddler."

Susanna opened her mouth to say, "You shouldn't begin

drinking so early," but cut the words off—he would only be angered by her interference. Instead she said, "I think Stephen came to show off his son. He and Ruth are very proud of Gideon's career."

"I suppose so. Do you think you can put up with Ruth's ways while they're here?" Thomas gave her a gloomy look, for he had not yet completely forgiven his brother Stephen for marrying a woman from the North. He agreed with his father that Stephen's decision to move to Washington and go into business was due to Ruth, his wife. The fact that he had done well there did nothing to placate either Thomas or his father. Both felt that Stephen had somehow betrayed his legacy as a Southerner.

"Oh, Ruth's all right, Thomas," Susanna said. "And they're right to be proud of Gideon. He's in the top 10 percent of his class at West Point, and he's been asked to stay on after graduation to help train the new cadets. That's quite an accomplishment." Then she added with a smile that didn't quite come off, "Gideon's quite good-looking, and in his uniform he'll have every girl in Richmond after him—even if he is a Yankee."

"Gideon's no Yankee!" Thomas drank the rest of the liquor in his glass, then came to take her arm. "He's a Southerner. You can't take that out of a man. Come on, let's go to the ball."

As they came to the staircase, a bedroom door opened. "Ruth, how nice you look!" Susanna said with a bright smile as her sister-in-law emerged, followed by Stephen. "That must be one of those new Washington fashions."

"Oh, I bought it to wear to the president's reception," Ruth said. She was a blond woman of forty-three, with quick brown eyes and a pronounced Northern accent. "President Van Buren thought it was nice, or so he said." She spoke of the president lightly, but both Thomas and Susanna knew they would hear of President Van Buren's opinion of Ruth's dress innumerable times. Stephen's wife was a ruthless socialite who structured her whole life by the political and social hierarchy that reigned in Washington. Her father had been in the House, and two of her brothers held office in the federal service.

As Ruth continued talking about Washington, Susanna listened but stole a glance at the two men at their sides. The difference between the brothers had fascinated her from the time she had first met them. Over the years she had watched these differences grow. Now she noted again how, physically, they looked very little like brothers. The term "Black Rocklins" fit Thomas very well—as it did Mark—for both of them were dark in coloring. But the other two brothers, Stephen and Mason, were fair like their mother. Thomas seemed much taller than Stephen, though actually he was only two inches over the other's height. The illusion came from the two men's builds— Thomas was lean and almost thin, whereas Stephen Rocklin was thickset and muscular. Because of this, Stephen's five feet ten inches seemed even shorter when he stood next to his taller brother. He had fair coloring like his mother, Charlotte, and possessed the only pair of gray eyes in the family. There was a solidness about him, not just physically in the thick shoulders and strong hands, but in the spirit, that impressed all he met.

As they reached the bottom of the stairs, Stephen turned and smiled at Susanna. "I want your first dance, Susanna. If I don't get that one, these young fellows will never give me another chance."

Ruth gave her husband a look of irritation. She never liked it when he paid attention to her sister-in-law. She was a quick-witted woman and had long ago realized that Susanna Rocklin and her husband were mutual admirers. Yet she said nothing, choosing to go at once to where the attorney general of Virginia was speaking with Noah Rocklin.

Stephen's dancing, Susanna thought as the two of them moved over the polished heart-pine floor, *is much like the man himself—competent and steady.* He had none of Thomas's flair, on the dance floor or otherwise, but he was a man women and men alike would trust.

"We've all missed you," Susanna said as they swung around in a stately waltz. "I've never ceased to be sorry that you moved to Washington. Though it's only a few miles from Gracefield, it's like another country."

"I miss this place. Don't think I'll ever get over my longing for the South," Stephen said slowly. "But Ruth would never be happy here."

"No, I don't think she would." Susanna avoided the subject of Ruth, for it was somewhat of a delicate matter. As was the matter of their daughter, Laura's, husband, Amos Steele. Amos and Laura had been married less than two years, and none of the Southern branch of the Rocklins could understand why such a sweet girl had married an abolitionist. Tactfully, Susanna said, "Laura's baby is precious. Isn't it nice that we both have new grandsons the same age?"

Stephen grinned suddenly, looking much younger. "It's pretty sad, I think, Susanna. All of us grandparents standing around bragging on each other's grandchildren, and thinking all the time how much handsomer *ours* really is!"

"Oh, Stephen! I don't do any such thing!" Susanna protested. Then, being an honest woman, she laughed ruefully. "You're right, of course. I guess we all feel that way. But your new grandson is every bit as handsome as mine!"

Stephen said with an unexpected burst of gallantry, "Well, Susanna, any grandson of yours would have to be handsome."

Susanna was taken aback by his remark. In all the years she had known him, he had never paid her such a compliment. "Why, Stephen, you're getting positively gallant!" Then she smiled at him, adding, "We're growing older, aren't we? At a fancy ball and talking about grandchildren! Let's talk about children," she urged. "I don't feel so old doing that. And let me say first how impressed I am with Gideon. You must be very proud, the record he's made at West Point."

"Ruth and I are proud of Gideon," Stephen agreed, nodding. "He's going to be a fine soldier." He lifted his head and glanced over to where Clay and his son were talking, one on each side of Melanie Benton. "Clay is the finest-looking young man here." Then he looked into her eyes and said seriously, "I heard about the duel. Too bad."

It was as close to being critical of Clay's behavior as Stephen would ever come. And he softened the remark at once by smiling. "I hope he doesn't challenge Gideon to a duel over Melanie. Arms are his profession."

The remark, lightly made and not intended to be serious, brought a line between Susanna's eyebrows. "I used to think that the two of them were just joking about their rivalry over her, but it's serious, Stephen. One of them is going to get a heartache sooner or later."

Even as she was speaking, Clay and Gideon were enduring some sly teasing over their rivalry. Taylor Dewitt, part of the group of young people that had clustered around Melanie and her two suitors, was saying, "Well now, Cadet Rocklin, looks like you got the inside track on all the rest of us." He winked at Tug Ramsey, the rotund nephew of the governor, adding,

"I never can get over how a uniform makes a woman blind to real quality!"

"Oh, you hush, Taylor!" Melanie said sharply. "You've had too much to drink already."

"Why, Melanie, there's no such thing as too much to drink!" Dewitt smiled. "Like there are never enough beautiful women. That's right, isn't it, Clay?"

His remark was a sly jab, and not without danger, for though Clay Rocklin believed exactly the same thing, he was touchy about having remarks made on it. Everyone glanced at him with a certain degree of apprehension, the memory of Clay's duel with Louis Waymeyer vivid in their minds. The fact that Dewitt was a daredevil himself made the situation even more explosive.

Fortunately, Clay chose to ignore Dewitt's gibe. "You old degenerate!" He grinned at Dewitt. "I resent your remark. It's an insult to Southern womanhood." His smile took the sting from his words, and he added, "Cousin Gideon doesn't need any uniform to attract women. He's always been a favorite with the fair sex." Then he turned to Gideon, who was taking all of this in with a faint smile. "Remember Lucy Ann Garner, Gid?" he asked. "I declare, that girl was so in love with you it was a shame!"

Melanie giggled then, for Gideon's solid features flushed and he looked very uncomfortable. "I remember that, Clay," she said, nodding, then explained, "Lucy was the daughter of the Baptist preacher who was here a few years ago. She was so taken with Gid that her father had to have a talk with him."

"I heard he brought his shotgun along for the talk," Clay said, his black eyes dancing.

"Oh, nonsense!" Gideon stammered. "You two always bring that poor girl up! She was like a sister to me."

A howl of laughter went up from the young men, and Dewitt cried out over them, "Ladies, look to your honor! When a dandy begins that old story about 'just being a brother,' it's time to flee!"

"That's right!" Tug Ramsey said, his blue eyes gleaming with fun in his round face. "As Dr. Johnson said, 'When a man starts talking a great deal about his honor, I start counting the spoons!'" Just then the music started, and Ramsey said, "Melanie, you can't trust either one of these two Rocklin boys, so I'll just claim this next dance."

He moved toward her, but suddenly Gideon was in front of him. "Ramsey, your uncle, the governor, has told my father some of the problems you've handed him. I don't think it would be safe for Melanie to be seen dancing with such a Don Juan."

He swept Melanie away while the group was laughing at the surprise on Tug's face, and only when the pair were swirling around the room did Dewitt say in surprise, "Well, I'll be dipped! I guess ol' Gid *has* learned something at West Point!"

"Learned what?" Clay asked at once, his dark eyes following the pair.

"Why, I guess he learned about maneuvering, Clay," Dewitt answered. "'Cause I surely don't see any of us dancing with Melanie!" Catching the look of irritation on Clay's face, he winked again at Tug Ramsey. "Maybe there is something in a uniform. Guess I'd better go sign up and get me one. Looks like that's what it takes to get the ladies around here!"

A small young woman who had walked up to the group in time to hear the last of the conversation said, "Taylor, that remark is an insult to ladies everywhere!"

Taylor Dewitt turned to her, a smile breaking across his lips. "I don't see how you can say that, Ellen. Everybody knows how

I revere the ladies." That brought a laugh from everyone, for Dewitt was a womanizer of infinite proportions. "But it does seem that a uniform draws pretty girls to a man."

Ellen Benton shook her head firmly. "It's not what a man wears that's important. It's what he is underneath." Her remark caught Clay's attention, and he studied her as she carried on a lively conversation with Dewitt. Ellen was Melanie's cousin, the daughter of Melanie's father's only brother. She had come to Briarcliff Plantation after her parents were killed in a steamboat accident in Portland. There was some sort of scandal attached to her family, but what it was no one quite knew. The Bentons never spoke of it. All anyone knew was that Melanie's father had cut all communication with his brother.

Wonder what her father did to get cut off from the family, Clay pondered, studying the girl. *She's good-looking, but pretty free with men.* Ellen was not beautiful in the sense that Melanie was, but she did have large brown eyes, a wealth of dark brown hair, and a fine complexion. And there was a certain quality in her looks and bearing that caused men to turn and stare at her. Yet none of the young men of the county pursued her seriously.

She's got what it takes to draw men, but none of us is quite sure what to do about it, Clay thought as he watched Dewitt and Ramsey and the others. *She's something else—if she were just any girl, it would be easier to pursue her. But she's the niece of James Benton, and it'd be a bad mistake to antagonize him.*

Suddenly Ellen turned to him. "Clay, ask me to dance."

"I was waiting for you to settle these callow youth," Clay answered at once, and soon they were whirling around the room. Several times she brushed against him, and the faint perfume she wore was sweet. She was not a tall girl, and when she tilted her head up to smile at him, he could not ignore the fullness of her lips.

As they danced, he was totally aware of her femininity, yet he was on his guard. Her free ways puzzled him, and he was aware that she was not a candidate for serious courtship. Of course, he was drawn to her physically—but she was, in one sense, a nobody. Despite her uncle's wealth, there was a cloud over her past and an uncertainty about her future. And she was not a Southern girl.

As the dance went on, Ellen glanced at Gid and Melanie, then looked up at Clay. "I suppose Taylor was right," she said. "About girls liking uniforms. I didn't like what he said, but you can't deny the truth of it, can you?"

"Maybe I ought to join the army."

"Don't do that, Clay!" Ellen said quickly, her hand tightening on his. "It may be all right for Gideon, but it wouldn't be for you."

He looked down at her, admiring the perfect skin and the smoothness of her shoulder. "Why not, Ellen? Don't you think I could be a good soldier?"

"You would be good at anything, Clay Rocklin," Ellen said instantly. "But you are different from Gideon. He doesn't mind the monotony and the formality of a soldier's life. You have a free spirit. A life like that would be misery for you."

He was startled at her perception but shook his head. "Father wishes I *were* a little more disciplined." He grinned briefly. "And Mother thinks my 'free spirit' is sinful. I'm a pretty big disappointment to them. Matter of fact, both of them wish I were more like Gid."

"As much as I admire your parents," Ellen said, "I don't think they're right in this case. The worst thing a parent can do is to try to make a child into something he's not. Wives make that mistake, too, don't they? A man has to be what he is, Clay. And what your parents don't see is that this is just a time for you to explore the world. Young people have to touch the world, and that means the bad as well as the good."

Clay was fascinated by her thinking—it was exactly the same thing he had said to himself many times. "What about you, Ellen?" he demanded. "What kind of life do you want?"

She smiled then, saying, "I'm like you, Clay. I want all that life has. It's soon over, isn't it? When I am old, I want to say, 'I've had an exciting journey. I didn't refuse life because I was afraid of what people would say.'" Then she laughed out loud, in a charming manner. "I've shocked you, haven't I, Clay? Women aren't supposed to even *think* such things, much less *say* them to a man!"

Clay suddenly pulled her closer, excited by her manner and by the pressure of her full figure. "You're quite a woman, Ellen," he whispered, and as they danced on, he forgot about Gid and Melanie, which was exactly what Ellen wished.

Melanie had not been at all displeased with the way Gideon had stepped in to take her out on the dance floor. As he held her, she was very conscious of the strength of his arms. "My, you've changed, Gid," she said with a smile. "You couldn't have done that two years ago. Are you sure you've been studying guns and marching and all that, and not courting those Yankee girls?"

Gid grinned suddenly. "My life's been one constant series of balls and picnics with beautiful women since I went to the Point," he said with a nod. "We have special classes in ballroom dancing and the fine points of courtship. Should have gone there years ago!" He pulled her closer, dropped his voice, and said, "Right now, page 84 in the manual on courtship would advise, 'As soon as you have wooed the young lady away from the lesser men, take her out to the garden for a breath of fresh air.'"

"Oh, I couldn't do that!" Melanie protested, but scant minutes later she found herself in the same arbor where she'd stood with Clay a few hours earlier. The night was so clear that the silver globe of the moon seemed huge against the velvety night sky. The music came to them, thin and faint, from the ballroom. The happy sound of laughter drifting on the wind was pleasant.

They stood there looking out over the rolling hills, and finally Melanie asked, "Well, what does your old manual say to do now?"

"This—," Gid said firmly and took her in his arms. It caught her off guard, for he had always been rather shy. She had known, in the way that beautiful young ladies know such things, that he liked her, but she had never been able to draw him out. As he kissed her, her idea that he had been without fire left her. There was nothing insipid in his manner now!

She pulled away, leaned back in his arms, and whispered, "Why, Gid! You've never done such a thing before!"

Gid stood there, taking in the beauty of her face, and then said slowly, "I was always afraid you'd laugh at me, Mellie. You were always the prettiest girl around. Every fellow wanted to be your beau. You could have had any of them. Still could," he added; then a light of determination came to his eye. "But you're going to have to run me off this time! I haven't read any manuals on how to court a girl, Mellie. There was never anyone I wanted. But I love you. Always have, I think, since the first time Father brought me to Gracefield. I was nine, and the first time I saw you, I think I just fell in love."

"Oh, Gid, that's not possible!"

"I think it is," he said, and there was a rocklike certainty in his manner that made her nervous. She was accustomed to light flirtations, but Gideon Rocklin, she saw, would pursue a woman with the same dogged determination he had used to get to the top of his class at West Point. "I guess that's about the only plan I have for courting you, Mellie," he said quietly. "Just to say I love you. And to promise that if you marry me, I'll do everything under God's heaven to make you happy." He shrugged slightly, adding, "I don't cut a very romantic figure. I know that."

Melanie understood at once that he was thinking of Clay, who cut a *very* romantic figure. The seriousness on Gid's face sobered her as she stood still in his arms. Finally she sighed, "Well, Gid, a romantic figure isn't everything." Then, knowing that it was time to break the scene off, she came up with a smile. "But I'll expect a little more in the way of courtship than a discussion of military tactics!"

Her remark brought a smile to his lips. Nodding, he said, "Maybe I'd better buy a manual on courtship, after all."

As she drew him down the stone walk, she glanced up at him. "No, you're doing fine, Cadet Rocklin. Do carry on!" They stepped inside and at once were engulfed by a world of music and color.

CHAPTER 2

A Cloud the Size of a Man's Hand

Gracefield Plantation was a little world dwarfed by the rolling hills of Virginia, yet it was complete in its workings. No tangible wall surrounded it, yet in some powerful spiritual manner, its limits were marked in the minds of the denizens who spent their lives within its boundaries. Even as a ship rolled onward over a trackless ocean with nothing to mark its progress, so Gracefield moved through time. The family and the slaves knew of the larger world outside Gracefield's borders, but for them its existence was vague and hazy—as was the distant shore to the sailor whose life was confined to the bobbing ship on the ocean.

Springtime and summer, fall and winter passed over the little world. Children were born; the aged died. Often songs of joy, such as the happy shouting of slaves in their Sunday meetings or the jig dances of the parties, filled the air. At other times the songs were slow and sad—when loved ones were lowered into the ground and covered over with the black earth, or when tragedy struck and the sound of weeping scored the long nights.

In all of this, though, there was order, for Gracefield was

a microcosm of the larger world of men. Noah Rocklin was the archetypal ruler: master, potentate, king, prince, emperor, congress, parliament, court. He ruled Gracefield with the power of a despot, and the Big House was no less the seat of authority than the Vatican or Buckingham Palace. Though he was growing old and the reins of power were slipping into other, more youthful hands, there was the certain knowledge that when Noah Rocklin loosened his hands for the last time, there would be no loss of the order he had kept. Others would be there to guide, to direct, to govern.

Nowhere was the order of Gracefield more evident than in the world of the slaves, whose sweat sustained the kingdom of the Rocklins. For within their ranks was a rigid hierarchy. Those who toiled in the long rows of white cotton were the base. Without them, there would be no Gracefield, for cotton and rice could only be grown by many hands. The field slaves had no need of skill; all that such work required were a strong back and endurance. In some minds, the less they knew, the better suited they were for the endless monotony of the task. What were dreams to a slave who went to the fields before dawn and picked cotton from a hunched position until it was too dark to see, with only a brief thirty-minute break to gobble down a dry piece of corn bread and swallow a drink of tepid water?

The second class of slaves consisted of those who had mastered some sort of skill. Such a slave was Box, a tall, strong Negro who was the best blacksmith at Gracefield. He was such a valuable part of the place that no one would have suggested he ever demean himself by going to the fields. As for his wife, Carrie, she enjoyed a status envied by the wives of mere field hands.

The aristocracy, however, of the world of the slave was the house slave—those who served as maids for the ladies of the Big House, cleaned the mansion, or cooked and served the meals for the white masters. These workers, it must be confessed, often were swollen with pride, feeling that the Negroes who worked the fields were far beneath them.

Still, even within the exalted positions of the house slaves, adamant lines were drawn. And Dorrie, a tall, heavy woman of thirty-seven, ruled with iron authority. Charlotte Rocklin had chosen Dorrie at the age of six, seeing in the child a quickness of mind that was lacking in others. As the years had passed, Dorrie had learned every skill of keeping a large house in order. She had served as cleaning maid, kitchen helper, ladies' maid, and cook. Technically, she was still the cook—but most of the actual cooking was done by a thin woman named Dulcie.

Charlotte Rocklin was, of course, the titular mistress of Gracefield, but it was Dorrie who saw to the seemingly endless details of the Big House. And it was a rare thing for the two women to disagree over matters, for if anything, Dorrie was far stricter in running the mansion than Charlotte herself. Dorrie was a shrewd woman who, over the years, had built up a system that worked well for her. She had married a tall, handsome field hand named Zander, and through careful and discreet manipulation had gotten him installed as butler. Their sixteen-year-old daughter, Cleo, worked in the kitchen; their other daughter, Lutie, was a housemaid. Their twelve-year-old son, Moses, was the stable boy.

The morning after the ball, Dorrie had driven the house slaves hard, so that by noon the house was clean and sparkling. Then, after a quick break, she routed them out again, her large eyes sharp and her voice sharper. Coming upon Cleo and Lutie sitting outside on a bench sipping lemonade left over from the ball, she lit into them.

"Git yourself in dis house! Whut you mean sippin' dat lemonade? You know dat ain't fo' you!"

"Aw, Mama," Cleo complained. "It was lef' over from the party!"

Dorrie snatched the pitcher from Cleo and cuffed her across the head. "De party ain't ovah yet, and you know it. Now you git them potatoes peeled or I'll do some peelin' my own self! And you, Lutie, go make up de yeller room."

"Who it for?"

Dorrie gave the fourteen-year-old an impatient shove. "Whut diff'rence it make? You just clean it up good." Then she relented, saying, "Marse Mark come dis morning, and Miz Charlotte tole me dat her baby boy comin' in anytime."

She had entered the kitchen as she spoke this, and Zander lifted his head to stare at her. "I didn't know dat." He was sitting on a high stool by the counter, carefully peeling potatoes, wearing a white apron over his black pants and white shirt. "Marse Noah threatened to run him off wif a shotgun do he come back."

Mark, the "baby" Dorrie had mentioned, was the youngest son of Noah and Charlotte Rocklin. He was twenty-nine years old, but to Dorrie he was still the baby. She had been almost a mother to him, and he had broken her heart as he had the hearts of his parents by his wild ways. A rebel from the time he could walk, he had brought such heartache to the Rocklins that Noah had finally thrown him out of the house. He had written from time to time and even visited, but his visits were always tense affairs for everyone in the family.

"Lemme see," Zander said. "Why, it's been three years since Marse Mark been heah, ain't it now?" He studied a half-peeled potato, carefully cut a peeling from it, then grinned. "Whoo, now! Whut dat boy been and done dis time!"

"You shut!" Dorrie said sharply, for she would never allow anyone to criticize the young man in her presence. "And you bettah get dat good silver polished—and we gonna have de good plates, too, for supper."

Zander stared at her curiously. "If Miss Marianne come, it'll be de fust time de whole family's et together in a mighty long time." A doubtful looked crossed his face, and he put down the bowl of potatoes, then said, "I hope dey ain't no big fuss lak de last time they all got together. Lawd! I thought dey was gonna start shootin'!"

Dorrie glanced around to where Dulcie and Cleo were working at the far end of the kitchen. "I tole you to shut!" she whispered. "They ain't gonna be no fighting."

Zander took off his apron, folded it carefully, then put it on the counter. He brushed the front of his shirt and pants, then straightened up to his full height. "Well, old woman," he said slowly, "if dem Black Rocklins gits through a meal without a fuss—it'll be 'bout the first time dat ever com about!"

Noah Rocklin's "study" was filled with a great many possessions—but few of them were books. One walnut bookshelf occupied a space along the west wall, and it was packed with books and magazines. Most were manuals dealing with some aspect of farming; the others dealt with history or law. The rest of the room was packed with mementos of Noah's lifetime. More than fifty guns, including rifles, shotguns, and pistols of all sorts, took prominence. The weapons gleamed in the afternoon sun that was streaming through the dormer window. It was Jacob's job to keep the guns well polished, and he took pride in this task. Paintings were hung randomly; most of them of family, but some of statesmen, generally from Virginia.

But Noah was not looking at his guns or souvenirs as he sat in his worn leather chair behind a huge flattop pine desk. He was considering his children. They were all there, all five of them, and it gave him a strange feeling to see them together. Glancing at Charlotte, who sat beside him in a straight chair, he saw that she shared that same feeling. Noah and Charlotte Rocklin were closer than most married couples. Always had been—but in the later years, their devotion had grown even deeper. She was, at sixty, more beautiful than she had been when he married her. Silver showed in her blond hair, and the dark blue eyes were not as bright as when they had married—but no matter! In Noah's eyes, his Charlotte was still the fairest of all women.

Sensing Noah's emotion at seeing all the family together, Charlotte reached out and put her hand on his forearm. Though they never spoke of it, she realized that he was a sick man. Steadfastly she refused to envision life without him and lived each day as if it were forever. Now she gave him a quick smile, then turned toward the children, her quick mind going over each of them—what they were, and what she and Noah longed for them to be.

Stephen, the steady one. The firstborn and the one she worried about the least. He was larger than she remembered, a solid man, strong and determined. His wife, Ruth, was an attractive woman, but she never had accepted the family. It had been a wrench when Stephen had left to make his life in Washington. Noah had grieved, but silently, speaking only to his wife of it.

Thomas, who could never find his way. Charlotte studied

the handsome face of her second-born, admiring his perfect features. If only he could settle down! He had always been jealous of Stephen. Charlotte thought that he longed for the steadiness in his brother, which was sadly lacking in himself. But it was not too late. He was only forty years old. Again the hope flared in Charlotte that somehow this handsome, gifted man would awaken to the potential that God had given him. Glancing quickly at Thomas's wife, Susanna, Charlotte gave a fervent prayer of thanksgiving, for from the moment Thomas had married her, both Noah and Charlotte knew that if Thomas Rocklin were ever to become a complete man, it would be this woman who would show him the way.

Mason, the lonely one. Lost because when his wife died, most of him died with her. Nothing had given Charlotte more satisfaction than Mason's marriage to Jane Dent. It was a pairing made in heaven. Then she died, along with the child she tried to bring into the world, and the life went out of Mason's dark blue eyes. *It's been seven years,* Charlotte thought, *and from all reports, he's never even looked at another woman.* He had fled Gracefield, and all the memories of Jane that it held, by going to join Stephen in Washington. But even his success in the business world had not given him any joy.

Marianne, the only daughter. She was blessed with Thomas's dark good looks and Stephen's determination. Tall and willowy, she could have had her pick of the youngbloods of Richmond. But she had married Claude Bristol. He was sitting beside his wife now, the French ancestry plain in his thin face. Too fond of cards and fast horses, he was dissatisfied with life at Gracefield, but tied to it by his inability to find anything more comfortable. "He's a weak man," Noah had once said to Charlotte. But he was Marianne's choice, and never did she by word or expression reveal any regret over her choice.

Mark, the wild one. At twenty-nine he looked exactly as his father had looked at that age: six feet one inch tall, with black hair and dark eyes. He was quick-witted, intelligent, charming—and lost! Of all their children, Charlotte and Noah knew this one the least. His early years had been a torment for them, and even now Charlotte felt a dull ache, looking at him and grieving over what might have been. She knew he was a gambler on a Mississippi riverboat, and that was less dishonorable than some professions he had followed. She had not seen him for three years, and although the marks of dissipation were not on his face, his eyes were empty, and there was a hollowness in his manner.

Jacob came in bearing a tray. He poured coffee from the massive silver pot, and Mark said, "Jacob, I hope this coffee is better than the stuff you used to make."

The wrinkled face of the old slave was immobile as he looked at the young man, but a light of humor came to his brown eyes. "I ain't had no complaints—not since you left, Marse Mark."

"Don't try to get one on Jake, Mark," Claude Bristol laughed. He had fine teeth and smiled as he looked at the slave. "He's the one who caught you and me gambling with the Huger boys out behind the slave quarters, remember?"

Mark blinked; then as the memory came back, he nodded. "I guess I do remember, Claude. I don't know what Father did to you, but he made an 'impression' on me that day!"

Noah's lips curved in a slight grin as laughter went around the room. "Not enough of one, I reckon," he said when it died down. "Maybe I should have used a bigger stick."

Charlotte was dismayed at the look that washed over Mark's face, knowing how he had resented all of Noah's attempts to curb his wild ways. But Stephen said quickly, "Not as big as the one you used on me, I hope, when I sneaked off to see the circus at Richmond." He smiled gently, adding, "I thought it was worth a licking to see my first elephant. Well, I guess the only thing I can say about the thrashing you gave me was that I was willing to quit a long time before you were!"

Mark relaxed as the others laughed at Stephen. He knew that it was the only thrashing Stephen had ever gotten, and he knew his older brother had spoken up to take the attention from him. He felt out of place, as always, in the family. But recently he had felt some vague dread. . .and though it was never quite clear in his mind, it had caused him to respond to his parents' urging to come home for the gathering. *They all have roots*, he thought, looking around at his prosperous family. *All except me.*

He looked at his father and saw that age had eaten away at him. The fine, erect figure was bent and stooped, and even the fierce determination that had been part of Noah Rocklin's being could not hide the pain that grabbed him from time to time. Mark was a good gambler, which meant he could hide his emotions well, but the first glimpse of his father's ravaged face and withered frame had broken that control. His father had seen his reaction, but neither of them could bring himself to mention the illness that was cutting the life out of Noah Rocklin.

"I wanted to see you all alone, before the supper tonight," Noah said suddenly, his voice cutting like a knife across the small talk of the children. He let his eyes run around the room, pausing on each of them as if weighing them in a balance, then added, "It's been a long time since we've been in the same room."

"Too long," Marianne said quickly. She patted Mason's arm,

saying, "It's not as far from Washington as all that, Mason!" She had always been close to this brother—and to his wife, Jane, before her death. "You just wait, dear brother, and see what plans I have for you!"

"I suspect it will be the same plan you use every time I come, Marianne," Mason said, humor in his blue eyes.

"Why, I never—!"

"Your plan," Mason interrupted her, "is to parade every lady looking for a husband in front of me." Marianne sputtered indignantly, but he reached over and put his hand over her mouth. "Do you have a new crop this time? Or is it the same old bunch?"

Stephen laughed at Marianne as she broke away from Mason's grasp, and he said, "She's got one new one, Mason. A very rich widow from Savannah is here, shopping around Richmond for a husband. A Mrs. Sterling. Trot her out, Marianne," he urged, "and have her bring her stock reports."

"Stephen, you are awful—and you, too, Mason!" Marianne said sharply. "Mrs. Sterling is *not* shopping for a husband!"

As the joking went on, Noah looked up suddenly, catching Jacob's eye. The old man was watching him carefully, and he let himself wink. They had been together for a long time, and Jake knew how much Noah needed this sort of thing. He let the talk between his children run on, taking little part but studying them all. From time to time he would respond when one of them asked a question, and he felt Charlotte's warmth as the hour rolled on.

Finally he said, "I guess you all know that I never was a man to mince words—and it's too late to begin now." A silence fell across the room, and he let it stand for what seemed like a long time.

"It's good to see you all here, but I'm thinking this may be the last time all of us are together." He felt Charlotte's hand suddenly grow tense as it lay on his arm, and he put his other hand over hers. His words had driven all the joy from the room, and now he smiled, a strange smile that touched his dark eyes.

"I hope I've brought you all up to face the truth. I've failed in so many ways. . . ." He paused then, dropped his head as he tried to find the right words. "Well, I've always been a stubborn man, but I'd like you to know that the one regret I have about coming to the end is that I could never say to you the things I wanted to say. So—let me say now that despite all our bickering and fighting, I've always loved you."

The huge clock in one corner ticked loudly in the silence. "Well, why it's hard for a man to say that to his children, I can't say. Maybe it isn't for some men. I hope all of you will learn to say it often to your own children. Don't put it off. It's something they need to hear."

Marianne said gently, tears in her eyes, "You've said it, Father."

Noah nodded but seemed sad. "It's easier to say to girls, I think. Harder to say to boys—and hardest of all to say to the boys who have become men."

Stephen said, "I think we all knew you loved us, Father."

"Did you?" Noah asked, looking up quickly at his oldest son as if for reassurance. "Still, it needs to be said." He shook his head firmly, then went on. "Well, I'm not dead yet, but this world is a pretty deadly place, and any of us can go at any time. So I wanted to talk to you, just you, without your children. Not a sermon, but not far from one either. . . ."

He began to speak, and it was not like anything any of them had ever heard from Noah Rocklin—not even Charlotte.

He was not a man given to long speeches, nor to talking about himself. But he did speak of himself, and it was of the dream he had cherished all his life. He told them how he'd begun even as a boy in Wales to dream of a place where he could grow and prosper and have his roots go down deep into the soil. The dream was to make a place that would last, a place of family where they could be free to build a world for the future.

As he spoke, each of his listeners sat silent, amazed. This was the part of Noah Rocklin that none of them had ever known—except for Charlotte. Never before had he put into words the dream that had brought him across the sea, but now that he was dying, the words seemed to come like a spring breaking free from a dam.

Finally he stopped talking, looked around the room, and said, "Don't ever grieve over me. I've had a long life and a good one. I've had the best woman I've ever seen"—here he squeezed Charlotte's hand—"a good place to work, good friends. God has been good to me!"

Then he shook his head, adding, "But a man can do only so much to make his world. I've done the best I know how to make one for you—for all of you. But some things are too big for any man. This country is changing, and I'm afraid of what those changes will do to all of you."

"Why, this is a new country, Father," Thomas said. "It's growing. Changes are to be expected."

Noah shook his head, saying at once, "I knew a man who was with Washington at Valley Forge, Thomas. That was a terrible time. He told me about the bloody footprints in the snow made by men with no shoes. But they were fighting an enemy from across the sea. Oh, Washington's men were Englishmen, I know, but this was America, the New World, and my friend said that it was that dream that kept them going."

"That's right, Father," Stephen agreed. "Men can stand almost anything if they've got the right cause."

Noah studied his hands, saying nothing, then looked up. "That's the change I've been seeing these last few years, Stephen," he said in a voice that was suddenly fragile and weak.

"You mean the problem over slavery?" Mason asked.

"It's not just slavery, son," Noah said. "That's the red flag that the abolitionists wave to get the crowd to shouting. But there's something lurking up ahead. It's not very big right now," he said slowly, then paused and seemed lost in thought. "It's like the story in the old Bible, when the prophet was praying for rain. I disremember where it is—"

"First Kings, the eighteenth chapter," Charlotte said promptly. Getting out of her chair, she went to a small table and picked up a worn, black Bible. She thumbed through it until she found the place, then read, "'And he said to his servant, Go up now, look toward the sea. And he went up and looked, and said, There is nothing. And he said, Go again seven times. And it came to pass at the seventh time, that he said, Behold, there ariseth a little cloud out of the sea, like a man's hand—'"

"That's it!" Noah exclaimed. "Something is coming to America. It's small now, but getting bigger every day. I saw it coming ten years ago. You remember, don't you, the debate in the Senate between Hayne and Webster?"

He referred to a head-on collision in 1830 over the matter of the tariff. But the issue went beyond that and became an arena when states' rights were thrown against national power. Robert Y. Hayne, a young, eloquent senator from South Carolina who was coached by John Calhoun, spoke in favor of the rights of individual states to govern themselves. Daniel

Webster rose the next day, and his reply—which took two afternoons!—was a remarkable speech that Northerners had quoted and revered for years.

"I remember what Webster said," Stephen said suddenly. "He said, 'Liberty and union, now and forever, one and inseparable!' "

Thomas suddenly lifted his head, disagreement in his tone. "If a state has the right to join the Union, she has the right to leave it," he said harshly. The two men had fought this battle many times. "You wouldn't think the Union was so great if you'd stayed here in the South, Stephen," he added. "The North is using our sweat to get rich. We grow the cotton; they pay us a pittance. Then they make it into clothing, and when we buy it back, it's for a king's ransom!"

It was not a new argument, and as usual, what was said for the next few minutes was not pleasant. Stephen and Mason, having gone North, felt that the changes of the South were not entirely unjust, but that the issues should be solved in Congress. Thomas and Claude Bristol disagreed. Mark said nothing but watched with sadness in his eyes.

"That's enough!" Noah said finally. He looked around the room, a bleak expression in his eyes. "You see how it is? If my own family is ready to come to blows over states' rights, how much chance is there that Congress can do better?"

"But you surely don't think it will come to a breakup of the Union, sir?" Claude Bristol asked.

"I think it might," Noah answered. "That's why I asked you all to come today. We may never meet again, as I said, and if we don't, I would like for you all to remember one thing." He paused, seeking the right words, then finally said, "If this small cloud that I see does get larger, and if there is ever a time when this country is torn apart—I want you all to remember that no matter how terrible the thing gets, you are all of one blood. And I don't mean just you five Rocklins and your children. I mean all of us who are Americans are of one blood. That's what Valley Forge was all about."

Noah turned away slightly so that his profile was caught in a shaft of clear white sunshine. The light was so bright that millions of motes danced wildly around the head of the old man, creating a profile that was almost spectral in appearance. This, those gathered around the table all felt strongly, was their source in the earth. Their very muscles and sinews came from the pair that sat quietly in the sunlight.

Finally Noah whispered, "May the God of all peace grant you His wisdom. For I know in my bones that you will need it in the days that are coming!"

Then he did something that none of them ever forgot—not ever! The head of the Rocklin family had been a nominal Christian during the latter days of his life, not given to much formal expression of his faith. But now he got to his feet and picked up his cane. With faltering steps, he moved around the desk and came to stand before Stephen. Slowly he put out his free hand until it rested on the head of his firstborn. He stood there, and Stephen bowed his head. They were like a statue, the two of them, so still did they become. Noah's lips were moving, but they could not hear what he said. Stephen only knew that his eyes were suddenly filled with hot tears, and then he heard his father say, "God bless you, my boy!"

Noah moved unhurriedly around the group, and when he had repeated the simple action with each of his children, he moved to the door. Jacob opened it silently, waited for Noah to pass through it, then closed it quietly.

They all heard the sound of the cane tapping down the

hall, and as it faded, each of them felt a stab of fear—there had been something in the nature of a farewell in the scene. No one wanted to speak. Finally Charlotte got up and left the room, pausing only to say quietly, "God bless you all. Your father and I love each one of you very much." Then she walked out, and the rest of them followed without saying a word. The only sound in the room then was the ticking of the old clock and the cry of a whippoorwill somewhere off in the distance.

CHAPTER 3

THE NEW PREACHER

*D*orrie, here's the seating arrangement for the dinner."

Dorrie, on her way from the dining room to the kitchen, paused long enough to take the list from Charlotte. She studied the paper, then nodded. "Yes, ma'am, I'll tend to it." A frown came to her face, and she shook her head, adding, "It ain't gonna make Marse Clay happy."

"Why not?"

" 'Cause you got him sitting across the table from Miz Melanie—and you got Marse Gideon sittin' right next to her, dat's why."

"Oh, don't be foolish, Dorrie," Charlotte snapped. "He's close enough to talk to her, and that's all that's necessary."

"He won't like it none, Miz Charlotte," Dorrie argued. "And I don't think you got the rest of it right, neither."

Charlotte had turned to leave but wheeled and stared at Dorrie. The two of them had ruled Gracefield so long that there were few disagreements, but Charlotte had learned to listen to the black woman, for she was shrewd. "Well, what's wrong with the seating?" she demanded.

Dorrie held out the paper and began pointing out various

guests and their positions. She could read as well as Charlotte and had taught Zander and their children. Her brow wrinkled with discontent as she pointed at the paper.

"Well, in the first place, you and Mistuh Noah is at one end of the table—and Mistuh Benton is away down at the other end. Now dat don't make no sense, Miz Charlotte! Mistuh Benton, he lak to talk to Mistuh Noah, and he kain't do dat way off down on t'other end!" She nodded emphatically, adding, "You and Mistuh Noah ought to be right across from the Bentons."

"Oh, Dorrie, we always put the honored guests at the other end of the table from where Noah and I sit! Besides, I've put Marianne and Claude down there to talk to them."

"Well, it doan make no sense," Dorrie said acidly. "And looky whut you done with the rest of it. You done got Marse Stephen and all his folks from up North on one side of de table, and on de other side you got all our own people."

Charlotte stared at the paper, then lifted her eyes to Dorrie, saying with considerable irritation, "They'll want to sit together!"

"Doan care whut dey wants! I says we needs to mix 'em all up! I 'spect dat oldest boy feel cut off enough, without lining him and his family up 'cross from de folks here like dey was all some kinda show!"

Staring down at the diagram, Charlotte saw what Dorrie meant. She and Noah were at the north end of the huge rectangular table, and to Noah's left she had placed the visitors: Stephen and Ruth; then their daughter, Laura, and her husband, Amos Steele; and past them she had put Mason and Gideon. *All from the North,* Charlotte thought, *and all set off as though they're nothing but guests.*

Across from them, at Charlotte's right, sat the people tied

to Gracefield: Thomas and Susanna; Amy and her husband, Brad; Marianne and her husband, Claude; then Mark and Clay. Across from Clay sat Melanie, right next to Gideon. Except for the new minister, Jeremiah Irons, who was seated between Mason and Gideon, one side of the table obviously represented the Northern branch of the Rocklins, the other the Southern.

"Never mind, Dorrie," Charlotte said wearily. "Just put the cards down. After we eat, we can go to the drawing room and they can talk to anyone they please."

"Whut about dat niece, Miz Ellen? You ain't got her down, but she'll be here, won't she?"

Charlotte hesitated, then said, "She won't be here. Mrs. Benton said that Ellen was going to a dance in Richmond with Taylor Dewitt."

"Dat girl has got a wicked pair of eyes, ain't she now? Gonna have all de men folks fighting duels ovah her!"

"Oh, she's just a child, Dorrie!" Charlotte said impatiently.

"Chile, my foot!" Dorrie sniffed. "She ain't got nothing but men on her mind!"

"Dorrie, don't meddle!"

Dorrie sniffed but said no more. Hustling back into the kitchen, she spent the next two hours harrying the cooks, the maids, and Zander. Jacob, who was to serve as a second butler, was above Dorrie's control. He sat in a straight-backed chair, smoking a corncob pipe and waiting patiently. When Dorrie had everything under control, she paused and fixed two cups of tea, then set one down before Jacob. He nodded, and he sipped the amber liquid as she related her grievance with the mistress over the seating. Finally she shook her head, her lips pursed together in displeasure, saying, "Miz Charlotte's gettin' old, Jacob. Time wuz when she could of fixed things better!"

Jacob closed his eyes, leaned back in the chair, and allowed a puff of blue smoke to escape his lips. He was tired, very tired, and the visitors from Washington had depressed him. The Rocklins were the only family he'd ever known, and he had grieved over the division that had come when Stephen and Mason had gone to live in the North.

"She's mighty tired, I reckon," he said finally. "So am I. But I don't see no way to make things bettah by swappin' folks around at the dinner table."

Dorrie sighed, sipped her tea, then nodded. "I know, Jacob. Breaks your heart, don't it? Might be bettah if dey hadn't come. I doan lak whut's goin' on. Clay and Gideon chasin' the same woman." She lifted her eyes to Jacob and asked softly, "Do Clay really want dat girl? He done chase aftuh so many, I kain't tell 'bout him."

Jacob thought of the two boys, then said, "Dorrie, you know Clay, how he is. Always been jealous of Gideon. Always tryin' to best him at everything. I been thinkin' he may be after Melanie Benton jest 'cause Gideon likes her. I hopes she turns both of them down." The two of them sat there talking quietly until the sound of voices rose from the dining room, and at once they began serving the meal.

The dining room was a large rectangular area, flanked on the outside wall by large windows. There was room at the huge table for exactly twenty people, and every seat was filled. As the soup was served, a pleasant low-pitched buzz filled the room, and Charlotte felt a weight leave her spirit. She had been worried about the dinner, wanting it to go well, not only for Noah's sake, but also for the rest of them.

They progressed through several courses, with Jacob and Zander moving quietly and efficiently through it all, both of them tall and dignified in their uniforms. The maids, well trained by Charlotte and Dorrie, saw to it that no glass was empty for more than a few moments, and the food was delicious.

James Benton, a large man with a shock of white hair over a round face, beamed and said in stentorian tones, "Why, Charlotte, this is excellent! Excellent!"

"Thank you, James," Charlotte said, smiling. "Not as fancy as your Richmond dinners, I fear."

Benton held up his hand in protest. "Not true! Your table at Gracefield is legendary, my dear. Noah, may I propose a toast? To the master and mistress of Gracefield—the epitome of Southern culture!"

Noah tasted his wine, then said, "I offer a toast. To our family and friends from Washington. Though miles come between us, may no distance nor difference sever us."

Murmurs of "Hear! Hear!" ran around the room, and after the toast, James Benton gave a quick glance at the man sitting between Mason and Gideon Rocklin. He had been introduced to the new pastor of the Baptist church before the meal, but a streak of curiosity ran through the planter. "Rev. Irons," he said, "would it be proper of me to propose a toast to you? Or as a man of the cloth, perhaps you might object to the use of ardent spirits?"

Rev. Jeremiah Irons was of medium height and wiry build. He was not handsome, though his direct brown eyes and neat features were agreeable. From time to time during the meal, he had spoken with those seated close to him, particularly to Marianne and Claude Bristol, but also to Mark Rocklin. Now he looked at Mr. Benton and said with a faint smile, "Well, sir, the first pay I ever got for my services as a clergyman was a gallon of homemade whiskey." A laugh went around the table, and when Mark asked, "Did you sample it, Reverend?" Irons shook his head and said, "I must remain silent on that subject, Mr. Rocklin."

"You come from Arkansas, Brother Irons?" Marianne asked.

"Yes, Mrs. Bristol. From so far back in the woods I'd never been to a town before I was twelve years old."

Marianne looked at the hands of Jeremiah Irons and saw that they were hard, brown, and calloused. It made her like him the more, and she said with an encouraging smile, "We are glad to have you, Reverend. Some of us have been praying for a revival at our church for some time."

Irons studied them for a moment, then said, "I'm glad to be here—but I must warn you of two things. One of them you'll discover as soon as I start preaching Sunday morning. I'm not an eloquent man. The other thing, I think you know, and that is that I didn't bring a revival in my bag when I came to Virginia. Only God can give a revival."

Amos Steele, Laura's husband, spoke up at once. "Brother Finney would not agree with you there, Reverend." Steele was a Congregational minister himself, a devout admirer of Charles Finney, the prominent evangelist. A tall man with a dark complexion and piercing hazel eyes, Steele was a striking figure as he leaned forward to peer down the table at Irons. "Mr. Finney insists that bringing a revival of religion is no different from bringing a harvest of corn. He states that there are 'laws' of the Spirit, and that if we do what God has commanded, the results must follow."

Irons answered, "I've read Mr. Finney's *Revival Lectures*. A great work, and he's a powerful man of God." He paused, then added, "He may be right, Rev. Steele. But even Mr. Finney says that no revival can come unless God's people repent and turn to God with all their heart."

Steele nodded his approval but made the mistake of saying, "I think if you can bring your church members to see the wrong in owning another human being, you might have a revival."

At once the room was charged with anger. Laura put her hand on her husband's arm, saying, "Amos, this is not the time to speak of that."

Steele gave her a direct look, then ran his gaze around the room. "It is always time to speak of righteousness," he said; then he seemed to brace himself, for the anger in the faces of those across the table from him was obvious. He felt a sudden regret that he had spoken, and indeed, he had promised Laura not to bring up the subject while at Gracefield. He was not a tactful man, but neither was he unkind. He had learned to admire and respect his father-in-law, Stephen Rocklin, as he did few other men. And he knew Mason Rocklin to be a man of high principle. But they had left the South—and presumably their Southern faith in slavery. Or so he had believed, but now he saw disapproval on Stephen's face, and it caused him to say, "I apologize. It was wrong of me to speak of my beliefs at this time."

Noah Rocklin said suddenly, "A man must hold to what he believes to be true, Amos." His simple words took the pressure out of the situation—for the moment. The dinner ran on, and nothing more was said about slavery.

Noah ate almost nothing but watched the little drama going on at the far end of the table. He could not hear the conversation between Melanie, Clay, and Gideon, but he saw the tension in the two men. And he saw also that the parents of both men were conscious of it. Certainly the Bentons didn't miss a word.

Alice Benton had said to Melanie before dinner, "I wish you wouldn't get those two young men stirred up. Wait until we get back home. You've got enough beaux there, heaven knows!"

Her words made no impression on Melanie. She was a fine young woman at heart, but who could resist the pleasure of having two men such as the Rocklin cousins vying for her hand? She sat next to Gideon—which caused Clay's eyes to burn with displeasure—and, as the meal progressed, showed her skill at handling suitors. Both men angled for the privilege of taking her to a party at a planter's house the next day; she neither encouraged nor discouraged either of them.

It had been Mark Rocklin who had started the conversation that led to the contest. "I saw something in Memphis last year that would have interested you, Gideon. Fellow named Colt who makes firearms gave a demonstration of his work."

"I met him, Mark," Gideon said. "He tried to get the army to approve his new rifle, but they turned him down."

Mark shrugged, saying, "Don't know about the army, but the rifle he demonstrated beat anything I'd ever seen. He called it the Ring Lever Rifle. Had a cylinder that took six bullets. Colt didn't do the shooting himself, but the marksman who did put six bullets in the bull's-eye in ten seconds. Fired so fast you couldn't even pick out the individual shots."

"Wish the army had bought them," Gideon said. "I'll probably be sent to the plains to fight Indians as soon as I graduate. Be nice to have men armed with those rifles."

"Better practice up on your shooting before you get there, Gideon," Clay spoke up. He grinned, adding, "At the last contest, I beat you pretty bad."

Stung, Gideon replied, "Yes, but I've had a little practice since then."

Clay shook his head. "I don't think practice helps much with shooting. Either a fellow has the eye and the hand, or he hasn't."

"Can't agree," Gideon said at once. "I've seen some pretty bad shots come to the Point, and they learned to hit the center."

Mark's dark eyes gleamed, and he said idly, "Why don't you two fellows shoot to see who takes the young lady to the party?"

Clay cried out, "Just the thing! What about it, Gid?"

"You'll have to ask Miss Benton," Gideon said at once. He thought she would put a stop to it and was surprised when she said, "Why, that would be fun!"

"I don't think it would be proper," Charlotte spoke up, seeing the danger of such a contest.

But Clay would not be denied. "Most of our crowd is coming here for breakfast tomorrow. We'll have the contest after that."

Mark suddenly said, "I shouldn't have proposed such a thing, Clay. Let's have the contest, but make the stakes a cash purse."

"I could shoot better for the privilege of escorting a Southern belle to a party than for a few paltry dollars, Mark," Clay said with a grin.

After dinner he said to his father, "I don't have a uniform to dazzle the ladies, but I could always outshoot Gid."

"Do him good to lose," Thomas said, smiling. "I never had any use for West Point, anyway."

❧

The following morning brought a group of young men on horseback and young ladies in carriages. There were nine new guests in all, and the house was filled with laughter and high-spirited talk during the breakfast. They devoured mountains of pancakes, sausages, battered eggs, and biscuits, and as they ate, Susanna tried to get Thomas to persuade Clay to abandon the idea of the shooting match. "It will cause hard feelings, I'm afraid."

"Nonsense!" Thomas said. He himself was excited by the match and had made a sizable bet with James Benton. He loved to gamble, and more than that, he wanted to see Clay beat Gideon. It was more than the simple desire of a father to see a son win. There was something much deeper than that. He knew it had something to do with the fact that he himself had never been able to best his older brother. He patted Susanna on the shoulder, saying, "It's just a bit of foolishness. The young people have to have their sport."

The shooting match had been mentioned at the breakfast, and at ten o'clock there was a parade from the Big House out to the south pasture. Jeremiah Irons had stayed the night, talking into the early hours of the morning with Amos Steele, whom he liked but disagreed with heartily. Steele and Brad Franklin had been impressed as judges for the match. It was a beautiful morning, and not only the young people who had come for the holiday, but everyone moved out to where a line of huge oaks formed a boundary for a grazing pasture.

"Don't either of you two hit one of my horses," Claude Bristol warned. He was enjoying the whole thing, for like Thomas, he was a man who liked the excitement of gambling. His wife, Marianne, did not like it and said so.

"I wish Mark had never thought of this foolish thing. He ought to know how competitive Clay and Gideon are."

"It'll be all right," Claude assured her. But Marianne saw

that her mother was worried, and she wished that the whole incident were over.

Several of the young men had clamored to get into the match, and Clay had said magnanimously, "Come on. None of you can hit the ground with a rifle anyway."

Jacob had brought a dozen rifles from Noah's study, and there was considerable time consumed as the young men argued over them. Zander was sent to nail a board to a tree, then to fasten to it a piece of paper with a cross in the center of it.

Jeremiah Irons found himself standing beside Charlotte Rocklin as the men drew for turns. He saw that her eyes were worried, and he said, "It's just a match, Mrs. Rocklin. Young people must have their fun."

Charlotte turned and looked into his eyes. "And how old are you, Rev. Irons?"

He saw she had him and said sheepishly, "Well, I'm twenty."

"The same age as Clay, and Gideon is twenty-one."

Irons felt uncomfortable but defended his position. "I guess I'm older than my years, you might say. Missed out on most of the things young people do." He looked down at his calloused hands and laughed ruefully. "Guess I was too busy working to learn how to play." Then he said quickly, "Not complaining, sister. But truly, your grandsons are fine boys. They'll be all right."

Charlotte did not answer, but she liked the preacher very much. They both turned to watch as six of the young men took shots at the target. After each shot, Zander put a circle around the hole in the target with an initial showing whose shot it was. Tug Ramsey, the rotund nephew of the governor, never even hit the target, but Taylor Dewitt and two others besides Gid and Clay did.

Mr. Benton called out, "Move back twenty feet for the second shot." In the next round two more dropped out, leaving only Dewitt and the Rocklins.

"Back another twenty feet!" Benton called out. They moved back, and it was Dewitt who dropped out that time. "Between you two," he said with a grin, stepping back.

They moved back again, and for the next ten minutes Clay and Gid took turns, each of them having three shots at the target. They stayed neck and neck, and Irons saw that the pressure was beginning to tell on Clay. *He thought he'd get an easy victory,* Irons realized. *I don't think he likes the pressure.*

It was true. Clay had expected an easy victory. He saw at once that Gid had improved a great deal, and the thought of losing to his cousin made him tense. At the beginning of the match, there had been a great deal of laughter and joking. When it narrowed down to Clay and Gid, most of that died away. A quiet fell on the field, broken only by the cries of the judges announcing the scores.

Gideon was heartily wishing that the thing had never begun. *Blast that fool Mark for thinking of such a thing!* he thought. He saw the pain in his grandmother's face and wanted to deliberately miss, but he found that it was not that easy. He had never loved a woman, and as silly as the contest was, it came to him strongly that the whole thing had become some kind of a symbol. He had glimpsed Melanie's face and saw that she was intent on the thing. So, calling himself a fool, he shot as well as he could.

The sun was hot, and the contest drew down finally to the last target. The scores were equal, and Mr. Benton said, "The man that comes the closest to the bull's-eye this time wins the match!"

The two men shot carefully, taking their time, and after each shot, Zander marked the result. After Clay sent his last shot home, Steele and Franklin took the target off and examined it. Then Steele cried out, "It looks like a tie!"

Clay nodded, his face grim, but Irons had been watching the faces of Noah and Charlotte. They were standing together, slightly to his left, and there was something fragile about them. Irons knew that Noah Rocklin was not well, and he admired him tremendously. He had already discovered that Charlotte Rocklin was one of the finest Christian women he'd ever met. He had been told this, and his visit had proven it to his own mind.

He was not a man to dominate, this young preacher, but the tension in the air and the potential for disaster made him step forward, saying, "Just a minute." They all turned to stare at him, and he took off his coat, saying, "I'm a little late to enter the contest, but I've got a good reason."

"What is it, Reverend?" Benton asked.

"Well, Mr. Benton, I was afraid I'd be embarrassed. I thought Virginia men could shoot. But I've got a twelve-year-old brother back home named Toby, and he could beat anybody I've seen here." He ignored the hard looks he got from the young men and added, "And *I* can beat Toby. So with your permission, Miss Melanie, I'd like to join myself to your other suitors."

Melanie Benton had a quick sense of humor. She liked the young preacher, and the idea of going to a party with him suddenly amused her. "I wish you luck, Rev. Irons," she said demurely.

"Put the target back up," Benton called to the judges, then turned to say with a frown, "I'm not sure it's proper for a man of the cloth to participate in such an affair as this, sir!"

"Oh, Jesus ate with sinners, Mr. Benton, so I suppose I can shoot with a few."

A tall young man named Bushrod Aimes nudged Taylor Dewitt. "He's a blowhard, ain't he, Dewitt?"

"Don't know until I see him shoot." A wicked light came into his eyes. "He better be as good as his brag. Otherwise he might get a ducking in the creek sometime or other."

Jake had loaded one of the Hawken rifles, and as Irons took it, he said softly to the preacher, "This is Marse Noah's personal rifle gun, suh. Pulls just a hair to the left."

Irons flashed the slave a quick grin, then swept the rifle up and fired the instant it reached shoulder level. There was no hesitation, and when Steele looked at the target, he yelled, "Dead center!"

There was no need for a second shot, for he had bested the efforts of Clay and Gideon. Gideon came up at once, his hand out and a smile of relief on his broad face. "Fine shot!"

Clay nodded, but he was not smiling as he said, "Good shot, Reverend."

Bushrod Aimes was staring at the preacher. "I guess he don't get no bath in the creek, does he, Dewitt?"

"Nope. Matter of fact, if I ever got in a bad scrap, that preacher would be a pretty good fellow to have around!"

Irons handed the rifle back to Jacob, saying, "Fine shooting gun. It does pull a mite to the left, at that."

Turning, he approached Clay, who was staring at the ground. "Clay, I'll tell you what," he said casually. "Why don't all three of us take that party in? You, me, and Gideon."

Clay looked up quickly at the minister. Disgust and anger marred his eyes, but when he saw the friendly expression on Irons's face, he swallowed hard and forced a grin. "That's decent of you, Preacher," he said. "We'll do it."

Noah and Charlotte were watching as Clay suddenly seemed

to lose his anger, and when the three men—Irons, Clay, and Gideon—went to Melanie, she laughed heartily and the tension seemed to dissipate. Irons left the others and moved to where the elder Rocklins stood.

"Where'd you learn to shoot like that, Preacher?" Noah demanded.

"Well, when you've got a single-shot rifle, a family of ten children, and a widowed mother to feed with what you shoot, you learn pretty fast."

Charlotte reached her hands out, and he took them without thinking. "Pastor, we are in your debt!"

Noah huffed and said, "Good to see a preacher can be of some practical use around the place!" But he nodded, his old eyes grown warm. "Glad to have you at Gracefield. I hope you'll be here often."

Irons watched as the two moved away, and he looked around to see Amos Steele, who'd come to stand beside him.

"That was good thinking, Jeremiah," Steele said with a warm smile. "It was fast becoming a pretty bad situation. Good thing you can shoot like that!"

"God was in it, Amos."

"You sound like a staunch Calvinist. You think God's in everything?"

"By Him all things consist," Irons said quietly.

"Well, I'm glad you've come to serve as pastor here. I love these people." Steele shook his head doubtfully, adding, "They don't care for me, because I'm an abolitionist. But they'll see the light one day. In any case, do what you can for them."

Irons said slowly, "Going to take more than a good sermon or two, Amos. The whole country is sitting on a powder keg. And the Rocklins are right in the middle of it."

Steele stared at the smaller man, a sober light in his hazel eyes. "It's a grand and awesome time, as the song says. I'm no prophet, Jeremiah, but as I've been told, Noah said yesterday there's a cloud the size of a man's hand on the horizon. A dark cloud that I can't quite understand—but I do believe it's going to get bigger, and all of us are going to be under it."

CHAPTER 4

THE CHOICE

July was hot and sultry that year. The heavens withheld the rains, and fine dust rose in tawny clouds as wagons and horses traveled the roads around Richmond. Noah Rocklin did not bear the heat well, and it was on a blistering Thursday afternoon that he said to Thomas, "I'd like to be up North. So hot around here it sears a man's lungs! And look at that dust over there! I feel like I got hot mud in my chest."

The two men were sitting under a huge oak in the backyard drinking tepid lemonade. Thomas glanced at the rising dust, then back to his father. He was worried, for Noah was exhausted, and the constant cough that had plagued him all summer seemed to grow worse day by day.

"Maybe I ought to take you to Maine," Thomas suggested. "You always liked it there. Ought to be cool, Father. I'd like to get some good sea air myself."

Noah shook his head, started to speak, then went into a spasm of coughing that racked his frail body. Thomas sat there, helpless, until the old man gained control. "No, I don't want to die anywhere but on my own ground." He took a swallow of the lemonade, and as Thomas began to protest, Noah said with a trace of irritation, "Of course, I'm going to die. I'm like an animal, Tom. Can feel it coming on." A flash of humor took him, his black eyes gleaming faintly. "Heard about a place in Africa once, where the elephants go to die when they feel it coming on. Seems to me there ought to be someplace for a man to go to and take care of it, too."

Thomas said nothing. He and the rest of the family recognized that Noah was growing weaker day by day, and there was nothing the doctor could do. Finally he said, "Maybe it'll rain. Cotton could stand it, and so could I."

Noah nodded, and the two men sat there very quietly. It was strange that the two of them had grown closer since Noah's illness. They had never been particularly close, for Thomas was not given to making Gracefield the greatest plantation in Virginia—which had been Noah's lifelong goal. Although Noah had never said so, he was deeply disappointed in the fact that none of his sons cared for farming. For a time Noah had hoped that Marianne would marry a man who could take over the empire he had built, but, like the others, Claude Bristol was more interested in fast horses and hunting than in raising cotton.

Noah thought of Amy's husband, Brad Franklin, who was as dedicated to the world of cotton as he himself had been. But Brad had his own plantation and could not leave it to come to Gracefield. Another spasm of coughing rose in his chest, but he quickly raised the glass and gulped the rest of the lemonade. He leaned his head back on the chair and mused quietly, "You know, Thomas, all this heat and dust we've had this summer, it reminds me of the election."

"You mean for president?" Thomas was quick of mind and caught his father's meaning at once. "Lots of heat and dust in the campaigns, you mean, Father? That's right. Who will win, do you think?"

"It won't be Van Buren," Noah said bitterly. "The country started going bankrupt the year he took office. The Whigs will win, and William Henry Harrison will be the president of the United States."

"He's a Virginian," Thomas noted with satisfaction. "He'll help us when he's elected. Lord knows we need it! I guess he's tough enough. An Indian fighter, isn't he?"

Noah suddenly smiled. "Don't pay any attention to the newspapers. They're saying that Harrison was born in a log cabin and loves cider. Trying to make him into a man the common people will love, like Andy Jackson. But Harrison's no bumpkin, Thomas. He's from a prosperous Virginia family, went to college and studied law. He'll win, and as you say, the South will have something to say about the way this country is going."

They spoke for a short time of politics; then Noah asked, "What's the latest report on the courtship?"

"Oh, I don't know, Father." Thomas shook his head with disgust. "It's gone too far, and if Melanie doesn't make up her mind soon, I think her father will lock her up for a year."

Clay and Gideon's rivalry had grown as heated as the climate and the political campaign. It had become, in fact, a form of joke around Richmond. A cartoon had circulated showing Melanie dressed in a hoopskirt juggling the two young men in the air. Neither James Benton nor Noah had thought it funny. The two men admired one another and wanted to see their families tied together—but both were heartily tired of the whole affair.

"I thought the Benton girl had more sense, Thomas," Noah said.

"Well, she's young, Father." Thomas shrugged. "Any young girl would be excited to have two attractive men after her. Can't blame her too much, I suppose."

"You'd like for Clay to win, wouldn't you?"

"Yes, I would. If she marries Gideon, Melanie will have to leave home and follow him to his stations. It's a hard life for a woman. Some of those forts out west are terrible places, I'm told. But if she marries Clay, it'll be a tie between Gracefield and Briarcliff. The Bentons don't have a son, so Clay would be master of the Benton empire sooner or later. That would give us more land and slaves than any other plantation in the South, I think."

"Not a very romantic approach to marriage," Noah said.

"I suppose not." Thomas shrugged, then said, "Stephen was always supposed to be the practical son, wasn't he? And here I am, the 'romantic' son, trying to gain more land by marrying my son into a wealthy family!"

Noah said carefully, "I've sometimes felt that you had hard feelings toward Stephen. Maybe I gave you some cause. I never wanted to show favoritism, but perhaps I did."

"We're not as much alike, you and I, as you and Stephen are," Thomas said slowly. "But I have no complaint, Father. Now that you mention it, though, I do think Clay feels a little antagonism toward Gideon. He's never said much about it, but I know him well. That's what worries me about this competition for Melanie. Clay's always tried to outdo Gideon in everything, and I've had the uneasy feeling that it's not altogether love for Melanie that's made him throw himself into this rivalry."

"You think he might want her just because Gideon's after her?"

"I hope I'm wrong, but Susanna and I have talked of it.

Whichever one of them Melanie chooses, it's going to be hard. All in the family, isn't it? And the loser will have to look at his cousin as a 'winner' as long as they both live."

"Too bad!" Noah said, sadness touching his voice. "I wish she'd drop them both. That would answer. But I don't suppose she will."

"No, Gideon's coming next week. Maybe he's tired of the game, too. I got that much from Stephen's last letter. He and Ruth feel much the same as we do about it. So with a little pressure from us, from Stephen, and from the Bentons, maybe it'll be settled." He got to his feet, stretched, and shook his head. "Clay hasn't been worth a dime this summer. Done nothing but chase around with his crowd. He's got to settle down."

Noah said quietly, "I've been proud of the way you've taken hold of the place lately, Thomas. You've done a fine job."

The unexpected praise brought a flush of pleasure to Thomas's face, and Noah wished suddenly that he'd been quicker in the past to praise this unstable son of his. Sadness washed over him as he realized it was too late. *I guess all old men come to this,* he thought. *Wanting to go back and change the past. But it's always too late.*

"I think I'll go to bed for a while, son," he said. "I'm a little tired."

❧

Washington had suffered from the blistering July heat no less than Richmond had, and as Stephen brought the buggy to a stop at the hitching rack outside of the Orange and Alexandria Railroad Station, sweat poured down his face. "Gid, if it's hotter in Richmond than it is here in Washington," he grunted, "you'll melt like butter in the sun."

Gideon stepped down, handed his mother to the ground, then answered soberly, "I'm not worried about the weather."

Ruth took his arm, holding on to him as if she planned to keep him from getting on the train. Ever since he had come in from West Point, stopping for an overnight visit on his way to Richmond, she had tried to get him to change his mind. Even now with the sound of the steam engine chuffing down the track, she pleaded, "Son, I wish you'd wait. There's no hurry about all this. Wait until fall, until you have more time to think about it."

Gideon looked down at her, smiling faintly. "You think if I stay away, Mellie will pick Clay, don't you, Mother?" Then he frowned, his square face growing sober. "That's what I'm afraid of. Clay's there all the time, and he's quite a romantic fellow. I'm just a plain soldier, and I'll be asking Mellie to leave her whole way of life."

"That's what your father and I are afraid of, son," Ruth broke in, nodding. "Southern women don't transplant easily. And the woman you marry will have to follow you all over the country."

Stephen listened as Ruth continued to plead, but said nothing. He had talked with his son alone and knew there was no hope of changing the boy's mind. He was, moreover, less resistant to the match than was his wife. He liked Melanie very much, feeling that under her facade of light foolishness lay a strong woman who would make an excellent wife for Gideon.

An earsplitting shriek rose from the engine, and Gid quickly kissed his mother. "Good-bye, Mother," he said, then took the hard hand his father offered. "Thanks for the extra cash, Father." He grinned at Stephen. "I promise not to spend it on anything useful."

"Come back as soon as you can, Gid," Stephen said.

Gid turned and, plucking his carpetbag from the back of the buggy, dashed toward the train, which was already in motion. He caught the steel handhold with his free hand, hauled himself aboard, then turned and waved as the train picked up speed. When his parents were out of sight, he moved into the car and found a seat. All the car windows were open, and though it was hot, the wind on his face was welcome. The cinders that floated in and stung his cheeks were not, but they were a necessary evil of travel on the Orange and Alexandria Railroad. The car swayed from side to side on sleepers that gave slightly, for much of the line was new.

Gid leaned back, relieved to have his visit with his parents behind him. He had felt constrained to go and, in a brief conversation with his father, had laid bare his intention. "I'm going to get this thing settled, one way or another," he had said after his mother had gone to bed. "Mellie's got to make up her mind. I can't go on in limbo, and I don't guess Clay can either. So after this visit, either you'll have a prospective daughter-in-law, or Uncle Thomas will!"

As the train moved on, Gideon watched the Potomac roll beside the tracks. He went over his decision again. He had been, he knew, almost useless at the Point—his mind was on Melanie, not his work. And he was honest enough to admit that he had little hope of success with her. As the train made a quick stop at Alexandria, then turned west, he reviewed his chances, finding them not very good.

She'd be better off with Clay, he thought painfully. *I'll only be able to offer her a bare room in some outpost in Nebraska or some other wild place. If she marries Clay, she'll have Briarcliff.*

The train chugged along, crossing Bull Run Creek, then

Manassas Station. As it roared over the bridge that spanned the Rappahannock River, Gid put his head on his chest and fell asleep. He awoke occasionally, but by the time the train pulled into Richmond, he had a painful neck and was bleary-eyed.

He made his way to a livery stable, rented a horse, and soon was on his way out of Richmond. Glad to be off the train, he kept the spirited bay at a fast trot, pulling him up now and then for a drink at one of the creeks that crossed the road. He passed the road that led to Briarcliff, then pulled the bay to a halt. It was growing late, and he was tempted to gallop right to the Benton place and put his cause to Melanie at once. But there was a solid patience in Gideon Rocklin, which some mistook for dullness. That was one of the characteristics that made him a good soldier. One of his instructors, Layton Fields, had argued this with another on the staff who thought Gideon was a plodder.

"Yes, he does plod," Fields had agreed. "But only until he is certain of his ground. When he knows the enemy and has assessed his own potential, he'll show enough dash. It's those fools who rush blindly toward the sound of the guns who scare me. Usually they manage to get themselves and their men promptly slaughtered!"

So it was typical of Gid that he would pause and consider every facet of the matter before he made a decision. *Clay,* he thought with a wry grin, *would not have hesitated for a single instant. He would have spurred the bay, arrived at Briarcliff with a spent horse, and flung himself toward Melanie without hesitation.*

"Maybe I am a plodder," Gid spoke aloud as he patted the neck of his mount. Then he shook his heavy shoulders, spoke to the horse, and galloped down the dusty road. The whippoorwills were calling faintly from the woods as he reached the entrance to Gracefield, and when he dismounted, Highboy, the oldest son of Box and Carrie, came out of the stable.

"Marse Gideon," he said, his white teeth flashing. "I thought you was off soljerin' somewhere." Catching the reins that Gideon tossed to him, he asked slyly, "You come courtin' Miss Melanie?"

Gideon laughed suddenly. "Yes, Highboy, I have indeed." He well knew that the activities of the Rocklin family were the chief topics of conversation for the slaves and thought wryly that there were no secrets in the world of Gracefield. "How's Mr. Noah?"

"Real poorly, Marse Gideon," Highboy said sadly. "De doctuh wuz here dis mawnin'. I heard my maw tell Miss Charlotte dat she better git some medicines from Granny Sarrie."

"Grain this horse, Highboy," Gideon said absently, then walked toward the Big House. Granny Sarrie was a black woman of indeterminate age who trafficked with herbs and voodoo in equal proportions. Charlotte sometimes used the herbs but scorned the rest of Sarrie's potions.

He was met at the door by his aunt Susanna and asked at once, "How is he, Aunt Sue?"

Susanna shook her head, saying, "Not well at all, Gideon. Come in." He followed her into the kitchen, where he was greeted by Carrie and given a glass of tea. "Most everyone's gone to Richmond, Gideon," Susanna said as he sipped it. "The Governor's Ball is tonight, you know."

"Forgot about it," Gid said. He looked at her carefully, then asked, "Can I see him?"

Susanna answered, "He was asleep a little while ago, but he wakes up often. Come along and we'll see."

He followed her to the bedroom on the first floor, and when they entered, they found Charlotte sitting beside the sick man. But Noah was awake and said at once, "Come in, Gid. And you two women can fix us a drink. A mint julep for me."

"I'll fix it," Charlotte said, and the two women left the room. Gid looked after them in surprise, for he knew that the doctor had forbidden liquor for his grandfather. *Not a good sign*, he thought, taking the chair beside the bed. *Almost as if they've given up.*

But he said only, "How do you feel?"

"Pretty bad, pretty bad," Noah said, then smiled faintly. "How come you're not at the ball?"

"Forgot about it."

"Well, you won't win any points that way," Noah said. He shifted in the bed, his thin hands pulling at his nightshirt. "How's Stephen and your mother?" He listened as Gid gave the news, then nodded. He examined Gid carefully. "You've got a look in your eye, Gid. What's on your mind?"

"Well, I've got to settle this business with Melanie," Gid said bluntly. He told his grandfather how he'd been practically useless, then added, "It's got to be one way or the other." A streak of curiosity touched him, and he asked, "Which way are you betting, Grandfather?"

Noah grinned faintly. "Not sayin', boy," he stated. "But I will say that if that girl takes you, she'll get a winner." He laughed silently, adding, "I must be going fast. Got to saying nice things to everybody. Never was broke out with that, was I?"

"I remember when I broke the leg of that promising colt," Gid said. "You told me I'd wind up picking cotton for a living." He saw the memory bring a smile to Noah's lips, then added, "But when I went to the Point, what you said when I came to say good-bye has been a real help to me. You said, 'Boy, you're a fool, but all young men are fools. When you get that out of you, the man that's left is going to do the Rocklins proud.'" Gideon suddenly reached out and took the frail hand in his thick one. It felt as fragile as the bones of a bird, but he said, "That meant a lot to me, Grandfather. More than you know. Sometimes when I was ready to quit, I'd think of that—and it kept me going."

Noah's eyes glistened as he patted the strong hand of his grandson. "Glad you told me about that, Gid," he said simply. "I'm proud of you, as I was proud of your father." He lay there quietly, and then he said, "Whatever comes to this country, Gid, don't let go of the part of you that's here at Gracefield. I'll have your word on that, as an officer and a gentleman."

Gideon saw the fire in the old eyes and at once said, "You have it."

Noah relaxed, and the two men talked quietly until Charlotte came back with two mint juleps. She handed one to Gid, then helped Noah sit up. After handing him the tall frosty glass, she stepped back, saying, "That's just about all the ice."

Noah sipped the concoction, then smacked his lips. "Gid, git out of here. Go give Clay a run for his money."

Gideon finished the drink, then rose to leave. "I'll see you tomorrow, Grandfather."

He left the room, and Noah said, "That's a good boy."

"They both are," Charlotte agreed. "I guess he's come to force Melanie to make a choice."

Noah was accustomed to her insight and merely nodded. "It'll be settled one way or another by the time he leaves. Which one will she have?"

Charlotte walked over and sat down on the bed. She

smoothed his silver hair back from his forehead, then smiled at him. "You used to be smarter, Noah, than to try to guess what's in a woman's heart. I don't think Melanie knows herself—but she will have to choose now."

The color of Melanie's gown reflected the royal blue of her eyes, and as she swirled about the dance floor with Clay, she threw her head back and laughed at something he had said. He was the best-looking man at the ball, dressed in fawn trousers and a rust-colored coat. His black hair and olive skin set off his chiseled features, and as he spoke, Melanie could sense the excitement that flowed through him. Aside from his good looks, there was a special quality that drew people to Clay. He seemed charged with some sort of energy, a life that seemed sadly lacking in most men. Though it was true that he often was quick to change direction, just now Melanie could feel her own spirit rising to meet his.

"I can't dance every dance with you, Clay," she protested. "You were absolutely rude to Lyle McIntire!"

"Let Lyle find his own woman," Clay said with a grin. "I've put the word out that I'll shoot any man who tries to dance with you tonight."

"You are awful!" Melanie exclaimed, but her eyes sparkled with excitement. "Very well, I'll sit out the next one, and you must ask Ellen to dance."

"She's got enough fellows chasing her." Clay cast a glance over his shoulder and, noting that Ellen had four of his friends surrounding her, laughed. "Look at them! Chasing after her like a pack of hound dogs with their tongues hanging out."

"Clay! Don't be crude!"

He was amused at her protest. "Mellie, any girl who wears a dress like Ellen has on wants to attract men."

Though she denied his words, secretly Melanie agreed. Ellen had appeared in a formfitting rose-colored dress, the front of which was cut extremely low. When Melanie had attempted to hint that the gown was immodest, Ellen had laughed at her. "It's what they're wearing in Europe, Mellie. I'm just introducing the newest styles. You'll be wearing one just like this at your next ball!"

Despite his protests, Melanie insisted that Clay dance with her cousin, so as soon as the dance ended, he handed her over to Taylor Dewitt, who saw Melanie to a chair, and went to Ellen. When he asked her to dance, at once she said, "Of course, Clay," and they waltzed off, leaving Bushrod Aimes staring after them in chagrin.

"Well, Tug, that is some stuck-up girl," Bushrod said half angrily. "Nothing but a Rocklin is good enough for her, I guess."

Tug Ramsey was wearing a tight collar, which made his round face red as a rising sun—though, to be honest, some of the color was due to the contents of a bottle that he and the other young men sampled from time to time. "If she wasn't as juicy as a ripe plum," Tug said with a grin, "I guess we'd leave her alone. Wonder if—" He broke off, saying in a startled voice, "Look, Bushrod! There's Gid!"

The two of them watched as Gideon, resplendent in dress uniform, came in through the double doors, looked around, and made his way to where Melanie was seated. They saw the astonishment steal over her face as she looked up at Gid. Then she arose and followed him through a pair of French doors that led to the outer court of the governor's mansion.

"Ol' Gid looks dead serious, don't he now?" Tug remarked. "I expect he means business."

"I'd better tell Clay," Bushrod said. He waited until the dance was over, then, as Clay brought Ellen from the dance floor, moved close to him. "Clay, did you see Gid come in?" he murmured.

Clay gave him a sharp look. "No. Where is he?"

Bushrod grinned brashly. "Out in the garden, boy, with Melanie—and you know what that means! Better get yourself into action."

Clay gave Aimes a look of irritation but said only, "I can't go busting out there now. Let's go have a drink. I'll head him off pretty soon."

But the drink turned out to be two drinks, then three. The pair of them were joined by Taylor Dewitt and Tug Ramsey, and the four of them got into a drinking contest. Dewitt, who could apparently hold any amount of whiskey with no discernible result, tried to caution Clay. "Better lay off this stuff, Clay," he said. "It's pretty potent. You don't want to get drunk."

Clay laughed rashly, tilted the bottle, and drank deeply. "I can hold my liquor, Taylor," he boasted. "You tend to your own business." He drank again and laughed as he handed the bottle to Bushrod. "Put it down like a man, Aimes!"

On the other side of the mansion, Melanie was in a state of shock. She had been glad to see Gid, but when she started to tell him what she'd been doing, he had said, "I didn't come to Richmond to hear about the balls you've been to, Mellie." His words sounded a little harsh, but his eyes were gentle. "I came to ask you to marry me."

Melanie smiled. "You've done that pretty regularly for the

past few months, Gid. In person and by mail."

Gid shook his head. The light that filtered through the French doors caught him, framing his solid shape and heightening the glow in his brown eyes. There was, Melanie saw suddenly, a determination in him that was somehow different than ever before.

"I'm worn out, Mellie," Gid said simply. "Life is difficult enough at West Point, and since I've had you on my mind, I've not done a blessed thing right. If something doesn't happen, I'll wash out." Then he took her hands and held them in his. "But that's not the point, Mellie."

Melanie was sobered by his manner. His hands were so large that her own were lost in his grasp, and she exclaimed, "Why, Gid, you're trembling!"

He looked down at his hands and laughed shortly. "I didn't think there was anything in the world that could do that to me, Mellie. Shows you how things are with me." He took one hand from hers and used it to draw her closer. "You're so beautiful, Mellie!" he whispered. "But that's not why I love you. I'd love you even if you lost your beauty."

It was a thought that had not occurred to Melanie, and the sudden strangeness of it shocked her. She relied on her good looks, even took them for granted. Sometimes she felt sorry for plain girls, and now the thought came to her, *What would happen if I got scarred?* And she knew at once the answer: Most men would turn from her.

"I really believe you would, Gid," she said softly. "You really would." In that moment, though she had known Gideon Rocklin all her life, Melanie saw the strength of the man. It made her feel strangely safe as she stood within the circle of his arms.

"You know me, Mellie," Gid said. "I don't change much. Guess I'm not very exciting. But I'll never stop loving you. Not even if you choose Clay. When we are both old and silver-haired, I'll love you."

His simple words did more to Melanie than any she'd ever heard before. If some other man had spoken them, she could have put them away—but not this man. He was not dashing, true enough, but Melanie realized with a start that what she wanted, more than dashing manners, was a man who would always love her.

"I—I love you, Gid," she whispered and stepped closer to him, reaching up to pull his head down. His kiss was sweet but not demanding. She sensed the longing behind the light pressure of his lips and knew that he was holding himself in tight rein, thinking of her. And she now knew that she would trust herself to this strong, solid man for the rest of her life.

"I'll marry you, Gid, if you want me," she whispered, drawing back from him so that she could see his face.

His eyes burned suddenly, and his lips grew firm as he took a deep breath. Then he laughed and caught her close. "Great guns!" he exclaimed. "I thought I'd lost you!"

They were both trembling, and for the next few minutes they simply walked around the garden, oblivious to everything except each other and the decision they had just made. Finally Melanie laughed nervously, saying, "I feel married already, Gid!"

"Well, you're not," he said practically, then kissed her.

"Let's go make the announcement!" Melanie said, taking his hand.

"No! That's not the way, Mellie!" Gid pulled her back, then said soberly, "We've got to think of Clay."

Melanie flushed and dropped her head. When she lifted it to look at him, she tried to smile. "You see what a selfish girl you're getting? Yes, we must think of Clay. But I must tell my parents now."

"Good! After that, you must take Clay someplace where it's quiet." Gid shook his head, adding, "It's going to be hard for him, Mellie."

"Oh, Gid, why did I ever lead you two on in such a senseless way?"

"That's past praying for, Mellie," he said gently. "The thing now is to make it as easy for him as possible. What I'd like to do is say nothing to anyone—except your parents, I suppose. Tell Clay you won't marry him, and don't even mention me. After he gets used to the idea, I can come courting again."

"Oh, Gid, that'll take forever!"

"But it's the best way, Mellie. Will you do it?"

Melanie nodded, then reached up and kissed him. "You're good, Gideon. Much better than I am!"

"That's true." He nodded with a twinkle of humor in his eye. "But you're young, and I can bring you up to my standards quickly enough. Now go and tell your parents."

Gideon's plan was good—but it never happened. Melanie found her father, and he was pleased enough with her choice. "He's a good, solid man, Mellie," James Benton affirmed. "He'll be a general one of these days. You'll see!"

Melanie kissed him, then went upstairs seeking her mother. In her excitement, she forgot to tell her father to keep the engagement a secret, and as soon as she was out of sight, Benton went to the governor, telling him the good news. The governor, anxious to please Benton, called for silence, then proposed a toast to the engagement of the couple.

Clay himself got the news when he came into the ballroom with his friends. His face was flushed and his speech was slightly slurred by the liquor. He was stopped by a friend who said, "Well, you gave it all you had, Clay. Too bad you got beat."

Clay stared at the man, a tall fellow named Christopher Potter. "What—you talking about, Chris?" he asked.

"Why, about Melanie's engagement to Gideon," Potter said; then he saw that Clay's face had turned white. "Oh, good Lord, Clay!" he apologized. "I thought you knew about it!"

Clay Rocklin stood there feeling the anger as it rose in him. He looked across the room for Melanie but did not see her. He did see Gid, however, and at that moment if he had had a gun, he would have shot his cousin through the heart.

Gideon saw Clay and started across the room. But as he drew near, Clay gave him one bitter glance of violent anger, then turned on his heel and stormed out.

"That was bad," Taylor Dewitt said to Bushrod. "We better go with him." The two of them left at once, and for the rest of the night they trailed along with Clay as he made his way through the lowest dives and brothels of Richmond. When he was completely unconscious, Dewitt and Aimes took him to a hotel room and put him to bed.

Looking down on him, Dewitt said, "I've seen Clay when he was mad, Bushrod. But this is different."

"He's crazy, Dewitt," Bushrod agreed. "Maybe he'll feel better about it when he wakes up."

Taylor Dewitt shook his head, a doubtful cast to his lean face. "I hope so—but Clay was mighty set on that girl. If only it could have been any other man! You know how he's always been jealous of Gid."

"I guess if it were any other man, Clay would call him out.

But he can't fight a duel with a member of his own family!"

"I don't know, Bushrod. . .just no telling what Clay will do. He's got a mighty wild streak." He suddenly struck his hands together and swore. "I wish Gid would take that girl and elope! Be better for everyone!"

But the pair knew that would never happen, and for a long time they sat up trying to think of a way to help their friend. But when the dawn came and Clay awoke, they saw the raw look of anger in his eyes. They both knew that there was not a single thing on earth they could do for Clay Rocklin.

CHAPTER 5

MELORA

I don't suppose you ever thought of deer hunting as a ministry, did you, Brother Irons!"

"I never try to figure out how God might want to work."

Rev. Jeremiah Irons looked over his cup of steaming coffee toward Susanna Rocklin. The two of them were sitting in Gracefield's kitchen, which was, for once, unoccupied. It was so early that it was still dark outside. A chill September wind had numbed the preacher's nose and stiffened his hands on the ride from the parsonage to Gracefield, and he had found Susanna waiting for him with hot coffee. Now as the two of them sat at the table waiting for Clay to come down, he thought about the past two months.

He had spent a great deal of his time at Gracefield, coming almost daily not only to visit Noah, who was usually confined to his bed, but to encourage Charlotte and Susanna. They were both pillars in his church, and both were in the valley of the shadow—Charlotte because she faced the loss of her beloved, and Susanna because of Clay's behavior. There was little he could do in a practical way for Noah and Charlotte, though his very presence there cheered both of them. But he had acted on

Susanna's request to make himself available to Clay. This was, to say the least, difficult, for Clay had gone sour since Melanie had accepted Gideon.

Every attempt that Irons made to help Clay in a spiritual way was rebuffed. Clay did his work on the plantation sullenly, staying away from the family and leaving for Richmond to drink and carouse as soon as his work was done. Reports of his wild behavior came to Thomas and Susanna, and it was this that prompted Susanna to call upon her pastor for help. "He'll never come to church, Brother Jerry," she had said in desperation, and it was then that Jeremiah had been struck with the idea of getting next to Clay in another way.

"Maybe not," he'd answered Susanna, "so let's try something else." His plan was to get Clay to hunt with him, for both of them were avid hunters. Susanna had agreed at once, and the plan had worked to some extent. Clay had curtly refused the first invitation, suspicious of the preacher, but the second time he had gone duck hunting with Irons. It had been a strange hunt, Irons reported later to Susanna. "He had a wall built around himself a mile high, expecting me to preach at him." The minister had smiled at her. "When I didn't say a word about how he's been behaving, and I didn't mention the Bible—I think it sort of disappointed him. He was loaded for bear, Susanna. Just ready to bawl me out and stalk off. When he saw I wasn't 'on duty,' so to speak, he relaxed and we had a good time."

Now Irons sipped his coffee and looked at Susanna. "Clay's running from God, but Jesus Christ is on his trail."

Susanna had circles under her eyes, and there was a droop to her shoulders. The double difficulty of taking over most of Charlotte's work while the older woman cared for Noah and bearing the burden of Clay's behavior had worn her thin. But when she smiled and said, "I'm glad you've found a way to get close to him, Pastor," there was a light of hope in her fine eyes. "I thank God for sending us a pastor like you, Brother Jerry!"

Irons flushed at the praise and started to protest, but at that moment Clay came in, his eyes bleary and a tremble in his hands. He stopped and stared at them, his eyes defiant. "I told you not to fix breakfast, Mother," he said crossly. "I don't want anything to eat."

Irons said quickly, "Well, I do, Clay. If you don't want anything, you can sit down and listen to me eat." He spoke lightly and began at once to eat the scrambled eggs and fried ham that Susanna set before him. As Irons had guessed, once Clay had made himself obnoxious—and when he saw that nobody was going to argue with him—he sat down and ate.

Susanna stood beside her son, saying, "Clay, you look like you've got a fever."

"I'm all right," he said shortly. "Just a cold."

When the two men were finished, Irons said, "Unless you know of a better spot, I thought we'd go over to Branson's Ridge. Buford Yancy got a big buck over there yesterday morning. He said there were plenty more he could have taken."

Clay nodded, muttered, "I don't care," and the two of them left the warmth of the kitchen. Taking care that Clay did not see, Irons winked at Susanna, and she smiled slightly in return.

Clay saddled a long-legged bay, and the two of them rode out of the stable. The air was chill and the horses were both spirited, so for the first mile they rode along at a gallop. Then they pulled down to a slower pace when they turned off the main road. Clay said nothing at all, but Irons spoke cheerfully of neutral things—mostly about hunting and horses and dogs.

They rode for an hour, then stopped at a rough house set

at the edge of a thick, dense woods. "Have to walk from here, Clay," Irons said. "Looks like none of the Yancys are up yet. I told Buford we'd leave our horses here. He said he'd take care of them if we were late getting back." Then he looked closely at Clay and remarked, "You look washed out, Clay. Why don't we call this off until you feel better?"

"Nothing wrong with me," Clay said stubbornly. In truth, he felt terrible—but he dismounted in silence and waited for Irons.

They put their horses in a ramshackle corral containing a cow and two mules, then plunged into the thick woods. At first the going was fairly easy, but soon the heavy trees seemed to close about them, slowing them down. They were both gasping for breath two hours later when Jeremiah pulled up, saying, "Here's the creek. I think we can pick up something here. Why don't you take this stand, and I'll go on down a quarter?"

"All right."

Clay watched as Irons faded away into the darkness, wondering how the man moved so quietly over dry leaves and dead branches. Then he moved to a large oak, put his back against it, and waited. The ebony sky was beginning to turn gray in the east, and half an hour later a rosy glow emanated through the branches of the tree he stood under.

As Clay stood there in the silence that was broken now and then by the scurrying of small animals or the soft cry of a bird awakening, random thoughts came to him. He had been drunk the night before, reeling up the stairs and falling into bed without removing his clothes. Flashing bits of memory touched his mind briefly, like reflections in a pool broken by ripples of water. Some of them were from other nights spent in the fleshpots of Richmond—the sound of a woman's voice enticing him, the clink of glasses in a bar, the crash of a chair thrown in a fight.

But there were other memories, too. . .memories that he hated even worse. Memories of Melanie. Her face seemed to flash before his eyes, the way she had appeared to him once when he had brought her a huge bouquet of daisies—eyes bright and lips parted with delight. He shut his eyes quickly, giving his shoulders an angry shake. But he could not blot the images out for long. That was why he had sought oblivion in a bottle for the past two months. That, and his resentment and bitterness against his cousin Gideon.

Time and again he had tried to pull himself up, ashamed that he had no more control. But the bitterness was a drug, no less potent or addictive than the rotgut he was drinking. Even as the dawn spread faint ruby gleams over the small creek that murmured a few feet away, he struggled again to cast the envy of Gideon away, but with no success. It ate at him like lye, and nothing seemed to make it more bearable.

Grandfather is dying, he thought, staring at the creek without seeing it. *My parents are worried sick about me. All I do is go around mean as a yard dog looking for somebody to bite!*

He glanced down the creek toward where he supposed Irons was stationed. *The preacher knows better than to say anything, but if he only knew the truth. . .that nobody hates those nights in Richmond worse than I do! But I can't quit!*

Suddenly a buck stepped out from behind a huge oak on the far side of the creek, his head held high and his ears working. As always at such a time, Clay's breathing seemed to stop as if a huge arm had tightened around his chest. He did not even blink as the buck stood there, suspicious, needing only a single movement to send him back into the woods. Time stopped for

Clay; the very creek seemed to pause as the deer waited, and the breeze in the tops of the branches of the tree Clay stood under seemed to stop as if the world held its breath.

Then the deer took a step, halted, listened again—and walked delicately to the edge of the brook. He dipped his head, and Clay, waiting for such a movement, lifted his gun and pulled the trigger. The explosion seemed to rock the world, and the deer leaped sideways in a tremendous jump that carried him to the edge of the trees.

But Clay's bullet was in its heart. All of the animal's actions were sheer reflex, and he dropped down lifelessly.

Clay gave a yell, dropped his gun, and plunged toward the creek, pulling his knife from his belt. He had no control at such times and, in fact, did not want to control the emotion that welled up inside him. He reached the creek, took two giant strides, his heart beating madly—and then his foot went into a crevice by the brook's edge and he fell headlong into the cold water.

A cry of pain was wrenched from him, for the hole was not soft dirt but solid rock, formed by large stones that had been brought together by the action of the water.

A shock of ragged pain flashed through Clay, for his full weight had been thrown against his ankle, which was held as in a vise by the stones. He pulled himself up, pulling his foot free as he rolled over. But when he looked down, he saw that the foot was bent at an unnatural angle—and the pain was like a knife.

Sitting there with the cold waters of the creek soaking him, he held his ankle, clenching his teeth against the waves of pure pain that scared him. It was so great, that pain, that for a few moments he could not even pull himself out of the cold water.

Then he tried to crawl, and a cry of pain escaped his lips.

"Clay! You get one?"

Irons's voice seemed to come faintly from far away, and it was all Clay could do to cry out, "Irons! Help me!"

He lay there on the bank, trying not to move the leg. Soon he heard Irons call out, "Clay? Where are you?"

"Over here!"

Then Irons was there, bending over him. "You didn't shoot your foot?" he asked in alarm.

"No—but I think I broke my ankle."

Irons began at once testing the leg with strong hands. "May be broken. But maybe not. I've seen some ankles twisted as bad as that without a break." Then he shook his head. "Got to get you out of here, Clay."

"I can walk if you'll let me lean on you, Preacher."

Irons looked doubtful, and when he had gotten Clay to a standing position, the first step brought a sharp grunt of pain from Clay's lips. "This won't do!" Irons protested. He helped Clay away from the stony creek bed and let him down on the soft earth. Standing up, he said, "I can't carry you, so you'll have to wait while I go for help."

"I'll be all right," Clay grunted. He cursed and slapped the ground with his palm. "What a stupid thing to do!"

"We all take falls, Clay," Irons said. He stripped off his coat and handed it to the injured man. "I'll build you up a fire." He quickly gathered a supply of deadwood from a fallen tree, kindled a fire, and got it burning.

"Let's dry your clothes out," Irons said. "It'll take me a few hours to get back here with help. Won't do that cold of yours any good to stay wet."

"No, I'll be all right."

Irons looked at him doubtfully, but Clay's stubborn face told him there was no use in arguing the point. He turned and left at a fast trot, disappearing into the brush like an Indian. Clay looked after him, then picked up a rock and threw it at the creek angrily. Carefully he settled back and began to wait.

And it was a long wait, made worse by the discomfort of his wet clothes and the pain of his injured leg. As the hours passed by, Clay was able to get the wood the preacher had pulled close without much effort, but soon he began to shake with a chill. Painfully he dragged the limbs to the fire, but no matter how close he tried to get to it, the chill seemed to grow worse.

Finally he used the last of the wood, and when that burned down to a blackened pile of ashes, he drew his coat around him and tried to sleep. He did doze off from time to time, but the chills became so violent they woke him up.

Finally the sound of voices came to him, and he opened his eyes to see Irons and another man coming down the side of the creek bank leading a mule. "Clay?" Irons called out. "Are you all right?"

Clay sat up and tried without success to keep his voice steady. "All right," he mumbled and was shocked at how feeble the answer was that came out of his mouth. As Irons came to where he sat, he tried to grin. "Had a little nap while I was waiting."

The preacher looked at him with alarm in his eyes, then shook his head. "We had to follow the creek. Woods were too thick to get the mule through." Then he turned, saying, "Buford, bring the mule up." As the man came up, he added, "This is Buford Yancy, Clay."

Yancy was a tall, thin man with greenish eyes, tow-colored hair, and a freckled complexion. He nodded slightly, saying only,

"Howdy." But his hands were strong as he and the minister helped Clay to mount the mule. When Clay was set, he took the hackamore and turned the animal, speaking to him in a flat voice. As they moved along the broken stones of the creek, Irons said, "Should have made you dry those clothes out, Clay. Didn't do you any good lying around wet all morning."

"I'll be all right when I get out of the woods," Clay said.

But by the time they got to the Yancy cabin, he was weaker than he thought possible. He staggered when he slipped down from the high back of the mule, and he heard Yancy say, "He can't ride that horse, Preacher."

Clay tried to protest that he could, but his head was swimming. Then he felt the two men, one on each side, guiding him across the yard, and they practically carried him up the steps.

"Mattie!" Yancy called out. "Git the bed ready for Mr. Rocklin."

Clay's vision faded as he went into the cabin, and he was lowered by the two men onto a rough bed. The mattress was rough cloth stuffed with corn shucks that rustled, but it felt better to him than the thick, fluffy feather bed he slept in each night.

"Be. . .all right," he mumbled, his tongue feeling thick and clumsy. "Jus' need to rest. . ."

The rustling of the shucks under him grew faint, and a soft blackness seemed to wrap him, like a warm ebony blanket. He felt secure as the sound of voices came to him from far away, like the faint cry of birds deep in the woods at evening.

Sometimes he was aware of light, but it was a watery sort of light, as he had seen when looking upward while swimming beneath the surface of the lake. The sounds, too, were muffled, as though he were deep underground in a warm cave sheltered far off from the harsh sounds of the world. Sometimes he would awake, and someone would always be beside him. Once he saw his mother, her face surrounded by an amber corona of light. She spoke to him, and he tried to speak back, but he was too tired. Hands would touch him, and the coolness that came to his brow and body was like balm.

Then, all at once, he opened his eyes and for one moment the room seemed fuzzy and out of focus. Then it changed, becoming clear and sharp. A young girl's face filled his field of vision. She had hair so black that it glistened in the lamplight like a crow's wing, and eyes that were large, almond-shaped, and of a peculiar greenish color.

"Hello," the child said, and she studied him so carefully that he thought she must be older than she appeared.

Clay tried to get up but found that his arms seemed too weak to hold him. Even so, the fever that had burned in him was gone. He licked his dry lips and whispered, "Water. . ."

The girl rose at once, picked up a glass from a table, and poured it full of water. Clay took it and drank thirstily, spilling some on his bare chest.

"Better not drink too much," the girl said. She picked up a cloth from the chair she'd been sitting in and, in a gesture much older than her years, reached over and mopped the water from his chest.

Clay blinked at her, then asked, "What's your name?"

"Melora Yancy," she said. "I've been helping take care of you."

"How old are you, Melora?"

"I'm six."

Clay peered at her, then ran a hand across his cheek, feeling a heavy growth of beard. He felt clearheaded but weak. "How long have I been here, Melora?" he asked.

"'Bout three days. Your ma, she was here right after you come. She brung the doctor with her."

Clay sat up carefully, noting that he wore only the bottom of a pair of underwear. Hand me my pants, will you, Melora?"

"You better wait, Mister Clay," she said quickly. "Doctor said for you not to rush nothin'." Then she said, "I'll bet you're hungry."

At her words, he was struck with a stab of hunger. "I sure am!"

"I'll feed you." She disappeared, and he managed to sit up in bed. His ankle was heavily bandaged, and when he tried to move it, he was pleased to find that though it was painful, it was not broken as he had feared. Carefully he got to his feet, but the room swayed in an alarming fashion, and he sat down abruptly, grabbing the side of the bed for support.

Melora came in with a plate, followed by a woman who had a cup in her hand. "You feelin' better, I see." She was obviously the mother of the girl, for she had the same dark hair and features. "You let Melora feed you, and I'll send my man to tell your folks you're all right."

"Hate to bother you, Mrs. Yancy."

Melora came close and handed him the bowl of stew, and he took a quick bite. It was rich and nourishing, and as he gobbled it down, the woman told him of the last few days.

"The preacher came back with the doctor, and he bound your ankle up," she said. "But you was so sick he was afraid to move you. He axed could we set with you until the fever broke, and we did. Your ma, she's been here, and the preacher, too."

"I'm in your debt, Mrs. Yancy."

"Well, Melora here, she stayed with you most of the time.

Fed you when you wuz awake and kept the cool cloths on you when the fever wuz burning." She gave Melora a fond glance, adding with a smile, "Reckon she's jest a natural-born nurse. Patches up every stray kitten and varmint that come on the place."

Clay suddenly grinned and stopped eating long enough to say, "Well, I fit in that category, I guess."

"Oh—I didn't mean you wuz a varmint, Mr. Rocklin!" Mrs. Yancy said in alarm.

"Been called worse than that," Clay said. After the woman left to get her husband, he said, "Melora, I'm going to give you all my business when I get sick."

Melora was very serious and said at once, "You kin have some of my guinea eggs for supper. I'll cook them for you myself."

He ate all the stew, then at once grew very sleepy. Melora pushed him down, then pulled the rough coverlet up, saying, "You sleep some more, Mister Clay."

When he woke up later, he felt stronger, and Melora fulfilled her promise by cooking him six guinea eggs, which he wolfed down. After he ate, she sat down and said, "I guess your ma will be comin' to git you, won't she?"

"I guess so."

Melora said wistfully, "I wisht you could stay awhile, Mister Clay. It's been nice takin' care of you."

Clay reached over and took her hand. "Tell you what, Melora, I'll come back and see you after I get well."

"Oh, you won't either!"

"Promise! And I'll bring you a present. How about a new dress?"

Melora stared at him wide-eyed, then shook her head. "I'd rather have a book."

Her request took him aback, and he asked tentatively, "Well, what kind of book?"

"One with knights in it, and dragons."

Clay was amused. "I think I've got a few of those myself. My mother never throws anything away. Seems like there's a box with all sorts of books I had when I was about your age. I'll pick out the best one and bring it to you."

Her strangely colored eyes glowed, and she hugged herself tightly. For the next hour she sat there talking to him. Clay had never been particularly drawn to children, but this girl's mind fascinated him. He discovered that her primitive world of cabin and field was small compared to the glittering world inside her small head. She told him tales that she had made up, composed of fragments of stories she had heard from her mother and from one book that contained a few romances—but mostly they were of her own imaginings.

Clay sat there for most of the morning, watching her small face as it glowed with excitement. He read to her out of the one book she possessed, then told some tall tales of his own. When his mother came in accompanied by Jeremiah Irons late that afternoon, he put his hand on Melora's shoulder, saying, "I don't know as I want to leave. My nursing has been so good here, I don't think I can expect as good at home."

Susanna was relieved to see that Clay's eyes were clear, for the doctor had feared pneumonia. She took a deep breath, then said, "Melora, thank you so much for taking such good care of my son. I'm sure God will reward you for it."

Clay walked out of the cabin and, finding Buford Yancy and his wife there with their other children, walked over and offered his hand. "Sorry to have forced myself on you two," he said, taking the man's hard hand. "I'm grateful to you all."

Buford Yancy nodded, saying, "Glad to be of help, Mr. Rocklin." His wife smiled nervously, and Melora came up to say, "Don't forget what we talked about, Mister Clay."

Clay stooped down and gave her a swift kiss on the cheek. "I sure won't! Be back soon as I can!"

As they rode back to Gracefield, Clay said, "That's some child, that Melora. Took care of me like she was a woman grown."

"What was she talking about when we left?"

"I promised to give her a book. Is that box still in the attic someplace, the one with the books all of us read when we were kids?"

"Yes. I'll get it for you as soon as you're able to go back." She hesitated, then said, "The wedding is next week. I don't know if you'll be well enough to go by then."

Clay said nothing to that, but he knew she was offering him an excuse to miss the event. That was not to be the case. He grew well rapidly, and when the day of the wedding arrived, he was there.

It was a big wedding, held in the Bentons' church in Richmond on Saturday morning. Clay felt like a fool, and his face was pale as he walked in with his family, but he had steeled himself for the affair. He did it so well that later he could remember little of the ceremony. He remembered going by to congratulate the couple, but it was a mechanical sort of thing. He shook Gideon's hand and even kissed the cheek of the bride, but the stares of the onlookers kept him stiff and unthinking.

"Thank you for coming, Clay," was all that Gideon said, and Melanie was too tense even to say that much.

As quickly as he could, Clay made his escape, avoiding

the reception. As he rode out, Bushrod Aimes said to Taylor Dewitt, "Well, there goes Clay to get drunk. Bet it'll be a stem-winder this time!"

Clay, however, rode straight home and changed his formal attire for more simple dress. He caught up a large bundle that was in his room and went at once to his horse. Balancing the bulky package on the saddle horn, he rode along the road, thinking of the wedding and wondering how he'd ever be able to deal with the thing. His accident had brought some sort of catharsis to the bitterness that had driven him, but as he rode toward the backwoods, he knew that nothing had really changed. He was like a man who had caught a wild beast in some sort of trap and was holding the door for his life. He feared that if he relaxed for one instant, the wildness that had raged in him would burst out.

The air was keen, and he forced everything from his mind as he drew near to the Yancy place. The one thing that had sustained him for the past week had been the pleasure he had found in going through the old books he had read as a child. His parents had been lavish with books, and Clay rediscovered some of the pleasures he had known in the stories of Washington Irving. He read *The Legend of Sleepy Hollow* and *Rip Van Winkle*, and he knew that they would be a delight to Melora. He also found a copy of *Gulliver's Travels*, with gorgeous illustrations of the little people in the land of Lilliput and the big people in Brobdingnag. He included this book, knowing that though Melora would not understand the text for some time, she would devour the pictures. The same was true of *Pilgrim's Progress*, which he reread from beginning to end in one day's sitting. It brought back the days when his mother would gather them all at the end of the day and read of Christian and Faithful and how they came to the Celestial City.

He had sorted out at least twenty books and packed them into a box, and now as he drew up in front of the Yancy cabin, Melora came sailing out the front door, shadowed by the other children. She didn't speak, but her eyes were bright as diamonds, and when he stooped down to kiss her, she threw both arms around his neck and held on with all her might.

"Told you I'd come back, didn't I?" Clay straightened up, and when he saw the Yancys come to stand on the porch, he grinned. "Came to settle my bill with my favorite nurse."

It was a fine hour, taking the books out one by one and showing them to the family. Buford stood with his back against the wall, his wife beside him, and though neither of them said much except to exclaim over one of the books now and then, there was a brightness in their expressions. They led a hard life, eking a living out of the earth; to see the pleasure on Melora's face was meat and drink to them.

When all the books were laid out on the table, Clay turned to the other children and asked, "Do you all have birthdays?"

Royal, age eight, stared at him as though he were dim-witted. " *'Course* we got birthdays!"

Clay laughed and said, "Come with me." He led them outside and took some small packages out of his saddlebag. "Happy birthday, all of you," he said, and he winked at Buford as they all tore into the presents.

"Mighty nice of you, Mr. Rocklin," Buford said, nodding.

Clay cocked his head, then reached into the saddlebag, coming out with something he handed to Yancy, and he said, "Happy birthday to you, too, Buford."

Yancy stared down at the revolver in the calfskin holster.

Slowly he pulled it out and held it in one hand. It was one of the new Colt .36 pistols, with a five-shot cylinder. They were rare as yet, and frightfully expensive. Buford Yancy lifted his eyes but could not say a word, for he well knew that he would never in years of work have earned enough spare cash for such a weapon. Finally he said, "I thank you, Mr. Rocklin."

Clay laughed it off, saying, "Small enough gift for saving my worthless hide, Buford. Now this is for you, Mattie."

Digging down into the other saddlebag, he pulled a bulky package out and handed it to the startled Mrs. Yancy. Winking at Buford as Mattie carefully untied the string and opened the package, Clay said, "Probably won't be worth a dime to you. I picked it out myself."

Mattie stared down at the folds of rich silk, green and crimson, in the package. She touched some of the buttons that Clay had gotten the clerk to include, then said without looking up, "It's right nice, Mr. Clay."

Clay wanted to ease the moment and said quickly, "Well, Mattie, if you'll make me a glass of that sassafras tea you do so well, Buford and I will go try out this new pistol. Then, Melora, you can show me how well you can read some of those books."

It was a fine day, and as Clay rode home at dusk, he wished that his own life were as simple and uncomplicated as that of Buford Yancy. But when he lay down on his bed late that night, he felt the magic of the afternoon slipping away. And as he tossed on the bed, he was plagued with bad dreams. Finally he got up and went to the window to stare out. The night was cloudy, and the oaks, stripped of most of their greenery, lifted clawlike branches to the dark skies. A rising wind keened around the house, then came to stir the tree outside his window. The branches clawed at the house and seemed to be trying to get at the sleepers inside. The moon slipped from behind a cloud, touched the tops of the trees with ghostly silver, then was covered as ragged clouds moved to cloak its brightness.

Clay stared out at the darkness for a long while, thinking of what might come. Finally he took a deep breath and went back to lie down on his bed—but he found no sleep that night. He lay there until dawn, and when the first rays of the morning touched his window, he rose and dressed with a heaviness of mind and spirit, finally going out to meet the day.

CHAPTER 6

A VISIT TO WASHINGTON

The snowflakes that fell on Washington on Election Eve of 1840 were heavy and larger than dimes. They fell on the Potomac so thickly that the river was like a moving white highway. By noon the streets were carpeted with a blanket six inches deep. The snow glittered like diamonds as Gid and Melanie sat in a carriage that carried them across town.

"It's beautiful, Gid!" Melanie exclaimed, taking in the glistening spires of churches that flashed in the sunlight. "Even the ugly old buildings look like palaces!"

"Too bad we can't have Washington covered with snow all the time," Gid answered. He put his arm around her and gave a hearty squeeze. When she looked up at him, he said, "I enjoyed my honeymoon."

A flush rose to color Melanie's cheeks, but she lifted her lips for a kiss, then pulled him close, whispering, "I—I did, too!"

"Why, you shameless creature!" Gid laughed. "Weren't you taught that women are supposed to be passive and free from passion?"

Melanie pushed him away, laughter edging her voice as she said, "I'll try to be more formal in the future, Mr. Rocklin."

"Don't you do it! Stay just the way you are, Mellie," he said, smiling at her. Then he looked down the street. The horse was forging his way steadily along, and the driver was carefully keeping his eyes turned to the front. "There's the house," Gid said, then frowned and shook his head. "I wish we could have our own place here, but it wouldn't make sense since we'll soon be at our first station."

"I don't mind, Gid," Melanie said quickly. Their honeymoon had been brief, and it would not have been feasible for them to get quarters. Gideon had to return to West Point in a few days, and there was plenty of room at the Rocklin home, a large brownstone in the downtown area.

They drew up in front of the house, and the driver got down to retrieve their luggage. As Gid helped Melanie down, the front door opened, and Pompey, the Rocklins' butler, came down the snow-covered steps. He was a lanky, limber man with skin the color of chocolate and a pair of merry brown eyes. "I been 'spectin' you, Mistuh Gideon," he said happily, nodding his head. "Welcome home, Miz Rocklin!"

It gave Melanie a queer pleasure to be called by her new name, and she smiled warmly, saying, "Thank you, Pompey. But I think there'll be one too many ladies named Rocklin, so you can call me Miss Melanie."

"Yes, ma'am, I will certainly do so! Now—" Taking the bags from the driver, he said, "I got a big fire in the parlor, so you two go on in. Delilah will be bringing you something hot to drink right away!"

A few minutes later, the pair were sitting on an upholstered sofa in front of a blazing fire, drinking hot chocolate brought to them by Pompey's wife, Delilah. The beverage was almost the same color as the plump servant who beamed on them as they both exclaimed that it was the best chocolate they'd ever had.

"We'll have the good silver and the Dresden china tonight, Delilah," Gideon's mother said. "And be sure there's plenty of food for our guests." When Delilah left, she smiled, adding, "I hope you don't mind, but I asked a few people for dinner tonight." The ivory-colored dress she wore was exquisitely tailored so that her extra pounds were not evident. Her hair was carefully and tastefully done, framing her round face in an attractive fashion.

"I warned Mellie we'd have company," Gideon said, grinning at his wife. What he'd actually said was, "Brace yourself, Mellie. My mother loves to give dinners. I think she'd give a dinner to celebrate the end of the world!" But now he went over to his mother and gave her a hug. "Who are we having tonight? Can't be a politician. They'll all be drunk."

"Oh, don't be silly, Gideon!"

"Fact. The losers because they lost, and the winners because they won."

"You know it'll take at least four or five days to get the votes counted," his mother chided. Then she turned to her new daughter-in-law, saying, "I know you're tired, Melanie, but I did want you to meet a few people. Amos is so excited, Gideon," she said quickly. "You've heard of Charles Finney?"

"The famous evangelist? Of course I have. Don't tell me he's going to be here?"

"Yes! He's not speaking as much as he used to, now that he's teaching at the college in Oberlin. But he came to Washington just to preach at our church, and Amos persuaded him to have dinner with us."

"He's a pretty stout character, from what I hear," Gideon said cautiously.

"Oh yes, indeed!" Mrs. Rocklin agreed, her brown eyes alive with excitement. "I don't think you'll be bored." Then she glanced at Melanie with a sly smile. "There'll be a surprise for you at dinner, my dear! I think you'll like it very much."

She refused to say more and left at once to attend to the details. "I wonder what she's got cooked up for you, Mellie?" Gid mused. He put his back toward the fire, soaking up the warmth, and shook his head. "I told you how it would be. Mother is kind, but she lives from one party to the next. I think she's the most sociable person I've ever known." He came over and sat down beside his wife. "If you get tired of all her parties, we'll get you a place of your own until I graduate."

"Oh no, Gid!" Melanie took his hands and held them. "I'll enjoy meeting your friends. And after all, it'll be good training for me, won't it? I mean, we'll always be moving from post to post, and an officer's wife has to know how to handle people with tact, doesn't she?"

"Well, Mother can get pretty bossy," Gid said but kissed her and grinned. "Do you good to learn how to hold your own with a strong personality." A thought came to him, and he added, "I'm looking forward to dinner. From what I hear of Rev. Finney, he's a potent sort of clergyman. Wouldn't put it past him to have us all on our knees."

"Oh, Gid! Don't be silly!"

They went upstairs and rested. Later in the afternoon they drove around the city, Gideon pointing out the sites of interest. They returned to the house just in time to dress for dinner. Melanie wore a powder blue dress, and Gid wore a dark blue suit. As she straightened his tie, he said, "Wonder what Mother's surprise is. Hope it's not something to do with more parties. I don't intend to waste all the time I've got left at boring dinners."

But Mrs. Rocklin met them at the foot of the stairs with a triumphant light in her eyes. "Now you step into the library, both of you."

Gid allowed Melanie to go first and heard her gasp, "Ellen!" in surprise. He stepped into the large high-ceilinged room in time to see Ellen Benton being embraced by Melanie.

"There!" Mrs. Rocklin cried. "I knew you'd be glad to see your cousin, Melanie!" Then she turned to her son, and there was a slight hesitation in her manner. "Gideon, look who came to escort Ellen from Richmond."

"Hello, Gid." Gideon turned to his left, shocked to see Clay standing with his back to the wall. There was a sardonic light in Clay's dark eyes, and he looked thinner.

"Clay!" Gideon said quickly, going at once to shake his hand. "By George, I'm glad to see you." That was the truth, for bad reports had come from Gracefield of Clay's behavior. *And they were not false*, Gid decided as he clapped his cousin on the back. The unmistakable signs of excess marred his handsome face, and he looked thin and drawn. But Gideon was smiling. "Can't tell you how glad I am that you've come!"

Melanie had disengaged herself from Ellen and came at once to greet Clay. Putting out her hand, she smiled nervously, saying, "Yes, it is good to see you, Clay. I hope you can stay for a while?"

"I'm just a delivery boy," Clay said with a shrug. "Your father didn't want Ellen to make the trip to Washington alone and asked me to escort her." There was no ease in his voice, and it was obvious to all of them that he was stiff in his greeting to Melanie.

"I engineered the whole thing, I'm afraid," Mrs. Rocklin spoke up. "I thought it might be good for Ellen to spend some time in Washington with you, Melanie. When Gideon goes back to West Point, it'll be lonely with just us old folks here."

Ellen said, "It was good of you to invite me, Mrs. Rocklin." She looked very stylish in a green woolen dress that showed her figure to good advantage. She stepped close to Clay and lightly put her hand on his arm, adding, "Of course, I couldn't have come if Clay hadn't offered to bring me."

There was, Gid saw, something possessive in Ellen's manner. He didn't know the young woman well, but the thought came to his mind that James Benton should have had better judgment than to trust Clay on such a mission. But he said only, "Well, now we can have some fun! I've got two days, and we can turn this town on its ear before I have to go back."

At that moment a knock at the door sounded, and Mrs. Rocklin said with some agitation, "That must be Laura and Amos with Rev. Finney. I'll go let them in myself."

Gideon winked at Clay, a wry light in his eyes. "Did you know who our dinner guests are, Clay?"

"No."

"The evangelist Charles Finney. He's pretty outspoken on the slavery issue, and he's made an ardent disciple of my brother-in-law. That's my mother for you, I'm afraid," he added, shaking his head in mock despair. "She brings in Clay Rocklin, a dyed-in-the-wool Southern planter, to have dinner with two abolitionists!"

Clay suddenly grinned. "Well, I hope we don't destroy each other, Gid."

"Just nod quietly and grunt every once in a while, Clay," Gid urged. "That's all I ever do at Mother's dinners. Makes life easier."

They waited somewhat awkwardly, but soon Mrs. Rocklin came in, shepherding her guests. She introduced Ellen to the

Steeles, then said, "This is Rev. Charles Finney."

Finney was the most famous preacher in America, with the possible exception of Rev. Beecher of Boston. He was a tall man, spare of form and with the most commanding eyes a man could possess—a pale blue that seemed to burn with energy. He listened to the names, then spoke in a firm but restrained voice, seeming rather less than his reputation. He was a lawyer by profession, who had undergone a dramatic conversion to belief in Jesus Christ. At once he had begun to preach, and his meetings had grown so large that few buildings could hold the crowds that came to hear him. He was not, however, universally admired—many traditional ministers deplored some of his practices.

The group went to dinner, and during the meal Stephen asked Finney about the opposition he had encountered. "Rev. Finney, I hear your methods have considerable opposition from your fellow ministers, but I don't know exactly what they oppose in them. They call them 'New Measures,' I understand."

Finney said evenly, "Why, some people call them that, Mr. Rocklin, mostly those who oppose them." He began to speak of his ministry, and it was obvious that he was not a ranting preacher, for he spoke fluently and well. Clay, who was not enamored of preachers as a breed, was impressed as the man said, "I pray for people by name in the service. After the sermon is over, I ask those who feel a hunger for God to come to the Anxious Seat."

"The Anxious Seat?" Gideon asked, puzzled. "What is that?"

"Why, just a chair or bench," Finney replied. "When God begins to work in a sinner's heart, there will be anxiety. It's God's way of drawing sinners to Himself."

"What happens when people go to—to the Anxious Seat, Rev. Finney?"

Finney gave a sudden smile, which made him look much younger. "Usually nothing dramatic, Mr. Rocklin," he said. "A minister or a believer will pray for him and read him some of the Bible. And then one of two things will happen—either he will repent and be converted, or else he will run away from God."

"Your critics mention that there's often what they call 'unseemly behavior' in your meetings, don't they?" Mrs. Rocklin asked.

"That is not a new charge, Mrs. Rocklin," Finney said. "Even in the ministry of Jesus, it was made. When the Savior was passing by and blind Bartimaeus began crying out very loudly for help, the crowd told him to be quiet, that his behavior was 'unseemly,' as we might put it. Every time a move of God comes to men, it is always the same. When John Wesley came and preached in the fields, men and women often were struck down by the power of God. The same was true with George Whitefield and Jonathan Edwards in our country. There are always those enemies of the cross to cry out that such things are not dignified." Finney's eyes burned, and his voice rose as he said, "Would it be better to remain dignified and let sinners go to hell? No! There have been excesses, certainly, but when God moves upon men, there will be brokenness—and that brokenness will often be displeasing to those who must have their religion in orderly rituals!"

It was a strange dinner, the strangest the Rocklins had ever attended. Finney had one burning interest, the gospel, and there was such power in the man that the other guests sat spellbound, listening to his words.

Dinner was over when Amos Steele asked, "Have you heard about Rev. Finney's innovation at Oberlin?"

"What is that, sir?" Gideon asked.

"He has opened the doors to females," Steele said proudly.

"The first college in America to do so!"

There was much interest in this, and Finney explained that in Christ there is "neither male nor female," so he was assured that both men and women were entitled to college training.

Clay suddenly asked, "Doesn't the Bible say there is 'neither bond nor free,' Reverend?"

Finney gave Clay a searching look. "You speak of the Negro race?"

"Yes, sir. Would you welcome them to your college?"

A sudden shock of silence filled the room, but Finney didn't hesitate. "The day will come in this country when we will see dark-skinned men and women in colleges."

"Not in the South!"

Amos said hotly, "The Negroes are human beings, Clay!"

Instantly Stephen said, "This would not be a good time to debate the slavery issue, I think."

Rev. Finney agreed. "No, but the time is coming when the question will have to be dealt with on a national level." Then he leaned forward, and a gentle light came into his stern eyes. He addressed Clay in a voice that was kind indeed. "Mr. Rocklin, no man has the wisdom to know how this matter should be handled, so I will not try to impose my political view on you, and certainly not my feeling about slavery. All I can say is that the first duty of all of us is to make our peace with God. And that can only be done through the blood of Jesus Christ."

Clay was prepared for an attack from the minister, so the simple words disarmed him. He flushed, nodded, and said merely, "You are certainly right about that, Reverend."

Later, when Gideon and Melanie were alone, preparing for bed, they spoke of Clay.

"He's been drinking a lot," Gideon said. "You can see it in his face."

Melanie gave him a quick glance, then said, "Do you think he hates us, Gid? I couldn't tell much about him. He was always so lively. There's a sadness in him now."

"Well, he lost you, Mellie. That's enough to make a man sad." Gid paused, then said slowly, "I'm surprised that your father let him bring Ellen here."

"Ellen has a way with Father. She can wheedle him into doing what she wants."

"Well, what she wants now is Clay." Gid's face was heavy, and he shook his head. "I see real trouble there for her. I don't think Clay will be interested in women for a long time."

Melanie nodded reluctantly, but there was a troubled frown on her face. "I suppose you're right, Gid—but she does have a way with men!"

CHAPTER 7

THE WRONG BRIDE

Clay Rocklin had never planned to stay in Washington for any longer than it took to deliver Ellen, but for some obscure reason not clear even to himself, he lingered in the city. He asked himself many times why he had come in the first place, for he was honest enough to admit he had not come simply to escort Ellen. She was well able to make the short journey alone, or her uncle could have found someone else to accompany her if he had refused the task.

He had no one to talk to, at least not about what was going on inside him. Except for Ellen, that is. The two of them had been thrown together much by necessity, and she had kept him busy seeing the city and attending the nightly parties that went on in his aunt Ruth's circle. It was due to Ellen that he stayed in the city, for she kept him busy, and Washington was more interesting than Gracefield in the winter. The two of them attended the theater more than once, and it was on the way home from an evening at the Ford Theater that she finally succeeded in getting him to speak some of the thoughts that had been bottled up inside.

The snow was still on the streets, and the air was biting cold as they drove through the silent streets late that night. A clock from the large Presbyterian church on Pennsylvania Avenue boomed out the hour as they passed. The sound was sudden, breaking the sibilant noise of the runners of the sleigh—and Ellen suddenly gave a start, grabbing at his arm.

"It's midnight, Clay!" she said, counting the strokes, then gave his arm a squeeze. "We'll be locked out."

Clay was feeling more relaxed than he had since coming to Washington, and the idea of having to wake his uncle and aunt amused him. "They might turn us away," he answered. "We'd have to spend the whole night in this sleigh." They had gone to a restaurant after the performance, eaten a late supper, then afterward sat there talking about the play. Clay drank liberally, and Ellen not a great deal less, so that when they finally left the restaurant, they were both giggling with their attempts to climb into the sleigh.

The sharp air numbed their faces but did little to sober them up. Suddenly Ellen moved closer to him, laughing up into his face. "I don't care if they lock us out," she declared. "We could sleep in the sleigh."

"Be mighty cold," Clay answered. They were passing under a streetlight, and the golden gleam of the lamp made Ellen look bewitching. Her eyes were half-lidded, which made them look sultry, and the rich swell of her full lower lip gave a sensuous cast to her face. He was acutely conscious of the pressure of her body as she leaned against him, and he thought again of what an attractive woman she was.

Without thinking about it, he suddenly leaned forward and kissed her. The alcohol had loosened them both, and she put her hand behind his head, drawing him closer. Her lips, softer than feathers, had a pressure of their own, and he drew her closer, savoring the kiss.

Finally they parted, and he said, "You're what a man needs, Ellen."

She did not withdraw fully but kept close beside him. "I know what it means to be disappointed, Clay," she said, her eyes dropping to study her hands. The kiss was not her first, for she had been pursued by many men, but it had shaken her. She had been drawn to Clay from the time she'd first seen him, and although she knew that he was a man who knew women well, she thought no less of him for that.

She didn't elaborate on her statement, knowing well that men didn't want to hear about the troubles of a woman. "You've had a bad time," she said instead. "But it won't last forever. Things change."

Clay studied her curiously. There was some sort of knowledge in her that most women lacked, and it appealed to him. He knew little about her past, save that there was some sort of tragedy concerning her parents. Whatever it was, it seemed to have given her a toughness, which he admired. Now he said, "I thought love was supposed to be eternal. That's what all the poets say."

Ellen stirred against him, turning her face to look at him. A smile curved the edges of her lips upward. "All the poets who write about love are men," she said. "And they really know better. Love is for now, Clay. Poets may write about a love they lost years before, but I'd guess most of them want more than a poem in their bed."

"Now that's speaking right out," Clay said, smiling at her frankness. "So you think love doesn't last?"

"I didn't say that," Ellen said. She thought about it as they moved along the dimly lit streets. The coronas of the streetlamps glowed, but the feeble rays were swallowed up in the darkness, and there was something surrealistic in the sight of the street so busy by day, now deserted. "Love can last," she said, "but it can die, too. Look at your uncle and aunt. They were in love once, I suppose. Now they just live in the same house. I can't imagine them being in love, can you?"

Clay shook his head. "No," he replied slowly. "But we all get old." He said no more for a few blocks, then suddenly began to speak of himself. He was not entirely sober, and the kiss had opened him up to her. "I can't figure out what I'm doing here, Ellen," he said. "I didn't have to come. Mr. Benton could have gotten someone else to bring you to Washington."

"I asked him to get you to bring me," Ellen said suddenly. "I wanted you to come and see Gid and Melanie together." She had thought about telling him this for some time, and now seemed the best time. "I saw what you were doing to yourself, Clay, with all the drinking and carousing. It was destroying you."

"And seeing Gid and Melanie is supposed to cure me?"

Ellen ignored his sardonic tone, saying, "It's better to look at things straight on, Clay. I thought it would be better for you to see them married than to eat your heart out thinking about it. Maybe I was wrong—but I meant well."

Clay thought about what she had said, then nodded. "Maybe you're right, Ellen. It hurts like fury to see them together—but somehow it's not as bad as thinking about it. So thanks for trying. Don't know why you fool with a sorehead like me!"

"Don't you, Clay?" Ellen said, giving him a slight smile. "Well, it's been good for me to have you here. I may be some company for Melanie after Gid leaves, but she doesn't need me now."

"He's going back to the Point day after tomorrow. Guess I'll go back to Richmond then." He sighed heavily, adding, "Not much going on at the farm this time of year."

Ellen had blinked when he announced his intention to leave, but she said only, "We'll have to make the most of our time, then."

❦

Gid and Melanie were too occupied with each other to give much attention to Clay, but on the morning of Gid's departure, they discussed him. Gideon was packing his suitcase, doing it methodically as he did most things, when Melanie came up behind him. Putting her arms around him, she held to him, pressing her face against his wide back.

"Oh, Gid!" she moaned. "I wish you didn't have to go! Or that I could go with you!"

He unclasped her hands, turned, and took her in his arms. His eyes were sober, but he allowed a smile to touch his broad lips. "That would make for an interesting life. Every one of the boys would fall in love with you." He stood there holding her, hating the idea of leaving but trying not to let it show. "You'll have Ellen for company, and it won't be forever."

"Yes, it will!" she pouted. "And Ellen is no substitute for a husband. Besides, she's always with Clay."

"She sure is." He drew back, his eyes thoughtful. "I guess he'll go back to Gracefield, won't he?" Moving away from her, he picked up his shaving equipment from the washstand and placed it in the suitcase, then shut it. "I'm surprised he's stayed this long. I don't think I'd want to do it."

"Do what?"

"Hang around and watch you being married to another man. If you'd chosen Clay, I'd have gotten as far away from you as I could. He's a peculiar fellow, Clay is. I don't really understand him." Then he looked at his watch, saying abruptly, "I've got to go. Don't want to miss my train."

His departure was an event, with the entire family going out to the carriage. His parents bid him a fond good-bye, and all the servants came to wish him well. Finally he shook hands with Clay. "I'm glad you came," he said simply. He wanted to say more, but others were listening, and he could not have said it in any case. "Take care of yourself, Clay," was all that came to him, and he hated the inadequacy of the bare statement. He had tried more than once to put his feelings into words but had not been able to break through the barrier that had risen between him and his cousin. He could not blame Clay, for he doubted he could have handled such a loss as well.

"Good-bye, Ellen," he said, taking her hand. "Take care of Melanie," he said, then got into the sleigh. "Let's go, Pompey!" He hated good-byes and had forbidden anyone to go with him to the station. He was actually relieved when the final words were spoken and the sleigh turned the corner, and he settled down in the seat, his face somber and thoughtful. He forced himself to think of his remaining days at the Point, wishing they were over and he was with Melanie at some distant station. But Gideon Rocklin was a practical man, not given to much wishing, and he left Washington determined to do his best at his job.

❧

For a week after Gid's departure, Clay remained in Washington. Each day he got up determined to leave, for somehow Melanie alone made his loss more bitter than when she had been with Gid. He grew morose and silent, and if it had not been for Ellen, he would have gone home the day after Gid left. But each morning she would meet him with a new plan, something that was taking place in the city that would entertain him. But it actually was something inside of Clay himself that kept him from fleeing Melanie's presence.

Stephen Rocklin pinpointed the young man's problem one evening after Clay had taken Ellen to a party. Melanie had gone to bed early, and he and Ruth were sitting in front of the fireplace. "I wish Clay would go home," he said abruptly, breaking into his wife's account of some problem with one of the servants.

Ruth looked at him in surprise. "Why do you say that?"

"He's mooning around like a lovesick puppy," Stephen answered. "The trouble with Clay is that he's gotten everything he wanted up to now. And that's not good for a man." He got up and went to peer out the window into the darkness. Framed by the window, he looked sturdy and powerful. Finally he turned, saying, "I may have to talk to him about leaving."

"Oh, Stephen, don't do that!" Ruth shook her head quickly, adding, "Clay needs a little time, that's all."

"He needs to get away from here, Ruth. I wish he hadn't come at all."

"Why, I thought you liked Clay."

"I do like him, Ruth. That's why I want him to go. He's not helping himself any hanging around here. He's drinking too much, and he's going to make a fool out of himself if it keeps up."

His words were not intended to be prophetic, but Clay had seen the disapproval in his uncle's face. "I've got to leave, Ellen," he said that night when they returned from the party. "I'm like a ghost at the party."

Ellen said quickly, "Well, not tomorrow. You promised to take me to see the Ethiopian Eccentricity—whatever that is."

She had seen a poster advertising a performance by Alex Carter's Black Face Minstrels and had forced him to agree to take her.

"Well, all right," he agreed, "but I'm catching a train out of here on Tuesday."

Melanie noticed that Ellen was in a strange mood all day Monday. She had none of her usual cheerfulness but seemed to be thinking of something else. "Don't you feel well, Ellen?" she asked as the other woman was getting dressed to go to the minstrel show.

"I'm fine," Ellen answered, but when she left with Clay, Melanie was worried about her. She knew that Clay would be leaving and was astute enough to know that Ellen would miss him. She felt sorry for her cousin but was relieved that Clay was going back to Virginia. The strain had been greater than she had anticipated, especially since Gideon had left. *Clay will be better off at Gracefield,* she said to herself firmly. *And maybe Ellen can see more of him when she goes back after her visit here.*

Ellen was bright and filled with excitement that evening. She carried Clay along with her, making him laugh at her outrageous comments on the minstrel show, which proved to be no better or worse than average. A pair of white artists with cork-blackened features clogged "Old Zip Coon," and the audience broke out into gales of applause. "Misto' Interlocutuh" wagged his preposterous woolly head and flung a series of conundrums to various members of his entourage. Mr. Alex Carter came on to sing, first "Blue Juanita," a long, sentimental ballad, and next a catchy tune called "Buffalo Gals." A pair of real Negroes then executed a very brisk buck-and-wing as a finale, to the evident enjoyment of the audience.

After the show was over, Clay and Ellen went out to eat,

and as usual Clay drank quite a bit. After the supper, he was feeling the effects of the liquor. "I'm drunk, Ellen," he remarked owlishly.

"No, you're just feeling good," she said at once. Then she leaned forward, smiling, to say, "Did you know there's a boxing match tonight?"

"A boxing match? No, I didn't know it."

"Well, there is. It's in a big warehouse down by the river. And we're going to see the match."

Clay laughed at her. "Women don't go to see such things, Ellen!"

"This one does!"

Shaking his head, he argued, "They wouldn't even let you in. No women allowed, I tell you."

"But I'm not going as a woman. Didn't you see the bag I put in the carriage? It's got men's clothing in it. I'm going to change this dress for a suit, put my hair up under a derby, and we'll be two young fellows at the fight!"

Clay stared at her. "You're not serious!"

"You just wait here, Clay Rocklin." Ellen grinned. "Give me half an hour; then meet me at the carriage."

She left at once, and Clay sat at the table, not believing what he had heard. He took several drinks from the bottle; then when the half hour had passed, he got to his feet—somewhat unsteadily—and went to pay the bill. When he got to the carriage, he took one look and laughed out loud.

Ellen had done exactly what she had said and now stood beside the carriage looking for all the world like a young man. "Hello, Clay," she greeted him in the deepest voice she could muster. "Let's go to the fight."

Clay grinned broadly, amused at her audacity. She had done a good job and looked like a young dandy. She had obtained a suit that was somewhat too large and a brown overcoat, so her figure was concealed. Her abundant hair she had managed to cover with a large bowler hat, and the effect was of a rather effeminate young man with large eyes and a smooth complexion.

She climbed into the buggy, saying, "Come on, we'll be late," and Clay got in and took the reins. "I even brought a flask," Ellen said, pulling a leather-covered bottle from her side pocket. "Have a blast, sport!"

Her attempts to emulate a young dandy brought a laugh from Clay. He took a drink, then said, "Here we go!"

The liquor was working on him, and he was delighted by Ellen's strange antics. He only wished that Taylor Dewitt and Tug Ramsey were along for the fun. It took some time to find the warehouse, and he stopped and refilled the flask at a saloon.

"You better keep that hat on," he warned Ellen as they entered the old warehouse. "This is a pretty rough place."

Ellen gave him a dig with her elbow. "Give me a drink, chum," she said roughly. Her eyes were sparkling, and he saw that she was having a fine time. She took a swallow of liquor, then said, "Let's get close to the ring."

Clay had seen many fights and knew what to expect. He thought at first that the coarse language of the spectators would offend Ellen, but she seemed to pay no heed to it. He was also apprehensive that someone would see through her disguise, but fortunately no one did. Clay paid little heed to the fight. By the time it was over, he had finished the flask and was almost too drunk to walk.

Ellen caught at him as he staggered getting into the carriage, and said, "I thought you could hold your liquor better than that, Clay Rocklin!"

The remark offended him, and he said belligerently, "Can drink all I want! Let's go—find a place. Not too late."

The rest of the evening was a blur to Clay. He was aware of going to a bar, then to another, but soon he lost all ability to make decisions. He laughed a great deal, hung on to Ellen for support, but the world began to lose focus.

He became dimly aware that night had gone. The morning sun was up, almost blinding him as they left one saloon, and he knew that he was supposed to do something. But he seemed like a man in a dream, and as he moved from one place to another, guided by Ellen's firm hand, he could not pull his thoughts together. There were some people around, and he spoke to them, but his words didn't make sense—even to him.

Finally he found himself being led into a room, and when the door was closed, the sound was faint and far away. Then he heard Ellen's voice, saying, "All right, Clay. We're here."

He didn't know what that meant, nor did he know where he was, and when her hands touched him, he fell forward. But the fall was never complete, and instead of touching the floor or a bed, he fell endlessly, never stopping until the warm darkness enveloped him.

❦

The darkness rolled back and Clay awoke slowly, sluggishly. A rough blanket was over his face, and he threw it off and lay there with his eyes closed, fighting a fierce headache, trying to think. Shreds of memories floated past his mind—a few snatches of conversations, a quick flash of one moment of the fight, Ellen's laughter as he tried to get into the carriage—but they all jumbled together in a meaningless fashion.

Then another memory came to him, and the abruptness of

it caused him to open his eyes and look around the room wildly. It was a strange room, with one large window through which the sun was filtered by an opaque shade. The wallpaper was white with small red flowers, and there was no furniture in the room except the bed and a washstand.

A hotel room, he thought. Then the memory came back, unmistakable, and turning his head, he saw that the pillow beside him was rumpled and dented.

Ellen!

He threw the covers back and got to his feet, ignoring the pounding at his temples. Moving to the washstand, he poured water into the basin with an unsteady hand, then splashed his face with the cold water. He found his clothing thrown on the floor. He grabbed his clothes and dressed as rapidly as he could, then moved to the mirror and stared into it.

His eyes were bleary, underscored by circles. He had no comb, so he tried to use his fingers to push his wild hair into place. Even as he was engaged in this, the door suddenly opened and he turned to see Ellen enter.

"Why, you're up at last!" she said at once. Her face was pale, and she looked drained. She was wearing the dress she had worn to the minstrel show and was carrying a tray with a white napkin covering the contents.

"Sit down and have some breakfast," she said nervously.

"Don't know if I can keep anything down," he mumbled. He felt as bad as he had ever felt, and worse than the physical misery was the knowledge that he had made a fool of himself. He could not bring himself to look at Ellen. In an attempt to disguise his self-disgust, he sat down on the bed and picked up the cup of coffee from the tray. It was hot and strong, and he muttered, "Thanks, Ellen. This is what I needed."

"Try some of the eggs," she said. "I've already eaten."

Clay picked up a fork and pushed the eggs around listlessly. The situation was abominable, and he wished he had never come to Washington in the first place. The Bentons were old family friends of the Rocklins, and he felt he had betrayed them.

Finally he said, "I've been a fool, Ellen."

She suddenly reached out and caressed his cheek, saying, "I guess we both were pretty carried away. But I'm not sorry."

Clay shook his head. "I took advantage of you. Wish I hadn't done that."

The apology seemed to hang in the air, but she sat down beside him. Putting her arm around him, she squeezed him, saying, "I'm happy, Clay. And you must be happy, too." She drew his head around, and her eyes were intense. "This isn't the way I planned to get married, but we have each other, so it doesn't really matter."

Clay sat there still as a stone, doubting his ears. "Married?" he asked hoarsely.

Ellen looked at him strangely. "Why, yes. Don't you remember?"

Clay shook his head, trying to free it from the cobwebs. His mind was reeling, and he wanted to run out of the room. "Ellen, marriage is a serious thing. What we've done was wrong, but it's not—"

"Clay! We are married!" Ellen rose and moved to pick up her coat. She retrieved a paper from the pocket and handed it to him. "Don't you remember?" She watched as he stared at the paper. "It's our marriage license. I wanted to wait, to have a nice wedding at Gracefield, but you wouldn't listen."

Dimly Clay remembered a trip to some office and an

argument with some official, but it was vague and fuzzy. "But—we can't be married!" he protested. "It takes more time than a single night to get the papers done."

Ellen shook her head. "You bribed him to set the dates back, Clay."

Suddenly Clay came to his feet, despair and confusion on his lean face. "Ellen! We've got to get it annulled!"

Ellen stood before him silently. Her eyes were enormous, and there was a vulnerability in her that seemed to make her smaller. "And do we annul what happened here?" She gestured at the tumbled bed, then quickly came to him. "Clay, I love you. Maybe you don't love me much, but I'll make you forget Melanie!" She began to weep, and suddenly she was in his arms.

Clay held her, feeling her grief, and for the next hour they talked. He tried to tell her that it would never work—but she clung to him, begging him not to leave her. The guilt that gripped him weakened him, and—despite his past—there was a strong steak of honor in Clay that wouldn't let him just walk away.

Desolate, defeated, he said wearily, "Ellen, we can't do this. I'd be ruining your life if we go on like this. I'm not fit for you."

But in the end, she had her way.

The next day they were on their way back to Gracefield. They didn't deceive Stephen and Ruth about being together the night before. Indeed, they didn't try. They only agreed to say nothing of their marriage. After listening to what had happened, Stephen had said only, "Clay, don't be hasty."

Later when they were alone together, Ellen urged, "Let's get married by the minister at Gracefield. We'll get a better start that way."

And that was what happened. A week after they returned, there was a wedding at Gracefield. Such a hasty marriage could not help but cause talk, but it was inevitable that people would say Ellen was getting Clay on the rebound.

Thomas and Susanna went through the ceremony with smiles, but when they were alone, they could not conceal their grief. Still, nothing could change what was happening, so they put the best face they could on it.

But it was Taylor Dewitt who spoke the sentiments of most people. As Clay kissed the bride, Dewitt leaned over and whispered into the ear of Tug Ramsey, "I hate to say so, Tug—but I'm very much afraid that Clay got the wrong bride."

PART TWO
Incident in Mexico—1846

CHAPTER 8

THE GUNS OF MONTEREY

A blistering gust of wind heated by the white-hot sun overhead washed over the face of Second Lieutenant Gideon Rocklin as he stared across a wide plain broken by a crooked arroyo. He looked down the line of blue-clad infantrymen, then took a sip of water from his canteen. It was tepid and tasted strongly of rubber, which was not strange since that was what the canteen was made of. The putrefying smell of decomposing corpses seemed to have somehow gotten into the water and even the food. At least, so it seemed to Gid.

Two hundred yards out on the rocks lay strange bundles— dead men who had turned black and swollen to such proportions it seemed that they had been pumped up like huge balloons. Their legs burst the seams of their pants. Many of them lay face upward, their arms lifted in eloquent gestures toward the pale sky that looked down on them pitilessly.

"You reckon we might move up again, Lieutenant?" The question came from Sergeant Boone Monroe, a tall, rawboned man of thirty from the hills of Tennessee. He had been with Gideon since they had left Texas as part of General Zachary Taylor's small force back in March.

"Looks like it, Sergeant," Gid said, nodding. Looking down the line again, he noticed the ragged uniforms and torn boots of the men. He looked at the men's faces, burned by the Mexican sun and thinned by poor rations. He hesitated, then said, "The men are pretty tired, Boone."

Monroe spit an amber stream of tobacco juice that hit a small brown lizard directly on the head. He admired his shot, grinned, and said, "Shore am glad those greasers can't hit with them artillery pieces like thet!" Then his face sobered. He shook his head slightly, saying, "We come a long way, Lieutenant, since we left Palo Alto." He studied the thin line of troopers carefully through half-closed eyes, then added, "Some of those boys we lost on the way here. . .it sort of eats at a man, don't it, Lieutenant?"

"They were all good men. None better."

As Gideon turned his gaze across the broken field, he thought of home, picturing the green grass and cool breezes of New York. But the war with Mexico had exploded—and had destroyed his world. He had known, they had all known, that the war was coming—but few of them were prepared when President Polk asked the Congress to declare a state of war in early May 1846.

Only four months ago, Gideon thought, his eyes burning from lack of sleep. *Seems like ten years! But I guess being in a war always does strange things to a man's thinking.*

He thought of how he and almost every other regular army officer had been gathered up with scarcely time to get their belongings together. No time for furloughs now! He had been stationed at Fort Swift in Dakota Territory and had barely been granted permission to take Melanie and their three boys back to his parents' house in Washington before leaving for Texas, where he had joined General Taylor's force. Officers were scarce, and Gid, like most of the other green lieutenants, was given command of troops with no experience in combat at all.

The experience had come soon enough. Taylor had driven his army to Palo Alto. The general was expecting a fight, but his small army, reduced by illness and desertions, now numbered only twenty-three hundred men. The Mexican army tallied over four thousand. Gideon thought of that fight as he stood beside Sergeant Monroe. He remembered how he had struggled with the unknown factor every new soldier faces in his first battle: *Will I fight—or will I run away?* Fear had been thick in his throat as he had led his men toward the battle, moving slowly with their supply train of two hundred wagons and the two eighteen-pound cannons that were drawn by twenty oxen each.

The scene came to him sharply—the Mexican line stretched a mile in length; infantry anchored on a wooded hillock to the right and extending left, interspersed with eight-pound cannons on massive carriages. To the left was a line of lancers, the sun glinting on their bayonets and on the razor-sharp lances from which bright pennants streamed.

He remembered General Taylor—"Old Rough and Ready," as he was called by the troops—sitting placidly on Old Whitey, his horse. Sergeant Monroe had looked at the general, then winked at Gideon as they had marched into the line of battle. "Looks like he's on a possum hunt, don't he, Lieutenant?" he had said. The easy manner of Monroe had braced Gid up, and he had grinned back, the fear gone.

But not for long. When the two armies had lined up no more than a few hundred feet apart, it had returned. When the bullets began to whistle past his ears, and when men began dropping abruptly out of the line, fear was replaced by a blind terror that weakened his legs and emptied his mind. Once again it had been Sergeant Monroe, who had stayed at his side whistling a tuneless melody as he loaded and reloaded his musket, who had kept him in place. Gid never knew if Monroe was aware of his lieutenant's fear. He suspected he was, but the tall Tennessean never referred to it.

There had been other battles, and the glamour of war, what little there had been for Gideon Rocklin, soon faded. There was nothing glamorous in what he saw. . .or what he did. Eventually he had learned to accept the terrible wounds, the sickness, and the constant presence of death.

The sound of a running horse came from behind, and Gideon took his eyes off the long hills that lay between the American army and Monterey. A smile creased his dry lips as a smallish man pulled his horse to an abrupt halt and came to the ground.

"Hello, Sam," Gid called out. "Glad to see you, but the rear is the other direction."

Second Lieutenant Ulysses Samuel Grant, a cigar clamped between his teeth, looked over, found Gideon, and came to stand before him. "Thought I'd better come and see the show." Grant and Gid had been classmates at West Point. Sam—as he was fondly called—had been a silent man who kept to himself, but he and Gid had become friends.

Grinning at Grant now, Gid remembered some of the times they'd shared in their relatively carefree days as cadets. Sam Grant was not a colorful soldier, but there was some quality in the man that other men respected. Now he looked at Gid, allowing a small smile to touch his lips. "Things are pretty bad when a quartermaster has to lead you dashing young infantry lieutenants into a fight, Gid."

"How'd you get out of your duty, Sam?" Gid asked curiously. Grant was under orders to serve as a quartermaster in charge of supplies. The stubby soldier had tried every way he knew to get out of the hateful duty but had not succeeded.

"My curiosity got the best of me, Gid," he said. "I couldn't stand being out of it all."

"You'll get court-martialed!"

"Well, maybe I'll get killed in this charge that's coming," Grant said lightly. "That would answer. Anyway, I had to come. This letter came for you yesterday."

Gid stared at the envelope that Grant pushed at him, then grabbed it and ripped it open. Just the sight of Mellie's handwriting brought her before his mind, and his hands trembled as he read the letter quickly, slowing down at the last paragraph:

My dearest husband, I miss you more than I ever thought possible! I am one of those women who lose themselves in their husbands, I suppose, and even after nearly six years of marriage, I still feel like a bride! I suppose that's foolish, but it's true, my dearest.

The boys are fine. You mustn't worry about them. I know your parents (and mine, as well) thought we should have waited to have children, but we did well. When I take the three of them out for a walk, people turn and stare at them. "Such fine boys!" they say. Tyler, Robert, and Frank all send their love. Every night we pray, our boys and I, and though they're only three, four, and five years old, I know their prayers for your safety will be heard! They all look so much like you it gives me a start!

I must close, with all my love. I enclose a letter I received

from Ellen. It is not good news, and I thought perhaps
I ought not to send it, that it might be a burden to you.
I know you are very fond of Clay, and according to Ellen,
he is not doing well at all. But I decided you should see it,
so I enclosed it with a prayer that he will wake up to the
terrible ruin he is making of his life. He has so much! Yet
he seems determined to throw everything away.

Be careful! Oh, be careful, my dear!

Your loving wife,
Mellie

Hastily Gid unfolded the other letter and scanned it. It was the letter of an unhappy woman, which Gid and Melanie had long known Ellen to be. It was three scrawled, poorly spelled pages, all with the same lament—Clay was acting like a fool! Gid let his eyes run over it, doubting if the situation was as bad as Ellen painted it. And yet he knew that his father had received similar word from Clay's father. He read a sentence: ". . .and not only does Clay neglect me, but he pays so little attention to the children! I hate to tell you, Mellie, but he's been seeing other women!"

"Looks like we're about to butt heads with them greasers, don't it, sir?"

Monroe's twangy voice brought Gid back to the present, and he looked quickly across the line just as a bugle sounded. Gid thrust the letters back into the envelope, shoved them into his inside pocket, and licked his lips. "All right, Sergeant, let's show the general what Company K is made of!"

"Mind if I go along, Gid?" Sam Grant stood before Gid, a dusty, insignificant figure, but with the light of battle gleaming in his dark eyes.

"Glad to have you, Sam," Gid said with a grin.

The charge sounded, and the two lieutenants moved forward, Gid shouting commands. Colonel John Garland led the charge, striking down the center between the Citadel on the right and La Teneria on the left. They had not gone far before they were caught on the front and at both sides by a shower of canister that whipped and tore the long lines. The men ran forward, hunching over, shoulders drawn in, clutching their muskets. The wounded fell with screams; the survivors jumped over bodies, stumbling, falling, seeing iron cut the dirt in front of them.

Gid yelled out, "Colonel Garland, we're taking a lot of hits!"

The colonel was a short, fat man with a red Irish face. Battle fury was on him, and he yelled, "Never will I yield an inch! I have too much Irish blood in me to give up! Forward, men!"

But he had not gone ten steps before a bullet took him in the stomach, driving him backward. Gid ran to him and held his head up, but Garland cursed him. "You're in command, Rocklin! Lead the men to the cannon's mouth!"

A gush of brilliant crimson blood spurted from his mouth, and his eyes rolled back in his head. Gid laid him down, called for two men to take him to the rear, then stood up and ran to where Grant was waiting. "Let's go, men!" Gid shouted and without a pause moved steadily into the musket fire. The Mexican front flickered up and down the line, and it soon became evident to Gid that they could go no farther without support. A thin line of rock lifted in front of where they stopped, a lip of basalt no more than a foot or so high, but it was something. "Take cover!" Gid shouted, and the men dropped behind it.

"Looks like they're moving toward us, Gid," Grant said. He had picked up a musket and laid it on the oncoming line of

Mexicans, then fired. He looked back over his shoulder. "Looks like we have help coming."

Two pieces of artillery were on the way, and soon the fire of the light cannons drove the Mexican forces back. Then it was time to charge again. Four times Grant and Rocklin led the men forward over the field, until they finally were forced to retreat before the artillery of the Mexican forces.

The air was thick with smoke, and the K Company was pinned down. "Be suicide to charge into that kind of fire, Gid." Grant shouted to make himself heard over the roar of musket fire. Then he stared at something to his right. "By the Almighty!" he said in awe. "Look! It's General Taylor."

Gid turned to look, but his attention was on something else. "Sam! Look out there!"

Grant turned to see what Rocklin was pointing to, squinted his eyes. "Why, that looks like Major Fields!"

"I thought he was dead," Gid said. He stared at the tall figure in blue who had risen to his feet. "He doesn't know where he is!"

"Must be hit pretty bad, Gid," Grant said. He peered through the smoke and said in alarm, "Look, they're coming!"

Gid saw the line of enemy troops at the same moment. And he knew, as every man in the company knew, that Major Fields was a dead man! The rest of the company had good cover, but Fields, standing tall in the sunlight, would be either shot or bayoneted within the next few minutes.

Gid could never remember what happened next. He remembered no conscious decision to get up and run through the hail of bullets that filled the air—but he found himself doing just that, leaning forward against the enemy's fire as a man leans against a hard wind.

Grant and Sergeant Monroe were both shocked into silence

for a moment, for there was no way a man could run into that kind of fire and live. Then Sergeant Monroe cried out, "Fire, boys! Give the lieutenant some help!"

It might have helped, for as Gid reached the major, who had slumped to his knees holding his side, he sensed that the line of Mexican infantry had faltered. He snatched the major up, throwing him up on his shoulders as if he were a rag doll. Just as he did so, he looked toward the enemy and found himself staring into the cold, black eyes of an enemy soldier. The Mexican had his rifle lifted, and Gid could see the creases on the man's brow. He was that close! He tensed his body, waiting for the bullet that could not miss—and then a small black spot appeared over the soldier's left eye and he went loosely backward, the shot he fired going into the air over Gid's head.

Quickly Gid whirled and ran back to the line of K Company, thankful for the great strength he had been blessed with. He ran in long, jolting strides, expecting each second to be struck in the back by a bullet, but it did not happen—not until he was five yards from Lieutenant Sam Grant and Sergeant Boone Monroe.

He saw the looks of amazement on the faces of both and knew that he had been a dead man in their eyes!

And that was the last thought he had, for suddenly he felt something like a blow of a giant's hand striking him in the back. He grunted, irritated at the blow, then fell forward, thinking, *I almost made it! I almost. . . !*

Within a fraction of a second, Monroe and Grant were at Gid's side, Grant shouting, "You men, take the major back to the ambulance!" He and Boone picked up the limp form of Gid Rocklin and moved toward the rear.

Suddenly a man on horseback was in front of them. "How is he, Grant?"

Lieutenant Grant looked up to see General Zachary Taylor staring down with concern in his eyes. The general seemed to be oblivious to the heavy fire that rented the air. He asked quickly, "Is he alive?"

Grant had felt the strong beat of Rocklin's heart. "Yes, General, he's alive." Then he gave Taylor a direct glance, a hard look that second lieutenants do not customarily give to generals. "If he doesn't get a decoration for this, General, I'll come back to haunt you."

General Taylor's lips turned up in a slight smile. He was not a man of much humor, but he found something amusing about Grant's attitude. "You're off your post, aren't you, Lieutenant? Aren't you supposed to be with the supply train?"

Ulysses S. Grant did not flinch. "Yes, sir," he said loudly, his head lifted in a defiant attitude.

The general held his gaze, then looked down at the still form of Rocklin. "Write it up, Grant. Send it to me and I'll put it through with my recommendation." Then he rode on, calling out, "Let's go see about taking Monterey!"

The long, ragged line of blue-clad infantry moved forward, following the general toward the low-lying hills that concealed the city of Monterey.

Sergeant Monroe and Lieutenant Grant delivered Rocklin to the ambulance, then walked back toward the line of battle.

"He'll do to tote the key to the smokehouse, won't he, Lieutenant?" Boone Monroe said, giving Rocklin as fine a compliment as any Southerner could give, for only the most trustworthy people were given a key to the smokehouse.

Grant stared at Monroe, nodded, and then the two of them moved across the smoke-filled battlefield.

CHAPTER 9

A DRAGON FOR MELORA

January 1847 was mild and benevolent. The year before, January had fallen on Richmond with all the ferocity of a half-starved timber wolf, freezing the rivers and drifting banks of heavy snow over the eyes of the houses. But Box, the blacksmith, assured everyone, "Gonna be nice and easy dis year. Shells on de acorns is thin as paper, and de woolly caterpillars ain't hardly got no fuzz at all!"

Box himself was a high, handsome man, a mulatto with smooth skin and hair that was straighter than most and tinged with auburn. His wife, Carrie, was black as night, an attractive woman of forty-seven. They were seated in the kitchen, visiting with Zander and Dorrie, helping with the preparation of the food for the birthday party of the twins, Denton and David, two of Clay and Ellen's children. The smell of fresh gingerbread wafting through the kitchen was pleasant, and all four of them were drinking hot chocolate.

These four were the heart of Gracefield in many ways. Zander—the butler—and Dorrie—the lieutenant of Miss Susanna—controlled the house, far more so than the white people suspected. Zander at the age of forty-eight was tall and thin, with a rich chocolate complexion. He was a man of tremendous dignity, rarely angry or upset, but stern enough to make the other house slaves flinch when he raised his voice. Dorrie, his wife, was somewhat heavy, in contrast to her husband's leanness. She had a pair of direct brown eyes and felt herself no less a Rocklin than any of the white people in the house.

If Zander and Dorrie controlled the house, it was Box and Carrie who stood first in the hierarchy of the field slaves. James Bronlin, the overseer, made a great deal of noise, but it was mostly sound and fury. The Rocklins had learned long ago that one word from either Box or Carrie would get more accomplished than a torrent of words from Bronlin.

"Dem chillun gonna catch dey death of cold," Carrie remarked, looking out the window to where the children were playing a game out in the grape arbor. The party had been scheduled for three in the afternoon, but it was after four and the shadows were beginning to lengthen.

"No, dey all right, Carrie," Box disagreed. "Lak I tole you all, we ain't gonna have no bad weather dis year." He picked up the cup in his massive blacksmith's hand, sipped at the rich chocolate, then asked, "Marse Clay, he ain't come back yet?"

It was an innocent question, but in some way it violated the unwritten code that existed in the world of the slaves of Gracefield. The white people were the main interest of all the slaves, but the house slaves felt a greater degree of sensitivity when the Rocklins were caught in some error. It was almost as though Zander and Dorrie were the protective parents of the Rocklins, quick to take offense at what they felt was any criticism of their "charges."

"Don't you be worried none 'bout dat!" Dorrie snapped at

Box, who blinked in surprise at her vehemence. "Marse Clay, he be comin' back in time for de party." She rose and went to the stove, opened the door to look at the cake that was baking, then slammed the door with unnecessary violence. She walked to the window, stared out, and said, "I reckon he got held up in Richmond."

"I guess so, Dorrie," Box said, understanding that he had violated one of the taboos of the little world he inhabited. To make his peace and show his good intent, he took a bite of gingerbread and commented, "Marse Clay is doin' bettah."

But this displeased Dorrie, too, and she gave Box an irritated glance. "You worry 'bout Damis, Box," she said, referring to Box and Carrie's oldest daughter, "and let Marse Clay take care of his ownself!" She glared at the muscular Box and, seeing the embarrassment in his eyes, sat down abruptly, saying, "My mouth is too big. Don't pay no attention to me, Box." She saw the reference to Damis had hurt them both and suddenly reached over and patted Carrie's hard, work-worn hand. "You know I didn't mean nothin', Carrie."

"Dat's all right, Dorrie," Carrie said heavily. But it was not all right, for Damis was a burden to her and her husband—and to Zander and Dorrie, as well, for their friendship went deep. Damis had been a problem since she was fourteen years old and had turned into a truly beautiful child. Too beautiful, really, for by the time she was sixteen, she had every male slave on the place watching her. And Damis had learned early in life that it was not just the slaves who noticed her, but the white boys and men who came to Gracefield, as well. It had been inevitable that she would be introduced to the lower lusts of men, and it came as no surprise that she became pregnant when she was barely seventeen.

The shock was that the baby, a boy, was obviously fathered by a white man. Such things were not uncommon on plantations, but the Rocklins, aided by Dorrie and Zander, Box and Carrie, had exercised such strict control that it was almost unknown at Gracefield.

And the silence of the girl was unnerving, for Damis would never name the father of her child. Privately, all parties thought that was best. How would it help to know? Such knowledge could only shame the father—and the rest of his family. Damis had been hastily married off to a middle-aged slave named Leon, but the marriage had not stopped her from chasing after other men. Her son, a sturdy six-year-old whom Damis called Fox, was far more white in appearance than black. His most striking feature was his eyes, which were not black or brown but a shade of gunmetal gray that sometimes looked almost blue. He was a fine little fellow, but set apart by his appearance so that his peers in the world of slavery had little to do with him.

The air in the kitchen had been made uncomfortable by Dorrie's unthinking remark. Box got up, and Carrie rose with him. Saying thanks for the treats, they left the kitchen.

"You shouldn't have said that, Dorrie," Zander said disapprovingly. "Dey can't help what Damis does—no more'n Miz Susanna kin help what Marse Clay does."

"I knows dat!" Dorrie said sharply, her face unhappy. "I'm jest worried 'bout Clay." She hesitated; then the words flooded from her lips. "When he gonna git ovah Miz Mellie, Zander? It's been six years since she turned him down for Marse Gideon, and he still mad as a bear with a sore tail!"

"Well, he don't talk 'bout Miz Mellie, does he?"

"And so dat make everything all right?" Dorrie shook her head, a sadness in her dark eyes. "You men! You think if nobody says anything, why, dey ain't nothing wrong. Jest cover it all up—and it'll go away!" She got up, went to the window, and looked out. "Look at dat, Zander." She waited until he rose and came to stand beside her, both of them looking at the group out in the yard. "Ain't dey a good sight? All dem chillun!" She named them off fondly. "There's Miz Marianne and Marse Claude with Marie. Ain't dat child a beauty! Jes' nine, but she gonna be a beauty! And Miz Amy and Marse Brad with them three fine chillun. Look like stair steps, don't dey, Zander? Little Les is two, Rachel is 'bout fo', and Grant is six. Dey may be named Franklins, but dey is all three Rocklins!"

"Fine chillun, Dorrie," Zander agreed. "But I reckon Marse Clay and Miz Ellen's crop is jest as purty." He named them with pride, having been active in their raising. "Look at dem twins, Dorrie! I nevuh kin tell which is Dent and which is David! Dis heah is their fifth birthday, and day bof big enough to be ten!"

"Well, dey may look alike," Dorrie snorted, "but dey sho' don't act alike! Dat David is de sweetest thing! But if somebody don't take a cane to Marse Dent Rocklin, he gonna be hung someday!"

"He is a mess!" Zander agreed sadly. "Take aftuh his daddy, I reckon. Look at Lowell, ain't but one year younger dan them twins, and ain't half as big! But look how he taking care of the baby. He do love that little Rena!"

They stood there watching the children, and finally Dorrie said, "You sees what it is! Dere's Miz Amy wif her husband, and dere's Miz Marianne and her husband. And where's the daddy of them four younguns? I tell you whar he is—he's drunk and wif some bad woman, dat's whar he be!"

Zander could not meet his wife's fiery glance, and his thin shoulders stooped. "Marse Clay, he's gonna put his mammy and pappy in an early grave, Dorrie."

"If Miz Ellen don't shoot him first!" Dorrie snapped. "I'm jest glad Marse Noah didn't live to see the way his grandson actin'!" Then she shook her head, saying, "Well, we ain't gonna make things no bettah by talking about it. Go tell 'em de cake and punch is ready."

"All right."

Ten minutes later, the dining room was filled with the treble sound of children's voices underlaid by lower, adult voices singing "Happy Birthday." The twins, Denton and David, sat at the head of the table, and when Dorrie brought in the three-layer chocolate cake with ten candles burning, they let out squeals of joy.

As the boys blew out the candles and the cake was cut, Amy said quietly, "Ellen, I'm sure Clay will be here." She was sitting beside Ellen, whose face was pale, and she tried to bring some assurance into her voice. "Perhaps the weather got worse."

Ellen Rocklin was no less striking than she had been when she married Clay six years earlier. The pink silk dress she wore for the party set off her figure, for even the birth of four children in that short period had not destroyed the lush curves. But there was a discontent in her brown eyes as she murmured, "Don't make excuses for him, Amy. I've done that long enough myself!"

"I know it's hard—"

"How can you know about it, Amy?" Ellen said, keeping her voice under control. "You've got a family. Brad is home with you and your children, which is what a husband is supposed to do, isn't it? And even Marianne, as sorry as Claude is with his liquor and women, doesn't have to put up with what I have to."

Across the room, Thomas and Susanna were very much

aware of Ellen's unhappiness. Indeed, they both felt Clay's inconsistencies keenly. Thomas moved his lips close to Susanna's ear, saying, "I never should have let him go to Richmond yesterday."

"It's not your fault, Tom," she answered. "He gave me his word he'd be back early this morning."

"His word!" Thomas said bitterly. "No such thing! Can't be trusted to do a single decent thing!"

Burke Rocklin, at sixteen, was the youngest child of Thomas and Susanna. He resembled his mother greatly in appearance, and he could see no wrong in anything his brother, Clay, did. "He'll be here," he said boldly to his mother. "Wait and see!"

"I hope so, Burke. The children are beginning to feel it," she answered sadly. "Dent asked me a minute ago why his father didn't like him." Her hand touched Thomas's under the table. "It made me cry, Tom! I didn't know what to say to the poor child."

The eyes of Thomas Rocklin were burning with anger. "Clay's not too old for a thrashing!"

"Yes, he is." Susanna spoke bitterly. "We should have seen to that when he was much younger."

Thomas felt the power of her remark, and though he realized she was speaking of the two of them, he said, "You're right, but it was my responsibility. I failed him, Susanna." Bitterness rose in his throat, and he had to force himself to keep the anger from showing on his face. The others, he realized, all knew what Clay was. Marianne, who loved Thomas more than the others, had tried to comfort him, but he had said, "Don't try to find an excuse for me, Marianne. I should have used the strap on him when he was younger. He's got a rebellious streak. All of us Rocklins have it, I think, but with Clay, it's almost like a demon!"

Thomas looked across at Marianne, saw her watching him. She always sensed his moods better than the others, and now he tried to cover his anger with a smile. She answered it, but both knew that the day was spoiled for most of them.

After the cake and punch, gifts were brought in, and the boys flew through them, sending the colorful wrapping paper flying. Both of them got exactly the same things, a few toys and some books. Marianne noticed that David snatched up a book and had his nose in it at once, while Dent was fascinated by a toy rifle. "That's sort of symbolic, isn't it, Claude?" she said to her husband.

Claude Bristol was of no more than average height, but he looked very much like the French aristocrat from whom he had descended. "David the scholar and Dent the fighter?" he remarked with a smile on his thin lips. "Yes, they are like that. Dent is like Clay, but I don't know whom David takes his quiet ways from."

"From his grandmother, I think. He's very like her." She looked toward the window, thinking of Clay but saying nothing.

"I should have gone with him," Claude said. Then he saw something in his wife's clear eyes that made him drop his own. "But that would be like sending a fox to guard the chickens." A slight bitterness touched his fine gray eyes, and he added, "Is that what you're thinking? That I'm very much like Clay?"

Marianne did not deny his words directly. But she touched his hand, looked into his face, and smiled. "You and Clay suffer from the same temptations. But you are man enough to struggle against them. Someday, Claude, you'll defeat them all. And you're a fine father!"

He shook his head slightly. "I try, my dear. And I will always try, for I love you very much."

At that moment, before Marianne could respond, Brad Franklin said, "Here comes Clay!" He had walked to the window and was staring out into the front drive. Now he turned and said evenly, "He's in time for the cake." Amy's husband was a smallish man, under medium height. He was lean, with fair skin and reddish-blond hair and a hungry-looking, intense face. He owned Lindwood Plantation twenty miles from Gracefield— closer to Richmond, which suited him, for he was up to his ears in politics. Now he moved to stand behind his wife, touching her shoulders, then stepped back to lean against the wall. He didn't like Clay, or more accurately, he didn't respect him. More than once in his rather intense fashion, he had told the younger man to his face that he was a sorry excuse for a husband and a father; Clay had taken it badly, and the two were always on guard when together.

"Daddy! Daddy!" The four children began to squeal excitedly and would have gone to meet their father, but Ellen said sharply, "Get back in your chairs, all of you!"

Three of them obeyed, but Denton ignored her and ran out of the room. Ellen rose to go after him, anger in her eyes, but Susanna said quietly, "Let him go, Ellen. You can speak to him later."

Clay came in, his eyes bright but his speech slurred. He had Dent in his arms and cried out, "Happy birthday!" as he entered. As usual he ignored Ellen, going at once to where David sat watching him with a pair of steady brown eyes. "How's my birthday twins?" Clay asked loudly, then picked them both up and squeezed them. Only then did he turn to face the others, and there was a defiant light in his dark eyes. "I got held up in

Richmond," he said briefly, which they all knew would be his only apology.

"Dorrie, bring some cake for Clay," Susanna said quickly. "Boys, show you father what you've gotten for your birthday."

Ellen said nothing, not to Clay, at least. While Clay exclaimed over the presents, she sat rigidly in her chair, her eyes fixed on him, unblinking and angry.

Claude said quietly to Brad, "Look at Ellen. She's mad enough to cut Clay's throat!"

"Guess she has reason," Franklin answered briefly. He got on well enough with Claude, but the Frenchman was too much like Clay and in Brad's opinion was partly responsible for Clay's lifestyle.

Claude said no more to Brad, and the two men stood back, letting the party wind down. Soon the children were hustled off to bed, and Thomas instructed Zander to have the evening meal set out. When they were all seated, Thomas asked the blessing. In his prayer, he said, "...and remember Gideon, Lord, and keep him safe from the enemy."

"What do you hear about Gid, Tom?" Brad Franklin asked, cutting the roast beef on his plate. "He over that wound he took at Monterey?"

"Stephen says so," Thomas replied. "Said he's going back to his unit in a couple of weeks."

"I don't believe in this war," Marianne said, her brow troubled. "Everyone knows President Polk brought it on, and it was Andrew Jackson who put him up to it." She took a bite of potatoes, then added, somewhat angrily, "Jimmy Polk never had an idea in his head that Andy Jackson didn't put there!"

"In that you are correct," Claude agreed, nodding. "Jackson was a man possessed when he was president. 'Manifest Destiny' was his creation, and he was convinced that God has given America a special place in history. He, and many others now, feel it's her right—her destiny—to take whatever lands she needs to become a great nation."

Brad nodded, his narrow face thoughtful. "He and Sam Houston were thick as thieves. Jackson needed Texas as a state, but he also saw it as a door to getting control of California."

"But Mexico owns California!" Amy protested.

"Of course, dear." Brad grinned. "And that's what this war is all about. Partly, anyway."

"The rest of it is slavery!" Clay said suddenly. He spoke thickly and was weaving just slightly in his seat.

"That's correct, Clay." Brad nodded. "The Missouri Compromise has got the North and the South in a bind." The now-famous act declared that slavery could not be introduced into any state north of the Louisiana Purchase territory. But the South had realized that there were more potential states in the northern area. Franklin said with a sudden passion in his voice, "Soon there will be more states in the Union that are opposed to slavery. They'll strangle us! So what Polk has done is open the door to more Southern states."

"You don't mean take Mexico!" Thomas said, a little shocked at his son-in-law.

Franklin hesitated. "That is not impossible. Some say Mexico is a natural extension of the South, good cotton country. But most thinking men of our part of the world are thinking of New Mexico and California. Mexico owns them, but they don't care about them. Already Polk has sent two forces to California to have our people in place when the Mexican War is settled."

Marianne was troubled. "Isn't that what we fought against England for, Brad? So we could have freedom?"

"Why, Marianne, there will be freedom! America must have that land; we must reach from shore to shore! And the good thing about it is that all this territory will become slave states!"

The discussion went on for some time, but finally Susanna said, "Well, I don't know about this war, if it's good or bad. But I do know that I'm very proud of Gideon."

Thomas added, "Stephen tells me the boy got a medal." A cry of approval went around the table, but Thomas noticed that Clay dropped his head to stare at the table.

"They don't give those away!" Claude said with admiration. "I read the report of the action in the papers. It was a bloody affair, taking Monterey. Do you have a report of what the boy did to get the medal?"

"Yes. I don't have the letter Stephen wrote, but it was a very courageous thing." He proceeded to relate Gid's rescue of the major and concluded by saying, "I'm glad a Rocklin is serving his country so well!"

Clay got up suddenly, looked around the room, then said, "So Gid's a hero! Well, soldiering is a pretty exciting life. Let him try to do something heroic around *this* place! He'd find it a little harder than playing soldier!"

He lurched away from the table and went to his bedroom, followed closely by Ellen. But when she started to berate him for missing the party, he said thickly, "Ellen, shut your mouth—or I'll shut it for you!"

"Go on, hit me!" she cried out bitterly, her fists clenched. She would have struck him but knew better. "Do you think that would hurt me as badly as what you do all the time?"

He threw his head back, his eyes bitter. He had long kept his tongue over the way they had gotten married. At first, he had done his best to make a real marriage of what they had. . .but he was haunted by the memories of Melanie. And the memory of Ellen's behavior had become a sickness with him.

"You wanted this marriage," he said in a deadly tone. "Well, you'll have to take what you got!"

"You never loved me!" Ellen whispered. "Do you think I don't know?"

"Know what?" he demanded, tired of the scene. It was like so many others!

"That you're still in love with Mellie!"

Clay stared at her, saying nothing. Their words seemed to have released a storm of emotions, a Pandora's box of buried thoughts that he had kept so deep that he had almost forgotten they were there. He thought of Mellie as she had been when he had courted her, and when he saw the twisted rage on Ellen's face, he knew he was doomed. There was no such thing as divorce in his family. *I will be married to this woman*, he thought bitterly, *as long as I live*.

Suddenly he wanted to strike her. He wanted to scream, "You've ruined my life! I'm trapped—and there's no way out!" Standing with his fists clenched, he almost let the wave of fierce anger overpower him, but then he wheeled and staggered out of the room.

She heard his steps pound unevenly down the hall and then down the stairs. A weakness took her, and she sat down on the bed. But there were no tears. She had shed them all long ago. Now there was only a barren anger that fed upon itself, and she sat there until she heard the sound of his horse leaving the stable, picking up speed until it reached the road and the furious drumming of the hoofbeats faded out.

I hate him, she thought numbly, sitting with her hands

clenched. *He'll go to Richmond, to those women! I smelled their perfume on him tonight! I hope someone shoots him at one of those places. I wish he were dead!*

⚜

Ellen almost got her wish exactly two weeks after the twins' birthday party.

It didn't happen, however, at a bordello. No, it was the jealous husband of a woman named Lorene Taliferro who shot a bullet exactly one-quarter of an inch away from Clay's right ear. And then Clay put a ball from his dueling pistol into the left side of Duncan Taliferro.

A light snow had fallen, cloaking the harsh dead earth with a beautiful coating of white. The two parties had met at eight in the morning at a spot just outside of Richmond. Clay could have stopped it all with a simple apology, but he had lived in a state of drunkenness since he had last seen Ellen. He could not live with the knowledge that his wife knew of his love for Melanie—and since he could not have the woman he loved, any woman would do—even a silly one like Lorene Taliferro!

Clay had stood quietly, giving Taliferro the first shot, which had missed. He thought once of tossing the pistol down and walking away; all honor would have been satisfied. But then, in a gesture that he never understood—never!—he aimed at the man's side and pulled the trigger. Watching Taliferro fall backward, the pristine snow suddenly turned a violent crimson, he was suddenly shaken as he had never been. A feeling of self-loathing swept over him, overwhelmed him, and he left the dueling field without stopping to see if the man was dead or alive.

For several days he tried to drown the knowledge of his

own heart in a bottle, but never succeeded. He discovered that everyone considered what he had done an act of cowardice. Even Taylor Dewitt, his best friend, had left him in disgust, saying, "My God, Clay! What a cowardly thing to do!"

He had not gone back to Gracefield, nor had he been sent for. The loose women and his drunken friends in Richmond had laughed at the duel, but this only made him feel worse.

Finally the pressure got to him. One gray morning he left Richmond, riding slowly along the rutted tracks of the road, unaware of the beauty of the countryside. He could have reached Gracefield before dark easily, but he dreaded the ordeal of facing his parents—and his children. He didn't care about Ellen, except that it was torture to be with her.

All morning he rode, his head down, his horse picking its way along the road. Blackbirds dotted the sky, making raucous cries, and a red fox came out of the brush, stared at him, then walked calmly away. Noon came, and by two o'clock he was sober. The sun was dropping and clouds were lowering in the west. He discovered that he had wandered onto a road that he didn't know, so he began looking for a house where he might ask for his bearings. It was nearly an hour later when he rounded a curve in the road and saw a child leading a calf. The yearling was not disposed to go, and the young person was having a hard time of it. Clay spurred his horse forward and brought him to a stop when he was ten feet away.

"A little balky, is he?"

The figure had a voice, and from it Clay deduced that the figure's gender was female. "Hello, Mister Clay."

Clay blinked, then peered at the shapeless figure. The girl was wearing men's trousers, a ragged bulky coat that was far too large, and a black slouch hat that came down to her eyes. He

147

tried to see her features, but they were covered by a green scarf pulled over them, which was tied behind her neck. "You know me?" Clay asked.

The girl loosed the scarf, pulled it away. "Why, certainly I do! It's me, Melora, Mister Clay!"

"Why—so it is!" Clay exclaimed. He had seen the child several times since she had nursed him to health, but time had slipped by. He remembered the books and asked, "Did you read all those books, Melora?"

Melora had a pair of remarkable green eyes, and they sparkled in her reddened face. "Lots of times," she said warmly.

Clay smiled, then said, "Calf stray away last night?"

"Yes, sir. Pa sent me to look this way."

"Well, it looks to me like he's more than you can handle. Give me that rope, Melora." He took the rope, then leaned over, saying, "Now you." She hesitated, and he said, "Not afraid of my horse, are you?"

"N–no, sir," she said. She lifted her arms and he put his right arm around her. She was larger than she looked, heavier and more filled out. He laughed, saying, "You're a grown-up woman almost, Melora! Another year or so and I won't be able to do that. How old are you now?"

"Twelve."

"Twelve." Clay twisted to smile at her. "Time sort of slipped by me! I thought you were about eight or nine."

"No, sir. I was twelve last month."

Clay touched the horse with his heels, gave the calf a jerk that nearly upended him, then began to question the girl. By the time they had reached the Yancy place, he had gotten a full report on her parents and the other children.

"Well—if it ain't Mr. Clay!" Buford Yancy had come from

the barn at the sight of the man on horseback, and there was a welcoming light on his face as he reached up for the rope. "Git down and be friendly!"

The warmth of Yancy touched Clay, coming after the cold treatment he was used to. "Might do with a cup of coffee if it's handy, Buford." He reached back to help Melora, but she slid to the ground on her own.

"Melora, go tell your ma to fry up some of that venison!" He ignored Clay's protest, saying, "No bother. Now you come and let's put this feller where he belongs—then we'll get us some grub outta my woman."

After the yearling was put into a corral, Buford showed Clay around the place. He had added several buildings since Clay had been tended by Melora, including a stout barn and several smaller additions. Yancy was proud of his place, Clay saw, as proud as any Rocklin was of Gracefield with its thousands of acres. Finally they went inside, and soon Clay was seated at the slab table eating fresh deer meat. He had eaten little for several days and suddenly was hungry as a wolf. It delighted the Yancys to see him eat, and he found himself feeling at home with them.

After the meal, he had to see how all the children were doing, and was impressed. Royal was fourteen, a carbon copy of his father, thin as a lathe and with alert greenish eyes. Zack, age ten, was more like his mother, short and sturdy. And Cora, at nine, was like Melora. The younger children resembled their father.

Melora, though, was a shock to him. Though only twelve, she was already possessed of the beginnings of beauty. She sat back from the fire, saying little that evening but taking in every word that Clay said.

Finally Buford said, "Well, I guess it's bedtime. Mattie's got you a bed made, Mr. Rocklin. Real feather bed! You take this room."

Clay was tired and said good night as Yancy and his wife retired to the single bedroom at the rear of the cabin. Melora herded the children up into the loft with practiced authority.

Clay drank the last of the coffee, then sat in a handmade chair, staring into the fire. He was so lost in his thoughts that he came to himself with a shock when Melora's voice came from close to his side.

"Can I get you anything, Mister Clay?"

"Why, I don't think so, Melora. I'm stuffed like a suckling pig right now." She half turned, but he stopped her. "I'd like to hear you read a little, if you're not too sleepy."

"Oh no!" Melora's face lit up, and at once she moved to a rough bookcase on one wall. She came back with a book, saying shyly, "This is my favorite."

He took the book, smiled, and said, "*Pilgrim's Progress*. I remember this one, sure enough!" He saw that the pages were worn and the back loose. It had been in good condition when he had brought it to her. "Read me your favorite part," he said, handing the book back to the girl.

Taking the book, she sat down at his feet, the pages illuminated by the flickering flames. "I like the part best where Christian fights with the fiend Apollyon." She started to read in a clear voice:

So he went on and Apollyon met him. Now the monster was hideous to behold: he was clothed with scales like a fish, and they are his pride; he had wings like a dragon, and feet like a bear, and out of his belly came fire and smoke; and his mouth

was as the mouth of a lion. When he came up to Christian,
he beheld him with a disdainful countenance, and thus
began to question him:
APOLLYON: Whence come you, and whither are you bound?
CHRISTIAN: I am come from the City of Destruction,
which is the place of all evil, and am going to the City
of Zion.
APOLLYON: By this, I perceive that thou are one of my
subjects; for all that country is mine, and I am the prince
and god of it.
CHRISTIAN: I was indeed born in your dominions, but your
service was hard, and your wages such as a man could not
live on, for the wages of sin is death.

As Melora read on, Clay was fascinated. She knew the
book by heart, and as she read, she threw herself into each part.
When she read the lines of Apollyon, she deepened her voice
and frowned angrily; when she read the part of Christian, she
spoke sweetly and firmly.

Finally she came to the section where the actual battle took
place between Bunyan's hero and the dragon:

CHRISTIAN: Apollyon, beware what you do, for I am in
the King's highway, the way of holiness.
Then Apollyon straddled quite over the whole
breadth of the way, and said, "Prepare to die; for I
swear by my infernal den, that thou shalt go no farther;
here will I spill my soul." And with that, he threw a
burning dart at his breast; but Christian held a shield
in his hand, with that he caught it, and so prevented the
danger of that.

Melora, Clay saw with wonder, was caught up in the old story, and he remembered suddenly that he had been the same when he was her age. When she was finished and looked up at him with her eyes alive, reflecting the fire, she whispered, "That's my favorite part!"

"I think it's mine, too, Melora." He smiled. "I must have read it a hundred times when I was a boy."

"Did you, sure enough?" she asked wistfully, her lips parted. "Ain't that nice, that we like the same part! Do you want to hear my second favorite part?"

"Sure I do!"

"It's the part about when Hopeful and Christian come to the Celestial City, but they can't get to it without they go through the River of Death first."

"I remember that part," Clay said, nodding. "It always scared me a little."

Melora began to read again, this time much more slowly, and her eyes were enormous in the firelight.

Now I further saw, that betwixt them and the gate was a river; but there was no bridge to go over, and the river was very deep. The pilgrims began to inquire if there were no other way to the City; to which they answered, "Yes, but there hath not any save two, to wit, Enoch and Elijah, been permitted to tread that path since the foundation of the world."

Then they asked if the waters were all of a depth. They said, "No, for you shall find it deeper or shallower as you believe in the King of the place."

Then they addressed themselves to the water; and entering, Christian began to sink, and crying out to his

good friend Hopeful, he said, "I sink in deep waters!"
Then said the other, "Be of good cheer, my brother; I
feel the bottom, and it is good!"

Melora lowered the book, and Clay saw that there were tears in her eyes. "I love Hopeful, don't you, Mister Clay? When his friend was afraid, he stayed with him and made him believe it would be all right. Ain't that grand!"

"Yes, Melora, it's a wonderful thing to make people feel good." He smiled suddenly, saying, "It's a thing you do better than anyone I know."

"Me!" Melora gasped, her hand flying to her throat. "Why, I don't do nothing like that, Mister Clay!"

Clay leaned forward and reached out for her hand. When it lay in his own, he said, "I think you do. Like when I was brought here so sick I could hardly breathe. It was you who took care of me. And like tonight. When I came here, I was feeling very bad, Melora. But you've made me feel very good."

Her hand was warm in his, strong and firm for a child's hand. He could feel the calluses that had already formed, young as she was. Then he released it, adding, "Thank you for reading to me, Melora. Do you like any of the other books?"

She was staring at him, overwhelmed by his compliment. She remembered clearly every detail of every encounter with him, and she knew she would never forget this night.

"Yes," she said. "Not so well as this one, though. But the ones about the knights and the dragons, I like them real well!" She ran to the bookshelf, and for the next hour, she read from the Arthurian romances that Clay had given her.

Finally she closed the book. "I like the part where the men go and kill the dragons that are killing the people, don't you?"

"Yes. I've always liked those stories."

She suddenly gave him an odd look, then giggled. "Know what, Mister Clay?"

"No. What?"

"When I saw you come down the road today, on your white horse and all, I thought you looked like a knight! I really did! And I pretended I was one of those ladies in the book and that you'd come to save me."

Clay smiled. "I'm not much of a dragon killer, Melora." Then a thought came to him. It drew his smile down, and the joy left his eyes. The thought of his life and its emptiness, and the futility of the years that lay ahead, laid its hand on him. He said quietly, "I'm not a good man like those knights, Melora. I'm a very bad man, as a matter of fact."

Her response startled him. She dropped the book and seized his arms with both hands, shaking him with all her strength. "You're not!" she cried, and he saw with absolute astonishment that tears were filling her eyes. "You're not a bad man!" she cried again, then turned, put her arm on the stones of the fireplace, and cried against it.

Clay Rocklin had never been so taken aback. He stared at the girl's slender form, shaking with a rage of weeping, and had no idea as to what it was all about. Standing there, however, a strange thought came to him. It was the most incredible thought he'd ever had, and at first he shook it off. But it came back even stronger. It filled his mind, and he told himself he was crazy, but it would not budge. Rather it grew into a full-fledged plan as he stood there staring down at Melora.

I'll go away from Gracefield, he thought. *I'll throw myself into something that will take all I have. The war! I'll join the army, go be with Gid. And if I'm any kind of a man at all, I'll find out about it. If I'm not—maybe a thing like that will change me! I'll do it, by the Lord!*

When the thing was settled, wild and fantastical with a thousand perils, he touched the girl's shoulder, turning her around. "Don't cry, Melora."

Tears left silver tracks down her smooth cheeks, and her eyes were half angry. "I don't like it when you talk like that, Mister Clay!"

"Well, I won't say it anymore." He hesitated, then said, "Melora, I've got to go away for a while, but I want you to do something for me."

"Me? What can I do?"

He took out his wallet and removed all the bills in it. "I want you to go into Richmond. Get your father to take you. And I want you to spend all of this money on books."

She stared at the bills, then looked up at him with bewilderment. "But what books?"

"The ones you like." He smiled. "Get a library for you and for the other children. When I come back, I want you to read them to me—like you have tonight."

Melora looked at him. "But—where are you going, Mister Clay?"

Clay took a deep breath, then smiled.

"Why, I'm going to slay a dragon for you, Melora!"

CHAPTER 10

THE NEW RECRUIT

The snow—not heavy and damp, but dry as dust—fell lightly on Washington, so lightly that it seemed the flakes played wild games, fluttering like miniature birds before coming to rest. Standing at the bay window, Stephen Rocklin felt a sudden unaccustomed twinge of fear as he watched Gideon playing in the snow with the boys. Stephen was not a man of great imagination; he spent little time speculating about the future. But as he watched his son make a snowball and toss it at Frank, the youngest grandchild, he suddenly was possessed of something like a vision. At least, it was as close to a vision as a man such as Stephen ever received. He suddenly saw Gideon lying dead on a battlefield in Mexico, his empty eyes staring blindly up into a merciless sky.

"What is it, Stephen?" Ruth had noted the sudden change of expression on his face. She was standing beside him, enjoying the sight of the children and their parents. "Don't you feel well?"

"It's nothing," he said quickly. They were not an overly affectionate pair, though the years of marriage had molded them into a solid couple. He had often envied the closeness that existed between his brother Tom and Susanna, the almost mystic relationship that they seemed to have. But he was content with his marriage. So he put her off with, "Just dreading to see Gid go back to Mexico."

Ruth's lips tightened, for the same thought was never far from her mind. Gid's convalescent leave had been so wonderful! His wound, not as serious as it might have been, had healed rapidly, and the house had been a happy place with him there. Ruth, for all her rather stiff mannerisms, had grown very close to Melanie, closer than she did to most people. She didn't know that Gid had told his wife, "Mellie, I know Mother is sometimes difficult, with all her parties and social climbing—but see if you can get close to her. She needs a real friend. Someone to talk to about something a little deeper than the next party."

Melanie had succeeded in this with little difficulty. She was a warm, outgoing young woman, and her years on the barren plains at Fort Swift had given her a desire to get closer to other people—and to Gid's parents. She came through the door now, snow sparkling in her blond hair. Her eyes were bright, and she was laughing as she entered the drawing room.

"Oh, my hands are freezing!" She had Frank in tow and thrust him close to the fire that burned merrily in the fireplace, filling the room with a faint scent of fragrant apple wood. "You're going to be a snowman yourself if you don't thaw out, Frank!" She began stripping the mittens off the sturdy boy, who protested, "Not cold, Mommy!"

The door slammed and Gid came in, anchored with the other two boys. "What about something hot for these fellows, Mother!" he demanded. His face was paler than usual, and he moved carefully as he began pulling the wool coat from Tyler, who at the age of five was insulted and insisted, "I can do it, Daddy!" He struggled with the buttons while the middle son, Robert, submitted docilely to his father's help. He was four, and already it was evident he would have his mother's slenderness. Tyler, however, was blocky, like his father and grandfather.

Ruth laughed and left for the kitchen, saying, "I don't think anyone could make enough chocolate to fill you all up!" She returned with a pot of frothy, steaming chocolate and a platter of sugar cookies, which the boys promptly fell on like small pigs. "Tyler, don't stuff three of those cookies in your mouth!" Ruth scolded. "There's plenty to go around." Then she looked at her son and laughed. "No wonder he eats like a pig, Gid, when you're stuffing yourself. Didn't they teach you any better manners than that at West Point?"

"Well, I may have had some polish at the Point," Gid said with a grin, licking his fingers and reaching for two more cookies, "but I lost them all in Mexico. No white tablecloths and polished silver there." He told them how he had joined with his sergeant, Boone Monroe, in a raid on a Mexican farm, nearly getting shot by an irate farmer as they tried for his chickens.

The boys all listened avidly, but Stephen laughed. "We sent you to West Point to learn how to steal chickens? I'd have expected a little more for a decorated hero!"

Gid flushed—as he always did when anyone referred to his medal—and covered quickly by saying, "Sergeant Monroe has more sense than most of the officers down there. I got a letter from him yesterday. He says the company's been sent to join General Scott's force."

The nature of the war had taken a sudden change during Gid's convalescence. President Polk, displeased with what he considered the snail's pace of the war, had named General

Winfield Scott to command a force that would bring the conflict to an end. The plan called for General Taylor to simply hold on in the north and send most of his men to join Scott, who would land an army at Vera Cruz and penetrate to the heart of Mexico.

A shadow crossed Melanie's face, but she quickly hid it. "Will you have to leave soon?"

Gid hesitated, then nodded. "Next week. My orders came yesterday."

"Oh, son, you're not fit to go back to the war!" Ruth cried.

"I'm fine, Mother," Gid said, going to give her a hug. "And it means so much to me that you and Father are taking care of Mellie and the boys while I'm gone."

His announcement dampened the joy of the day. Even the boys realized what was happening, and Tyler asked, "Daddy, take me with you. I can kill those old Mexicans!"

Gideon took the sturdy form of the boy, holding him close. "I hope," he said quietly, "that you never have to kill anyone, Tyler."

The family spent the day together, going out for a sleigh ride in the afternoon, and when they returned, Pompey met them as they came into the house. "Marse Clay is here, Mr. Rocklin."

A look of surprise passed across Stephen's face, but he said, "Well, where did you put him, Pompey?"

"In the library, sir."

Gid caught his father's glance and said, "Well, let's go welcome him."

Melanie took Gid's arm, holding it tightly, and he felt the tension running through her. When they entered the lofty room where Stephen kept his books, they saw Clay standing at the window, staring out. When he turned, Melanie noticed that he was thinner than she remembered and that he seemed very nervous. That was unusual for Clay, and somehow she was sorry that he had come. She forced a smile, however, and noted that he didn't look at her after his first glance.

"Clay! What a surprise!" Gid said, stepping forward to give his cousin a hearty handshake and slapping him on the shoulder. "You should have let us know you were coming."

"Well, to tell the truth, Gid, I didn't know it myself until two days ago." He thought of the storm of resistance and shock at his announcement that he was going to join the war, then forced the memory out of his mind. "Everyone sends their best to all of you."

Ruth's social skills came in handy, for she bullied them all into the dining room for dinner as soon as possible. It was her notion that food could solve any problem—if properly served in the right setting. Or at least, it could put off any problem for a time.

The dinner went well, though Clay's remarks about Gracefield held a significant omission: he spoke of everyone except Ellen. They all noticed that he was under some sort of strain, eating little and speaking too rapidly. After the meal, he said quietly, "Gid, I've got to talk to you."

"Come to the library," Gid said at once. "Pompey, bring us some coffee." He led the way and made no attempt to force Clay to speak. When the two men had their coffee and Pompey closed the door with a sibilant sound, Clay said at once with a grimace, "Sorry to bust in on you like this, Gid."

"What's wrong, Clay?" Gid asked at once. "Trouble at home?"

"Yes, but I guess the trouble is mostly in here," Clay said, giving his chest a slap. He got up, striding back and forth, his face pale and his mouth grim. "I want to ask you for something, Gid—but before I do, let me tell you what's been happening to me."

Gid sat there quietly, listening to Clay's rapid words. He had learned much about men from his tour at Fort Swift; he had been forced to deal with the problems of his men constantly. As a result, he had become a good listener, which gave men confidence in him. He knew now that if he said little and waited long enough, a man would finally wade through the minor problems and come to the big one.

As Clay spoke frankly—and with disgust—of his life and his failures as a parent, Gid listened. When Clay said, "I've made a mess of everything, Gid!" he knew Clay had left something out, but he did not force it.

"We all do things we're sorry for, Clay," Gid said. "But you're a young man. There's time to make it up to Ellen and the children."

Clay shook his head stubbornly. "Not at Gracefield, Gid. I've got to get away and make a new start. Too many failures stare me in the face there."

"Leave Gracefield?" Gid was startled. He knew the feeling that Rocklins had for the land, and he shook his head. "You belong there, Clay. Running away won't solve anything."

Clay stared at him, then flushed. "I've got to get away, Gid. For a while, at least. When I get some order and peace in my life, maybe I can go back. And that brings me to the favor."

"Anything, Clay. You know that."

Clay stared at him. "You really mean that, don't you, Gid? Well, here it is—I'm going to enlist in the army. Can you fix it so I'll be in your company?"

Gid Rocklin was a hard man to shock, but Clay had succeeded in doing just that. He had imagined his troubled cousin saying all sorts of things, but nothing like this! He tried to collect his thoughts, getting up to face his cousin. Instinctively he felt Clay was making a mistake, but he saw the stubborn pride on Clay's handsome, sensitive face and knew he must not fail the man standing before him.

"I think it's a mistake, Clay—" He saw the hurt and anger begin to form in the eyes of the other man, then added with a smile, "But I'll do what I can." He threw his arm around Clay's shoulders, adding with a laugh, "It'll be good to have two Rocklins in the company!"

Clay trembled slightly, the warmth and weight of Gid's heavy arm feeling good to him. "I—I won't let you down, Gid! I swear it!"

"Of course you won't!" Gid saw emotion building up in Clay and wanted to break the tension of the moment. "Let's go tell the family that you're going to be going along to keep an eye on me, Clay. They'll be happy to hear it!"

"Gid—thanks!"

"No thanks to it." Gid smiled. "You'll wind up hating me, I expect. Most new recruits don't love their officers too much. But I've got a job in mind for you that you'll be good at."

"What job, Gid?"

"I'll put you on a horse." Gid smiled. "Make a courier out of you. You were always the best rider in Virginia, so we'll put that talent to work for the U.S. Army. Look out, Santa Anna!" he added.

The idea fired Clay, and at once he felt the tension running out of him. *It's going to be all right!* he thought. *I knew Gid wouldn't let me down.*

162

The next two weeks were exciting for Clay. He spent every day with the Sixth New York Calvary, learning the rudiments of military drill. He was careless about most of the restrictions, which displeased the sergeant in charge. But he was such a fine rider that his lax disciplinary habits were overlooked. He was popular with the men, too, being likable and, as a Southerner, an interesting specimen.

Still, though he enjoyed his time with the Sixth, he felt strangely restless when at "home" at the Rocklin mansion. He knew, of course, that the cause of his unease was being around Melanie—but he would never have admitted it. He simply kept his distance from her, physically and in every other way. Melanie realized what was happening, but she seemed to be the only one. Gid and the rest of the family seemed oblivious. Once Melanie tried to bring the subject up to her husband.

"Do you think it might be best if Clay stayed with the unit?" she asked one night after they had gone to bed.

"With the men?" Gid had been thinking of the day of his departure—dreading it—and the question caught him off guard. "I don't know. Do you think he's unhappy here?"

Melanie hesitated, then said, "He's a restless man, Gid. He's going to be unhappy wherever he is." She tried to find a way to say what had been troubling her but could not find the words.

"What is it, Mellie? Something's bothering you."

"Gid. . .Clay still feels something for me."

A brief silence, then, "He hasn't—"

"Oh, nothing like that! It's the way he doesn't say anything to me, Gid. He barely speaks to me. If he were over being in love with me, he'd be more natural."

"Poor fellow!" Gid lay there thinking, then sighed. "Well, we'll both be gone next week. He'll just have to get over it. I was hoping he and Ellen would make a better job of it."

"They were never suited. Oh, Gid, I hate to see you go!"

"I'll be back soon. This war won't last long." He reached for her then, and they forgot about Clay and the war and everything else but each other.

A week later, the two cousins were on their way to join General Scott's army at Tampico, a staging point for the invasion of Vera Cruz. As the train pulled out of the Washington station, Gideon threw himself down in the seat beside Clay. He had just endured a painful farewell with his family, and his mood was definitely gloomy. "This is the worst part of being a soldier, Clay," he muttered, staring blindly out the window. "Leaving your family."

Clay felt the pinch of guilt, for he felt like a young boy off on a hunting trip. He missed his children, but not much. The idea of a new challenge was like wine to him, and he said only, "It's hard, Gid. But we'll come back with chests full of medals."

Gid gave him a sudden hard stare. "Get that idea out of your head, Clay. War isn't like that. It's not romantic and thrilling. It's an ugly, painful business that no man in his right mind could enjoy. I just pray we get back alive and not maimed!"

Clay agreed at once, but he was thinking of the sound of guns, the waving of banners. *When I get back with a medal or two,* he thought, *things will be different. I may even get a promotion to second lieutenant.* He had a sudden picture of himself wearing the blue uniform of an officer, being met at Richmond by a brass band and everyone cheering his name. *I'll show the folks who the real soldier is! Maybe Gid has a medal or two, but I could always outdo him!* His thoughts went back to the night he'd spent at the Yancy cabin, and a smile came to him as he remembered Melora and her idea about knights. She had mistaken him for one—well, he'd be one for her sake. Surely there was a dragon somewhere waiting for him in the dusty land of Mexico!

So the two men went to war—together physically, but far apart in every other way.

CHAPTER 11

DEATH AT CERRO GORDO

Clay's dreams of cavalry charges with flags flying did not last long. When he and Gid got off the ship near Brazos Santiago, they were separated at once. Gid was thrust into the job of whipping K Company into fighting trim, while Clay was given the responsibility of grooming horses. At first he went at the task cheerfully enough, but there was no challenge to it—nothing but dirty work. By the end of the first week, he was sick of it.

A young lieutenant named George B. McClellan arrived at the Brazos Santiago, having made the move with his command from Taylor's force. He and Gid had been classmates at West Point, and the two of them had a good time over supper. McClellan, a small, erect man of a dapper appearance, spoke of his journey. "There was some hardship, Gid, but we made our own fun. You never saw such a bunch! We sat around and criticized the generals, laughed and swore at the mustangs and volunteers, and it was a nice outing."

"When you get to be a general, George," Gid laughed, "you'll know from experience just what the men are saying about you."

McClellan laughed in response—but years later, he would

recall that remark with some chagrin. "You say your cousin is here with your company? Not an officer?"

"No, Mac. To tell the truth, he's running away from troubles at home. I got him in for a short enlistment. He would never make a career soldier. Too independent."

"Well, Gid, I don't know what sort of trouble he's running from, but he may have jumped from the frying pan into the fire. I hear Vera Cruz is bristling with cannon. Beats me how General Scott thinks we can take it with ships. Those shore batteries have thirty-pound cannon, some of them capable of firing hot shot. If a ship takes just one of those red-hot balls, it'll go up like tinder!"

"Well, we've got to get there first," Gid said. "With this weather, I don't know if the ships can transport this army to Tampico, much less Vera Cruz."

His words proved prophetic, for of the forty-one ships that Scott had requisitioned to ferry his troops and munitions to Vera Cruz, seventeen were delayed for a month by terrible weather. Another ten ships that were to sail to Gulf ports and embark troops for the expedition were canceled by mistake. Other ships simply never appeared. Despite these factors, by the first of March—eight weeks later than he had hoped—Scott concluded that he would never be readier.

There were seasoned men in his army, including two regular divisions—one headed by General Worth, who had led the attack on Monterey—and the robust old cavalry commander who would fight a circular saw. Sprinkled through this army were some familiar faces: Ulysses Grant, the reluctant quartermaster; a newcomer worth watching—a middle-aged junior officer named Robert E. Lee; and Lieutenant P. G. T. Beauregard, a swarthy soldier from Louisiana.

If Clay had known action was immediate, he might have avoided the problem he found himself in just before the invasion. While Gid spent much of his time with the officers, Clay was thrown into a rough company—a profane, hard-drinking bunch of volunteers who were looked down on by the regulars with barely veiled contempt. One of the volunteers, an Englishman named Rodney Hood, was a remittance man—which meant that his family in England paid him to stay away from them! Hood was a hulking man, twenty-eight years old, black-haired, and beetle-browed. He organized gambling among the enlisted men, scrounged liquor to sell to them, and pretty much did as he pleased among the enlisted men. Being an expert gunner, he was tolerated by the officers, particularly since they were not overly concerned about the volunteers.

Hood had run head-on into Clay in an argument over cards. The larger man started for the thin young Southerner to pound him into the ground with his massive fists. He had awakened sometime later with a lump on his head. Clay had simply pulled out his heavy Colt and brought it down on Hood's head.

"Well, want to try it again, Rod?" Clay asked, smiling as the big man struggled to his feet.

Hood touched his head and stared at Rocklin with admiration. "No, bucko," he said, grinning. "I admire any man who can put me down. Let's shake on it." The two of them became friends, making a strange pair indeed! It was Hood's influence that kept Clay involved in constant drinking and gambling. And in an indirect manner, it was Hood who eventually led Clay into more serious trouble.

The pair of them, at the insistence of Hood, had slipped off into a Mexican cantina for a night's carousing. When they returned, they were hailed as they stumbled to their tents. Hood, wise in the ways of the game, slipped off into the darkness, but Clay was caught.

"Hold it!" It was Sergeant Boone Monroe coming out of the darkness, a lantern in his hand, his eyes hard. He had been instructed by Lieutenant Rocklin that no exceptions were to be made for his cousin, and he said, "Left the camp without permission? Well, you'll be sorry for that, I reckon. Come on, soldier."

Clay was just drunk enough to resent Boone's hand on his arm, and he swung, catching the tall soldier on the neck with a wild blow. The next instant he was driven to the ground by a tremendous hit that caught him in the temple. Lights flashed before his eyes, and he grew sick from the bad liquor. When he had finished vomiting, Monroe pulled him to his feet with an iron grip. "Come along and take your medicine."

Gid and McClellan were together in the tent they shared when Monroe called out, "Lieutenant!" They both stepped outside, and Gid kept the shock that ran through him from showing on his face. "One of the men, Lieutenant. I caught him sneaking back from the saloon. Private Rocklin, it is, sir."

McClellan took the situation at once. Rocklin had told him enough about the cousin from Virginia to let him know how touchy the situation was. He stepped forward before Gid could speak, saying, "All right, Sergeant. Put him in the guardhouse for three days, bread and water. Give him lots of exercise, though. Let him clean up after the horses."

"Yes, sir!" Monroe hauled Clay off at the end of his long arm, and Gid stood there silently staring after them. Finally he turned and gave McClellan a smile. "Thanks, Mac. I was in a pretty tough spot."

"May be what he needs, Gid," McClellan said with a shrug.

"I hope so. He's a good rider, I guess, but a courier has to be dependable. Better have a little talk with him, off the record."

Whether or not McClellan's advice would have been effective, Gideon never knew, for the next day he was ordered to take a patrol out to screen Scott's action from the enemy. The order came so suddenly that he had no time for even a brief visit with Clay. It troubled him, but he thought, *It will only be a few days. Clay will be more reasonable when I get back. We'll talk it out then.*

But the patrol lasted a week, and Clay had other counsel during that time. Rodney Hood smuggled liquor in to him for the three days of his confinement. When Clay was released, Hood welcomed him like a lost brother.

"You see how these officers are?" he said angrily. "Your own cousin, and he lets you rot in that filthy sty of a guardhouse!" Ordinarily Clay would have had nothing to do with a man like Hood, but the shame of his confinement with drunks and deserters cut into him deeply. Hood's constant tirades concerning officers and the army in general had sunk more deeply than Clay realized into his spirit. And when Gid finally returned from patrol, his cousin was in a vile temper.

"How's my cousin doing, Sergeant?" Gid asked Monroe the morning after his return. He was worn thin, and his wound was giving him some trouble, enough so that he was weary of spirit and not as sharp as usual.

"No disrespect to you, sir," Boone answered bluntly, "but he's poor stuff! Been hanging around with Hood and the others who cause most of the trouble in the outfit, acting like a snapping turtle, ready to bite anything that moves."

Gid soon discovered for himself the accuracy of that description. He found Clay brushing a tall bay and tried to joke the thing away. "Well, how's the veteran doing? Ready for the invasion?"

Clay looked up, his eyes cold with resentment. "I'll hold up my end, I reckon." He took a swipe at the horse, then turned to face his cousin. "I didn't sign up to clean stalls, Gid. And I thought you'd do better than to have me put in the guardhouse."

Gid stared at him, trying to find a way to get inside the man. Clay had always been touchy, and the discipline of army life was no place for that. "Clay, if Lieutenant McClellan hadn't spoken up—and he did it to save me embarrassment—you'd have gotten more than three days in the guardhouse! Sergeant Monroe told me you hit him. For that alone I'd have nailed your hide to the wall!"

"Sure you would!" Clay shot back. "You'd do anything to keep me from showing you up!"

Gid struggled to keep his own temper in check. "That's not so, and you know it, Clay. I want to see you do great things, and I know it's in you. But I'm an officer, and you're an enlisted man. Do you think the whole company's not watching to see if I give you special treatment?" Gid hated the scene and wanted to cut it short. He tried to smile. "Let's put this behind us, Clay. There's a big job ahead of us. You'll be needed, and I'll do all I can to help you."

Clay could not get the resentment out of his system. He ignored the frank words, saying in the same cold voice, "I'll take care of myself, Lieutenant."

It was useless. Silently Gid stared at his relative, wishing he knew how to do better with him—but there was no way. He was locked into his rank, and his responsibility to his men and to his superiors made any concession to Clay impossible. "Very well, Clay," he said evenly, then walked out of the stable.

For the next few days the invasion was poised, and finally after a risky voyage through rough weather, Scott's armada arrived offshore from Vera Cruz. Scott surveyed the coast; from what he could see of Vera Cruz, the defenses were impregnable from the sea. The city was enclosed by walls fifteen feet high, and on the land side they extended from the water's edge south of the town to the water again on the north. A massive granite seawall protected the waterfront, and more than a hundred pieces of heavy artillery—most of which had been cast in an American foundry across the Hudson River from West Point—were aimed seaward.

Every man on the transports was dreading the moment when they would have to row ashore in small boats and face those terrible guns. But on March 9, when the invasion began, a minor miracle took place. The nine-mile ride to the beach began, the tall ships of war sailing along under their topsails. The ships' decks thronged in every part with dense masses of troops whose bright muskets and bayonets were flashing in the sunbeams, and bands played loudly.

Gid, standing in the stern of one of the flatboats that was to deliver the troops through shallow water, expected the huge cannons to fire at any moment. He turned to George McClellan, saying, "No reason why we can expect to get ashore alive, is there, Mac?"

"None that I can think of," McClellan answered jauntily. At that moment a shot whistled overhead, and he added, "Here it comes! Now we'll catch it!"

But the shot had come from the other direction. An American ship was having a go at scattering a few Mexican dragoons who were visible on the shore. And there were no more shots from the land batteries! History would never explain why the

Mexicans did not blow the American ships out of the water. Whatever the reason, the landing was made without a shot being fired, which pleased the general very much—but puzzled him and his staff, as well.

When the troops were all disembarked, Gid was in a small group of junior officers directing the placement of the mortars. He looked up to see General Winfield Scott approaching, accompanied by some of his staff. Scott spotted McClellan and said, "Lieutenant McClellan, how does it look, the lay of the mortars?"

"Fine, General Scott," McClellan answered. As he pointed out the spots on the wall that would be the best places to attack, the dark-haired officer who stood close to the general walked around to survey the walls of the city from a different angle. When McClellan finished, the officer came back and Scott said, "Captain Lee, you'll be glad to meet a fellow Virginian. This is Lieutenant Gideon Rocklin, from Richmond."

Lee was the handsomest man Gid had ever seen. He had perfect features, and his form was tall and erect. "From Richmond?" Lee said with a smile. "I expect we have mutual friends, Lieutenant. I have many acquaintances there. Do you know the Chesnuts?"

"Yes, sir, very well." Gid nodded. "Fine people."

Lee stood there speaking quietly, and before he left, he faced Gid directly. "Lieutenant Rocklin, I read the report from Monterey. As a matter of fact, I submitted General Taylor's recommendation for decoration to General Scott. It gave me a great deal of pleasure that a man from my state performed so well." Lee's quick eyes saw that his remarks embarrassed Rocklin, so he said only, "I'll be seeing you, I expect. My congratulations, sir."

"I never met anybody like him," Gid remarked as Lee walked back to the group of officers with the general.

"There is something about the man," McClellan agreed. "General Scott thinks he'll command the entire Union Army before he's finished."

🙟

The capture of Vera Cruz was relatively simple. For some reason, the Mexican command decided to pull its main forces out, and morale inside the city collapsed. Scott kept the mortars firing, and on the twenty-sixth of March, his army marched into the city. His victory had been swift and unblemished. His losses were minimal, by the standards of war—only thirteen killed and fifty-five wounded. At once he began preparing for the march into Mexico. Still, it was almost two weeks before the first of his troops set off. His immediate goal was Jalpa, seventy-four miles up the national road to Mexico City, four thousand feet above sea level.

Santa Anna had pulled his army together and chosen a spot twelve miles coastward from Jalpa where the national road passed between commanding hills as it climbed into the highlands. He established his headquarters near the sleepy town of Cerro Gordo, or "Big Hill." It was named for the mountain that dominated it, which the Mexicans called El Telegrafo.

Company K found itself under the command of General Twiggs, and they marched rapidly toward Cerro Gordo. Twiggs was eager for action and didn't seem to notice that many of his troops were collapsing in the heat. On April 11 they reached the bridge across the Rio del Plan, about three miles downstream from Cerro Gordo. The next morning, Gid and the other officers were called to a staff meeting. Twiggs informed them that about four thousand Mexicans were dug into the hill that lay in front of them.

"We'll wait for General Scott," Twiggs informed them. "Get your equipment and men ready. I think it'll be a hard fight."

Scott pitched camp near the bridge on April 14, but instead of attacking, he began a careful three-day reconnaissance of the Mexican positions. He learned that Mexican cannon occupied the high ground on both sides of the road. A frontal assault would be suicidal.

On the American left, the Rio del Plan ran through a gorge five hundred feet deep, which made an advance in that direction impossible. Scott's best hope was to find a way to attack on the right—the weak side of the Mexican position. Scott gave the job of blazing a trail in this direction to his engineers, who included Robert E. Lee, P. G. T. Beauregard, and George McClellan.

It was early in the morning when Captain Lee came to the tent McClellan shared with Gideon. The two men looked up, and Lee said, "I need one of you for a mission General Scott has assigned me. The General tells me that you are busy, Lieutenant McClellan, so I would appreciate it if you could help me, Lieutenant Rocklin."

"Yes, sir! Of course!" Gid grabbed his gear and followed Captain Lee toward the edge of camp. He spotted Clay holding a horse in readiness and waved toward him, but got no response.

"We've got a difficult job, Lieutenant," Lee said. He explained the need for finding a hole in the Mexican line. With a smile, he added, "I thought a Virginian might be good at sneaking through the rough country. Did you ever do any stalking?"

"Yes, Captain Lee, but I should tell you, I'm not really a Virginian. What I mean is, my parents moved to Washington some time ago, but I have a cousin serving in the ranks whose family is in Virginia. Thomas Rocklin is his father."

"I know of him. But in any case, we've got to crawl through some rough country. Get your sidearm loaded and we'll start right away."

Gid never forgot that wild trip. He and Lee soon outdistanced the small escort and about midmorning came upon a small spring ringed with trampled ferns. "Somebody's been here, Captain," Gid said, then stopped, for the sound of voices came to them.

"Quick, behind this log!" Lee whispered, and the two of them dropped behind a huge log near the water. A troop of Mexican soldiers appeared, drank from the spring, then sat down on the log, laughing and chatting. Ants and spiders began to chew on Gid, and he saw that Lee was in the same condition. They lay motionless for hours, scarcely daring to breathe, and it was almost evening before the soldiers left. The two men stood up, stiff and burning with insect bites, then made their way back to camp.

"Thanks for your company, Lieutenant Rocklin," Lee said. "I think we'll be able to attack tomorrow." His eyes were bright, and afterward Gid remembered how the prospect of battle had excited the stately Virginian.

"Thanks for letting me go with you, sir."

Basing his plans on Lee's report, Scott called for a two-faceted attack for April 18. General Twiggs's division of regulars, reinforced by Shield's brigade, would cut the Jalpa road in order to trap the bulk of Santa Anna's army. At the same time, General Pillow's brigade would mount a diversionary attack designed to convince Santa Anna that the American main effort would come exactly where he expected it—against the strongly defended promontories between the road and the river.

"I believe he'll fall for it, Lee," General Scott said, staring at the map in front of him. "Be sure that we have good communication. If any of our people get pinned down, we'll need to know about it right away."

"Yes, General. I'll see to it."

And see to it he did, by hunting down the best couriers available—one of whom was Clay Rocklin. As it happened, Lee came by the headquarters of Company K and found Gid hard at work. "I need your best courier," Lee said at once. "He must be dependable."

If Clay had not been there, looking on with hope in his eyes, Gid would have chosen another man. But he gave way to an impulse. "I have a Virginian for you, Captain Lee. This is Clay Rocklin from Richmond."

Lee looked toward Clay, saying with a smile, "Private Rocklin, I'm glad you're with us. We'll expect you to do the Rocklins proud, as your cousin has."

"I'll do my best, sir!"

As Lee left, Gid said, "It's a big attack, Clay. Be careful."

"I can take care of myself!"

Clay stalked away, resentment in every line of his body, Lee's remark about Gid burning in his ears and his heart. When he got back to his tent that night, his excitement over the prospect of seeing action was dampened by Lee's obvious regard for Gid.

He slept poorly, and early in the morning he had a frightful nightmare. He dreamed that he was dressed in armor, like a knight of the Round Table, and he was facing some dark, terrible creature. He could not see what it was, but a woman was weeping, and a great desire to help her came to him. He pulled the visor of his helmet down, lowered his lance, and rode full-tilt at the beast, still not able to see the creature well. As he drew near, his horse suddenly reared up, and he was thrown to the earth. Unable to rise because of the weight of his armor, he saw the grisly beast emerge from a darkling wood—yet he was not afraid. Struggling to his feet, he drew his sword and cried out, "Come to me, and I will kill you!"

But when the beast drew near, he saw to his horror that though it had the body of a grisly beast, the face was his own! "I have come for you," the beast whispered, and it threw terrible arms around him, crushing him and filling his nostrils with its foul breath! Closer and closer the monster drew him to its rank body, and he felt the life flowing out of him. Despair filled him as he heard the woman still crying, and he began to die.

Clay awoke with a wild cry and sat bolt upright in bed. The sun was already breaking the darkness, and Hood, awakened by his cry, muttered, "What's happening, Clay?" He got out of his bed, then peered at Rocklin. "Bad dreams, eh? Well, we all have 'em, I suppose." He leaned down and fumbled for something, then found it.

"Take this with you on your little jaunt, Clay."

"Where'd you get it, Rodney?" Clay asked, staring at the quart of whiskey Hood had given him. "I thought you were out of the stuff."

"Got it off a Mexican last night. He says it'll take your skull off, so be careful. But a man's got to have a drink, now, don't he?"

Clay put the bottle in with his other things, saying, "Thanks, Hood. Don't get in the way of any bullets, you hear?"

"Not bloody likely!"

Clay mounted his horse and fell behind the line of infantry that moved slowly toward the Mexican position. The air was still that morning, and the flags hung limply on their staffs as the men marched out. There was no cheering, and Clay was depressed by it all. He had expected more than this.

The going was hard, with ravines so steep that men could barely climb them. Artillery was let down each steep slope on ropes and pulled up on the opposite side. Men grew thirsty and drank from streams, and many were limping by the time the action started.

Gid heard it first, then Boone Monroe. "That's rifle fire," Gid said with a nod. "Sounds like some of our advance parties have made contact."

They had indeed, for a rifle company on a reconnoitering mission at the base of the mountain had clashed unexpectedly with a troop of Mexicans. At once Twiggs commanded three companies to rescue the rifle company. Gid called out, "K Company, forward! Private Rocklin, stay fifty yards behind us."

The men followed Gid, and soon they chased the attacking enemy down the mountains—and straight into three thousand Mexicans. Outnumbered twenty-five to one, Gid saw there was no hope without reinforcements. He waved for Clay, who came pounding forward. Gid was watching the enemy and didn't notice how unsteady Clay looked or how flushed his face was as he reined up.

"Ride back to General Twiggs, Clay!" Gid yelled. "Tell him we've got more Mexicans than we can handle! Tell him if he comes in from the south, he'll wipe them out! We'll do our best to hold—now ride!"

Clay tore out, and Gid turned back to the fight, which was not going well. All afternoon they fought, and when darkness fell, Gid was shocked at their losses. "If we don't get help by morning," he said in quiet desperation to Sergeant Monroe, "we'll be chewed up and swallowed." Then he added, "But Clay is the best rider I've ever seen, and he's studied the ground. He won't let us down."

The fragile hope Gid was trying to keep alive would have died completely had he been able to see his cousin at that moment. For Clay was lying on the trail, halfway back to General Scott's headquarters. The Mexican who had sold the whiskey to Hood had sold several other bottles of the vile stuff to the men of K Company—and it was pure poison. Two of the men went raving mad for a time, and another lost his vision for three days. Everyone who drank it was hard hit. The liquor Clay had drunk had attacked his nerves. He had begun to lose his vision and finally had fallen from his horse. His stomach cramped, and he blundered along the trail, unable to see. Finally he passed out, facedown, on the trail.

❦

General Scott's advance scouts found Clay Rocklin at noon the next day. They took him to headquarters, and Scott said sternly, "You're drunk, Private!"

Clay gasped out, "Send troops. . .to Lieutenant. . .Rocklin!" It was all he could do, for his stomach cramped and he fell to the floor in agony.

Scott stared at him, a merciless light in his pale blue eyes. "Place this man under arrest. Now! Lock him up!"

"He's pretty sick, sir," one of the scouts suggested.

"He's drunk on duty! Put him in irons." As soon as they

removed Clay bodily, he called out, "Lee! I want you!"

Captain Lee came at once. "Yes, General?"

Scott related what had happened, adding, "It's probably too late, but send a relief column to help Rocklin."

Lee nodded, saying only, "I regret this, General. I picked Rocklin myself."

Scott stared at him, then forced himself to relax. "No blame on you, my boy. We have to trust men—and sometimes they fail us."

"Yes, sir, but Lieutenant Rocklin is too valuable a man to be wasted. I'll get the relief column at once, a cavalry troop. They'll be there in two hours."

When the troops arrived, they found one hundred men dead, shot to pieces. The reinforcements drove off the Mexicans, and at once the commander began to call, "Lieutenant Rocklin!"

"I'm here, Captain." The captain whirled to see a dusty officer step out from behind a large rock. "Glad you made it. But it's too late for most of my men."

Captain Steele said at once, "The courier didn't get through, Lieutenant. We found him just a few hours ago—dead drunk." His voice was thick with disgust, and looking around at the pitiful bodies in the clearing, he swore and cried out, "I'd like to be on the firing squad that shoots him!"

There was no firing squad, though. Word of the bad whiskey got about, and that was taken into account. And although no one mentioned it, the members of the court-martial all felt tremendously sorry for Gideon Rocklin. It was that, plus admiration for the lieutenant, that motivated the officers who stood in judgment over Clay Rocklin to bring in a verdict of guilty, but with a mild sentence: immediate dishonorable discharge.

Clay stood at attention as the verdict was read. He felt the eyes of Robert E. Lee, who was on the court, upon him and could not meet them. When the sentence was read and he was dismissed, he moved blindly to his tent. He knew the men hated him, blamed him for the senseless deaths of so many of their number. But none of them blamed Clay as much as he blamed himself. They had no idea of the shame he felt, a shame that turned the world black for him.

He left without seeing Gid, though his cousin looked for him. He moved slowly, like an old man, and as he boarded the boat that would take him home, he felt like a man who was condemned for life to a prison cell far under the ground. The court could let him go free, but it could not take away the guilt that burned in his belly like fire.

And he knew it would never stop. He had killed those men as surely as if he had shot or bayoneted them himself. And he could never bring them back to life. He could only live—for the rest of his life—with the knowledge that he was a murderer.

As the boat moved across the dark waters, he stared down into the depths, longing to throw himself overboard. But he did not. Instead, he left the deck and stumbled to his cabin, where he drank himself into a stupor.

CHAPTER 12

THE END OF A MAN

*W*ell, the scripture says seven is the perfect number—and it looks like that's what you ladies have here!"

Reverend Jeremiah Irons had come for his twice-weekly visit with Charlotte Rocklin and, taking a shortcut from the stable to the house, had encountered what seemed to be a miniature school. Actually it was Ellen Rocklin with her four children and Melanie, Gideon's wife, with her three. Irons stood beside the two women, admiring the yelling band of children, all of whom were so much alike in appearance that it was almost comical.

"They'll never be able to deny their Rocklin blood," the preacher remarked.

Melanie smiled suddenly. "They call us the Black Rocklins, Rev. Irons." She was looking pretty in her blue dress, and her blue eyes sparkled in the August sunlight. "Can you point out which are mine and Gid's and which are Ellen and Clay's?"

"I never let myself get trapped into a discussion of people's children," Irons said with a grin. "In Arkansas where I come from, some folk get almost as upset if you insult their children as they do if you bad-mouth their favorite coonhound." He studied the children, who were engaged in some sort of game involving a wagon filled with rocks. They were trying to hitch a sad-looking bluetick hound to the wagon, but all he would do was lie down and scratch.

Those children certainly do look alike, Irons thought as he watched. *All of them have the same dark hair and dark eyes. And they're all the same age, or almost so. Fine-looking children. . . How sad that Clay's are in far more trouble than they know!*

But he said only, "I used to lie when women showed me their babies. I'd say 'My, that *is* a beautiful child'—and the baby would be ugly as a pan of worms!"

Melanie laughed in delight. "Do you still lie, sir?"

"Oh no," Irons said, his brown eyes filled with humor. "Now whenever a mother brings out her baby and it looks like seven pounds of raw hamburger, I point at it and say in my most admiring voice, 'Now *that* is a baby!'" He laughed at himself, then said, "I didn't know you were here, Mrs. Rocklin."

Melanie said quickly, "Oh, I wanted the children to have some time with their Virginia grandparents while Gid is gone."

That was not strictly the truth. She had come at Gid's suggestion. *"Go for a visit to Gracefield,"* he had written. *"They're probably worried sick about Clay, and you could encourage Ellen. Take the boys and make a holiday of it."* So she had gathered up the boys for the visit.

When Melanie arrived, she had found Thomas and Susanna sick with grief. Clay had not been heard from since his dishonorable discharge. As for Ellen, she was as angry as a woman could be. Melanie sensed that Ellen's feelings went deeper than Clay's disgraceful act; somehow the fragile marriage of the pair had been destroyed. Melanie had tried to counsel Ellen to be forgiving, but the rage in Ellen was white-hot, and the best she could do was spend time with her children.

Irons gave Melanie a careful look. He traveled over the country a great deal, holding evangelistic meetings and visiting other ministers. The story of Clay Rocklin's dishonorable behavior was spoken of everywhere he went, and since he was known to be a close friend of Clay's, he was often asked about the matter. He never said one harsh word about Clay but defended him as well as he could. Now he said carefully, "Well, I'll expect you and your brood in church Sunday. And I'm giving you the job of bringing Miss Ellen and her children with you."

It was a mild rebuke, but Ellen flushed with irritation. "If you had to be father *and* mother to four children, Rev. Irons, you might not have so much time on your hands!"

Irons said gently, "I realize you have heavy responsibilities, Ellen, but the scripture urges us to let the Lord bear our burdens."

"The scripture teaches that when a man breeds children, he's supposed to stay home and take care of them, too!" Without another word, Ellen whirled and walked angrily toward the house, slamming the door as she entered.

"I'm sorry, Brother Jerry," Melanie said. "She's not herself."

"No word at all on Clay?"

"No. For all we know he may be dead."

"Oh, I think it's not that bad," he said quickly. *More than likely off on a monumental drunk*, he thought to himself, then said, "But he can't stay gone forever. He'll have to come home sooner or later."

Jeremiah Irons was no prophet, nor even the son of a prophet, but just as he had predicted, Clay Rocklin finally came home.

It was not the homecoming he had dreamed of. No medals. No crowd at the station to meet him. Which was just as well, since he made a sorry figure when he got off the train—his suit was torn and dirty, and he had not shaved in a week. His step was unsteady and his eyes were red-rimmed as he made his way toward the stable across from the railroad station. He kept his hat pulled down low over his eyes, fearful that he might be recognized, and when Harvey Simmons, the hostler, greeted him, saying, "Hello—something for you?" he realized that Simmons didn't recognize him.

"I need to rent a horse, Harvey."

Simmons leaned forward, peering at Clay more closely, and could not hide the shock as he said, "Why, Mr. Rocklin! I didn't know—" He broke off quickly, saying, "I'll saddle up the bay for you."

Clay did not miss the furtive looks that Simmons gave him. He knew Harvey to be the biggest gossip in Richmond. *Well, I won't have to announce my homecoming in the paper. Harvey will see that the news gets out,* he thought dryly.

He mounted the horse when Simmons brought him up, saying, "I'll bring him back tomorrow, Harvey."

"Sure, Mr. Rocklin." Simmons struggled to contain his questions, but he'd had little practice doing such a thing. "What was it like, Mr. Rocklin? Down in Mexico in the war?"

Clay settled himself in the saddle, then turned to give the hostler a hostile glance. "It was dandy, Harvey. You ought to go see for yourself."

As Clay rode out at a gallop, Harvey scowled. "Somebody ought to make that man give a decent answer!" Then he whirled and hurried down to the Hard Tack Saloon, announcing as he entered, "Hey, Clay Rocklin's come back!"

The sun was hot, and the liquor Clay had drunk on the train brought the sweat pouring down his face, and the jolting of his horse made him sick. Pulling the animal down to a slow walk, he thought sourly about the weeks he had spent in Dallas—that was as far as he had gotten after getting off the boat—and none of his memories were good. Being a fair gambler, he had managed to stretch out his money and his stay for two weeks. Finally a bad night at cards had left him with barely enough for train fare, and he had reluctantly bought his ticket, along with a bottle to numb his memories.

He rode slowly, wanting to sober up before he got home. He finally decided to time his arrival after the family went to bed. He could clean up and make his appearance in the morning. To that end, he walked the horse at a slow gait all afternoon, almost going to sleep more than once. It was after four when he came to the cutoff that led to the Yancy place. He thought suddenly that he could go there and clean up before going home, and on a sudden impulse, he turned the horse down the narrow road.

The air grew colder as the sun went down, but he had a raging thirst and stopped once to drink from a shallow creek that crossed the road. He washed his face in the clear water, then tried to push his hair into place, using his fingers for a comb. Then he looked down into the shallow water, saw his reflection, and stopped dead still. He stared at the image—saw the hollow eyes, the sunken cheeks—and knew that if someone looking as bad as he did turned up at the back door of Gracefield, he'd send him down the road.

Despair filled him as he sat back on his heels. A bird was singing close by, a happy, joyous sound, and the rippling water over the stones was a merry note. But the happy world around him only amplified the unhappiness within him. For a long time he sat there, his face buried in his arms. Finally he got to his feet wearily, then mounted his horse, his face set. "They'll probably run me off the place," he muttered, but driven by some impulse, he made his way to the cabin.

Smoke curled out of the chimney, and he saw Melora at once. She was feeding some hens, throwing the grain with a graceful motion. As he rode up, she glanced his way, not knowing him, he saw. Then when recognition came, she came running to stand behind the horse. Her eyes were enormous in the gathering twilight as she looked at him.

"Mister Clay!" she whispered with a tremulous smile. "You came back!"

Clay's lips trembled, for he saw that she was glad to see him. "Well, I didn't kill any dragons, Melora."

"That doesn't matter," she said. "I was afraid for you."

Clay would have answered, but her parents had come out on the porch, and he looked at Yancy as he came closer. He saw the surprise in the man's careful green eyes, but there was no condemnation.

"Why, Mr. Rocklin!" he said quickly. "Git off that critter! You're worse than a preacher for gettin' to a man's house just in time for supper!"

Yancy, Clay saw, was trying to put him at ease, but he was sure that they all knew about his sorry part at Cerro Gordo.

"Like to wash up, Buford," he said with an effort. "I'm dirty as a pig."

"I'll heat you some water, Mister Clay," Melora said quickly. "We got a tub you can use."

"Don't want to be a trouble," Clay mumbled.

"How could you be that?" Melora asked, then turned and

walked into the cabin.

Clay still sat on the horse, the shame cutting him like a knife inside. "Buford, you may not want me in your home after I tell you what I've been doing."

In letters, Buford Yancy was an ignorant man—but he was wise in things that mattered. He had heard about Clay's discharge, but he came from a line of men who held friendship sacred. He said quietly, "Get down, Clay. You can use my razor."

The simplicity of the rough mountain man's acceptance brought a mist to Clay's eyes, and he got down, trying to hide his emotions. He didn't have to say anything, for with a natural tact, the family cared for him. He took a long bath in a tub placed on the back porch, shaved with Yancy's razor, and put on one of Yancy's shirts while Mattie washed his own. It dried by the stove as they ate a supper of roasted rabbit, collard greens, and freshly baked corn bread. The buttermilk, cool from its home in the springhouse, did more to cool Clay's burning throat than anything he had tasted.

After supper, he and Buford sat on the front porch. Yancy did almost all the talking. Mostly he talked about hunting and fishing, about his children. He sensed that Clay needed to say little and took the burden of the conversation.

"You gotta see them books that Melora bought with the money you gave her!" He added proudly, "She's done read every one of them!"

Finally Clay rose and went inside, where Melora showed him the books, and he commended her choices. But when he caught sight of the tattered copy of *Pilgrim's Progress*, he grew silent.

Finally he put on his clean shirt, which was not quite dry. He looked fairly presentable, but he felt a reluctance to leave.

There was an ease, a happiness in the humble cabin that he knew would be lacking at Gracefield. And he also knew whose fault it was.

"Got to be going," he announced. The family followed him out, and as he rode away into the darkness, they all called after him. And he was able to pick out Melora's sweet voice as she cried out, "Come back soon, Mister Clay!"

In the years that followed, Clay Rocklin often wondered what would have happened if he had gotten home an hour later. It was a fine point, but his life was changed by the fact that he arrived at Gracefield at nine thirty.

For if he had come just one hour later, he would not have encountered Melanie alone. He would have seen her in the morning at breakfast. If not there, then someplace else—but someplace where they would have been with other people.

Melanie wondered with grief much the same thing in the years that followed. She went over it a thousand times. . .how she stayed up late, which was very unusual for her. . .how she had gone downstairs to the library to read, not being able to sleep. She had never done that before, but that night she was worried about Gid.

She had put the children to bed fairly early, and being tired from a hard day's play, they had gone to sleep almost at once. Then she had sat down and talked with Charlotte, who was much weaker these days. Melanie did not think the woman would ever recover, and she spent as much time as possible with her.

Charlotte Rocklin had gone downhill quickly after Noah died. It was as if there were an invisible cord between the two, and when that was snapped by Noah's death, Charlotte lost her vitality and her will to live. She was feeble, and the thought of Clay was heavy on her heart. She had not been told of his behavior at Cerro Gordo, but still she was a wise woman and knew that things were ill with him.

"Noah worried so about him," the sick woman whispered. "But he always believed that God would bring him back. There's a verse in the Bible about it. Noah found it one day. I remember it so plain! He came running in where I was making a cake and said, 'Look here! It's in the Bible about our grandson Clay!' He was so excited that day!"

"Do you remember the verse, Mother Rocklin?"

"Of course. It's in Isaiah, chapter 54, verse 13. It says, 'All thy children shall be taught of the Lord.' And Noah never forgot it, Mellie! One of the last things he said before the Lord took him was, 'Clay! Clay's going to come to the Lord!'"

"That's wonderful!" Melanie said, and for a long time she sat there as the old woman spoke of her children and grand-children. Finally she dropped off to sleep, and Melanie tiptoed out of the room.

"You ain't in bed yet, Miss Mellie?" Dorrie was in the kitchen, cutting up the last of a chicken as Melanie entered.

"I've been with Miss Charlotte."

"Poor thing! She ain't got long, has she? Jesus gonna come for her soon!"

"I think so, Dorrie. And she'll be glad to go."

"She been like a lost chile ever since Marse Noah was took."

The two women talked for a time, neither of them mentioning Clay, and finally Dorrie finished and left.

Still not sleepy, Melanie went to the library. She chose a book, then sat down in one of the horsehair chairs and began to read. It was not a good novel, and she was about to put it down when she heard a horse come down the drive and go to the stable. She looked out the window, wondering who could be moving about so late.

She turned the lamp down and left the library. Then as she crossed the foyer, the door opened and a man stood there. Startled, she asked, "Who is it?"

The answer sent a shock running through her.

"It's me, Mellie—Clay!"

"Clay!" Melanie went to him at once, holding out her hands. "I'm so glad!"

Clay took her hands, his mind reeling. It was like witchcraft, for he had been thinking of her as he rode from the Yancy place, of the days of their courtship and how sweet, how beautiful she was.

And now she had come to him, appearing out of the night like a phantom—a beautiful phantom, for she wore a light rose-colored robe of silk, and her eyes glowed warmly in the dark.

"Come to the library," she said quickly. "I want to talk to you."

He allowed her to pull him down the hall, and as soon as they were in the dim light of the library, she asked, "Clay, are you all right?"

"All right?" he asked in confusion. "Why, I guess so."

"We've been so worried, Clay! Not a word from you since you left Mexico!"

Clay stood in the darkness, listening to Mellie's voice, unable to think. For years he had kept his distance from Mellie, for he was still in love with her. Though bitter that she had chosen Gid, he could not forget her sweetness, and as they stood there whispering in the dim light, every nerve was painfully conscious of her beauty. She looked up at him, her lips rich and full, and he suddenly reached out and took hold of her.

"Clay!" she cried in alarm. "Don't—"

But he was like a man who was caught in one of those terrible, vivid dreams in which reality and fantasy are so fused that he can't separate the two. He clutched her in his arms, and his lips sought hers. She was so soft and fragrant, and he forgot his family, forgot that she was another man's wife, forgot everything except that she was all he had ever wanted.

Melanie, shocked and outraged, fought against him, but he was far stronger. Her cries, though, did not go unheeded, for suddenly someone was standing in the door, and Melanie cried out, "Help me, please!"

Thomas had heard Clay's horse approach and, getting out of bed, had caught a glimpse of the rider as he crossed to the stable. "I'm going down, Susanna," he said to his wife.

"Is it Clay?" she asked quickly.

"Might be."

Thomas struggled into his clothing and went down the stairs, leaving Susanna as she searched for a robe. When he got to the foot of the stairs, he was startled by a cry from the library. Not sure of what he would find, he picked up the iron poker that rested against the fireplace.

What he saw as he came in the door sent such a wave of rage through him that he could not control himself. He saw his son Clay forcing Melanie—his nephew's wife!—toward the couch.

Years of frustration and rage suddenly spilled out, and with a hoarse cry, Thomas lifted the poker and brought it down twice on Clay's unprotected head.

Melanie almost fell as Clay went to his knees, the sleeve of her gown ripping at the shoulder. She drew the gown together and, seeing Thomas raise the poker again, his eyes mad, ran to him and threw herself against him.

"No! Don't kill him!"

"The dog!" Thomas cried out, trying to disengage her clinging hands. At that moment Susanna rushed in. Taking in the scene, she joined Melanie in restraining Thomas.

"You must not!" she said, holding him tightly. The two women were hard pressed to hold him back, and Clay got to his feet, blood streaming down his cheek. The first blow had taken him on top of his head; the second had caught him as he turned and had opened a cut from his eyebrow to his cheekbone. Stunned by the attack, he stood there, his eyes blank.

Slowly Thomas regained control. He took a deep breath, then tossed the poker to the floor. "I'm—all right now," he said with a trembling voice. "It's a good thing you were here. I would have killed him!"

Clay blinked, felt the blood running down his cheek, and raised one hand to touch it. He stared at the blood, then at the three who stood in front of him. He could not think clearly, but the look in his father's eyes told him that nothing he could say would matter.

Then Thomas spoke to his son in a voice as cold and hard as his eyes. "Get out of my house! You are no longer my son!"

Clay licked his lips, trying to reply, but there was no mercy in those eyes. He shook his head, then turned and walked out of the library. As his feet sounded on the steps, Susanna clutched at Thomas, saying, "Oh, my dear, are you sure—?"

"He's not our son, Susanna!" Thomas said in an iron voice. "He is dead—and I never want to hear his name again!"

Melanie, Susanna, and Thomas stood there, and soon the sound of a horse's hooves came to them. They waited until the echoes died away, and to all of them the sound of it was like a death knell.

PART THREE

Prodigal's Return—1859

CHAPTER 13

THE SLAVER

A fierce gale had torn the tops out of the *Carrie Jane* and—even worse—had snapped the mainmast ten feet above the deck. Ignoring the biting wind that numbed his fingers and stiffened his face, Clay Rocklin drove the deckhands aloft to set the new canvas. He would have gone up himself, but one of the first things he had discovered when he had come aboard the ship was that he had little head for heights. He had mastered every other aspect of seamanship, and it grated on his nerves that young Carlin, who was only sixteen, could scamper aloft into the swaying tops, while he himself was confined to the deck by some bad gene.

"Better get every inch on her you can, Mr. Rocklin." Clay turned to find that Captain March had come from the wheel to look at the tattered canvas. He was a thick-bodied man, his white hair set off by a ruddy complexion. Though well over sixty years old, the captain could work any of the deckhands into a stupor. It had been the fact that he could not outwork Clay Rocklin that had drawn his attention to the young man.

Clay had been stranded in Jamaica, totally destitute and with no prospects. The *Carrie Jane* had glided into the harbor under half sail, beautiful in the sparkling sunshine. That night Clay had met Captain Jonas March, and the other man had gotten the outline of his story. "Never too late for a man to change," he had said. "God can do what you can't."

Clay had resisted his preaching but had signed on as a deckhand for a run to Africa. "You know our cargo?" March had asked. "No? Well, it's black ivory, mister."

"Slaves?" Clay had asked in surprise. "That's against international law."

"It ain't against God's law! The pay's good, but it's the Lord's work, too. It's all there in the Bible, in black and white... the sons of Ham, bondservants, the sweat of their brow. We're spreading the Lord's seed, mister!"

Clay had soon discovered that Captain March held with the ideology of most of the planters he knew, that the black man was blessed by slavery. That his lot as a slave in the South was better than the life he would have had in a hut in Africa. Even more important, this new life would expose the black man to the gospel, which would save his soul.

The crew of the *Carrie Jane* was a poor lot, but March had some education. He invited Clay to his cabin often, and they had become friends by the time the ship touched on the African continent. March had said, "You're young and strong, Rocklin, and you're smart. Now let me tell you, if you apply yourself, you can make something of your life. I'm no spring chicken, you know! And I been keepin' my eye out for a good young man. Don't see why you can't be him. I'll teach you the sea and ships, and you work hard. Sooner than you think, you'll be a fine seaman, and you can buy an interest in the *Carrie Jane*."

As the wind whipped across his face, Clay studied the face of Jonas March. Things had happened exactly as the old sailor had predicted that night in his cabin. Clay had applied himself, discovering that he had a natural gift for the sea. The years had gone by swiftly, and now he owned one-half of the ship and had a large bank account besides.

The pay was good, as Jonas had said—but life had not been easy. Even now, Clay could hear the moaning of the blacks below deck. He always heard it these days, even in his sleep. The years had hardened him to the sight of men, women, and children being chained and packed below deck like animals. He had learned to block what he was doing out of his mind. He had even reached the point where he could ignore the awful smell of filth and disease that clung to the ship. After he had become master's mate, he simply concentrated on counting his money, dreaming of the time when he would leave the ship.

The land summoned him, for—despite his abilities—he was not a sailor. He longed for the fields, the trees, and the rivers of Virginia. More than once he had almost taken the plunge, but then he would think, *Where would I go? Back to Gracefield? I can't do that! They've written me off forever.*

Clay looked toward the stern, noting that the sails of the British frigate were slightly closer. "She's gaining on us, Jonas." He spoke loudly over the sound of the keening wind. "I don't think even with the topsails repaired we can outrun her. Not with the mainmast down."

"Try it." As he said this, Captain March stared at Clay, a thought in his head. But he decided the time was not right and simply said, "Get the canvas on her, Clay!"

An hour later, the topsails were all in place, but it was obvious that the frigate was not going to be shaken off.

"What'll happen if they catch us, sir?"

Clay looked around to see young Carlin staring at the warship, his eyes big with fear.

"They'll confiscate the ship and throw us all in a rotting prison for the rest of our lives," he said harshly. "That's what you were told when you signed on. It's the risk you take on as a slaver." Then he said in a softer tone, "Maybe she'll lose some of her sails. Ordinarily we could run away and leave her, but not without a mainmast."

Clay had no hope, for he was seaman enough to know the truth—they could not outsail the frigate with the sails they had. He knew another truth, too: He would never go to prison, not as long as he had a pistol in his cabin. Life was bad enough, but he knew enough of the English prisons to know it would be better to die than go to one.

He was standing on the deck when Captain March joined him. "She'll be up with us in two hours, Jonas," he remarked.

"Aye, she will." A strange look was on the face of the old captain, and he said in a tight voice, "Get all the blacks up on deck."

"On deck? What for?"

"Just obey the order, mister!"

A thought crossed Clay's mind, but he put it quickly away. Captain March had been a slaver for many years; perhaps shifting the slaves around would give the ship another knot or so an hour. He obeyed the order, and twenty minutes later the deck was packed with the captives. They were terrified, of course, as they always were from the time they stepped on board.

What must it be like, Clay wondered, not for the first time, *to be snatched from your village, from your home? To be chained and whipped and driven away from all you've ever known? And*

198

then to be put on a ship, taken thousands of miles to a strange land where nothing is familiar. No wonder so many of them just give up and die!

The wind was rising as Clay stood there staring at the pitiful captives. There were mothers with babies, and children so young they could barely walk. And there were the men, whose bodies were striped by the whips of the slavers who had brought them to the ship. He saw one young woman, a beautiful girl of no more than sixteen or seventeen. She had a child, and she clung to it fiercely, her arms around him to cut off the cold wind. She was dressed in rags, as they all were, and the cold January wind must have chilled her to the bones.

Then he heard Captain March say, "Over the side with them, Mr. Rocklin!"

Clay's mind seemed to turn to ice. He stood absolutely still, refusing to believe that he had heard the captain's order correctly. The young woman with the child was staring at him with huge eyes, and he could hear the keening of the child, a thin cry that seemed to tie his stomach into knots.

"Did you hear me, Mr. Rocklin?" Jonas March's face was fixed in a flinty expression. "Quick! You know what will happen if that frigate takes us with this cargo!" The hand of Captain Marsh grasped Clay's arm, and his voice was harsh. "We have no choice!"

Still Clay stood there, transfixed, his mind reeling. It was like a terrible dream, the face of the young woman growing larger and larger, the sound of the child's crying thin and faint.

Then Jonas yelled at the second mate. "Over the side, Jenkins!"

As Clay watched, the burly Jenkins lifted the man on the end of the chain and flung him over the side. The man screamed, and the weight of his body jerked the slave next to him over the side. Immediate horrible screams rent the air, drowning out the wind whistling in Clay's ears.

The young woman had her eyes fixed on him when the chain around her waist caught her, dragging her to the rail, and she clutched her baby tightly. Her eyes were filled with panic, but she didn't scream. She stared at Clay as if she expected him to do something, but he stood there unable to move.

Just as she went over, her body striking the rail, she took one hand from her baby and lifted it in a strangely eloquent gesture for mercy, and her eyes were fixed on him as she disappeared from his sight. He took one horrified glance toward the stern and saw the line of writhing bodies sinking into the churning wake of the *Carrie Jane.*

Then he whirled and ran to the bow, where he vomited so violently that he thought his rib cage would be torn apart.

The rest of the voyage was strange. The British frigate finally overtook the slaver and boarded her. The British captain knew what they had done, and in his cabin he excoriated Captain March and Clay, cursing them with every invective he could manage. But he had no evidence, and in the end he had to let them go.

March said little for the next two days. It was clear that his partner was in bad shape. Finally he sought Clay out, saying, "It was unfortunate, my boy, and we both grieve over the loss."

"How much money did we lose, Jonas?" Clay's voice was harsh as a raven's caw, and he stared at the captain with haunted eyes. "How many dollars went down to the bottom?"

Jonas March stood there, his eyes hurt. He was not a dishonest man. He lived according to what he thought was right—but the sight of those black bodies had shaken his theory, and now he said, "I—I wasn't thinking of dollars, Clay."

Clay stared at him, his body tense; then he saw the pain in the eyes of the old man. "I'm sure you weren't, Jonas," he said wearily. "But this is the end for me."

And so it was at the end of the voyage that Jonas bought back Clay's half-interest in the ship. The two men parted at the bank where they had settled the legal side of the business.

"Jonas, I thank you for your goodness to me. You've been more than generous."

March waved his hand. "No, my boy, no more than just. You've done more than I expected." He paused and asked before turning to go, "What will you do, Clay?"

Clay shrugged his shoulders in a gesture of helplessness. "Try to forget," he said, and he walked out of the bank.

CHAPTER 14

THE END OF THE TETHER

$\mathcal{M}$r. Warren Larrimore sat back in his tan leather chair, framed a steeple with his fingers, and stared at the man across the desk from him. Larrimore was a lean man with a large head and a full black beard that concealed most of his features. In fact, that was precisely why he wore the beard—as a banker he had to make hard decisions, decisions that sometimes went against his own desires. As a young man he had allowed his naturally generous nature to dictate his business decisions, but a lifetime of dealing with men and money had taught him something.

"Tom," he said quietly, his mild voice more like that of a choir director than a banker as he spoke, "we've been over this before. Although I hate to remind you of it, you've gone against every bit of advice I've ever given you. I'm accustomed to that, for most men think they know more about their business than a stodgy banker. But I like to think that our relationship has been a little more than just banker and depositor. I've considered you a friend for a long time."

Thomas Rocklin sat across from Larrimore, his face pulled tight and his heart beating too fast. He tried to smile but made a bad job of it. "Certainly, Warren! I feel that way, too." His collar seemed too tight, and he pulled at it nervously, trying to find a way to say what he hoped would change Larrimore's mind about the loan. "And you're right about the rest. I should have listened to you. But I thought the price of cotton would go up—and I still think it will. Where else is England going to buy cotton for her mills?"

Larrimore shook his head with a sharp impatience. "Tom, you're like all the rest of the planters. You think the world runs on cotton!" The blindness that Southern planters had developed about cotton was an old story to the banker. He had explained the problem to Rocklin before, but he tried once again. "It's always an evil to be tied to one source of income, Tom. You're bound to it and helpless in the long run. What can you do if the price goes down? Hold your cotton? No, because almost every planter I know borrows to the hilt to get the crop raised. So you'll take whatever is offered. And if there's a war, what will you do with it? You can't eat it, and you can't make cannon or shells out of it."

"England will buy it," Thomas said stubbornly. "She has to."

Larrimore gave up, and though nothing showed in his face, he was sickened over what he had to do. But there was no way out—a fact he had known from the beginning. Drawing his eyes down to a stare, he said, "Tom, I've got to call your loans. It's not my decision, you understand. I have a board of directors to answer to. When the loan committee met, I tried everything I could think of to get them to extend the loans, but they voted me down unanimously."

"But, Warren, there must be something you can do!" A cold sweat appeared on Rocklin's brow, and he clenched his hands to control the tremor that suddenly came to them. "I'll lose Gracefield!"

"I think I can maneuver the thing so that you'll come out with something, Tom," Larrimore said. "Not much, but enough so that you and Susanna won't have to worry." He tried to put a good face on the thing, saying in an encouraging tone, "After all, it's time you took things easy. You can travel some, maybe buy a little place in town, just big enough for you and Susanna and for the grandchildren to visit."

Thomas blinked his eyes nervously. The thing he had dreaded had finally come, and he felt as though he were in a terrible nightmare. More than anything in his life, he wanted Warren Larrimore to suddenly laugh and say, "Now, Tom, I was just trying to give you a scare! Cheer up! You can have the loan!"

He knew, though, with a sickening certainty, that no such thing was going to happen. He sat there trying not to let the fear that clutched him show, but Larrimore saw it. A Christian man, Larrimore had more compassion than was prudent for a banker. "Tom," he said, "I've told you before, there's one way out of this. Ask your brother to help you. Stephen is a wealthy man. He's your older brother. I think he'd be glad to help you."

"No!" The banker was shocked at the vehemence in Rocklin's answer. "I won't do it!" He got to his feet, picked up his coat, and started for the door. He stopped abruptly, turned back, and added, nodding, "I'll find a way out of this, Warren. There are other banks!"

As the door closed, Larrimore sat at his desk, grieving over the tragedy of the Rocklin family. None of them was fitted for the world of business—except Stephen, of course. Burke Rocklin, Thomas's younger son, was no help. He had hated farmwork from the time he was ten years old. Thomas had spent a fortune educating him, and at the age of twenty-nine,

Burke was still "trying to find himself." Then there was Clay Rocklin...

The door opened and a tall, heavy man with a smooth face and a pair of direct gray eyes came in. George Snelling was chairman of the board. He asked at once, "You tell him, Warren?"

"Yes," the other replied heavily. "He didn't take it well."

"Too bad! But it's been inevitable. You did all you could to help him, Warren. But a man's got to stand on his own two feet." He went to the window and watched the traffic, then asked, "He understands that he's got to vacate at once?"

"I gave him a month, George."

Snelling frowned. That was not what the board had instructed Larrimore to do. But then he smiled. He was a hard character himself, but he had learned to trust the small man sitting at the desk. "Well, you know best, I suppose." He studied Larrimore, then said again, "Too bad," and left the room. Larrimore did not move for more than five minutes. He sat there staring at the wall until, in a rare gesture of anger, he suddenly raised his fist and struck his walnut desk an angry blow that sent papers flying. Then he took a deep breath, shook his head, and began to gather them up in a logical fashion.

Susanna knew that something was wrong with Tom the minute he returned. She saw him from the kitchen window where she was helping Dorrie. "Finish the rest of these potatoes, Dorrie," she said and went at once to meet him, but he came in through the side door and went upstairs. When she went into her room, she was shocked to find him sitting on the bed, his face twisted as though he was having some sort of attack.

"Tom! What is it?" She rushed over to his side, and he suddenly reached for her. She held his head against her breast, fear beginning to rise in her. In all their years of married life, she had never seen him like this! "Is it your heart?"

"No!" He pulled himself back and stared at her, his dark eyes blinking. She saw that he was on the verge of losing control.

She said nothing but put her arm around him. He clung to her until, finally, he grew calm. He took a deep breath. "I've been to see Warren Larrimore," he said.

Susanna understood. "He's not going to renew our loans?"

"He said he wants to, but the loan committee turned us down." He bit his lip, then broke out, "Susanna, we're going to lose everything!"

Susanna knew at that moment that she was stronger than her husband. But then, she had always known that. "We'll be all right, Tom," she said evenly.

"All right? How can we be 'all right'?" he demanded, his control slipping. He stopped, put out his hand, saying, "I'm sorry. I'm just not myself."

"We've seen it coming for a long time."

"I know—but I thought something would happen!" He groaned and pulled at his hair nervously. "How am I going to tell the children?"

"Just tell them," Susanna said practically. The thought of leaving Gracefield was a sharp pain in her bosom, but she would never let Thomas or anyone else see it. "A family is more than a house, I do hope," she said. "The Rocklins have good stuff. We'll be all right."

Tom shook his head. "I talked to Brad yesterday. I thought he could help, but he's had a bad year, too. Oh, he offered what he could, but it wasn't nearly enough."

"We can't take the money from Brad and Amy," Susanna said at once. "They're in debt as deeply as we are. Brad expanded too fast." After a while, she got Tom to sit down and talk. It was, Susanna thought with some bitterness, the first time they'd talked so long in years. *It takes a tragedy to get us together for an hour,* she thought. But all she said was, "We'll tell the family tonight, after supper."

"All right. It'll have to be done."

That night Thomas ate almost nothing. Susanna looked around the table at each face, wondering how they would take the news. She sat at one end of the table, Thomas at the other. To her right sat Ellen with the twins, Dent and David. On her left Burke sat next to his father, and beside him, Lowell and Rena. *Four out of the eight are Clay's,* she thought suddenly, then resolutely closed her mind to the image of her oldest child.

The talk at the table centered on the strain between the North and the South. As usual, Dent and Burke were the loudest. Burke was not more than five feet ten inches tall and looked remarkably like Susanna; he was the only one of the children who resembled her. He had a round face, smooth brown hair, and gray-green eyes. Actually he cared little for politics, but he loved to tease Dent, who was easily stirred. They were arguing about a series of debates that had taken place a few months earlier between two politicians in Illinois—Stephen A. Douglas, a man of national prominence, and Abraham Lincoln, a lesser-known figure.

"Steve Douglas is our man, Burke!" Dent said, waving a fork with a large chunk of roast beef impaled on it. "He's got the right idea—popular sovereignty!"

"And what's that?" Burke prodded.

"Why, the right of a state to tend to its own business!

You just wait, Burke," Dent said, his dark eyes burning. "Steve Douglas will be the next president of the United States!" Dent, at the age of seventeen, looked so much like Clay had at that age that it pained Susanna to watch him. He was like Clay in more than looks, too. . . .

Burke sipped his buttermilk, then said, "No, Lincoln finished him off in those debates. I hear the rail-splitter is about as homely as a man can get, but he does have a way with words! People listen to him. Why, I can quote you what he said about all the trouble we're having in this country over slavery. 'A house divided against itself cannot stand. . . . I believe this government cannot endure permanently half-slave and half-free. . . . I do not expect the Union to be dissolved—I do not expect the house to fall—but I do expect it will cease to be divided. It will become all one thing or the other.'" Burke had always had a fine memory, and he had recited the words with evident relish.

"If Lincoln means that," Rena said suddenly, "we'll have a war." She was tall for a girl of thirteen, and her dark brown hair formed the perfect frame for her fine complexion.

"You don't know anything about it, Rena!" Ellen snapped. "There can't be a war!" Ellen was on one of her diets, struggling to keep her figure. She was an attractive woman, but her features had sharpened as her figure had grown fuller over the years. That she was here at all was unusual, for she spent more time in Richmond with friends on extended visits than she spent at Gracefield.

The argument went on for several minutes; then Lowell got up, saying, "I'm going over to the stable. It's time for the new colt to come."

He was caught when he was halfway to the door by his

grandfather's voice. "Lowell! Come back. I have something to tell you."

Lowell at once showed a stubborn streak, going back to his seat and flinging himself into it. He was fifteen and a throwback to his great-grandfather Noah. He had all the good traits, such as kindness and generosity, and some less admirable traits—mostly a tendency to be bullheaded!

Thomas looked around the table, cleared his throat, then said, "I have some news for you. I'm sure you'll not like it. I didn't! But we have to face up to it."

"What is it, Thomas?" Ellen demanded

"Well, I'm afraid that we're going to be leaving Gracefield." He saw the blank looks with which they regarded him—all except Burke—and went on lamely. "Times have been very bad ever since Buchanan took office in '57. We've had a depression that's shaken the whole country. And we've had poor crops for the last two or three years. So we're going to have to sell out."

"But—where will we go, Grandfather?" Rena was a quick child. She picked up on the uncertainty in Thomas at once, and her own voice had a thread of fear.

"We don't know yet, Rena," Susanna said quickly, "but God will take care of us."

"Is it the bank?" Burke asked quietly.

"I'm afraid so, Burke." Thomas tried to put a good face on it. "We'll look around and find a nice place. Not as large as this, of course. Maybe we'll move to the coast. You've all liked our vacations there."

Susanna saw that all of them were frightened. Little wonder, for the one fixed point in all their lives had been Gracefield. Ellen, she saw, was pale, and her lips were trembling. Since Clay had left, Susanna and Thomas had provided for her—and

Ellen had been far from inexpensive. Now she was faced with being a woman with four children and no income.

Dent was staring at his grandfather, speechless for once, and David looked stunned. He was the quiet one, the thinker, and Susanna knew he would not sleep all night. He would lie awake and think about the future—but then, she would do the same, she realized suddenly.

"We'll talk about it later," Susanna said quickly. "We don't have to move tomorrow. And God will take care of us."

"Will God let us stay here in our home?" Dent said, his voice hard. "Doesn't seem that's too much for Him to do."

"Don't speak like that, Dent!" Susanna said with a direct stare. Then she said, "We'll talk more about it later."

They left the table, quiet and subdued.

For the next week, Thomas walked around the plantation like a man in a dream. They all talked, of course, but no one knew what to do. Finally on Saturday night, after they had gone to bed, Susanna said, "Tom, are you certain you don't want to ask Stephen for help?"

Tom seemed to freeze, and she knew it had been the wrong thing to say. She had always known that Tom resented his older brother, but not until now did she know how deeply rooted that resentment was.

"I'll *never* ask him!" Thomas said between clenched teeth. "I'd rather die!"

She hugged him tightly. "We won't die, Tom. God won't fail us. You'll see!"

CHAPTER 15

A VISITOR FROM THE PAST

The tall man in the fawn-colored suit looked to John Novak as though he might be business. Novak had been hired by Stephen Rocklin years ago, when the foundry had occupied an old carriage house on the outskirts of Washington. A scrawny boy of fifteen with eyes that looked huge in his hungry, lean face, Novak had been thrilled to find a job, though it was only as a lowly clerk. He came from a family of fifteen, his parents still speaking English with a thick European accent. Novak always smiled when he recalled how, three mornings in a row, Stephen Rocklin had run him away. But persistence was a family trait for the young immigrant, and on the fourth morning, Rocklin had studied the lad carefully. "You want to work, boy?" he had asked.

"Yah, I work, mister!"

And Rocklin had believed him.

The boy had attacked work like a hungry dog attacks raw meat. Nothing was too hard, no work too dirty for him. Stephen admired the boy's eagerness, and his belief in him became strong. He had paid for Novak's schooling, and the boy soaked up learning like a sponge! As the Rocklin Foundry grew, John

Novak grew with it, so that now Stephen often said, "No need to worry if I die. Novak would keep the place running without missing a day!"

Novak knew every job in the foundry, and his post as assistant to Mr. Rocklin required, in part, that he filter out visitors who wanted to see the owner. Gifted with a natural ability to discern a person's intent and motives, John Novak turned many people away. But there was something about the man who had appeared suddenly at eleven o'clock on a Tuesday morning and asked to see Mr. Rocklin.

Novak noted the fine suit, the expensive black leather shoes, and the diamond that glittered on the visitor's right hand. He noticed the hand, too; it was brown and calloused but well cared for. The man's face was strong—more handsome than a man's face should be, perhaps—and it was saved from any look of weakness by the tough line of the lips and the firm jaw. Novak considered a person's eyes "the window of the soul," and the visitor had a pair of the darkest eyes he had ever seen, with a direct gaze that took in the office and Novak carefully.

"May I ask your business, sir? Mr. Rocklin is quite busy this morning."

"Tell him an old friend from the past would like to see him for a few minutes."

Novak hesitated, then nodded. "I'll tell him, sir."

Novak entered the door behind him and found his employer engaged in studying a rifle that had been disassembled and carefully laid out on a pine table. He looked up with a trace of impatience, but his voice was even. "Yes?"

"A gentleman to see you, Mr. Rocklin. He won't say why, but he's top drawer." Novak shrugged his thin shoulders. "Says he's an old friend from your past."

"Blast it, I don't want to see anyone, John!"

"Might mean money," Novak said mildly. "He's got some."

Suddenly Rocklin smiled. "I sometimes think you can smell cash, John! Well, show him in—but come back in five minutes and tell me I have to do something. Can't waste much time on my 'old friend.'"

Novak nodded but had already decided to do just that. He stepped outside and, holding the door open, said, "Please step in, sir."

Stephen had bent over the rifle, having put on his glasses to study the fine work of the firing mechanism. He was aware that his visitor had entered but did not want to drop the screw that he was trying to put into the tiny hole. Finally he got it started, laid the part down, then looked up, saying, "Now then, sir, what can I do for you?"

The sunlight from a window was in his eyes, and he saw only the outline of a tall man who stood quietly in the center of the room. He blinked, adding, "I'm Stephen Rocklin."

"How are you, Uncle?"

Rocklin gave a start, then moved to one side so that he could see the man clearly. "Clay!" he said, blinking with surprise. "My Lord! Is it you?"

Clay smiled but did not offer his hand or move any closer. "I'm afraid it is. Bad penny turning up again."

But the shock that had gone through Stephen passed, and he came forward at once to throw his arms around his nephew. He felt the lean body grow stiff, but gave him a hearty hug, then stepped back, saying, "By Harry, it's good to see you, my boy!"

Clay's face was stiff with the effort of concealing the emotion that had washed through him as his uncle embraced him. Stephen was older, thicker in body, and his face was lined.

Otherwise, he seemed to be unchanged in appearance. Clay slowly relaxed, saying quietly, "I've been here in Washington nearly a week." His wide mouth turned upward in a faint smile. "Most of that time I've been trying to get up enough courage to come and see you."

Stephen waved his thick hand. "Why, there was no need for that, my boy! You should have come at once!"

"That's—kind of you, Uncle. But you were always that way."

Stephen saw that Clay was uncomfortable and said briskly, "Well, by Harry, this *is* fine. Now first we've got to go out and have lunch. I've got the inside track on the best chef in Washington, Clay! He thinks I'm more important than I am, and I allow him to think so. Novak—!" He began to pull on his overcoat, and when the secretary came to the door, he said, "This is my nephew, Clay Rocklin. My brother Tom's oldest boy. We're going out to eat."

"Glad to know you, Mr. Rocklin," Novak said, perfectly aware of Clay's history but allowing no emotion to touch his smooth, dark face. "But you have an appointment with the board at one, Mr. Rocklin."

"You meet with them, John," Stephen said with a grin. "You always think you know this business better than I do."

Novak protested, but Rocklin grabbed Clay's arm, saying, "Come on, Clay. Let's get out of here!"

An hour later they were finishing steaks at the Arlington House, the finest restaurant in Washington. Stephen had kept up a rapid-fire account of the family, including Gideon's promotion to major and a detailed description of his grandchildren. He said, "It was hard, losing Mother." Then he stared at Clay. "You didn't know? She died about a year after you left." Then, seeing Clay's sadness, he said quickly, "Gid's stationed here, Clay.

He'll be glad to see you."

Clay had said almost nothing, but now he set down the glass of sherry he had been sipping and looked at his uncle candidly. "You're a clever man, Uncle Stephen. You've made me feel—well, like a man again. But I won't be seeing Gid. . .or Melanie."

His voice faltered as he pronounced Melanie's name, and Stephen studied him carefully. He was not the same immature, rash man who had disappeared twelve years ago. He was thirty-nine now, but older in more ways than in years. A little heavier, but not much, and his olive skin had been darkened to a richer tone. He was strong and fit, and Stephen had noticed that he had a sailor's walk, as if contending with a deck that rose and fell. Clay's eyes bothered him, though—for in their dark depths he read a pain that ran deep. Now he said quietly, "I'm a fool to chatter on like a magpie, Clay. But I wanted you to feel at ease." Leaning forward, he shook his head, adding, "Melanie would like to see you. She's spoken of you many times. We all have."

"Even after I attacked her?"

Stephen ignored the harsh, brittle tone. "Clay, that was one act. You don't judge a man by one act, but by his whole life."

"Like when I let Gid's company down at Cerro Gordo? You think I could face Gid after that?" Clay's face had grown hard, and the memories that came to him brought a torment into his face. "No, I just wanted to see you, Uncle."

"Have you been in touch with your family at all, Clay?"

"I didn't write for years. I pretty well hit bottom, but then after I got on my feet, I wrote to my father."

When Clay broke off abruptly, Stephen asked quietly, "Did he answer you?"

"He—sent my letter back unopened."

"That was a mistake. I've tried to talk to him about it several times."

"I sent money, Uncle Stephen, and he sent that back, too. I did get one letter. A year ago I wrote again, asking if I could come and see them, but he sent back one line—'Don't come to my house ever!'"

Just then a waiter came to say in a low voice, "Will you gentlemen have anything else?"

Clay looked up and, after studying the face of the man, said in a sardonic tone, "No, thanks. I've had enough."

Suddenly a thought entered Stephen's mind, an instant impression that seemed to grow into a full-fledged plan in a matter of seconds. It was what some call an epiphany, referring to a sudden insight that comes by something other than logic or even conscious thought.

Stephen was not accustomed to such thoughts, and it rattled him somewhat. He made an affair of lighting a cigar, and not until he got it going and sent a cloud of aromatic blue smoke in the air did he decide the idea was sound, even if it had come almost like a mystic vision.

"Come back to my office, Clay." He saw a refusal forming and added quickly, "I have something there you should see. It won't take long, and there'll be no chance of meeting any of the family, if that's what you're thinking."

Clay stared at him curiously, then shrugged. "I have no place to go, Uncle Stephen."

On the way back through the raw weather, Clay wondered what awaited them at his uncle's office, but did not press for any information. Stephen told him about the factory—how it was booming, always behind in orders.

"I suppose," Clay offered, "if the war comes that everyone's talking about, you'll make a lot of money."

"I'd rather not make money off the lives of people," Stephen said, and he happened to be looking at Clay as he spoke. He saw with surprise that his remark struck his nephew hard, for Clay's face grew pale and his lips contracted into a thin line. *I said something wrong*, Stephen thought, but he had no idea what it was.

Novak met them in the outer office, saying, "The board voted—"

"Later, John," Stephen said briefly and led Clay into his office. "Have a seat," he said, going around to sit in his chair. He opened his desk drawer and took out an envelope. "I got this two days ago, Clay," he said. "It's bothered me more than anything has in a long time. I just don't know what to do about it. It's from Warren Larrimore. Do you know him?"

"The banker in Richmond?" Clay asked, opening the letter.

"Yes. He's a good man."

Clay read the letter indolently; then he drew a sudden breath. "Why, this is terrible!"

"It will kill your father, Clay," Stephen answered grimly. "It's the end of everything for him."

Clay finished the letter, then lifted his eyes to meet the steady gaze of his uncle. "I don't understand. What happened? How did things get in such a mess?"

"It's the curse of the South, Clay, as Larrimore points out. A one-crop system is economic suicide. And cotton planting is tied to slavery. It takes an enormous number of low-skilled people to make the crop, and the price of slaves has gotten exorbitant. I know you're from the South and feel differently, but in my mind slavery is an albatross around the neck of the Southern people! A damnable thing that's not only financially ruinous, but morally wrong!" He cut his words off with a brief apology. "Sorry, Clay. I know you don't want to hear that sort of talk from a Yankee."

To Stephen's surprise, Clay said slowly, "No offense, Uncle. As a matter of fact, I agree with you."

Stephen blinked his eyes, surprised. "Well, that's good to hear. But of course, your father and almost all the planters feel differently. And that's why we're on a collision course in this country!"

Clay was only half listening. "This can't happen, Uncle Stephen! It must not!"

"I'd help in an instant. As a matter of fact, I've offered. But as Larrimore says, your father won't take help from me." He shook his head, sadness in his eyes. "It's been a grief to me, Clay, the way your father resents me."

Clay said slowly, "You're everything my father would like to be—and never can be."

"That's not so! Tom is one of the finest men I know!"

"He's not a man to get things done, as you are." Stephen didn't answer, for he knew deep down that this was true. He was, however, surprised to hear Clay voice such a thing. Then Clay asked suddenly, "Why have you shown me this?"

Stephen leaned back in his chair, thinking about the matter. "I think a lot of your family, Clay. I love your father, and I've always been fond of you. You've gotten off on the wrong track, but that can happen to any man, my boy. I don't ask what you've been doing for the past few years, but I am interested in the years that lie ahead of you."

"I don't have a life, Uncle Stephen," Clay said. "Not in the past, nor in the future." He leaned back in his chair, his eyes half closed. "Some things a man can repair, but I'm past all that. I'm like Humpty-Dumpty. All the king's horses and all the king's men couldn't put Clay Rocklin together again."

Stephen hesitated, then said, "God can put any man or woman together, Clay." He did not press his argument, for he saw that Clay was not ready for it. He only added, "Jesus Christ will come to you one day. When that happens, promise me you'll stop running and let Him have His chance with you."

"If Jesus ever comes, I'll remember what you say. But I think Christianity doesn't work for some of us." Clay shook his shoulders, then asked again, "Why did you show me the letter?"

"Haven't you guessed? I think you have."

Clay stared at his uncle with a strange intensity. "I think you believe that I can rescue Gracefield and save the family."

Stephen nodded. "I believe God has sent you here at just the right time. You need your family, and God knows they need you!"

"Why, my father would die before he'd take my help!"

"No, I don't think so. I believe all this has come upon my brother to save him from the bitterness that's been eating him alive ever since you left. He would never have given up on that bitterness as long as he had a choice, but now he has none. Or rather, he has one, and that's you, Clay."

Clay was half amused and half angry. "You think God is interested in all of this? With a universe to run, you think He cares about keeping track of a scoundrel named Clay Rocklin?"

"We're all scoundrels, Clay. Some may put up a better front than others, but inside we're all lost." Stephen came around the desk and put his hand on Clay's shoulder. "It's your last chance, Clay, just as it's your father's last chance. Will you do it?"

A hammer was ringing on an anvil, a rhythmic, pleasant sound. The clock on the wall in Stephen's office was ticking quietly. Neither man spoke, and the silence between them ran on. Finally Clay got to his feet, and there was a look of grim determination on his face.

"Uncle Stephen, I hope you've got faith in this thing—because I think it's insane." Then Clay suddenly brushed his hands across his eyes, and when he looked at Stephen again, he was as sober as a man could be.

"I'll do everything I can. If it were just a matter of money, it wouldn't be so bad. But you know it's more than that."

"I know, I know, my boy," Stephen said, a great happiness filling him. "You'll have a hard way. You'll not be welcomed back. Your family won't accept you. Your friends will all remember your failures—and they'll be waiting for you to make more mistakes. You'll be all alone." Then he threw his thick arm around the young man's shoulders, saying with a hearty voice, "But you'll do it, Clay! I believe God's in it, and when God gets in a thing and we let Him do what He wants, why, that thing is settled!"

"Well, all they can do is kill me, Uncle Stephen," Clay said with a slight smile. "And since I'm dead already, that won't hurt too much. Come on, let's see what we can do with the Rocklin clan!"

CHAPTER 16

THE HOMECOMING OF CLAY ROCKLIN

It amused Clay that Harvey Simmons met him at the livery stable, just as he had twelve years earlier. But this time, Clay saw, Simmons had risen in the world, for the sign over the barn read SIMMONS LIVERY STABLE, not JACOB ESSEN'S LIVERY STABLE as it had those long years ago. Clay had taken the Orange and Alexandria Railroad from Washington, arrived at the station just after seven in the morning, and spent the morning walking around the bustling city.

He had expected the city to stay as he had left it, but since 1847, many changes had come, mostly commercial. New construction was sprouting up everywhere, and the streets were alive with people going to work. *Couldn't expect the old town to stay just as it was,* he thought as he wandered along the side streets. *And I guess I've changed even more than it has.* Every street held memories, some of them good and some bad. He saw that the Blackjack Saloon had fallen into even worse disrepair. The paint was peeling and the windows were filled with cardboard, but the same sign with the ace of spades over the name still swung in the wind. He thought of the night that he, along with Taylor Dewitt and Bushrod Aimes, had tackled a gang of hoodlums over a woman, and all of them had come out of the scrap looking like raw hamburger. *I expect that pair is respectable now.*

He had taken lunch at the Harley House and recognized only one or two people. One of them was the manager, Nolan Finn. But Finn had not noticed him, and Clay did not speak to him. *I'll meet him soon enough*, Clay thought as he left the restaurant and moved toward the livery stable.

He had spent the last month with his uncle Stephen—not at his home, for Clay refused to go there. He had taken a room at a hotel, and the two of them had kept the mails hot with letters to Warren Larrimore. It had taken a great deal of doing, for Thomas's affairs were in such sad condition and so many creditors had to be satisfied that it took every effort on the part of the banker to achieve what Stephen and Clay had asked.

Stephen had written explaining the situation, asking him to keep Clay's name out of any conversations with the family. He had requested that Clay be allowed to buy the paper mortgages, but this proved to be impossible. Some of the men who held the notes would not sell them back, for Gracefield was a good property and they didn't want to lose their chance at gaining possession. Also, Clay didn't have enough money to pay all the notes and finance another crop. In the end, Larrimore wrote, *"We will have to agree with some of the demands of the creditors and, I might add, with my board. The creditors want the place, and my board will not renew the note we hold if Thomas is in control. I persuaded them to renew, and they agreed only on the condition that Clay be responsible for the financial end of the plantation. I don't know how Thomas will take this, but it was the best I could do."*

As Clay approached the livery stable, he thought of the nights he had lain awake, dreading the moment when he would have to return to his home. More than once he had almost fled

Washington, but Stephen Rocklin had sensed those times and had stayed closer than a barnacle until they passed.

Even now he wanted to go back to the station, get on the train, and put Gracefield far behind him. But he did not. Deep inside, he knew that this was the only chance in the world for him, and he hailed the owner of the stable with determination in his voice. "I need to rent a horse."

Simmons stared at Clay uncertainly. The bright noonday April sun blinded him as he came out of the darkness of the stable, and he hesitated. There was something familiar about the tall man who stood there, but he couldn't put his finger on it.

"Know you, don't I, sir?"

"You did once, Harvey."

Simmons blinked, and as his vision cleared, he gasped. "Why, it's Clay Rocklin!"

"What's left of him. You're looking prosperous, Harvey. Own the business now, do you?"

"Well, yes. Old Man Essen died five years ago, and Mr. Larrimore at the bank helped me buy the place." He shook his head, staring at Clay in disbelief. "Most people think you died, Clay."

"Have to disappoint them. Let me have a good horse, Harvey."

"You going out to Gracefield?"

"Yes." *Where else would I be going?* Clay thought.

"Well, you don't need to rent a horse, unless you want to. One of the niggers from your place is in town. Boy named Fox."

"I remember him. His mother was Damis."

"That's the one. He come in early this morning for supplies. He's coming back here to pick up Mr. Burke's saddle any minute. You could ride back with him if you wanted to."

Clay hesitated but then shook his head. "I'm in a hurry, Harvey."

"All right. I'll give you the best we got."

Clay waited until Simmons brought out a tall buckskin, and soon he was riding through the streets of the city. The town had edged out, taking the countryside, and he was impressed at the growth. A huge building, the Tredgar Ironworks, had grown like a mushroom since he had left. Other businesses filled the busy streets. It was not Washington, of course, but it was impressive.

He passed into the countryside, enjoying the feel of a good horse much better than the rise and fall of the schooner. Traffic was heavy for a time, the road crowded with wagons bringing produce to market, farmers bringing their families into town, and a surprising number of people on foot making their way into Richmond.

There was something about the journey to Gracefield that made him uneasy, and as he rode along, he decided that it was the fact that he was going over the same ground he had followed twelve years ago. That time he had come home drunk and half out of his mind over his failure at Cerro Gordo. Now he was on the same road, going to the same house. And if the guilt over the dead soldiers he had murdered in Mexico had been heavy, the scene of the slaves going overboard into the freezing sea to drown was much worse. Ever since he had left the *Carrie Jane*, he had experienced terrible nightmares, especially one that involved the young mother and her baby. Even now, with the sun shining overhead and the beauty of the Virginia countryside surrounding him, the sight of her face tried to form in his mind. He shook his head and galloped his horse for a quarter, driving the image away.

A strong urge took him as he passed the turnoff to the Yancy place. As always, the thought of the Yancys gave him pleasure, but he steadfastly refused to turn his horse in their direction.

At four he passed onto Rocklin land and felt strangely at home. Despite all that had happened, there was a mystic pull in this black soil that he felt at once. It had always been there, no matter how far he sailed to distant lands, and now it came back—along with memories of many things and many people.

He slowed the horse as he approached the drive leading to the house, uncertain even now of how to proceed. Most of all, he dreaded seeing Ellen and the children. The memory of the children had been strong in him all his years of wandering, but he knew from what little Stephen had told him that Ellen had brought them up to despise him.

No matter—or, more accurately, no cure for it now. As he turned down the curving drive, he had a sudden thought and pulled his horse off sharply, crossing into a grove of water oak that rose to the east of the house. Anyone approaching the house by means of the drive would be seen at once, but there was another way. One hundred yards into the grove, there was—or had been—a tiny house, a cabin really. Only two rooms, but snug and comfortable. The summerhouse, as it had been called, had been used for visitors and by the children for playing games.

He was pleased to find it still there and in fair condition. Stepping out of the saddle, he tied the horse and stepped inside. There was no lock, and he found that the inside was in poor shape. Evidently the roof had some leaks, for the furniture was warped and there was a decaying smell to the place. He turned and walked down the path, which was overgrown, coming to the side of the house. He glanced at the scuppernong arbor where he'd courted Mellie in the old days. The vines were still there, but thin and wilted in the heat. There was, he noted, a general deterioration about the place. Fences sagged and were patched just enough to hold together, and the sheds had not been whitewashed in some time. Even the Big House was in need of paint and some repairs—but it was not as bad as he had expected.

Coming to the side door, he hesitated, uncertain as to his next move. He wanted to avoid all the family except his parents, but if he stepped inside the house, he could encounter anyone.

Suddenly the door opened and he found himself looking at Zander. The tall black man stood stock still, his eyes sprung so wide the whites were enormous. "Marse Clay!" he whispered.

"Hello, Zander," Clay said and moved closer. Zander, he noted, had grown white-headed and was overweight. But he was still sharp, for the brown eyes of the slave were studying him carefully now that the shock was over. Clay said quickly, "Zander, I need to see my parents—but nobody else. Are they here?"

"Yas, suh, they here. They both upstairs."

"Anybody else in the house?"

"Everybody gone. Camp meeting over at Spring Grove, and a party at Miz Amy's house." Zander stared at Clay, questions in his eyes, but he said, "You want me to tell them you're here?"

Clay hesitated, then said, "I'll go to the library. Go ask them if they will come down and meet me there, Zander."

"Yas, suh."

Zander went back into the house, and Clay walked around to the door that led into the hall. The library was stuffy, and he moved to open one of the windows. He could hear someone speaking down the hall and supposed that it was Dorrie or some of the other house slaves.

He forced himself to stand quietly, looking out of the window, but he felt his hands trembling. Quickly he slapped them together, then tried to make his mind stop fluttering. Never could he remember being so tense, and he was glad when the door opened.

His father came in, followed by his mother, and for one brief moment they all three seemed to be frozen. *We could be a picture entitled "The Return of the Prodigal,"* Clay thought. He was shocked at his father's appearance. The black hair he remembered was sprinkled with gray, and his face was worn and etched with lines. He was still a handsome man, but worry and care had struck him hard. Clay's mother, on the other hand, seemed little different than when he had seen her last.

Thomas said in a voice tight with emotion, "I thought I made myself clear about your presence here."

"Very clear, sir," Clay answered. He saw that his mother wanted to come to him, but knew that she would not do so—not with her husband in the room. "I would have respected your wishes, but I felt I had to come." He hesitated, then got right to the matter. "I've been in touch with Warren Larrimore, Father. About the difficulties with the loans."

"I'm surprised you'd find that of any interest!"

"You have every right to think that," Clay said evenly. "I've given you occasion to think it."

"I'll ask you to leave, sir!"

Clay said quietly, "I will leave—if you will give me ten minutes."

Thomas had been stunned when Zander had come with the news that Clay was in the house. He had thought at first the butler must be mistaken, but Zander had been adamant. His mind had reeled, and the bitterness that he had nursed over the years welled up. He had started for the door, but Susanna caught at him.

"Don't go to him like this, Tom," she whispered.

He had stood there, keeping a tight hold on his anger. Now he said, "Very well, you have your ten minutes. No more."

"Yes, sir." Clay had thought out what he wanted to say, and Stephen had helped him with how to say it. "We'll arrange it with Warren," his uncle had said. "Keep my part out of it. You just found out about the problem and wanted to help. If you mention me, it'll just get his back up even more!"

Speaking slowly, Clay now said, "I've been out of the country for many years. But when I came back last month, I heard a rumor that you were having trouble with finances."

"Who told you this?" Thomas demanded.

"Oh, just a fellow who knew the county. He said that quite a few planters were having trouble meeting their loans because of the low price on cotton." He evaded the question easily and saw that his father was satisfied. That kept Stephen in the clear. If only the rest could be as easy.

"After I left here," he said, "I went to the bottom. You wouldn't want to hear about it. But I met a man who liked me. He taught me his trade and gave me every opportunity to rise. The venture prospered, and I made considerable money from it."

"What venture?" Thomas demanded.

"Why, shipping. I owned half-interest in a schooner. But I never really liked it, so I sold out last month." Clay hesitated, troubled by what was sure to come. But there was no way to put the thing except to come right out with it: "When I heard that you were having problems, I wrote to Larrimore, telling him I'd like to help."

"He never said a word to me!"

"I asked him to keep it confidential. I wasn't sure how the thing would go. But when he wrote and put all the facts before me, I made a decision. You won't like it, I'm afraid."

"What decision? And why should I be involved?"

"Larrimore said that you were going to lose Gracefield. I didn't want that to happen. So I asked him if I could help with the notes."

"You had no right to do that!" Thomas was about to launch.

Susanna spoke for the first time. "What sort of arrangement did you make, Clay?"

Clay explained that he didn't have enough money to get the place clear, but that he had worked something out with Larrimore. "He actually did all the work, of course," Clay said. "I wanted to be able to get the place clear, then just leave the country. But Warren could only make the arrangements if I agreed to be responsible for the financial side of the operation."

Thomas turned pale, and his voice was reedy. "So you've come back to be lord and master over us—is that it?"

It was the most dangerous time, and Clay said carefully, "Nothing was farther from my mind. The only way I could help was to take the bank's offer. But I won't be your master, sir! Never!" Then he lowered his voice, pleading as he never thought he would. "Let me do this thing, Father, please! Just let me stay until the place is clear of debt. Then I'll sign it over to you, and you never have to see me again!"

Susanna looked quickly at Thomas and saw the rejection that he was forming. "Clay, leave us now. It's too sudden, all of this. Come back tomorrow morning."

"Of course, Mother." Clay left the room at once, and when he got outside he discovered that his heart was thumping harder than it ever had in battle or in a storm at sea! He made his way at once to where his horse was tied but decided to sleep in the summerhouse. *I might be making only one more trip to the house,* he thought grimly.

Thomas and Susanna stayed up late, talking. At first Thomas was adamant—Clay would never come back to Gracefield! Not while he was there! But Susanna knew this man better than he knew himself. By the time they fell into bed, exhausted, she had won the day.

Thomas had agreed, but with iron terms. "He'll be no son of mine, Susanna! He can stay, and he can help. It's only right, for it's been his family he's hurt the worst. But I'll never forgive him!" Later he said, "Ellen will never have him back. And she's spent years drumming into the children's heads that their father is the scum of the earth. They'll never accept him, Susanna!"

Susanna did not argue. There was time for that later—and long after Thomas went to sleep, she lay awake, her hot tears falling to her pillow. *My son is home!* her heart said over and over. *Thank God! My son is home!*

Susanna Rocklin was the pillar that held Gracefield together. She was at work by candlelight and sometimes in the dead of night smoothing out troubles, watching the baking, the sewing, the soap and candle making, the births and deaths in slaves' cabins. Her manner was gracious, and she seldom raised her voice to a servant. She knew her Bible and trusted God. She was a woman of charm and grace, with inner strength of tempered steel.

Now she was faced with a monumental task—to prepare the way for Clay's return to Gracefield. Thomas should have been the one to do this, but he withdrew from the matter, saying, "You'll have to tell Ellen and the children." So she had, and Ellen had stared at her as if she had announced that the world was going to blow up. "Clay? Coming here? No, Susanna, I won't have it!"

However, when Ellen discovered that Clay had come up with the money to save Gracefield—and thus preserve the comforts of her life that went with it—she submitted. "He needn't think I'll take him back! But he owes it to you and Thomas and to the children to help."

"He'll come to supper tonight," Susanna said. "Do you want me to tell the children?"

"Oh yes, Susanna! I'm too nervous—and you know how to handle them!"

"I'll send him to see you first, Ellen," Susanna said. "Try to work things out with him."

So it went, with Susanna's deft hand guiding them all. She spoke to the children, together at first, then separately. They were astonished, angry—and tremendously curious. "Give him a chance," Susanna told each of them. "He's probably more nervous than any of you."

When Clay came at five, Susanna met him at the door. No one else was there, and she held up her arms. He crushed her in a strong embrace, and the tears came to his eyes. He didn't try to hide them when he drew back, and she whispered as she wiped them away, "Welcome home, my own dear son!"

"Mother—!" was all Clay could say, and then she said, "It will be hard tonight. They'll all want their little bit of revenge. But you can stand it, Clay. Now go to Ellen."

231

His audience with Ellen was short but far from sweet. She was not the woman he remembered at all; the years had not been kind to her. She was overweight, the slim curves he remembered now being hidden beneath pampered flesh. She still would be considered attractive to men, but there was a predatory look about her that he did not admire. At once he said, "Ellen, there's no point in my making apologies, but let me say I'm deeply grieved at the sorrow I've brought you."

She stared at him, then snapped, "You needn't think I'll have you back, Clay, so you can stop begging. . . !"

The rest of the interview consisted of her telling him what a rotter he was, then listing the things he would have to do if he were permitted to stay on. He listened without comment, wondering at the changes in her. Finally he said, "You won't be troubled by me, Ellen. I'll be busy with the work here."

Downstairs, the children gathered in the dining room, all of them trying to talk at once. Dent said loudly, "Well, I must say he's got brass! Stay away from us for years, then come breezing in as if nothing had happened!" He was angry and intended to give no quarter to his father.

David shook his head, saying moderately, "Dent, let's hear what he has to say. He may have had more problems than we know."

Lowell scowled, then muttered, "It's rotten! Why did he have to come home?"

Rena was so tense that her voice was strained. All her life she had dreamed of a father, which meant she had learned to resent Clay for not being there. Now she was like a cocked pistol, just waiting for her chance to tell the man who had robbed her of what every girl should have exactly what she thought of him.

But when she looked up and saw her father enter with

their mother, she could not say a word. She had been only a baby when he had left, and the pictures she had seen were suddenly worthless. Clay stepped to the table, and he looked first at her. *He's so handsome*, was Rena's first thought. He was tall and very strong, with hair black as a crow's wing and a pair of eyes that seemed to see right into her. She stared back at him, and he smiled. Then she dropped her head, unable to meet his gaze. But as he took his eyes from her, she watched him avidly.

Thomas and Susanna entered but did not sit down. They were all standing, and Clay said at once, "I know you're all embarrassed. Not so much as I am, though." He met Denton's hard gaze, then said, "Long ago I forfeited the right to be called your father. So the one thing you don't have to fear is that I've come back to make all sorts of demands on you. Your grandparents and your mother have done all the hard work of raising you, and I didn't come to take over."

"Well then, why *did* you come?" Dent demanded, his face pale.

"That's a good question, Dent."

Suddenly David asked, "How did you know he's Dent? Maybe I'm Dent."

"No, you're David." Clay smiled briefly, then added, "Dent was always the one to attack. And you were always the quiet one." Then he said, "I've come back to serve my father. You know, I suppose, that things haven't been going well with most plantations. My father has had to bear all the burden since I ran out on him. Now I want to do what I can to help him make it through this crisis." He stopped then and looked straight at his father. "Your grandfather is master here—of all of us, but especially of me."

Susanna touched Thomas's arm, and he said hurriedly, "Now

that's the way it is. So let's have something to eat." Truthfully the words of his son had struck him hard, as had the look in Clay's eyes. *Can he possibly mean all that?* Thomas asked himself as he sat down. A faint flicker of hope ran through him as he looked at Clay, and he saw that Susanna had tears in her eyes.

The mood, of course, was strained. Clay said nothing at first, but when David said, "You've been outdoors a great deal, sir," he opened up. He told them about the schooner—omitting the fact that she was a slave ship—and told a story about a storm off the coast of Chile. He was a good storyteller, always had been, and despite their suspicion, the children listened avidly.

When the meal was over, they were all glad of it. Clay made no attempt to go to any of them, but as they stood up, he said, "It's late for me to say this, but if I can help any of you in any way, it would be my privilege." Then he turned and left the room.

"Where's he going to stay?" Rena asked.

"In the summerhouse," Susanna answered.

Rena said stubbornly, "He's not my father, Grandmother! Not my real father!"

Susanna bent down and took Rena's face between her hands. "He'll be what you let him be, my dear. If you'll let him, he'll be a father to you. If you won't—there's nothing he can do about it."

Tears rose in Rena's eyes, but she blinked them away. She was confused and angry. "I don't need him. I don't!"

When she ran through the door, Susanna went to stand in front of Thomas. She leaned against him, weak from the tension that had built up. "It's not going to be easy, Tom!"

"We'll see. I don't think he's changed, Susanna. He's weak, as he always was. Oh, he's a charmer. I'll give him that! But he's not solid!" Then Thomas straightened his back, and sadness touched his eyes. "He gets that from me, my dear!" he said, then left the room at a fast walk.

CHAPTER 17

THE OLD MAID

*W*ell, shoot! What's he want to come back for, anyway?"

It was early, and Rena was in the yard looking for bantam eggs. The miniature chickens were allowed to roam free and found strange and bizarre places to deposit their eggs. The tiny eggs were delicacies that Thomas loved, and he assigned Rena the chore of finding them. Usually she liked hunting them. "It's like an Easter egg hunt every day," she confided to Susanna.

But today a cross frown marred the smooth perfection of the girl's brow, and she shoved Buck away roughly. The big dog ignored her and pushed his huge head close to lick her on the face. He was a formidable animal, a deerhound of almost mythological fame, but he was devoted to Rena, who treated him as if he had two legs instead of four. Her grandparents had found it deliciously funny, coming upon them playing when Rena was only four years old. She had dressed him in one of her father's old shirts, and the two of them were sitting at her small table having tea!

Rena had no close girlfriends. Her cousin Rachel Franklin lived close by, but Rachel was seventeen, and between that age and Rena's thirteen years a great gulf is fixed! Rena played with the slave children, but they had their work. Besides, it was becoming clear to Rena that an even greater gulf existed between herself and Maisie, the slave girl of her own age who had been brought into the house to learn the mysteries of being a lady's maid. Rena was close to her brother Lowell, but he was a boy, and that was another gulf.

So that left Buck, and more and more she spent her time with him, roaming the fields, dabbling in the creek—even sneaking him into her room to spend the night whenever she could manage it. If the dog could have talked, he would have informed the adults of the house that Rena was in need of attention. He knew all there was to know about the child, for she had formed the habit of talking to Buck aloud—and she did so now as he nuzzled her neck.

"Get away, Buck!" she said crossly, pushing at him. But he weighed almost as much as she did, and it was like shoving a tree. She sighed and surrendered. Handing him the basket she had trained him to carry by the handle, she said, "Come on, let's go down to the barn. I'll bet we'll find some eggs there." She ran across the front yard, the big dog loping at her side easily, keeping the basket between his great jaws. When they got to the barn, she slowed down, probing here and there in her search for the tiny eggs, talking with the dog.

"He's been here two weeks, Buck," she said with a frown. "And nobody ever sees him. None of us, I mean." She paused, picked up two eggs that were behind an old grindstone, and put them in the basket. "He stays with the slaves most of the time. Lowell said he likes them better than he does his own family. But I don't care! Do you, Buck?"

Buck said, "Woof!"—which Rena took to mean he didn't care either—and wagged his tail.

"I asked Dorrie why he didn't eat with us, and she said he worked all the time, that he came in lots of times after we were all in bed, all dirty and tired. She said she saves him a plate from suppertime." She paused long enough to go over the fence and scratch Delilah's ears. The huge sow groaned happily, and Rena sat there, continuing her recitation. "I told Dorrie I didn't like him and wished he'd never come home, and she said I was a fool! I told Grandmother on her, but do you think she whipped Dorrie? No, she took her part! Blamed old nigger!"

Buck caught the displeased tone in her voice and began to whine. "Oh, I'm not mad at you, Buck!" Rena laughed, throwing her arms around him. "It's just that. . .everything's changed!"

What Rena didn't realize was that it was not the plantation or her relatives that had changed, but she herself. She longed for the simplicity of the past, when she had played with her dolls or with Buck and roamed Gracefield at her grandfather's side. In those days she had given little thought to the world outside her own sphere. That had been a happy time for Rena. Her mother had been gone most of the time to Richmond, but Susanna had been always there—and Dorrie, who, in some ways, was closer than her own mother.

But changes in Rena's body and in her emotions had come, and now she was confused and moody. Susanna and Dorrie had recognized her unhappiness but could do little to help her. Dorrie had spoken their mutual thoughts only once. She and Susanna had been shelling purple-hulled peas on the porch late one afternoon, and Rena had walked by, her head down, with Buck at her side.

"Chile misses havin' a momma and daddy," Dorrie had murmured. "Gonna be a hard time comin' for her."

Susanna had not commented, for she knew well enough that all of Clay's children lived under a cloud. Their friends all had parents; but Ellen was no mother, and with the shadow over their father, all four of the children had grown thick shields around their hearts without knowing it. Dent bluffed it out, swaggering as a front, letting it be known that he didn't have any concern about his parents. David tried to do the same but, being more sensitive, could not quite bring it off. Lowell was hard to read. He had the tough self-assurance of his great-grandfather Noah Rocklin, but Susanna saw the needs in the boy. It was Rena, though, who was the most vulnerable. Susanna had discovered the girl's longing for a mother and father when she read stories to her, for Rena always loved those stories best that featured a child who had a father and mother who loved and were there.

The sun was rising quickly, peering at Rena over the top of the grove of water oaks where the summerhouse was located. Rena hesitated, then said, "Come on, Buck. We might as well go over to the grove. Some of these durned banty chickens may have found that place."

None of the chickens ever had wandered as far away as the summerhouse, but Rena insisted to the dog that they might have, and Buck gave her no argument. The two of them walked across the lawn, and the shade was cool under the trees. A startled possum scurried away as the pair surprised him, which made Rena laugh with delight. "Did you see her babies, Buck? They were all hanging to her tail! They looked like little pink mice!"

The sight of the possum cheered her up, for she loved the wild things of the woods. She always had some pet or other in a cage made by Box. Once it was a baby raccoon, which grew up to be the worst pest on the place, getting into everything, its clever little hands able to open any door or lock! Once it was a fox, another time a yearling deer. She always cried when they returned to the wild, but forgot her grief promptly when another wild pet came along. And so the circle of certain loss would begin again.

When she got to the summerhouse, she was surprised to see that the yard had been cleared and that new paint had been applied to the small frame structure. Cautiously she approached the cabin almost on tiptoe, ready to wheel and flee if her father should suddenly appear. But when she got to the window and peered inside, she saw that no one was there. He could have been in the bedroom, of course, but she didn't think so. Her eyes were caught by a stack of books that were strewn on the table helter-skelter. She loved books and tried to see the covers but could not. Temptation suddenly came, and she struggled with it dutifully—but the sight of the books was too much, and going to the door, she pushed it open and walked inside.

It was a favorite place for Rena. She and her brothers had used it for a playhouse for years, but the boys had outgrown it and Rena herself had not been here much since the previous fall. Carefully she advanced to the table and was delighted to see several magazines with pictures. She picked one up, gave a fearful look at the door, then, satisfied that there was no danger, began to look through the periodical. She was a great reader and soon was lost in the pictures—so lost that she came to herself with a start when Buck made a huffing sound. It was his way, she well knew, of announcing that someone was coming. In a sudden panic she threw the book down and dashed to the door, Buck right beside her.

Opening the door, she dashed outside—and ran smack into

someone who said, "What the devil—!"

Rena in a blind panic bounced off the newcomer and gave a small cry of fear.

"Why—it's Rena!" Clay looked down at her with startled eyes, but that was all he had time to do—for Buck had heard his beloved Rena cry for help, and he launched himself at the tall man with a terrifying snarl.

Clay had time only to push Rena to one side and get his hands up before the huge dog bit him in the chest, driving him backward. He stumbled, then sprawled to the ground and felt the fangs of the dog rip his hand. He caught the dog by the fur on each side of his head, but the animal was so strong that it was all he could do to hang on. The two of them rolled over and over on the grass as Clay tried to get away, and he knew that sooner or later that dog would break his grip.

Rena had been shoved to one side, but when she caught her balance and saw Buck going for her father's throat, she was petrified. She had seen Buck fight other dogs and knew that he was terrible when aroused. At once she threw herself at the pair, getting her arm around the dog's neck and screaming, "Buck! Buck, don't!"

The dog lifted his mighty head, and his terrifying snarls cut short. He twisted his head and saw Rena, whereupon he began to whine and try to get to her.

Cautiously Clay held on, but when he saw that the dog was no longer trying to tear his throat out, he released his grip. At once Buck turned to Rena, trying to lick her face, for she was crying in a hysterical manner. Clay looked down to see that his hand was deeply cut by the dog's jaws and took out a handkerchief. Wrapping it around his hand, he said, "It's all right, Rena."

The girl looked up, tears running down her face. She couldn't speak, so great was her fear, and Clay said, "It's all right. I'm not hurt."

Rena dashed the tears from her eyes, but then as she released Buck, who watched Clay with a steady gaze, she saw the crimson stain on his hand. "Oh, he bit you!"

"He got me a little, but it'll be all right. I'd better clean it out, though." He moved around the pair, keeping his eye on the dog, and entered the cabin. Going to a pitcher of water, he filled the basin and carefully unwrapped his hand. It was a deep gash, and the water was soon stained crimson. He reached for a bottle of weak lye solution that he had found in a box nailed to a wall. As he sat down and opened the bottle, he glanced up to see that Rena was standing at the door, uncertainty on her youthful face.

"That's a good bodyguard you have there, Rena," he said gently and smiled. Then as he took the lid from the bottle, he said, "Come on in. You can help me do the bandaging."

Rena hesitated but then came into the room, saying, "You stay here, Buck!" She came to stand stiffly in front of the table, and when she saw the deep gash, which was still bleeding freely, she gasped.

"It's not all that bad," Clay assured her. "I got lots worse than this on board the *Carrie Jane*." He poured the lye solution into the cut and gritted his teeth while it burned into the wound.

"I'm—I'm sorry!" Rena whispered. She edged closer, her face pale at the sight of the wound.

"Don't worry about it," Clay said quickly. "I'm glad you've got a good fellow like Buck to take care of you. He thought you were in trouble, and he helped the only way he knows how. He may not like me very much for a while, but I'm glad you have a friend."

"He's the best friend I have," Rena said. She watched as he rose, went to a chest, and took out a shirt. When he tried to tear it, she asked, "Are you going to make a bandage out of that?"

"It's just an old one."

"I can do that," Rena said. "I always help Grandmother make bandages out of old underwear."

Handing it to her, he smiled. "I can't do much with one hand. Maybe you can use my knife, since we don't have any scissors." He fished out his knife and managed to get it open. While she cut the shirt into narrow strips, he put more antiseptic on the cut, but actually was watching the girl. *She looks like Ellen did when she was younger,* he decided. But there was a delicacy in Rena that her mother had never had. Rena was slender, like the Rocklins, and already her girlish figure was beginning to become more womanly. She had a beautiful face with deep brown eyes and long eyelashes, and her lips were rosy and expressive. *I'm a stranger to her,* Clay thought. *She'll be a woman soon, and I've missed out on it all!*

"I can bandage your hand, if you like," Rena said diffidently. "Last year Buck got a bad cut on his paw and I bandaged it all the time."

"If you're a good enough nurse for Buck," Clay said, smiling, "you're good enough for me!" As she took his hand carefully and began to wrap the strips of cloth around it, he saw that her skin was so fine it was almost translucent. When she tied the knots firmly, he lifted his hand and admired it. "Why, Rena, that's a professional job! Maybe you ought to consider being a nurse. You'd do fine at it!"

"I'd rather be a doctor," she said firmly. Then she blushed. "I know there aren't any women doctors, but I used to pretend to be a doctor when I was a little girl."

"Well, someday there will be women doctors, I expect," Clay predicted. "And I don't see any reason why you can't be the first one." Seeing her fertile imagination beginning to work, he added, "I've got a book somewhere about medical work in Africa. May be a little dull for you—?"

"Oh no, I like dull books!" she exclaimed, and seeing his smile, she blushed again. "I mean, I like all kinds of books, not just stories."

"You do?" he asked with mock surprise. "Well, that's odd—because I do, too. Spend half my money on books!" That was true enough. He had not been much of a reader as a young man, but the long voyages of the ship had been made endurable only by books, and he had collected many fine editions. He waved at a box that had come by train from Washington. "Maybe you'd like to help me unpack all those. Might be some you'd like."

Rena said quickly, "Can I really? I never get enough books!"

Two hours later Clay looked over the pile of books scattered on the floor and table, than glanced at Rena, who was sitting cross-legged, deep into one of his travel books. He said, "Rena, does your mother know where you are?"

A startled look came into the girl's eyes, and she scrambled to her feet. "Oh, I forgot! I'm supposed to be gathering the banty eggs! Grandmother will kill me!"

"Maybe I'd better go along and take the blame," Clay suggested. He got to his feet, and Buck rose at once, still alert, his eyes fixed on Clay. The three of them made their way to the house, where they found Susanna upset and exasperated. She started to chastise Rena, but Clay said quickly, "Take it out on me, Mother. I kept Rena so busy working on my books, that's why she's late with the eggs."

Susanna saw the thankful look Rena shot at Clay; then her

eyes fell on his hand. "What's wrong with your hand?"

"Just a little cut, Mother."

"Come in and let me see it."

"No need for that." Clay winked with a conspiratorial air at Rena. "The doctor's already taken care of it." He gave his mother a smile, adding, "Rena's going to help me arrange all my books as soon as I get a bookcase. That all right with you?"

Susanna felt a thrill of joy in her heart at the sight of the two. "Yes, Clay, that's fine with me!"

Taylor Dewitt, keeping his eyes on the door that separated the bar from the restaurant, was paying only slight attention to Bushrod Aimes. The two men met often at the Harley House; it was the focal point for the planters who came to Richmond. The bar was only half filled, for it was still early afternoon.

Bushrod, who at thirty-eight was a prosperous planter, had been telling Taylor about a new horse he'd bought. It didn't take long for him to see that the other was paying no heed. "Might as well talk to a tree as you, Dewitt!" he grumbled. "What's eatin' on you?"

"Thinking about Clay Rocklin."

He was not alone, for the return of Rocklin had been a staple item of gossip for three weeks. There was plenty to gossip about, too. Ellen Rocklin had been a fixture in Richmond for years. She still had that aura of sexuality about her, but she was a discreet woman. She had managed to keep her standing as a respectable woman intact, so that she still had entrance into the lower echelon of Richmond high society.

"Wonder if Ellen will go back to him?" Bushrod asked aloud, echoing what had been on most people's minds. Then he shook his head, answering his own question. "I don't think so, not after the way he's acted. She's got too much pride for that!"

Taylor knew Ellen better than his friend, and a sardonic look swept his face. "Not sure about that, Bushrod. Ellen likes her fun, but she's gettin' a little long in the tooth."

"Why, she's about the same age as you, Taylor—or me, for that matter."

"Well, we're not getting any younger. Clay's not either. He's what? Thirty-eight or thirty-nine, isn't he? Wonder what he's been doing all these years?"

"Nobody knows, but he came back with money. Bought back all the paper his father had on Gracefield, with plenty left over—"

"There he is now," Dewitt interrupted Aimes, then straightened up in his chair as Clay Rocklin came into the room and headed toward them at once. Both men got up, and Taylor put his hand out to greet his old friend. "Clay! Why, you look great!"

"Hello, Taylor, Bushrod." Clay smiled at the pair, shook his head, and said, "You two sure you want to be seen in public with a reprobate like me?"

The question made both men feel a little uncomfortable, for although neither had voiced it, each had thought that it might be embarrassing to pick up their old friendship with Clay Rocklin. Taylor, however, grinned suddenly. "Maybe we'll be a good influence on you." Then some of the old memories of his good times with this man came back, and he suddenly threw his arm around Clay's shoulders and said, "You old bandit! By the Lord, but I'm glad to see you!"

The three sat down, and as soon as a white-coated waiter took their order, Clay said, "Go on and ask me."

"Ask you what, Clay?" Bushrod lifted his eyebrows at the question.

"Ask me where I've been, how much devilment I've been into, how much money I brought back with me, if I'm going back to Ellen, and if I'm going to behave myself!"

Both Aimes and Dewitt broke into laughter. "You are a caution, Clay Rocklin!" Bushrod said finally. "Haven't changed much, have you? You look good, Clay! How come you're still lean and tough while ol' Dewitt and me are getting fat?"

"Clean living and a pure heart. But you two look fine," Clay said, and he meant it. Both of them were older, of course, but Taylor had not changed—still lean with an unlined pale face and the lightest blue eyes Clay had ever seen. He was well dressed, as was Bushrod, and Clay knew from talking to Dorrie and Zander that these two were among the leaders of the young aristocracy in the county.

Both men were thinking that Clay had become a different sort of man. He looked older but was still smooth-faced and hawk-eyed. It was his manner that was most different. Clay had always been reckless and forward, but now there was a solid quality about him, and assurance emanated from him.

Taylor said, "Everybody wants to know about you, Clay. Tell us what you want us to know. But first, I apologize for the way I let you down." He shook his head at what was a painful memory. "When you plugged Duncan Taliferro in that duel, I came down on you too hard."

"Forget it, Taylor."

"No, I was so blasted self-righteous! Then right after that you went off to Mexico and got in another mess. I always felt like if I'd not been such a self-righteous prig, it might have made a difference."

Clay shook his head, stared fondly at Taylor, but said, "When a man's bound and determined to make a fool out of himself as I was in those days, he'll do it one way or another. So forget it. Now let me tell you about what I've been up to, and what I'm trying to do. Then you won't have to go to Benson's Barber shop to get the gossip. . . ."

He told them as much of his story as he thought wise. He told them he'd come back with some money and was trying to help his father make it over a difficult time. And he said bluntly, "Ellen wouldn't have me back, so I'm staying in the old summerhouse at Gracefield. My children don't like me much, and my father thinks I haven't really changed. My mother forgave me before I even got here, but she'd forgive Judas and Attila the Hun. End of story."

Both men knew there was more to it than that, but they accepted it as what Clay wanted to have known. "Glad to have you back. Now maybe we can have some fun," Bushrod said.

"Well, not the kind we used to have," Taylor said with some regret. "All three of us are married and have children. Still, Clay, we get together with Tug Ramsey and some of your other old friends and have a friendly poker game every week."

"Friendly!" Bushrod cried out. "Call it that if you like, but it's the biggest bunch of cutthroats since Captain Kidd was in business!"

The three men sat there, and Clay relaxed. He had missed these men. It had been years since he had had anything even close to the camaraderie this group had enjoyed. He drank the frosty mint julep placed in front of him, then another, and finally Bushrod said, "Going to need you, Clay. Things are going to get tough around here."

"I thought they already were."

"If Lincoln gets elected next year, it'll mean a war," Taylor said evenly. He sipped his drink, then added, "We may as well get ready to fight, for the North isn't going to give us any choice."

"Why, it won't come to that, Taylor!" Clay said at once. He had heard such talk but didn't believe it could ever happen. "They've got a little sense up North! When they see it's going to mean a war, they'll lower that blasted tariff and give the South some freedom from the pressure."

"No, we'll have to fight," Bushrod insisted doggedly. Then he said something that Clay was to get sick of hearing. "Any Southerner can whip six of those Yankee boys!"

"Besides, England would like to see the Union divided," Taylor said. "And she needs our cotton to run her mills. The North wouldn't dare risk another war with England when she comes in on our side!"

Clay listened carefully but finally said, "Well, I didn't come home to fight a war, but to save Gracefield if I can. And I didn't know until I came here how much I missed you fellows. Thanks for taking me back."

Both men protested that it was too early for him to leave, but he laughed, saying, "You rich planters can loll around swigging mint juleps all day, but us poor workers have to be in the fields. I'll be at that poker game on Thursday. I can use some extra cash, and I could always trim you two!"

He left the Harley House, feeling better than at any time since coming back to Virginia. Several people hailed him as he went into Dennison's General Store to pick up supplies, but several more whom he recognized ignored him. He loaded his supplies, then reluctantly drove to the small rooming house where Ellen stayed most of the time. It was a large home, a mansion, really, that had been built by J. P. Mulligan, a prosperous stockbroker. But Mulligan had lost his shirt in the depression and, after blowing his brains out, was discovered to have left his widow, Harriet, nothing but debts. She had more fortitude than J.P. and made a good living renting out rooms to the better sort of clientele.

Clay was met at the front door by the landlady, and she smiled at him. "Clay! It's good to see you! Come in." She was a tall woman of fifty, plain but with a warm manner. "I've thought about you often. It's good to have you home."

Clay nodded, warmed by her friendliness. "I was sorry to hear about J.P., Harriet. I always liked him."

"Thank you, Clay." She hesitated, then said, "Ellen isn't here now. She left an hour ago. I'm afraid she won't be back soon." She was not a devious woman, but there was a strange hesitancy in her manner that puzzled Clay. Then he suddenly realized the woman knew something about Ellen that she didn't want to mention. Nor did he want to hear it.

Clay nodded. "Could you give her a message for me?" He wrote a quick note, saying only, *"Ellen, here's the cash you asked for. Clay."* Putting both the note and the money in an envelope, he handed it to Mrs. Mulligan, bid her good-bye, and left the house. For the rest of the afternoon, he drove around Richmond, taking care of business matters. It was three o'clock when he turned the buggy toward the edge of the city.

It was a perfect June day, not too hot, but warm enough so that he removed his coat. The clouds scudded across the skies in huge, billowy masses like moving mountains, and the countryside was alive with wildflowers. He looked down at his hand, smiling as he thought of Rena. She had come to his place the next evening, and the two of them had sat up until Susanna sent Maisie to get her. It was the one gain he'd made, so far as the children were concerned. David and Lowell were so dominated by Dent that they had come to feel it a weakness to show any warmth to Clay. Dent himself used every opportunity to show his insolence.

Clay's father had shown no sign of bending. Clay took every decision to him and received only a gruff approval for most of them. His mother said little, but her smiles kept Clay going, and he had become a good friend to many of the slaves—especially to Fox, the mulatto son of Damis. At the age of eighteen, the young man was far and away the brightest of the help. Though he had been standoffish with Clay at first, when he saw that the new master was fair, he had become invaluable. He not only knew the practical things about actual farming—such as when to plant and when to hold off planting—but he had been trained to do some of the bookwork for Thomas. This irritated the overseer tremendously, and he had become the implacable enemy of Fox.

Clay let the horse pick his own pace, and it was almost dark when he came to the small store where the poor whites did most of their buying. It was called simply Hardee's Store by most. The Rocklins did a little business with Lyle Hardee, a transplanted Yankee from Illinois, but his prices were higher than those of the larger stores in town. However, Clay remembered that Susanna had asked him to bring some quinine home, and he remembered it only as he saw the store. Hitching the horse to the rail, he walked up the steps and met a woman and two children who were coming out. All of them were carrying large sacks, he saw. The woman had turned to lock the door, and Clay asked, "Can you let me have a little quinine before you close?"

The woman turned quickly to look at him, then hesitated.

"Sorry to be a bother. Guess it can wait," Clay said, and he turned to leave.

"No, it's all right." Unlocking the door, she went in, saying, "You and Toby wait here, Martha. I won't be long."

The only light in the store was a tiny flame in a single lantern, so that Clay could see almost nothing. Then she turned the wick up and turned to him. "How much quinine do you need?" she asked. The lamplight threw its amber glow over her face, and he saw that she was a young woman. Young and very attractive. So attractive with her enormous eyes and beautifully shaped lips that he said tardily, "Why—I don't know." He laughed ruefully. "That sounds dumb, doesn't it? How much would you think a lady with a large house and a hundred or more slaves might use?"

"A quart." Her manner was assured, but she stood there examining him, as though waiting for him to add to the order.

Her self-possession brought a slight sense of embarrassment to Clay, which was unusual. Her lips were full in the center, and as he watched, the edges of them curved up in a half smile. Her eyes smiled, too, he saw. "I'm Clay Rocklin," he said suddenly. "I've just come back. Guess I'll be seeing you here from time to time."

Still she watched him, and he could see a strange expression in her eyes, which appeared to be green. "Will that be all?" she asked finally.

"I guess so." Clay watched her as she took a very large glass jug from a shelf, then an empty bottle from beneath the counter. The jug was heavy, and she had trouble holding it. "Here, let me help you, ma'am," he said quickly. He reached over the counter, took the jug, and added, "Just hold the bottle for me, if you will."

She held the bottle, and when it was full, she put the cork in it. Then she took the jug, put it back on the shelf, and turned to say, "That'll be a quarter, please."

He fumbled in his pockets, coming up with no change. Then he discovered that he had no small bills. She stood there watching him as he searched, then said, "I'll trust you for the quarter, Mister Clay."

Mister Clay! He looked up, startled.

The moment she said his name, he knew her and cried out, "Melora!"

"I've been hoping to see you ever since I heard you'd come home," she said with a smile.

Clay could not believe it. He stood there staring at her, finally saying, "I guess I expected you to stay twelve years old, Melora. You're—!" He was going to say, "You're beautiful!" but changed his words. "You're all grown up." She was beautiful. Now that he knew who she was, he realized she had not changed all that much, for she had been a beautiful child. But the years had made a woman of her. "How old are you?" he asked suddenly.

Melora laughed, a delightful sound. "Wherever you've been, Mister Clay, they didn't teach you how to talk to a woman! Never ask a woman's age!"

Clay shook his head. "You're twenty-four or twenty-five." This was a greater shock than he had thought it would be. This young woman was not the thin girl who had fed him soup and read to him out of *Pilgrim's Progress*. He felt sad in some strange way, for he had missed her growing up. He voiced this, saying, "I'm sorry I haven't been around to watch you grow up into such a fine young woman." He looked around the store, asking, "Do you work here, Melora?" Then the thought of the two children came to him. He glanced at them, asking, "Or did you marry one of Hardee's boys?"

"I'm just filling in once in a while."

"Oh. Well, I'm keeping you." He stepped back, and she came with him to the door, pausing to lock it. "I suppose these are yours?" Clay said, for they looked much like her, both the boy who was about eight and the girl she'd called Martha who must have been about ten.

"No, this is my brother and sister, Toby and Martha." She paused, then said, "Well, it's been good seeing you, Mister Clay."

"Do you live far?"

"The same place."

"You're still with your folks?" Clay asked in surprise, thinking that something must have gone wrong with Melora's life. She was too attractive not to be married and yet was still at home. Perhaps her husband had moved to the home place. Then he asked, "It's getting late. I suppose you have a wagon to come to work in."

"Just a mule," she said. "We make it fine, don't we, Martha?"

The girl nodded shyly, but Clay said, "Well, I've got a whole buggy seat and some room in the back. Tie your mule on, and I'll get your things loaded."

"It would be a help, Mister Clay—but it's out of your way," Melora said.

"Be glad to see your folks," Clay said. "I've meant to come before this."

Soon the children were in the backseat, sucking noisily on two cherry lollipops that Melora had provided. As the buggy moved smartly down the road, Clay gave the abbreviated version of how he'd come home—heavily edited, as he had learned to do.

She sat there listening, and in the twilight shadows he saw

that her face had the same stillness it had had when she was twelve—or when she was six, for that matter. She did speak from time to time, telling him a little about the farm, but said nothing about her own life.

"I guess you're married," Clay said finally.

"No, I'm an old maid, Mister Clay!"

Astonishment ran through Clay, and he blinked at her. "Well, I can't understand that," he said finally. "The men around here, they've all gone blind?"

"Mother died when Toby was born," she said. "When I saw that Daddy would never marry again, there was nothing to do but take care of the little ones." She laughed at his expression. "I'm really a widow with nine children, Mister Clay, so my prospects aren't too good!"

"Nonsense! Royal must be—how old now? Twenty-six or -seven? And Zack and Cora are full-grown."

"But the rest of them are sixteen down to eight," she reminded him. "They need me."

He said no more but was very quiet as they rode along the dusty road. When they got to the cabin, Melora said quickly, "I do have one suitor. I think you might remember him—Rev. Jeremiah Irons?"

"Why, of course I do! But didn't I hear that he was married with two children?"

"His wife died three years ago, Mister Clay." She got out of the wagon, saying, "Martha, you and Toby wake up. We're home." Clay helped the children to the ground, then, as they stumbled toward the house, picked up the bundles.

She took one of them from him, saying, "That's Rev. Irons's horse tied there. He comes to court me." A humorous smile came to her, and she said, "Most of his congregation are against his choice—especially young widows or families with marriageable daughters. As a matter of fact, most people around here think he's lost his mind. He could marry anybody, instead of just me."

Clay took a deep breath, thinking hard. Then he said, "Melora, remember when I rode out of here years ago to slay a dragon for you?"

"I—I remember."

"Well, I didn't do any dragon killing—but you turned into a lovely princess, just like those in the stories we used to read!"

The warm darkness hid her face, but her voice was husky when she finally said in a whisper, "Thank you for saying that, Mister Clay!"

Then she turned abruptly, lifting her voice to cry out, "Daddy! Look who's come to see us!"

CHAPTER 18

MELORA'S VISITOR

A whiteness of snow. Whiter than the breasts of pigeons and stretching out to infinity.

This was one of the scenes that came, but it was spinning and wheeling so that the dazzling whiteness blinded him. He tried to shut his eyes, but the lids were frozen, or so it seemed, and he could do nothing but stare at the endless stretch of pale snow.

But then the unrelieved purity of the snow was broken by a single flaw, a speck of crimson. Clay stared at it, and as he stared, it began to swell, spreading over the snow in an obscene blot of scarlet horror. He knew that it was blood and tried to shut his eyes, to run—but he was paralyzed, unable to move so much as an eyelid.

And then he saw him. A man was lying there, and it was his blood pumping out of a terrible wound that was staining the snow. At first Clay thought the man was dead, but then he lifted his face, and Clay saw that it was Duncan Taliferro! His eyes were pleading, and he lifted a bloody hand from his wound in a hopeless gesture.

And even as he did so, Clay was suddenly aware that he and Taliferro were being observed. He lifted his head and saw that they were in a huge amphitheater and that thousands of people were watching, and all of them had great, staring eyes. Some of them he recognized—his father shaking his fist; Taylor Dewitt shaking his head; his mother weeping. All of them were crying out, "Shame! Shame!"

That was one scene, and he wrenched himself away until the snow seemed to melt, and all the figures faded into a mist, and Taliferro became a specter, then vanished.

But another vision was already forming, and he knew what it would be. He began running, and he ran over a thousand plains, but the farther he ran, the more terrified he became— for he heard the sound of the sea moaning in his ears.

The sky darkened, and he cried out as he felt himself torn from the land. He shut his eyes, praying that it would not come again. But it did come. Opening his eyes, Clay saw the lifting waves, capped with frothy white, and he saw the sails of the ship overhead, swelling in the wind that howled like a demented soul.

He tried to dig his way into the deck, but an iron hand caught him up and he found himself looking into the face of Captain March.

"Overboard with them!" the captain cried in a voice like thunder.

"No! No!" Clay whispered, but his voice was snatched away by the wind. And then he knew it was going to happen.

He saw the young woman with the baby. Her eyes were fixed on him, and she turned the ragged cloth back, then held the infant up for him to see. Her lips were forming the words, "Help me!"

But March was shouting, "Overboard with them!"

As he had done so many times, he moved to the woman. She

watched him, hope in her eyes, thinking that he was coming to free her from the iron chains around her waist.

Then he put his hands on her, lifted her high over his head, and flung her and the child into the sea!

She sank at once, and the long line of slaves who were attached to her by the chain began to be pulled overboard. One by one they went, screaming as they plunged over the side and into the black depths.

Then March was laughing like a maniac and screaming, "Overboard with you, Clay Rocklin!"

Clay looked down—and saw the chain around his waist.

And then he knew. . .

He was one of them! He was part of the living chain that was sinking into the sea. Suddenly he felt himself jerked wildly toward the rail, caught by the weight of the dying blacks who had already been dragged overboard.

He hit the freezing water, and the darkness came as he died. But it was not so dark that he could not see the line of living beings as they kicked and waved their arms wildly in the murky depths.

Then he saw the woman again, but now she was laughing—and all the others had suddenly turned their sable eyes on him, and their mouths were open like gargoyles as they laughed and screamed.

"You dead, too, white man! You dead like we are! Come down, come down to hell—!"

Clay began screaming, but the dark water filled his throat and his nose, so his screams were silent as he sank deeper and deeper, toward the hideous black hole that was opening up beneath him.

"No! No!"

Clay awoke with a start to find himself drenched with sweat and crying out in utter terror. He came off the bed as though it were white-hot iron and staggered toward the door. When he lunged outside, he stood there taking great gulps of the cool night air. He was trembling so hard that he had to move to the maple tree and lean against it. The bark was rough, and he pressed against it, needing the sense of reality after the nightmare.

Finally he began to breathe normally, and the tremors stopped racking his body. He wiped the sweat off his face and stood there in the silence of the night. His cry had alarmed the night creatures, silenced the frogs that boomed their bass voices from the pond, and cut off the high-pitched singing of the crickets and katydids. The only sound, other than the heavy beating of his own heart, was the whine of mosquitoes.

With a moan of despair, he struck the maple, then turned and went back into the house. Finding a match, he lit the lantern and then stared at the bottle of whiskey. It was almost empty, and his throbbing head told him he was beginning to feel the aftereffects of a drunk.

He grimaced at the sight of it, then went to the stove and poured cold coffee into a cup and drank it down. It was tepid and bitter, but better than whiskey. Glancing at his watch on the table, he saw that it was only three o'clock. At least two more hours until the world came alive.

He washed his face, dressed, and went outside, walking slowly down the path that led to the pond. The moon was huge in the velvety black sky, and he could see his way clearly. When he got to the pond, he stood there staring at it, the silver surface rippled in spots by fish moving or by water striders. The stillness flowed into him, and he felt the weariness that came from loss of sleep.

For more than a week, he had not slept more than a few hours. The bad dreams had started without warning, coming every night, so that he dreaded to go to bed. He had never been a man to dream much, and there was something about these dreams that he knew was abnormal. They were so brilliantly clear! Not fuzzy and vague as most of his dreams had been. The sheer terror of them was beyond anything he had ever known in the real world. *There is something almost evil about them,* he thought as he stared at the water.

His eyes were burning from lack of sleep, and he knew that the day would be terrible. He had not mentioned his lack of sleep to anyone, and he had continued putting in long hours in the fields and about the place. But he was getting weaker, and finally he had given in to a desperate hope that liquor might make him sleep. But it had only made things worse—as bad as anything he had ever known.

"Can't go on like this!" he said aloud.

A frog at his feet hollered, *"Yikes!"* and hit the water with a lusty splash.

Clay stood there for half an hour, wondering what to do, then walked around the pond slowly. He went back to the house, shaved, and made his way to the Big House at six. The sky was just beginning to turn pink, and he found his mother in the kitchen alone.

"Why, good morning, Clay," she said in surprise. "You are up early this morning." She smiled, but then something in his face made her ask, "What's the matter? Don't you feel well?"

"I'm all right. A little tired, I guess."

She stared at him but said nothing until she had poured

him a cup of hot coffee. "You're working too hard."

"That's why I came."

She moved to sit beside him and, after a moment's awkwardness, put her hands on his, the one that was bandaged. "You've done so well, Clay!"

He could not help saying, "I wish Father thought so."

"He'll come around. As the children will. Look how close you've gotten to Rena!"

He looked at her and mustered up a tired grin. "Well, that makes two of you I've won over. Only about ten thousand more to go in the county."

"That's not so!" she said. "Amy and Brad are so pleased with you, and the slaves think you are wonderful!" A question came to her eyes, and she asked it carefully. "You never liked the slaves before, Clay. Now you're so kind to them. What made you change?"

His hand tightened around the cup, and he evaded her question. "Just got older, I guess."

Then Dorrie came in, her eyes taking him in. "You ain't getting enough rest, Marse Clay! I gonna tie you in bed! See if I don't!"

Clay and his mother laughed, and he said, "I guess I'm like the boy they put in college. They put him there, but they couldn't make him think."

"What's dat got to do with you?"

"You can tie me in bed, but you can't make me sleep, Dorrie," Clay said.

"I'll fix you a toddy tonight," Dorrie said emphatically. "My toddies make anybody sleep."

Clay thought of the bottle of whiskey he'd downed the night before but said, "Thanks, Dorrie. That'll probably do it."

Dorrie fixed breakfast, but Clay could not eat, at least not enough to please the two women. When he left, Dorrie said, "He ain't happy, Miz Susanna."

"No. Did you see his eyes? He hasn't slept for several nights."

"Fox says he's giving up. Says he's got something goin' on in his head that's gonna kill him if it ain't took care of!"

Susanna said quietly, "It's not in his head, Dorrie."

The slave was very quick. "You right about dat! He's needin' a good case of ol' time gospel salvation!"

"That's what Rev. Irons says, Dorrie. He's been to talk to me about Clay. He says about the same thing you do, that if Clay doesn't get some peace, he won't make it."

Dorrie nodded firmly. "Dat preacher has got some sense! Whut he say he gonna do? Git him to come to one of his meetin's?"

"No, he said Clay wouldn't come. And he's right. But he did ask me to pray that he'd have a chance to give him the gospel in some way."

"Well, we gonna believe Gawd for dat!" There was nothing timid about Dorrie's faith, and she took Susanna's hand and the sound of her fervent prayers could be heard as far away as the slave quarters!

❧

Jeremiah Irons was aware that Melora was laughing at him, though the only hint of this was a sly twinkle in her green eyes. Even worse, he strongly suspected that at least five of the other seven people who were sitting in the big room of Buford Yancy's cabin were also amused at him. He was sitting in a rocking chair made by Buford, listening to his host give his opinion on the heresy of universalism.

Scattered around the room in various positions were the rest of the Yancy clan, except for Royal, Zack, and Cora, the married children. As Buford droned on, Irons shifted his eyes around the room at the children, all with their father's tow hair and greenish eyes: from Lonnie, who at sixteen was a younger edition of his father, down to Toby, the youngest. In between, in rather a stair-step fashion, Bobby, Rose, Josh, and Martha were examining the good reverend as though he were some sort of alien specimen.

Melora was washing the last of the supper dishes when she turned and gave him a certain look—that was when Jeremiah sensed that she was amused at him, and her humor had been picked up by all the rest except for Toby, who was asleep, and Buford, who was wading through the heavy seas of Calvinistic theology with a knitted brow.

"...a man can't find nothing like that in the Bible, kin he, Parson?"

Irons suddenly realized that he had tuned Buford out and tried to fake it. He knew the arguments well but was not inclined to argue over fine theological points of doctrine. "Well, Buford," he said, clearing his throat, "as I've said so often, the universalists do what most do with the scripture. They take a truth, close their eyes to what the rest of the scripture has to say about the matter, then blow that single truth up until it's swollen like a huge balloon. In this case, men take a verse such as Colossians, first chapter, verses 19 and 20. 'For it pleased the Father that in him should all fulness dwell; and, having made peace through the blood of his cross, by him to reconcile all things unto himself; by him, I say, whether they be things in earth, or things in heaven.' Well, the universalist jumps on the phrase 'reconcile all things unto himself.' "

Buford blinked; then he brightened up. "That's it! They claim that means that every soul who's ever been created will be saved, that nobody will be lost."

"They go farther than that, I'm afraid," Irons said. "They claim that even the devil will be saved at last."

Such a thought had never occurred to Buford Yancy's simple mind. He sat there staring at the minister blankly, then said with indignation, "Well, I'll be dipped! Can't they read, Parson? The whole Bible talks about people who go to hell!"

Melora had finished the dishes and took pity on the preacher. She knew her brothers and sisters thought it was funny that Rev. Irons kept coming to call on her and was always trapped in the single room with half a dozen small Yancys and forced to listen to her father discuss the Bible.

"I've got to go check on the new calf," she announced.

"I'll jist go along with you, sister," Lonnie said with a gleam in his eye.

"You'll do no such thing, Lonnie," Melora announced firmly. "You'll do the rest of those problems on page 34." She gave the others a straight, hard look that shut down the works before they even started. "The rest of you finish up your work, too."

Irons got up hastily, saying, "I'll go along, Melora. I always like to see a new calf."

"They are a sight to behold, ain't they now," Lonnie exclaimed with a grin. "I allus like to go down five or six times a day and see the new calves!" Then he caught his father's warning glance and sat down suddenly and lowered his head over his arithmetic book.

When Melora and Irons left, his father said, "Lonnie, if you make fun of Rev. Irons and his courtin' one more time, I'll peel your potato, you hear me, boy?"

"Yessir," Lonnie mumbled but gave a merry wink at Bobby and Rose, who giggled. "But, Pa, there's something downright comical about it, ain't they, now? I mean, I never thought of an old man like Rev. Irons courtin' a lady—and 'specially not Melora."

Buford Yancy did not allow a flicker of an emotion to show in his steady gaze, which he fixed on Lonnie. But he had felt more or less the same way when he had first discovered what was happening. When the minister had started calling, Buford thought Irons was making a pastoral call. But the man kept coming over a period of several weeks. Finally Yancy had remarked to Melora one evening after Irons went home having stayed most of the evening, " 'Pears like the reverend likes to talk theology with me, don't it, Melora?"

"He's calling on me, Daddy," Melora had said, and she had laughed outright at the comical expression on his face. "How'd you like to have a preacher for a son-in-law?" she had teased him, but then had shaken her head and patted his arm. "It won't come to anything. He's just lonesome—and he wants a woman to help him raise Asa and Ann."

Now as Melora walked along the path to the barn, she knew that Irons was frustrated. "You ought to give up, Jeremiah," she said frankly. "I don't think any other man in the world would put up with such a thing—courting a woman under the eyes of such a mob."

Irons suddenly chuckled, for he had a keen sense of humor. "I do it because it gives such fun to your brothers and sisters," he said. "And it's one way I can irritate some of my congregation without fear of getting run off."

They came to the wooden fence then, and Melora leaned on it, watching the calf come wobbling to her call. She put her hand out and enjoyed the rough texture of the beautiful creature's tongue. "You're a beauty, you are," she murmured, running her hand over the silky coat of the young creature.

Jeremiah watched her, the red-gold rays of the setting sun washing over her glossy black hair, the blackest hair he'd ever seen. Her skin was creamy and smooth as silk, and her large almond-shaped eyes were filled with delight at the calf. Irons was not a poetic man, but now he said without meaning to, "You're the beauty, Melora."

Startled, she brought her gaze up to meet his, and a slight flush tinged her cheeks. "You've been a long time coming to that, Jeremiah," she remarked.

"I'm a slow man," he said. "I was a slow child, a slow young fellow, and now in my old age I'm as slow as ever."

"You're not old," Melora said quickly, almost defensively.

"I'm thirty-eight; you're twenty-five."

"That makes no difference. You married Judd Harkins to Della Mae Conroy last January. He was sixty-two and she was only seventeen."

"I thought Judd made a fool out of himself, too." Then he took her hand, marveling at the strength and smoothness of it. "But you go on talking like that, Melora. I need somebody on my side." Then he dropped her hand, took her gently, and pulled her forward. Her lips were cool and tender, and he thought once that he felt her respond to his kiss. But there was a reserve in Melora Yancy, which he had long admired—most young women were too forward. He had watched Melora coolly receive several young men, some of them substantial and sound. The community had been offended when she refused them all, giving as a reason that she could not leave her brothers and sisters.

Now as she pulled back slightly and looked up at him, he saw that the kiss had not moved her—as it had him. She was watching him soberly with a steady gaze. "I'd like for you to marry me, Melora," he said quietly.

"I know, Jeremiah," she said slowly. "But I don't love you—not in that way."

"That can come later."

"I'd be afraid to gamble on such a thing. What if it didn't come? Marriage is forever. I can't think of anything worse than sharing a house and a bed with a man I didn't love with all my heart."

Her forthrightness made him blink, and he was suddenly out of words. Finally he summoned up a smile of sorts. "I'm slow, Melora, but I'm stubborn. You think I'll be so embarrassed by your refusal that I'll let the matter drop. But you don't know me as well as you think."

She smiled and patted his cheek. "Perhaps not, Jeremiah. But I hate to see you wasting your time." The humor that lay just beneath the surface of her lively mind leaped out at him. "You'd pass up the Widow Hathcock for a chance to marry me? And her with five hundred acres of prime land?"

"Oh, Melora!" Irons groaned. "She's a fine woman, but she must weigh three hundred pounds!" Then he saw that she was teasing him, and he laughed despite himself. "A man would never be bored in a marriage with you!"

The moment had passed, and they sat down on a stile, talking freely. He came finally to speak of Clay Rocklin. "He's in big trouble, Melora," he said, shaking his head. "He's given his best shot to reforming his life—and it's not working." He had gone hunting with Clay once since his return, and Clay had spoken tersely of his bad dreams and his doubts of anything ever coming of his return.

"He's trying very hard," Melora said quietly. "Pa says the

same as you, that he's not going to make it."

"I think he's at a crossroads, Melora. He's got to find God now, or I don't think he ever will."

"You've talked to him, haven't you, Jeremiah? You're a preacher, but you're better, I think, face-to-face."

"I tried, but Clay's got the idea he's sinned away his day of grace. Some idiot put the idea of an 'unpardonable' sin in his mind, and he thinks he's crossed the line." He sat there silently, thinking of Clay, and finally he said, "I think you ought to talk to him, Melora."

"Me? Why, I couldn't tell Clay Rocklin what to do!"

"Yes, you could." The certainty grew in him, and he turned to face her. "He doesn't need complexity of any sort, Melora. No complicated theology—such as your father loves to talk about. I've heard you talk about your love for Jesus and His love for you. The power of God is in you when you do that. That's one big mistake people make. They think that the power of God comes when a preacher is up on a platform, yelling with all his might! Well, sometimes it is, but far more often I think people sense God when somebody like you speaks of Jesus."

"I—I want so much to see him find his way, Jeremiah!"

"You two are great friends, aren't you?"

"I've always felt close to him somehow. When I was a little girl, I thought he was wonderful. Even when he went bad, I knew there was something good in him—and I prayed for him all the time he was gone."

"Talk to him, Melora. Perhaps, like another young woman, you've come to the kingdom for such a time as this."

❧

When Clay Rocklin rode his big buckskin into the front yard

two days after Irons had urged her to speak with him, Melora had one of the strangest feelings she had ever experienced. For one thing, she was absolutely alone, which had not happened more than half a dozen times in her life. A circus had come to Richmond, and her father had bundled the whole family up and taken them to see it. It was not a thing he had planned, but for some reason he felt constrained to do it. "By gum, every child ort to go to the circus once, and you young'uns are going if it harelips Virginia!"

Melora hadn't been feeling well and felt that the quiet would do her more good than all the excitement of a circus. But when Clay rode in, she began to tremble, for she had promised God that she would talk with Clay if God would make the arrangements. She was a woman of faith, and this was beginning to look as much like a miracle as anything she had seen. As she went to greet him, she was agitated in her spirit.

"Hello, Melora," Clay said, pulling a package from one of his saddlebags. "I brought the worm medicine Buford asked me to pick up for the stock. Is he inside?"

"N—no, they're all gone to Richmond."

Clay saw that she was upset, the first time he had ever seen her shaken. "What's the matter, Melora?" he demanded.

Melora stared at him, tempted to let the moment pass, but she remembered Irons's words—and she remembered her promise to God. Her voice was not steady, and her lips were tight as she said, "Mister Clay, can I talk to you?"

"Why, certainly!" Clay felt that she was struggling with a personal problem and thought, *She's got nobody to talk to. I hope I can help.*

Melora turned and walked into the cabin, and when he followed her, she said, "Let's sit down at the table." When he sat down with his black eyes fixed on her, she walked to the bookcase and returned with the big black family Bible. It was worn thin and dog-eared, the pages brown with age. She put her hand on it, said a quick prayer, then gave him a tremendous smile, saying, "Mister Clay, I've always loved you."

Clay blinked, his jaw dropping. He could not speak, so shattered had he become.

She continued, "You've done so much for me, ever since I was a little girl!"

"Why, Melora, I've done very little!"

"Maybe you think so, but I don't. So I'm thanking you for the books and everything." He tried to protest, but she shook her head. "But that's not what I wanted to talk about. Mister Clay, you're having a terrible time, aren't you?"

"Why—I'm no worse off than lots of others, Melora!"

Melora shook her head, and there was something fragile, yet very strong, in her firm jaw. "You're dying, and unless you get some help, you're not going to make it. Isn't that the truth?"

Clay stared at her—this young woman knew what was happening to him. How? He couldn't tell, but he said heavily, "I guess you're right, Melora. I never really thought it was going to work, my coming back here. I guess my father is going to make it—but I'm going away."

"You mustn't!" Melora cried out, and the smoothness of her face was marred by pain. "You can't run away! You've got to stay!"

"It just isn't working, Melora," Clay said, defeat in his eyes and despair in his voice.

"Mister Clay," she said quickly, "can I tell you about what happened to me when I was fifteen years old?" She waited for his nod, then began to speak slowly. "I was so afraid that I could never be happy. I was all legs and arms and thought I was so ugly. And we were so poor! I wanted to have nice dresses and go to school. . .but I knew none of it was ever going to happen."

For a long time Melora went on, speaking softly, her eyes fixed on his. He sat there, seeing for the first time the life of the child he had thought was so happy and content. It had simply never occurred to him that Melora had problems that went so deep.

Finally Melora said, "I was so miserable, I prayed that God would take my life." She smiled then, saying, "But God was there! It was in this room, Mister Clay, right at this table. Everyone was in bed asleep, but I'd stayed up crying over my life. And then a wonderful thing happened. I was sitting right here in this chair, when I suddenly felt—oh, I don't know how to say it! Have you ever been alone, maybe out in a field, and had the feeling that you're not really alone, that someone is watching you even if you can't see anyone?"

"Many times, Melora!"

"It was a little like that, but different, too, somehow. My mother was living then, and she was always so busy with all of us, but once when I was no more than seven or eight, I woke up after a nightmare, crying and scared to death. She came to me, took me in her arms. . .and all the fear left me! It was a little like that, Mister Clay. I just felt that God was in the room, and I began to read the Bible. Right off I read a verse that said, 'Sirs, what must I do to be saved?' and then the next verse said, 'Believe on the Lord Jesus Christ, and thou shalt be saved, and thy house.'" Melora's eyes suddenly flooded with tears, and she brushed them away with one hand. "I didn't know what to do. I'd been so scared and lonely, and all I knew to do was ask God to do what my mother had done. I just said, 'Lord, I want to be saved! Will you please save me?'"

Clay watched her and saw that she was choked with emotion. "What happened then, Melora?"

Diamonds were in her eyes as she looked across the table at him. "Nothing really. I mean, I didn't hear any voices or anything. But something happened to me right here in this chair. Ever since that moment, Mister Clay, I've loved God. Jesus Christ has been as real to me as you are. And I've never been afraid or lonely."

Clay saw that she was finished and said, "That's a wonderful story, Melora. You've got such peace, more than anyone I know."

"Would you like to have that sort of peace?" Melora asked at once.

"Why, of course, Melora. But it's not for me. You don't know what I've done, the wrongs that—"

"Jesus died for those sins!" Melora insisted. "It says so right here." She opened the worn Bible and read a verse: " 'Who his own self bare our sins in his own body on the tree, that we, being dead to sins, should live unto righteousness: by whose stripes ye were healed.'"

For some reason that Clay could not understand, he became extremely nervous. There was no reason for it, for Melora was speaking in a very moderate voice. But it was similar to the time before a battle, when a man's hands would begin to sweat and his stomach would tighten. If it had been Jeremiah Irons, he would have given a list of reasons why he could not trust Jesus Christ. But Melora was different. She was no preacher, had nothing to gain from him. He felt free with her in a way he never would have with a preacher or a member of his family. "Melora, I can't understand it. How can a man dying two thousand years ago do anything for me? I'll never understand such a thing!"

"No, you won't," Melora agreed. "It's not a thing a person can understand. I didn't understand when my mother came to me and my fears all left. We never understand love, do we, Mister Clay? You love your mother, but can you explain what that is? No, but it's real, more real than some of the things you can understand, isn't it?"

Clay stared at her, then slowly nodded. "Yes, Melora. It is. But—surely it's not as easy as that. Surely a man has to do something before God will have him!"

"Do what?" Melora demanded strongly. "If a person could do something to get rid of his sins, why would God send Jesus to die on the cross? Most of the Bible is about people who thought they could do something to make God love them. But God just loves us, Clay. We don't have to earn it. I think all love is like that. Suppose you went to Rena and said, 'I'll love you, but only if you do certain things!' You would never do that! You just love her, don't you?"

Melora had touched a nerve, and Clay suddenly wet his lips. He clenched his hands to keep them from trembling. Suddenly he realized from her simple words what a thousand sermons had failed to make clear: God did love him! He dropped his eyes, for he could not hold her gaze. "Melora, I've been so rotten!" and then without planning it, he told her of his experience on the *Carrie Jane*. It was the first time he had spoken of it to anyone, and the bitterness of it all flooded over him. He spoke of the young woman and the baby, and when he got to the part when they were dragged overboard, his throat grew thick and his eyes burned with unshed tears.

He looked up, expecting to see disgust and rejection in her—and saw that she was weeping. He cried out suddenly, "Melora! I'm a murderer! God help me! I can't forget those poor people I killed."

Clay Rocklin had never wept, not since he was a child, but now his body was racked with great sobs. He stared at her helplessly, tears running down his cheeks.

Melora saw that he was paralyzed by his guilt, and at once she got up and went to him. She took his head, holding it against her breast for a moment. She felt the terror that was shaking him and waited for a few moments. Then she drew back and knelt beside him.

"You can't undo the past, Clay. Those who died are in God's hands. But you can't carry such a load!"

"Melora. . .what *can* I do?"

"You've been a proud man, but now you've got to do the one thing that's hardest for a strong man. You *must* do it!"

"Do what, Melora?" he asked thickly.

"You have to receive, Clay. God wants to give you a precious gift. He wants to give you life. Life in Jesus Christ. You've already confessed you've been a sinner. Now will you ask God to put your sins on Jesus? And will you let Jesus come into your life? That means more than going to church. It's like a marriage! You'll be part of the bride of Christ, and a bride loves and honors her husband above all things. Will you do that, Clay?"

Clay Rocklin felt that he was standing on a tremendously high precipice. He felt that he must turn and run or he would fall off. Yet somehow he knew that his only hope for peace was to throw himself off the cliff. As Melora continued to speak to him, not of doctrines or creeds, but of Jesus Christ, the man of Galilee, he felt a rising faith that was like nothing he'd ever felt in church. It was a quiet and powerful thing, as real as the earth or sky.

Suddenly he knew he had no choice—not really. He lifted his head and, in a husky whisper, said, "I'll do it, Melora! I'll follow Jesus as long as I live!"

Melora said, "Let's pray, then, and you tell God that you want to receive the gift He's giving you. . . ."

Three hours later, when Clay walked into the kitchen at Gracefield, he found Dorrie and his mother there, planning the meals for the next week. When he entered, the greeting on his mother's lips died, and her face turned as pale as paper. Dropping the book she was holding, she ran to him, crying out, "Oh, my boy! My boy!"

As he held his mother, Clay saw Dorrie throw her hands into the air and heard her shout, "Glory to God! Glory to God! My chile's done come home! He's found de glory!"

And then she began to do an ecstatic dance of joy around the kitchen. It was not a graceful sort of dance, but it was the most beautiful dance Clay Rocklin had ever seen!

PART FOUR

Thunder over Sumter—1860

CHAPTER 19

THE WINDS OF WAR

Late in the afternoon of October 16, 1859, John Brown reached the Maryland Bridge of Harpers Ferry. Brown, looking much like an Old Testament prophet—and believing himself to be the chosen vessel of God for freeing the slaves—had come with a grandiose plan for a deathblow against slavery. For two years he had waited, raising money to set his dream in motion. Now the time had come. His lips compressed, his eyes shining like polished steel, Brown marched at the head of his "army"—which consisted of sixteen whites, four free blacks, and one escaped slave.

"Men, we will proceed to the Ferry," he proclaimed, a fanatical light in his great staring eyes. He led the group through a cold drizzle, crossing the Potomac River on a covered bridge leading into the town; then the party moved toward the U.S. arsenal on Potomac Street.

It all went with remarkable ease. The watchman at the arsenal was taken by surprise; then the raiders captured the nearby Hall's Rifle Works. Next, Brown sent a few of his men to seize some prominent hostages, particularly Colonel Lewis Washington, a prosperous slaveholder and a great-grandnephew of the first president. Following explicit instructions from Brown, the contingent brought back not only Colonel Washington, but also a sword belonging to him that had been presented to George Washington by Frederick the Great. Brown strapped the weapon around his waist and waited, expecting slaves by the thousands to rally to him. Once he had armed them from the arsenal, they would march on in his campaign of liberation.

But the slaves did not come. Instead the town roused up and began to fight, and soon telegraph wires all over the East hummed with exaggerated reports like "Negro insurrection at Harpers Ferry! Fire and raping on the Virginia border!"

Several militia companies formed, and when they got to the town, they pinned Brown and his men down in Hall's Rifle Works. The raiders suffered the first casualty. Dangerfield Newby, a black, was killed. Townspeople dragged his body to a gutter and cut off his ears and let hogs chew on the corpse.

The battle went on all afternoon. At one o'clock, Brown sent two men out to negotiate under a truce flag. They were shot down. The battle went on, with several of the raiders shot or wounded. In the melee, the mayor of Harpers Ferry was shot dead, and in drunken rage the townsmen hauled out a raider whom they had captured that morning, killed him in cold blood, and used his body for target practice.

Word soon came that a company of marines from Washington was on its way. As the night wore on, Brown and his men spent a cold, hungry night in the engine house, listening to desultory gunfire and a drunken ruckus in the town. By then, Brown's son Oliver had been wounded, and he lay beside his brother Watson, both of them dying in terrible pain. "If you must die, die like a man," Brown replied in cold anger. Some time later he called to Oliver and got no reply. "I guess he is dead," said John Brown.

"What is it, Gid?" Melanie came out of the bedroom, pulling a green silk robe around her shoulders. She had awakened at once when the banging on the front door came, but waited until Gid threw on his own robe and went to answer it. There was some muffled talk that she did not understand, and when she heard the front door close, she went to meet him.

Gid's hair was mussed, but his eyes were wide open, and she saw that he was aroused. "I've got orders to go to Harpers Ferry, Mellie," he said. "Help me get ready."

As he shaved, she pulled his kit together, listening as he told her what little he knew. "Some maniac named John Brown has captured the arsenal at Harpers Ferry," he told her. "That's about all I know. I'm ordered to go with the marines to capture the raiders."

Melanie always dreaded such moments. They had been stationed in Washington for over a year, and it had been a wonderful time for her, for both of them. But now he would be facing danger, and when he left her, she kissed him and held him with all her might, saying, "I'll be waiting."

"It won't be long, I think. You'll have to tell the boys." Then he was gone, and she watched as he moved out into the darkness, his body strong and upright in the blue uniform. When she could no longer see him, she went back to bed—but not to sleep.

When Gid got to company headquarters, he received another shock. Colonel Barrington, his commanding officer, met him, saying, "You made good time, Major. Now come with me. I want you to meet your commanding officer." He led Gid across the yard where men were running about in what seemed to be wild confusion, but was only the normal manner of men called into sudden action. Barrington led Gid inside the quartermaster's building and moved to where two officers were leaning over a map on the desk.

"Colonel Lee, this is Major Rocklin. He'll accompany you as an aide."

Lieutenant Colonel Robert E. Lee turned and faced Gid and at once recognized him. A smile came to his lips, and he nodded. "Well, Major, it's been a long time since our venture in Mexico."

Gid returned the smile. "Yes, sir, I'm glad to see you again."

"This is Lieutenant Stuart of the First U.S. Cavalry, Major. He'll be in our command." Lee waited until the two men shook hands, then said, "We'll move at once." He hesitated, his eyes on Gid, and said, "Well, it's always good to have a man who's been decorated along." When Gid moved his shoulders slightly, he said contritely, "I remember now. You never did like to hear anyone speak of your medal. But in any case, I'm glad to have you."

Later as they rode rapidly at the head of the column, Lee mostly kept his silence. Once, though, he did ask, "I don't want to bring up unpleasant things, Major, but what became of your cousin, the one we had to discharge?"

Gid explained briefly that Clay had led an unfortunate life, then added, "He's back in Virginia now, helping his father with the plantation. I have hopes he'll do well."

"Men can change, sir," Lee answered, and he said no more until they arrived at the arsenal. He took charge at once, spoke with the officer in charge of the militia, then sent Jeb Stuart under a white flag to demand surrender and promise protection for the raiders. Gid was standing slightly behind

Lee and watched as Stuart talked to Brown at the door. After five minutes, Stuart jumped aside and waved his hat as a signal for the marines to charge.

It was soon over, but Gid always remembered the charge. He had led the way and heard the familiar sound of bullets singing in the air. He pulled his Colt and fired at the door and was with the first two or three men who crashed through to confront the raiders. The rifle shots rattled around the bricked-in engine room like firecrackers set off in a stone jug, and there was the harsh stink of sweat and powder.

Brown fired and missed, then fell to his knees, the sword in his hand bent double. A private snatched it from Brown and rained blows about his head.

From beginning to end, the charge took only fifteen minutes. Later as Lee, Stuart, and Rocklin stood watching the soldiers put irons on Brown, Stuart said, "Well, that was easy! But I'm glad it's over."

A shadow crossed Lee's face. He said quietly, "It's not over, Lieutenant. In fact, I'm afraid this is just the beginning."

Lee was correct. Brown was hanged forty-five days later and promptly became a martyr to the abolitionist cause—and a dark omen to the South. He inspired the North, and the day would come when men would march off to fight, singing, "John Brown's body lies a'moldering in the grave...."

❧

For over a year John Brown's body did molder in the grave, but when the election of 1860 came, the cause for which he died was very much alive. The nation seemed to be poised on the brink of some climactic change, and when the announcement was made that Abraham Lincoln was the new president, both

North and South reacted strongly. Springfield, Illinois, went wild, and there was dancing in the streets in Washington.

In the South, there was a strange reaction. The general populace felt a deep anger and a sense of being abused by the North. But there was also a sudden sense of release, a sense of some sort of bondage being lifted.

The Rocklins felt it as they drove to Richmond for a dress ball. The election was still in progress, though they were expecting to hear the results before the night was out. Clay drove Ellen and the children, and he was strangely oppressed as they drove through the crowded streets of the city. Ellen seemed oblivious to Clay's mood, as did the children. There were bands on the streets and buildings were decorated.

Ellen said with satisfaction, "It's so exciting! And Mr. Breckinridge will surely come to Richmond after he's elected."

"He won't be elected, Ellen," Clay said. He had explained to her twice that the Democratic Party had committed political suicide by its refusal to agree on a candidate. Instead the Party had divided into camps favoring three men: J. C. Breckinridge, John Bell, and Stephen A. Douglas. "Lincoln couldn't beat any one of those, but when the party split three ways, he couldn't lose," Clay had explained.

But Ellen said, "If you were a true Southerner, you wouldn't talk like that!" Then she began to talk to Dent, who agreed with her. She was wearing a new dress that was far too youthful for her and much too ornate. The fact that Clay was coming to the ball with her at all was some sort of a victory. Since his return, he had not shown any inclination to join the social life of Richmond. But she had insisted, and Susanna had said mildly, "I think it would be nice if you'd make an appearance with the family, Clay. For the sake of the children."

So he had agreed, but as he helped Ellen down from the carriage and led her into the ballroom, he was wishing he had not. Since his return to Gracefield, he had been isolated completely from her—especially after he made his conversion known. Ellen had laughed at him, saying, "It's just another of your fancies, Clay. It'll never last!" But somehow, as the months passed and Clay worked away doggedly at restoring Gracefield—and slowly gained the respect of the community—she resented the change in him. It was as though she wanted him to fail, and Clay soon began to realize that was her true desire.

The ballroom was beautifully decked. Flanking its long sides were chairs of all descriptions and degrees of comfort, with scarcely an inch between them. Here and there the line of chairs was broken by stands of Boston ferns. The ferns had been washed to look fresher, and the stands were sashed in broad bands of colored silk tied with elaborate bows. Large branches of magnolias with dark brown limbs and dark green leaves were set in tin tubs that had been tinseled over and so gave back the light of the huge chandeliers and the two hundred candles that brightened the hall.

There were already people everywhere, and soon the dancing began, but only waltzing; the formal sets had not yet been called. There was a general air of coming and going, and spectators staked jealous claims to the chairs that would afford the best views of the dancing and flirting. The ladies did much traipsing up and down the stairs with the excuse of leaving wraps or repairing hair and faces.

Ellen proved to be very popular, which did not surprise Clay. She was still an attractive woman, if one liked the lush type. She was claimed at once by a man he didn't know. As she floated off, he left the dance floor and made his way to the billiard room, where he found, as he expected, some of the men with whom he played poker. Bushrod Aimes was talking, as usual, waving one hand around wildly and holding a glass in the other. He spotted Clay and cried out, "Clay, come and wet your whistle!"

Clay moved forward and took a glass of wine from one of the white-jacketed waiters. He had learned long ago that it was easier to take one drink of the mild wine and nurse it along for hours than to fight off the constant demands of his friends that he join them in drinking.

Taylor Dewitt grinned at him. "You look pretty as a picture in that outfit, Clay. Now if you drop dead, we won't have to do a thing to you, except stick a lily in your hand."

"What's that I smell?" Clay frowned, ignoring Taylor's words.

"That's me!" Tug Ramsey said proudly. "Ain't it elegant?" He was as fat as a bear but still had the baby face he'd had at eighteen. Shy to excess with women, he had remained a bachelor, the only one of the old group who had done so.

"He got that lotion from a Frenchman on Bourbon Street in New Orleans," Taylor explained, grinning.

"I did not either!" Ramsey protested indignantly. "I bought it at a fancy store right here in Richmond!"

The mood of the room was light, and Taylor Dewitt stood there thinking, *Well, it took over a year, but old Clay has made it! Never thought it could happen!* He, along with the rest of the close-knit world of wealthy planters, had expected Clay to do well for a time. But it had come as a pleasant shock when he had kept to the task of restoring the fortunes of Gracefield. Dire prophecies had gone forth, stating that sooner or later he would break out, as he always did. But it had not happened. And Taylor was convinced that Clay was over the terrible part of his life. Oh, he had no life with Ellen, that was plain, for Taylor knew that she was unchanged. He himself kept his distance from her, but one of his friends, a boastful fellow named Jake Slocum, had informed him that the Rocklins did not live together as man and wife. Slocum, a stallion of a man with bulging arms and legs, had nudged Taylor in the ribs and given a sly grin, saying, "Woman's got to have a man, ain't that right, Dewitt? If Rocklin can't take care of his woman, reckon it's all I can do for him to take the chore myself!"

Slocum had taken a savage pleasure in throwing pointed gibes at Clay on the rare occasions when they were in the same company. Taylor had been alarmed on the first of these occasions. He had taken Slocum aside, saying, "Jake, I wouldn't take that line with Clay. He's been known to plug one or two fellows who took liberties with him."

"Rocklin! Aw, Dewitt, ain't you heard? He's on the glory trail! A good Christian like him can't take a shot at a fellow, can he, now?" Slocum had taken every opportunity to push at Clay, and most of the crowd had been disappointed in Clay's reaction.

"You want him to shoot Jake, Bushrod?" Taylor had asked the fiery Aimes, who had expressed his wish to see Rocklin put a stop to Slocum's gibes. "That's just what Clay needs, isn't it? A duel! That's what got him off on the wrong foot in the first place, you blockhead!" Then he had said thoughtfully, "I might call Jake out myself."

Bushrod had stared at him. "What for, Taylor? He ain't insulted you."

"I may shoot him for being so stupid!"

The talk came around to the election, but Clay took no part in the heated discussion. He found a seat behind the wall, had the waiter bring him a cup of hot coffee, and relaxed. The sound of music drifted in from the ballroom, and for the next hour he sat and enjoyed the company. Though he refused to talk about politics, he did talk about farming. He shocked the small group that gathered around him by his remark that he was changing from cotton to corn, at least partially.

"Why, Clay, there's not the money in corn that there is in cotton!" Devoe Tate exclaimed. He was a short, muscular man of thirty who had become friendly with Clay over the past few months. "And this is cotton country. Too hot for corn."

"Tell you how it comes out next fall, Devoe," Clay said with a shrug. But when Devoe pressed him, he finally said, "Not going to tell you your business, Devoe, but corn would really be even better for you than for Gracefield." When Devoe pressed him, he went on to explain, a little self-conscious because several other men had gathered around to listen. "Well, you've got a smaller place, for one thing, and not nearly so many slaves. Cotton wears land out fast, which we all know, and it takes lots of hands to make the crop."

"Well, I was thinking of buying more slaves and more land," Devoe said, scratching his chin.

"You could do that, but do you know the price of a prime field hand?"

"About three thousand dollars, I reckon."

"How much cotton would he have to raise before you make three thousand dollars clear?"

Devoe did some rapid calculation, then said, "I'd say about fifty bales, Clay, maybe more. But I'd have him for years."

"If he didn't die or get sick."

Clay sipped his coffee, and Tug asked, "Are you against slavery, Clay?"

"I'm against losing money, Tug," Clay remarked, turning the question away. Then he went on, "Devoe, you wouldn't have to buy another acre or another slave to raise corn. Maybe you wouldn't make as much cash. I can't say about that."

Devoe looked a little embarrassed. "You know, my folks moved here from Missouri. Know what they did there? They raised corn and fed hogs, then sold the hogs. Did real good at it." He sighed, adding, "Pa told me the last time he was out of debt was back in Missouri. Said the first slave he bought put him in debt, and he's never been out since!"

Bushrod laughed and slapped Tate on the back. "You going to be a pig farmer, Devoe? You can't court that Debbie girl of yours smelling like pigs!"

A laugh went around the room, with Devoe Tate laughing at himself, but Clay noticed that he was sober the rest of the evening. As they all moved out of the billiard room later, Devoe said quietly, "Clay, be all right if I come over and talk to you this week?"

"Anytime, Devoe."

The ball was in full swing, with the dancers moving across the floor to the sound of music. To Clay's surprise, Ellen came to him at once, demanding, "Dance with me!"

He had no chance to refuse, for she had practically thrown herself into his arms. She was a marvelous dancer, and as they moved around the floor, she was humming along with the waltz tune. There was a happy expression on her face, and in the candlelight she looked much younger. Suddenly she looked at him, asking, "Why are you staring at me, Clay?"

"Didn't mean to, Ellen," he apologized. "I'm not much of a dancer, you know. Have to keep my mind on it or I'll be walking all over your feet."

"You're a good dancer," she answered. She had forced him to dance with her simply to make their charade more believable. One of her women friends had taunted her, "That good-looking husband of yours doesn't pay enough attention to you, Ellen. You better keep a tighter rein on him, or he might run off with one of these Richmond belles!"

This was the closest she had been to her husband since he'd returned to Gracefield, and it gave her a queer feeling to be in his arms. *He is fine-looking*, she thought, looking up into his face. But then, he always had been the best-looking man she'd ever known. He was one of the tallest men in the room, and his coal black hair gleamed richly, complementing his rich tan. His face was still smooth and unlined, his features strong and clear.

His arms were strong, and more than once he pressed against her in the dance, causing her to examine him carefully—but he had a preoccupied look on his face. When he had come home, she had assumed that he would eventually come back to her. She had informed him that she would never have anything to do with him, but as the weeks wore on, she had known she would relax as he tried to make up to her. Finally she would permit him back into her life and into her bed. That had been her plan, but it had never happened.

He had remained in the summerhouse, fixing it up, adding on to it, and giving every indication of staying there on a permanent basis. He was always polite and even considerate to her, but never showed the least interest in her as a woman. This had irked Ellen, and once or twice she had pressed against him on some pretext, but he had never seemed to notice. She feared that he had heard of her affairs in Richmond, but he never mentioned it if he had. Then she began to watch him closely, suspecting that he was seeing some woman, but it was obvious that he was not. He never went anywhere except to church, and then always with his parents, and with their own children when he could persuade her to send them.

He looked at her, smiled, and said, "It's a nice dance. And you look very attractive." His compliment gave her an unexpected pleasure. She moved closer to him, but then the dance was over and he took her to the refreshment table.

He was getting her a glass of punch when there was a muffled shout, and when they turned to look, Sam Decosta, the editor of the *Richmond News*, came running into the room, his hair wild and his eyes wilder.

"Lincoln has won!" he shouted, waving a telegram over his head. "It's all over! Lincoln is the new president."

The room was alive with talk but not with cheers. A man shouted, "Let the baboon be president! He won't be *our* president! We'll take care of that!"

A roar went up, and for the next hour there was bedlam. Clay marveled at what was happening. The entire South hated Lincoln, and many leaders had vowed that if he was elected they'd lead their states out of the Union. Yet here the people of Richmond were, shouting and yelling and drinking toasts as if they had won a great victory!

He spoke with his uncle Claude Bristol about it. He had always liked Claude, preferring him to Brad Franklin, his hotheaded brother-in-law. "I just don't understand it, Claude," he said, speaking loudly to be heard. "What's everyone so excited about? Don't they know this probably means war?"

Claude cast a weary eye over the crowd. He was fifty-five years old, and years of hard living had worn him thin. He had been a sorrow to Clay's aunt Marianne, for there was little substance to him. He was, at the core, a degenerate—but there was a genteel quality in his manner that caused him to be so discreet in his affairs that they never became public. He had charm and, surprisingly, some insight. "It's a release, Clay," he said. "The tension is gone. Nobody knows what the future will bring, but at least the pressure is gone. From now on the South knows what it will do, and it's always easier when you've made up your mind."

Clay was depressed, and as soon as he could, he collected his family and took them back to Gracefield. He sat glumly as Dent spoke excitedly about the future. *Was I ever that young and so sure of everything?* he wondered, feeling about a thousand years old.

His parents were still at the ball, and Clay was glad that Highboy, the oldest son of Box, the blacksmith, was there to unhitch the team. "Good night," he said and moved away down the path that led to his house. It was not, he thought as he entered, *the summerhouse* any longer, but *Clay's house.* The slaves called it that, and the family had taken it up.

He built up a small fire and made a pot of coffee. He removed his suit, then put on a pair of old cotton trousers and sat down at the table. He was tired but not sleepy, so he worked on the books for the next hour.

The sound of tapping on the door startled him, and he came to his feet quickly. It was unusual for anyone to come to his house this late, so he picked up the pistol he kept on top of the mantel and demanded, "Who is it?"

"It's me—Ellen. Let me in, Clay."

He opened the door, and she came in at once. "What's wrong?" he asked, turning to replace the pistol.

She was wearing a thick wool coat, and her cheeks were

flushed. She looked around the room, saying, "I haven't been here in a long time. We stayed here once, you remember? When we had the reunion and the house was full."

He nodded but asked, "Is something wrong, Ellen? One of the children sick?"

She seemed embarrassed and shook her head. "No. Nobody's sick. I just wanted to talk to you."

He studied her thoughtfully, thinking it strange that she would come so late. "Well, sit down. I've got some coffee on."

He got her a cup of coffee, but when he brought it to her, she took only a sip, then set it down absently. She began to talk of the ball and how exciting it had been. Her cheeks were red, and Clay knew she had been drinking, but he said nothing.

Finally she said, "It's hot in here, Clay," and threw off her coat. She was wearing only a cotton robe over her nightgown, and when he stared at her, she said quickly, "I was in bed, but I couldn't sleep, so I just threw on my overcoat and came here."

Then she got up and began walking around the room, talking aimlessly about the books, the furniture, and how well he'd fixed the place up. She seemed nervous, which was unusual for her. She had taken extra care with her hair, and she smoothed her hand over it as she spoke. Finally she seemed to run out of words. She bit her lower lip, then came over to stand in front of him. He got to his feet, and she suddenly leaned forward.

"Clay—!" she whispered, pulling at him. "I'm your wife! Doesn't that mean anything to you?"

It was a trying moment for Clay Rocklin, for he had lived a long time without women. Her body lay against him, and her lips were parted as she whispered, "Love me, Clay! Like you used to!"

Clay knew that Ellen had no love for him. He guessed that

she saw him as a challenge, that she wanted him only to prove that she was still desirable. And she *was* desirable, no denying that! Clay stood there struggling with the hungers that he had kept under strict control for so long. There was nothing wrong with taking her; she was his wife, after all.

Yet he knew instinctively that he must not touch her. She represented a way of life he could not share. If he resumed his relationship with her, he would be in a bondage that he knew he could not endure and would never escape. She would devour him, as a female praying mantis devours her mate.

"Ellen, we're past all that," he said and stepped away from her. He tried to make his rejection less harsh by saying, "You don't need me. I'd make you miserable. It's better if we keep on just as we are."

If he had touched her with a hot iron, the effect would not have been greatly different. She turned pale, and after one moment of standing before him in shocked silence, not moving at all, she suddenly drew her hand back and slapped him across the face, screaming curses at him.

Clay stood there, not moving, and she slapped him twice more. Then she grabbed her coat and ran out of the house. He could hear her curses as she ran down the path. They grew faint, and still he stood there, until finally he turned rigid. He knew this was not the end of it. She would never let him have a moment's peace, not now.

Finally taking a deep breath, he picked up the Bible he kept on the table and began to read.

❧

When Deborah Steele heard that her uncle Gideon was going to move his family to Virginia, she immediately mounted a crusade to get herself invited. Deborah, at the age of eighteen, had learned to get what she wanted as a rule. She got some of that from her father, Amos, who was a minister but also an abolitionist. He had taught his three sons, Patrick, Colin, and Clinton, and his daughter, as well, that it was displeasing to the Lord to go at anything halfheartedly. "Whatsoever thy hand findeth to do, do it with thy might," was a scripture that had molded his own life. He had managed to pass that message along to all his children except Colin, who took life less seriously than his father liked.

Deborah had been educated at Rev. Charles Finney's Oberlin College, where she had become an admirer of the great evangelist. The two strongest men she knew were both devoted to freeing the slaves, and it was not surprising that she became an abolitionist at an early age.

When she had gone to Oberlin at the age of sixteen, she had been one of the youngest students. If her father had not been one of Finney's strongest supporters for years, she would not have been accepted. Even then, the president had examined her long and hard, testing her morals, her intelligence, and her determination. In the end, he had admitted her.

Life at Oberlin had been exciting; Deborah had met the men and women who were at the head of the abolition movement, including William Lloyd Garrison, Frederick Douglass, and Theodore Parker. Deborah's youth and beauty made her stand out, and when she proved that she could hold her own intellectually with the best at Oberlin, she was busy and happy.

But college was over now, and Deborah found that there was no excitement in being a former student. She accompanied her father to meetings, but he was a busy man, and she felt that she had been marooned on a desert island.

Then her cousin Tyler, Uncle Gideon's oldest son, had told her that his father was being transferred to South Carolina, and his mother was going to visit Uncle Thomas and Aunt Susanna before joining Gideon at Charleston. It was like a light coming on in a dark room!

I'll go with them and study the terrible lot of the slaves firsthand! Deborah's fertile imagination at once pounced on the germ of a thought, and within two hours, her plan was fully grown. She had to convince her own parents and her uncle and aunt, but she had no doubt of success. Being a very honest young woman, she freely acknowledged that she had learned early to get her own way. Being the only girl among six boys (counting Gideon and Melanie's three boys and her own three brothers), she had been a spoiled pet all her life. It had not ruined her, but she had learned that there were certain things she could do to get her own way. Though she had never formulated this knowledge into a written code, she practiced the principle of it on certain occasions.

In this case, success fell to her like a ripe apple. She had simply gone to her father and smiled at him, twisting the button on his coat, and said, "Father, do you think I could be of any help to the movement by doing some primary research on the terrible life of the slaves?" He had thought she meant in a library, but she had fluffed his side whiskers, saying innocently, "That's been done, hasn't it? But do you know what I thought of? I could go to Richmond with Aunt Mellie. She's always begged me to go with her for a visit. Perhaps I should do it. Then I could see slavery firsthand, and just think of the material I could get done for your book!"

Amos Steele could handle a large congregation, an angry

mob, or almost anything else—but he was easy pickings for his daughter. Before she was finished with him, he was totally convinced that the whole thing had been his idea! He plunged in with his abnormal energy, and before the sun went down, he had convinced his wife that Deborah should go; visited his sister-in-law Melanie Rocklin and admitted that he had been wrong to prevent Deborah from visiting her family in Richmond; gained Gid's permission for Deborah's visit; and bought a new set of luggage for her.

Deborah threw her arms around his neck and kissed him warmly. "Oh, Father, you're so wonderful!"

Steele hesitated, then said, "Deborah, you know the scripture says a beautiful woman without discretion is like a jewel of gold in a swine's snout. So you must be discreet while doing your work there for the movement."

"But, Father, they know I'm an abolitionist!"

"Yes, but you don't have to wear a sign that says in bold print, 'I am here to study the cruel treatment of slaves'!"

Deborah got a sudden vision of herself wearing that sign and giggled. "Of course not, Father. That would be silly."

"I'm serious, Deborah. You could do great harm to our relatives there if anyone found out about your study. You are a very impulsive young woman, and you'll see things there that will anger you. You'll want to step in and right the wrongs. But you must not! You must always remember that you can serve the best interest of those poor people by taking the long view. The book will stir the people of our country, both in the South and in the North. There need not be a war, for the South can be reached and won without bloodshed."

"I'll remember, Father," Deborah said, nodding.

She left the next week, on the twenty-first of November,

never suspecting as she got on the train with the rest of the family that her uncle Gideon had been assigned to serve under Major Robert Anderson. And she did not know that Major Anderson was ordered to man a fort located at the entrance to the harbor of Charleston, South Carolina.

Nor did she know that this fort—Fort Sumter—would be the first place to feel the winds of war.

CHAPTER 20

KISSING COUSINS

$\mathcal{D}$eborah Steele came to the South with an adamant pre-disposition to dislike everything there, but she found that she could not do it. For one thing, the Rocklins of Gracefield were such open, warmhearted people that she could not help liking them. The twins, David and Denton, were gone on a hunting trip, but she found Lowell and Rena to be as well bred as any Yankee children their age. Her great-aunt Susanna Rocklin was especially charming, and by the end of three days at the big plantation, Deborah felt that she had known the older woman forever. She liked Thomas Rocklin, too, but realized almost at once that he was a man to be pitied. She was too close to strong men, such as her father and her uncle Gideon Rocklin, to miss the fact that the head of Gracefield was a weak man—but she could not deny his warmth and generosity.

It was Clay Rocklin, though, who fascinated the young woman. She had heard stories of his wild youth, his long exile, and his dramatic return. A lover of novels, Deborah was possessed of a powerful imagination, and the drama of Clay Rocklin's life would have made an excellent novel. He even looked like the hero of a romance, lean and darkly handsome.

Strangely enough, it was Deborah who discovered the rather unusual friendship between Clay Rocklin and Melora Yancy. It happened quite accidentally, actually. Deborah had always loved horses and had her own mare in Washington. When she lamented one morning that she missed her horse, Clay said at once, "That's no problem. Come along with me." He had led her to the stables and to her delight assigned a beautiful mare named Lady for her use while visiting at Gracefield.

"Oh, what a beauty!" Deborah cried out with delight. "May I ride her now?"

"Get dressed and I'll give you a tour of the place."

Deborah had dashed away at once, borrowing one of Susanna's riding habits. Soon she and Clay were riding across the fields. Clay watched her carefully, aware that the mare was spirited, but soon he was satisfied that the young woman would have no trouble.

"You're a fine horsewoman," he said. "Lady's been known to throw her rider a time or two, but I can see you can handle her." The fields were dead and brown, filled with the brittle cotton stalks from the last harvest. "I wish you could see this field when the cotton is ready to harvest, Deborah," Clay said. "It looks like fields of snow."

"Maybe I can come back for a visit then," Deborah said, smiling. She gave him a glance, admiring his rugged good looks, and added, "It's a lovely place, Mr. Rocklin. And everyone is so nice."

He suddenly turned his head and gave her a shrewd smile. "You didn't think we would be, did you? Nice, I mean." He laughed at her expression. "The daughter of Amos Steele and a graduate of Oberlin College wouldn't be expected to like Southerners. I expect you thought you'd find some pretty grim monsters.

Beating slaves to death every morning before breakfast."

"Oh no—!" Deborah protested, then laughed, though she was blushing. "You're pretty clever, Uncle Clay." She smiled. "I suppose that *was* what I expected." She sat on her horse, unaware of what a picture she made. She had hair that was almost blond, the only light-colored hair in her family, and her eyes were large, well shaped, and a beautiful pure violet. She had a heart-shaped face with a widow's peak and a beautiful complexion. Even in her aunt's riding habit, her slim but well-curved figure was evident. For all her beauty, though, Deborah was not a vain young woman. Her mirror—and many young men!—had told her that her appearance was good, but she did not trade on it.

That was what made Clay admire her. It was unusual for such a beautiful young woman to ignore the tricks that most of her sort used on men. As they talked during that ride, he quickly discovered that the reports he had heard of her intelligence had not been exaggerations.

She looked at him now and asked directly, "Do you ever beat your slaves, Uncle Clay?"

"No." Clay thought about the thing, then shook his head. "I hate slavery, Deborah. If I had my way, I'd set every one of the slaves here at Gracefield free today."

His simple statement stunned Deborah. She stared at him but saw that he was completely serious. "I wouldn't have believed it," she said finally. "But you're not a typical Southern planter, are you?"

"No, not really. But there are more like me than you think. Robert E. Lee, for example, feels the same way. Of course, most planters are blind to the evils of slavery, just as they're blind that our peculiar institution is leading us to economic disaster." He talked quietly as they rode over the plantation, and Deborah was forced to rethink her position on the question of the Southern slaveholder. She sensed a generous spirit in Clay Rocklin, which did not fit with her previously firm opinion that all slave owners were cruel men.

Clay led them down a narrow lane lined with first-growth fir trees that arched over them. "Somebody I want you to meet," he said as they turned toward a cabin that lay in a clearing. "You've met the so-called aristocracy of the South. You've met some of the slaves on the place. But I want you to meet another class of people. I think you'll like them."

Deborah asked no questions but was soon being introduced to the Yancy family. Buford Yancy welcomed Clay and, when introduced, beamed a welcome to Deborah. "Come in, Miss Deborah. Always glad to meet Mr. Rocklin's kin."

Deborah tried to sort out the children, who only stared at her shyly at first, then came out of their shells as she smiled and began to talk to them. All of them looked like Buford. "You have beautiful children, Mrs. Yancy." Then she was startled to hear the Yancy children all break out in giggles. Buford Yancy grinned shyly, saying, "Now I hope you take notice of that, all of you. Your pa looks so young he gets mistook for his own daughter's husband!"

"Oh, I didn't—" Deborah blushed, throwing a horrified glance at the dark-haired woman. She was no more than twenty-five, and she was a beauty. But there was a twinkle in her green-gray eyes.

"Melora *is* a mother to the children—a second mother," Clay said with a fond look at the young woman. "Actually, she's Buford's oldest daughter."

"Don't be embarrassed, Miss Steele," Melora said, smiling.

"You're not the first to think as you have." Then she turned to Clay. "I don't think you've ever come here anytime except just before mealtime, Mister Clay."

"My mama didn't raise no fools," Clay said, grinning.

Soon Deborah was seated at the crowded table. She tasted what Melora called "winter crab gumbo," which she dipped from a large aromatic pot onto a bed of freshly steamed rice. There also was cold ham and cheese with toasted biscuits. The fresh milk was rich and sweet, and when Melora set down a huge slice of pumpkin pie, she held up her hands, protesting, "Please, Melora—no more! I've got to get into my clothes when I get home!"

After the meal, Buford said, "Clay, I've got a new litter of pigs from that big red boar of yours. Turned out real good. Come on, I'll show you." The men left, and Deborah offered to help clean the dishes. Melora protested that they could wait, but soon the two of them were elbow-deep in the soapy water. As they worked, Deborah probed at her hostess. She was very good at such things, but Melora was equally adept at keeping her own counsel.

"How do you like the Rocklins?" Melora asked, and that kept Deborah talking for some time. She gave more information about herself than she knew, and as they finished, Melora said, "You haven't met Mister Clay's oldest boy, Denton. He's the one who's most like his father, but—" She broke off, and Deborah picked up on the fact that something lay between Clay and his son. By the time the men returned, the children all began prompting their father to take them to see the beaver dam as he had promised. Buford groaned, saying, "Seems funny to me that you kids can forget everything I say about the work around here, but you jist let me mention some kind of holiday in a passin' kind of way—and you'll nag a man to death." He finally agreed, and when the children all had donned their heavy coats, he asked, "Don't reckon you'd wade across twenty acres of briars to see a beaver dam, would you, Miss Steele? No, I didn't think so. Well, come on, you kids!"

Melora set a cup of coffee out for Clay, then poured two more for herself and Deborah. Clay sipped his carefully, then asked, "Got anything for me, Melora?"

A quick flush touched the smooth cheeks of the young woman, which aroused Deborah's curiosity. "Oh, not now, please. Miss Deborah doesn't want to waste her time."

Deborah was intrigued and asked at once, "What is it?"

"Can I tell her, Melora?" Clay asked. When he got a slight nod, he said, "Melora has a real gift for writing, Deborah. She lets me read it from time to time." He turned back to Melora. "Let's see it. What have you got?"

Melora gave a helpless look at the pair, saying, "Oh, it's nothing. Just things that come to me." At their urging she went to the bookcase stuffed with books of all sorts, then came back with an inexpensive notebook. She handed it to Clay, but he shook his head. "Read it to us."

Melora gave Deborah a shy look but opened the notebook and began reading in a clear, easy voice. It was a very simple essay, more like an entry from a journal, and at first Deborah thought, *What does Clay see in this?* But as the young woman went on, she began to find a beauty in the prose. Deborah had read Emerson and Thoreau, and Melora's style reminded her a little of Thoreau. It described a visit Melora had made to take some cool springwater to her father as he plowed in the fields. As Melora read on, Deborah realized that this young woman had a rare gift! She could smell the rich loam of the earth or see the ragged clouds race across the sky. When she described finding a young raccoon with his paw caught in a steel trap and confessed how she had released him, Deborah was deeply moved. Then Melora read on, speaking of a coon as some sort of symbol of all men—and Deborah knew for certain that Melora had that special genius that was given to only a few: the ability to communicate truth and honest emotion.

As the three sat there, Melora reading and the other two listening, Deborah suddenly became aware that Clay was different. She had seen him with his family and soon discovered that he and his wife were totally alien. There was no mistaking the harsh light in Ellen Rocklin's eyes when she looked at Clay—nor the lack of any affection at all in Clay toward her.

Now, Deborah saw, Clay was totally absorbed in Melora. His coffee cup rested in his hand, forgotten, and his dark eyes were fixed on her face. He had built a wall around himself, Deborah knew, but now the wall was down. He had forgotten that Deborah was there, and suddenly the girl from the North knew that Clay Rocklin felt a great deal for Melora Yancy— perhaps even more than was proper. She knew instinctively that this was a scene that had been repeated many times, the two of them together. Melora had spoken briefly of how Clay had been kind to her even when she was a child, bringing her books and small gifts.

Suddenly Melora lifted her eyes to look at Clay. She had forgotten the third party in the room, Deborah saw, and her face was open, filled with something that she kept hidden when she was aware of it. But it was evident, at least to Deborah, that her feelings for Clay Rocklin went deep—a fact that perplexed Deborah. Clay was so much older, and the young woman was attractive enough to have found a husband long ago. Deborah resolved to probe deeper, her romantic spirit and natural curiosity alerted.

"Oh, that's enough of this!" Melora laughed shortly, gave a quick glimpse toward Deborah, and got to her feet. "I feel like a fool reading my scribbling to you," she said, coming back to sit at the table. Her eyes gleamed with a sudden humor, and she said, "I'll write a part for you, Mister Clay. You can be the innkeeper. You can rant and roar and throw poor Joseph and Mary out into the cold."

"Just let me at it!" Clay grinned. "I'll tear a passion to tatters! The stage missed something when I decided to be a cotton farmer, but now's my big chance!" He ran on, laughing at his own foolishness, the first time Deborah had seen him in such a mood, and she marked it as another piece of evidence that he was one man when he was at Gracefield, and another when he was at the Yancy cabin.

Soon they left the cabin, and on the way back home, Deborah spoke of the Yancys. "They don't own any slaves," she remarked. "Is it because they think it's an evil—or are they just too poor?"

"Both, I guess." Clay shook his head with a puzzled air. "It's odd, Deborah. Buford has told me many times he'll never own a slave, but he's also told me that nobody is going to tell him that he can't own a slave. There are lots of men like that in the South. If it came right down to it, they'd fight for the right to do as they please. That's what states' rights is all about, isn't it?"

When they arrived at Gracefield, she thanked Clay and insisted on taking the saddle from Lady and giving her a rubdown. She was engaged in this when Rena came in, dressed in a pair of overalls that had obviously belonged to one of her brothers. "Hello," she said shyly. "Did you have a good ride?"

"Oh yes! Lady is a wonderful mount, isn't she? And your father showed me all over Gracefield. I expect he takes you riding pretty often, doesn't he? You're lucky to live here, Rena, with horses to ride and lots of things to do."

Rena gave Deborah a strange look and came to stand closer. "I guess so." She sounded so uncertain that Deborah gave her a closer look, and at once she saw that the girl was unhappy. Quickly she said, "I'm through with Lady. Why don't you show me your room, Rena? I'll bet it's nice."

Rena looked surprised but brightened up at once. "It's not much," she said diffidently. But when Deborah insisted, she led the way to a bright, cheerful room on the corner of the second floor. The room had a large dormer window and was decorated with white molding, which set off the yellow wallpaper. It was a child's room, with several stuffed animals on top of the furniture and the wallpaper featuring small ducks and white geese. Deborah made much of it, saying, "It's the very nicest room I've seen in the whole house, Rena!"

Rena looked around with surprise, as if it were a room she'd never seen before, and then said, "Would you like to see some of my pictures?" The two of them sat down on the bed, and Rena pulled out canvasses and sketch pads filled with drawings. They were very good, revealing a talent for drawing that Deborah praised. "I can't draw a stick, myself," she laughed, "but you have real talent. Do any of the rest of your family paint or draw?"

This led Rena to speak of her family, and she revealed a great deal of herself in her description. She spoke warmly of her brothers, but hardly mentioned her mother. When she spoke cautiously of her father, her eyes revealed what Deborah recognized as a deep longing. Deborah soon had the whole story, how Ellen Rocklin had in effect abdicated her responsibility as a mother years ago. If Clay had abandoned his family physically, Ellen had done the same emotionally and spiritually. Although Rena didn't realize it, she revealed to the quick mind of her guest how she had missed having a mother and how she had hated her father for leaving them. The story of Buck's attack on Clay came out, and Rena's eyes grew warm as she spoke of how her father had let her help him fix his books and how he sometimes read to her. Then she said uncertainly, "Maybe I shouldn't spend so much time with him. Dent says it's wrong. He says that he doesn't deserve to be trusted."

What an awful, pompous boor Mr. Denton Rocklin must be! Deborah thought with a stab of contempt, but said, "Oh, I don't think that's right, Rena. I like your father very much."

"You do?"

"Why, certainly. He made some bad mistakes, but we have to give people a second chance, don't we? You know what I think?"

"What?"

"I think your father is a very lonely man. And I think it's fine that you're spending a lot of time with him."

A look of relief washed across Rena's face, and she smiled at Deborah, saying, "He's really changed! I know he has! And I'm going to tell Dent to mind his own business!"

Good for you! Deborah thought but said no more. Then Rena asked, "Would you do something for me? Something really big?"

Deborah hesitated, but when she saw the eager look in the girl's eyes, she said, "If I can, Rena."

"Ask Mama if I can go to the Christmas party in Richmond with you." She began speaking quickly, as if to forestall any arguments. "Mama thinks I'm such a baby! She says I'm too young for a ball, but I don't think fourteen is too young, do you, Deborah?"

"Well, I don't think so, Rena—but I can't go against your mother on something like this."

"She doesn't really care! She just doesn't want to have to watch after me. But if you tell her that you want me to go and that you'll watch me, she'll say yes. Oh, please, Deborah! I don't want to stay home by myself!"

Deborah's father often said, "Daughter, your spiritual gift is meddling!" And she realized that it was true. Something told her not to get involved with the internal affairs of the Rocklin family, but she was not far enough away from the age of fourteen to forget what a trying time it was. The pleading expression on Rena's face was more than she could bear, so she suddenly laughed and hugged the girl. "We'll do it, Rena! And you can get your father to give you a new dress."

"Oh, he'd never do that!"

"Fathers will do anything for their daughters, Rena," Deborah said confidentially, nodding. "But you have to butter them up a little."

"Butter them up how?"

"Oh, sit on their lap, run your fingers through their hair, tickle their ears. They like that a lot." She laughed at Rena's expression and hugged her again. "It's something you can work on. Now let's go talk to your mother."

❦

Major Robert Anderson was a lean, clean-shaven, graying veteran, noted both for an excellent combat record in the Black Hawk and Mexican wars and for a mildly bookish quality that was somewhat rare among army officers. He was also a Southerner, of Virginian ancestry, and some of the officers at Fort Sumter told each other that he had been chosen by Secretary of War Floyd because he was proslavery.

Gideon stood with his commanding officer on the battlements of Fort Moultrie in Charleston Harbor. It was cold, with a stiff wind pushing against them, and Major Anderson had to raise his voice as he explained the military situation to his newest officer.

"A poor way to spend Christmas, Major Rocklin," Anderson said, "but we've got no choice." He went on to explain carefully what he was doing in Charleston, most of which Gid knew already. "South Carolina seceded from the Union, as you know, five days ago. The next step they will make is to take over these Union forts."

"You really think they'll attack, sir?"

"No doubt about it. And look at what we have—our main base here at Fort Moultrie is completely vulnerable to land attack from the rear." Anderson turned to face his subordinate, remarking, "My father, Captain Richard Anderson, defended this fort during the Revolution. Now I have to defend it from our own people—and it cannot be done!"

"I take it you have a plan?"

"Yes. Clearly the most advantageous place to make a stand is Fort Sumter. It's an island fort, only about three miles from Charleston, but we have heavy guns there. Since we can't hold Fort Moultrie, we'll shift all the men to Fort Sumter."

"Yes, sir. When are you thinking of moving?"

Anderson was a sober man, burdened with an awesome responsibility, but he smiled slightly as he answered Gid's question. "Tonight."

Gid was startled. "On Christmas night?" Then he nodded.

"No one will expect us to do such a thing. And I remember what Tom Jackson said when we were in Mexico—always try to do what your enemy will never suspect!"

Anderson nodded absently, then said quietly, "Take charge of loading the equipment, Major Rocklin." He turned to go but hesitated, then said, "Merry Christmas, Major."

" 'And God bless us every one,' as Tiny Tim put it," Gid replied, and then the two men moved away from the biting sea wind.

⌁

"I don't see why I have to keep track of an old abolitionist!"

Denton and David had come back from their trip late in the afternoon, and Dent was informed by Susanna that he would be expected to escort his cousin Deborah Steele to the Christmas ball. Dent had other plans—he had been engaged in a lively contest with Jackie Terrel for the favors of Mary Ann Small. "She's probably as ugly as homemade soap," he grumbled, then brightened up as he thought of a solution. "Let David take her, Grandmother."

"He's taking Lorella Ballentine," Susanna said briskly. An impish thought came to her, and she said, "It will be a good deed for you, Denton. The poor girl is rather homely. I'd venture a guess that she never had a real live young man to take her to a ball. It's Christmas. You can bring some cheer into a dreary life. Isn't that what Christmas is all about?"

Dent grumbled, but he knew that he was doomed. He could get around his mother, but he had never been able to circumvent any plan that his grandmother decided on. He went off to dress, and Susanna quickly told the other members of the family what she'd done. David fell to laughing at once, and the others thought it would serve Dent right. He was always playing some practical joke on others, and it was only fair for them to get him back!

Susanna went to Deborah's room and said, "My dear, I've done a dreadful thing. . . ." When she told her story, Deborah laughed out loud, delighted at the chance to see young Mr. Denton suffer. Susanna said, "I'll come in and help you fix your hair. I want you to look like an angel tonight!"

David was not given to practical jokes, but he entered into this one. A few minutes before time for the carriage to leave, he went to the bedroom he shared with Dent. Putting a somber look on his face, he said, "Well, Dent, one good thing about this—you won't have to do it but once. I mean, Christmas only comes but once a year. And she'll be going back to Washington pretty soon, I suppose."

Dent stared at him. "She's pretty ugly, David?"

"Well, look at it like this, Dent," David said with a pained expression, throwing himself into his role. "Beauty is only skin-deep."

Dent swore, then gave the desk before him a sound kick. "Well, why don't you go skin her, then?" He was deeply depressed and raved about what an awful woman his grandmother was to force him into such a thing. Finally he was ready—at least, he was dressed—but he stood there, his lip sticking out mulishly. "I don't think I'm well, David. Just go tell Grandmother—"

"You know that won't work," David broke in, shaking his head. "Come on, Dent. Might as well get it over with. Tell you what, I'll dance with her twice myself! Now there's brotherly love for you—considering what she looks like!"

Dent followed David down the stairs and found the rest of the family waiting at the foot of the great staircase. "Well, why don't you go on and laugh!" he exploded when Lowell tried to stifle a giggle behind his hand and Rena grinned at him broadly. "Fine family you are!" he burst out bitterly. "Spoiling my whole Christmas!"

"You've got to learn to take your medicine with less fuss, my boy," his grandfather said. Thomas could scarcely keep his face straight, and when Dent looked down with a scowl, he winked at Clay. "I understand that the young lady makes up in scholarship what she lacks in personal attraction, Clay."

"Why, that's correct, Father," Clay said blandly. "She's quite a marvel in theology, I believe. Dent, ask her about her views on hyper-Calvinism and a second work of grace. I think you'll benefit from her knowledge."

Dent gave both of them an angry look, and then Lowell said, "There she comes!"

Dent was aware that the entire family was having a great time at his expense, and he hated it. Determined not to give them any satisfaction, he didn't even look up, but stared out the window. "Dent, this is your cousin Deborah Steele. I know you'll take good care of her at the ball tonight," Susanna said.

Dent knew that he'd have to look at the girl. He couldn't avoid that, of course! He lifted his eyes and, at the same time, started to mutter some fitting remark—but he could not get it out of his mouth.

The girl who stood before him was the most beautiful thing he'd ever seen in his life!

He felt as if he had been struck a blow in the pit of the stomach, and his brain seemed to go dead. His eyes were working, however, and he stared at her while waiting for his voice and mind to come back to life.

Deborah was wearing an evening gown of magenta silk,

which was cut slightly lower than the going fashion. She had picked it out because she knew her father would never permit her to wear it, and even Susanna had been a little apprehensive. But the gown suited her somehow, bringing out her flawless complexion, and the tiara she wore was a dramatic touch that drew the eye at once. Her strange violet-colored eyes looked enormous, and her lips were full and rosy as she smiled at Dent.

"How do you do, Mr. Rocklin?" she asked demurely.

"Uh—fine!" Dent stammered. He was not usually shy, but the beauty of this girl affected him strangely.

"Your family has told me how much you've looked forward to taking me to the ball—"

Deborah never finished, because Thomas Rocklin let out a great whoop of laughter at the comical expression on Dent's face, and then all of the family joined in. Only Ellen didn't laugh, for she had not been in on the joke.

Dent stared around wildly, thinking his family had gone mad—and then it came to him. A rich crimson color came to his face, and then it ebbed, leaving him pale. He had the impulse to turn and leave the room, but somehow he could not do it. He saw that his grandmother was smiling at him, and managed to say reproachfully, "I didn't think you could stoop so low, Grandmother!"

The look on his face sent them all off into fresh gales of laughter. Finally Deborah said, "I won't hold you to such a bargain, Mr. Rocklin. Practical jokes are always a little unkind, aren't they?"

Dent looked very uncomfortable and managed to say, "I think I understand that now for the first time. I'll be very cautious about pulling one in the future." Then he said, "But now that the joke is over, I'm delighted to meet you."

Thomas found his grandson's reformation amusing. "You young devil! Miss Deborah, I suggest that you cast this fellow aside. I'll find you a suitable escort when we get to the ball."

Deborah smiled, and Dent was intrigued at the two small dimples that appeared in her cheeks. "Thank you, Uncle Thomas. That's very gracious of you." She didn't look at Dent as she added, "I suppose all Southern men can't be gallant, can they?"

Dent straightened his back and determined to escort the girl if it snowed ink! "Miss Deborah, I confess that I've behaved very badly. But you'll surely give me an opportunity to redeem myself? I ask it as a favor."

You are a devil! Deborah thought. *And good-looking as sin! Better-looking even than your father, and that's saying a lot. I think you haven't suffered enough yet—* "Why, that's very gallant, sir." She smiled and took the arm Dent offered. "While we're on the way to the ball, let me tell you about some of the latest doctrinal problems that have come up in these trying days. . . ."

Dent knew she was tormenting him, but he didn't care in the least. He had completely forgotten that he was supposed to be contesting with Jackie Terrel for the favors of some girl—whatever her name was!

Deborah Steele was the belle of the ball. She was a Yankee and, some said, an abolitionist—but as one young man noted, "She can be a retarded Buddhist for all I care! With a face and figure like that, I'd just 'bout be ready to join up with the Yankees if that's what she wanted!"

Deborah had a wonderful time, enjoying the antics of the young men who vied over her dances. She tormented Dent fully, but she gave much of her time to Rena. She had helped the girl with a dress, and the two of them sat and giggled as often as Deborah could fight off her admirers.

She forced Clay to ask her to dance, then said, "It would be nice if you would ask Rena to dance, Mr. Rocklin."

Clay smiled. "I don't even know if she can dance."

"Of course she can! All fourteen-year-old girls can dance. It's born in them. And you two would look so nice!"

"I'll do it!" Clay stared at her, then shook his head. "Miss Deborah Steele, you're a caution!"

Deborah hesitated, then said daringly, "I can tell what you're thinking. Did you know I can read minds?"

"What am I thinking?"

"You're wishing that I were Melora Yancy!" Clay stiffened, and she saw that she had overstepped her bounds. At once her hand tightened on his arm, and she whispered, "I'm so sorry! I'm a witless fool!"

Clay blinked, amazed to see tears glisten in her eyes. She really was sorry, he saw. "I want to see Melora have something better," he said finally. "One of the finest men I know wants to marry her. It would be good if she'd take him."

He said no more, but the joy was gone out of his face, and Deborah was sorry she'd mentioned Melora. When the dance was over, she found Dent at her side, demanding a dance. But before it got well under way, he maneuvered her out of the ballroom into a hallway that led to a small sunroom with huge glass windows. It was empty, and he said at once, "I brought you out here to ask you to go to a ball with me." He was wearing a gray suit, and his black hair and fine figure made him quite dashing. "Next week, at my aunt's house. Will you go?"

"I don't think so," Deborah said. "We laughed at you for not wanting to take a homely girl to a ball. I suppose that's common, so I don't really blame you for that. But I still won't go to the ball with you."

Dent was stung. "Am I too Southern for you?"

"Probably. But that's not it either." She looked up at him coolly and said, "I like your father very much. I think he's a fine man."

Dent stared at her. "Well, what's that got to do with going to a ball with me?"

Deborah said clearly, "I don't like the way you treat him, Mr. Rocklin. He made a bad mistake, but you're making a worse one. He abandoned his family, which is a terrible thing to do. But you're standing in judgment on him, refusing to forgive. That, in my opinion, is a worse thing to do."

Dent turned pale and said bitterly, "Easy for you to make judgments, isn't it, Miss Steele? But aren't you judging me, just as you said I'm judging my father?"

"Don't you see the difference? I'm a stranger to you. A few more weeks and you won't see me again. But Clay Rocklin is your father. You'll never have another one. I think you're headed for a terrible fall, Dent," she said. "Anyone who won't forgive is going to have problems."

Dent was furious—and deep down, he was terribly ashamed. He had struggled with his bitterness, but it had been a silent struggle. Now this snip of a girl had laid it bare!

Her very beauty made it worse! He stood there, fists clenched, then suddenly reached out and pulled her close. Her eyes opened wide with shock, and then he was kissing her. It was an angry kiss on his part, something to hurt her. If she had been a man, he would have struck her with his fist. But since that was out of the question. . .

And yet, even as his lips bruised hers, he felt something sweet in her. Despite all her puffed-up knowledge and wrong ideas, he felt himself change, loosening his tight grip but keeping his lips on hers. Finally he thought he felt her respond, and when he pulled back, he said in an unsteady voice, "Deborah, you're an awful person in lots of ways, but you've got something that gets to a man!"

Deborah Steele had been kissed before—but never had she felt such a powerful emotion. She stared at Denton, wanting to hurt him, and finally said, "Well, we're kissing cousins, it seems! And I can tell you've had a great deal of practice."

"Deborah—!"

"Never mind. Let's go back to the ballroom."

Both of them were shaken by the experience, and both were angry. Clay saw them return and said to his mother, "I think our Dent got his feathers singed!"

The ball went on.

Far away in Charleston, Gideon Rocklin was in a boat with a full load of soldiers. The water was cold, and the men were doused by the high waves that threatened to swamp the boats.

By dawn the next morning, Gideon said wearily, "All the men are disembarked, Major."

Anderson looked at him, his own face gray with fatigue.

"Very well, sir. Now we'll wait for them to come!"

CHAPTER 21

"I CAN BE ALONE!"

The year of 1861 did not come in gently for America. Ferment in the North and in the South stirred, and angry men on both sides pushed the two sections closer to the brink of war. President Buchanan, never a strong leader and now a lame duck, was so out of touch with things that it was Senator Jefferson Davis who had come to his office and broken the news to him that Major Anderson had spiked his guns at Fort Moultrie and moved his garrison to Fort Sumter. The senator had added, "And now, Mr. President, you are surrounded with blood and dishonor on all sides."

But Buchanan seemed to be completely paralyzed and did nothing but wait for Lincoln to assume the burden. On January 5, General Scott sent the *Star of the West*, a merchant vessel, with two hundred troops to reinforce Major Anderson at Sumter. But the ship was driven off by cannon fire aimed by a South Carolina battery and had to make her way back home with the troops. All that had been accomplished was to pour oil on the fire. Robert Barnwell Rhett, the fire-eating editor of the *Charleston Mercury*, wrote that "powder has been burnt over the degrees of our state, and the firing on the *Star of the West* is the opening ball of the Revolution. South Carolina is honored to be the first thus to resist the Yankee tyranny. She has not hesitated to strike the first blow, full in the face of her insulter."

Major Anderson had not even been informed that reinforcements were coming, and when he had joined his staff at the sound of cannon fire, none of them knew what was happening. When they learned that their reinforcements were not coming, Anderson said bleakly, "Major Rocklin, our enemies may not have to take our position by attack. If supplies don't arrive soon, we'll be starved out!"

"They'll come, Major," Gid said confidently.

But they did not come, and the weeks passed with an agonizing slowness for the little company on the island fortress. The Southern states began to coalesce, with Mississippi voting eighty-four to fifteen in favor of secession, and ten days later, on January 10, Florida joined Mississippi and South Carolina. A day later Alabama left the union. Finally in February, the secessionist delegates met in Montgomery, Alabama, to set up their Southern nation. Jefferson Davis was elected as the first president, and when the word of his election came to him, his face paled. He said then and repeated later that he had not wanted the office. Rather he had hoped for command of the Confederacy's army.

So it went, ponderously at first, like a juggernaut. From time to time, Melanie would ride out to Sumter and spend time with Gideon. She gave him reports on the boys. She told him of Deborah's visit at Gracefield, which had been extended.

"It can't go on like this, Mellie," Gid told her one cold February morning as she waited for the boat to take her back to her rooming house in Charleston. "It's like a powder house, and sooner or later one spark is going to set the whole thing off!"

Back at Gracefield, Clay was running into problems, too. He had made many friends since coming back to his home, but now he was losing them fast. He tried to be moderate, but after one of his oldest friends left him angrily, Clay said to Jeremiah Irons, "It's like the last judgment, Jeremiah. There are only sheep and goats—nothing in between. A man's either got to be all-out for this war and slavery, or he's a Yankee abolitionist."

Irons studied Clay carefully. They were riding toward the Yancy place, meeting Buford for a hunting trip. For both of them it was an escape from the pressures of life, for the minister was in little better shape than Clay. He had tried to speak of patience, of trying to work things out with the North, and had been branded a traitor by some of his most prominent board members.

"What will you do, Clay?" he asked suddenly. "If war comes, you'll have to decide. As you say, there's no such thing as neutrality in this thing."

"I have no idea, Jerry. What will you do?"

Irons shrugged, and the two men rode on silently, both deep in thought. "I've got fine friends in the North, Clay," Irons said finally. "Hate to think about fighting them."

"And there are Rocklins who'll be wearing Union uniforms. How can I shoot at my own family?"

It was a discussion that was going on all over the country, and no one ever reached an answer. In the end, the two men veered away from the subject. "That young woman, Deborah, has certainly plowed up a snake!"

"You mean with Dent? She sure has. I expect those two will

have to be separated before they shoot each other! They get into those awful arguments about slavery that serve no purpose. I like the girl, but she ought to go home."

Irons thought about it, then remarked, "Melora says she's attracted to Dent."

Clay stared at him, then laughed. "Well, she takes a funny way of showing it! Dent's been pretty cool toward me since I came back, but I feel sorry for the boy. He's so besotted with that girl he can't see straight, but he's got as much chance of getting her as—as—"

"As I have of getting Melora," Irons finished gloomily.

Clay glanced at his friend, not sure what to make of that remark. "Don't give up, Jerry," he said quietly. "Melora's worth waiting for."

"Clay, I don't think she'll ever marry."

They got to the Yancy cabin and found Buford ready to go. To their surprise they found Melora dressed in her old overalls, obviously ready to join the hunt. "I'm not getting left behind this time," she declared.

"Who's going to watch the kids?" Clay asked.

"Lonnie and Bobby, that's who!" Buford declared grimly. "They don't deserve to go with growed-up men!" He refused to say what the boys had done to disgrace themselves, but it must have been serious. Buford shook his head, saying, "Do them good to learn to act like grown people instead of babies!"

They all got in the wagon that carried the tents and the supplies, and they drove for hours. The deep woods began to close about them late that afternoon, but they pressed on until dusk. Pulling the team up, Buford said, "You two fellers get the tents up. I'll do the important things—like catching some bullhead catfish outta that crick."

Clay and Jeremiah began to set up the tents but made such a mess out of it that they began to argue, each convinced that the other was incompetent. Melora came over from where she was building a fire to cook the hypothetical fish that her father was to bring and began to laugh at them. "Two grown men, and you can't put up a tent!"

"Well, if the preacher would just do what I tell him to do—!" Clay sputtered.

"I was putting up tents when you were in diapers!" Jeremiah snapped back, which seemed unlikely since the two men were the same age.

Finally the tents were up. Buford returned with a fine string of catfish, which he cleaned, and in good time they were sitting around the fire eating fresh fish and hush puppies, washing it all down with strong black coffee.

"I think a few of those big black bugs hit the grease the fish were in," Melora remarked. "It was too dark to see."

"Anybody who objects to a few black bugs in his fish don't deserve no consideration," her father pronounced. Then he proceeded to ask Jeremiah, "What's the meaning of the beast that came up out of the sea in the thirteenth chapter of Revelation, Reverend? The one with the seven heads and the ten horns?"

"Buford, don't you start on me with your endless questions about prophecy!" Jeremiah protested. "Let's just hunt and fish and rest."

Buford was offended. "Well, it's important, ain't it? Wouldn't be in the Bible if it wasn't!"

"Yes, yes, it's important, Buford," Jeremiah said wearily, "but I just don't know what the blamed beast means!"

Clay and Melora looked across the fire at each other, smiling at the pair. They had often laughed at the dogged manner in which Buford asked question after question on the more obscure sections of the Bible, while Jeremiah was interested in more practical things—such as how to get his members to stop gossiping!

The four of them sat around the fire for a long time, listening to the occasional cry of a night bird and, more than once, the plaintive wail of a coyote. Melora kept the coffeepot going, saying little, listening as the men talked. Mostly they didn't speak of the war or of politics. Instead they discussed farming, horses, and dogs—simple things that men enjoy. Jeremiah told stories of his boyhood in Arkansas, of the hard life in the back reaches of the Ozark Mountains where shoes were a luxury.

Finally they went to bed, Melora in the small tent and the three men in the large one. Wrapped in blankets up to her eyes, Melora lay there, listening to the night sounds for a long time. Then she dropped off to sleep. She awoke to the smell of bacon and fresh coffee. When she emerged from her tent, she found her father cooking eggs in the bacon grease. "The preacher and Clay took off 'fore dawn," he remarked. "Thought they might get a shot at a buck down where we seen them big tracks. Here, pitch into this bacon, daughter."

Melora took the plate, ate bacon and eggs, then sat back to drink coffee. The air was cold, but she liked it that way. "Funny the way you decided to come along on this trip," Buford said. "But I'm glad you did." He was watching her as she drank the coffee, and thoughtfully he remarked, "You ort to get married. I feel bad that you've spent your whole life taking care of the kids." He tossed the stick he was whittling onto the ground, his face as sober as she had ever seen it. He was not a man of deep thought, Melora realized, but something was troubling him. He sought for what was inside him, then said simply, "I should have got married again when your mother died. I could have done it."

"Why didn't you, Pa? Most men would have."

He was embarrassed at what was in his heart, and he struggled with it. Finally he said, "I never seen a woman I liked as much as I did your ma. She was. . .special, you know?"

Melora realized that poets had been writing about love that never died for thousands of years. But it was a rare thing, she understood. Now, here in the deep woods, she found it—not in a prince, but in Buford Yancy, with his stubble of a beard, rough hands, and rougher speech. She said quietly, "That's real sweet, Pa."

Yancy was embarrassed and hurried to say, "Well, I don't know about that, but I do know I've robbed you of your youth, daughter." A question came to his lips, but after glancing at her, he seemed awkward and ill at ease. Finally he voiced it. "The preacher wants to marry you right bad."

It was, she realized, his way of asking her to share her feelings with him. But it was not easy—for she herself was confused about the thing.

"I wish he would find somebody else," she finally said. Now it was her turn to search for words. Like her father, she had difficulty putting into words the deep feelings that ran through her. Finally she said, "I like him so much, it'd be easy to just give up and marry him. The kids are old enough now so they aren't much trouble. I could help him with his two, and I guess I could learn to be a preacher's wife—but not a good one."

"Why not? You're a good Christian girl."

"Not the same thing, Pa," she said slowly. "I've been free all my life. Oh, I've had to do my work and watch the children, but a preacher's wife doesn't have much freedom." She smiled at him, adding, "For example, I don't think I ever heard of a minister's wife going hunting with a bunch of men!"

He said, "You could do it if you set your mind. I'd feel better about you, daughter."

She got up and went to him and, bending over, kissed his cheek. "Don't worry about me, Pa." She left him at the fire, and there was no more discussion with him on that subject. But she knew that he was worried—and hated to cause him grief.

The weather warmed up, and for two days the four of them had a fine time. Melora didn't want to shoot anything, but she enjoyed walking through the woods. She had brought her notebook and filled it with her "scribbling" during that time.

On the third day Jeremiah took it into his head that he had to have a wild turkey. They had bagged everything else: coon, possum, a fat deer, even three ducks from a pond. "I've got a special feeling for wild turkey," Irons announced on the morning of the last day.

"Wild turkey's about the slyest thing in the woods, Preacher." Buford said, shaking his head. "Offhand, I don't think I see but one feller in this camp who can git one."

Both Jeremiah and Clay at once began to deride him, and after breakfast they all set off for a place that was stiff with wild toms, according to Buford. They made a bet that the one who got the biggest turkey got to tell the other two what to do. "I got some fencing that needs to be put up," Buford said with a grin. "I can see now that you two boys are just the pair to do it."

They left right away, riding the two mules that had pulled the wagon, Clay and Buford sharing one of the animals. Melora began to pack some of the gear, but about ten o'clock she took a line and went fishing in the stream. The fish were uneducated, and she caught enough for supper in thirty minutes. She went back to the camp, and ten minutes after she arrived, she was surprised to see Clay come riding in on one of the mules.

"What did you forget?"

"I forgot to watch where I was walking," Clay said. He slid off the mule and hopped painfully toward the fire, his face drawn with pain.

"What's wrong with your foot?" Melora asked.

"Stepped in a hole and twisted my ankle," he said in disgust. "We stopped down by the river and poked around looking for bear sign. I stepped into a hole and darn near broke my leg! Your dad and Jeremiah wanted to turn back, but I wouldn't let them. No reason why my clumsiness should keep them from having a good time."

"Let's get that boot off," Melora said. "I'll heat some water."

The ankle was not badly twisted, but it was painful. As Clay looked at it stretched out before him, he remarked, "I always forget if you put cold compresses or hot cloths on a sprained leg."

"Hot," Melora announced. She had heated the water and began to put the hot cloths on the injured leg. "Be still!" she said. "You behave worse than Toby!"

"Well, those things are too hot," he complained. He watched as she held the compress in place, then said, "You've had to treat just about every sort of sickness and accident, haven't you, Melora?"

"Oh yes. Most doctoring is just common sense." She knelt at his feet, holding the compress and speaking of some of the aches and pains the children had had. He admired the firm set of her jaw and saw that she had a faint line of freckles across her nose that he'd never noticed. She was a slim woman, but there was a pleasing roundness to her. Despite the rough clothing, there was a grace about her, and Clay said suddenly, "Been a long time since you fed me soup and nursed me. You're all grown up now, but I still remember that little girl. All eyes and as somber as a tree full of owls. I'd never been around children then, and I thought you were normal."

She laughed then, her green eyes glinting in the sun. "Why, I *was* normal!"

"No, you were never normal," he said. "You've always been different, Melora." She looked up at him quickly and saw that his eyes were half closed. "All those years I was gone, I dreamed a lot about home, but mostly about you. I guess I can remember every moment of those times. I went over them again and again. It was like—like having an album filled with pictures, Melora, those times with you. And I'd go over and over them, until I guess they became clearer to me than anything else in the world."

Melora stood up and held the compress in her hands. Her eyes fell, and she whispered, "I did the same."

"You did?" Clay said quickly. "I never knew that!"

"I was always a romantic thing, I guess. Remember how I always wanted books about knights and castles? Well, life was pretty drab, I suppose, so I remembered your visits and how we read *Pilgrim's Progress* and *Gulliver's Travels* together."

She came to stand beside him, saying, "You've got to keep off that foot. Come on. I'll help you to your tent."

Clay struggled to his feet, saying, "If you'll get me a stick—"

"I will, but first you need to lie down and keep the weight off that foot. Lean on me now."

Clay put his right arm around her shoulders, and she bore most of his weight as they moved to the tent. When they went inside, he started to let himself down, but his leg gave way, and the suddenness of it made him grab at her for support. He pulled her down as he fell and hit the ground with a grunt, still holding on to her.

Melora was lying across his chest, and when she lifted her head, she started to laugh. "You're clumsy—," she said, then broke off. His face was only inches away from hers, and she suddenly read the longing in his eyes. She caught her breath but seemed unable to move. The pressure of her soft body on his was both a torment and a delight to Clay.

It was as though time had stopped for both of them. Clay was thinking, *No, this is wrong!* but at the same time, he was realizing that he had wanted to reach out and touch this woman for years. It came as a shock to him, for there was a picture in his mind of a child who fed him soup, or a girl of twelve who loved books. Now he knew that he could never think of her in quite the same way again.

And Melora was thinking, *At last he knows I'm a woman! He's always ignored the fact that I grew up. But I can see in his eyes that he's thinking of me as a man thinks of a woman.*

Then without thinking she lowered her head and put her soft lips on his. It was as natural to her as breathing, for she meant only to show how she cared for him, was grateful to him. That was the beginning, but it was not the end, for slowly she became aware that this was not the caress of a child. Something powerful and strong began to form within her, and she could feel his recognition of the same force. His arms tightened, and the pressure of his lips grew more demanding.

How long that kiss lasted, she never knew—nor did he. Nor did they ever know which of them first realized the potent danger of what was happening. But however it was, Melora reluctantly moved her head, and then she stood to her feet. But she did not leave. Something kept her there, and then Clay said, "That was very wrong of me, Melora."

"Wrong of me, too, Clay," she said quietly.

He struggled to a sitting position. "Come down here. I can't talk with you up there." He waited until she was kneeling and studied her face. With one hand he reached out and brushed her hair from her forehead. "Don't be upset by this, Melora. It's not your fault."

Melora said slowly, "I think you'd better know. I'm in love with you, Clay. I have been for years."

"Melora!" He cried out as if she had struck him. "You mustn't say such a thing. It's not true!"

She looked at him, her eyes enormous in the gloom of the tent. "You may not love me. But I'll always love you."

He stared at her helplessly, then suddenly groaned and pulled her to his chest. "God help me! I love you, too, Melora!" He held her for only a moment, then released her. She watched him calmly, and he said, "It's a sad thing, Melora, for both of us. In the first place, I'm too old for you. And besides that, I'm already married."

Melora said, "Yes, I know that. Not that you are too old. But that you have a wife. She's no wife to you; I know that, too. I know how lonely you get. I get lonely, too." She bit her lip, adding, "Clay, don't let my love be a burden to you. It's the finest thing in my life—the most real thing. I can never have you; I know that. I've always known that. But it helps to know. . .that you care for me."

She got up and turned to go, but then his voice caught her. "Melora, marry Jeremiah! Be a wife to him! He loves you."

Melora shook her head. "No. I'll never marry Jeremiah—or anyone else."

"You can't be alone!"

"Yes, I can be alone. I'm strong enough for that, Clay. I have God, and now I know that you love me. That's all I need."

She left the tent then and went into the woods. For an hour she walked under the thick foliage. Then she came back and found him sitting in front of the fire, his leg stretched out. When she spoke, her voice was without strain. "Let's be friends. As we've always been. We can have that, can't we? If we can't have anything else, let's have that."

"Wouldn't we have to be on guard? Wouldn't it feel odd?"

"No. Let's talk about books, and you listen to me read out of my notebook. Come and see Pa, and sometimes we'll meet at the store. We'll smile and talk, and then you'll leave. Let's have that much, Mister Clay!"

He smiled at her use of the name she'd used when she was a child. Somehow the strain was gone, and he said, "You are my best friend, Melora. And I'm yours."

She took a deep breath, and then a smile touched her wide lips. "I'm glad I came on this trip." She said no more, but he knew as she rose and went about building up the fire that neither of them would refer to what had happened in the tent.

And he knew, just as certainly, that neither of them would ever forget it.

CHAPTER 22

BEFORE THE STORM

As the air sometimes grows utterly still before the power of a hurricane is unleashed, so a time of peace came to Gracefield. Susanna commented on it as she and Deborah were walking across to the slave quarters. The two had become quite close, and the younger woman had learned to trust the heart of the older, even though she did not agree with her ideas on slavery.

Susanna said as they passed Box, who at the age of sixty-nine was still able to do some work at the forge, "I feel so strange, Deborah. The whole country is falling apart, with all the politicians screaming of war. And yet everything seems so peaceful." As they came to the row of cabins that housed the slaves, she added, "I'm afraid, for the first time. There's something ominous about this time."

Deborah nodded, saying, "I am, too. I got a letter from my father yesterday. He wants me to come home."

"I'll miss you, Deborah." Susanna turned a smile on the girl, adding, "But if you don't go home, you're going to drive Dent crazy. I've never seen anyone so lovesick. It's like something out of a bad romance."

Deborah didn't return the smile. "Aunt Susanna, I...I haven't told anyone, but..."

She paused, but the older woman nodded at once, her face gentle and filled with a sudden concern. "I know. You feel something for him, don't you, Deborah?"

"It's insane, of course," Deborah said quickly, her face slightly tinged with a flush that made her look very young. "We don't agree on a single thing, I suppose. Every time we get together, it winds up in a blazing row." She fell silent and then, after a moment, said with a burst of honesty, "But you're right, Aunt Susanna, I do feel something for Dent! It's not that he's fine-looking. I don't care about that. He's bursting with all this Southern pride. . . . 'Any Southerner can handle six Yankees!' But I have this feeling that beneath all that bluster, there's something very real about Dent."

"You see his father in him," Susanna suggested. "You're very fond of Clay. Anyone can see that. And Clay's got the same stuff." Her eyes grew nostalgic, and she said, "When Clay was nineteen, he was exactly as Dent is now. Unfortunately, Dent's got the same weaknesses that Clay had then—he's too impulsive, too self-centered."

"But Clay got over all that."

"Yes, but God only knows what hell he had to go through to do so. And he's still paying for some of it."

"He and Ellen, do you think they'll ever put their marriage together?"

"I doubt it. They were never suited from the beginning, and she's grown...more careless over the years."

Deborah hesitated, then said, "I think he's fond of Melora Yancy."

Susanna was startled by the young woman's perception. She

had long known that Clay was half in love with the woman, but she had said nothing to anyone. "It can never come to anything, Deborah. I know you won't say anything to anyone."

"No, of course not. I just feel bad for them."

Susanna gave her a sudden hug. "You're a kind girl, Deborah. I wish Dent were more mature."

"Maybe I could marry him and raise him right! Housebreak him and all."

"Never try that!" Susanna said with a wry smile. "If a man doesn't change before a woman marries him, she'll not be able to do anything with him afterward. These Rocklin men are stubborn anyway. They have to beat their heads against a stone wall to get any sense knocked into them. Now come along, and we'll get all the chores done, then go into Richmond for a wild shopping spree!"

Jake Slocum was a man of little sensitivity. He did, however, have pride in one thing: his ability to handle women. From his youth, he had known how to get women to surrender to his attentions. Certain women, that is—and it galled him that he was being denied by Ellen Rocklin.

He had pursued her for some time before she had agreed to meet him, and of all the women he had known, she was the one he prized most. For one thing, she was of a higher class than most of his women. Slocum was a small-time planter, with only eight slaves on his relatively small plantation. He blustered and shoved his way into the small group of prosperous planters who owned the really huge plantations and hundreds of slaves. But he knew they only tolerated him. He had pursued several of the wives and daughters of these men, finding more pleasure in the fact that he was irritating the men than from his flirtations with their women.

Though Slocum was not a handsome man, he was powerful and bold, and some women were drawn to this. He was a large man, six feet two, and weighed 220 pounds. Always dressed in the finest clothing, which he bought in New Orleans, he was an impressive man physically. He had a shock of heavy, slightly wavy blond hair and a pair of aggressive blue eyes. His face was broad and his mouth wide in a sensual way. His reputation as a womanizer was equaled by his reputation as a fighting man. He steered clear of pistol duels, preferring to be known as a bruising fistfighter. It was what he liked best, and he had destroyed many men with his massive fists.

But Slocum was unhappy now, for his conquest of Ellen Rocklin had backfired. He had won her after a long pursuit, longer than he normally gave to most of his conquests, but it had been worth it to him. Slocum had little taste for finer qualities in women, and Ellen proved to be more troublesome than he had expected. She had been adamant about their meetings, controlling them so they never became publicly known. This had displeased Slocum, who wanted the world to know of his victory in charming the wife of a prominent planter, but she had refused to be seen with him in public.

And now, without warning, she had dropped him, which was a severe blow to Slocum's pride. He had persuaded her to meet him in Richmond, and she had finally agreed. He had taken a room at a third-rate hotel, where the clerk could not have cared less who made their way up the rickety staircase to the seedy rooms on the second floor. He had given scarcely a glance at Slocum and Ellen as they had gone upstairs, but had leaned back and dozed off.

When the door closed, Slocum got a rude shock, for when he came over to put his arms around Ellen as she stood there, she said, "Jake, I'm not coming to you like this anymore."

He blinked; then anger rose in him. He turned her around, kissed her hard, then said, "Sure you are! You're as crazy about me as I am about you."

But she had simply waited until he released her, then turned and said in a sharp tone, "It's too risky. And I'm sick of these awful rooms."

"We could go to my place," he said. "It's a fine house, and nobody would know."

"Yes, they would," she said calmly. "You've got slaves and a housekeeper. Word would be out in Richmond the next day."

"What difference does it make? Who cares what the hypocrites say?"

"I care, Jake." Ellen turned away from him, thinking quietly for a moment, then added, "You men can do what you please and still be accepted. It's a matter of pride, how many women you have. But it's different with a woman. Clay and I are nothing to each other, but as his wife I'm accepted in the best homes in the county."

"People know you haven't been a saint," Slocum growled.

"They may think it, Jake, but they don't know it. Because I've been—discreet. That's why we can't meet anymore. At least for a while. You talk too much, and much as I like you, I'm not about to give up everything for you. Now if you want to marry me—," she said, turning to look at him, but his expression gave him away, and she laughed harshly, adding, "No, you want your fun, but you want me to pay for it. Well, you'll just have to wait until it's safer."

"I don't have to wait for a woman!"

"For this one you do." Her face was set, and she adjusted her coat, a beautiful silver fox. "It's not going to be easy for me. Clay's not much, but at least he's safe. He doesn't need me, but he doesn't want any other woman either."

Slocum gave her a rough grin. "Don't be too sure about that, Ellen."

She had started to turn but stopped to stare at him. "What's that supposed to mean?"

"You don't know about your husband and Melora Yancy?" Slocum saw the sudden shock on Ellen's face and knew he had found a way to bring her to heel. "I thought you knew," he said casually. "He's been chasing around after her for a long time."

"That's ridiculous! She's poor white trash!"

"I guess maybe she is, but she's mighty gorgeous trash."

"Clay's got better sense," Ellen argued. "He's no fool to chase around after a girl like that. Why, he's old enough to be her father."

"And you think men never make fools of themselves over a younger woman?" Slocum retorted. "Happens all the time," he said, then threw in carelessly, "especially when a man's been married a long time. His wife can't satisfy him, so he goes out and gets him a young woman. You've seen it happen enough, Ellen. Don't see why you should be surprised."

A smoldering rage began to rise in Ellen. She had been filled with hatred for Clay since the night she had gone to his cabin. His rejection had cut her to the bone, but it had never once occurred to her that she was rejected because he had another woman. Now, standing there motionlessly, she began to remember that Clay did make a great many visits to the Yancy place. She had thought it was to hunt with Buford Yancy, but now as she called up a vision of the daughter, she was instantly convinced that Slocum was telling the truth. It was impossible for her to believe that men and women could simply enjoy each other's company, for she herself never had such simple motives. As she thought of Melora's youth and beauty, she wanted to kill her.

"You're wrong," she said, trying to convince herself.

"Why, honey, he went out in the woods with her for three days! You think they was hunting all that time?" Buford had shot a record turkey and in casual conversation had mentioned to a group of which Slocum was a part that his daughter had been on the hunt. He had said also that Rev. Irons had been along, but Slocum altered the story to rouse Ellen's wrath, which it did, of course.

"He can't make a fool out of me!" Ellen grated. She stared at Jake, and he could almost see the workings of her mind. And she did exactly what he had known she would. "Jake, you've got to do something! He doesn't pay any attention to me, but I want him hurt!"

Slocum knew he had his way. He smiled and came toward her. "I'll take care of it, honey."

"Don't fight a duel with him," Ellen warned. "He'd shoot you dead, Jake."

"There's better ways," he murmured. Then, slipping her coat off, he grinned, saying, "You're not in that big a hurry, honey...."

The shopping trip to Richmond was a bittersweet experience for Deborah, with far more of the bitter than the sweet. She and Susanna were joined by Dent, who invited himself along.

"I've got a few things to buy," he said blandly, and it secretly pleased both women, for he was at his best. He kept them entertained all the way to the city, telling tall tales of his escapades at Virginia Military Institute, some of them concerning one of his instructors, Thomas Jackson. "He knows Uncle Gideon well," Dent said. "They were in Mexico together."

They shopped in the morning and had lunch at a fine restaurant; then Susanna left the young people and went to visit a sick friend. "Don't get into one of your terrible arguments," she warned.

"No chance of that," Dent agreed cheerfully. "A man would be a fool to argue with anyone as beautiful as this woman!"

"You're out to charm me, aren't you?" Deborah asked. She was wearing an attractive dress of gray and pearl stripe, but pulled on a royal blue woolen coat as they got up to leave the restaurant.

"Certainly!" he agreed. "I've got fine manners you've never even seen. Come along now—we've got a lot to see and do."

All afternoon they wandered the streets of the city, and Deborah had a wonderful time. Dent knew the city like the back of his hand and introduced her to so many people that she lost track.

It would have been well if they had not made their last visit, and later both of them wished they had not.

They were walking down Walnut Street when a crowd moving into a large building of red brick caught Deborah's eye. "What's that, Dent?"

"Oh, nothing much," he said and spoke so diffidently that she knew it was something he didn't want her to see. She looked at the front of the building as they walked by and saw a poster proclaiming that a firm named Ellis & Livingstone was conducting a sale of Negroes.

There it was. The evil she had heard about all her life; that her father had devoted his life to destroying; that her teacher Charles G. Finney had spoken against with great passion.

"I want to go inside," she said impulsively.

Dent tried to dissuade her. "It's mostly men, Deborah. You'd be very uncomfortable."

"Dent, I'm going inside." Deborah's lips were tight, and her head was held high in a stubborn gesture. "You can come with me or not."

Dent followed her reluctantly into a large room where the sales took place. He had been there many times, but now he was apprehensive. He was also on the defensive, for he knew her feelings and was aware that the slave market would only harden her views.

The room into which Deborah stepped was about fifty feet square, and it was bare of all furniture except for a few scattered chairs and benches. The whitewashed walls, which were about twelve feet high, picked up the light from the mullioned windows. A pair of steep staircases made of rough oak led to the floor overhead, and a single door at the back led, apparently, to some sort of holding room where the slaves were kept until they were brought out.

Two classes of people were in the room, and Deborah at once recognized that they might have been beings from two separate worlds! There were many men in the room who were dressed in dark suits and wore broad-brimmed hats. They were walking around smoking cigars, talking to one another and examining some of the second group—slaves who were either standing or sitting on benches.

As Deborah moved around the room, she saw many of the planters give her a startled look; more than one of them made remarks of some sort to the other men but, seeing Dent standing behind her, kept their remarks muffled. Dent himself was unhappy and kept his chin high, ready to resent any sort of insult.

At the front of the room was a small raised platform, occupied by the auctioneer, who was watching a woman mount the three high steps. She was wearing a red dress with a white apron over it. When she got to the top of the platform, the auctioneer began the bidding.

"Here now, look at this prime specimen, gentlemen! Only nineteen years old and never had a sick day! She's healthy and ready to breed, so what am I offered?"

The bidding started at fifteen hundred dollars but rose rapidly. The young woman was a mulatto and very pretty. She dropped her head as the bidding went on, and once a man stepped up to the platform and took her jaw, forcing her to open her mouth while he examined her teeth. He ran his hand over her body, then stepped down and raised the bid.

The woman was sold for forty-two hundred dollars. And Deborah heard a man close to her say, "That's Bartlett from New Orleans. He buys the pretty ones up for the bawdy houses there."

Slightly sick to her stomach, Deborah stood there watching. She saw a child sold to one buyer. The mother, who was sold to another, fought to keep her little girl but was cuffed into submission, and the little girl was picked up bodily by a tough-looking man and carried out of the building screaming.

"Take me out of here, Denton!" Deborah whispered. She swayed, and he took her arm quickly, holding her firmly as they left the auction house. When they were outside, she said, "I want to go home."

Dent said quickly, "It wasn't something for you to see,

Deborah. I shouldn't have let you go in there."

"Would it not go on if I didn't see it?" Deborah asked. They walked along the street, not speaking. She was almost beyond thought, so revolted was she by the terrible sight she had just witnessed. As for Dent, he was well aware that what had just occurred could be death to their relationship.

They found Susanna waiting for them, and she took one look at Deborah's stricken face, then asked, "What is it, child?"

"I—went to the slave auction."

Susanna glanced at Dent, who was stiff-lipped, and said, "We'll go home now, Dent."

"You two go on. I'll come later."

He accompanied them to the carriage, handed them in, and nodded as Susanna spoke to the horses and they left him at a fast clip. The day had turned sour for Dent, all the more so since—before the incident at the auction—he had seen a warmth and acceptance in Deborah that he had sought ever since meeting her.

Frustrated and angry, he turned on his heel and made his way to the Water Hole, a favorite haunt of the young bucks of Richmond. He found several of his cronies there and almost at once began to drink. He was not much of a drinker as a rule, but the whole group was excited, two of them being in the militia and expecting to be off to war soon. They sat around black-guarding the North until a poker game claimed their attention. Dent was a good card player, and he sat there for several hours, not realizing how much he was drinking. Finally he noticed that he was losing hands and laughed, "You boys are pretty sharp. You know the only way to beat me is to get me drunk!" They protested, but he took his winnings, stuck them in his pocket, and left the saloon with a promise to come back and let them have a chance to win some of it back the next day.

He made his way down the street, walking carefully, for he was at that stage of drunkenness when the earth is somewhat unsteady and the curbs do not remain stable. Suddenly he remembered that he had no way to get back home, since Susanna had taken the buggy. *Have to stay in town tonight*, he thought and made his way to the Harley House. The room clerk looked up, a smallish young fellow named Dixon Morgan.

"Need a room for the night, Dix," Dent said. "Got stranded with no way to get home."

"Your father's in the bar, Dent," Morgan said. "He came in for supper with Taylor Dewitt and some others. Expect he'll be heading out pretty soon."

Dent stood there irresolutely. He didn't want any company—especially his father's—but he didn't want to spend the night in a hotel room either. "Thanks, Dix," he finally said. "You just missed a customer."

He entered the bar, a large room with what was reported to be the longest and finest bar in the South along one wall and tables in the center. White-jacketed bartenders and waiters moved about serving the customers, and Dent spotted his father at a table with several of his friends. He walked over, and when his father looked up with surprise at seeing him, he asked, "Got room for me when you go home?"

"Sure, Dent," Clay said. "I brought the small wagon in. Be ready to go pretty soon."

"Take a seat, Dent," Taylor Dewitt said. He had noticed that Dent was speaking in that careful way that a man will use when he's been drinking and is aware that his speech is slurred. "Saw you squiring that Yankee girl around this afternoon." A grin scored his thin lips, and he winked at the others. "First thing you know, she'll have you converted. I can just see you now going around the North giving lectures on the horrors of slavery!"

A laugh ran around the table, and several of the men offered ribald suggestions to the younger Rocklin. Dent managed a sour grin but said only, "Seems like you fellows have all the answers. Maybe you ought to hunt Jefferson Davis up and tell him how to get the Yankees out of our hair. Or maybe Abe Lincoln."

There was a congenial air around the table, and Dent had taken no offense. But suddenly a voice said loudly, "You Rocklins don't have much luck with your women, do you?"

Dent turned to find Jake Slocum grinning at him, and it was not a pleasant grin. At first he thought he had heard the man wrong, for his hearing was fuzzy. His senses were drugged with alcohol, and sounds came to him hollowly, as if he were in a steel drum. But as he focused on Slocum's broad face, he saw that the man was deliberately provoking him.

"Keep your mouth shut, Jake," he said angrily. The frustrations that had been boiling in him all evening suddenly rose like a tide, and he glared at the huge man with anger in his face.

He did not know that Slocum had been pushing against Clay for some time. Never offering a direct insult, but so insolent with his words and expression that Taylor had said, "Jake, you're offensive. Either straighten up or go find some other crowd." He had gotten a rough glance from Slocum, who had said only, "You're not president of anything, Dewitt."

Taylor had gone to the bathroom with Bushrod Aimes and taken occasion to say, "What's Jake up to? He's got some kind of wild hair."

"Dunno. But if he says much more to Clay, it'll mean a shooting."

Slocum had prodded Clay Rocklin steadily, determined to start trouble. But he was smart enough not to let it become a shooting affair. He was aware of Clay's skill with a pistol and had no intention of dying for any woman. He wanted to use his fists on the man but had had no success in stirring Rocklin. Clay Rocklin was a steady man and was hard to provoke. But Slocum was determined that the provocation would come, so that when he smashed Rocklin beyond recognition, no one could accuse him of being the instigator. Now, however, he saw in young Dent Rocklin a new opportunity.

"What's the matter, Dent?" Slocum asked. "You can't get that Yankee girl's attention? I did a little better than that with your ma! Maybe I better give you a few lessons—"

Dent came out of his chair and lunged at Slocum, who was waiting for just such a move. He brushed off the wild blow aimed at his face and drove his huge fist into Dent. The wicked blow caught the boy on the forehead and dropped him to the floor senseless.

At once Clay came to his feet, his face contorted with rage. He recognized what Slocum was doing and knew that he was falling into a trap, but for one instant the volatile temper he'd always had flared up. But as he moved toward Slocum, Bushrod caught him, saying, "Watch it, Clay! You know how Jake fights! He'll gouge your eyes out! You can't fight him with fists!"

"That's right, Clay," Taylor said instantly. "Let it be pistols!"

Fear came into Slocum, but out of the fear he managed to say the one right thing, the thing that would inflame Clay Rocklin.

"He can't even take care of his own wife! He's too busy chasing around after that Yancy girl!"

A coldness came to Clay then, and he shook off Bushrod

and came to stand before Slocum. Something told him he could not shoot the man, and he knew that he could never beat him in a roughhouse fight. But he was ice-cold now, and with a sudden motion, he picked up a bottle of whiskey, almost full, and before Slocum could move, he brought it down over the man's head, lifting himself on his toes to put more force into the blow.

Slocum was driven to the floor as the bottle struck his head. It broke as it struck, cutting a jagged slash across his skull. A muffled cry went up from his thick throat, and then there was a sudden silence in the saloon as every eye turned to watch.

The blow would have knocked a lesser man out, but Slocum had a thick skull, and he came to his feet, his eyes glazed and a bright river of crimson blood flowing down his cheek. He was confused, but still a formidable figure. His huge muscles bulged against his suit, and his neck was so thick that his head seemed to be perched on his broad shoulders. Some of the men watching looked at the frightening bulk and—remembering how he had nearly killed men in this sort of fight—shook their heads. "Clay ain't got no show!" one of them said quietly. "Slocum will get him down and kick his head off!"

Clay Rocklin was the same height as Slocum, but lean rather than heavily muscled. He looked almost fragile against the hulking man. But there was a quickness about his movement, and he picked up a chair, raised it in the air, and brought it down over Slocum's head. It was a frightful blow, smashing the chair and knocking Slocum to the floor. He moved slowly, thrashing his arms like a man underwater as he shoved at the broken fragments of the chair, but then he slowly came to his feet.

"That's all right, Clay!" he said thickly. "That's all right! I'm going to get you now!"

The endurance of the man was unbelievable! He should have been unconscious, but he was advancing with his great arms outstretched. Clay picked up another chair and drove it with all his force into Slocum's face. One leg caught him in the mouth, knocking out teeth and driving his head backward. He staggered, spat out teeth and blood, then, with his eyes dulled, moved forward, saying, "That's all right, Clay!"

"I guess we're even now, Jake," Clay said. He caught Slocum with a driving right that stopped him dead in his tracks. But Slocum was not out, and he caught Clay full in the mouth with a right hand that sent sparks reeling before his eyes. It was a disaster that shook Clay to his heels, and as he fell backward, Slocum cried out, "I got you!"

Clay sprawled flat on his back and saw the madness in Slocum's eyes, and he knew. . .he knew if he fell prey to those massive arms, every rib he had would be broken. He was helpless, but as Slocum launched himself to fall on him, he did the only thing he could. He raised his leg and, with all his strength, sent his heel into the face of Slocum.

It caught the man full in the face, breaking his nose and driving his head back at an acute angle. He fell on Clay, who scrambled frantically to get free, but Slocum was out.

Clay stood there, his mouth bleeding from the blow he had taken, his breath coming in rasps. The saloon was absolutely still, and there was something like fear in the eyes of some of the men.

"Clay!" Taylor burst out. "I think you broke his neck!"

"I hope so," Clay managed to say, then moved over to where Dent was struggling to get to his feet. Putting his hands under his son's arms, he hauled him to his feet. "Are you ready to go, Dent?" he asked.

"Y–yes." Dent had regained consciousness in time to see the last of the fight, but was still confused. He let Clay hold him up, and the two left the saloon.

"I never saw anything like that!" Bushrod said. He bent over Slocum, staring at the ruin of the man's face. "He ain't dead," he announced. "But he won't be a lady-killer any more. Not with that face!"

"Clay should have killed him," Taylor said. "He'll have to now, sooner or later!"

The two Rocklins got into the wagon, Clay helping his son. Then they left town, saying nothing.

Finally Clay said, "I wish that hadn't happened, Dent."

Dent took a deep breath of the cool air. It was all like a bad dream, and all he could hear was the taunt of Jake Slocum about his mother. He had long been aware that she was not a good woman, but to have her spoken about in such a way, in a saloon, made it unbearable. He was hurt and confused, and he struck out at Clay blindly.

"It's all your fault! Why did you have to come back? You've brought shame on my mother!"

The unfairness of it struck Clay like a blow, but he said nothing. Hot words came to his lips, but he bit them back. There was, he knew, nothing that he could do to make peace with Dent. So he kept his hurting to himself.

When they reached the house, Dent fell off the wagon and lurched off blindly into the night, leaving Clay to stare after him helplessly. Finally he unhitched the team and went to his house. He was met by Buck, who had befriended him long ago. The dog whined and licked his hand, but Clay only spoke to him absently, then went inside and lay down.

He stared at the ceiling, despair welling up in his mind. He'd wanted to kill Slocum! He felt again the fury that had risen in him when the brute had spoken of Melora. He'd thought he had overcome his temper, and since becoming a Christian, he'd had little problem. Now he despaired knowing that word would get back to Melora, who would be scarred by it.

And Dent was in even worse shape. He was shattered by the experience. Finally, after walking for what seemed like a long time, he came back but could not stand to go into the house. Making his way to the scuppernong arbor, he slumped on one of the benches inside. He did not even see Deborah, who had been standing at one end, shaded from his view by a winter hedge.

She turned to go, not wanting to speak to him—and then she stopped dead still, for she heard the sound of sobs. Turning quickly, she saw in the moonlight that Dent's head was bowed and his shoulders were shaking. The weeping came in great gasping sobs, and they went to her heart. She had struggled all evening with what had happened and had made Dent the villain of the piece, throwing all the anger and bitterness that had come to her on him.

Now as she stood there, amazed that the bold young man who seemed so hard and tough was weeping, something came to her. Deborah was a compassionate woman, tender of heart, despite the manner that she sometimes wore. And she had seen in the wild young Rocklin something of this side of his character. Now the great sobs tore at her, and she moved toward him.

"Dent—what is it? What's the matter?"

He looked up, startled, his eyes staring and the tears streaming down his face. "Deborah!" he whispered. But he could say no more. He was ashamed at being discovered with his defenses down and could not say a word. Yet her face, he saw, was not filled with contempt for his weakness, as he had feared. Rather her expression was soft with compassion as she came to sit beside him.

She took his hands and asked softly, "Can I help, Dent?"

"No, there's no help!" he said, unable to take his eyes from hers. Then he suddenly told her what had happened. When he finished, his voice was unsteady. "I. . .love my mother, Deborah. I know she's not. . .good."

He paused, unable to go on, and she answered him out of a full heart, for his brokenness had somehow washed away her own pain and bitterness. "I'm glad, Dent. And you must love your father, too."

Dent sat there, then said, "I love *you*, Deborah."

"No, you mustn't!" she said quickly. "We can never be together. You must know that." She stood up, shaken by his simple statement. When he stood up with her, she touched his cheek, adding, "I—have to go home, Dent. This is good-bye."

Dent Rocklin had led an easy life, with only minor problems. Now he was suddenly aware that without this girl, he would never be complete. A flash of desperation ran through him, and he caught her in his arms. She was sweet beyond anything he had ever dreamed, and he whispered, "I can't let you go, darling! I can't live without you!"

Deborah lifted her face to reply, but his lips fell on hers and there was such a desperate intensity in them that she felt her will grow weak. She felt her hands go behind his head, pulling it down, and for one moment she forgot all the mountains that lay between them. Then they came rushing back, and she pulled away.

"You'll forget me, Dent. . .and I'll have to forget you. Good-bye!"

Dent stood there, the silver moon washing the arbor with warm waves of light, watching her float away into the darkness. He had never felt so lost and alone in his life.

Finally he took a deep breath, looked toward the house, and said quietly, "War or no war, slavery or no slavery—I'm going to have you for my wife, Deborah Steele!"

CHAPTER 23

THE CANNON'S ROAR

*O*n March 4, 1861, Abraham Lincoln took his oath of office as the sixteenth president of the United States. He had addressed the South in conciliatory tones. "We are not enemies, but friends." He concluded with urgency in his voice, "We must not be enemies."

But he was in office for only one day when the simmering Fort Sumter crisis boiled over. He received a letter from Major Anderson declaring that his position was nearly hopeless; that he needed twenty thousand more troops to hold the position in Charleston Harbor; that even if Sumter were not attacked, his dwindling food supply would soon force him to choose between starvation and surrender.

Lincoln had made a public pledge to defend Federal property, but members of his cabinet sabotaged his efforts to reinforce Sumter. On April 4, the president informed Major Anderson that a relief expedition was coming, but that it would consist of supplies only, no troops.

The letter reached Fort Sumter on April 9. Early that morning, Major Gideon Rocklin was standing on the parapet of Sumter speaking with Private Daniel Hough when his commanding officer received the letter. Gideon listened as Hough spoke of his home and family, but his eyes were on Major Anderson, who was tearing open the sealed envelope handed him by a messenger who had come on a small boat.

"So as soon as I get discharged, Major," Private Hough was saying, "I'm going home and get married." Hough, a towheaded young man of twenty-two, had a cheerful smile and was a favorite of officers and enlisted men alike. During the long months of siege, the young Michigan private had never complained of the shortage of food, even though he was so thin that his uniform hung on him. "Did I tell you I was getting married, Major Rocklin?"

Anderson was disturbed by the news, Gideon saw. He was staring at the message glumly, his mouth turned down. "No, you never mentioned it, Daniel," Gideon said. He gave the thin young man a quick glance, wondering what he thought of what was happening. It was hard to tell, sometimes, with enlisted men. "What if the war starts? Will you still get married?"

"Why, sure I will, Major!" Hough said, his smooth face showing surprise. "Me and Carrie got it all planned. We've got us a little place my pa gave me, got a nice cabin, and we'll be startin' a family pretty soon. My enlistment's up in two months, so it won't be long."

Anderson beckoned to him, but Gideon lingered to ask, "But if the war comes, you'll serve your country, won't you?"

Private Hough said, "Why, Major, didn't I tell you? Carrie, my girl, she's from South Carolina. Got a houseful of brothers, and all of them's been real friendly to me." His brow wrinkled in a frown, and he shook his head. "No, Major, I'm going to farm, me and Carrie."

Anderson was giving him an impatient look, so Gideon said,

"Well, I hope you and Carrie have a fine marriage, Private." He hurried over to the commanding officer, saying, "What is it, Major?"

"President Lincoln says he's sending us supplies." Anderson's eyes were weary, for the three-month siege had worn him thin. He looked across the bay to Fort Moultrie on Sullivan's Island, adding, "Beauregard's guns will blow any ships out of the water that try to relieve us."

"They could do it, I'm afraid," Gideon agreed, nodding. "My report is that he's got some big guns in place. Five of them that fire twenty-four-pound shot, some long-range cannon, and some heavy mortars."

"And he's got plenty of firepower on James Island, as well. Not to mention about six thousand men to storm our base. To tell the truth, Rocklin, we're in a tight spot."

Anderson was right, for Sumter was in no condition to fight a battle. The fort was solid enough—brick walls five feet thick rising forty feet above the water, designed to carry three tiers of guns. Anderson had forty-eight guns in position, but some of them could not be brought to bear, and there were not nearly enough men to fire the guns. He had only 128 men, 43 of them civilians. Anderson and his officers had done what they could to get ready for an invasion. The wharf was mined and could be blown to bits at a moment's notice, and various infernal machines loaded with kegs of gunpowder were ready to be dropped on the invaders.

"We'll give a good account of ourselves, sir," Gideon said. "The men's morale is high."

"Yes, and I give you and your lieutenants credit for that, Gideon," Anderson said with a sudden smile. "You've done a fine job with them. But we can't go on for long." The food was practically gone, and they both knew that if the relief expedition didn't arrive soon, they would have to surrender. "Well, we shall see," Anderson concluded and left to go below.

The next day, April 10, at one o'clock, Gideon heard one of the guards call out, "Boat coming from shore, Major!" He turned to see the same boat that had brought Lincoln's message coming across the choppy waters. There were several passengers but no women, which disappointed him. He had hoped that Mellie might come, but she had told him it was getting more difficult to get permission from the officers in charge. He walked along the stones, thinking of her, dismissing the boat from his thoughts. Every spare moment now, day and night, he was taxing his brain, trying to find a way to defend the fort. Over and over he thought of the difficulties, looking for solutions but finding few.

"Hello, Gid," a voice said, and he whirled to see his cousin Clay Rocklin, who had come to stand beside the wall.

Gideon threw his head back, blinking with the shock of the meeting. But he recovered at once and moved forward. "Clay! By all that's holy! I can't believe it!" He gripped Clay's hand and stood there taking in the face of the other man. "It's been a long time, Clay," he said finally.

"Maybe not long enough," Clay said. He was searching Gideon's face, looking for a sign of displeasure. Gid was older, weathered by sun and storm, but otherwise he was the same— thick-shouldered, solid, and with the same square face, which was as open and honest as ever. "Gid, let me have my say; then you can ask me anything. I've come to ask you to forgive me." Clay's expressive lips tightened, and he shook his head, saying sadly, "For all of it. For what I tried to do to Melanie, for killing all of your men in Mexico. . ." He paused, then added, "Ever since I became a Christian, I've wanted to come to you. And lately I've felt it more strongly. Then last week it came to me that you could get killed in this place, and. . ."

Clay paused, his voice thick with emotion, and Gideon suddenly put his arm around his cousin. "Clay—I'm glad you're here. For years I've wanted to see you. Prayed for you. Forgive you?" He gave Clay's shoulders a mighty squeeze. "Why, I did that long ago! Long ago!"

The two men stood there, and some of the men watched with curious eyes to see their officer hugging the tall man. Clay smiled, saying, "That's like you, Gid! But I'm only halfway home. With your permission, I'd like to go to Melanie. I want to ask her forgiveness, too."

"She's in the Foster Hotel, room 221," Gideon said at once. "She's been praying for you, too, Clay." He looked suddenly across the bay, saying, "I'm worried about her, Clay. She wouldn't listen to me when I tried to tell her it could be dangerous here. This thing is going to blow up any day now, and there's some pretty wild Southern fanatics in Charleston. Anything could happen."

Clay laughed out loud. "I don't think Melanie would welcome me as a protector, Gideon."

"Yes, she would. Soon as you leave here, go see her. Right away."

Clay stared at him. "It's not that close, is it? These South Carolinians are hotheads, but I'm still hoping it won't come to a shooting war."

Gideon lowered his voice. "I think it'll come very soon. Lincoln is sending a fleet to relieve the fort. And the secessionists know it. Those leaders who want a war know about it, and they'll never let it happen! I think they'll begin firing in two or three days."

"What will happen?" He listened as Gideon told him what he thought. The two men walked around behind the guns slowly, and by the time they had made a circuit, Clay was depressed. "It's insane, Gid!"

"Yes. War always is. There haven't been any sane, logical wars." Gid suddenly said, "Mellie and I have been keeping up with you. Your mother's told us how well you've done since you came home. My father's more pleased with you than I've ever seen him!"

Clay ducked his head, then smiled wryly. "I wish my father was as optimistic."

"He'll come around!"

"I doubt it, Gid. He was pleased, but when this war started shaping up, things changed in Virginia. Every man who's not ready to grab a musket and charge to Washington to shoot the Yankees is a traitor! And that's pretty well what Father thinks of me. And a lot of others think the same thing."

"What will you do, Clay?" Gideon asked quietly.

Clay said gloomily, "I honestly don't know, Gid. I hate slavery, but I love my state. Right now I'm in limbo."

"Well, so are lots of others—including Robert E. Lee," Gideon pointed out. "I've made my choice, but then, it was easier for me. I don't have the land in my blood—Virginia land—as you do."

"Everyone knows what your choice will be, Gid. And how can I pick up a musket and fight you?"

Gideon was silent, and both men knew there was nothing they could say to make the terrible choice any easier. They walked for an hour, and then the boat handler called, "Passengers for shore!" Clay said, "I'll see Melanie. And if she'll let me, I'll look out for her. Any message?"

"Nothing very original," Gid said, grinning. "Give her my love." The two men parted with a final gripping of hands. "I'll write your father, Clay," Gideon said as the boat left the wharf. "He'll come around!"

Clay waved but didn't answer, for he had little faith in winning his father's approval. When the boat docked, he went at once to the Foster Hotel, but going into the lobby, he suddenly was struck by a fear that Gideon might be wrong. It was Melanie he'd attacked, after all, and a sensitive woman would not shake off such a thing easily.

"It's got to be now," he muttered, straightening his shoulders. "I told Gid I'd watch out for her." He walked resolutely up the stairs, paused one moment before room 221, then knocked on the door.

"Just a minute!" He stood there bracing his shoulders, and then the door opened. She was as beautiful as ever, he saw as she opened the door. She stood there, her mouth open in surprise, her eyes startled. Then she said quietly, "Come in, Clay." When he stepped inside, she closed the door, then asked, "Have you been to see Gid?"

"Yes, I have." Clay was nervous and began at once with his plea for forgiveness. She let him speak, listening carefully. He was far more nervous than he had been with Gideon, but this made her warm toward him all the more. When he had finished, she said, "Clay, when we do a wrong thing, there are two things we can do about it. We can cover it up. Keep it inside. When we do that, it grows. And that's what's happened. What you did was wrong, but you've nursed that bad memory in your mind for years. Of course I'll forgive you! But if you'd asked years ago, you wouldn't have had this on your heart all this time."

Clay wiped the perspiration from his forehead. His limbs were strangely weak, and his head felt light—but he felt free. He nodded. "Thank you, Melanie. You're right, but I was too big a fool to do anything so simple as just asking for forgiveness in those days."

"Now that's over," Melanie said with a smile. "Please tell me about Gid. They wouldn't let me go to the fort today."

Clay gave his report, passing along Gid's final word, and the two of them sat there talking about the dangers. He saw that she was tense, and after what Gid had told him, he did not try to soothe her with false comfort. "I'm going to stay around for a few days," he said. "Maybe I can get a room here. I understand the war fever gets out of hand."

"Gid asked you to take care of me, didn't he? Well, to tell the absolute truth, Clay, there have been a few unpleasantries. The wives of the Union officers aren't particularly popular in Charleston right now."

"I'll go see about a room. Then maybe you can show me a good place to eat."

The room clerk, a tall, sallow-faced man with a fierce set of whiskers, insisted there was no room available, but when Clay let a twenty-dollar bill be seen in his palm, he suddenly remembered a vacancy. Clay checked into the room, washed his face, then walked around the city until suppertime. At six o'clock he returned to the hotel, where he found Melanie waiting for him. "It may be hard to find a place to eat," he remarked as they stepped out on the street. "The streets are packed."

"There's something in the air tonight, Clay," Melanie said with apprehension in her voice.

She was exactly right. The excitement and patriotic passions that had been building up since secession in December had reached fever pitch. Neither of them was hungry, and as they walked around the city that night, long parades snaked through the streets, drums rolled, horses' hooves clattered, and the leaping flames of great bonfires made dancing shadows.

Charleston that night was no place for moderation, no setting for trepidation. Charleston was in the hands of the fire-eaters. Clay and Melanie stood under a balcony, surrounded by a screaming mob, listening to Roger Pryor, a Virginian, speaking to the seething crowd.

"You have at last annihilated this accursed Union, reeking with corruption and insolent with excess of tyranny. Not only is it gone, but it is gone forever. As sure as tomorrow's sun will rise upon us," Pryor shouted, "so it is sure that old Virginia will be a member of the Southern Confederacy! Strike a blow! The very moment blood is shed, old Virginia will make common cause with her sisters of the South!"

Clay said, "Let's get out of this crowd, Mellie." She nodded, and with some effort they made their way down the street toward the hotel. When they arrived, she said, "There's a balcony with some chairs. Let's sit and talk for a while, Clay."

The balcony was small, and as they took two of the chairs, Melanie said, "I sit here quite often at night. It's cool and you can smell the ocean." For a time they sat there speaking idly; then Melanie said, "Your mother has written me several times. She's very proud of you." Then, being a very direct woman, she turned to face him. "How are you, Clay? Susanna told us about the fight you had with the man who insulted Ellen. Was there any more trouble with him?"

Clay shook his head. "Not with him, Mellie. I carried a gun for a few weeks, but he never tried to take the thing further." He hesitated, then said painfully, "Ellen blamed the fight on me." He looked at his hands, and his silence told her much. Finally he began to talk, speaking of his life and the difficulties that had risen in the past few months. Finally he said, "I guess I've come to the end of the road, Mellie. My family doesn't have much use for me. Can't blame them much, for I've treated them shamefully."

"Not all of them, Clay. Susanna tells me you've become very close to Rena."

He smiled and nodded. "My one victory. But the others haven't forgotten that I ran out on them. Especially Dent."

"He's in love with Deborah, Susanna says. She's a favorite of mine, you know. We spent a great deal of time together when we were stationed in Washington."

"A beautiful girl," Clay said. "I like her very much. But she's an abolitionist, and Dent's just the opposite. They'd make each other miserable!"

"What about Melora?"

The question caught Clay off balance. His fists clenched, and he closed his mouth suddenly. When Melanie said nothing, he relaxed. "I guess Mother's been writing you more than I knew." He sat there looking down on the street, then began to speak of Melora. His voice grew gentle as he went over how he'd known her from childhood and how when he'd come back, he'd expected to find her married.

"I wonder why she didn't marry?" Melanie's voice was casual, but she was watching Clay carefully. "It's unusual for a beautiful young woman to stay single."

Clay made no answer to that but said at once, "Mellie, I've not said anything to a soul, not even to my mother. I love Melora, but it's hopeless. Ellen is my wife, and that's all there is to it. As a matter of fact, I've told Melora she ought to marry the minister who's proposed to her. He's a good man, and she needs a family."

Clay said no more, but Melanie sensed the heaviness of his spirit. She longed to encourage him but could not get around the truth that he had spoken. Ellen *was* his wife, though she brought him no pleasure and likely never would. Finally she said, "God knows our ways, Clay. You are doing the right thing—painful as it is for you. He won't forget that!"

They sat there listening to the cries of the people, and finally Melanie rose, saying, "I'm going to bed, Clay. Not that I'll sleep, but I need the rest. Good night." She suddenly leaned over and kissed his cheek. "I'm glad you're here. I feel much safer!"

Clay sat there for hours, listening to the city, thinking of many things. Finally he went to bed, weary in body and mind, but also with a small feeling of triumph.

੭

At noon of the same day Clay had met with Gideon, three men had stood before Major Anderson and his aide-de-camp, Major Rocklin. They were Colonel James A. Chisholm, Captain Stephen D. Lee, and Colonel James Chesnut. The two Union officers had been formal, as were the visitors, but they all knew that this was the ultimatum. Major Anderson withdrew, discussed the situation with his officer, then wrote out his response.

The next day, Chestnut and his party came again at one o'clock. Anderson and his officers debated once more. At three o'clock in the morning, Anderson handed the envoys his response, which was not acceptable. When Anderson escorted the Confederates back to their boat, he shook hands with each one, saying, "If we never meet in this world again, God grant that we may meet in the next."

The bells of St. Michael's in Charleston were pealing four o'clock in the morning as Chestnut's party rowed up to Fort Johnson. Chestnut ordered Captain George S. James to fire the signal shell that would open the bombardment at four thirty.

Everyone was waiting. Roger Pryor was offered the honor of firing the signal gun, but said, "I will not fire the first gun of the war." It was Lieutenant Henry S. Farley who jerked the lanyard that sent the signal shell arching high into the sky over Fort Sumter.

All day and into the night the crowds had gathered at the beach, looking out over the sea, waiting for something to happen. Clay and Melanie were there, and as the signal shell exploded, a great cheer went up from the crowd. But Melanie whispered, "Oh, God! It's started! It's started, and no one can stop it!" She turned to Clay blindly, and he held her while the crowd lifted great cheers. Then she pulled back and with her handkerchief wiped away her tears. "I mustn't cry! It's too late for weeping, isn't it, Clay? Everything is out of control, and no one can stop it. Not Anderson or Lincoln or Davis. But God is still in His heaven!"

Gideon Rocklin did not flinch when he saw that signal shell. Nor did he falter during the entire action. It was a strange, tentative, melodramatic fight that bore practically no resemblance to the cruel headlong battles that would come later. The first Confederate shot hit the wall of the magazine where Captain Abner Doubleday and one other officer had only a scanty supply of powder bags. For hours the shells fell on Fort Sumter, and no effort was made by the Union forces to answer the bombardment. At six, the men ate a meal of salt pork, and then Major Anderson directed the return fire. It was

Doubleday, at about seven o'clock, who fired the first Union shot, which was a miss.

For hours the duel went on, and noontime found Sumter withstanding the bombardment well. Gideon moved from gun to gun, directing the fire. Once he passed by Private Daniel Hough, and the young man gave him a smile. "Well, Major, I guess I'll be telling folks what a hero I was when I get back to Michigan!" he said, then turned to his gun, whistling "Buffalo Gals."

The exhausted Federals slept as they could that night, and in the morning they breakfasted on a little salt pork and some rice. By now the Confederate gunners were firing hot shot, and fires were beginning to break out. By ten o'clock the fire was nearly out of control, and Gideon had the men move their small supply of powder. His eyes burned, and many of the men lay prostrate to avoid the smoke.

Finally a Confederate shot knocked down the flagpole and Beauregard sent out three aides to give Anderson and his forces a chance to surrender.

"We can hold out, Major!" Gideon insisted, his fighting blood aroused.

"No, we must save our men, Major," Anderson said quietly.

At one thirty Major Anderson ordered his men to raise a white cloth.

And that was it.

Fort Sumter had fallen.

The next day, April 14, 1861, the defenders of Fort Sumter were allowed by General Beauregard to fire a hundred-gun salute. Gideon had to scrape the bottom of the barrel to find enough powder, but he found it. The salute began about two o'clock that afternoon. Thousands watched from boats in the harbor, among them General Beauregard.

Gid was walking down the line of guns, watching as each one was fired. His heart was sick, and he wished that the whole terrible thing were done.

Suddenly an explosion rent the air—not of a cannon being fired, but something else. Gideon turned to get a glimpse of men being lifted and thrown into the air like dolls!

One of the gunners had rammed another cartridge into his gun before the sparks from the previous round were thoroughly swabbed out. The spark prematurely ignited the cartridge, and the explosion had blown the crew to the ground.

One body fell not five feet from Gideon, rolled over twice, and came to rest almost at his feet. His face was black, and his right arm was missing. Scarlet blood pumped steadily from the raw wound. Gideon fell to his knees, pulled out his handkerchief, and, knowing it was useless, pressed against the gaping hole in the boy's side.

"Major—"

Gid started and looked carefully at the blackened face. It was Private Daniel Hough!

"Major?"

"Yes, Daniel, what is it, son?"

Hough's lips were blistered, and his tongue was burned. He tried to raise himself, his eyes pleading. "Am I—pretty bad, Major?"

Gideon bit his lip, then nodded. "I'm afraid so, Daniel."

The life was ebbing, and the voice faded so that Gideon had to lean forward to catch the words of the dying boy.

"Tell—Carrie—tell her—"

And then the body went lax as Daniel Hough died.

He was the only casualty of the battle of Fort Sumter, but

never did Rocklin forget that moment, nor the agonizing cry of the boy for his sweetheart. There would be others to die, many of them. But up until the moment that Daniel Hough died in his arms, the war had been abstract for Gideon.

Now he knew.

There would be thousands of Daniel Houghs dying.

There would be many, many Carries weeping wildly for their men.

Before the end came, the land would be red with blood—and perhaps some of it would be his.

CHAPTER 24

AFTER THE DARKNESS, THE DAWN

Long shadows of a darkness that was just beginning enveloped the land as spring turned into summer. The untaught armies were gathering, small fights were erupting on the fringes like ominous flashes of lightning, and here and there people died. One of them was Stephen A. Douglas, the Little Giant and legendary opponent of Abraham Lincoln.

Stephen and Ruth Rocklin were informed of his death by Amos Steele at supper. Ruth had brought the family together. Gideon and Melanie with their three boys were there, along with Laura and Amos and their four children. It was the irrepressible Pat, the oldest son of Laura and Amos, who looked around the table and grinned. "There are thirteen of us. That's unlucky. We better send somebody away."

"Or get somebody else and make fourteen," Gid said.

And then it was Clinton, age seventeen, who put his foot in his mouth. He grinned at his sister, Deborah, saying impulsively, "Hey, Deborah, maybe you could send for that rebel cousin of ours!"

It was a false note, and Clinton—who was very fond of Deborah—saw from the look on his sister's face that his remark had given her pain. He fumbled with his napkin in the silence that followed his statement, trying to find some way to cover up his awkwardness.

Laura glanced at Amos, both of them still sensitive over Deborah's behavior. She had come home from her visit pale and not herself. Both Amos and Laura had tried to talk with her, but she would say nothing about what had happened. Amos had said, "I think seeing the evils of slavery up close has been a shock to her, Laura. She'll come out of it." But he was mistaken, and finally Laura learned the truth from Susanna. She had gone at once to Deborah and discovered that her daughter was shattered, not over slavery, but over an attachment to Dent Rocklin.

Now as Laura watched her daughter, she thought, *It's not getting any better, but it will have to. She can't marry a man who's likely to be shooting at her brothers!*

Amos Steele felt Deborah's reticence keenly. The two of them had been very close, and he sensed that Deborah was pulling away from him. Looking at her, he saw that she was pained over Clinton's thoughtless remark and said quickly, "I forgot to tell you. Stephen Douglas died last night."

Stephen said at once, "I'm sorry to hear it. He was a gifted man."

"Do you know," Gid said thoughtfully, "he could have been president instead of Lincoln? Just a few votes the other way, and he'd have been in office."

"I wish he had been," Melanie said. "He was more moderate on slavery and states' rights than Lincoln. Maybe he could have kept us out of this war."

"No, he couldn't have done that," Stephen said sadly. "It's been building up for years—decades even—and no one man could have stopped it."

"I think that's right," Gid agreed. He sat back in his chair, and Melanie noticed that he had gained back some of the weight he had lost at the siege of Sumter. "There's a line of a song that keeps going through my mind—'We are living, we are dwelling, in a grand and awesome time.' I think that's true. Grand and awesome enough, but inevitable. We've had two nations here, headed in different directions. And now we're going to have to fight a civil war to decide exactly what sort of country this is going to be."

His words fell across the room, sobering them all. "Well, Father," Tyler said, "it won't be a long war. The South can't last long." At the age of nineteen, Tyler was already broad and strong, as his father had been at that age. He was also pugnacious and stubborn, and he thrust his chin forward, stating emphatically, "Why, it's ridiculous! The South doesn't have any factories, and wars are fought with weapons. And we outnumber them, too."

"That's right enough, Tyler," Gid said. "But they have some advantages. In the first place, they don't have to win the war."

Deborah looked at him curiously. She looked very pretty in a red-and-black-striped dress. Her clear eyes, however, were troubled. "What does that mean, Uncle Gideon?"

"Why, it means that they don't want to invade us." Gid shrugged. "They just want to be left alone. So they'll be fighting a defensive war on their territory. We'll have to invade them, and that means enormous supply lines in enemy territory. And we in the North are fighting for an idea, but they'll be fighting for their homes."

"And they'll have better leadership in the army," Stephen added. Seeing the shocked looks on the faces of his grandchildren, he explained, "The best of the West Pointers have resigned from the United States Army to go fight for the Confederacy."

"I'm afraid you're right, Father," Gid said soberly. "General Scott practically begged Robert E. Lee to stay and take command of our army, but he refused. So have a lot of other good men." He shook his head. "I don't envy the general who has to attack Robert E. Lee on his own ground!"

As Gid continued to speak of the difficulties of conducting a war against the South, Stephen was swept with a sudden sense of gloom. Looking around the table, he surveyed Gideon's sons—Tyler, nineteen; Robert, eighteen; and Frank, seventeen. Then he glanced at the three sons of Laura and Amos—Pat, twenty; Colin, nineteen; and Clinton, seventeen.

All so young! he thought sadly. *The old men will bring the war on, but it'll be the young men like these who'll shed their blood.* Then he thought of Clay's sons, and Amy's—all young men, the same as these around his table. "Have you heard from Clay since you got back from Sumter?" he asked when Gideon finished.

"Yes, twice," Gid answered, nodding. A frown crossed his brow, and he shook his head. "No good news, I'm afraid. Clay is against the war. He thinks it's a lost cause before it begins. You can imagine how that goes over in Virginia right now! He doesn't complain, but I know what such a thing can be like."

"But what will he do, Gideon?" Ruth asked. "Will he leave Gracefield? I wouldn't think he could stay there."

"He'll never leave his home." They all turned to look at Deborah, who had spoken. "It's all so sad! He'd made such a wonderful recovery—and then this awful war came along!" She got up suddenly and left the table, her lips pale and tense.

"She was very disturbed by what she saw in Virginia," her father said quickly. "The slave auctions and that sort of thing."

They all knew there was more to it than that, but were careful not to mention Deborah's problem. A sense of impending gloom fell across the room, and they all hastily rose and left the table. The Steeles left as soon as they could, and when Stephen and Gideon spoke later, neither of them was optimistic about the future.

"Are you pleased with your new assignment, son?" Stephen asked as they sipped coffee in the library. Gideon had been ordered to report to General Scott at once. The wording of his orders was vague, and Gideon shrugged pessimistically. "The general just wants me around to get my ideas on how the South is feeling—will they fight and that sort of thing. Mostly because I'm from Virginia, I think. But I won't be with him long." He smiled slightly, adding, "I've been doing a little politicking. A number of new brigades are being formed. They're putting several older units together, and I'll be joining them as soon as the general has pumped me dry."

"I suppose promotion will come quicker that way." Stephen drummed his fingers on the table, then said, "I'm worried about Deborah. About Clay, too. About all of us."

Gideon looked at his father, noting with surprise that he seemed much older than usual. *He's only sixty-two, and he's still strong—but he feels the same as I do,* he thought. "It's going to be a hard thing," he said gently. "Wars are all terrible, but a war between brothers is the worst of all."

The dinner at her grandparents' disturbed Deborah, though she tried not to show it. For the next three days, she threw herself into her father's work, staying up late and accompanying him on two speaking engagements. Amos was pleased, but Laura was not. "She's going on nerve, Amos," she said to her husband. "She can't go on long this way."

The next day was Friday, and Steele had an engagement in Philadelphia. He wanted to take Deborah, but Laura discouraged this, insisting that the girl needed rest. "Very well, she can work on the book," Amos conceded, and asked Deborah to do so. She agreed, and when he left the next morning, she kissed him good-bye, saying, "I'll have a lot for you to see when you get back."

All day she labored in the library, working from the notes she had made while in Richmond. More than once a note brought a memory before her that caused her hand to stop—but at once she would press on with vigor.

"Deborah, you've got to rest," her mother scolded that night. It was after eight, and Deborah had not eaten supper. "Now I've fixed you a late supper. You come and eat right now!"

Deborah protested, but Laura was adamant, so she surrendered. She haggled the steak her mother had saved, eating a few bites, then sat with her mother briefly. Finally she said, "I think I'll take a walk before I go to bed, Mother."

She kissed her mother, then put on a light coat and walked out of the house. It was a mild night, and the stars were putting on a glittering show overhead. The streetlights threw their gleam across the walk, and for an hour she walked the streets of Washington. She was not a moody young woman, and for that reason the black depression she had suffered since her return home had taken her by surprise. All her life she had been able to identify a problem, then attack it with all her might—and in almost every case she had been able to overcome the problem.

But she could not seem to shake off the unhappiness that had come to her, and she knew that it was more than the war—terrible as that was. No, it was both lesser and greater than the war. In one sense there was nothing she could do about the war, except her duty, of course. For a long time she had fought with others against slavery, coming to believe that the evil would never be struck down except by force. But that was an idea, an abstraction. Now she was painfully aware of the flesh-and-blood element. Her great-aunt Susanna had grown to be very dear to her during her brief stay. . . . Her world would have to be destroyed. *How do you destroy a person's world without killing that very person?* she wondered, turning finally down the street to her home.

As she approached the house, she thought of the night all the Rocklins had met for Thomas's birthday party. It had been a lighthearted, happy affair, with all the children and grandchildren gathered around the big table to celebrate the event. In her mind's eye, she saw the older relatives and then the younger family members. And she felt despair close about her as she thought, *They'll never survive this war! Never!*

Then she turned into the walk that led to the front door, and as she did so, someone moved out of the shadows and called her name.

"Who are you?" Deborah cried out, startled and suddenly afraid. Washington was not quite the place it had once been, and the man who suddenly appeared out of the shadows was not familiar.

"It's me, Dent Rocklin."

Deborah stood still, her heart beating as rapidly as a bird's "Dent! What are you—"

"I had to come, Deborah!" he whispered. He was wearing a dark suit and a broad-brimmed hat that shaded his eyes. He took it off and stood before her silently for a moment. Then he said, "I didn't mean to frighten you."

"I was startled—but what are you doing here?" Deborah was taking in Dent's face, noting even in the feeble, pale light of the streetlamp that he looked worn and tired. She wanted to reach out to him but knew she must not. "Have you been in the house?"

"No. I was afraid your parents might not let you see me."

"Well, we can't talk here," Deborah said. "Come around to the side of the house." She led him quickly to the small garden framed by hedge and then turned to face him. "Dent, you shouldn't have come."

"I know that," he said wearily. He was changed, she saw at once. He had lost that lighthearted air that had made him so attractive. The dim light cast his face into strong planes, his high cheekbones and deep-set eyes giving his face a sculptured look. "Deborah, I'm in the Confederate Army."

"Dent!" Deborah whispered. "You'll be shot if they catch you here in civilian clothes! They'd say you're a spy."

"I'm not carrying any papers they could shoot me for," he said with a shrug. "I don't even have a uniform. My company won't be mustered for a week, and I had to see you, Deborah!"

She was not thinking clearly. His sudden appearance had unnerved her, and she tried to regain her composure. The very sight of his face had brought back the memories of his kiss, and she said unsteadily, "You can't stay here. It's too dangerous."

Dent suddenly grinned, his teeth very white against his tan. "Here I am going into the army to face shot and shell, and it's 'dangerous' to come and see my girl."

"It's not funny—and I'm not your girl!"

"Yes, you are." He suddenly grasped her arms and leaned down. "Now it's time for you to tell me that it'll never work. Tell me that I'll probably get my head blown off. Your family would never agree. My family would never agree. Then tell me I'll be fighting against your brothers. Give me a dozen reasons why we can't have each other. Go on!"

Deborah was trembling in his grasp. "It's all true! Everything you say is true!"

Dent's face grew gentle. He suddenly put his arms around her, ignoring her struggles. "I know it is, Deborah. But I know one more thing. Something you've overlooked."

"What—"

He pulled her close and kissed her, cutting off her words. Again she felt the stirrings that had shaken her when he had taken her in his arms in Virginia. There was a wild sweetness in his caress, and she lay in his arms passively at first, then added a pressure of her own to the kiss.

He lifted his head but held her close, whispering, "That's what you've forgotten, Deborah!"

Suddenly tears came to her eyes, and she laid her face against his chest. Everything that was in her longed to say, "I love you, Dent! We'll make it somehow!"

But she could not. The obstacles were too overwhelming. She seemed to see a huge set of balances, the sort with two thin plates hanging from opposite ends of a hinged beam. In one of the plates she saw her family—parents, brothers, and others— and all that she believed in and had worked for, including the freedom of black people.

In the other plate was Dent.

And she knew that all the joy that she felt in his arms was not enough. She could not deny her family and her faith, not even for the love she felt for him.

Drawing back, she forced herself to say quietly, "I can never turn my back on my family, Dent."

He stared at her, his face pale and tense. "You don't love me, then."

"There are all kinds of love. Sometimes one kind of love works against another."

If it had been another man, Dent could have fought, but he was stopped by the look on Deborah's face. He wanted to take her in his arms again but knew that she would not respond.

Finally he said, "Deborah, I love you. And I know you love me." A hardness came into his tone, and his jaw clenched. "I've got to go, but this isn't the end. When the war is over, I'll come for you."

"I can't promise you anything, Dent," she said, hiding the misery that rose in her at the sight of his anger.

He seemed not to have heard. Looking up at the stars, he seemed to be lost in thought. Finally he put his hat on, then said almost harshly, "I'll be coming for you. But first I've got this war to fight. And until it's over, there's no mercy in me."

Deborah cried, "You see what's happening?"

"I see that I've got one thing to do, and I'm going to do it no matter what it costs me or anyone else." He whirled and walked away but paused and gave her one look, and his eyes were filled with regret. "Don't forget me, Deborah. After it's over, I'll be coming for you!"

Then he was gone. Deborah stood peering into the darkness. Overhead the full moon looked down on her, pouring silver bars of light across the arbor. And then a ragged cloud racing across the sky covered its face, and she turned and walked slowly into the house.

❧

"Oh, isn't it exciting! I declare, Leona, that Denton Rocklin is the handsomest thing in his uniform I've ever seen!"

A group of young ladies had pushed their way (in a most

unladylike fashion!) to the forefront of the city square. All of Richmond seemed to be gathered there for the commissioning of the Richmond Grays, and the air was filled with the brave tunes played by the band and the smell of coffee furnished by the ladies of Richmond.

Dent, in his ash-gray uniform, black boots that shone like a well-rubbed table, and a fine tasseled scarlet sash, was at the head of the formation, his second-lieutenant bars gleaming in the sunlight. He caught the eye of Lily Duprey, who had just commented on his appearance, and nodded, smiling slightly. "Lily! He's watching you!" Maybelle Saunders whispered. "I hear that Yankee girl he was so taken with went back home. What Denton needs now is a good Southern woman."

Dent, however, was not thinking of a woman, but of his company. He called it "my company" to himself, for he had a queer possessiveness about the Richmond Grays. The unit took the place of Deborah in his mind, and in pouring himself into the company, he forced the images of her back into the secret part of his being.

And he was content that fine June afternoon. Very content! Looking down the lines as the men waited for the president to come and address them, he was pleased with what he saw. The lines were straight, the uniforms sharp, and the men alert. But he realized that they should be impressive, for it was an elite body of men. As soon as James Benton had announced his intention of organizing and equipping a company of young men, there was virtually a stampede to enlist. Oh, there were other companies being formed all over the South, some of them with ferocious titles: Lexington Wild Cats, Yankee Terrors, Southern Avengers, and Chickasaw Desperadoes, for example.

But the Richmond Grays were different. The ranks were

filled with the cavaliers, sons of the cream of Richmond society. Choosing the officers had been most difficult, for there were only a handful of positions, of course, with dozens of young aristocrats who longed for the officer's uniform. There were elections, and James Benton was the colonel. Brad Franklin was the major, which was no surprise, since he had borne half the expense of equipping the troop. The captain was a man named Brandon Coldfax, owner of a fifty-thousand-acre plantation north of Richmond. At the age of sixty, he was the only one of the officers with any military experience at all, having served in the Indian wars and under Zachary Taylor in Mexico. The lieutenants were Taylor Dewitt, Bushrod Aimes, and Denton Rocklin. Not all of the volunteers were wealthy, of course, but the flavor of aristocracy was strong in the Richmond Grays.

"Look fine, don't they, Dent?" Bushrod, standing to Dent's right, had pride in his voice. "They're ready to fight anything the Yankees send our way!" Aimes and Dewitt had been somewhat taken aback at the way that Dent Rocklin had thrown himself into the work of whipping the Grays into fighting trim. They both knew he had made some sort of trip, and though Dewitt had an idea it was to Washington to see the Yankee girl, there was no evidence of that.

"Whatever happened, it sure did put gunpowder in his blood!" Aimes had exclaimed. True, Dent had made himself cordially disliked for his hard drilling sessions, but he seemed not to notice. Day and night he had been hard at work, and all the officers had given him full credit, especially Captain Coldfax, who had said, "That young man puts us all to shame, Colonel Benton!"

Suddenly a hush went over the crowd, for a tall, erect figure on the platform had risen and begun to speak. Jefferson Davis, the president of the Southern Confederacy, looked like a hawk with his lean cheeks, sharp features, and piercing eyes. He spoke slowly at first, but at the last of what was a stirring speech, he cried out, "I am ready to march with you, shoulder to shoulder, to shed the last drop of my blood for our holy cause!"

The crowd went wild, and the Richmond Grays lifted their rifles, cheering their leader. Dewitt noticed that Dent frowned at this breach of discipline, and he whispered to Aimes, "The boys will get it for that! Look how mad ol' Dent is!"

As Rev. Jeremiah Irons, the chaplain of the Grays, came to pronounce a prayer, Dent looked over the crowd. The men had all pulled their hats off, and suddenly he spotted his father standing with his mother. He frowned quickly, the joy of the event turning sour. When Irons pronounced the amen, the company was dismissed. "There's a lunch for all heroes at the Dixon House, Dent," Taylor said, grinning. "Let's go show how well we can eat!"

The dining room of the Dixon House was crowded, and the tables were laden with food. Thomas came at once to Dent, saying, "My boy, I am very proud of you!"

Dent said, "We haven't done anything yet, sir. But give us time." He noticed that his own father was holding back, and he asked suddenly, "Did you think the company looked well, sir?"

"Yes, I did. You've all done a fine job."

They found a place to eat, across from Colonel Benton and Rev. Irons. Benton said, "This son of yours is a slave driver, Clay! The Yankees can't be any tougher than he is!" A laugh went around the table, and Benton added, "Thomas, you ought to join my staff."

"I'm a little old for that, James! Besides, all I know how to do is raise cotton. You can't fight the Yankees with a cotton stalk!"

The colonel joined in the laugh but said, "Why, you're no older than I am, or Captain Coldfax! As for that, the captain is the only officer we have with battle experience. I wish we had more like him."

Suddenly a man in civilian clothes, a tall, dark, lean individual, spoke up. "Well, what about your son, Mr. Rocklin? He's had military experience, I understand."

The remark brought an end to the ease of the dinner. The speaker, whose name was Rafe Longley, was a close friend of Jake Slocum. He seemed to enjoy the discomfort he had created, and he added, "Of course, your service wasn't of high quality, Mr. Rocklin—but perhaps you've matured a little since those days."

Clay sat there pressing his feet against the floor. Longley was insulting him publicly, daring him to take up the insult. And there was a desire to do just that. But he suddenly caught the steady gaze of Jeremiah Irons, who shook his head very slightly. He had told Clay earlier, "You're a sitting duck, Clay. As long as you don't join in with the crowd, somebody's going to take his shots at you. And if you fight them, you've dug your own grave."

Carefully Clay said, "I'm not proud of that time, Mr. Longley. What I did in Mexico was dishonorable. It certainly wouldn't qualify me to serve with these brave young men in the Richmond Grays!"

It was the right answer, and Colonel Benton said instantly, "It takes a strong man to face up to his mistakes. We've all made them, and I for one have been happy to see Clay Rocklin come back and make amends as best he can!"

The moment passed, but Thomas noticed that Clay ate almost nothing. Afterward, the three of them walked out of the hotel together. They found the women waiting beside the carriage, and when they got there, Susanna asked, "Was it a nice dinner, Tom?"

But Thomas had no time to answer, for Denton took an aggressive stance facing his father. His face was pale, but his voice was clear as he said, "How much longer are you going to keep this up, may I ask?"

Clay looked at his son and made no pretense of misunderstanding him. "I know I'm an embarrassment to you, Dent. But you'll have to give me a little time."

"Time for what?" Dent asked sharply, his lips thin against his teeth. "Don't you know all our friends and half of Richmond are watching you? Do you have any idea what they are saying?"

"Probably that I'm either a coward or a traitor," Clay said evenly. "But I can't let public opinion force me to make my decisions. I would be a coward if I let that happen."

"Dent, don't make a scene!" Ellen snapped. "Haven't you learned yet that your father's a weak man? Don't count on him for help!"

Thomas said at once, "Stop this! I won't have it! It's unseemly and undignified. Dent, if you have anything to take up with your father, this is no place to do it. We have a home, and you well know where it is. Come along and we'll talk this out in private."

But his words did not touch Dent. Standing straight as a ramrod, he said, "Sir, I apologize to you—but to you, sir," he said evenly to Clay, "I have nothing at all to say. Except that it was a sorry day for the Rocklin family when you came back!"

He turned and left, leaving the family staring after him. "He'll get over it, Clay," Susanna said quickly, taking his arm.

"No, I don't think he will," Clay said, his eyes brooding. "Even if I join the Confederate Army and kill a thousand

Yankees, Dent will never get over it."

"Let's go home," Susanna whispered, and they got into the carriage and drove through the streets of Richmond. The sound of the band music playing floated on the air, and cheers rose as they left the city.

༜

Clay knew at once that something was wrong. He was helping Box shoe his horse when David, Dent's twin, came walking into the blacksmith shop, his face pale. At once Clay said, "I'll finish this job, Box. Why don't you go get some of the cool buttermilk Dorrie keeps in the springhouse. Bring me some, too."

"Yas, Marse Clay." Box could read faces as well as his master, or better. He'd been reading Rocklin faces before Clay was born, and he knew trouble when he saw it. Going to the kitchen, he said, "Trouble." When Dorrie stared at him, he shook his head. "Gimme some buttermilk!"

Clay asked, "What's wrong, David?" This boy was the bookish Rocklin, the thoughtful one. Identical to Dent in appearance, he was almost the opposite in his ways. He was easygoing, but because he accepted Dent's leadership, he had not allowed Clay to come close to him.

He stood there, unable to find a way to say what had brought him to the blacksmith shop. He fumbled with the button on his shirt, as he always did when he was nervous, and finally said, "Sir, I—I don't know how to tell you!"

"It's never easy to give someone bad news, David. The easiest way is just to speak it out."

Still the young man faltered. Finally he swallowed hard, then said, "It's about—Melora Yancy."

Shock ran along Clay's nerves, but he let nothing show on

his face. "What's wrong with her? Is she sick?"

"N—no, sir, not sick. But I'm afraid that Mother. . ." He paused and had a wretched look on his face. Clay saw that he was tremendously embarrassed. Taking a deep breath, David said, "Mother got the idea that—that you were having some sort of affair with the young woman."

"David, I want you to know that's not so," Clay said evenly.

David gave him an astonished stare. "Is that the truth, sir?"

"With God as my witness, there's nothing between us."

David bit his lip. "That—makes what Mother did even worse!"

"What's happened? Tell me."

"Mother got to drinking, I'm afraid. And she went to the store where Miss Yancy works. She cursed her out in front of the customers, called her awful names, and then she started slapping her. Mr. Hardee pulled her off her and brought her home." David closed his eyes, trying to shut out the memory of what he had witnessed. "The servants had to carry Mother into the house."

Clay stood there until the anger that had blazed up in him ebbed. He was aware that David was watching him carefully, waiting for him to speak, to act. "Thanks for coming to tell me, David. Better to hear it from your own." He saw a new light come to his son's eyes and added, "Your mother is a bitter woman, son. We'll have to be patient with her."

David's only thought until that moment was that his father hated his mother. Now he saw grief in the dark eyes that regarded him, but no hatred. "Yes, sir. Can—can I do anything?"

Clay said, "I'm going to ride over to the Yancys, David. Buford Yancy's been a good friend to me. I want to look them all in the eye and tell them your mother was mistaken. I'll make her apologies. Later your mother and I will talk."

"Yes, sir, that would be best." David hesitated; then he said slowly, "I'm sorry this happened, sir—but one good thing has come of it."

"What's that, David?"

"Well, sir—I've been wrong." David dropped his eyes and twisted the button. "I've never given you a chance, not since you came back. I'm sorry for that!"

Clay's eyes lit up, and he did what he would not have dared to do before. He put his arm around David's shoulder, saying, "That means more to me than anything in the world, David!" Then he saw that the boy was shy, and so he said, "I'll talk with you when I get back."

"Yes, sir!"

Clay rode the black horse hard, and it was almost dusk when he got to Hardee's Store. He swung out of the saddle, tied the sweating horse to the rail, and went into the store. Lyle Hardee was behind the counter, along with his wife, Sarah. Lyle peered at Clay over his silver-rimmed glasses and said in the flat Yankee twang, "Mr. Rocklin, I wish you'd leave my store."

Clay stopped, studied the pair, then said, "I apologize for my wife. She'd been drinking, I understand. What she said was wrong, and what she did was wrong. There's no finer girl on this planet than Melora Yancy, and I'm on my way to speak to her family right now. I thought she might still be here."

Hardee stared at him. He had been as angry when Ellen Rocklin had abused Melora as he had ever been in his life—but he saw the naked pain in Clay's eyes and revised his opinion of the man. "Maybe I was a bit hasty, sir," he said. "I don't like to lose my temper, and your wife made me do just that. However, I can see you're as upset about this as I am. . .probably more so.

Well, Melora left twenty minutes ago, walking."

"Thank you, Mr. Hardee," Clay said, then left the store. He mounted the black but went at a slower pace. Before long he saw her walking along the side of the road, and as he drew near, she turned and stopped to wait for him. As he dismounted he saw the scratches Ellen had left on her cheeks and fought down the rage that came to him.

"I thought you'd come," she said.

"I'm going to talk to your father," he said quietly. "Are you all right?"

"Yes." She was wearing a simple gray dress and a thin cotton jacket. Her hair was blown by the late breeze, and she tucked a curl in, adding, "It makes things hard for you, Clay."

"No, it doesn't." He stood there in the failing light, looking at her face. He dropped the reins of the black, knowing that the animal was too tired to run away. "Let me walk with you," he said.

"All right." They began to walk, and for a time neither of them spoke. Overhead the purple martins performed their acrobatics, and from the woods came the sudden barking of a dog. The air was cool, and from the distant range of mountains, a line of light seemed to grow.

Finally he said, "Melora, I have to tell you something."

She stopped and looked up at him, her green eyes wide. "I know, Clay."

"You do?"

"Yes." A smile touched her lips, and she reached up and touched his cheek gently. "You're going to tell me that we can't see each other."

Clay set his teeth, his jaw clenched. Nodding, he whispered, "I can't bring more shame on you, Melora. And I have a family."

Dropping her head, she turned to look toward the distant mountains. Everything was still, except for the cry of a bird who made it back to her nest just in time, before the darkness caught her.

Melora said, "It's getting dark, Clay. But after a while, the sun will come up again, and it'll be a new morning. That's God's way, I like to think. Darkness and cold—and then the first streaks of light in the dawn. And soon the darkness disappears and the world is bright again."

He knew she was telling him to be patient, and he suddenly wanted very much to believe her.

"Do you believe that, Melora? That despite all that's happened—and all the darkness that lies in front of us—that somehow we'll see the sun again?"

Melora nodded, whispering, "Yes, Clay. I believe it with all my heart! I don't know how, but God will bring us through all this."

"Then—I'll believe it, too, my dear!" He hesitated, then slowly and with great care leaned down and kissed her lips. They were warm and soft, like a child's lips.

"That was good-bye, wasn't it, Clay?" Melora said evenly.

"Until the sun comes up again," Clay answered simply.

Melora nodded; then she said, "Well, we're not going to have a funeral service! Come on, Mister Clay! I want to read you some of my scribblings! Come on now."

Melora laughed, and Clay smiled. "All right. Let's see if you can stay on this horse behind me. I never could abide a woman who couldn't ride!"

He mounted, and using the stirrup, she swung up behind him. "Here we are, the knight and his lady!" she said. "Remember those stories, Mister Clay?"

Clay Rocklin felt strangely happy. Nothing had changed outwardly, but the spirit of this woman had lifted him.

"Dragons, you all look out!" he called, then kicked the horse in the ribs. Melora clung to him, and a red-eyed possum scurried out of the way as the black horse trotted down the road in the moonlight.

GATE OF HIS
ENEMIES

PART ONE

Washington

❦

CHAPTER 1

MR. PRESIDENT

Washington was dark as Deborah Steele walked slowly down the street that led to her home. The clock in the belfry of the Congregational church her father pastored sounded out nine times, but the voice of the bronze bell seemed muffled by the darkness and the fog that enveloped the city like a thick mantle.

Deborah was tired. The news of the fall of Fort Sumter in South Carolina had brought a heaviness to her—as it had to Washington and the North. Some of her fellow abolitionists were celebrating the event, rejoicing that at last a blow could be struck that would set the slaves free. Most felt it would be an easy matter: Send a few of our fine Northern troops down and teach the Rebels a lesson! Won't take thirty days—then we'll have a land free from the awful bondage of slavery!

Somehow Deborah had sensed that the war would not be like that, and a heaviness had quenched her lively spirit. Though the April night was not cold, the dampness of the air and the thick canopy of fog sent a shudder through her. Finally she reached the walk that led to her home and paused for a moment, gazing into the darkness, remembering.

It wasn't that long ago, only a few nights, that she had come home on a night very much like this one—and a man had moved toward her out of the shadows, calling her name.

Deborah remembered how the sudden appearance of the man had sent a startling fear through her. Washington, since the fall of Sumter, had been filled with crowds drinking and celebrating the beginning of the war. Deborah knew there had been several nasty incidents.

"Who are you? What do you want?" she had demanded. The reply had astounded her.

"It's me, Deborah—Dent Rocklin!"

As she relived that moment, Deborah closed her eyes, feeling once again the shock that had rolled over her. Dent had moved toward her, telling her that he'd had to come, had to talk with her. Even in the murky darkness broken by a pale yellow gleam from the streetlamp, she had been able to see the tension in his lean face. He was the best-looking man she had ever known—tall, lean, with the blackest hair possible and strongly formed features.

That night, though, he had looked worn and tired. She had wanted so much to reach out to him. . .but had known she must not.

Deborah moved restlessly. She did not want to remember any more. Passing a trembling hand over her eyes, she wished things could have been different. But it had seemed, from their very first meeting, as though Deborah and Denton had been destined to fall in love.

She remembered vividly every detail of her visit with her uncle Gideon's family, of her time in Richmond and at Gracefield, the Rocklin family home just outside of that city. She clearly recalled how startled she had been by the powerful attraction that had sparked between Dent and herself. Even the fact that Dent was a fiery advocate of slavery and secession while she had been active as an abolitionist hadn't weakened that attraction. There had been some violent arguments between them, and finally, to avoid the strong feelings that Dent was creating in her own heart, Deborah had fled back to her home in Washington.

In a scene that could still tear her to pieces, she had said, "You'll forget me, Dent—and I'll have to forget you!"

She had left then and come home. Once back with her family, surrounded by all that was familiar and safe, she had been sure that was the end of her encounter with Dent Rocklin.

Then, a few nights ago, he had shown up, right here by the gate in front of her home.

She had scolded him, telling him he should not have come.

"I know that," he had said wearily. Looking at him, Deborah had noted that he was changed somehow. He had lost his lighthearted air. Then he had spoken the words that struck her heart a fierce blow. "Deborah, I'm in the Confederate Army."

Deborah breathed deeply, struggling with the tears that suddenly threatened to overcome her. The Confederate Army. Dent was in the Confederate Army. How could she love a man who would be fighting to destroy everything she believed in?

She had sent Dent away that night, but not before he had grasped her arms and leaned down, his eyes fierce. She could still hear his words ringing in her ears.

"Now you can tell me it'll never work. Tell me I'll probably get my head blown off. Your family would never agree. My family would never agree. Then tell me I'll be fighting against your brothers. Give me a dozen reasons why we can't be together. Go on!"

Trembling in his grasp, Deborah had answered, "It's all true! Everything you say is true!"

"I know it is, Deborah. But I know one thing more. Something you've overlooked."

"What—"

And then he had pulled her close and kissed her, cutting off her words—and filling her with the same stirring that had shaken her back in Virginia. Despite herself, Deborah had responded to Dent's caress.

When he had finally lifted his head, he had held her close, whispering, "That's what you've forgotten, Deborah!"

Everything within her had longed to say, "I love you, Dent! We'll make it somehow!"

But she could not. The obstacles were too overwhelming. There was more than just their love at stake. There was her family—parents, brothers, and all the others—and all that she had worked for, including the freedom of the slaves.

She had told him that, told him she could never turn her back on her family, told him that there were all kinds of love. . . and sometimes one kind of love works against another.

She had known Dent had wanted to take her in his arms again, but he had not. Instead he spoke to her simply with a great determination.

"Deborah, I love you. And I know you love me. I've got to go, but this isn't the end. When the war is over, I'll come for you."

He had whirled and walked away, pausing a few feet away, almost hidden in the shadows, to say, "Don't forget me, Deborah. After it's over, I'll be coming for you!"

Then he had disappeared, swallowed up by the shadows. Deborah now stood peering into the thick grayness where he had disappeared and struggling with the emotions sweeping over her. Then a break in the sky allowed the full moon to appear. It poured down a silver bar of light. . .until a ragged cloud racing across the sky closed it off, and the darkness moved across the land as Deborah turned slowly and walked into the house.

૭

"Amos, I'm worried about Deborah."

The Reverend Amos Steele looked at his wife over his coffee cup, startled by the abruptness of her statement. He was a tall man with a pair of piercing hazel eyes, which he fixed on his wife, Laura. "Why, what's wrong with her? Is she ill?"

Laura Steele gave him an impatient look. She was a small woman of forty-three, still well formed and in almost every way the opposite of her husband. Her round face and dark blue eyes concealed a streak of humor, and she was quick in both emotion and action.

"Amos Steele," she said with a trace of asperity, "if you'd get your head out of your theology book and look around at the world, you'd be—"

She paused so abruptly that he looked at her with surprise. "I'd be what?" he asked. Then he sighed and put his cup down. "Well, you might as well say it, Laura. I'd be a better father. And a better husband, too, I expect."

Laura jumped to her feet and ran around the table. Throwing her arms around him, she cried out, "No! That's not what I meant! You've been a good father and a fine husband!"

But Steele, shaking his head, put his arm around her and said, "I know I get too caught up in my work, Laura. But I'm not so blind that I don't know what you mean about Deborah." He rose and walked to the window, staring out at the pale sunshine that was tinging the fog with a trace of color. Without turning to look at his wife, he said, "She's in love with Denton Rocklin."

Laura came to stand beside him, slightly surprised at his quickness. She knew him for a man who got so deeply involved in the work at hand that he forgot to eat. And for ten years the work at hand had been the abolitionist movement. Laura believed in the movement, too, and had worked at her husband's side, but she was aware that he had sacrificed much for the cause. Now she said in a voice edged with worry, "Yes, she is. Or she thinks she is, and that can be just as bad."

"Denton's a fine young man," Amos said slowly, "but—"

He didn't finish. He had no need to. Laura had been a Rocklin before she and Amos had married, and that family had divided into two branches. Thomas Rocklin, Denton's grandfather, had founded a dynasty at Gracefield Plantation outside Richmond. Thomas's older brother, Stephen, had left the South and founded the Rocklin Ironworks. Laura, Stephen's only daughter, along with her brother, Major Gideon Rocklin, formed the Northern branch of the Rocklin family. Stephen and Thomas had their differences, like any brothers, but these were minor compared to those that the clouds of a civil war had brought in the past few years.

The worst situation that had faced Laura and Amos was the attraction of their daughter, Deborah, to Dent Rocklin. When Deborah had accompanied her uncle Gideon and his family to Gracefield, nothing had been further from her parents' minds than a love affair between their daughter and a staunch Southern firebrand. But it had happened. They had not spoken of it much, as though leaving the thing alone would cause it to go away. But unfortunately, it was still very much alive.

"It would be tragic for both of them," Amos said heavily.

He was a stern man—or at least was possessed of a stern manner—and he knew a great deal. But the one thing he had not known was how to get close to his children. Now that they were all grown, or almost so, the minister felt a gnawing regret that he had not done more with them. He turned and put his arms around Laura in a gesture that surprised her.

"With God all things are possible," he said quietly. "We'll trust Him to bring Deborah—and Denton, too—through this thing." Stepping back, he said, "I have some papers to take to Gideon. I thought it would be good if Deborah went along." He hesitated, then added, "We could talk, perhaps."

"That would be very good, Amos," Laura said and smiled. "Perhaps you'll get to see the new president. He stays very close to Gideon's commanding officer, General Scott."

"He's very busy, Gideon says. Sucked dry by office seekers." Amos shook his head, adding, "Mr. Lincoln's got a heavy load to bear. We must hold him up in prayer." Then he kissed Laura on the cheek and smiled. "You've held this family together, my dear. Don't think for a moment that I don't know that." Then, embarrassed by the scene, he gave a half laugh and left the room. "We'll be back for dinner early," he said over his shoulder.

When Amos found Deborah, he noted how tired she looked. But she was ready enough to accept his invitation. The main thoroughfare of the city was four miles long and one hundred sixty feet wide. The Capitol, with its unfinished dome topped by a huge crane and encircled by scaffolding, blocked the straight line of Pennsylvania Avenue, which led eastward from the expanding Treasury Building and the Executive Mansion, as the White House was called.

Deborah thought of the gracious streets of Richmond as she and her father drove past the Center Market at Ninth Street, a place that was taboo for the elite because the brothels and gambling houses there operated more or less openly. As Amos drove, he kept well away from sections such as Swampoodle, Negro Hill, and the alley domains that were inhabited by rabble-rousers, thieves, and cutthroats. Fortunately they did not have to pass the iron bridges that linked the two sections of the city. He couldn't avoid, however, passing along the Old City Canal, a fetid bayou filled with floating dead cats and all kinds of putridity and reeking with pestilential odors. Cattle, swine, sheep, and geese ran at large everywhere. Only two short sewers served the entire city, and often they were so clogged that their contents backed up into cellars and stores on the Avenue.

Steele drove into the open area beside the Executive Mansion, got down, secured the team, then helped Deborah down. "General Scott has a temporary office here so that he can be close to President Lincoln," he said as they walked down the broad sidewalk. "That's the War Department over there." He motioned toward a square building off to their left. "But Gideon says the president wants to know everything that's going on in the military."

He led her up the steps of the two-story building, past the massive columns of the semicircular portico. They were met by a sergeant wearing the flamboyant dress of a Zouave. As he inspected Steele's pass, the father and daughter took in the soldier's scarlet pants held up by a crimson tasseled cord, the short, richly embroidered vest, and the tasseled fez that perched on the man's head. After he had allowed them entrance into the mansion, Deborah said, "He looked more like a music hall entertainer than a soldier, Father."

"I think so, too, and so does your uncle Gideon," Steele agreed. "He's one of Commander Hawkins's Zouaves from the

Ninth New York Infantry Regiment—or so Gideon told me. He says lots of outfits have gone wild over the French uniforms." He led her down several halls, up a long stairway, and finally to a door marked MILITARY ADJUTANT.

"This is General Scott's office," Amos said. "I hope Gideon is here."

The two of them entered, and a corporal sitting at a desk covered with papers asked for their pass. Then he rose, saying, "Major Rocklin is meeting with his new commanding officer, Mr. Steele, but I think he'd want to see you." He disappeared into one of the doors leading to an office, then came back at once, saying, "Go right in, Mr. Steele. And you, too, ma'am."

Deborah stepped into the room, which was much plainer than she had expected. There was only a desk, four chairs, and a walnut bookcase against one wall. Two officers, one of whom was her uncle, were standing by a large map on the wall. Gideon came to Deborah at once, holding out his hands. "Well now, this is fine! My favorite niece!"

Deborah had always idolized her uncle Gideon. He was an intensely masculine man, strongly built and straight as a ramrod. A heavy-duty man with big hands and legs, Gideon was well able to overwhelm any soldier under his command. He was a fine soldier, decorated for courage in Mexico. But what was more important to Deborah was the fact that he had always been partial to his niece, spoiling her whenever he got the chance.

Taking his hands, she swiftly reached forward and kissed his cheek. "You owe me a visit." She smiled impudently. "Don't think you can get out of taking me to the next review with a little old compliment!"

"You'll have your own way, of course," Major Rocklin responded, smiling fondly. "You always do." Then he turned toward the tall officer. "I'd like you to meet my new commanding officer, Colonel Laurence Bradford. Colonel Bradford, this is my brother-in-law, Rev. Amos Steele, and his daughter, Deborah."

"I have heard of your work, Rev. Steele. It's a pleasure to meet you." Bradford shook hands with the minister, then bowed to Deborah, a smile on his lips. "And you, too, Miss Steele."

Deborah put out her hand impulsively, and he took it at once, his long fingers closing around it firmly. He was, she thought, no more than thirty-five, which was young for his rank. He had a sharp, aquiline face, with a pair of large brown eyes overshadowed by heavy brows. He was not tall, but his erect posture made him seem so. As he released her hand, he said, "Your uncle is a godsend, Miss Steele. I asked General Scott to give me a man who knew everything about the army, who was patient with new commanding officers, and who would keep me from any fatal blunders. I didn't request that he have an attractive niece, but happily, Major Rocklin meets all the requirements, even that one."

"Colonel Bradford has been commissioned to raise a new regiment," Rocklin said, nodding. "I might add he is doing so out of his own pocket."

"Actually, I'm just a dowdy businessman," Bradford said with a shrug. "But I want to do my part in this war that's coming up."

"Most commendable of you, sir!" Amos Steele said warmly. "I am certain that God will bless your efforts and your battalion."

"Father may not like it so well," Gideon said with a sudden grin. "Colonel Bradford and I are going to his plant to make an appeal for volunteers to serve with the new unit. He'll hit the ceiling when we entice some of his best workers away."

"Do you think they'll volunteer?" Deborah asked. "Leaving a settled job for a chance to get killed isn't very prudent, is it?"

"It doesn't seem to work that way, Miss Steele," Colonel Bradford said. "Most men are sick of their jobs anyway, and the chance to put on a uniform and play soldier—well, a lot of them like the idea. They'll only enlist for three months, you know. They can go to summer camp and let all the pretty girls fuss over them. Most of the men we've recruited so far are worried that the thing won't last long enough for them to see any action."

"They don't have to worry about that," Rocklin said soberly. "It won't be like that at all."

Colonel Bradford laughed and winked confidentially at Steele and Deborah. "The major is the best soldier General Scott could find, but he's also the gloomiest! Come now, Rocklin, you know what the South is like. Some of your people are there, you've told me. Now how can a mob of half-civilized mountain rubes be made into a trained army?"

"Ask my niece," Rocklin said at once. He was taking very seriously the instructions of his commanding general that Colonel Bradford was to be humored.

"He's worth thousands, Rocklin," Scott had growled. "Gave an enormous sum to President Lincoln's campaign fund. Now he wants to play soldier. Well, sir, he's paying well for the experience—but you keep him from getting our people killed!"

Gideon Rocklin fully understood politics of this sort and had gotten on well with the new colonel.

"So, Miss Rocklin," Bradford said, fixing his large eyes on Deborah, "did you see any of the South's military?"

"No, not really." The subject was painful to Deborah, so she added only, "But they're a very determined people, Colonel. Don't underestimate them."

"Certainly not," Bradford said, smiling. "Not with Major Rocklin to keep me from doing so."

"When will your regiment be ready, Colonel?" Amos asked.

"Very soon. If we can get a good response at Mr. Rocklin's factory and a few other places, we'll have a full complement by next week." An idea came to him, and he turned to face Deborah. "Miss Steele, I must call upon you as a patriot for a very important military service!"

"Sir?"

"Next Friday, you really must come to the rally at your grandfather's factory."

"Oh, Colonel, I couldn't!"

"Maybe you should, Deborah," Major Rocklin interjected. "The only man who spoils you worse than I do is my father. I'll need all the support I can get if we take his best men away. Come along and soothe him for us."

"Father? Do you approve?"

"Certainly! And, gentlemen, if you'll pardon my pride, I must point out that my daughter has been a most effective speaker at our abolition rallies. You might let her give a patriotic speech and see what happens."

"Excellent!" Colonel Bradford cried, slapping his hands together with pleasure. "It's settled, then. Now if we can—"

He was interrupted as the door burst open, and the corporal on duty scurried in, excitement making his eyes large. "Sir! It's General Scott—and the president is with him!"

"Well, show them in, Corporal!" Colonel Bradford snapped at once. As the corporal disappeared, he said, "Well, Major, perhaps our little talks with the general weren't all wasted, eh?"

The door opened and Deborah recognized the two men at once. General Scott was an old man, worn from his service to his country. He had been a hero of the War of 1812 and again during the Mexican War, but time had marked him, and now he was a huge whale of a man, weighing more than three hundred pounds. His face was lined and flushed with the effort of movement.

But it was the other man who drew the gaze of everyone: Abraham Lincoln, president of the United States. He was very tall, Deborah saw, and as awkward as rumor and a hostile press had stated. But he was not ugly. His face was homely as a plowed field, but there was such strength in the cadaverous cheeks and such compassion in the deep-set brown eyes that Deborah could not think of him as ugly.

"General Scott, this is Rev. Amos Steele and his daughter, Deborah." When Scott rumbled his greeting, Gideon said, "Mr. Steele, Miss Steele, the president."

Deborah put out her hand and found it swallowed in the huge hand of the president. He held it gently, his warm eyes seeking hers, then said, "Major Rocklin, you'd better have a guard for this young lady. She's much too pretty to be wandering around our rough soldiers unchaperoned."

"I'll do that myself, Mr. President," Colonel Bradford said at once. "Miss Steele has just come back from Richmond, I understand. She's going to attend our rally next Friday."

"You've been in Richmond?" Lincoln picked up on Bradford's statement. "A fine city. What was it like, Miss Steele?"

Deborah was so flustered she could hardly think. The lean face of the president was turned on her, and she knew that he was not making idle conversation. "It's a very disturbed city, Mr. President. People are. . .well, they're not what they were when I was there a few years ago. It's like a fever."

"Yes, that's it," Lincoln agreed, nodding. "It's here in Washington, too. Good people, but they've lost their balance." Then he shook off the gloom that had come to his gaunt face, saying, "Tell your grandfather I will be expecting a great many rifles from him, Miss Steele. He's a fine man, strong for the Union."

"Yes, sir, I'll tell him."

Tactfully Gideon said, "Well, Mr. Steele, thanks for stopping by."

"Oh—yes!" Amos said hastily. He pulled a sheaf of papers from his inner pocket and thrust them at Gid. "Here are the papers you agreed to look over, Gideon. Now we'll be going."

❧

"I'll be by to pick you up for the rally next Friday, Miss Steele," Colonel Bradford said quickly. "Will two o'clock be convenient?"

He was, Deborah realized, a clever man. He had caught her in a position that would have made a refusal awkward, even unpatriotic.

"Two will be fine, Colonel." She nodded, then added with a glint of humor in her eyes, "I suppose it will be all right if I bring my mother along?"

"Why—ah, yes—" Bradford stumbled over the words, and when the pair left, Lincoln gave the new officer a knowing grin.

"You were outmaneuvered that time, Colonel. You'll have to study up on your tactics."

"I propose to do so, Mr. President!"

As Amos and Deborah left the building, Deborah said thoughtfully, "He's had considerable success with women, the colonel."

"How could you know that?" Steele asked, giving her a startled glance.

"I just know it, Father."

Steele studied her, a baffled look on his face. "Well, are you going to the rally, knowing that?"

"Oh yes. He's Uncle Gideon's commanding officer. I have to be nice to him. Besides, perhaps I really can be of help."

"Help in getting men to volunteer?"

"Yes."

"And what if you do convince a man to volunteer—and he gets killed?"

She did not answer, and he said quietly, "I'm sorry, Deborah. I shouldn't have said that." They didn't speak again until they were in the carriage, and then Steele said, "This isn't going to be just a soldiers' war, Deborah. All of us are going to be touched by it."

They drove by the Washington Monument, which was just a stubby base. Suddenly, for no reason she could think of, Deborah said, "I'll bet George Washington would have hated all of this!"

CHAPTER 2

DEBORAH'S RECRUIT

Will Kojak's shack was squeezed between two other shabby frame buildings that were no better than his own. Living cheek-to-jowl with the Sullivans and the Millers created tensions that grated on his temper, but the battered three-room house he rented was so frail that it was kept from falling only by his neighbors' shacks. Every time he paid the monthly rent of ten dollars, he cursed the landlord's representative harshly, vowing that he'd move if improvements weren't made. But they never were, and he never did.

The landlord, a wealthy politician named Jennings, attended a large downtown church and kept himself and his family well away from the Swampoodle district. This section lay on the south side of Pennsylvania Avenue and was composed of slums, brothels, gambling clubs of the worst sort, and a scattering of small, grubby shops and businesses. On the north side of the Avenue were the dwellings of the respectable people of Washington, along with the offices of government.

Pennsylvania Avenue itself was a massive Sahara of dust during the dry seasons and a river of mud and filth during the wet days. It served not only as a street, but as a metaphysical line, as well—for those who lived on the south side in the Swampoodle district were as isolated from the well-to-do segment of Washington's populace as if they lived on the moon. They might cross the Avenue to attend the presidential inauguration—as they had done by the thousands a few weeks earlier—but they turned back to their side of the Avenue when such things were over.

A thin, pale light outlined the city at dawn on Friday, April 19, 1861, just as Noel Kojak, Will's eldest son, appeared at the door of the house. The boy paused and admired the symmetrical rise of the skyline. He had come to get wood for the cookstove, but it was typical of Noel to momentarily forget his task in admiring something he considered beautiful. There was nothing in his appearance to attract attention, for he was no more than average height, and his features, though regular, were not handsome. His short nose and high cheekbones evidenced the European roots of his family, but the steady gray eyes and shock of light brown hair came from other roots.

Old Red, the rooster kept in a small pen in the backyard, broke the silence of the morning with a shrill clarion cry, and the suddenness of it shook Noel from his rapt attitude. Walking over to a pile of wood, he picked up an ax and, with quick, economical movements, split the cylinders of beech into small wedge-shaped slices. It was a task he liked, for with each sharp blow of the ax, the short lengths of beech fell as splinterless as a cloven rock. Noel didn't stop when he had enough for the first fire, but cut enough to last the day. He knew that his mother would have to chop the wood if he didn't, and to help her any way he could was as natural to him as his habit of staring at things that seemed unusual or beautiful.

Piling his arms high with wood, he went back into the

house and deposited the load in the wood box. Quickly he built a small fire. When it was blazing nicely, he picked up a book and began to read by the dim light filtering through the single window that broke the wall on the east side.

At once he was lost, unaware of anything except the words on the page. He had that sort of mind, one that gave him the ability to lose himself in books. Noel had never heard of Coleridge's words about enjoying literature, that one must cultivate "the willing suspension of disbelief," yet he was adept in applying the principle. In an instant, he could leave the shabby world of reality in which he was trapped, entering instead the world of the imagination. When he read Sir Walter Scott's romances, he was in a world of romance and color, far away from the grubbiness of Washington with its dust and mud and poverty.

The fire crackled, but Noel did not look up. If he had, he would have seen a bare room with rough planks adorned only with a few cheap prints. He would have seen Sarah, his seventeen-year-old sister, asleep on a shabby horsehair couch, and fifteen-year-old Grace swathed in a dirty blanket along one wall. The stove occupied a space on one wall, and a table and an assortment of patched-up and rickety chairs took up most of the space. There were two doors on the back wall, one leading to a small room where Noel slept with four brothers, and the other leading to his parents' bedroom. There was no grace or comfort in the place, but Noel's family seemed not to miss those things. Noel had realized that he himself was aware of the shabbiness of life in Swampoodle only because he had caught a glimpse of other things in the world of literature.

A woman came into the room, pausing to look at the young man. Though she was only in her late thirties, her brown hair was streaked with gray, and her brown eyes had the look that chronically ill people sometimes have. Too many children and too little comfort had worn her down, though there were still faint traces of beauty in her worn face. She was thin and slightly stooped, but as she spoke there was no evidence of discontent.

"What a nice fire!" she exclaimed; then she moved over to pat the shoulder of the boy, who lifted his head, startled. "You don't know how nice it is to get up with a fire already made, Noel," she said. For one moment she stood there, her worn hand on his sturdy shoulder, looking down on him fondly. There was a special bond between these two—always had been since he was a small child. Except for six-year-old Joel, her other children, for the most part, were not demonstrative. Anna Kojak received little thanks and few gestures of affection.

Then, as if embarrassed by the scene, the woman laughed, saying, "Better get breakfast. It's late." As she began to prepare the meal, the two of them talked quietly. He spoke of the book he had been reading, and she listened, smiling as his face grew animated with excitement. The smell of the food began to fill the room, and one by one the sleepers awoke. "Better go get your brothers, Noel," Anna said.

Noel said, "All right, Mother," then rose and went into the small room, where he found Joel awake and staring at him with enormous eyes made larger by the thinness of his face. "Breakfast, Joel," Noel said, ruffling his fine brown hair. As the boy arose and pulled on his ragged clothes, Noel spoke to Peter and Holmes, ages sixteen and eleven. They occupied a double bunk bed and came tumbling out with sleepy protests. Ignoring them, Noel turned to the large bed where Bing lay, his face up, his mouth open, snoring loudly.

"Breakfast, Bing," Noel said loudly, but Bing only snorted, flopped over, and buried his face in the thin pillow. "Come on, boy," Noel said, pulling at his brother's thick shoulder. "Got to get moving. We're going to have to hurry to get to work on time."

"Lemme alone!" Bing thrashed about, striking at Noel's hand. When the older boy kept at him, he said angrily, "All right, all right! I'm awake." He shook his head, which brought a streak of pain that pulled a groan out of him, then swung his feet to the floor. "Bring me a cuppa coffee, will you, Noel? I've got the granddaddy of all hangovers!"

Noel said, "Sure," then went to the kitchen and poured a cup of black coffee into a chipped mug. Taking it back, he handed it to Bing, who took it with an unsteady hand. Moving slowly, he swallowed the black liquid carefully, keeping his eyes shut. Noel watched to be sure his brother was awake. At nineteen, Bing was the most handsome one of the family. He was tall and muscular, with a shock of wavy black hair and a pair of large brown eyes set in a well-shaped head. "Better get to the table before it's all gone," Noel warned, then left the room.

When he got back, his father came stumbling in, his eyes red, a tremor in his hands. He had been with Bing at the taverns until early morning and was in a surly mood. He slumped down at the table and grasped the coffee that Anna put before him, saying nothing to anyone. Nor did anyone speak to him, for he had a terrible temper when he'd been drinking.

"Sit down and eat while it's hot," Anna said, and then as they found their places and waited, she bowed her head and said a brief blessing in a hurried voice. When she finished, Will Kojak stared at her with a hard look in his dark eyes, half inclined to belittle her. But his head hurt too much to bother, so he began stuffing the scrambled eggs into his mouth.

The rest of the family ate hungrily, for there was never

enough. Sarah was a dark-haired girl, already shapely and giving evidence of real beauty. She began begging her parents to let her go to a dance that was being held, but Anna said sharply, "No, you're too young, and I know what sort of men will be there." Sarah slammed her knife down, her dark eyes bright with anger, but one sharp word from her father brought her to a sullen silence.

Grace, at fifteen, could have almost passed for a boy. She kept her dark auburn hair cut short and wore the cast-off clothing of her older brothers. Now she stuck her tongue out at Sarah, her dark eyes sparkling as she taunted, "Now poor old Jimmy Sullivan won't have a girl, will he?"

"Keep your mouth shut!" Will Kojak said harshly, then looked at Anna. "Any more eggs?"

"Just a little," Anna said, and she gave him what was left in the bowl. Noel looked at her sharply, knowing that she had given her own breakfast to his father.

Will had just finished wolfing them down when Bing came in and sat down. He complained when his mother gave him two pieces of bread and some gravy, but his father said, "Get to the table if you want to eat."

"Wouldn't do any good." Bing dipped the bread into the gravy, put half of the piece of bread into his mouth, then said, "Guess we'll get something to eat at the rally today."

"What's a rally, Bing?" Joel asked, his head barely clearing the table.

Bing grinned at him despite his headache. "It's a meeting where the bigwigs try to get dunces like me to go into the army."

"You're going to b–be a soldier?" Pete asked, his mouth open with surprise. He was a thin, gawky boy, so plain and awkward that his father often said he was worthless. He stuttered slightly, which embarrassed him so much that he usually kept quiet. Many thought he was slow of mind, but actually he was rather bright.

"No, stupid, I'm not going to b–be a soldier," Bing mocked him. "I'm not dumb enough for that. I can make more in one fight than a soldier makes in six months." Bing, whose real name was Michael, had been a street fighter since he was twelve. Then he had been taken up by a sharp operator, and before long he'd had four professional fights and won three of them. His purses weren't enough to live on, but he was certain that day would come.

Anna stared at him, then asked her husband, "Will, do you think many of the men will volunteer?"

"Yeah, I guess so. Dumb dogs!"

"Why are they dumb?" Sarah demanded. "Ain't we got to go down and whip the Rebels?"

"What do I care what they do down South?" Kojak snapped. "Let 'em own all the slaves they want to. Most of them live better than we do." The thought seemed to anger him, and he was off on one of his tirades. "Look at this swill we have to eat. Down there they got fresh vegetables and plenty of meat. Just work a few hours in a cotton field and then it's back to a nice warm cabin. I say let Abe Lincoln go down and get himself killed if he's got such a bleedin' heart for the poor old slaves!"

He raved on, then got to his feet, saying, "Come on. We ain't gonna fight in no war, but there'll be plenty of food and maybe a little whiskey at that rally!"

As he put on his hat, Anna came up to him and asked nervously, "Will, I need a little money to buy some food—"

He pushed her away so roughly that she stumbled and would have fallen if Noel had not caught her. A sudden flare of anger showed in Noel's eyes, and seeing it, his father scowled. "You gonna do anything about it?"

Noel hesitated, then shrugged. "No," he said quietly, but after his father and Bing left, he reached into his pocket and found a few coins. Slipping them into his mother's hand, he said, "Today's payday, Mother. I'll have more when I come home tonight."

She blinked back the tears, saying, "You never have a penny to spend on yourself, son."

He smiled easily, looking very young, then kissed her. "When I'm rich, I'll buy you the prettiest blue dress in Washington," he said, then turned and left the room.

The three Kojak men joined the other men who were trudging along the dusty street, all headed toward the factory section. Bing and his father spoke of the fun they'd had the night before, but Noel kept silent. His mind was far away, reliving what he'd read before breakfast.

❧

"You're looking lovely today, Miss Steele. . .or may I call you Deborah?"

Colonel Laurence Bradford looked with frank admiration at his passenger. He was accomplished in the art of charming women, and as soon as he had handed Deborah into a carriage driven by a smartly dressed sergeant, he had begun his campaign. He studied the young woman as a soldier might study the terrain and measure the strengths and weaknesses of an opposing force. It was an old game with him, the only one—except for making money—that he truly enjoyed.

What he saw sitting next to him was a young woman of nineteen who was dressed in a deep blue crinoline dress trimmed with pink satin ribbons. She had a heart-shaped face and a pair of eyes such as he had never seen before. Large, almond-shaped, and shaded by thick lashes, they were a beautiful violet color. Her lips were red and shapely, and her complexion was smooth and beautifully set off by thick blond hair. A beauty!

Bradford had become satiated with the professional and slightly worn beauties of the stage. Now, as he glanced at Deborah Steele, he saw her as a refreshing change—as well as a challenge to his masculine pride.

"Why, yes, and I'll call you Colonel Bradford," Deborah answered him with a smile. She was aware of the man's charm, and equally aware that he was a man who had captivated many women. She had agreed to come at the urging of her uncle but was now looking forward to the rally. She gave Bradford a steady look as he protested that she should call him Larry, interrupting to say, "You must be very proud of your new life. I know you've been successful in business, but serving in the army is very different."

"Oh, I'm proud of my regiment, Deborah," he said with enthusiasm. "It'll be a refreshing change from business."

"Have you thought much about the danger?" she asked. "Men do get killed in wars, you know."

"You just don't know how tough the world of business is!" he shot back, laughing. "It's worse than any war."

"Oh, not really," she objected. "On the battlefield men are going to be killed. Even officers."

"I fancy I can take care of myself!"

"What about our men?"

"Why, you can't make an omelet without breaking a few eggs, Deborah," he said with a careless wave of his hand. "Some of the boys are going to take a bullet, but that's to be expected."

As he went on, it seemed to Deborah that he took the war too lightly. Still, she did not argue with him.

"There's my grandfather's factory." Deborah pointed out a low brick building with tall smokestacks that belched huge puffs of rich, black smoke. "The rally will be around on the other side, Grandfather said." She directed the colonel down a side street, noting that the large area next to the factory was already swarming with men. Bradford found a place for the buggy, got out, and helped Deborah to the ground.

"There's Grandfather over there with Uncle Gideon," she said, and the two of them made their way through the crowd to where the men stood.

"Well, granddaughter, you're all dressed for the occasion." Stephen Rocklin gave Deborah a kiss and smiled at her fondly. He was a thickset man of sixty-two, with a pair of steady gray eyes in a face characterized by blunt heavy features. There was something ponderous about him, not only physically, but in other ways. He was slow to make up his mind, but once his decision was made, nothing could stop him. He had come to Washington from Richmond as a young man, knowing nothing but how to grow cotton. From his first job as a janitor at a small foundry, he had progressed steadily in the business world—and now the Rocklin Ironworks was one of the most profitable factories in the North.

"This is my commanding officer, Colonel Bradford. Sir, this is my father, Mr. Stephen Rocklin," Gideon said.

Bradford took the strong hand that was offered, saying, "An honor, sir! Your son must have told you that I'm the most inept officer in the army, but he's taking good care of me."

Stephen Rocklin studied the officer for a moment, as was his custom, then smiled. "Not at all, Colonel. Gideon is very pleased about your new endeavor. And I congratulate you on your spirit." A shadow fell across his broad face as he added, "I'm afraid it's going to be hard on all of us, this war."

"Oh, I hope for better things, sir!" Bradford smiled confidentially, looking very official in his dress uniform. "All we need are good men—such as some of these fine fellows here." He waved his hand at the crowd milling around in the large open space. "Very generous of you to allow us to make our appeal to them."

"Well, the decision is theirs," Rocklin said. "I understand it's an enlistment for only ninety days. I've told the men that those who enlist can count on having their jobs back when their time is up."

"Splendid!" Bradford exclaimed. "We should have the Rebels properly thrashed long before that time."

Bradford did not catch the look that passed between the two Rocklin men, for he was looking out over the crowd. Deborah, however, saw that both her grandfather and her uncle were skeptical of the officer's judgment. She herself had been reading the writings of Horace Greeley, the powerful owner and editor of the *New York Tribune*. Greeley was totally confident that the Northern military forces would crush the Rebels, and he was already printing large headlines that said "ON TO RICHMOND!"

"Would you like to address the men now, Colonel? Or perhaps you'd rather let them get the eating and drinking out of the way?" Stephen asked.

"Let them eat and drink, by all means," Bradford responded. "They'll be more ready to volunteer on full stomachs. While they're doing that, there's a matter of firearms I'd like to discuss with you, Mr. Rocklin—an idea that I've been toying with."

"Certainly, sir." Stephen went to the raised platform and

called for quiet, and as soon as the talk ceased, he said loudly, "Men, there's plenty of food and refreshments. Eat hearty, and when you've finished, we'll hear a word from Colonel Bradford and my son, Major Rocklin. But now let's enjoy the food. Rev. Stoneman, will you ask the blessing?"

After a tall minister said a prayer, the men moved at once to the long tables laden with sandwiches of all kinds, barbecued beef, fresh pork, and vegetables of all sorts. The men ate and drank, talking at the top of their lungs and enjoying the break from the hard labor of the foundry.

Colonel Bradford took the mill owner off to one side, speaking in an animated fashion, and Deborah's uncle said, "Come along, Deborah. Let's get something to eat."

He led the way to one of the tables, and when the roughly dressed working men saw them approach, they stood back, making a place for them. A short, thickly built man with a pair of sharp dark eyes was serving the men, but he paused long enough to say, "Right here, Major Rocklin. Let me fix you and Miss Steele a plate." This was John Novak, Stephen Rocklin's secretary and second in command. Piling the plates high with food, he smiled fondly at Deborah, whom he knew well from her visits to the foundry. "If you give me another smile like that, Miss Deborah, I may forget myself and be one of the first to enlist as a soldier."

"Why don't you, Mr. Novak?" Deborah dimpled at him. "It would do you good to get away from your dusty old books. And Caroline would marry you if you came home with a chestful of medals!"

Major Rocklin laughed with delight, for John Novak's pursuit of Miss Caroline DeForest was one of the longest-lasting on record. "Better do it, John," he said, taking his plate.

"No woman can resist a uniform!"

The men around the table were taking in their conversation, and as soon as Gideon got his food, one of them began to question him. "Think it'll be a hard fight, Major?"

Gideon began to speak, and for a time Deborah stood there awkwardly balancing her plate. It was impossible to eat with a plate in one hand and a glass of tea in another. The men were managing, some of them, by placing the glasses of beer provided for them on the ground and swooping to pick them up to wash the food down from time to time—but that would not do for her.

She moved away from the table, threading her way through the men, but found no place to sit. Most of the men were gathered into small groups, enjoying their food as they talked, but she could not join any of those groups. Finally she saw a lone figure sitting on the low platform that had been built especially for the speakers. It was located on the far end of the open space, far from the tables, and the man looked isolated and somehow a little lonely. Balancing the glass, she walked toward the platform. As she approached, he looked up with a startled glance, then came to his feet.

"Hello," Deborah said with a smile. "I can't seem to manage all this food standing up. May I join you?"

"Oh—yes, miss!" He was, she saw, a young man with a round face and a pair of large gray eyes. He glanced at the seat. "It's a little dusty, I'm afraid. Let me clean it for you." He whipped out a handkerchief that was none too clean and used it to remove most of the dust. "That's about the best I can do, miss."

"Thank you. That's very nice." Deborah sat down, put her glass down, then started to eat, only to notice that the young workingman was still standing, staring at her uneasily. "Oh, do sit down!" she urged. "My name is Miss Steele. What's yours?"

"I'm Noel Kojak." He sat down gingerly, then picked up his plate and began to eat.

"Have you worked here long, Mr. Kojak?" Deborah asked. She did not see his reaction, nor would she have understood it. In all of his twenty years of life, nobody had ever called Noel *mister*, and he could not believe that this beautiful young woman would do so. He felt more uncomfortable sitting there than he had ever felt in his life! He had never been in the presence of anyone from the upper class, much less in the company of a beautiful and wealthy young woman. He had read about such women, but now that he was in the presence of one, he had the strange feeling that he had stepped out of the real world and into one of the romances he had read.

Belatedly he realized that he had not answered her question. "Oh, I've been working here for eight years, miss."

Deborah turned to look at him more closely. "Why, you must be much older than you look!"

"I'm twenty, ma'am."

"But—" Deborah did some quick arithmetic, then said with some surprise, "You can't have come to work when you were twelve years old, surely!"

"Oh yes, miss! That's what I was, twelve."

Deborah had never spoken with a workingman of Noel Kojak's class before. She had read of some of the abuses of the working class and had been indignant over them. But those were stories; this young man was flesh and blood. Forgetting her food, she stared at him—which made him more nervous than ever. "You were only a child! What could a child do at an ironworks?"

"Oh, there's plenty to do, Miss Steele," Noel replied. "I was a wiper when I first come to Rocklin's. I cleaned the machinery and oiled it."

"Isn't that a little dangerous?"

"Oh, a little, I suppose. Fellow has to watch what he's up to." Noel paused, and a thought came to him, making his face serious. "My best friend, Charlie Mack, he got caught up in a crane when he was only ten. Pulled his arm off right at the shoulder."

A vivid picture of what the young man had just related flashed before Deborah's mind, which caused her to put down her sandwich suddenly. "I see," she said evenly. "So you didn't get to finish school?"

"Finish?" Noel smiled for the first time. "Bless you, miss, I never even got to start!" Then he saw the look of dismay in the strange violet eyes of the girl and said hastily, "But I learned to read and write. My mother taught me. She's a fine scholar, my mother!"

Deborah was intrigued by Noel. She would never have noticed him in a crowd, and without meaning to, she pictured the young workingman with his shabby clothing and hard, calloused hands beside Dent Rocklin. At once she told herself she was a fool. Dent was one of the most handsome men she had ever met, and it was foolish to put this young man who had had no advantages alongside the Southern aristocrat. It was a bad habit she'd fallen into, thinking of Dent too much, and she grew angry with herself. "What do you do at the mill now?" she asked quickly.

Noel was ordinarily a quiet young fellow. He lived a secret life through his books, and no one except his mother had ever shown any interest in hearing about what he did. At first he spoke in monosyllables, but Deborah had learned much from her father on their trips to meetings around the country, and she was very good at drawing people out. Now she began to encourage the young man, and as he got over his hesitancy and began to speak, she found a picture beginning to form in her mind. A picture that, had it been put on a daguerreotype by the photographer Matthew Brady, might have been titled "Portrait of a Poor Workingman."

Noel painted a vivid picture of poverty, of the everlasting battle for enough bread to live on and for keeping some sort of roof overhead. His words showed Deborah the lack of anything more than the bare necessities of life, the starchy diet and the hunger for something sweet and rich to break the monotony. He opened her eyes to long, weary days of standing at a machine and working until dusk, only to plod home to a shack without any conveniences whatsoever. As he talked, she envisioned life without the finer things to which she had become so accustomed, things that she accepted as thoughtlessly as the air she breathed.

It was a disturbing picture, and when Noel's voice trailed off, Deborah did not know how to respond. To gain time she asked, "What do you think about this war, Mr. Kojak?"

"I—I'd like it better if you'd call me Noel, Miss Steele," he said nervously. Then he thought of her question, and his answer surprised her. "Well, I don't know much about it, of course. But I don't think it's right for one man to own another. I guess if it takes a war to stop that..."

Deborah stared at him speechlessly. This was the philosophy she and her family had struggled so to share, yet it was brought down to the simplest statement. This crude young man had said more than all the speeches and books; his simple words had eloquently framed what she believed.

"And you'd risk your life for that cause?"

Noel hesitated. He had never seriously considered going into the army—he bore such a heavy responsibility at home—but the woman's words stirred something in his spirit. An awareness that he had long ago buried began to rise and became a fervent desire to do something that mattered, something with color and life and excitement!

"If it wasn't for my mother, I'd go in a minute," he said, his eyes steady. "She'd—she'd have a hard time without me."

Deborah waited, and he spoke of the hard, bitter life his mother endured. He said nothing about his father, but the girl could guess what the woman's life was like. As he spoke, something came to her—an idea that she tried to ignore but that kept returning. Finally Noel said hopelessly, "I'd enlist right off, but my family would go hungry without my wages."

Deborah hesitated, then suggested carefully, "Noel, if you really want to go, I'd be glad to help your mother with expenses." She saw the shock and refusal in his face, then added quickly, "It's not so much to do. I have an income, and what I want most is for men and women to be free. I can't fight as a soldier, but I'd feel like I was doing my duty if I made it possible for a man to do so."

Noel was dumbfounded. This conversation was stranger than anything he had ever read in fiction! He sat there thinking hard and slowly began to discover that the desire to enlist had been deep inside of him. He longed to do something worthwhile, to be a soldier, to fight for what was right!

"I'll do it, Miss Steele!" he said suddenly, his lips pressed together firmly. "It's only for three months, and if you can help my mother until I get back—"

"Oh, Noel, are you sure?" Deborah asked at once. "It might seem romantic, but you could be killed or maimed!"

Such things were far from Noel's mind. The decision had come so suddenly that he scarcely believed what was happening, but he knew that it was going to happen. "I know, but some have to risk that," he said simply.

A rush of excitement swept over Deborah, and she stood up. Noel rose with her, and she put out her hands. As he took them, she felt the hard calluses and the strength of his hands. "I'll pray for you every day, Noel, and I'll write you, too—and you won't have to worry about your family! I'll see after them!"

Noel had never felt anything like Deborah's hands. They were softer than he had known hands could be. As he held them and looked into her violet eyes, he could not speak for a moment. Then he said huskily, "I'll do my best, Miss Steele. I won't let you down, nor the army either!"

They stood there, two people so far apart in birth and breeding and every circumstance that it would have been difficult to picture them ever having anything in common. But somehow Deborah knew that this young man was tied to her from that very moment on!

CHAPTER 3

THE WASHINGTON BLUES

I think it's about time to make our appeal, Colonel."

The rally had been a tremendous success. At least, the men had eaten and drunk incredible amounts of food and beer, and Gideon felt that it was time to get on with the matter. "Some of them have drunk so much beer they'd volunteer for a trip to the moon," he commented dryly to Bradford.

"All the better, Major," Bradford said cheerfully. He was in excellent spirits, having gotten what he considered to be a good response from Stephen Rocklin. Looking over the milling crowd, he nodded confidently. "Suppose you say a few words first. Being the son of the owner, you should have some influence. Then I'll come on and make the appeal."

"Very well, Colonel." Gideon and Bradford made their way to the platform, where they found Deborah talking with a young worker. "Come on up here, Deborah," Gideon said. "Time to get this thing moving." He helped her up onto the low platform, then turned and held his hands up, calling in his best parade-ground voice, "Attention! Will you all move in toward the platform, please." When the crowd had moved forward and was standing quietly, he said in a more moderate voice that carried easily to the outer edges of the crowd, "Have you enjoyed the refreshment?" When they roared back, "Yes!" he grinned and glanced at his father, who had remained on the ground. "You can thank my father for that, and for the time off from work. Let's give him a round of applause, for Colonel Bradford and I are grateful, as well."

The crowd was feeling expansive, and they lifted a cheer for the owner.

"Fine!" Gideon said, then began his remarks. He spoke simply, reminding the men that the country was facing a crisis and that it would take a sacrifice from all its citizens to meet it. There were no promises. Gideon made it clear that the life of a soldier was not an easy one.

Finally he said, "Men all over the North are rising up to meet this crisis, and none has done so with more honor or spirit than the man I introduce to you now." He sketched Laurence Bradford's career as a successful businessman and politician, then said, "It would have been easy for this man to just sit back and let others do the job, but he did not. He left the profitable world of business and, out of his own pocket, is raising a regiment, the Washington Blues. It gives me great pride to introduce my commanding officer, Colonel Laurence Bradford. Will you give him a warm greeting and listen carefully to what he has to say? I know you will!"

The men burst into hearty applause as the tall officer stepped forward, but quieted down as he began to speak. "Men, the country needs you!" he began, then swept into a passionate appeal. Deborah stood there beside her father, listening carefully. She had heard many fine speakers in the abolitionist movement—from the fiery Lloyd Garrison to the famous black orator Frederick Douglass—so she was a good judge of speakers. Bradford was quite good, she decided. He had been a man of power for a long time and had learned how to move the minds of men. Now he proved that he also knew how to stir their emotions.

He had, she knew, been listening to the opponents of slavery, for he used some of the more graphic examples of the evils of that system. After he gave several classic examples of terrible beatings, of families being torn apart and sold to different owners, of the misuse of black women by white owners, the crowd responded as Bradford expected: They grew angry and restless. Then he began to outline the future of the Washington Blues, and what a rosy picture he painted! Beautiful uniforms, marches in parades, comradeship with other good men, a military life that was colorful and exciting—all these things Colonel Bradford set forth in glowing terms.

Gideon leaned forward and whispered to Deborah, "Sounds sort of like a summer picnic, doesn't it? Makes me want to enlist myself!"

Deborah shushed him quickly, for she was caught up in the colonel's rhetoric. From time to time she let her eyes fall on Noel Kojak, who stood far off to one side of the crowd. He was listening carefully to the speech, his eyes glowing with an inner desire. Deborah thought of their talk, and a feeling of pride came to her that she had been able to do something to help the cause.

Finally Bradford said passionately, "I call upon you to follow the flag of your beloved country. And I promise you, men, that as the flag goes forward against the enemies of our nation, I will be with you! I will be in the first line, and if necessary, I will shed my blood to defend this great nation of ours!" He looked around with flashing eyes, then lifted his voice, crying out, "Are you with me? Will you help me put down this terrible rebellion?"

A shout went up, and at once Bradford said, "Fine! You are heroes! Now my sergeants have a table over there, and the papers are all ready. If you'll go there, you can enlist right now."

The ranks of the workmen broke, and many headed for the table, where the trimly dressed sergeants waited. Bradford turned to say, "Well, it looks as though it went very well, doesn't it, Rocklin?"

"Yes, I think we'll get some good men," Gideon agreed. "I think I'll go over and help the sergeants, if you don't mind."

"Certainly! I'll be here with Deborah if you need me." Bradford waited until Rocklin left, then turned to say, "Well, you didn't get to make your speech, did you?"

"Oh, I didn't really expect to. The men need to hear from soldiers, not from women."

"I disagree," Bradford said as he shook his head. He was still heady with excitement from the speech and put his hand on her arm, saying, "A man needs a woman to fight for, Deborah. That's what it's all about, isn't it? When you strip everything else away, what's left is what men and women feel for each other. Isn't that true?"

"The war is over slavery, Colonel, not love."

"Why, Deborah, don't you think that men and women should be free to love where they will?"

"Why—of course, but—"

"And slaves are not free, are they?"

"Well, no, they're not."

"So the war is about love!" He pressed her arm, adding, "I'm just a businessman turned soldier, Deborah, but what I need most in the world is a woman's love. All men need that, and I think you know it."

Deborah found herself unable to answer. He was, she realized, a clever man, as well as a most attractive one. She smiled faintly but said only, "Love is important, Colonel. All women will admit that." Then because she felt he was in some way pressing her, she said, "Let's go down where the men are signing up, Colonel."

"All right, but only if you stop calling me Colonel." He grinned suddenly, adding, "I feel like an impostor as it is. Men like your uncle have earned their ranks with years of service, and here I come, just a rank impostor. So if you'll call me Larry, I'll feel a little less uneasy."

He seemed so genuine that she agreed. "Very well. Let's go meet some of your new soldiers, Larry!" He took her arm possessively, helped her down to the ground, then led her through the throng across to the tables.

Noel had listened to the speeches intently, and his resolve was strengthened by Colonel Bradford's words. As soon as the call to sign up came, he moved at once from the edge of the crowd toward the tables. He was not the first—both tables were surrounded by men clamoring for attention. He stood there as the sergeants, smiling but firm, said, "All right, we'll have a line, men. Right here, now, and don't worry—we'll get you all into the Washington Blues soon enough!"

Noel moved to take his place in the line forming in front of one of the tables, but as he did so, a hand suddenly grasped his arm. His father's voice rose above the talk of the men: "What the devil do you think you're doing!"

Will Kojak had been drinking freely from the barrels of beer that had been provided. He had told Bing, "We can eat anytime, but this is good beer!" During the speeches, he had stood at the back of the crowd with Bing, scoffing at the words of both officers, laughing at the response when the call to enlist came. Then he had caught sight of Noel in the line, and his anger flared up. "Get yourself out of that line, you young idiot!" he snarled, yanking at Noel so powerfully that the boy was jerked off balance.

Noel pulled himself up, very much aware that his father's voice had drawn the attention of the crowd. His face flushed, and despite himself, there was a tremor in his limbs. He had always been an easygoing boy and, unlike Bing, had never crossed his father. But now he could not give way.

He faced his father and said in a voice that was not quite steady, "This is something I have to do."

"Have to do? What the devil do you have to do with the slaves?" Kojak's anger was always just below the surface, and something about Noel's refusal made it boil over. He had given up trying to force Bing to do anything, for the young man could put him on his back with ease. But Noel had never challenged him. Until now.

Kojak began to curse, and he moved to grab his oldest son by the collar, intending to drag him off bodily.

"Better stop that, Rocklin!" Bradford said quickly. "He's going to destroy the spirit of the recruiting."

Gideon agreed and moved toward the pair but was shouldered aside by his father. Stephen Rocklin had already decided what to do and, heavy as he was, moved quickly to stand beside the father and son. "Kojak," he said quietly, but loudly enough for the crowd to hear. "You've got a right to do as you please. But you won't quench the spirit of any man who wants to fight for his country, not as long as you work for me."

Kojak glared at him, his brutal face blazing with wrath. Deborah was standing to the left of her grandfather and could see the anger burning in Kojak's eyes. Wondering if the man would strike out at his employer, she thought of what Noel had said about his mother and was filled with anger that the woman had suffered mistreatment at her husband's hands. She half hoped Kojak *would* strike out at her grandfather or at least curse and quit his job.

But Will Kojak was aware that jobs were scarce. He struggled with his anger briefly, then said, "Well, a man has to look out for his son, don't he?"

"Your son is old enough to make his own decisions," Stephen Rocklin said. "Now I won't have you disturbing this meeting. Either stay quiet or go back to work. If you can't do either of those, go draw your time."

Kojak said at once, "I'll say no more." Turning on his heel, he stalked away toward the factory.

"All right, men, you can go on with the recruiting," Rocklin said. "And remember, when your enlistment is up, you'll have your place back here at the factory."

Good humor was restored at once, and the sergeants began writing furiously.

"He never was any good," Stephen said to Gideon and Colonel Bradford. "Comes to work with such a hangover he can barely see straight. The boy isn't like him, though, far as I know."

"You saved the day, Mr. Rocklin," Colonel Bradford said warmly. He looked at the long lines, then said, "This may hurt you some. You'll be losing some good men."

"You do the fighting, Colonel Bradford, and we'll take care of things here at home."

"Well said, sir!" Bradford exclaimed. "And we'll do exactly that, won't we, men?"

As he raised his voice so that the crowd could hear, Deborah saw that her uncle's face was a study. She moved closer to him, asking, "What's the matter, Uncle Gid?"

"Why, nothing, Deborah," he answered quickly, but then added, "Bradford's quite a fellow. Good at motivating men. But he's always been in charge of everything. No soldier is that much in control. There's always someone above him. I'm just wondering if our commanding officer will be able to take orders as well as he gives them."

Deborah stood talking with her uncle, waiting for a chance to speak to Noel. Enlisting was a slow process, but finally he finished, and she caught his eye. He nodded and would have passed, but she said, "Uncle Gideon, I want you to meet someone."

"Oh? Who might that be?" her uncle asked in surprise, but he allowed her to lead him to where the young Kojak was standing.

"This is Noel Kojak, Major Rocklin," Deborah said. "We had lunch together, and he's going to be one of your fine soldiers."

Gideon studied the young man, noting the honest gray eyes and sturdy body. *Better type than his father,* he thought and said with a smile, "Glad to have you in the Washington Blues, Kojak. I know you'll do well."

Noel swallowed, managing to say, "I'll do my best, sir. I don't know much about soldiering, though."

"You'll get good training," Gideon said, then noted that Bradford had come over to stand beside them, a curious look in his eye. "Colonel Bradford, this is Private Noel Kojak, the newest member of the Washington Blues."

"Glad to have you in the regiment, Private Kojak," Bradford

said, then seemed anxious to leave. "Are you ready, Miss Steele?"

"Yes, of course." Deborah paused long enough to say to Noel, "The matter we spoke of, don't worry about it."

"Thank you, miss." Noel nodded, then turned and left.

"Seems to be a nice young man," Gideon remarked.

"Have to keep your eye on him, Rocklin," Bradford said sternly. "Seems to be a little weak, allowing his father to make his decisions and all that. Well, come along, Miss Steele, if you're ready."

On the way back to her home, Bradford asked, "What did you mean by what you said to Kojak?"

"Oh, he was reluctant to enlist because his family would suffer. He comes from a large family, and they depend on his wages to survive. I told him I'd help his mother from time to time until he got home."

He shook his head but smiled at her. "You have a strong mothering instinct, I suspect, Deborah. But you can't be responsible for the family of every soldier I recruit. Most of them are just lazy anyway."

Deborah stared at him. "I don't think that's true of many of them, Larry."

He was a man who was accustomed to women agreeing with him, and Deborah's comment annoyed him. Then he shook off his resentment and grinned. "You're a strong-minded young woman, Deborah. A man would never be bored with you."

He took her home; then at the door he took her hand and kissed it, saying, "Dinner tonight? I insist! You must let me have my way sometimes, Deborah!" She agreed, but as he left and she moved inside the house, her thoughts were more about Noel Kojak than about the colonel.

Noel had gone back to work, but for the rest of the afternoon he had dreaded getting off for the day. He knew that his father had been intimidated by Stephen Rocklin, but he also knew that the anger would be building up in him. Noel tried to brace himself for the explosion that was sure to come.

And come it did, as soon as the three Kojak men began their walk home. Will Kojak began cursing and reviling Noel, keeping on even after they got home. All night long he raved, and the entire family, except for Bing, came in for a share of his abuse.

Noel had wanted to break the news to his mother gently, but there was no chance of that. It was not until after supper, when Bing and his father went off to the tavern to get some liquor, that he had a moment alone with her. The children were all outside seeking relief from the heat of the summer night, and he came to sit beside her after the dishes were done.

"Mother, I wanted to talk to you, to tell you," he said, putting his hand on hers, "but there was no time."

"Is this something you feel is right, Noel?"

"Yes, Mother!"

"Then you must do it." She picked up a worn, black Bible that lay on the battered table, found a verse, then read it. " 'Whatsoever thy hand findeth to do, do it with thy might.' " She closed the Bible, then sat there quietly. "You came to know the Lord Jesus when you were only eleven years old, Noel," she said quietly. "And you've been faithful ever since. I don't think I could have lived if you hadn't stood with me! Now promise me that you'll be faithful while you're in the army. It will be hard, for there'll be many wild young men. Promise me you'll keep yourself free from the sins that soldiers are likely to fall into."

"Why, I promise," Noel said, somewhat surprised. "A man doesn't have two selves. I mean, if a man is a Christian, he's a Christian when he's away from home just the same as he is at home."

"That's exactly right, Noel!"

He spoke of his absence, then said awkwardly, "Mother, I made a friend today. It will be hard for you to do without my wages, so you'll be getting some help."

"Oh? What's his name, Noel?"

"Well, actually it's a young lady, Mother. Her name is Miss Deborah Steele. She's the granddaughter of Mr. Stephen Rocklin, the factory owner." Noel told her of his meeting with the young woman and of the agreement that had taken place. When he was finished, he said, "She took your address, so you'll be getting some money from time to time." He hesitated, then added carefully, "I suppose it might not be best to tell Pa about this. Just use the money for food and for the things the others need."

"This young woman, Noel, is she a Christian?"

"Why, I don't know, Mother," he said, then added, "But she did say she would pray for me."

Anna Kojak nodded, thinking of the strangeness of it all. "I think she must be, Noel. And I praise God for the way He's worked this all out. When will you leave, son?"

"The day after tomorrow, the sergeant said. Tomorrow will be my last day at the ironworks."

"You'll be back soon, only three months," his mother said. Then she put her hand on his and held on to it possessively. "It's going to be hard to let you go, Noel, but I believe God will bring you back safe. If you should fall in battle, well, you belong to God, so you'll be in a better place!"

They sat there quietly, each of them thinking their own thoughts. Eventually Anna broke the silence.

"I wonder how many mothers in this country are saying good-bye to their sons. And some of them for the last time on this earth."

He had no answer for her. He could only clasp her hand, praying that God would protect her while he was gone.

CHAPTER 4

A VISIT TO CAMP

All through April, Washington was hot, dusty, loud, and packed with a confederation of frantic seekers of all sorts. The new administration of Abraham Lincoln had drawn office seekers from all over the North, and their continual swarming around the presidential mansion almost drove the tall rail-splitter to flight. They laid wait for him in every conceivable location—not only in the White House, but on the streets as he tried to get some exercise, and even on the Sabbath in St. John's Episcopal Church near the White House, where Lincoln sometimes worshipped.

Some of the men who thronged the city were not friendly to Lincoln, for the presidential campaign had been bitter. Some in the North had become angered during the campaign, but even more bitter were the Southerners in the city who carried their pride and anger over Sumter like a flag—John Hatcher was one of these angered Southerners. A handsome man, six feet six inches tall, he was with one of his friends from South Carolina when a line of people formed to shake hands with the president. "I'll never shake the hand of old Abe Lincoln," Hatcher said.

His friend responded, "I'll bet you a suit of clothing you will. You can't pass by Mr. Lincoln."

"Agreed!" said the tall and handsome John Hatcher. The two fell in line, Hatcher in the lead, his head erect and determination showing in every line of his face. The retiring president, Mr. Buchanan, took Hatcher's hand and shook it cordially. After receiving Hatcher's name, Buchanan turned to introduce the man to Mr. Lincoln, but the Southerner removed his hand, let it drop to his side, and began to move on without greeting Mr. Lincoln or even looking upon his face. Lincoln grasped the situation instantly and, with a smile, said, "No man who is taller and handsomer than I am can pass by me today without shaking hands with me."

As they left, Hatcher's friend said, "John, I have won the suit of clothes."

"Yes," Hatcher replied, "but who could refuse to shake hands with a man who would leave his position and put his hand in front of you as Mr. Lincoln did?"

"Well, I have won the suit of clothes fairly," replied his friend, "but I won't take the wager, because you surrendered like a courteous Southern gentleman and shook the hand of our new president, as all Americans should do."

Abraham Lincoln took the office of chief executive at the most critical time in the nation's history, and it was with acts such as his encounter with John Hatcher that he began to win the hearts of his people. The nation sensed that grand and awful times were coming. Crowds of young men flooded into Washington to find their part in the coming war. Every hotel was packed, and private homes were invaded by young relatives coming to the capital to get into the cauldron of excitement. Most of them were afraid that the war would be over before they could get in on it, a sentiment that came close to driving Major Gideon Rocklin to despair.

"The young fools!" he said to his brother-in-law, Rev. Amos Steele, as the two of them left the War Department late one afternoon on the last day of April. "They don't have the faintest idea what they're getting into!"

"Do you think it will really be that bad, sir?" Steele asked cautiously. "I mean, after all, we have the Regular Army on our side. The Rebels have nothing to match it, surely?"

Gideon had picked up his hat, but he paused to stare at Steele. "The Old Army, yes, we have that, Amos. But it's not what people think. Do you have any idea at all how small the Old Army is? No more than sixteen thousand men at most, and scattered all over the continent. And no more than eleven hundred officers of all grades."

Steele was shocked. "I had no idea!"

"And of those officers, many will fight for the South. I got a letter from Captain Winfield Scott Hancock yesterday, from his post in California. They had a supper for a few friends, including General Albert Sidney Johnston, Lewis Armistead, George E. Pickett, Richard B. Garnett, and others—all of whom are leaving to take commissions in the Confederate Army!

"I know for a fact, Amos, that General Scott spoke with Robert E. Lee and asked him to be commander in chief of the Federal Army. And he refused! Said he couldn't take up arms against his native state. The very cream of the crop of West Point officers have gone to the South to fight against us." Jamming his hat down savagely on his head, he growled, "And these young firebrands think we can run down South, fire a few shots, and the Rebels will run for cover. Well, let me tell you, men like these don't run!"

Steele walked quietly to the carriage with his brother-in-law, and it was not until they got almost to his house, where Gideon's family was invited to dinner, that he said, "You know, Gid, I feel guilty about this war."

Amos Steele was a man of the firmest convictions, and his confession caused Gideon to stare at him in surprise. Ever since he had known Steele, the minister had pursued the cause of freeing the slaves unswervingly. At times Gideon had tried to warn him that he was sacrificing his family to his work—but he never pushed the point since he felt that he himself was somewhat guilty of the same offense.

"I've been so determined to see the black people freed," Steele said in a painful manner, "that I never thought what it would cost to bring it about."

"You should have listened to your hero, old John Brown," Rocklin said. "He warned us all that it would take bloodshed for slavery to be eliminated in this nation."

"I know, Gid, but that was something far off, something distant. Now it's here with us—and it's going to be bad."

The two men found out exactly how bad that evening at dinner. The large dining room was filled with Rocklins and Steeles, and the table was covered with food. At first, the meal went well. Gideon sat at one end of the table with his wife, Melanie, at his right, and their three sons—Tyler, Robert, and Frank—ranked on her right. Amos Steele sat at the other end of the table with his wife, Laura, on his right. Beside her, across from the Rocklins, were their three sons—Pat, Colin, and Clinton—along with Deborah.

Melanie Rocklin was wearing a crimson dress of silk, and her hair was as blond as it had been when she had married. She had been the beauty of Richmond society in those days and still was a most attractive woman. Looking at her, Gideon wondered how he had ever managed to get her as his wife. It was Colin Steele, wondering much the same thing, who precipitated the difficulties of the evening.

Colin was a short young man of twenty, not as smart as his brothers, but very likable. He was a brash young fellow, saying whatever came into his mind, and now as he looked at his Aunt Melanie, he blurted out, "Aunt Melanie, I suppose you're glad you didn't marry that Rebel, aren't you?"

A dead silence fell on the table, and Colin flushed. He tried to patch up the damage his remark had wrought by stammering, "I mean—well, after all, if you'd married Cousin Clay when him and Uncle Gid were courting you, why, you'd be down in Richmond about to take a licking from us, wouldn't you?"

Never had Gid Rocklin admired his wife more, for she showed no sign of the agitation she must have felt. Instead she smiled at her nephew, saying, "Colin, Clay Rocklin is a fine man. But there was no man for me but your uncle."

As Melanie spoke, the painful memories of her courtship came back to her. She had been courted by Clay Rocklin, the son of Thomas and Susanna Rocklin, and had fancied herself in love with him. She had thought at one time that she would marry Clay, become mistress of Gracefield Plantation, and reign in Richmond society. Then Gideon had come into her life, and she had fallen in love with him. Never for one moment had she regretted her choice, but she did grieve over the way her marriage to Gid had affected Clay.

As a young man, Clay Rocklin had been strong and handsome, with all the natural gifts one could desire. But he had been completely undisciplined, unable to control his passions. When Melanie had refused him, he had married her cousin

Ellen Benton, and they had known nothing but unhappiness together. Clay had tried many things to resolve his restlessness, including joining Gideon's company during the Mexican War—but that, too, had been a failure. Dishonorably discharged from the army, Clay had disappeared without a trace for years. He had returned about two years ago, but from what Gideon and Melanie could discover, he was still not happy with his marriage.

Colin's hapless question reminded the entire family of the situation. It was Pat, the Steeles' twenty-one-year-old son, who suddenly asked, "What will they do, Uncle Gideon? Our family at Gracefield?"

Gideon gave the tall young man a careful glance. Pat had the same intensity as his father, along with the same hazel eyes and sharp features. "They'll do what we'll do, Pat," he said. "Fight for what they think is right." He added heavily, "Clay won't serve in the army. He seems to have mixed feelings about the war. Melanie got a letter from Clay's mother, Susanna, last week."

"She said," Melanie spoke up, "that Clay was very unpopular, that anyone who questioned the war was being persecuted." She gave Deborah a glance, then added, "What makes it worse is that Clay's son Denton is a lieutenant in the Confederate Army."

At this, everyone at the table stared at Deborah, for they were all aware that she and Dent Rocklin had been in love—or at least that Dent had courted Deborah while she was in Richmond. Deborah's cheeks reddened, but she said only, "Yes, I got a letter from Uncle Clay's daughter, Rena. She's only fifteen, but we grew very close while I visited there."

"I hate to think of it," Laura Steele said. She was Gideon's only sister, and the two were very close. She was a small woman with a wealth of auburn hair and a round face. A thought came to her, and she gave her brother a startled look. "Gid, you might have to fight Denton."

"I hope not." Gid Rocklin's face was sober and his eyes hooded as he looked down. It was something that he knew would become a burning issue in many families. "Even so, I must do my duty."

"Exactly right!" Pat Steele spoke up so loudly that they all turned to look at him. Pat gave his father a direct look. Then, lifting his head in a stubborn gesture, he said, "I guess this is as good a time as any to let you all know. . . . I joined the Washington Blues this morning."

Amos Steele blinked, caught completely off guard. His lips grew white, and he said sharply, "I don't recall that we talked about your decision."

"Yes, sir, we talked about it," Pat said quietly. "I said I wanted to join the army, and you said I couldn't. That was the whole discussion, sir." He was a handsome young man with a firm will, but it was the first time he had ever directly disobeyed his father.

"We'll talk about it at a more convenient time," Steele said sharply.

"Sir, I'm twenty-one years of age," Pat said stubbornly. "We can discuss the future, but I will be leaving in the morning to take my place with my company."

Tyler Rocklin had observed the clash between his cousin and his uncle silently, but now he gave his parents a steady look, then said, "Father, Mother, I'd planned to talk to you tonight when we got home."

Gid suddenly felt a warning go off in his spirit. He glanced at his son, then at Melanie. Slowly he asked, "Have you joined the army, too, son?"

"No, sir, I haven't. But I want your permission to join the New York Fire Zouaves."

"That's Colonel Ellsworth's unit, isn't it?"

"Yes, sir. He's come to Washington at President Lincoln's request. I want to join his regiment."

Colonel Elmer E. Ellsworth, a favorite of Lincoln's, had been busy for several years organizing his unit. The men were wonderful at close-order drill, and Ellsworth, though he had absolutely no military experience, was a fine organizer. With Lincoln's support, he was becoming a nationally known figure.

Gideon Rocklin was too wise a man to make an issue of the matter. He said only, "Ellsworth's unit might not be the best choice, Tyler. Why don't you come to my office tomorrow and we can see what's available."

Tyler nodded at once, relief washing over his face. "I'd like that very much, sir," he said.

The suddenness of this news had taken both sets of parents unaware, though they had expected that the young men would eventually want to go. After the Rocklins left, Amos went to his study with Pat. Colin said to his sister, "Boy, I'll bet Pat's catching it!"

"I hope not," Deborah said quietly. "Pat's determined on this thing, and the more anyone tries to change him, the more stubborn he's going to get."

Colin thought about it, then said, "I may enlist myself. I'm twenty, the same age as Tyler. Maybe I will."

"You're too lazy," Deborah said. "Do you think your sergeant will fix your breakfast like Mother and I do?"

Colin grinned at her, then came over and squeezed her till she gasped. "I'll take you along, Deb. I heard that some of the Rebs are taking their black servants along to wait on them while they're in the army. I'll just take you along. You can press my clothes and cook for me."

"You'd like that, wouldn't you?" Deborah tried to pull away from him, but he held to her tightly. "Let me go, you monster!" The two of them wrestled around the dining room, joyfully laughing. Colin was the best-natured of Deborah's brothers, the one with whom she had played as a child. Now she gave him a hug and a kiss. "Don't enlist, Colin," she said, a serious look in her large violet eyes. "I couldn't bear it if anything happened to you!"

"Oh, shoot!" he grumbled, embarrassed by her concern. "No ol' Rebel's going to hurt me!" Then he gave her a curious look. "What about you and Dent? You still going to let him court you?"

Deborah pulled away from him, her face growing tense. "He won't be thinking about me now, Colin," she said quietly.

Colin stared at her, his large blue eyes considering her. "Bet he will, Deb," he said quietly. "Any man would be a fool to give you up!"

Deborah quickly kissed him, then ran from the room, saying, "Don't you sign up, Colin! You'd be miserable!"

❦

"Come on along, Deborah. You might find yourself a handsome beau to come courting!"

So Pat had said to Deborah on the first day of May 1861. He was getting ready to head for his camp. His excitement and enthusiasm had infected his sister.

"All right, Pat," Deborah said at once, and the two of them had left the house after breakfast. On the way she asked tentatively, "Was your talk with Daddy very bad, Pat?"

He considered the question for a few moments, then shook his head. "You know, Deb, it wasn't all that bad. Oh, he was hurt because I enlisted without talking it over with him, but he seemed all right." He glanced out at the streets, which seemed to be filled already with busy people. Then he said slowly, "I think he feels that he hasn't been a good father to us. He said he wished he'd spent more time with all of us. But I guess it's too late for that."

"No, it isn't," Deborah said at once. "It won't be easy, but you've got to make an effort. All of us do."

"Sure, I'll do that." The two of them had not been close, but now that he was leaving, Pat felt somewhat nervous and spoke with vigor of how wonderful the army was going to be. There was, Deborah sensed, an apprehension in him, and she did her best to encourage him.

As soon as they got to the camp—a large area filled with parade grounds full of drilling men and a small city of Sibley tents in neat rows—they got directions and made their way to regimental headquarters. Inside the large tent, they found that the commanding officer and his adjutant were present, but not in the happiest of moods.

Colonel Bradford's face was flushed when he turned to greet the visitors, and it was obvious that he was not happy. He greeted them with a smile that seemed forced, saying, "Well now, this is a pleasant surprise!" When Pat informed him that he'd come to volunteer, Bradford said, "Well, I'm pleased, of course. Did you recruit this young fellow, Miss Rocklin?"

"No, I can't claim any credit for it, Colonel." Deborah smiled. "It was all his own idea. But I came along to see that you give him the best of treatment."

"Private Steele, you couldn't have picked a better advocate,"

Bradford said. "What company do you suggest, Major Rocklin?"

"A Company might be the best, Colonel," Gideon said at once. "Captain Frost is pretty hard-nosed, but he's a professional."

The remark, both Pat and Deborah saw, irritated Bradford. He snorted impatiently, saying, "Oh, Major, you've got a fixation on the Regular Army! You don't give the militia and the volunteers a chance. But you'll see what fine fellows we have soon enough."

Gideon started to speak but then seemed to change his mind. "Shall I take Private Steele to his new company?"

"Yes, do that, Major," Bradford said. "I'll take Miss Steele out to see some of the drill."

Gideon said, "Come along, Private," and the two left the tent. Soon Pat was being introduced to Captain Hiram Frost, a hard-bitten individual of forty-five. "Captain Frost will be watching you very closely, Private," Gideon said. "Captain, I know you will make a good soldier out of my nephew."

Frost nodded slightly, then turned to a bull-shouldered soldier who was wearing sergeant's chevrons. "Sergeant Cobb, take Private Steele to the commissary. Get his equipment; then get him settled in. Put him in Lieutenant Monroe's platoon."

"Yes, sir." Frost waited until the pair had left, then asked abruptly, as was his manner, "Well, Major, did you make any headway with the colonel?"

"Afraid not, Captain," Gideon said, shaking his head. He and the captain—who was an ex-lobsterman from Maine turned Indian fighter—had been unhappy with the training of the men. Both of them wanted to see less close-order drill and more marching and firing practice. "I tried to talk to him just now, but he won't hear of it."

The captain rested his weight on one foot and stood there, a heavy shape in the morning sun. There was a ponderous quality about him that made him seem slow of thought, but his friends soon learned that once he did make up his mind, he could act as fast as any man in the army. Now he added, "The men like it, all the exhibitions in the city. It's flashy enough. But the first time one of them drops with a Rebel's minié ball in his gut, all those fancy drills won't help them much."

While the two men were speaking, Bradford was explaining the situation to Deborah. The two of them were walking along the dusty lanes between two large fields, and he pointed out the fine execution of the men as they drilled. "Your uncle and I have had a bit of a disagreement over the training of the men," he had explained. "Now, he knows the army, but I think I know something about what makes men tick. He wants to toughen them up with long forced marches and short rations. Well, that's important, of course. But I know what's equally important, and that's pride." His eyes flashed, and he looked very handsome in his blue uniform.

Finally he smiled, slightly embarrassed, saying, "I expect you think I'm very opinionated, don't you, Deborah?"

Deborah said quickly, "I think you're both right. You need both qualities. I'm sure you'll be able to work it out." She looked around at the men, then up at him. "You must be very proud, Larry. This is a fine thing you're doing."

Bradford was used to the praise of women, but his eyes lit up at her compliment. He would have spoken, but just then a lieutenant came to say, "Sir, the meeting with the staff—?"

Irritation swept across Bradford's face, but he said, "Oh, blast! Deborah, I've got to speak to my staff. I won't be long. Would you like to go back to my headquarters?"

"No, I'll just watch the drill." She saw that he didn't like to leave her, but when he did turn on his heel and leave the drill ground, she felt more at ease. For a time she watched the lines move across the dry grounds, raising clouds of dust as they performed their intricate maneuvers.

Then as she began to walk slowly down the dusty pathways, a sergeant came toward her. "The colonel said you can get out of the sun if you like, miss," he told her.

"Oh, I'm fine, Sergeant." She hesitated, then asked, "Do you know where A Company is? My brother is with them."

"Come along, miss," he said, his eyes filled with admiration for her. "I'll take you to their area."

He led Deborah through the labyrinth of tents. Finally he stopped. "There's Captain Frost's tent. He'll be glad to help you."

"Thank you, Sergeant." Deborah smiled at the young man, who at once fell in love with her; then she turned and walked toward the tent. She passed along the line of tents and was surprised when one of the soldiers working with a detail called out to her, "Miss Steele—?"

She turned. Noel Kojak was standing a few feet away, an ax in his hand. At once she exclaimed, "Why, it's you!" She went to him with a smile on her face and, without thinking, held out her hands to him.

Noel blinked with alarm but took her hands, releasing them almost at once, aware that his fellow soldiers were not missing any of the action. "Noel, are you in A Company?"

"Yes, I am, Miss Steele."

She smiled at him, exclaiming with delight, "My brother will be with you. His name is Pat, Noel. You two will have to become friends."

"Yes, I'd like that." Noel was wearing a blue uniform and had a forage cap pulled down almost over his eyes. He was watching her with a pair of warm gray eyes and said at once, "I got word from my mother about the money you sent, Miss Steele. It was such a help, she said."

Deborah said uncomfortably, "Oh, Noel, it was nothing."

"That's not so," he insisted. "It means a lot."

Deborah changed the subject. "How do you like the army?"

He laughed at that. "It's easier than working in the plant. Good food and not much work."

The two of them stood there talking, Noel forgetting that he was on a work detail, lost in the pleasure of her company. She was wearing a pale blue dress with a white bonnet that framed her heart-shaped face. She was so pretty that he had to remind himself not to stare—but could not seem to help himself. He had thought about her constantly, though he had not said a word about her to anyone in his platoon.

Deborah was enjoying the moment. It pleased her to think that Pat would be in the same company as Noel. She had said little to anyone about what she was doing, but resolved to ask her brother to befriend Noel.

Finally he said, "I'm worried about Ma. She's been sick. I hope it isn't this flu that's got everybody down. Some families are hard hit. Everyone down at the same time."

The two of them were so lost in conversation that neither of them heard the approach of Bradford, who came up to say, "Well, here you are, Miss Steele. I thought you were lost."

"Oh no, Colonel," Deborah said, turning with a smile. "I came over to meet my brother's captain—and I found an old friend. You must remember Noel Kojak? He was one of the men who worked in my grandfather's factory."

"Yes, of course." Bradford gave Noel a brief nod, then took

GILBERT MORRIS

Deborah's arm. "Come along, I'll introduce you to your brother's officer."

"Thanks again, Miss Steele," Noel called out as the two left. Then he went back to the woodpile.

Manny Zale, a hard-faced man of twenty-seven, was waiting for Noel, a grin on his thick lips. "Hey now, Kojak. I didn't know you moved in such high company. Who's the doll?" When Noel just shook his head, Zale grabbed the younger man by the arm, his hand closing like a vise. "You psalm singer! Don't clam up on me! Who was she?" Zale had been the leader in the small group that made fun of Noel. They were a godless bunch, and when they discovered that Noel prayed and read the Bible, they had delighted in making his life as miserable as they could.

Corporal Buck Riley had been watching what was happening between the two men and said at once, "Zale, if you got enough energy to do all that arguing, I'm glad to hear it. You can cut some more wood after dinner."

Zale turned angrily, but Riley was a tough one himself, so the burly private just muttered, "You won't always have somebody around to baby you, Kojak!"

Noel knew that he was in for a bad time down the road— Manny Zale had a vicious streak and seldom forgot offenses. But as Noel went back to chopping wood, he could think only of a pair of violet eyes.

Chapter 5

Epidemic

When Pat and Tyler enlisted in the army, it brought the grim reality of war home to the Rocklins and the Steeles in a way nothing else had. Of course, both families had been caught up in the events of the times—the Steeles in the abolition movement, the Rocklins in the military—but with the departure of the young men, life changed for all of them. For Rev. Amos Steele, his son's absence was a continual reminder that he had failed as a father, at least in his own mind. Steele was an honest man, and when he faced up to the fact that he had neglected his family, he admitted it to his wife, Laura.

"If he dies in battle, Laura," he said in a strained voice, "I'll never know a moment's peace!" She had tried to comfort him, telling him that he had given much to his family. He just brushed her off, saying bitterly, "Don't try to make excuses for me! As a minister of the gospel, I, of all men, should have been a good father. And I will be, Laura, the best I can, but the children are all grown. Pat is twenty-one, Colin is twenty, and Clint is eighteen. And Deborah may be only nineteen, but she is a grown woman."

"It's not too late, Amos," Laura insisted. She came to stand before him, putting her arms around him and lifting her face to kiss him. "You have love in you. You've always been afraid to show it."

"Not to you."

"No, dear," she said with a smile. "Not when we're alone. But even with me you're afraid to show affection in public."

Staring at her, Amos said slowly, "My family was never demonstrative. I don't ever remember seeing my father kiss my mother. Even now none of my brothers and sisters show emotion. I was taught such things were a weakness." Then he shook his head, adding almost angrily, "Well, those who taught me that are wrong! And with God's help, I'll give more of myself to the children from now on!"

"Now don't go falling all over them!" Laura warned, a light of pride in her eyes. She had yearned for years to see this stern husband of hers break out of his rigid mold. "You'll scare them to death."

"Well then, I'll just practice up on you!" Steele pulled her to him and kissed her so forcibly that she could scarcely catch her breath. When he released her, she laughed at him. "Now remember, I'm an old married woman, Amos!"

"You're a child!" he said, and from that moment—though he wasn't sure just why—he found it easier to be more expressive in his relationships with his children. He spent much of his time with Clinton, taking him fishing, something they both loved. The lad was strong and agile, and Amos loved watching him. By the time the two of them had been together on two trips, he had opened up to his father in a way he never had before.

As welcome as this was, it was a sorrow for Steele, for the thing Clint shared with his father was that he wanted nothing so much as to be a soldier. He had finally come out with this as they were wading a trout stream. The swift water bubbled over their feet, and their creels were full of fish.

"Pa, I want to be a soldier," Clint had said without preamble. It had been on his mind for years, but he had not dared to mention it to anyone.

Steele had restrained the impulse to flatly squash the notion, which was what he would have done not long ago. Instead he laid the fly line down on the water with an expert motion, then, getting no strike, said as easily as he could, "Because of Pat's decision to enlist?"

"No, sir. I've always wanted to be a soldier. Like Uncle Gideon, in the Regular Army."

"It's a hard life, son."

"I know it is, but it's all I want." Clint's square face was set as he added, "I want to go to West Point. For a long time I've wanted to ask you to try to get me an appointment." At that moment, a trout took Clint's fly. For the next few moments he played the fish expertly, his face alive with pleasure. He removed the fish, admiring the red and gold stipples on its sides, then slipped it into the creel at his side and turned to face his father. "Will you do it?"

Amos Steele stood there, everything in him longing to deny the boy's request. He hated the world of the military, or at least what it stood for in its ultimate purpose, which was to destroy an enemy. Yet the past few days had brought changes to him, and he knew that he had no choice. Slowly he nodded. "If it's what you really want, Clint, I'll try to get you an appointment."

Clint Steele stood transfixed for a few moments, staring at his father's face. Then he suddenly splashed through the knee-deep water and threw his arms around his father. Holding on to him tightly, he gasped, "Oh, Pa! Pa!"

Tears rose in Steele's eyes as, for the first time since his son was a child, he held him in his arms. *And it took a war to teach me how much this means!* he thought bitterly. Then he slapped Clinton on the back, saying, "Well, we'll have to tell your mother—and your uncle Gid, too. I expect he'll like it better than she will!"

The two of them went that afternoon to see Gideon, who received the news with less surprise than they had expected. "You've always been fascinated by the army, Clint." He smiled at the boy. "You've read everything there is, I guess, about the service, and sometimes you've pestered me to death with your questions. I thought it might come to this."

"Can you get me into West Point, Uncle Gideon?" Clint asked eagerly.

"Well, that takes a congressional appointment, and I'm just a lowly major. But I'll work on it. You've got a little time to wait." Smiling at Clint, he said, "Maybe you'll change your mind and decide to become an actor."

"Oh no!" Clint said, shocked by the very idea.

Gid laughed, then turned to Amos. "Tell you what, Amos. You bring your whole brood over to our house for supper tonight. Clint can make his big announcement about his plans to become a general to all the family."

"I wish Pat could come," Clint said. "But I guess he can't get away."

"Well now, that's one of the advantages of having an uncle who's a major," Gid said. Then he added with a sly glance at Steele, "But if you'd really like Pat to come, you might have Deborah ask Colonel Bradford. I think he's about ready to do whatever she asks."

"I'd rather you did it, Gideon," Steele said at once. He did not amplify his remark, but the soldier understood.

"Of course, Amos. I'll bring him along."

The Rocklin home was not as large or as expensively furnished as the Steeles' home, for a soldier had to be ready to move at a moment's notice. But the old brownstone, located just off Pennsylvania Avenue, was large and fairly comfortable. After the cramped, miserable quarters that Melanie and Gideon had occupied at Fort Swift in the Dakota Territory, the house seemed a palace!

Melanie and Laura, with some help from Deborah, worked on the meal, running into each other at times in the small kitchen. Meanwhile, the men sat in the parlor and talked. When the pot roast was done, Melanie said, "Well, the food's ready, so let's see if we can sandwich ourselves into the dining room."

They all crowded into the dining room, a cheerful space with yellow wallpaper and a large bay window that admitted a slight breeze and bars of yellow sunlight. The six Steeles and four Rocklins squeezed themselves into place. "We can't eat much, that's for sure," Clint piped up, pinched between Pat and Colin. "All squoze up like this, there's not much room for food!"

"That's right, Clint," Gid said, grinning. "Part of our strategy to live on a lowly soldier's pay! Squeeze 'em in so tight they can't hold much grub!"

"Well, it won't work with me, sir!" Pat said at once. "I've missed home cooking so much, just don't anyone get his hand too close to my plate or he's likely to draw back a stub!"

"Ask the blessing, will you, Amos?" Gid said.

"Oh God, we thank Thee for the food, which is Your

provision. But we thank Thee even more for each other, for our family. You set the solitary in families, and we ask Your protection on every member of this family." Steele hesitated slightly, then added, "And we ask Your protection and blessing on our family at Gracefield, on the grandparents, the parents, and the young ones there. In Jesus' name, I ask it."

"I'm glad you did that, Amos," Melanie said as they began to fill their plates. "We need to remember Thomas and Susanna. I miss them so much, and now it looks as though we may not see them for a long time."

"Father says Thomas isn't well," Gid remarked, carving the roast with a long knife and laying neat slices on the plates that came to him. "He said that if Clay hadn't come back when he did, Gracefield would have been lost. Clay took all the money he made while he was gone and paid the notes off."

Deborah took a bite of fresh biscuit, then said slowly, "It's strange, isn't it? Clay made all that money in the slave trade and it saved the family home. Now he hates slavery, and everybody there is angry at him because he won't enlist in the army so that slavery can be preserved. It must be hard on him."

"I'm very proud of Clay," Gid said warmly. "He started out making such a wreck out of his life, but he's come back and done all he can to put things right. Not many men can do that, and it's sad that some people in his world don't seem to realize it."

As the meal went on, they talked across the table, enjoying the food and the company. When Amos asked about Tyler, Gideon shrugged. "He likes it very well in the New York Zouaves. Since Virginia seceded, the president sent eight regiments across the Potomac to seize Alexandria and Arlington Heights. Colonel Ellsworth's Zouaves were part of that force."

"That's really the beginning, isn't it?" Robert asked. At

nineteen, he was more like his mother, Melanie, than his father. Always a quiet boy, he had grown up to be a studious young man, thoughtful and curious about everything. "It's the first invasion of the South, isn't it, Father?"

"Yes, it is, Rob," Gideon said, and a sadness touched his dark eyes. "It won't be the last, though." Then he shook his head and said with a smile, "Well, what about your announcement, Clint?"

Clint stammered, "Well. . .I'm—I'm going to be an offic—uh, in the army. Father has agreed, and Uncle Gideon's going to get me an appointment to West Point!"

His announcement brought cries of surprise from everyone. Pat grinned at him, saying, "Well, you son of a gun! I'll be taking orders from my own brother!"

"Not for a while, Pat," Clint said, pleased with the attention. "I can't get into the Point for a while. By the time I get out, the war will be over."

After the meal, they were all drinking coffee when Pat suddenly snapped his fingers. "Hey, I almost forgot! I have a message for you, Deborah—from one of your admirers."

"Must be Colonel Bradford," Amos grunted. "He's been at the house twice."

"No, the colonel doesn't send messages by lowly privates," Pat said, grinning. "But it's right handy having the commanding officer stuck on your sister! Makes you kind of special."

"Bet you wish Captain Frost was in love with Deborah, don't you, Pat?" Gid said with a slight smile. "You'd never have to dig a ditch!"

Deborah sniffed. "Oh, don't be silly! A message from whom, Pat?"

"Noel Kojak. He said to tell you thanks for the help you

sent to his mother."

"What's that?" Amos asked, surprised, and Deborah flushed. She explained, "Oh, I encouraged the young man to enlist, so I'm helping his mother a little until his enlistment is up." Wanting to change the subject, she asked, "Is he a good soldier, Pat?"

"Better than I am, for sure!" Pat grinned ruefully. "Matter of fact, he's the best in the platoon. Always up first and keeps his equipment polished and clean. Never makes sick call." He scowled at Deborah, saying, "You might tell him he could make life a little easier on the rest of us if he'd mess up once in a while!"

"The working class makes the best soldiers," Gid said. "They've had hard lives, so soldiering is easy. Spoiled characters, like Pat here, have to get weaned from Mama before they can function as troopers. The same in the South. The farm boys like the army because they have better clothes, more fun, and less work than they've ever had in their lives."

"Well, Noel is in trouble enough with some of the fellas in the platoon," Pat said. "Mostly because he insists on letting his religion show."

"How's that, Pat?" Amos Steele asked at once, his eyes alert.

"Oh, Noel reads his Bible all the time, it seems like, and every night he gets down on his knees and prays."

"And you don't, Pat?" It was his mother who asked the question, and Pat was embarrassed.

"Well, I can pray just as well in bed, Mother. When a fellow shows too much religion, it makes the men think he's showing off." The conversation bothered Pat, and he changed the subject. "By the way, Deborah, Noel told me something else. He said his family's down with the flu, and he wants you to pray for them."

"Bad epidemic," Gid stated. "We've been blessed, but quite a few of the men have been down, and Father tells me many of his men and their families are in bad shape."

The evening ended soon, but Deborah did not join in much of the talk. On the way home, Clint said, "You're worried about this fellow's family, aren't you, Deb?"

"Yes, I am."

"Well, you'll have to do what he asks," Clint said practically. "You'll have to pray for them."

Deborah did pray that night after she went to bed, but by the time she went to sleep, she knew that prayer wasn't going to be enough. She dropped off to sleep, a plan hatching in her mind. That night it was only a vague notion, but by morning it was fully developed.

❧

The Swampoodle district announced itself to Deborah first by the almost overpowering stench that issued from the hundreds of ramshackle privies behind the crude shanties. It had rained during the night, and the moist air seemed heavy with the rank odor.

The visual impact of the area offended the eyes almost as much as the smell offended the nose. There was no trace of beauty to be found, not anywhere. Line after line of shacks, unpainted and scoured to a leprous gray-brown by wind and weather, met Deborah's gaze. Drying clothes hung from a crisscross of lines and billowed in the breeze, but the clothing had no more color than the shacks. There was no attempt at decoration, no flowers or fresh curtains—all was crude, plain, and depressing.

Deborah drove her buggy down the muddy streets, doing her best to miss the pigs and chickens, most of which were as scrawny and lean as specters, that were crossing in front of her. The children who watched her pass stared at her, eyes large in their thin faces. They seemed to have been born exhausted, too tired to play as children should.

A trio of men leaning against a stark building with the single word SALOON over the door looked up as she approached. Deborah resisted the impulse to whip the horse up, and when one of them leered at her, saying, "Hello, girlie. How about a little drink?" she did not even look at him. The man made a coarse remark as she moved on, her heart beating rapidly, but he did not follow.

A small general store at an intersection drew her attention. She got down, hitched the horse to a rickety rail, then walked to the board sidewalk. Stepping inside, she blinked to adjust her eyes to the gloomy darkness. A single room with an assortment of cans on shelves made of rough lumber, and barrels of pickles and crackers on the floor, met her gaze.

"Help you?" Deborah turned quickly to face a short, fat man who was smoking a cigar. It had burned down so far that the ruby glow seemed to touch his lips. He was sitting on a cane-backed chair and made no move to get up.

"I'm looking for a family named Kojak," she answered.

The man studied her, then removed the cigar and studied it. "Which one?"

"Oh, why, I don't—"

"Three Kojaks I know of around here."

"The one with a son named Noel. He's in the army."

"Yeah, well—that's Will." Replacing the cigar between his lips, the owner drew on it, and in the gloom the glowing end made a vivid period under his stubby nose. "What'cha want with 'em?"

Deborah stared at him, stopped dead still by his abrupt question. "I have something for Mrs. Kojak," she said.

"Down this street five blocks, then go right for two blocks. Ask some of the kids you see where Will Kojak lives."

Deborah said, "Thank you," but as she turned to leave, an idea came to her. "I'd like a few groceries." The man got to his feet quickly, his eyes brightening. His stock was pitifully small, and Deborah cut that by a full quarter before she was through. He found an old box, packed it with tins of canned food, then stuffed fresh vegetables into old newspapers. He had some hard candy, and she took a large sampling of that, as well as some staples of flour, sugar, and coffee.

"Comes to nine dollars and sixty-six cents," the thickset man said, looking at her fearfully, as if afraid that the price might overwhelm her.

Deborah counted out the money, and he poked it into his vest pocket with aplomb, then said, "Lemme put this in your buggy, ma'am." When the goods were loaded and she got into the buggy, he lifted his hat, saying cheerfully, "Top o' the morning to you, miss!"

Deborah smiled at him. "Thank you," she said, then made her way down the street. As she followed his directions, she thought of how a few dollars had made the man civil. It wasn't just the money, she felt, although she was sure that her order had been a large one for the owner. The sale had brought cheer and hope into the man's countenance, and it somehow shamed her that she had come to think so little of the abundance she'd lived in all her life.

The section she came to was, if possible, even worse than the collections of shanties she had passed already, but she pressed on. A group of children, none over seven or eight, stood watching her listlessly. When she pulled up and asked, "Do you know where Will Kojak lives?" none of them answered. Finally one of them pointed to one of the shacks and piped up, "Right there."

"Thank you." Deborah flicked the reins, and when she reached the house the youngster had indicated, she got down and hitched the horse to a sapling that had somehow survived. As she approached the door, her courage almost failed her. But she lifted her chin and made herself knock on the door. There was no response at first. Then she heard a faint rustling. The door opened slowly, and the interior was so dark that Deborah could see nothing. Uncertainly she said, "Hello? Is anybody here?"

A voice came from somewhere. "Yes. I'm here." She looked down and saw a small boy staring up at her. He was wearing only a tattered shirt, and his eyes were frightened.

"Is your mother here?" Deborah asked.

"She's sick."

"Oh. Well, are any of your brothers and sisters here?"

The boy nodded. "They're all sick."

Deborah stood there nonplussed, for the situation was beyond her. But the boy didn't move, and she had to do something. "Can you ask your mother to come to the door?"

The child disappeared, and Deborah stood there wishing she'd never come. He was gone so long that she was ready to leave, but then he was back. "Mama says you come to her."

Deborah said, "Well, all right." She stepped inside and was almost knocked down by the incredible, fetid odor of unwashed bodies and worse.

I can't do it! she thought desperately, gasping and standing stock still in the dark room. The only illumination came in from

460

two small windows. Deborah struggled with the overpowering stench, longing for a breath of fresh air, but the boy said, "Back this way."

A door led into another room. When Deborah stepped inside, she was able to see, by the light of one small window, a woman lying in the bed that took up most of the space. She was sick, more so than anyone Deborah had ever seen. Her face was shrunken to a skull, and her eyes were dull and lifeless. The hands were little more than bones, and Deborah could see that the woman was in danger of dying.

"Mrs. Kojak...," she said tentatively. The head on the soiled pillow turned, and a faint light came into the woman's eyes. "I'm Deborah Steele, Mrs. Kojak. I think Noel's told you about me."

The shrunken lips moved, but no sound came. Deborah saw a pitcher on the table and filled a chipped cup with tepid water. "Let me help you," she said and reached down to help the woman raise her head. The terrible smell of human waste smote her, and she closed her eyes, trying not to faint. Then with all the resolution she could muster, she opened them and concentrated on the task of holding the glass steady. When Mrs. Kojak had drunk a few swallows, Deborah lowered the woman's head, saying, "Noel sent word that you were sick, but I didn't know how bad." She put the glass down, then asked, "Are all the children sick?"

"Yes." The single word seemed to take all the strength the sick woman had. After a moment she nodded and whispered, "Thank you for coming."

Deborah had never been at such a loss. What little nursing she had done had been with doctors on hand, not to mention clean linen, medicine, and food. She tried to organize her thoughts, but her brain seemed to be paralyzed. She glanced about her, searching for any available supplies.

There's nothing here to do anything with, she thought, almost in a panic. But there was a stubborn streak in Deborah Steele that came down the generations from her grandfather Stephen—or perhaps from his father, Noah Rocklin, who was, according to every report, a tartar. Now in the gloomy room, with every instinct telling her to get out, she felt that inbred stubbornness begin to rise. It swelled until she said suddenly, "Mrs. Kojak, you've got to have help. Do you have any family coming, or are there any neighbors who could help?"

"No."

Deborah was launched into action by that hopeless monosyllable. "Well, I'll do what I can now; then we'll see. First I'm going to get you all cleaned up."

The simple act of bathing Mrs. Kojak was a monumental task, but Deborah did it. There was no hot water, but she found a small basin and filled it with water from the well in back of the house. For soap there was only the coarse, powerful lye soap used for washing clothing in the big black pot outside the back door. Even so, she managed. She found one gown that was not soiled, and when she had put it on the woman, she looked down, saying, "Now I'm going to fix you something to eat."

The cupboard was bare, she discovered when she moved to the kitchen. She was grateful that she had brought some things from the small store. The two girls in the larger room were in need of bathing, but Deborah thought that food was the number one priority. Finding some small sticks, she managed to get a fire going in the ancient stove and put together a meal of sorts. It was difficult, for there were few cooking vessels. Those that she did find were caked with old food, so that she had to scrub them at the pump. She managed, though, to brew a pot of tea and make a broth out of the stores of rice and tinned chicken.

When it was ready, she said to the two girls who were watching, "I'll feed your mother; then you girls can eat."

She got Mrs. Kojak into a sitting position, and the sick woman ate half a bowl of the broth and two cups of sugared tea. When she was finished and Deborah laid her down, she lifted a hand and caught at Deborah. "God bless you! I've been praying that He'd send someone. Praise His name!"

Suddenly tears rose in Deborah's eyes, and she said, "Try to sleep, Mrs. Kojak. I'll take care of the children."

She left the bedroom and, for the rest of the day, threw herself into a frenzy of work. Mr. Kojak, she discovered by talking with the two girls, had been taken sick first, and he had nearly died. Then as soon as he had recovered and gone back to work, the rest of the family had gone down within three days. "All but Bing," the older girl, Sarah, said. "He left soon as we got sick." Then she cursed her brother with a terrible oath and lay back, bitterness on her face.

Somehow Deborah got them all cleaned and fed, even the two boys. She gathered all the soiled clothing into a pile, the stench of which gagged her when she hauled it out to the backyard. Finding some small sticks, she started a fire under the blackened wash pot, built it up, then filled the pot with water and added lye soap. It took three pots to do enough clothing for the whole family, and she dried them on the single clothesline that ran between a tree and the house. After the clothes were done, she washed the ragged sheets. By that time it was growing dark.

Sarah, the oldest of the girls, seemed to be the fittest of the family. She had come outside to sit on the step and watch while Deborah labored over the washing. When Deborah came inside and was putting the clean bedding down, she followed, watching with wary eyes. As Deborah cooked supper, she asked suddenly, "Who are you?"

"Why, I'm Deborah. A friend of Noel's."

The answer only puzzled the girl, who sat watching silently for a time, then asked, "Why are you doing all this stuff for us?"

Deborah looked up from where she was mixing biscuits. The girl was pale, but she had dark hair and a pair of beautiful dark eyes that made her very attractive. "Because you need help, Sarah." That was no better, Deborah saw, for the girl was still suspicious.

When supper was ready, consisting mostly of biscuits and battered eggs, Deborah sent Sarah to get the two boys to the table. While the four children ate, Deborah took some food to the sick mother. "How do you feel, Mrs. Kojak?" she asked, sitting down and picking up the bowl of broth.

"Better, much better. It feels so good to be clean." She ate the broth—some of it, at least—then sighed. "My stomach's shrunk. But it's so good! How are the children?"

"Sarah seems almost well, and the rest of them feel better."

Anna Kojak watched the young woman with faded eyes as she sipped the tea. She had been almost delirious when the girl had come earlier, but now she felt able to think more clearly. "You don't know what all this means to me, Miss Steele," she said suddenly. "We've been so grateful for the money, but this is different." She hesitated, then said, "You must be a Christian."

"Well, my father's a minister," Deborah said, nodding. "And I promised Noel I'd look after you while he's gone to the army."

"He's such a fine boy!" Anna's eyes filled with pride as she spoke of Noel. "Never a minute's trouble all his life. And such a dedicated Christian boy, too."

"I like him very much. And my brother Pat says Noel's the best soldier in the company."

"You don't tell me! But I'm not surprised. Noel always was one to work at whatever he put his hand to. His writing, for example."

"You taught him to read and write, he said."

"Oh, I taught him his letters, but I mean his story writing. He done all that himself. Never had a soul to teach him."

"Noel writes stories?" Deborah was surprised. "What kind of stories?"

"Stories about people. He didn't tell you? Well, no, he wouldn't, I suppose." She was growing tired and said, "Look over in that drawer. There's a tablet there with some of them. Take them with you."

"All right." Seeing that the woman was growing sleepy, Deborah found the tablet, looked inside to see it filled with the most beautiful handwriting she'd ever seen, then left the room.

As she gathered her things together, the door opened and Will Kojak walked into the room. He had seen the buggy outside and could not guess whose it was. Even he, Deborah saw, was not over his sickness. His eyes were still hollow, and he had lost so much weight that his clothing hung on him. Quickly she said, "Hello, Mr. Kojak. Do you remember me? I'm Stephen Rocklin's granddaughter."

He blinked at her, then looked around the room, startled by the changes he saw. "What you doing here?" he demanded.

"I heard that your family was sick, so I came to help out a little." Deborah knew the man had a frightful temper and said nervously, "I've cooked some supper. Why don't you have some eggs while they're hot? I really have to run."

"It's good, Pa," Grace Kojak spoke up. "It's real good!"

Kojak stared at the food on the table, then back at Deborah. "I don't understand this," he said.

"Sit down and eat," Deborah said, then turned to go. But she paused long enough to say, "I thought I'd come back in the morning and help a little more. Would that be all right with you, Mr. Kojak?"

The face of Will Kojak was a study in bewilderment. He had nearly died with the flu and had gone back to work too soon. When he had left that morning, he had half expected to find some of his family dead when he got home. The sight of the clean sheets, the food on the table, and the improved condition of his family seemed to stun him. Biting his lip, he looked around the room, then back at Deborah. For a long moment he studied her; then finally he spoke.

"I guess. . .I guess it'll be all right."

CHAPTER 6

NOEL

*M*ajor Gideon Rocklin was confronted with two requests the moment he walked into his office on the morning of May 25. The first was actually a command rather than a request, but it was the easiest of the two to handle. Sergeant Benny Thomas rose as the major entered and said at once, "General Scott wants you in his office for a meeting right away, Major."

"Very well." But just as Rocklin turned to leave the room, he almost ran into his niece, who practically ran through the door. "Oh, Uncle Gideon!" she cried breathlessly. "I have to talk to you."

Gid Rocklin looked down at her, admiring her clear eyes and clean-cut features. "Of course, Deborah," he said, "but you'll have to wait. General Scott wants to see me right away."

"Oh, he can wait for a minute," Deborah said, and her remark brought a burst of laughter from Benny Thomas.

Rocklin gave him a withering glance that wiped the smile from his face; then he himself had to smile. "Well, he *is* the ranking general in the United States Army, but I guess I can keep him waiting for a little while." Not having any daughters of his own, Gid had been partial to Deborah all her life. He delighted in buying her the girlish things she liked and was well pleased with the way she had grown up. "What's the matter?"

Deborah said, "It's Noel's family, Uncle Gid. They're all down with the flu. I did what I could for them yesterday, but they need more help. I want you to give him a pass so we can get them through this illness."

"Noel? Who's Noel?" Rocklin could not place the name, but when Deborah mentioned the young man she'd recruited at the rally, he said, "Oh yes, I remember. But I can't give one of the men a pass because his family is sick, Deborah."

It was true—he couldn't. He knew that.

But somehow he did.

Deborah stood there looking up at him, her lips parted with concern, her voice pleading and insistent, and in the end he walked to his desk, scribbled out a note, then shoved it at her, growling, "There it is; now go on, woman! I've got a war to fight."

"Oh, thank you, Uncle Gid!" she cried ecstatically, throwing her arms around him and kissing him soundly.

She ran out of the office, and Rocklin turned to see Sergeant Thomas grinning broadly. "Not one word out of you, Benny!"

"No, sir, only—"

"Only what?"

"Well, sir, I don't blame you a bit! I guess that young woman could get just about anything from any man when she wants to." He sighed, adding, "I just wished she wanted me to do something, Major!"

"Get on with your work, Sergeant!" Rocklin snapped, but he had to smile as he left the room to meet with the general.

He's right about that, Benny is! Gideon thought. But he was somewhat worried about Deborah—had been since she had fallen in love with Denton Rocklin, his cousin Clay's son. He hoped that was over but wondered what she was doing chasing around after a private in his regiment.

He had to shelve that problem, however, as soon as he stepped into the general's office and saw that the president was there with several members of his cabinet. Gid knew something was terribly wrong.

"Come in, Major Rocklin," General Scott said. "Have you heard the news?"

"News? No, sir. I've just come in."

Lincoln looked haggard, and his dark eyes were hooded with grief. "It's a tragedy for all of us, Major. Colonel Ellsworth is dead!"

Rocklin stared at him. "My son is with his command, sir. Was there an engagement with the Rebels?"

"No, nothing like that," Scott grunted. "He was murdered by a secessionist." Scott quickly gave the details—Ellsworth had led his troops into Alexandria and had seen a Confederate flag flying on a flagpole above the Marshall House. It was obviously a challenge, and Ellsworth, followed by some of his men, went inside the hotel, up to the roof, and cut down the flag. Going back down the stairs in a shadowy hallway, the colonel met the proprietor of the inn, a Virginian named James T. Jackson. Jackson had lifted a shotgun and killed Ellsworth, then was himself killed by one of Ellsworth's Zouaves, who first shot the man, then ran a bayonet through him.

Lincoln, Rocklin saw, was hit hard by the news. Ellsworth had been only twenty-four and had won the affection of the president. Now he was dead—the Union's first casualty. Lincoln moved to the window, staring down silently, and there was a moment's silence in the room.

It was broken by William Seward, the secretary of state—he was a tall man with a wild crop of white hair and a terrible temper. "Now we see what sort of men we are fighting!" he said angrily. "Butchers and murderers! Mr. President, surely now it's clear that we must strike the Rebels!" Lincoln didn't move, and Seward continued to argue for a quick blow that would destroy the fledgling Confederate forces. "One quick blow, drive them back to Richmond; then we can put an end to this thing!"

General Scott stared at Seward—Scott was an old man now, sick and obese. He could no longer mount a horse, and just moving from one place to another tired him. . .but he was still an astute soldier and perhaps the best military mind in the world. Now he grunted angrily and stated flatly, "It cannot be done, sir! Our men are untrained, and you cannot move a military force of untrained men."

Seward argued angrily that the Confederates were also untrained, and the air grew thick as the argument raged. Finally Lincoln turned from his place at the window, saying, "We must see to the burial of our brave young Ellsworth." When Seward tried to press him, a flash of irritation showed in the president's eyes. "I know you think you should be the president instead of me, Mr. Seward, but you are not! Now we will bury our dead; then we will proceed with the war."

Lincoln walked out of the room, followed by the cabinet members. As soon as they were gone, Scott slapped his hand on his huge thigh, growling, "Pack of fools! Especially Seward!"

"He's wrong, sir," Rocklin agreed. "We have good men, but they've never been put under fire. Of course, the Rebs haven't either, so it would be a toss-up as to which bunch would run."

"I won't have the future of this country settled by a toss-up, Major! I've put too much into it to allow such a thing." The two men spoke of what must be done, but as they worked, Gid felt depressed and thought to himself, *We can do all the planning we want, but it'll be Horace Greeley and his newspaper that decide when we'll fight. Him and the politicians like Seward!*

Noel had slipped out of his blankets early, earning a muffled curse from Manny Zale as he stumbled around getting dressed. The round Sibley tent was packed with men. Supported by an upright center pole, its fifteen occupants slept with their feet toward the center and their heads near the edge, like the spokes of a wagon wheel. The sky was still black, and Noel had to walk carefully to avoid falling over tent stakes as he made his way to the parade ground. It was a vast ghostly plain at this hour, but one of the few places where a man could be sure of solitude. After spending so many miserable hours drilling there, the men hated the sight of it.

It was here that Noel came every morning to think and pray. He had found it almost impossible to find any quiet place other than this, for the army was a noisy organization. Now the best times of his day were these cobwebby times of the early morning, and he walked slowly around the field, enjoying the silence. He prayed and thought, remembering his family and his new friends in the company. There were only two other Christians in his platoon, and they were not too strong. The rest of the group were not bad fellows, Noel believed, just careless and open to temptation. He prayed for the men he knew, and then he gave a special prayer for his mother, who must bear the whole load of the family. He also prayed for his father, who did not know God.

Finally he heard the brassy sound of reveille and went at once

471

back to the camp. The corporals were busy waking up the men, and soon the camp was a beehive of activity. Some commanders allowed their men to answer roll call in any sort of dress, but Colonel Bradford insisted that his men turn out in full dress. Noel joined the sleepy soldiers as Cobb, the first sergeant of A Company, called the roll. Then the men were allowed to return to their tent for thirty minutes. Next came breakfast call, followed by sick call.

At eight o'clock the musicians sounded the call for guard mounting, at which the first sergeant of each company turned out his detail for the next twenty-four hours. Usually that meant digging latrines or chopping wood, but Cobb gave his men a careful look, saying, "All right, this morning you'll fall in at the firing range for target practice."

A cheer went up, and Jim Freeman exclaimed, "About time we got to do some shooting, ain't it, Noel? I joined up to shoot Rebs, not to dig latrines!" Jim, a towheaded, happy-go-lucky young man of eighteen, was usually in trouble for minor infractions such as failing to make his bed. He was a Christian, but not a very dedicated one. Now he chattered like a magpie as the platoon trudged toward the rifle pits. His comments got on Manny Zale's nerves.

"Shut your face, Freeman!" Zale growled. His temper, bad at the best of times, was like a land mine in the morning. He scarcely spoke before noon, unless it was to curse anyone who got in his way. Jim gave Noel a baleful look, then dropped his head to stare at the ground.

It took some time to issue the weapons, but as soon as the men had them, Cobb said, "All right, listen to me. The weapon you're holding is a Springfield rifled musket. It weighs nine and three-quarter pounds, including the bayonet, and fires a .58

slug. By the time I get through with you, you'll be able to get off three shots a minute. Right now, we're going to find out who can shoot."

He took a few minutes to show the men how to load the muskets, then said, "All right, there's the target." He pointed to a log barricade some distance away. A white target about one foot square was affixed to the barricade. Cobb said, "I'll take the first shot." Lifting his rifle, he got off his shot, which clipped the outside edge of the target. "All right, who's next?"

All the men clamored for the chance to shoot, and Cobb said, "Armstrong, take a shot." Armstrong, a short, trim man with a lean jaw, aimed carefully—and missed the whole barricade! A howl of derision went up, and Armstrong stepped back with a red face.

Noel stood back as the others shot, keenly interested in the affair. He had never even held a gun in his hand and was certain that he'd do no better than Tate Armstrong. Several of the men did very well; Manny Zale put his bullet within two inches of dead center. He grinned wolfishly at the others, boasting, "That's the way to plug the Rebs!"

Finally Cobb said, "All right, Kojak, take your shot."

As Noel stepped forward, Zale said, "Why, it won't do no good to let the preacher shoot, Sergeant! He's too good a Christian to kill anybody. Ain't that so, Preacher?"

Cobb said irritably, "Shut up, Manny. Now just squeeze that trigger easy, Kojak."

Feeling very awkward with the eyes of the squad on him, Noel stepped forward and lifted the musket. It was heavier than he had thought, but years of hard work in the foundry had given him a set of formidable hands and forearms. He leveled the piece and held it true on the target. Somehow, though he had never held a rifle, it felt right. He squeezed the trigger, taking the kick of the piece with his shoulder.

"Dead center!" Cobb yelped. He turned to stare at Noel with wide eyes. "You done a lot of shooting, Kojak?"

"No. That was the first time I ever shot a gun."

"Beginner's luck!" Zale snorted.

"We'll see," Cobb said. "Load up and take another shot, Kojak." He watched carefully as Noel loaded the musket. Cobb was aware that his men would, on the whole, be poor shots. He needed a few good men to serve as sharpshooters. Zale was a good shot but a bad soldier. Oh, he was plenty tough, but he was always truculent and in fights.

One thing was certain—they were heading for some serious battles. Cobb and the captain had been concerned about leadership in the ranks. Now, as Noel brought his musket to bear, the first sergeant found himself hoping the young man's shot hadn't been a fluke. Kojak was a model soldier in some respects—always ready to do whatever the sergeant ordered, took good care of his equipment, and got along with the men. He was a Christian, but Cobb was willing to put up with that if he could bring some sort of steadiness to the company.

Noel took his second shot, and this time the slug hit not one inch away from the other. "Hey, that's shootin'!" Jim Freeman yelped, and Sergeant Cobb said with satisfaction, "Good shot, Kojak. You can give the rest of the boys some pointers."

Noel shifted uncomfortably. "I'll have to learn a lot more than I know now before I can do that, Sergeant Cobb." He hated being the center of attention and was glad when practice went on. He got only one more shot, though, for Sergeant Locke from regimental headquarters came up to give a note to Cobb. The sergeant studied it, then called out, "Kojak—fall out of rifle practice." When Noel looked at him in confusion, Cobb held up the note. "Go by the adjutant's and pick up a pass. You got three days' leave."

As Noel left in a daze, Manny Zale glared after him. "What's he get a leave for? He ain't done no more than the rest of us."

"Why don't you go take that up with Major Rocklin, Manny?" Cobb said with a grin. "If you don't like his answer, dress him down." Then he turned to the squad, booming out, "Get that rifle out of the dirt, Freeman!"

Noel hurried to his tent, put on his uniform, then presented himself at regimental headquarters, where a lieutenant gave him a pass, saying sourly, "You'd better be back right on time, Kojak!"

"Yes, sir!" Noel saluted and left the area hurriedly. It was seven miles from the camp to the city, but he managed to catch a ride with a civilian teamster who'd just delivered a wagonload of supplies to the quartermaster.

"Think you boys will be movin' out to stomp the Rebs pretty soon?" the driver asked. He was a cheerful middle-aged man with huge hands that held the reins expertly.

"Guess so," Noel said, then sat there listening for the rest of the trip as the teamster outlined the best strategy for overcoming the Confederacy. When they got to the outskirts of Washington and Noel stepped off, he said, "Git a few o' them Rebs for me, sodjer!"

Noel grinned and thanked the man, then turned to make his way through Negro Hill. As he passed through the area, he tried again to find some explanation for his leave, but nothing came to him.

Passing into the Swampoodle neighborhood, he was greeted several times by acquaintances. More than once he had to stop and give a brief greeting to those who insisted on speaking to him, but finally he arrived at his house. He saw at once the horse and buggy drawn up outside. *Must be the doctor*, he thought, then froze for a moment when he realized it might be the undertaker. Many people had died of the flu, and fear fluttered through him as he hurried forward to enter the house.

As he moved down the walk, the door opened, and a large black woman with a red bandanna around her head came out of the house, pausing to stare at him. She stopped abruptly, staring at him with a pair of careful brown eyes. "What you want?" she asked directly.

"Why—I live here," Noel said, faltering. Then he asked inanely, "Is somebody dead?"

"Daid! I reckon not!" The black face gave him a scornful look. "Whut fo' you talk lak dat?"

At that moment the door opened again, and Noel was astonished to see Deborah Rocklin come sailing out of the house. "Noel!" she cried out, coming to meet him. "I've been waiting for you forever! Now come on and see your mother!"

Noel felt her hands on his as she greeted him, but there was a sense of unreality as he passed through the front door. Deborah was wearing a simple brown dress with a white collar, and the sunlight made her hair seem more golden than it really was. Her eyes were sparkling as she pulled him inside, where he got another shock.

The room he knew so well was gone—or rather, transformed! There was nothing really new in it, except for some dishes he'd never seen before on the shelves and on the table, but it was spotlessly clean. The floor was whitewashed and the walls were clean. The pots and pans were hung neatly on hooks instead of being piled haphazardly on the table. Most striking of all were the yellow curtains that framed the windows.

He stopped, looking around the room, a startled expression on his face. Then he saw Grace and Sarah sitting on a bed with a quilted coverlet on it. "Hi, Noel!" Grace said. "Deborah said you'd come today." Noel went to her, noting how thin she was, but she said at once, "I've been real sick, but I'm fine now!"

He touched her hair, which was, he noted, clean and brushed. Deborah pulled at him impatiently. "You can talk to Grace and Sarah later." She pulled him into the bedroom, and he saw that the same magic had touched his parents' room. It was his mother, though, who caught his eye. She was sitting in bed and was dressed in a white gown, her hair neatly done.

"Noel!" She spoke to him, and he went to her at once, bending over to kiss her. She clung to him, and he felt the thinness of her trembling body. "Are you all right, son?"

"I'm fine," he said, then straightened up. He turned to look at Deborah, who was watching with a smile from the doorway. "I've been wondering how I got a leave. But I guess I know now."

"She's done everything, Noel!" Anna Kojak said, her eyes fixed on Deborah. "We were about gone. I think I would have died if she hadn't come."

Noel stared at the girl who looked so unlikely to be in such a place as this poor shack. She flushed at his look, then shook her head. "Oh, nonsense! You'd have been fine, Anna!" Then she turned and left the room, saying, "You two visit. Delilah and I have work to do."

Noel sat down beside his mother. "Tell me," he said, and for the next half hour Anna told him how Deborah had arrived and thrown herself into the battle to save them.

"She worked like I never knew a woman of her class could work, Noel! You know how dirty it is taking care of sick people, but she done it all. And the next day she brought a doctor and her family servant, Delilah. And that woman is a saint! She's stayed here and nursed us all night and day. Them women have took care of us like we was their own kin, Noel!"

Noel sat there, his mind numb. He could not grasp what had happened, for it was something outside of his experience. Finally he saw that his mother was getting sleepy. "I'm better, son, but I sleep like a kitten—all the time taking little naps."

She dropped off to sleep, and Noel looked down at her, reaching out to replace a strand of her hair that had come loose. Then he turned and left the room. "Go see your brothers," Deborah commanded from where she sat with Delilah shelling peas. For the next hour Noel talked with his brothers and sisters, finding them all weak but obviously on the mend. He didn't have to pry information out of them about their rescuer, for they could talk of little else.

"She went out and got us all new stuff to sleep in, Noel," Joel piped up, pointing at a red nightshirt with pride. "I told her we just slept in whatever we had, and she went right out and come back with new clothes!"

Finally he went to where the two women were cooking on the ancient stove, saying, "Anything I can do?"

"Why, yes, Noel," Deborah said. "I've got to go buy a few things. You can drive that cantankerous mare of mine and then carry my things to the buggy."

He followed her outside, helped her in, then got in beside her and took the reins. "Go to the general store first," she commanded, and he turned the horse back toward the business district. On the way, she spoke lightly and easily of his family.

"What about Bing, my brother?" he asked.

Deborah hesitated, then said, "He came to the house once. But he's staying with somebody downtown." When he didn't respond, she said, "I had some difficulty with him, Noel. You might as well hear it from me. I thought he behaved badly, leaving the family alone, and I told him so."

"You told Bing that?"

"Yes, and he told me I was a meddlesome woman, and then he—"

She broke off abruptly, and when Noel looked at her, he saw that her face was flushed. "Well, he tried to kiss me—and I hit him with a stick of stove wood!" she finished defiantly.

Noel laughed out loud. "Good for you, Miss Steele! I hope you laid him out!"

"Oh no, nothing like that. It made him so mad he went off, cursing me."

"I'll talk to Bing." Noel sat there silently, then finally said, "Miss Steele, it's—hard for me to say what I feel."

"Oh, Noel, I hate thank-you speeches!" Deborah turned to face him, adding, "You swore an oath to serve your country, didn't you? Well, I made you a promise that I'd help your family while you were doing that. And that's what I've done."

Noel struggled with the things that were inside him, but saw that she was speaking the truth. "All right, I won't say any more, Miss Steele—"

"Noel, my name is Deborah. I think we're friends enough for first names."

They spent more time than was necessary buying the things she'd come for. She made him tell her all about his experiences, and to his amazement he was talking more than he ever had in his life. He found himself telling her about the rifle practice, about his difficulties with Manny Zale, and about his efforts to keep Jim Freeman out of trouble. He was amazed when they arrived at the house. Helping Deborah down, he shook his head, saying ruefully, "Gosh, I don't think I ever talked so much in my whole life!"

"It's been fun, Noel," Deborah said. "I guess all of us wonder what it's really like, being in the army." A thought came to her, and she said, "Before I leave, there's something I want to talk to you about. But not now. You get some wood chopped, and I'll see how Delilah's doing with the cooking."

It was a fine day for Noel. He chopped enough wood to last a week, then spent hours with his brothers and sisters, telling them about the army. Finally his father came home, and Noel was shocked to see how thin and pale he was. "Glad to see you, Pa," he said, going to meet him as he came down the walk. "You've had a hard time."

Will Kojak stared at his son, taking in the neat blue uniform, the tanned face, then nodded. "It ain't been no picnic." He paused, trying to think of some way to ask what had been on his mind for days. Finally he said, "That woman who's been comin' around here—old Rocklin's granddaughter? What's she doin' it all for? Taking care of your ma and the kids and buyin' no end of stuff?"

"Why, she just wants to help. She's done a lot, hasn't she?"

Kojak stared at the ground. He was a rough man, in form and in manners. The sickness had been his first illness, and he had been frightened by it. Always before he had been strong enough to meet whatever came, but the flu had nearly killed him. Now he was feeling his own mortality, and the appearance of the Rocklin girl had confused him greatly. His was not a world that was filled with people who were willing to give. It was a dog-eat-dog existence, and he could not get the girl out of his mind. Now he looked up and asked abruptly, "She want to marry you?"

"Marry me!" Noel stared at his father, shocked at the suggestion. "Land no, Pa! She's a fine lady. That's crazy!"

"I guess so." Kojak shook his head wearily. "She had a row of some kind with Bing. He says she's no good."

"Well, you know Bing, Pa. Come on in. Supper's on the table."

Kojak said little at the table as Delilah moved around efficiently, keeping all the plates full. He watched her cautiously but said nothing. Finally, when the meal was over and Delilah had washed the dishes, it was growing dark.

"I'll drive you part of the way," Noel said. "This is a rough neighborhood."

"All right," Deborah said. "Delilah, I think this is the last night you'll have to stay. I'll take you back home tomorrow."

The night was warm, and Noel insisted on driving Deborah all the way through the worst district. She protested that it was too far for him to walk home, but he only laughed at her. The streets were filled with people out for late walks, but by the time he reached the better neighborhoods and pulled up, the stars were faintly shining.

"Don't get out, Noel," Deborah said. "I want to talk to you about your writing."

"My what?"

"Your stories." Deborah grew serious, her lips firm and her eyes glinting. "Your mother gave me some of them. I hope you don't mind."

"Why, no, Deborah—but they're just stuff I made up for my own pleasure. Can't think why they'd interest anyone else."

Deborah had not been anxious to read the stories. She had not, as a matter of fact, touched the tablets for several days after she had taken them from the drawer. But once Delilah had come and the work was done, she found time one afternoon and took out the tablet, thinking to scan it. She well knew that she would have to comment to Anna on it and wanted to be able to say, "That's nice," or something that would please the woman.

But it had not happened like that. She had begun to read rather carelessly, admiring the fine penmanship but not at all excited about reading what she assumed would be a crude type of amateur fiction. Deborah loved literature and had at one time considered becoming a writer herself, but she quickly discovered that it was one thing to appreciate good writing and quite another to produce it. She was honest enough to see that she did not have the gift and had resigned herself to reading. She read everything, but fiction was her first love, and as she began to read the story titled "No Hope for Emily," she was rather blasé about it.

Almost at once she became aware that this was not an ordinary composition. There was a roughness about it, to be sure. Some misspelled words and some awkwardness of sentence structure. But there was something else that seized her at once.

The story was about a sixteen-year-old girl named Emily who lived in the Swampoodle district. The plot was simple enough: A young girl longed to find a husband and have a good home. But there was such a graphic quality in the description that Deborah entered into the story fully. Noel had caught the essence of the poverty and hardship Deborah had seen during her days in the district. He had brought to life the coarse food, the barren houses, the dirt that never got cleaned up, the grinding labor that wore men and women out by the time they were barely out of their teens. All of this was there, in a simple prose that fixed everything on the page.

And the girl—Emily—was real. Deborah somehow sensed that Noel had known her and had liked her. She was no creature of fiction, for by the time Deborah finished the story, tears were in her eyes. The girl had struggled to keep herself pure, but the world she lived in had been inexorable. She had turned bad, going through the worst of her world, ending her own life in despair at the age of nineteen.

Deborah had read all the stories and now knew that Noel was the most gifted writer she'd ever met.

"Noel, you don't know what you have," she now said earnestly. "I'm no expert, but I've read a lot. God has given you a great gift."

Noel stared at her, for such a thing had never entered his head. "Why, Deborah, you're just being kind. I just write down stories that are in my head. I mean, I just write about things I've seen."

"That's what makes you different," Deborah insisted. "People can learn to write, up to a point. They can learn the techniques, how to make chapters and things like that. But most of us can't put any life into the things we write. Did you know your Emily?"

"Yes. She lived two houses down from us. I—liked her a lot, Deborah. Made me feel so bad when she went the way she did."

"And when you put what you felt in your story, it made me feel the same way!" Deborah said. "That's what great literature is, Noel. Great writers like Dickens and Cooper, they make us *feel*."

Noel was struck by her remark. "You know, Deborah, I never thought of it until right this minute," he said thoughtfully, his face broken into sharp planes where the yellow glow of a streetlight reflected on it. "But the times I seem to be most alive are when I'm writing about people." Then he laughed shortly, adding, "But I could never be a real writer."

"You *are* a real writer, Noel!" Deborah insisted sharply. In her desire to get through to him, she took his arm and held it tightly. She had the feeling that somehow she was responsible for the young man. He had a talent that the world needed and might never do a thing with it unless someone helped him develop it. "What you've done proves it," she insisted. "You didn't write to make money or to see your name in print. You write because it's what's in you, because you want to share what you think and feel with others."

"Well, I guess the others are Ma and you. Nobody else has seen them."

"But they should see them, Noel." Taking a deep breath, she paused, then said, "Noel, I've been thinking a lot about this. You're going to be a soldier. My uncle thinks this will be a long war, a terrible war. Who's going to write about it, to let the world see it as it really is?"

"Why, the writers, I guess."

"That's right—and where will they be? Cooped up in their study in Boston! They'll never hear a cannon fire or hear a young man gasping his last breath on earth, will they? But you will, Noel! You've got to write about it!"

Noel was stunned by Deborah's intensity. He sat there in disbelief, then finally shook his head. "Even if I could write it, Deborah, who would read it? You have to be somebody big to get a book published. Even I know that!"

Deborah shook his arm, saying fiercely, "Noel Kojak, you are somebody! You're a soldier in the United States Army! You're a young man with a great talent! Don't ever let me hear you say you're a nobody, you hear me!"

Suddenly Noel smiled. "I hear you all right, Deborah—and I guess everybody else on this side of Washington hears you, too. Do you know you're shouting at me?"

"Well, I don't care!" Deborah lowered her voice, then sat there quietly. She had been waiting for the chance to talk with Noel ever since reading the stories, and now she feared she had done it badly. Finally she said, "I know all this is new to you, Noel, but you've got to let me help you. Would you let me take some of your stories to a man who can help? His name is Langdon Devoe. He's a publisher right here in Washington."

"Why, sure, Deborah," Noel said. "What kind of books does he print?"

"Oh, all kinds. He did a lot of publishing for the movement, the abolitionist movement, I mean. He likes me and he knows good writing when he sees it. I'll see him as quick as I can, but you have to promise me something."

Noel stared at her in the glimmering darkness. "I've been wishing there was something I could do for you, Deborah."

She looked at him sharply, hearing something in his voice that hadn't been there before. "Well, Noel, this is for both of us. You write all the time from now on. I know you'll be busy and it'll be hard. But make yourself do it. Write about the drills, the men in your company. The bad ones and the good ones. And make it honest. Don't try to make it literary. There'll be lots of people writing that sort of thing." She thought hard, then added, "Write it like the one about Emily."

"I'll do it," Noel said at once.

She put her hand out, and he took it readily. "It's a bargain, then," Deborah said. "You do the writing, and I'll do the rest."

He found her hand soft and somehow enticing—and he

was suddenly totally aware of the beauty of the girl who sat beside him. He became so engrossed with admiring the smooth loveliness of her cheeks and the lustrous darkness of her eyes that he unconsciously held on to her hand.

Deborah, too, was suddenly aware of Noel for the first time as a young man who admired her, and she did not know what to do. She had, at first, thought of him only as an object of pity. Now as she looked into his face, she was aware that this was an unusual young man. There was a clean strength in his even features, in the sweeping jawline that denoted determination and the steady gray eyes that were warm and honest. There was, she understood, no trickery in this young man, and she suddenly felt very close to him.

"I–I'm glad we're going to be good friends, Noel," she said, and when he released her hand, she smiled at him. "I'll see you in the morning."

He got down and looked up at her. "It sure has been a strange time for me, Deborah. When I got up this morning, I never imagined I'd be here with you tonight. I—I know you said not to mention it, but I got to thank you for all you've done for my family." He said no more, but she saw the gratitude in his eyes. Then he ducked his head, and when he lifted it, he grinned. "About me being a writer, I got to say that I'm doing it because of you. Good night, Deborah!"

"Good night, Noel."

He turned and disappeared into the night, but as Deborah Steele watched him go, she had a premonition. She had never had one before, but as she sat there in the buggy, something deep within her seemed to tell her that Noel Kojak would play a big part in her life. It was very real, and as she drove homeward, the impression grew stronger. Finally she looked up into the stars, wondering what it all could mean. But the stars had no answer. They were impressive enough, winking like diamonds in the deep velvet sky, but they had nothing to say.

"We'll see," she said to the mare, who perked her ears, nickered twice, then picked up her hooves and started down the dusty road at a fast pace.

PART TWO

Richmond

❧

CHAPTER 7

A SMALL ISLAND

The pearly morning light that spilled over the distant treetops pleased Clay Rocklin. He had risen before dawn, saddled his gray gelding, and made his way to the fields where he now sat. The sight of the broad fields that made up Gracefield, his plantation, always filled him with pleasure. Sitting hipshot in the saddle, he achieved a moment's stillness that was uncharacteristic of him.

He was a man of loose, rough, durable parts. Like a machine intended for hard usage, he had no fineness and little smoothness about him. He was one of the Black Rocklins, those of raven hair, olive skin, and dark eyes. His long mouth was expressive when he smiled, and he had the darkest of eyes, sharp and clear.

All of this made a face that, in repose, reflected the mixed elements of sadness and rash temper. A scar shaped like a fishhook was at the left corner of his mouth, the relic of a fistfight he'd had when he was younger and eager to indulge in action. Now, at forty-one, he had better control of himself.

Clay could only remain still for so long, and with an impulsive tug at the reins, he touched the gray with his heels.

The large animal responded by throwing himself into an enthusiastic gallop and following the edge of the mile-long field. The soft warmth of May had bathed Virginia, and by the time Clay had circled the edge of the field and made his way through a first-growth thicket of towering water oak, he was beginning to feel the heat. He pulled King to a halt at the edge of a sea of emerald sorghum and removed his light jacket, stuffing it into a saddlebag. Clay's deep chest swelled against the thin white cotton shirt, and his considerable physical strength, gained through years at sea, was evident in his corded wrists and square, powerful hands.

Once again he paused, pleased by the fields. It had been his idea to plant sorghum. His father, Thomas, was adamantly certain that planting anything except cotton was a waste of good land. Clay was equally certain that planting only cotton was a sure way to ruin. He had seen the mountains of cotton bales on the docks and was sure the market was headed for a glut. Already the rumor was rife that the new president of the Confederacy favored an embargo against Britain. The hope was that the refusal to send cotton to England would draw the British into giving aid to the new nation being birthed in the South.

When Clay had first heard his brother-in-law Brad Franklin state this, he had stared at the man, saying, "Brad, we're not the only country that grows cotton. Besides, England's got a good supply in their warehouses. What we'd better do is ship every bale we've got to England right now, because you can bet the first thing the Federals will do is blockade our coasts. Then what will you do with your cotton...sell it to the Yankees?"

Brad had only laughed at him, saying, "Cotton is king, Clay. You'll see!"

Ever since planting had begun, Clay had carried on the

same battle with his father, the older man resisting every innovation his son tried to make. Clay had kept his temper for the most part, for he had no desire to anger his father. Actually, Gracefield belonged to Clay more than to Thomas Rocklin. Clay had returned two years ago after a long exile from his family, just in time to save the great plantation from financial ruin. It had been difficult for him to return.

The reason was perhaps natural, for Clay had abandoned his wife and children after a wild and misspent youth, leaving them at Gracefield to be provided for. As he sat now atop his horse and watched the sea of green shoots waving in the breeze, he thought of his youthful, rash love for Melanie Benton, who was now married to his cousin Gideon. Quickly he shook that off, for it was painful to think how he had allowed his raw passions for the beautiful young girl to drive him into ruin— and into an imprudent marriage to a woman he did not love. Saving Gracefield meant coming back to face all that he had run from. . .and that had been most difficult indeed.

Clay also struggled with guilt over the fact that he had made his small fortune in a dirty business: slave running. And it was that ill-made fortune that he had used to reestablish the plantation. Even now, two years after he had sold his share of the ship, he awoke at night crying out in fear and disgust at the thought of the terrible suffering the black men and women— and children—had undergone in the passage from Africa to the States. He still felt dirty and unclean at times. Though he knew he was forgiven by God, he wondered if the shame he felt would ever go away completely.

As the sun rose over the oaks surrounding the fields, Clay turned King's head north and made his way slowly around the field. He was in no rush to get home for breakfast, so he let the horse pick his way slowly through fields still damp with dew. He passed a line of slaves, led by Highboy, headed for the fields. Highboy greeted him cheerfully as always: "Hi, Marse Clay!"

"Hello, Highboy. Better take care of that twenty acres over by the pond today." Highboy gave him an indignant look, whereupon Clay smiled suddenly, his teeth making a white slash across his tanned face. "But you know that better than I do," he said, knowing it to be true. The tall son of Box and Carrie knew every blade of grass on the Gracefield earth. "See you later, Highboy," Clay said, touching his heels to the horse. The gray responded at once, breaking into an easy run. Clay let him go, enjoying the motion of the animal. As they covered the ground, the man's eyes moved constantly over the fields, missing nothing.

Finally he rounded a cornfield and took a barely discernible trail through a small forest of loblolly pine, pulling the horse to a walk as he emerged into the wide clearing where the Rocklin mansion sat. The sight of the house always stirred Clay; the long years of alienation at sea had whetted his love for the place. Smoke was rising from the kitchen chimney, and though he knew that Dorrie would have breakfast waiting, Clay sat there for a moment, savoring the silence and peace of the morning.

Gracefield had been built by an Englishman who had incorporated in his creation more than a few of the characteristics of the fine homes of England. The house was an imposing Greek Revival plantation home, and it glittered white in the morning sun as Clay sat there admiring it. It was a two-story house with a steep roof adorned by three gables on each side. The most striking feature was the line of rising smooth columns, which ran across the front and down both sides, enclosing the structure within the imposing white shafts. The ground behind the house held the outbuildings. Large grape arbors flanked the main house on both sides. The front lawn was a flat carpet of rich green broken by a sweeping U-shaped driveway filled with oyster shells.

As Clay moved out of the grove and toward the house, he thought suddenly how similar Gracefield was to an island. The plantation, surrounded by others like it—as well as by hills, fields, and streams—was almost self-sustaining. Almost all the food the Rocklins ate was grown in their own fields, and up until recently, communication with the outside world had been tenuous. Riding down the sweeping driveway, Clay remembered how as a boy he had thought that Gracefield was all the world. Longingly he thought, *I wish it was! There are worse things than being marooned on a desert island.*

He dismounted and tossed the reins to Moses, Dorrie and Zander's oldest son. The boy grinned at him, saying, "You better git in to brekfuss, Marse Clay, 'fore Dorrie have her a fit."

Clay grinned at Moses. Dorrie had been a house slave at Gracefield since she was six and was more or less the general of the mansion, second only to Susanna, Clay's mother, in power and authority. And she did not look with favor on anyone who flaunted her well-orchestrated schedules, even "Master Clay," who had always been a favorite with the dark woman.

Clay fished in his pocket and found a piece of hard candy wrapped in paper. Tossing it to the boy, he said, "Walk King for me, Moses, then let him graze in the meadow." He left the boy sucking ecstatically on the candy and entered the house by the front door. Two of the house slaves, both young girls, were polishing the heart-pine floor, and he spoke to them as he passed by the massive stairway that led to the second floor. The family was gathered in the dining room, already eating as he entered.

"Whar you been?" Dorrie demanded, staring at him out of a pair of sharp brown eyes. "You sit down and eat 'fore them eggs freeze!"

"Sorry, Dorrie," Clay said contritely, taking his place across from his mother, just to the right of his father, who sat at the head of the table. "Good morning," he said, taking the plate of eggs his mother handed him. "Sorry to be late." He filled his plate with grits, eggs, ham, and biscuits, then said, "The sorghum looks good. We'll be eating our own syrup next fall."

"How do you make it, Father?" It was typical that David would ask, for he was the one of Clay's sons with the sort of mind that had to know things. Dent, his twin, had never shown any interest in the workings of the plantation, nor had Lowell, the youngest boy. David, however, had put his nose into a book as soon as he could read and had poked into every nook and cranny of the place, insatiably curious about everything. At nineteen, he was the best student in his college, and Clay had to smile as he answered, "Don't know, David. We'll have to go over to the Payson place. They've got a sorghum mill over there. I guess you can draw a plan of the thing."

"Yes, sir." David nodded, brightening at once. "Then Box and me will make it."

"Don't see any need of such a thing, Clay." Thomas Rocklin was shoving his food around on his plate. Clay glanced at his father and noted how ill he looked as he added, "We don't eat much of the stuff, and we can buy what we need from Payson. We could get five bales of cotton off that land."

"Why, Grandfather," Rena said, "We can't pour cotton over our pancakes!" She was the only daughter of Clay and Ellen and, at the age of fifteen, was caught in that awkward period between childhood and womanhood. She had deep blue eyes, dark brown hair, and a sweet expression.

Thomas stared at her, snorted, and said almost harshly, "You can't make cloth out of sorghum, either, miss! And England wants cotton, not syrup!"

Clay said quickly, "We'll have a good cotton crop, sir. But the land needs a rest from too much cotton."

Denton put his fork down with a violent gesture. He was wearing his new uniform of ash gray with polished leather and straps. "This is no time to worry about such things. We're in a war!" Denton and David were identical twins, but few people ever mistook one for the other. Both were fine-looking young men, but there was a fiery manner about Dent that his brother lacked. Some of that raw impatience came out now as Dent stared across the table at his father. "When we've whipped the Yankees, it'll be time to worry about rotating crops."

"Right, my boy!" Thomas Rocklin gave an approving thump to the table. He was a tall, thin shape at the table, and as his wife, Susanna, looked at him, she thought how much he had been like Denton as a young man—rash and impulsive. He had lost that ramrod-straight posture of his youth and was now bent. His once-black hair was tinged with silver, and his shoulders were thin. Yet despite the ill health that had plagued him for the last year, he was still handsome. For all his good looks and powerful personality, though, Thomas Rocklin had been a poor husband. But Susanna had remained true to him.

Susanna Rocklin was the driving force of Gracefield, inside the house at least. She was an attractive woman of sixty, her auburn hair darker than when she was younger, but still glossy and full. She had a pair of even, greenish eyes, which were now fixed on Clay.

He's done so well since he came back! she thought. But it would not do to say so in front of Thomas, for her husband still harbored a black streak of anger toward his son. He had never forgiven Clay for what he felt was rank disloyalty to the Rocklin family. His feelings had smoldered over the years, and when Clay had finally returned, it had taken much persuasion from Susanna to get him to let Clay stay.

Suddenly Susanna looked at Ellen, Clay's wife, and a startling thought flashed across her mind as she studied the woman's face: *She hates Clay. She never loved him—but now it's worse.*

As if she had sensed Susanna's thoughts, Ellen Rocklin turned and looked across the table at her mother-in-law. At nineteen Ellen had been a lush beauty, but there had been something predatory about her even then. It had come as a shock to Thomas and Susanna when Clay had brought her home from Washington to announce their engagement. Something had happened there, Susanna had always known, but neither Clay nor Ellen ever spoke of it. One thing Susanna knew for certain—it had something to do with Melanie Rocklin.

Susanna remembered how Clay had been wildly in love with Melanie and how devastated he was when Melanie had chosen Gideon, the son of Stephen Rocklin, Thomas's older brother. Somehow, in the midst of that devastation, Clay and Ellen had come together. Susanna had worried that the marriage was a mistake...and there was little even now, so many years later, to prove that worry wrong.

Clay and Ellen's marriage had been stormy enough before Clay had abandoned them all. Now that he was back, it was different. Not better, just different. Clay did not even stay in the big house but kept his quarters in the summerhouse. Ellen stayed in Richmond most of the time, coming back to Gracefield when her funds ran low. They shared none of the closeness of man and wife, as Susanna—and everyone else—knew.

"Clay, I need to talk to you," Ellen said, breaking into Susanna's train of thought. Susanna watched as the woman rose and left the table. Clay, after giving his wife a strange look, rose and followed her. She went into the library, then turned at once and said, "Clay, I've got to have some money."

Clay gave her an even look but shook his head firmly. "There isn't any right now, Ellen. I told you when I gave you your allowance it would have to do you."

She stared at him, the anger in her eyes plain to see. "You've got to give it to me!" She was forty now and still attractive. There was a certain quality in her lips and figure that caught men's attention. She had begun to use too much makeup and wore clothes that were too young for her, yet men were drawn to her. She had worked hard keeping her figure and her reputation, though the latter was more difficult. Still, she had entrance into some of Virginia's plushest homes.

But nothing could change the one overriding factor in her life: her hatred of her husband. That hatred was based on two things, two things for which she had never forgiven Clay—for loving Melanie Benton and for abandoning her. She always insisted that it was his abandonment of the children that was the basis of her anger, but it was not; Ellen was a woman who had to possess things, and Clay had refused to let her own him. She knew that his flight was as much from her as from his hopeless love for his cousin's wife.

"You love to make me beg, don't you, Clay!" she cried, her voice rising. "If it were your precious Melanie, you'd hand out the money fast enough!"

Clay stood there, his heart cold and barren as polar ice.

Whatever he had felt for Ellen had died long ago. She had tricked him into marriage, and it had been wrong from the start. He had hoped that the children would make it bearable, but finally he had gone over the edge and fled his home. Now he half wished that he had never returned, but he kept his voice even as he replied, "Ellen, that's absurd and you know it. Melanie's nothing to me but a fine friend. As for the money, I've told you the truth. Things are tight. . .and they're going to get tighter. All we have to sell is cotton, and as you've probably heard, it's going to be impossible to sell cotton if Davis and the Congress go through with their plan to cut off sales to England."

She glared at him, then raged as he stood there regarding her. Finally he said, "Your hotel bill is paid. If you've spent the rest of your money, you'll have to stay here—or eat with your friends in Richmond."

Instantly she laughed, her lips contorted. "You'd like to know who takes me out to dinner, wouldn't you?"

"No, I wouldn't." Clay turned and walked away, going out the front door, sickened by his brief interview with Ellen. He knew that she hated him. That had become clearer than ever after an incident that had occurred months earlier. When he had first returned, Ellen had slashed at him, warning him that he would never be a husband to her. Clay had expected that, and it relieved him greatly. He did not want anything from his wife, especially physical intimacy. But when Ellen saw that he seemed uninterested, she paradoxically began to try to gain his attention. Finally she had come to the summerhouse late one night to see him alone. When Clay had rejected her, she had cursed him like a madwoman. From that time, she had made little or no effort to hide her hatred, and Clay had been forced to endure her tirades as best he could.

Clay headed for the summerhouse. It was a small structure, only two rooms, but Clay had made himself a cozy bachelor's quarters out of it. Decay had been at it, but he had taken pleasure in working hard with the help of Highboy and a few others to make it into a very attractive place. Now as he walked down the narrow lane that led to it and entered the sequestered area under tall pines where the house rested on a slight rise, he felt a sense of despair.

Entering the house, he sat down and stared blankly at the floor for a long time. Thinking of the problems that loomed ahead for him, he felt drained and tired. He thought of the war that was on the horizon. No battles had been fought since Fort Sumter had fallen, but they would come. There were too many fire-eaters in the Southern camp, and the people of the North were bound and determined to keep the Union intact. He saw nothing but ruin down that road, for he had been in the North and knew that it was a sleeping giant, with factories, coal, steel mills, and industrial might as yet unrealized. His own life, too, was a shambles. His marriage was a farce, and Denton, he well understood, resented him for his long absence. The other children had forgiven him as best they could, but he had robbed them of a father, and that he could never restore.

"Daddy?"

Clay gave a start, then smiled as Rena opened the door and peered in tentatively. "Daddy, can I come in?"

"Come in, Rena," Clay said, and his mood lightened as the girl came to stand before him. She had been withdrawn and hostile when he'd first returned to Gracefield, but he'd found out that she was really starved for affection. It had gladdened his heart as she had slowly opened up to him, and now he smiled at her fondly. "What's on your schedule today? Finding more sick animals to take care of?"

Rena made a face at him, for it was something he teased her about often. She had something in her that made her want to help when sickness came to humans or animals. That desire most often found an outlet in taking care of any animal that became ill on the farm, or any injured or ailing wild animals that were brought to her. Not long ago Clay had brought her a small raccoon with a broken leg. "How's Bandit?" he asked.

Her expressive face brightened as she replied, "Oh, Daddy, he's almost well!"

As she went on to tell about her care for the wounded animal, Clay thought, *If everyone were as sweet and gentle as this child, it'd be a good world.* Finally he said, "That's good, Rena, but don't get too close to Bandit."

"Why not, Daddy?"

"Because you'll have to part with him sooner or later."

"Can't we keep him as a pet?"

"No, he's not a tame animal. He's wild, and sooner or later he'll have to go back to his own."

"But—I don't want him to go," Rena protested. "I love him!"

Clay reached out and drew the girl closer, his arm around her. She did not hold back as she once would have done. "I know," he said gently, "but it wouldn't be best for Bandit. Wild things aren't happy in cages, and that's what you'd have to keep him in." He hesitated, then added, "You have to learn to let things go, Rena. We all do."

She was very still in his embrace, her features troubled. She was the most sensitive thing Clay had ever known, and his love for her was beyond measure. Finally she whispered, "I won't have to let you go, will I, Daddy?"

His grip on her tightened, and he realized suddenly that Rena was more deeply scarred than he had guessed. The shame of abandoning her cut into him like a razor. She was afraid he would leave again. More than anything he wanted to give her security, but he knew better than to make any promises that went beyond his power to keep.

He drew her closer and kissed her cheek. "You'll never lose me if I can help it, sweetheart," he said huskily. "Lots of things are happening, but I'll do my best to stay close to you always."

"Will you really, Daddy?"

"Really!"

She lay against him, seeming to soak up the love that she sensed in him, but finally she asked tentatively, "Daddy, will we ever. . .be a family again?" It was not quite what she wanted to ask, and she pulled back to look into his face. "I mean, will you and Mother ever be together?"

Clay wanted to assure her but knew that he could not. "I don't know what's going to happen, Rena. But one thing I do know—I love you, and I won't ever leave you if I can help it. And I'll always help your mother as much as I can."

Clay had no idea how much Rena understood about him and Ellen—probably more than he had thought—but he could say no more.

She seemed content to stand there with him, not replying. Finally she looked up at him and smiled. "I'm glad you're here, Daddy. I was so lonesome for you while you were gone!" Then she seemed to feel uncomfortable, or at least her mood passed. "Daddy, can I go to the ball in Richmond next week?"

"You're too young for balls," he told her with a smile, relieved at the change of topic. "Besides, you're getting too pretty. Some young fellow might try to steal you."

"Oh, Daddy!" Rena flushed with pleasure, then began to beg him to let her go. Clay had already decided that he would take her, but he let her wheedle him, taking pleasure in her bright eyes and eager voice.

Finally he said, "All right, but you can only dance with me or your brothers."

"Oh, thank you, Daddy!" She kissed him with a loud smack, then ran off, saying, "I've got to get Grandmother to help me with a dress!"

Clay stood there watching her fly up the path to the Big House; then he moved back inside. If only he could win the hearts of others as easily as he'd won Rena's.

CHAPTER 8

THE YANCYS

The Reverend Jeremiah Irons had some of the quality of his name in his character. Not that he was a weeping prophet like his namesake in the Old Testament, but there was something of a stubborn streak in him. In fact, so strong was this streak that some of his parishioners called him "Old Ironsides"—the nickname given to Oliver Cromwell, who had ruled England with an iron fist.

Despite the shared nickname, Jeremiah Irons was nothing like the dour Cromwell. Rather, the pastor of Grace Congregational Church fully appreciated a good joke. This fact and his renown as a crack shot made Irons a popular man with the hunters of the county. He was always welcome on a hunt—though he steadfastly refused to join them in a drink of the fiery liquor that usually accompanied them on such expeditions.

But there was no sign of humor on the minister's broad lips as he drove his buggy along the road leading to Gracefield on Friday afternoon. His fifteen-year-old daughter, Ann, sat beside him, chattering away about things that mattered to her. From time to time he would put in a question, but his mind was elsewhere. A man of no more than medium height, Irons was still as wiry at the age of forty-one as he had been when he had left the hills of Arkansas at the age of sixteen. He was not a particularly handsome man, though he had neat features and agreeable brown eyes. He was the despair of a large segment of his congregation—that segment made up of single young women, women with marriageable daughters, and widows looking for a second go at marital bliss.

When his wife, Lorraine, had died, he had stubbornly insisted on rearing their two children alone. It had been a difficult time for him, as well as for the children, Asa and Ann. They had, he had always known, missed their mother and had fully expected him to remarry. Now Asa at the age of sixteen and Ann at fifteen were still showing signs of resentment over his refusal to marry. Asa had said nothing, but Ann had more than once questioned him closely about his singleness. Looking at her now, her face illuminated by the afternoon sun, he felt guilty over his failure.

His elders at the church had often expressed their displeasure over his single state. When he had quoted St. Paul's maxim from scripture, "I say therefore to the unmarried and widows, it is good for them if they abide as I," they had frowned, indicating that that was very well during biblical times, but the pastor of Grace Church needed to set an example for his congregation. Irons's refusal to marry had been a touchy subject, and at the last meeting Elder Rufus Matlock had said bluntly, "Rev. Irons, if you can't see your way clear to marry, it would be best if you found another congregation."

Irons had stared at the elder with a pair of direct brown eyes, knowing that this was a final warning; the two had clashed over this matter many times. As the pastor drove along the dusty road, then turned into the oyster-shell drive of Gracefield, he knew that in a power struggle against Elder Matlock, he would lose. Irons had no patience with political maneuvering, and his direct preaching had not been calculated to make him popular. He had offended many with his direct bombshell hits on sin, and if the matter came to a vote, he knew that he would be without a congregation.

He glanced at the Rocklin mansion as he drove closer. As always, he admired the lines of the house and the way it overlooked the expanse of green, but his mind was on things other than architectural beauty. He was a man who never flinched from a hard task, but the occasion of his visit to Clay Rocklin was especially difficult. He and Clay had been friends for years; there was no man who admired Rocklin's determined efforts to rebuild a shattered life more than the pastor of Grace Church. Irons was closer to Clay than any other man, and the pastor knew that hard times lay ahead for Clay Rocklin because of his stand against the war.

Now he was coming to add to the big man's burden.

Irons pulled the buggy up to the front porch and handed the lines to Moses, then moved with Ann up the steps. They were met by the mistress of Gracefield, Susanna Rocklin. "Come in, Brother Irons, and you, too, Ann. My, what a pretty dress!"

"Thank you," Ann said with a nod. Then she asked at once, "Is Rena here, Mrs. Rocklin?"

"She's down at the summerhouse, Ann. Why don't you run on down, and you two can have some time together. You're staying for supper, I trust, Reverend?"

There was no table that Irons enjoyed more than the one set by Susanna Rocklin, but an uncertainty moved in him. When he hesitated, Susanna was surprised. It was so unlike Irons to show any sort of doubt that she knew at once he was struggling with a problem. "Of course you will!" she said quickly, taking the struggle out of his hands. "You've been neglecting me lately, so tonight you've got to give me some of your time."

"All right, Susanna." Irons smiled, knowing that she had noted his uncertainty. He turned to his daughter. "You run on to see Rena, Ann. Have a good time." As she ran down the steps, Irons followed Susanna into the house.

She led him into the small parlor she used for sewing and said, "You sit right down. I'll have Dorrie make us some fresh tea—no, you like coffee better—and Dorrie made a cake this afternoon. It won't spoil your supper to sample it."

As she moved away, Irons relaxed on the horsehair sofa and looked out through the mullioned windows. A small crew of slaves were barbering the green lawn just outside. They moved slowly, clipping the grass carefully, and the sound of their lazy laughter floated on the air.

Why didn't Harriet Beecher Stowe put that in her book? he thought with a stab of irritation. He himself hated slavery and made no bones about it, but he knew full well that the North deceived itself, believing that freeing the slaves would bring them into an Edenic state. He had no answers to offer for the nation's conflict—but thought of the words of the fanatic John Brown, who had said before being hanged, "This thing called slavery can only be washed away by blood."

The pastor sat there in the quietness of the room, trying to find some way to avoid talking to Clay. But he was grimly aware that there was none. He was trapped by his position as minister, and Clay was bound by other forces. Now he could do no less than meet the thing head on.

"Now you eat this, Brother Irons," Susanna said, returning with a silver tray filled with coffee, tea, and cake. "I can bake a better cake than Dorrie, but she refuses to admit it. I'm sure you'll agree." She smiled at him, pouring his coffee into a fragile china cup that looked small in the pastor's hand. "Remember that chocolate cake I sent to you last month?"

Irons smiled at her but said, "Susanna, I'm bound not to say who's the best cook. An old bachelor like me can't afford to offend anybody who can cook." His lips parted in a smile, and humor lit his brown eyes. "Now between ourselves, I'll admit you're the best cook in Virginia, but I'll never repeat that in front of Dorrie."

"You're a fine minister!" Susanna cried out in mock horror. "Dorrie just told me you said she was the best cook in the whole state!"

"I'm just a poor sinner," Irons said mournfully, shoving a huge bite of the cake into his mouth. "Especially where cake is concerned, Susanna. Got no character at all."

She smiled at him, and he was touched by her warmth. Their close friendship had begun almost as soon as he had come to Grace Church as pastor. He had made enough mistakes to get ten preachers run off, and it had been Susanna Rocklin who had brought him through the difficult years. She had smoothed ruffled feelings among the congregation while she taught Irons that a pastor could be strong and tactful at the same time. He had discovered in the woman a strength that was lacking in her husband, Thomas. It was to her that he often came with his problems.

Finally, after they had talked quietly, enjoying each other's company, Susanna asked, "What's troubling you, Jeremiah?"

He looked at her with a smile. "I never could hide anything from you, could I?"

"You can't hide much from anyone," she said. "You're a direct man. It's hard for you to cover things up." Susanna sipped her tea, then asked quietly, "I suppose it has something to do with the Rocklin family?"

"Well, yes—" Dissatisfaction stirred the shoulders of Irons, and he gripped his hands together, which Susanna recognized as a sign of agitation. "I'd rather be whipped than come here with this, Susanna."

"What is it?"

"It's about Clay," he said evenly. "And Melora Yancy."

Susanna did not speak but let her eyes remain on the preacher's face. She had been expecting something unpleasant, and now it was here. The silence ran on, and finally she said, "It's especially hard for you, Jeremiah."

In that one phrase she said a great deal. In it, she indicated that she was aware that Jeremiah Irons was in love with Melora Yancy, which was no secret, since most people suspected it. Susanna had known for a long time of the minister's love for Melora, though he had never spoken to her of it. Still, Susanna had seen it in his attitude toward the woman, in his eyes when he looked at her, and in the gentleness he always manifested toward her.

Susanna knew, perhaps better than anyone else, the loneliness in Irons. She was lonely in much the same way. His wife was dead; her husband was removed and weak in many ways. She could no more get close to Thomas than Irons could get close to his dead wife.

"The elders...they insist that I speak to both of them." Irons rose, walked to the windows, and peered out, seeing nothing. After a moment, he came back to stand and look down on her. "I ought to resign from the church, Susanna."

"What would that accomplish? Whoever came to follow

you wouldn't be God's man for Grace Church."

"He wouldn't be all tangled up in his own harness, either!" Irons said almost bitterly. "How can I talk to Clay about this? Or Melora?"

Susanna rose and took his hands. "You'll talk to them as you talk to everybody, Jeremiah. Honestly and without guile. Do you think they don't know there's been talk about them?"

The preacher's face flushed, and he shook his head. "I nearly punched the jaw of Elder Matlock when he came to me and said Clay and Melora were too close."

"He's only repeating what others have said," Susanna said gently. "You can't go around punching the jaw of every gossiper in the community, can you?" Then she said, "Sit down. We must pray about this."

Irons sat down and said quietly, "Yes, we'd better pray, Susanna. Because only God can do anything about this thing. It's beyond me—beyond anybody!"

Rena Rocklin and Ann Irons were best friends. They seldom had much time together, so the afternoon was a pleasure for them both. At fifteen, both girls were filled with the fears and anticipations of that particular age. They had grown up together, sharing the same tutors who had come to Gracefield and attending the same church all their lives. Often they had spent the night together, alternating between Gracefield and the parsonage, where the Irons family lived.

All afternoon they talked eagerly as they roamed the fields together and retired into the summerhouse. Rena found plenty of snacks, and as the two ate cookies and drank fresh milk, they giggled and laughed outright. Rena showed Ann the new drawings she had made, brought her up to date on her "hospital" of sick and wounded animals, and listened in turn as Ann talked about the Jennings family, a new family that had moved into the community and joined the church. She said so much about one family member, a boy named James, that Rena finally grinned, saying, "I think you've got a case on him, this James Jennings."

Ann stared at her, then cried out, "Oh, Rena, I like him so much—but Papa goes into a fit if I even eat a bowl of ice cream with him at a sociable! I wish I were dead!"

Rena, well accustomed to the overreactions of her friend, comforted her as well as she could. "Tell me about him, Ann. Is he tall? How old is he?" When she had absorbed all the details, she nodded, saying, "Listen, my birthday is in two weeks. I'll make Daddy ask him to my party. Then you can eat all the ice cream you want with James Jennings."

Ann was ecstatic. She hugged Rena and walked around the room making plans for the unknowing young man. Rena was glad she could do so much for Ann, for she was fond of her. But unfortunately, she blundered into the one topic that brought Ann's joy to a halt. Forgetting that Ann was the daughter of a minister and therefore was unable to attend dances, she mentioned that her father had just told her that she could attend the Officers' Ball in Richmond the following week. She was so excited at the prospect that it escaped her notice that the more she spoke of the ball, the more Ann Irons turned gloomy.

Finally Ann cried out, "It's not fair! You have all the good times, Rena! I never get to have any fun!"

Rena was caught off guard, but when she saw the resentment on Ann's brow, she grew a little angry. "What do you mean I have all the good times? I've just told you how I'm going to get that old boy to my party, and just for you!"

"Who cares about your old party?" Ann snapped back, not meaning a word of it but mortified and stung by Rena's attack. "What's a silly old party next to the Officers' Ball in Richmond?"

"Well, if you feel like that, you don't have to come to my party yourself!" Rena regretted the words the moment they left her lips. She was a gentle girl and hated to hurt anyone. She was about to apologize and put her arms around Ann, but she was too late.

One thing that Ann Irons had inherited from her mother was a quick temper, and it rose up in her at once. "I wouldn't come to your old party!" she cried out. "My father wouldn't let me. He doesn't want me having anything to do with the daughter of an adulterer!"

The words hung in the air, both girls shocked into silence.

"Oh, Rena—!" Ann exclaimed, horrified at what she had said, but at that moment the door opened and her father walked in, along with Clay Rocklin.

The two men had been walking slowly down the path from the house. They had had their talk, and it had been very painful for both of them. Irons had put the matter simply: "Clay, I know you and Melora are innocent, but people are talking. They're saying that you spend too much time with an unmarried young woman. The elders asked me to speak to you about it, and they'd like you to meet with them. I've done that now, so I'll say no more."

Clay had flushed, an angry retort rising to his lips, but when he saw the pain in his friend's face, he swallowed the words. "It's hard on you, Jerry," he had said. "I'll pray about it."

That had been the extent of their conversation, and both of

them were saddened by it. Clay had known for a long time that Irons had refused to marry because he was in love with Melora. More than once he had urged the minister to press his case. But Irons had said evenly, "In Melora's eyes you're the only man in the world, Clay." Since then, the two had steered clear of talk about the situation. The fact that they remained close friends despite all this was evidence of the depth and strength of their bond.

Now as they entered the summerhouse, they looked at the girls. Both men had heard Ann's angry cry, and Irons said firmly, "Ann, you will apologize for your remark. It's not true, and you certainly never heard me say any such thing."

Clay saw the humiliation on Ann's youthful face. At once, he went to her and put his arm around her, saying gently, "Don't make her do that, Reverend. Ann didn't mean it."

Ann looked up at him, tears running down her cheeks. She threw her arms around Clay and whispered, "No! I never did!"

Catching Irons's glance, Clay shook his head slightly, and the other man understood. "Well, sometimes we all say things we don't mean. Don't cry, Ann."

Ann left Clay's embrace and flew to Rena. The two girls were weeping, and Rena said, "It's all right, Ann. You mustn't feel bad!"

It was a tense time, and Irons made his departure as soon as possible. Rena called out as they were well away from the house, "Don't forget my birthday party, Ann!" Then she turned to her father, who was watching her strangely. Rena felt awkward, and there was a heaviness in the room, but she looked up and said, "I'm sorry you had to hear what Ann said, Daddy."

"I'm sorry you had to hear it," Clay said. He gave her a careful look, then asked, "You've heard it before—talk about me and Melora Yancy—haven't you, Rena?"

Rena flushed and wished she'd never listened to the gossip. She had heard it from one of the girls at church, a daughter of Elder Swinson, and it had angered her. Then she had heard some of the slaves talking about it, but they had not known she was listening. She had wept herself to sleep over it more nights than one but had never mentioned it to a living soul. Now she lifted her head, her youthful innocence plain to see. "Is—is it so, Daddy?"

Clay shook his head instantly, more glad than he could say to be able to look his daughter in the eye. "No, Rena. It's not so. You know Miss Melora. There's no finer woman on earth than her, and she'd never do what people are saying."

"Oh, Daddy! I'm so glad!" Rena went to her father, and he held her closely. The strength of his arms comforted her, and finally she drew back with a frown on her face. "You ought to shoot whoever starts those old stories, Daddy!"

Clay smiled in spite of himself. "Hey, that's no way to talk! In the first place, I'd run out of ammunition," he said, making a joke out of it. Then he paused, his lips growing firm as he said, "It hurts me that I've been the cause of harm to Melora. I don't think we'll be able to see her much anymore." He had taken Rena with him to the Yancy place more than once, and the girl had taken to Melora instantly. The two of them had become fast friends.

Clay looked down at his daughter. "Don't let this make you hate anyone, Rena. Never let anything do that." He kissed her, then looked into her clear eyes and said quietly, "I let hate and bitterness get into me once. And it cost me the dearest thing in the world."

Rena understood instantly that her father was speaking

about whatever it was that had taken him away from Gracefield for so many years. She nodded, her eyes suddenly filled with love for her father. "I promise, Daddy!"

That was all. Except that when Rena left to go back to the Big House, she asked, "Daddy, when you see Miss Melora, will you tell her why I won't be coming to see her?"

"I'll tell her. She'll understand."

Clay stood at the head of the path that led through the trees, watching his daughter make her way between the huge trunks. The scene had torn at his insides, but now he faced something even worse.

Tomorrow I'll go tell Melora.

The thought was painful, and that night he slept little, knowing that it must be done yet dreading it with all his heart.

❧

Clay Rocklin was no man to put off an unpleasant chore, so he saddled King and left Gracefield early the next morning, just after dawn. The distance was not far and he walked the horse most of the way, but it seemed when he came in sight of the Yancy house that the ride had been very brief. Buford Yancy was working in his barn, shoeing a nervous mare, and he called out as Clay dismounted, "Come in here and help me with this animal, Clay! She's more likely to shoe me than t'other way around!"

"Fine mare, Buford," Clay said, taking the horse's head and holding her firmly. "Out of Thunderhead, if I remember?"

The two men talked as they worked, but Clay was thinking back over the years. Buford Yancy was one of the innumerable poor white farmers who filled the South. He was, at the age of fifty-four, stronger and more active than most men half his age. He was six feet tall and lean as a lath, with a pair of quick, greenish eyes and a head of tow hair that he hacked off with a knife when it got in his way. He was as independent as a lion—and proud as one, too.

Clay thought back to how the two of them had become friends. Clay had been a young fool, filled with pride and arrogance. Then a hunting accident had felled him when he was hunting with Jeremiah Irons, and he had been brought to the Yancy cabin while the minister went for help. Clay smiled as he thought of how he'd learned that it was not the aristocrats who had real pride, but men like Buford Yancy!

He thought, too, of the small girl who'd taken care of him, how womanlike she had been though she was just a child. Melora. . .he'd been taken with her childish ways and the wisdom she often displayed that seemed so far beyond her years. The days he'd spent there had taught him much about children—at least about one of them. Melora was bright as a newly minted coin, and when he'd asked her what she wanted for taking care of him, she'd told him she wanted a book.

That had been the beginning. It had gone on like that, and his delight in bringing her books and reading the difficult ones to her was the chief solace in his troubled life. Her favorite had been *Pilgrim's Progress*, and when he'd left to go to the Mexican War, seeking glory to equal that of his cousin who'd married the girl Clay loved, he'd said on his last visit with the child, "I'll slay a dragon for you, Melora!"

But he had slain no dragons in Mexico. He had disgraced himself by getting drunk and allowing the men of his company to be butchered by the enemy. He was dishonorably discharged. No sooner had he gotten home than he disgraced himself further by forcing his attentions on Melanie, Gideon's wife. That had been the end of it. His father had driven him from Gracefield, and he'd wandered the world, a drunken derelict. Finally a ship's captain had seen something in him, taken him aboard, and trained him. Clay had risen in that business—the slave running business—until he grew sick of heart and soul at what he was doing and came back to Virginia.

Now, looking down at Buford as the man worked, Clay felt a quick flash of affection. No matter how many of his old friends—or his family—had shunned him, Buford Yancy had not. He had watched Clay carefully for a time; then one day he said easily, "Glad you come back, Clay." That had been all, but to Clay Rocklin it had been the equivalent of a brass band and a dozen speeches. Since then he and Yancy had grown close. Clay had found great solace in the friendship he shared with Buford. And with Melora.

If Buford was one of his closest friends, Melora was...well, she was probably the one person who really knew Clay, really understood him. It had been she, with her quiet ways and solid faith, who had finally lifted Clay out of the blackness that he had thought would destroy him—by leading him to the Lord.

As Buford's long figure rose from his work, Clay watched him, then said, "Buford, have you thought about what we talked about last time?"

"Shore. It's okay with me, Clay."

Rocklin was surprised. He had come a week earlier to convince Buford that he should plant corn and raise hogs instead of raising cotton. Clay had been expecting to have to overcome the tall man's objections. "You made up your mind already?"

"Makes sense to me. Cotton ain't gonna feed nobody this fall. Can't eat the blamed stuff." Yancy's green eyes gleamed with humor as he added, "To tell the truth, Clay, I've always hated cotton—blasted stuff!"

Clay laughed but warned at once, "People will say you're a fool. They've already said as much about me. They say it's not patriotic to raise anything else."

"I never thought it made a man a patriot to raise cotton. Now let's figure some on this corn business. And how we gonna hold them hogs? Take a heap of fencing, won't it?"

The two men went out and sat under a spreading ash as they talked, and it was a pleasure for Clay. He'd been called a fool and a traitor by so many for wanting to break with cotton. Now he knew that he was right. There was an inborn shrewdness in Buford Yancy, and Clay had grown to trust his judgment on anything concerning farming.

Finally Clay paused, looked at Buford, and said flatly, "Rev. Irons came to see me yesterday."

"Thought he might," was Yancy's comment. "About you and Melora, I expect."

His quickness stopped Clay for a moment, but he nodded. "People are talking. I've got to do something about it."

"You do whut's right, Clay. And in my mind they ain't nothin' right about lettin' a bunch of long-tongued busybodies run your life."

Clay said soberly, "Not worried about myself, Buford. It's Melora who's getting the worst of it."

"Wal, here she comes. Tell her about it; then you do whut you got to do." He got up and went across the yard, disappearing behind the house.

Clay stood up and turned to Melora, who had left the cabin and was walking across the yard. "Come for breakfast, Clay?" She laughed, a tinkling sound on the morning air. "You always manage to show up here at mealtime. You're bad as a preacher about that. Breakfast is almost ready. We'll have to wait for the biscuits."

Clay smiled slightly. "You're as bossy as you were the first time I ever saw you." His eyes crinkled with humor as he added, "You weren't more than six or seven, and you bossed me around like you were a sergeant in the army." He paused, then added thoughtfully, "I think of those days often, Melora. More than you'd know."

He watched her smile answer him. The morning air had roughed her cheeks and put sparkles in her eyes. She had a beautifully fashioned face, all of its features graceful yet generous and capable of robust emotion. She was a girl with a great degree of vitality and imagination, which she held under careful restraint. He saw the hint of her will—or of her pride—in the corners of her eyes and lips.

She looked at him now, her green eyes shining. "I think of them, too, Clay."

They stood there, and finally he took a deep breath. "Melora, I need to stop coming here." He watched for her reaction and was astonished when she showed little emotion. "I said—"

"I heard what you said."

He stood motionless in the bright sunshine, her presence hitting him with a jolt. She saw what was happening to him, but she stood still. Within her own chest she felt a sudden heavy undertow of feeling starting to unsettle her resolution and turn her reckless. She made a sharp movement to break that moment and wheeled away. Clay stood still, and presently she turned back to face him, her face almost severe. For a moment they watched each other, completely still. Then she lifted her chin and took his arm.

"The biscuits will be ready. Come to breakfast."

He held her back for one moment. "But what about the talk, Melora?"

"If you stop coming to see me, you'll be saying that they're right. I don't like to see you run from anything, Clay."

He shook his head slowly. "It's you I'm worried about."

There was pride in the woman's eyes, and her lips were firm as she answered him. "Before God, we have done nothing wrong. You can run if you like, but I won't do it!"

Admiration ran through Clay, and he said, "By heaven, Melora, you're right! Come on, let's eat breakfast!" She smiled at him, and the two of them entered the cabin.

CHAPTER 9

THE OFFICERS' BALL

*T*he war fever that struck Richmond following the fall of Fort Sumter was, in many respects, like an epidemic. It reached into every home, from the palatial mansions of the wealthy planters to the unpainted shacks of the poor whites scattered in the deep woods. The young men flocked to Richmond to enlist, their greatest fear being that the great battle would be over before they could become a part of it. The term *war fever* was not inaccurate, for the populace behaved as though they were infected, rushing around from rally to rally, faces flushed, shouting war slogans.

Volunteer companies sprang up like mushrooms, most of which bore names reflecting their patriotism and the terror they sought to inspire: Baker Fire-Eaters, Southern Avengers, Bartow Yankee Killers, Cherokee Lincoln Killers, and Hornet's Nest Riflemen. A few titles even had an occupational flavor, such as the Cumberland Ploughboys or the Cow Hunters.

Almost constantly the city held ceremonies full of staging and flourish designed to thrill the hearts of the home folk. The speeches became almost as stereotyped and platitudinous as the high school valedictories of later years.

When Clay brought his family to Richmond on Friday morning, he found such a celebration going on. The main streets were so packed with wagons and buggies that he had to hitch his own rig several blocks from the center of town. "I'd better keep an eye on you two," he said to David and Lowell as he handed Ellen down from the rig and they all made their way through the shouting throng. "You might get carried away with all the excitement and join up."

Rena glanced at her brothers, wondering if they might do just that. David merely grinned and shook his head, but Lowell was looking at the crowds, taking in the spectacle. He was seventeen years old, and several of his close friends, no older than he, had already signed up and were urging him to join their outfits. Lowell was a throwback to Noah Rocklin, the founder of the family. He was thickset and stubborn—and it was that which made Clay keep his eye on the boy.

Got to watch him, he thought as he led the way to the raised platform where the speakers were already winding up. *He's too much like Grandfather—and like me, I guess*, he thought wryly.

Clay and his family found a good spot close to the platform and watched as a battle flag made by the ladies of Richmond was presented with great ceremony to the new company, which had the rather ferocious name of Southern Yankee Killers. The volunteers stood in ranks, their eyes fixed on the speakers, who gave them a flowery tribute. Then the color sergeant advanced with his corporals to receive the flag, rising to the occasion with an impressive response:

"Ladies, with high-beating hearts and pulses throbbing with emotion, we receive from your hands this beautiful flag, the proud emblem of our young republic. To those who will return from the field of battle bearing this flag—though it may be tattered and torn—in triumph, this incident will always prove a cheering recollection. And to him whose fate it may be to die a soldier's death, this moment brought before his fading view will recall your kind and sympathetic words; he will bless you as his spirit takes its aerial flight."

On and on went the speech, and others much like it. Finally, though, the oratory stopped long enough for the soldiers to receive liberal offerings of cake, cookies, punch, and coffee from the young ladies, all of whom were adorned in their best dresses. Along with the refreshments, kisses were sometimes added, and David nudged Clay with an elbow, whispering, "Makes me want to sign up, Father. Let's both of us join the company!"

Clay grinned rashly at him, but Lowell said soberly, "Joke all you want, David, but those fellows are doing something."

David snorted impatiently. "Yes, swilling down lemonade and eating cake and kissing girls. As soon as the train leaves to take them to camp, that'll be over."

Clay nodded his agreement but saw that the two of them were in the minority. He had made his own position on the war clear, but only David agreed with him. The carnival atmosphere that so effectively whipped up the spirits of the crowd did nothing but depress him. Finally he said, "Dent's company is giving a drill exhibition on the green. Let's go watch."

Making their way to the large area adjacent to the courthouse, they arrived just as the Richmond Grays were beginning their drill. The square was packed, and as the Grays went through their paces, there were cheers of admiration.

"They are pretty good, aren't they, Daddy?" Rena said, her eyes bright with excitement. "And Dent is the most handsome of all the officers."

Ellen was standing close to Clay, wearing a bright yellow dress and a broad-brimmed white hat adorned with blue flowers. She liked the excitement, for she was a woman who could not be happy in solitude. Now she pressed against Clay as she said, "It's so exciting! I never saw such handsome young men!" Then she pulled away and gave Clay a critical look, whispering, "You should be proud of your son! He's a patriot, serving his country. Why don't you at least try to look like all this is important?"

Clay shrugged his shoulders, saying, "Sorry, Ellen. I'll try to do better." And he did try. All afternoon he took his family to the drills and ceremonies, even taking time to visit the officers of the Grays. Colonel James Benton greeted him effusively. "Clay, glad to see you! Isn't this a fine group!" Benton was Melanie Rocklin's father, Gid's father-in-law, but the man never mentioned either his relationship to the woman Clay had once loved so foolishly or Clay's past conflicts. Now he seemed almost majestic, albeit overweight, in his new uniform. He had no military experience at all, but he had raised the regiment at his own expense, and now his life was nothing but the military. He spent all his time making speeches, studying strategy from officers of the Regular Army, and talking about the war.

Clay spoke with Taylor Dewitt, captain of the Grays and one of his oldest friends. "You look great in your uniform, Captain Dewitt," Clay said with a grin, then added a barbed comment. "Now if you drop dead of excitement over being an officer, we won't have to do a thing to you except put a lily in your hand."

Taylor flushed, then laughed loudly. "You could always puncture any kind of pride I had, Clay!" Taylor was a tall, erect man of thirty-eight, aristocratic to the bone. "You son of a gun!" he said, thumping Clay's shoulder, "I wish you were in this thing with me. I don't know any more about soldiering than I know about Chinese painting. None of us do."

As he spoke, the pair of them were joined by Bushrod Aimes, another old crony of Clay's. He wore the insignia of a second lieutenant and looked sheepishly at Clay, saying, "Taylor's right about that, Clay. We none of us know a thing. Talk about shoving off to sea in a sieve!"

"You'll do fine, both of you," Clay said, nodding and looking fondly on the pair. The three of them shared some very fine memories of their youth, when all had been golden and there had been nothing but fun on the horizon. Clay spoke what the three of them were feeling. "Maybe I never said so, but you two have always been pretty special to me. We've had some good times."

Dewitt gave him a rash grin, saying, "That sounds like an epitaph, Clay. Don't be so confounded sentimental!" Then his thin face grew sober, and he looked at the milling figures of the company surrounding them. "Well, all kidding aside, I've thought of those days myself. They were fine, weren't they?" A shadow crossed his face, making him look tired and older. "They go pretty quick, the good days. Now we're walking into a rough time. Not all these boys will be here when the shooting's over."

Bushrod Aimes shook his head, for he was a careless fellow who had always refused to think of unpleasant things. "My gosh, Dewitt, you're worse than Rocklin here! We're going to do fine!"

Dent chose that moment to step up to the trio. "Like to speak to you, sir, when you've finished," he said to Clay.

"Why, now's fine, Dent," Clay said. He nodded at his two old friends, saying, "I'll be careful to pray for you fellas." Then he followed Dent, who was making his way through the crowd.

Bushrod stared at the two, then shook his head. "Pray for

us! Boy, that sure don't sound like the Clay Rocklin we grew up with, does it, Captain Dewitt?"

"No, but I think it's the real thing." Taylor's face was thoughtful as his eyes followed Clay. "Guess he'll need all the religion he can get, Bushrod. Right now, it takes a lot less courage to be a soldier and take a chance on a bullet than it does to stay out of the army. Clay's taking a lot of abuse over his stand—and it'll get worse, I reckon."

Clay shouldered his way through the crowd, following Dent off the green. There had been a tense look on Dent's youthful face, and when he reached a relatively uncrowded spot near the firehouse, there was an edge of temper in his voice as he spoke. "I've been talking to Mother. She's very upset."

"About what, Dent?"

"About the miserably small allowance you dole out to her. You've got to give her more money!"

Clay clamped his lips firmly together, choking back the hot retort that leaped to them. He drew a steadying sigh. "I've talked to her about that, son. She can't seem to understand that things are very tight right now—and likely to get worse."

"Things aren't that bad," Dent said, a stubborn air in the jut of his chin. "Isn't it bad enough that she had to survive all the years you weren't around? Do you have to punish her now that you've got control of all the money?"

Clay wanted to remind Dent that Ellen had lived very well during the years he was gone and, in fact, that the bills she had run up then were a large factor in the financial ruin he had found when he had come back. But Dent was in no mood to hear the truth. Besides, Clay felt the old streak of guilt over his past, so he merely said, "Dent, if you'd like to go over the books with me, I'd be happy to have you find some extra money. But

I'm telling you now, there isn't any. As a matter of fact, I may as well tell you—the way this war is shaping up, we're going to have to cut back even more. The first thing to go will be the personal expenses of all of us. That means the room your mother keeps rented here in Richmond will have to go, I'm afraid."

What followed was as unpleasant as anything Clay had endured since his return. His son had a fiery temper, and for the next five minutes, Clay had to endure the worst of it. While Dent stood there, pale with anger and resentment, speaking bitterly about what a pitiful excuse for a husband and a father he had been, Clay could only stand and hold his tongue.

More than once he'd had to fight down the impulse to strike out or to turn and walk away from his son's invectives, which burned as they fell on him. There had been a time when he would not have been able to endure such things, for his pride had been every bit as high as his son's. Now as he stood there enduring Dent's torrent, he took some small comfort in the fact that he was able to hang on to his temper—he knew it was not in him to endure such a thing, and that, as much as anything that had happened, convinced him that his life had been touched by God.

Angrily Dent clamped his lips together. There was a wild look in his eyes, as well as exhaustion. He was like a man who'd run himself out and was now at the end of his resources. Since the day his father had come home to take over Gracefield, a bitter streak of resentment had galled Dent. Now, here in the bright sunlight, he had let all that lay within him spill out. Yet it had not brought relief. It would have been better if his father had struck out at him; nothing would have pleased him better than a rousing battle with blows and shouts. But his father did no more than stand there quietly, looking at him with pain in his eyes, making no defense.

Finally, drained and bitter, Dent said, "I'll never ask you for anything again!" then turned and stalked away. He didn't look back, but if he had, he would have seen the anguish on Clay Rocklin's face that he had so longed to put there. He had not really expected that his father would do anything for his mother. In fact, down deep he was ashamed of his tirade, for he had already spoken to his grandmother, who had told him the same thing he had just heard from his father. Even so, something in him had driven him to seek the confrontation—some demon that seemed to eat away at him.

Now he moved away, stiff with anger and bitterness, and went into a saloon and ordered a bottle. For the rest of the afternoon he sat there, ignoring those who came to clap him on the shoulder and acclaim him as a patriot. The darkness that was in him seemed to deepen, and as he slumped in his chair, sullen in the midst of the laughing crowd, he wondered why he could not forget his father and get on with his life.

Colonel Benton had rented the ballroom of the Capitol Hotel for the Officers' Ball, and when Dent arrived, the floor was already filled with couples spinning around the room. The amber light from the glass chandeliers picked up the brilliant colors of the women's dresses, and the brass buttons on the gray uniforms of the officers winked merrily as the music beat out a steady tune.

Bushrod Aimes had found Dent drinking alone and had practically hauled him bodily to the affair. "What's wrong with you, Dent?" Aimes had demanded. "No sense paying for your own liquor. It'll be free at the ball. I hear Colonel Benton bought out the bar for tonight. Come on, let's go let the ladies make a fuss over us!"

Dent had decided not to go to the ball, for he was still filled with anger, having spent hours brooding over the scene with his father. But the liquor he had consumed had dulled the edge of his anger, so he allowed himself to be bullied by Aimes. When the pair arrived, he suddenly became the center of attention for several lovely young ladies. Some of them he knew well, and for the next hour he was able to thrust the memory of the quarrel with his father from his mind.

One newcomer was a beautiful girl named Leona Reed. Mrs. Mary Boykin Chesnut, the leader of society in Richmond, had led the young woman up, saying, "Lieutenant, you must meet one of our distinguished guests. You've heard of her father, Samuel Reed, I'm sure. Miss Reed, I present to you Lieutenant Denton Rocklin, one of our fine officers from the Richmond Grays."

"Thank you, Mrs. Chesnut," Dent said instantly. "May I have this dance, Miss Reed?"

"Of course, Lieutenant."

She stepped into his embrace, and as they spun around the floor, he was captivated by her beauty. She was not tall, but her bright orchid dress set off a trim figure. Her blond hair was done up in a coronet around her shapely head, and the sweep of her cheeks was intensely feminine. A pair of large blue eyes and beautifully formed lips made her an attractive girl. But as taken as he was with her beauty, he was aware almost at once that she was a fiery patriot, for she spoke of "the Cause" in a fervent tone.

That was natural enough, for her father, Samuel Reed, was

one of the Southern senators who had led the South down the pathway to secession. Reed was a wealthy man who had gone into politics in his forties and had been as successful there as he had been in the field of business.

When the dance was over, Taylor came over to say, "You're starting at the top, Dent, old boy! Brains, beauty, and money! But you'll have to edge out half the officers in the regiment to get her."

Dent grinned rashly. "She's a woman, isn't she? I'll turn my fatal charm on, Captain." And at once he went away to demand another dance, noting that Miss Reed was not disappointed when he came.

As he spun her out on the floor, Mary Chesnut said to Colonel Chesnut, her husband, "They make a beautiful couple, don't they?"

Colonel Chesnut cast his look on the pair, then shook his head. "Mary, will you give up this eternal matchmaking?" But he added later, "They do look well. But a soldier's got no business thinking of women before he goes to battle."

Mary Chesnut moved her shoulders angrily. "You have no more romance in you than a cabbage, James!"

As the night wore on, Dent Rocklin maneuvered himself into every dance he could with Leona Reed. It was a matter of guile, for she was highly sought after. When he wasn't actually dancing with her, he was at the refreshment table imbibing the liquor that flowed quite freely. By ten o'clock, he was beginning to feel the effects of the liquor. When he danced he was not nearly so smooth as he thought, and he laughed more loudly at things that were not really funny.

The colors of the dresses swirled in front of his eyes in a kaleidoscopic fashion—reds, yellows, and greens. His dances with Leona Reed were as intoxicating as the liquor he consumed, for she spoke of his company urgently and with pride. When she praised him for throwing himself into the glorious struggle to preserve the South they all loved, he felt a glowing sense of exaltation that blotted out all else.

After eleven o'clock, he was unable to get another dance with Leona. He was on the verge of leaving when Mrs. Chesnut appeared and asked, "Lieutenant, you see that young woman sitting alone? Would you talk to her for a few minutes?"

"Of course, Mrs. Chesnut," he said. He moved toward the girl. When he reached her, he bowed and asked, "May I have this dance, miss?" He was surprised when the young woman hesitated. She seemed preoccupied, and he thought that she had not heard him. "My name is Denton Rocklin," he said in a louder tone. "I'd like to dance with you."

The girl looked up with a faraway look in her eyes. "I—I don't dance very well, Mr. Rocklin," she said in a small voice.

"Oh, that's all right," Dent said at once. "I'm not any prize-winner myself. But that's a good band." He put out his arm, but she seemed to ignore it, so he simply put his arm around her and swept her out on the floor.

It was a slow waltz, and Dent was aware that the girl was not a good dancer. She did not move easily with him, seemed not able to anticipate his movements. At first it was a matter of steering her around on the floor, and she whispered, "I don't think I can do it, Mr. Denton."

"Oh, sure you can! Be a good time for you to practice." He looked down at her curiously, for all the girls he knew were accomplished dancers. It was the one skill they made certain to attain! She was, he saw, not over average height, no more than five feet four. Her head was down so he could not see her face plainly, but she looked lovely in her pale blue dress. When she did look up slightly, he saw that she had an attractive heart-shaped face and that her eyes were dark blue. She was not, he decided, a raving beauty, but she was pretty enough. "I didn't hear your name," he said when she had begun to dance with more assurance.

"Raimey Reed," she said quietly. She kept her head down, seeming to concentrate on her feet. Her hair was long, auburn, with a glint of gold where the light from the chandeliers touched it, and he could smell a hint of lilac scent. She had a beautiful complexion, rich and smooth as a child's.

"Raimey? Never heard of a girl named that," Dent muttered. "Or a boy, for that matter."

"It's my mother's maiden name."

Dent blinked as a thought came to him. "You said Reed? I just met a girl named Leona Reed."

"My sister."

Her answers were brief, which was somehow disturbing to Dent. He was accustomed to girls who talked much. He began speaking of the war and how glad he was to serve in the Richmond Grays. When she said nothing, he added, "Your sister is a great patriot. I suppose you are, too?"

Raimey Reed hesitated somewhat awkwardly, then shook her head, the motion sending the mass of auburn hair shimmering over her shoulders. "No, I'm afraid not, Mr. Rocklin."

At first Dent thought he had misunderstood her. Looking down he said, "I beg your pardon?"

"I said I'm not a patriot. I think this war is a terrible blunder."

Her words came to Dent clearly, and his reaction was anger. He stopped dead still, leaned back, and snapped, "A blunder!

You think it's a blunder for a man to fight for his country?"

A flush came to the girl's face. She looked up at his harsh tone but said only, "I don't think this is the proper place to discuss it, Mr. Rocklin."

Dent stood there, trying to sort it all out. His thoughts came slowly, and all he could do was say angrily, "Miss Reed, you're a disgrace to Southern womanhood! I think you should listen to your sister. She's the kind of woman a soldier can be proud of!"

At that moment, a wave of dizziness caught up with Dent, and he was afraid he was going to be sick. "I'll just leave you here, Miss Reed. I don't think you'd care to dance with a simple soldier who's about to offer his life for his country!"

The speech sounded pompous and stilted even to his own ears, but Dent wheeled around and walked away, leaving the girl standing alone in the center of the floor. Anger boiled up in him, and he muttered, "Little snob! Let her dance with some Yankee!"

He reached the edge of the dance floor and started for the door, but he was halted when Mrs. Chesnut barred his way, her face stern.

"What are you doing, Lieutenant?" she demanded. "You've left Miss Reed alone!"

Dent stared at her, standing very straight, and said, "Miss Reed is not sympathetic to the cause—," he began, but he was cut off by an angry gesture from the woman.

"Go back and get her at once!"

"I won't dance with a—a—"

"You fool!" Mary Chesnut said, her usually gentle dark eyes sharp with anger. "Go at once and get her!" She leaned forward and whispered in a tight voice, "She's blind!"

Dent blinked and turned his head as if the woman had

slapped him. He turned and saw that the girl was trying to make her way through the throng of dancers. Her hands were held before her, and her eyes were staring straight ahead.

"My God!" Dent groaned and at once plunged into the crowd. He upset several couples as he shoved his way toward her, getting rough looks from some of his fellow officers. His legs were unsteady and a cold sweat broke out on his brow, but he did not stop until he got to where the girl was struggling to find her way off the floor.

He took her arm, saying, "Miss Reed—!"

"Leave me alone, Mr. Rocklin!"

He noted that she turned her face to him as she attempted to pull away. He held her firmly. "I've got to talk to you!" he muttered, and ignoring her attempts to pull away, he moved her across the floor, sheltering her from the dancers. He was aware that people were looking at them strangely, but it was too late to remedy the thing. He didn't stop when he got her to the side of the floor, but continued to pull her along. He had been outside earlier and knew that a small balcony lay to the side of the ballroom. He pulled the door open and led her out into the open air, then closed the door.

"Where is this?" Raimey asked at once. "Please, take me back!"

"In a few moments, I will." Dent stood beside her, taking deep breaths of the air. The music came to them, muted by the door, and he could smell the aroma of the firs that flanked the building. A large magnolia tree grew twenty feet from the balcony, and one of the branches dipped so low that he could smell the sweet richness of the blossoms.

Finally he released her arm and, turning to face her, said, "This is a small balcony just outside the ballroom."

"I want to go back inside."

"All right, but first you have to let me say something."

Raimey Reed cocked her head very slightly. In the relative silence of the secluded balcony, she heard Denton Rocklin's voice clearly for the first time. She had known from the first that he was drunk, or almost so. Now she seemed to grow calm. She turned and faced the open lawn, saying nothing. Dent waited, trying to frame some sort of apology, but everything he thought of seemed stupid.

Suddenly she said, "I've never danced before. Not at a real dance."

Dent stared at her, not knowing how to answer. Finally he said carefully, "You did very well for your first time. With a little practice, you could be very good."

The air caressed her cheeks as she turned slightly and said evenly, "I'm not likely to get much practice. I should have warned you. It wasn't fair to you."

Dent said stiffly, "Miss Reed, anything I say will sound downright dumb, but I am sorry."

He stood there, knowing that he had treated her abominably, almost wishing she would turn and rail on him. But she did no such thing. She suddenly lifted her face and smiled. A deep dimple appeared in her left cheek, and it was impossible to tell from her eyes that she was blind. "Let that be a lesson to you, Mr. Rocklin, against taking up with strange women." Then she said, "Don't let it upset you. I'm not hurt—and I did get to dance, didn't I? That's something, isn't it?"

He blew his breath out, saying, "I feel rotten!"

"That's because I'm blind," Raimey said with no particular note in her voice. "You've probably treated girls much worse than you treated me, haven't you?"

"Why—!" Dent was absolutely floored at her matter-of-fact question. Then he laughed shortly, nodding. "Yes, I have."

"Well, you don't have to add your impoliteness to me to your list of sins. I forgive you."

Dent was feeling very strange. "I'll accept that on one condition."

"What condition, Mr. Rocklin?"

"That you dance with me again."

His request disturbed her. Her full lips tightened, and a shadow fell across her cheeks. "You say that because you feel sorry for me," she said in a voice that was not quite steady. "I'm used to it. People often don't know that I can't see, and they make mistakes. Like yesterday a woman came up and asked me to read an address for her. She couldn't read herself, and when I told her I was blind, she acted as though she'd done something horrible. You don't have to dance with me. That's just something you want to do because you feel guilty."

Dent said patiently, "You can argue all you want, Miss Reed, but when you run out of argument, I'm going to be standing here waiting for you to dance. Maybe you're right—that I just want to wash out my guilt. Well, give me a chance to do it, then, will you?"

Raimey stood there, uncertain for the first time. She had thought that her words would drive Rocklin away, but now she felt his sincerity. She was adept in dealing with people who were awkward about her handicap, but now she felt awkward. Finally she laughed. "All right, just one dance to show that I'm not angry."

"Fine!"

He led her to the floor, and she came into his arms readily. She was not afraid now, and by the end of the dance, she was moving around in his arms with confidence. "Now this next one will be a little faster," he said. "We'll see how you do with it."

"You said one dance," she rebuked him with a smile.

"I lied," he announced calmly. For the next three dances they moved around the floor.

Then she said, "I think four dances ought to blot out your guilt, Mr. Rocklin."

"I do feel much better," Dent said and escorted her to the seats. He found Leona waiting for him.

"Well, I see you've met my sister," she said, looking at him strangely.

"Yes, Miss Reed." Dent nodded. He guided Raimey to her chair, then bowed. "I must be off, I'm afraid. Drill begins early. Thank you both for the dances."

He moved away, and Leona asked, "How in the world did that happen? You've always refused to learn how to dance."

"I don't know. He just asked me and I said yes." She lifted her face to her sister. "What does he look like, Leona?"

Leona sat down and took her sister's hand. "He's the best-looking man I've ever seen. Black hair and dark, soulful eyes." She smiled, a dimple exactly like Raimey's peeking out of her cheek, then added, "And he's got a body like mortal sin!" She laughed when Raimey rebuked her, then grew serious. "I'd think you two would have little to talk about. He's going off to fight for a cause you think is dead wrong."

Raimey said, "It scares me, Leona. To think that he might be killed, along with thousands of others like him. And it can't make any difference! So many dead, for nothing!"

Leona had argued with Raimey too many times over this, so she simply said, "Let's go home, Raimey. It's late."

"All right." Raimey allowed Leona to lead her to the carriage.

As she passed across the lawn, she caught the rich smell of magnolia, and she knew that whenever she smelled one of those blossoms, she'd think of her first dance and the man with whom she had shared it.

CHAPTER 10

"BECAUSE I'M DIFFERENT!"

*D*ulcie was an excellent reader. She had a smooth, clear voice and had been trained by a noted teacher of diction, but she could not disguise her disgust with what she read. The mulatto slave girl loved romances with knights in armor and maidens who were rescued from fire-breathing dragons. She could not understand why her mistress had her read a dull poem again and again. She held the old copy of *Graham's Magazine* and stared at the top of the page at the title, "The Arsenal at Springfield." Noting that it was written by some man named Henry Wadsworth Longfellow, she began reading:

> *"This is the Arsenal. From floor to ceiling,*
> *Like a huge organ, rise the burnished arms;*
> *But from their silent pipes no anthem pealing*
> *Startles the villages with strange alarms."*

She waded through several stanzas, all dealing with war and battle, then lowered the magazine and protested, "Miss Raimey, do I have to read this old poem again? I don't see no sense in it!"

But her mistress, lying on the floor, said, "Read it." So Dulcie, giving her head a disgusted shake, went back to the poem. When she finished and was about to close the book, she heard a muffled voice. "Read the last two stanzas again, Dulcie." Knowing that argument was useless, she read the words:

"Down the dark future, through long generations,
The echoing sounds grow fainter and then cease;
And like a bell, with solemn, sweet vibrations,
I hear once more the voice of Christ say, 'Peace!'
Peace! and no longer from its brazen portals
The blast of War's great organ shakes the skies!
But beautiful as songs of the immortals,
The holy melodies of love arise."

Raimey gave a slight shiver as the last line fell across the quiet of the room. She had been lying flat on her stomach, her face buried in a pillow, listening to the slave girl read. Now she sat up abruptly, exclaiming, "Isn't that a marvelous phrase, Dulcie? 'The holy melodies of love arise.'" Her rich auburn hair fell down her back in masses of curls, and there was a look of pleasure on her wide mouth as she repeated the phrase.

"I don't see what's so great about it," Dulcie snapped. "I don't see why people can't say what they mean instead of usin' this poetry! I don't think it means anything!" A sudden irritation brought creases between her brows, for she took more liberties than any other Reed slave. This stemmed partly from the fact that she had been taught to read as a child, but it came even more from the fact that her duty went far beyond that of the ordinary lady's maid.

When Raimey Reed had become blind at the age of seven, Samuel Reed had spent a fortune on doctors, attempting to find a cure for his daughter. When he finally resigned himself that a cure would not be found, he turned his energies to making Raimey as able as she could be to live in the world. Dulcie had been his most successful move. Dulcie had learned to read by "accident." She had merely sat with the girls while their tutor went over the letters and, to the shock of everyone, learned much faster than Leona. This shook the bottom out of Sam Reed's theory about black people, which was that they had no soul and were incapable of learning anything except to pick cotton and perform other menial tasks. Reed was, however, a flexible man. When he had Dulcie tested and found out that she was extremely intelligent, he'd made her Raimey's maid at once.

The choice had been wise, for Dulcie had become everything to the blind girl. Not only did she function as Raimey's maid, keeping track of her clothes and fixing her hair, but she served as the girl's eyes. The two were inseparable, and as Dulcie saw, she spoke. It was through her that Raimey received much of her impression of the world. She could not have had a better guide, for Dulcie was alert and had a natural flow of rather poetic language, enabling her to make anything she saw come alive for her mistress. She could describe things—such as the sweeping flight of a kingfisher swooping down to scoop a minnow from a pond—so graphically that Sam Reed once said, "Blast my eyes! That Dulcie can see more and say more in less time than any human on God's green earth!"

Dulcie loved to read. She did it well, and Samuel Reed had filled his home with books of all kinds to feed Raimey's voracious hunger for knowledge. Every day the smooth, beautifully cadenced voice of the maid could be heard in the Reed house, and Raimey's mother had said more than once,

"Sam, what would we have done without that girl Dulcie?"

"I don't know, but she's got enough gall for ten Caesars!" her husband often replied ruefully. "She's got us, Ellie! She knows we can't do without her and she does as she pleases. And there's not a blessed thing we can do about it!"

Dulcie continued to argue about the poem and finally threw the magazine down with disgust, just as the door opened and Miss Leona Reed dashed into the room.

"Raimey, you're not even dressed yet! Dulcie, why haven't you helped your mistress!"

Now as Leona stood looking at the pair, Dulcie showed no fear. "I told her to get ready, but you know how she is. I had to read this old poem to her ten times!"

"Well, it's nearly time to go," Leona snapped; then she shrugged. "Come on, I'll help you, Dulcie. We have to be at the Chesnuts' in an hour." The two girls began at once, and together they were able to get Raimey into her dress and her rebellious curls in some sort of order by the time they heard their father roaring outside the door, "Come on or get left, you two!"

The sisters scurried down the stairs and were handed into the carriage by their father, who complained, "You two girls will be late for the Resurrection!" as he climbed in and settled himself heavily next to his wife. "Whip up those horses, Job!" he called to the driver, and the matched grays leaped at the touch of the whip. Reed settled down, pulled a cigar from his inner pocket, lit it expertly, then leaned back and looked at his daughters. He was a tall, corpulent man of forty, success written in his every inch. "You look very well. How much did I pay for those dresses?"

"Oh, Father, they're old as the hills!" Leona said. "All my good dresses are at home. Mother, we've got to go shopping tomorrow. I'm ashamed to wear this old thing to meet the president!"

Ellie Reed, a calm woman of thirty-three who had smooth brown hair and large eyes, said, "I think President Davis will be thinking of more important things than your dress, Leona." Then she glanced out the window, took in a troop of soldiers drilling on a field, and began to describe them. "What funny uniforms!" she exclaimed. "They're wearing some sort of puffy scarlet trousers. What are they, Sam?"

Reed took a look, then said, "They're Colonel Field's Louisiana Fire Zouaves. A bad outfit, or so I hear. The sweepings of the worst of New Orleans riffraff." He took up the description from his wife without thinking, describing the lean, evil faces under the tasseled hats, which were much like the Persian fez, and the garish colors of the uniforms. It had become second nature to all the family to speak what they saw, creating the world in words for Raimey's sake.

Raimey sat upright beside Leona, listening carefully as her father described the troop. She was as aware of sound as a fox, her ears recording the creaking of the carriage, the shout of some man yelling, "Stop that, Craig, or I'll bust you!" and the slap of the hands of a group of drilling soldiers on their muskets as their drill sergeant called out sharply, "Present—arms!" Deprived of sight, Raimey had developed her other senses to extraordinary degrees. She smelled the acrid odor of tar as the carriage wheeled by a barrel that was smoldering slightly. Instantly she recognized the sharp smell of a blacksmith shop, smoky and vaguely metallic, and over the open carriage came the scent of magnolia—bringing instantly the thought of her encounter with Denton Rocklin.

Listening to her family describe the bustle of Richmond's

streets with one ear, she allowed the memory of that evening to flow through the other part of her mind. She was gifted with a keen imagination, and her blindness had sharpened even that so that she could recall an event clearly, recreating it quite vividly. As the carriage turned and her father said, "There's the Chesnut house, Job, the white one with the green shutters," she had the strongest possible memory of Rocklin's every word, of the touch of his hand on her waist as they had gone around the floor. She had thought of it constantly since that night, for there had been something in his touch and in his presence that had been different from that of any other young man.

Now the carriage pulled up, and Leona moved close to her so that as they moved down a brick walk and up three steps, Raimey did not need to take her arm at all. By merely brushing her sister's gown, she was able to walk into the house, for Leona was able—as were the other members of the family, and Dulcie most of all—to measure distances so that Raimey would not bump into objects or doorjambs. So well did they do this that strangers meeting the family for the first time often had to be told that Raimey was blind.

"Mr. Reed, Mrs. Reed, come in with your girls." Raimey recognized the voice of Mrs. Chesnut instantly. The sound of a voice to her was like the sight of a face to others; once she heard the voice of man, woman, or child, she recognized it instantly, no matter how faint it was or how long it had been since she had heard it last. Now she stood there listening as Mrs. Chesnut and her parents exchanged greetings, smelling the fresh wax, listening to half a dozen conversations going on inside a large room off to her left, and sensing the bustle of servants moving busily over the smooth wooden floors.

"You young ladies come with me," Mrs. Chesnut said, and

Raimey knew by her tone she was smiling. "The officers are waiting for you. I've told them that the two most handsome young ladies in Richmond are to be here. Now be on your guard, both of you. You know how these soldiers are!"

Leona laughed, and as they moved from the foyer into the large drawing room, Raimey sensed the size of the room. She had been told that James Chesnut was a very wealthy planter from South Carolina who had recently moved to Richmond because he was a member of the brand-new Confederate Congress. He was an amiable man, but it was his wife, Mary Boykin Chesnut, who was the magnet that drew the cream of Southern society to her house—even the president of the Confederacy, Jefferson Davis.

Mrs. Chesnut was not a raving beauty, as several had told Raimey, but she was one of those women whom men liked. She was thirty-eight years old, a small woman with black hair and lustrous dark eyes. Now she said, "Mr. President, may I present our two young guests, the daughters of Mr. Samuel Reed. This is Leona and her sister, Raimey."

Feeling a touch on her arm by Leona, Raimey put out her hand, which was taken instantly. Davis's hand was thin but strong, and he said in a pleasant high-pitched voice, "Where do you find all these beautiful young ladies, Mrs. Chesnut? Your house is filled with them."

Raimey felt the touch of a light kiss on her hand; then a woman's voice said, "Now, sir, be careful! You know I only allow you to kiss one fair hand in the evening."

"Oh, Varina!" Davis said to his wife, humor in his voice— an unusual thing, for this new president had little of that quality. "You mustn't be jealous of two staunch supporters of our cause."

Sam Reed spoke up very quickly and rather nervously, for he had a sudden fear that Raimey might speak her convictions against the war on the spot. "Is General Johnson here this evening, Mr. President?"

"No, but General Lee is here. You ladies will excuse me? I'm sure the gallant officers of our fine troops will entertain you."

Raimey and Leona were surrounded at once by several officers, all trying to gain their attention. Leona spoke lightly, laughing at their eagerness, and Raimey spoke with one or two of them. She recognized the instant that one of them became aware that she was blind. He broke off suddenly, his speech faltering, and then he picked up the threads of his thought, speaking more loudly.

This was something that Raimey had experienced many times, and it no longer troubled her. On the contrary, it made her conversation much easier. But she had never learned quite how to handle the matter of letting strangers know she could not see. She had once said plainly, "I'm blind," but that had so embarrassed the man she was speaking to that she never repeated that tactic.

For the next hour, Raimey spoke with several of the officers, mostly of things other than the war itself. But the war was the center of all things now, she realized, and the light voices and the warm ease of the men were somehow an omen to her. For each one who stood beside her, pressing refreshments on her and laughing at the frivolous jokes that ran around the room, was on his way to something dark and grim—something more ominous than any of them seemed to realize.

Then as she was speaking with a youthful captain, she heard the door to the foyer open and close. A man's voice, low as it was, came to her, and she recognized it at once as Dent Rocklin.

She didn't move and continued to speak with the captain, but she was acutely aware of Rocklin's presence in the room. She heard him speak to Colonel Chesnut, and as the two of them spoke, she wondered if he would come to her.

He did come, almost at once. She heard the sound of his boots on the pine floor; then he said, "Miss Reed—?"

She turned to face him quickly, saying with a smile, "Hello, Lieutenant Rocklin. How are you this afternoon?"

Her instant recognition of his voice caught Rocklin off guard. He had gone over the strange experience of their meeting again and again. She had gotten into his thoughts, and now he said, "I didn't know you'd be here this afternoon. It's good to see you."

She nodded, and they stood there talking of unimportant things. As they spoke, he studied her carefully. He realized that though she was not beautiful, she was most decidedly pretty. There was a freshness in her youthful skin, which glowed like translucent pearl. Her eyes were blue, large, and well shaped. There was, he noted instantly, no sign of damage to them. On the contrary, they were quite beautiful, marred only by the fact that they did not focus. Her lips were wide and well shaped, mobile, and firm. The heavy mane of auburn ringlets that hung down her back was beautiful indeed, and the white dress with yellow lace at the throat set off her trim figure.

There was an innocence about this girl that Dent had never seen before. And Rocklin knew women very well. They had provided a game for him, one that he had learned how to play well. Most women played the game as well as he, but what had worked with other young women seemed wrong and out of place with Raimey Reed.

For the next thirty minutes he stayed close beside her, sharply observed by Mary Chesnut, who whispered to Raimey's mother, "Better be careful, Ellie. Denton Rocklin is quite a ladies' man."

The room buzzed with talk and laughter; then Raimey heard the president say, "And this is the daughter of Mr. Reed. Miss Raimey, may I present General Robert E. Lee."

"I'm happy to know you, General," Raimey said and put out her hand, which was taken at once. Lee's hand was square and very firm. "Only last week I read your account of the action at Cerro Gordo in Mexico."

Lee was amused, they all saw. His deep-set eyes gleamed with humor, and he said, "I wish I could have gotten the cadets at West Point to read as easily, Miss Reed. But that must have been dreary reading for a young lady!"

"Not at all." Raimey smiled then, the dimple in her left cheek appearing. "But I must confess my maid got very tired of it. I made her read it twice, and she went to sleep the last time."

Something changed in Lee's eyes. He had just realized, Dent noted instantly, that the girl was blind, and Dent spoke up quickly to cover the moment. "My uncle didn't grow tired of it, General Lee. He was with you when you found the way through the mountains." Catching Lee's attention, he said, "That was Lieutenant Gideon Rocklin, General."

Lee nodded at once. "A fine officer. Very dedicated." Then he asked with a slight hesitation, "Will he stay with the Union, Lieutenant?"

"Yes, I'm afraid so, General Lee."

"Well, each of us must decide about that. It's not an easy choice. Give your uncle my best regards when you write him."

Lee and Davis passed on, and Rocklin told Raimey, "My uncle says Lee is the finest soldier on the planet. It almost broke my uncle's heart when Lee chose to stay with Virginia. It hurt Lincoln, too." Then he said, "I've got to get back to camp."

"We'd love to see the camp, Lieutenant Rocklin!" Leona had come up while Lee was speaking, and now her eyes were alert. "Father would like to go, too."

"All of you are welcome," Dent said but added, "There's not much to see, I'm afraid. Just dull duty and drill."

But Leona insisted, and Dent asked, "Would you like to go, Miss Raimey?"

"Yes."

"Very well. I'll invite your father."

Samuel Reed declined the invitation but offered the use of his carriage and driver to bring the girls home. They left at once, and as soon as they got to the camp, Dent took the young women to meet his staff. Almost at once, Leona was invited to watch target practice, and she left with Second Lieutenant Bushrod Aimes and Third Lieutenant Tug Ramsey. Dent put his hand on Raimey's arm, saying, "You might be more interested in watching some close-order drill, Miss Raimey."

Raimey said, "Of course," and the two of them walked along the dusty lanes between the rows of Sibley tents. Dent put himself close to her, and she put her hand on his arm at once. The air was still hot, and when they had come to the drill field, Rocklin explained what was happening, watching the movements of the men carefully. Raimey faced the field, the sun making a golden candescent gleam on her smooth cheeks. Listening to the shouted commands, some of them profane when the men faltered, she asked, "Is this important? I mean, when men go into a battle, they don't keep step, do they?"

"Not as they do in Europe," Dent said. "But it's important for the men to learn to obey quickly." He saw that she was really interested and said, "Let's get under those trees, Miss Raimey. This sun is too hot for you." Fifty yards past the field was a grove of tall pecans, and as soon as they moved under their shade, Raimey asked, "Where's the brook?"

"The brook?" Dent had not known there was a brook. Looking around, he said, "No brook, I'm afraid."

"Yes, it's over here." Raimey moved toward the deeper part of the woods, and soon Dent heard it too. "That's such a nice sound!" Raimey said. "Is it deep?"

"No, I don't think so." Dent led her to it, saying, "It's a pretty little creek. Full of small fish, I'd guess. I used to catch redear perch from one just like it when I was a boy."

Raimey said, "I'd love to wade in it!"

Denton was amused. "Why don't you? It's not deep, and it looks cool."

"Turn around while I take my stockings off." He turned at once, a grin on his face. Soon she said, "Now you can turn around." She was moving, even as he turned, toward the creek, and he stepped forward, afraid she would fall. But she guided herself using the feel of the moist earth and the sound of the gurgling water. Lifting her skirts above her calves, she began to wade back and forth. She made a pretty picture standing there, with the sun coming through the tops of the high trees, flecked and barred on her face as she laughed softly.

I wish I were a portrait painter, Dent reflected. *I'd like to keep this forever.* But he realized at once that no painter on earth could do more than suggest the beauty of the scene.

For ten minutes Raimey walked on the rounded stones of the brook, delighting in the cool water and the smell of old moss. She grew bolder, going down the creek in search of deeper water. Dent followed along the bank and, noting an ebullience in the stream, warned, "Better be careful, Miss Raimey—that looks like a pretty deep pool there."

But he was too late, for Raimey stepped into a sudden drop-off, threw her hands wildly around in a vain attempt to gain her balance, then plunged headlong into the pool. Dent cried out and went splashing into the creek in waist-deep water. Raimey came to the surface, her hair plastered to her head, her hat floating downstream, and he caught her by the arm. Then as she gasped for breath, he swept her up into his arms and waded out.

When they got to the shore, she sputtered and wiped her face with her hands. Then she began to laugh. It was a delightful sound, completely natural and without inhibition. Dent suddenly grinned, then chuckled. He knew that any other young woman of his acquaintance would have been horrified at her appearance, but this one didn't seem to care.

He stood, holding her for a moment and watching her, when suddenly she realized that she was in his arms. She caught her breath, waiting for him to put her down. When he made no move to do so, she asked with a smile tugging at the corners of her mouth, "Are you trying to guess my weight, Lieutenant?"

A redness touched Dent's cheeks, and hastily he let her down. "Are you all right?"

"Oh yes. It caught me off guard. I swim in the river near our house every day in warm weather." She plucked at her wet blouse, saying, "But I'll look like a fool going back to camp."

"I'll bring the carriage around here with some blankets. No one will see you, Raimey."

"Thank you." Raimey had noticed his unconscious use of her first name and smiled. "Let's just sit in the sun for a little while. Leona won't want to leave so soon. Is there a sunny spot where we can't be seen?"

"Sure. Right over here."

Again she took his arm, saying, "Let's get my stockings. At least I'll have dry feet on the way home." Her hand rested on his arm, and when Dent had retrieved the stockings, he led her to a sunny spot at the edge of the field, cut off from the camp by a low rise covered with second-growth timber. "Here, sit on my coat," he said, stripping off his jacket and placing it on the grass. She sat down and he joined her, facing her two feet away.

"The sun is nice," she said, holding her face up, and he noticed that she closed her eyes as she faced the sun. He wondered why and reclined on his elbow to watch her. She was in a good humor, made so, he realized, by the fall into the creek. It had been an adventure, one that took no vision to enjoy, and she was excited and pleased with it.

They sat there, and the event seemed to have freed some constraint that he had always been aware of. She asked about his duties, then about his home and his family. As he spoke, slowly and casually, her hair began to dry, curling rebelliously so that it became a mass of curls, with red and golden tints in the red rays of the late afternoon sun.

He thought he spoke guardedly, but he soon realized that this girl heard more than words. When he had traced his family for her, mentioning all of them briefly, he paused and saw that she was thinking hard. A single line appeared between her brows, and she asked quietly, "You don't get along with your father?"

Dent stared at her, for he had said nothing to indicate the conflicts he had had with his father. Then he realized that it had not been the words, but something else. She could not see his face, but she must have had heard some bitterness in his voice. It could be nothing else, and it troubled him.

"You're very quick," he murmured. "No, my father and I don't agree." He intended to say no more, but somehow he began to speak, diffidently at first, tracing his father's history. He mentioned how Clay had abandoned his family. As he finally came to the present, he said, "You and Father would get along. He thinks the war is wrong just as you do." Then he shook himself and tried to laugh. "Good grief! I've talked you to death, Raimey! Sorry about that. I'm not usually such a chatterbox."

"It's all right."

As he looked at her, he saw the sweetness on her lips and the goodness in her face. Her skin glowed in the sun with a diaphanous quality, fine and clear. "I've never talked with a girl like this."

"It's because I'm different, Dent," she said with no trace at all of pity. "You're always on your guard with other girls, because they're out to get you to marry them."

He stared at her with amazement. "Why, not all of them!"

"Pretty much so," she said with a nod. "It's the only way for a young woman to live, doing all she can to find a good husband. It's what all women study and train for."

"Good night! I can't believe you're saying these things!"

Raimey smiled and picked a blade of grass. She tasted it, then turned her head to one side. "That's sour," she commented, then added, "Even if a young woman isn't out to catch you, you think she is. I suspect all handsome young men feel that way."

"How do you know I'm handsome?" Dent was amazed at the play of their words and asked the question without awkwardness.

"Leona said so." Then she paused, a thought coming to her. "May I touch your face?"

"Why—I guess so." Dent sat still as Raimey leaned forward and touched his chest, then let her hand rise to his face. Her hand was soft—and her touch was the softest thing he could imagine.

"You have a wide mouth," Raimey murmured. "And a strong jaw." As her hands moved over his features, she cataloged them all. "Broad forehead, deep-set eyes—very black, Leona said—high cheekbones, small ears. Very thick hair—black as night, she said." Then she removed her hand and sat back.

"Yes, you're very attractive, Dent." He was so speechless that she laughed at him. "Never had your face pushed and probed by any of your young ladies, did you? I'm sorry. But it helps. I know what you look like now." Then she added, "But you've been so free with me because you feel none of that pressure with me that you feel with other girls. You're safe."

Dent stared at her. "Maybe you're right."

"I am right," she announced with a brisk nod. Then she said in a different tone, "I wish you'd make it up with your father. Even if he's wrong, you'll be sorry if you don't." A breeze lifted a lock of her hair, and she pushed it back with a quick gesture. "There are only two things on this earth that really matter, and your family is one of them."

"What's the other?"

"Why, God, of course!"

Dent nodded. "I know you're right about that, Raimey, but I just don't have it in me to forgive him. He's hurt us all too much." He expected her to preach at him, but she sat there quietly. She seemed to be listening to something he could not hear, and finally he grew nervous. "I guess that sounds pretty feeble to you. But I'm just a weak character, Raimey. You strong Christians can turn the other cheek, but fellows like me, why, we just can't manage things like that." A strong memory of his last argument with his father came to him, turning him sour. "I'll go get the carriage," he said. "Just stay here. Nobody will trouble you."

He left abruptly, and she stood up as he left her. She wanted to cry out to him, to warn him of the peril of hating his father—but it was too late.

She waited until the carriage came back. Leona was put out with her, but Dent had calmed down. As he held Raimey's hand and put her into the carriage, he said, "I'll stop by tomorrow to apologize for letting you fall in the creek."

"Come for supper, Lieutenant, six o'clock sharp," Leona said instantly. "And bring that handsome Captain Forbes of D Company with you." Without waiting for his answer, she said, "Let's go, Job!" and the carriage leaped ahead. Denton stood there, staring after it, then went over and picked up his jacket. As he put it on, he suddenly shook his head, a look of admiration in his dark eyes. "She's some girl. I couldn't handle a thing like that!"

He returned to the camp, found Forbes, and the two of them made their plans to go into Richmond. When Dent asked Captain Taylor for permission, the captain gave him a careful look. "Better get your running around done quick, Dent. And get the men ready. Something's happening. When orders come, we'll have to move fast." He drummed on the table with his fingers, then remarked, "Fine-looking girls, the Reed women. Too bad about the younger one."

"Yes," Dent said, then left the tent.

CHAPTER 11

A HOUSE DIVIDED

As May gave way to June, summer fell across the land, wrapping it with a mantle of blistering heat. The field hands at Gracefield endured the white-hot sun patiently, larding the fields with their sweat; but for Clay Rocklin the sultry heat was one more irritating factor he didn't need. By nature he was a hard-driving man in the physical sense, and he had always been able to override any sort of trouble in his mind by hard work or play. Now, however, no matter how many hard, long hours he labored in the fields, when night came he tossed restlessly on his bed, getting up hollow-eyed and tired.

"You don't look well, Clay," his mother said as he came to the big house late one night. It was after eleven, and she had found him in the kitchen eating a piece of cold chicken from the cellar. "You're working too hard."

"I'm all right," he said briefly, but his face was slack with fatigue as he chewed listlessly on the cold meat. "The black mare had her foal tonight, but she had a hard time. I thought Fox and I were going to lose them both for a while, but she had a fine colt. What are you doing up so late?"

"Oh, I just couldn't sleep."

Clay glanced at her sharply. "Father's not doing well?"

"No. I'm worried about him, Clay. He's been poorly all winter and spring, and this heat seems to make him even worse."

"What does Dr. Medlin say?"

"He doesn't know." Susanna brushed her hair back from her forehead with a weary gesture. The pressure of running Gracefield was heavy, and Clay noted that new lines had come to her face. "Those terrible stomach pains frighten me—him, too, though he won't say anything. I guess we both are thinking of Noah, your grandfather. He had the same kind of trouble before he died."

They sat at the table, talking slowly, letting the time run on. The grandfather clock in the hall ticked on with a stately cadence and loudly struck one reverberating, brassy note to mark the half hour. Susanna felt close to this tall, sunburned son of hers, perhaps because—of all of her children—he was the one closest to God. Or perhaps it was because he had been lost for so many years, and when he had come back, she had received him as a gift from God. He was, she thought as she studied his aquiline features, a strong man—stronger than his father or any of the other Rocklin men. The genes of Noah Rocklin, her husband's father, ran strong in Clay and were evident in the same streak of stubborn individualism that Susanna had so much admired in Noah.

The sound of a horse coming down the drive at a trot broke through to them, sharp and clear. "That's Denton, I expect," Susanna said.

"What's he doing away from his company?"

"He took those Reed girls over to Brad's to visit with Amy." Brad Franklin was married to Amy, Clay's sister. They lived twenty miles away on Franklin's large plantation, and the two families were very close. Their sons had grown up together, even though Brad's son Grant was older than Clay's twins.

"I wish Brad had stayed out of this war," Clay said, frowning. "He's not cut out to be a soldier—and he's got plenty to do on that place of his."

"I know, but he's caught up in it," Susanna agreed. Then as footsteps sounded on the side walkway, she lowered her voice to say, "Dent's getting pretty thick with those Reed girls. He's been to their house two or three times, and now he's taken them to Brad's."

"Maybe he's getting over Deborah," Clay said, but then steps sounded on the porch and he fell silent until the door opened. "Hello, Dent."

Dent stopped at the sight of Clay at the table, but nodded at him briefly, then said, "Hello. You two are up late."

"How are Amy and her brood?" Susanna asked, listening as Dent gave a brief report. Dent was wearing his uniform, and he looked very dashing in the yellow lamplight. He was, Susanna saw, uncomfortable with his father. That grieved her, but there was nothing she could do about the situation. Finally when he paused, she asked, "When are you going to bring those young women by for me to meet, Denton?"

"Oh, maybe day after tomorrow. That's what Aunt Amy said, I think." He hesitated, then walked over and got a drink of water from the pitcher. There was a restlessness about him that kept him in motion, and he said briefly, "I have to be back for drill. Good night, Grandmother. . .sir." He left without a pause, and the echo of his horse's hoofbeats came to Clay and his mother on the night air.

"I'm sorry he feels as he does, Clay, about you."

"He thinks I'm unfair to Ellen. And he's never really forgiven me for leaving you all in the lurch." Clay's expression turned heavy, and he got to his feet. "Better get to bed, I guess." He moved over to Susanna, leaned down, and kissed her cheek. "Good night, Mother."

"Good night, Clay." Reaching up, she patted his cheek. "It'll all come out. God is still with us."

"Yes, He is." Clay turned to go, then hesitated. "I'm worried about Lowell. He's restless."

"Most of his friends have joined the army. He feels left out."

"I know. Do what you can to keep him out of it."

"You know how stubborn he is, Clay."

The corners of his mouth twitched. "Like me? Well, I'm going to spend more time with him. Maybe if he stays busy, he'll be content. We've got up a hunting trip tomorrow. We'll leave before dawn, so you'll be asleep. May stay two or three days, but things are in pretty good shape here now. Good night."

He left the house and went at once to his own place, slept poorly until four in the morning, then rose and dressed. He walked to the Big House, entered the kitchen, and started coffee. Lowell was a heavy sleeper, so Clay had to go into his room and shake him thoroughly before the boy got out of bed.

"I'll fix some breakfast," Clay said when he was sure that Lowell was really awake, then went downstairs. Ten minutes later Lowell stumbled into the kitchen, bleary-eyed with sleep, and the two of them sat down and ate the bacon and eggs. The food brought Lowell out of it, and when they finished, they cleaned up the kitchen and left for the stables. Soon they were on their way down the road, leading two mules that would pack the meat back. The cool air lay across the earth, and fragments of gossamer clouds drifted across the pale moon. By the time they had reached Wilson's Creek, the sun was up.

As they moved westward, the flatland began to break up into small rises covered with scrub pine. By midmorning they were in the foothills and stopped long enough to eat some sandwiches and make coffee. The sun was hot, but Clay was glad to see that Lowell was enjoying himself.

Should have done more of this with all my boys, he thought. *If I had, maybe Dent and I wouldn't be so cut off from each other.* He resolved to throw himself into his family, and as they moved on toward the higher ranges, he drew Lowell out, trying to understand what was going on in his mind.

Lowell was quite different from the twins, in both appearance and manner. He was shorter, more muscular, and had little of the darkness of the other men—the Black Rocklins—of his immediate family. His hair, darker in his youth, was now light brown, thick and full, and he had a set of clear hazel eyes. His complexion was fair, like his mother's, and while he was no scholar like David and had little of Dent's impulsiveness, he had a quick mind and always finished what he started. That had been clearly evident even when the boys were young. Clay had noted that when David and Dent gave up on a project, it was Lowell who forged ahead with a dogged patience until the thing was completed.

As they rode through large stands of virgin pine, Lowell began to speak freely. At first he talked about his horses, for he was the best horseman of them all and had shown great perception in breeding good stock. But inevitably he spoke of the war. It came out as he spoke of his cousin Grant. "Grant's going into the cavalry—did you know?"

"No, I didn't."

"Well, he is. Uncle Brad tried to get him to join the Richmond

Grays, but Grant says he'd rather ride than walk." A smile touched Lowell's lips, and he shrugged. "Guess he's right about that, but the Grays are a good outfit. Dent's been telling me about how good they are." When his father said nothing, Lowell gave him a quick glance. "I guess you know I've been thinking about it a lot."

Clay nodded slowly, thinking of the best way to respond. If he turned the boy off with a curt refusal, he knew he would be closing a door that he'd not likely open again. Still, he yearned to keep Lowell out of the army. Finally he said, "Sure, I know. All your close friends are signing up, and you feel left out."

Lowell nodded quickly, a little surprised at his father's understanding. "Yes, sir, they are. And I feel like a quitter—like I'm letting them down and letting my country down, too." He hesitated, then added, "I know how you feel about the war, but what's going to happen to us if the Yankees take over our place? We'll lose everything!"

Clay let Lowell talk, aware that the boy's head had been filled with war talk and propaganda of all sorts. Some of it was true, much of it was not, but at the age of seventeen, Lowell was not going to be able to sort it all out. If men such as Robert E. Lee had trouble, how could a mere boy do better? Clay had had second thoughts himself—many times. He believed the war was an invitation to tragedy for the South. Still, he was a Virginian, and the idea of failing his own was a bitter one to him.

"Nothing's much worse than being left out, Lowell," Clay answered thoughtfully. "And when you're seventeen, to be on the outside is just about unbearable. I was a lot older than you are now when the Mexican War started, but I was itching to join. Gideon was in the army getting ready to go, and lots of my friends were rushing to sign up." As he spoke of those days, the memories came back to him, and Lowell listened avidly, for his father never spoke of that time. "I couldn't stand it, Lowell, so I signed up, too. And for me it was a bad decision."

Lowell listened as his father told of his time in the army. It was not a pleasant story, and Clay Rocklin did not spare himself. He spoke of how he had been weak and unsteady and far more interested in personal glory than in serving his country. Bitterness scored his lips as he related how he'd failed his unit at the most critical hour. He didn't add that it was not altogether his fault, but shouldered the entire blame for the loss of life that had come when he failed his duty.

Finally he stopped, and after a moment of silence, Lowell said, "Thanks for telling me, sir. I—I know it wasn't easy."

"Never easy for a man to talk about his failures," Clay said evenly, then added, "I've not been a good father to you, Lowell. I wish I had been, but I've made many mistakes."

Lowell recognized instantly that his father was referring to his relationship to his mother and looked at him quickly. It had been difficult for him to accept his father when he had returned, but he had come to have hopes that his father and mother would be happy together. Lowell knew more about his mother than he would ever voice, for her reputation in Richmond was unsavory, and there was no way he could have failed to hear of her affairs. He loved his mother but was keenly aware of her shortcomings. Glancing at his father, he had a sudden insight into what a travesty his parents' marriage had been.

"We all make mistakes, sir," he said quietly and was glad to see that his remark had pleased his father. "And maybe it would be a mistake for me to go into the army—but how's a man to know what to do? Everybody is saying that it's right, that we've got to defend the South. And you know better than most what happens when a man refuses to go along. You've taken a lot of abuse because of your views on this war. How do you know you're right? Can you tell me?"

"I wish I could give you a formula," Clay said slowly. "It would be nice if everything were clear-cut, but most things aren't that way. The North has been wrong for years, burdening the South with unfair economic policies, but the South is wrong, too. At least, I think so. Slavery has to go, Lowell. Men like Lee know that, but they're part of the system the North has saddled us with. As for states' rights, well, I don't know. Most of us in the South say that if a state agrees to join the Union, it can decide to withdraw. But Lincoln and others like him feel that if that happens, this country will die; break us up into a lot of tiny nations and America will cease to be."

Lowell listened carefully, then sighed. "I don't know what to do, sir." Then he asked, "Would you agree to let me enlist, if that's what I decide is right?"

"If you decide it's the right thing, Lowell," Clay said, "I guess I wouldn't stand in your way. But lots of men are signing up just for the thrill of it, some to get out of boring work, others because they've been shamed into it. I wouldn't want to see you go unless you knew it was for a better reason than some we've seen."

Lowell was thoughtful as they went deeper into the woods, but said no more. Clay didn't know if what he had said was a help to his son, but he had done his best. They made camp, hobbled the animals, then went hunting. The woods were stiff with game, and Lowell brought down a fat buck with one shot. Lowell's youthful face was aglow with pleasure, and Clay enjoyed the kill as much as the boy. They dressed the deer, cooked up huge steaks over the fire, then sat back and enjoyed the night, talking until the stars glittered overhead. When they finally rolled into their blankets, Lowell went to sleep at once. Clay lay on his back, watching the opalescent gleam of the stars as they wheeled around in their old dance. Then, after saying a brief prayer, he dropped off to sleep.

❧

The next day they hunted the ridges all morning, taking small game, but at three o'clock, Clay said, "Let's go over to Blackwell Peak. Your grandfather might like some fresh bear meat. He was always partial to it." Lowell had never shot a bear, so he was eager to go. They broke camp, moved across the upper reaches of the Mogolla Mountains, and came to the foot of the Blackwell range late that afternoon. Clay knew the country well, and as they came into a small valley, he said, "Looks like somebody beat us to it, Lowell. But we can move on around to the other side of this ridge."

But as they drew near the camp, where a fire was sending a thin line of white smoke almost straight up in the still air, Clay smiled, saying, "Guess we won't have to move on. It's Buford Yancy." As they rode in, he called out, "Don't shoot, Buford! We're friendly."

Yancy had been squatting at the fire, cooking a chunk of meat in a blackened skillet, and he rose at once, calling out, "Well, dang me, if it ain't Clay Rocklin! Come and eat, you fellers! How are you, Lowell?" Without waiting for an answer, he commanded, "You, Bobby! Git them animals tied up, will you? Come and set, both of you."

Clay and Lowell dismounted at once and went to greet Yancy. "You located some bear sign, Buford?" Clay asked, then looked at the meat. "I see you have."

"They're plum thick this year, Clay." Yancy grinned. "And bold, too. Won't even run from you. Feller could hunt 'em with a good-sized stick." He looked over his shoulder toward the tent. "Melora! Come outta there and wait on these fellers!"

Clay looked startled as Melora stepped out of the tent. She emerged with a pleased look on her face. "How are you, Clay? And you, Lowell?"

She was wearing a pair of worn jeans that had belonged to one of her brothers, a faded blue shirt of Buford's, and a pair of low, worn boots. She looked trim, her full figure set off to good advantage by the rough clothing. Clay noticed that Lowell spoke briefly, and he felt a pang of regret.

He's heard the talk about Melora and me, Clay thought, but said only, "Came to load up on bear meat. Mother says bear fat makes the best soap, and Father likes a bear steak real well."

"Too late to go after bear today," Buford announced. "Bob wants to go for coon after dark. That's for young folks, fallin' all over your feet in the dark."

"Come along with me, Lowell. We got some good dogs—a new one that can track a coon over runnin' water." Bob Yancy, at the age of seventeen, was a carbon copy of his father. He knew Lowell fairly well, though they came from different backgrounds. They'd met at church, and several times Lowell had gone hunting with the Yancys.

"Sure, Bob," Lowell agreed. "I promised Dorrie I'd bring her some fresh coon. She can sure cook it good, too. Let's see that new dog."

The young men went off, talking dogs and guns, and Clay sat down, leaning against a tree. He watched as Melora moved around, putting a meal together. The two men spoke quietly, mostly of farming and horses. Finally the meal was ready, and

Melora called the younger men to the fire. She served them all fresh bear steaks, sweet potatoes cooked in hot ashes, and black coffee. When the men were served, she fixed a plate for herself and sat on a blanket with her father. As they ate with gusto, Buford asked, "Why does grub taste so much better outdoors than in a house?"

"Must be fresher, I guess," Clay ventured.

"If this meat was any fresher, it'd still be on that ol' bear!" Bob Yancy said with a grin and spun out the story of how he'd tracked the bear and shot it. When he was finished with that tale, Buford told about a mountain lion he'd shot the previous week. For a long time they sat around the fire, drinking the strong black coffee and listening to the stories. Finally Bob said, "Let's go for them coons, Lowell," and the two young men got their guns, whistled up the dogs, then plunged off into the growing darkness.

Melora cleaned the dishes as Clay and her father spoke of their venture with corn and hogs; then she came back to sit on the blanket again. They talked intermittently, pausing to listen to the dogs, whose howls scored the night with sharp crescendos. Buford nodded when one long, drawn-out note floated to them on the night air. "That's Bess," he said. "That dog is death on a cold trail!" Finally he asked, "Whut about this war, Clay? You still agin it?"

Clay leaned back against the tree, and for some time they talked about the war. Both of them had sons who were vulnerable; in fact, one of the Yancy boys, Lonnie, had already enlisted in the Richmond Grays.

Melora saw that Clay was weary over it all. She spoke little herself but listened carefully, as always treasuring any time in his presence. She was now twenty-six, ready for marriage and feeling a strong desire for children of her own. But she knew that her love for this tall man sitting across the fire would spoil her for any other man. She had often thought of marrying and had not lacked for suitors. Rev. Jeremiah Irons had long waited for her to turn to him, but Melora knew that she could never bring what she felt for Clay Rocklin to another man. And the thought of concealing her feelings for a lifetime from a husband she could never fully love was repugnant to her. She had called herself a romantic fool often enough, but still, there it was. She could not shake off what she felt for Clay as she would shake off an old garment. She could only choose not to act on her feelings—and this she had done.

The night wore on, and finally the hounds' clarion cries grew nearer. Buford, always the hunter, could stand it no longer. Rising and picking up his rifle, he grinned. "Them young fellers don't know much about coons. I better go give 'em a hand."

He disappeared into the dark shadows, and Melora laughed. "Pa's never satisfied with anyone's hunting but his."

"Best man in the woods I ever saw," Clay said. Then he looked across the fire at her. "How have you been, Melora?"

"All right," she said, smiling. Drawing up her feet, she rested her chin on her knees and regarded him. "Tell me about everything, Clay."

"Big order—everything."

"Tell me about what you've been doing."

"Working, mostly." He sat there, the firelight playing on his face, speaking slowly of himself. The peacefulness of the night was on him, and in Melora's presence he relaxed—as he always did. He dropped his head, thinking of all the problems that loomed ahead of them, and then looked up. "Sometimes

I wish life were as simple as the stories you used to love, about knights and maidens—where there's always a happy ending. Seems like in real life, things usually go wrong."

"Don't give up, Clay," she said instantly. Her eyes were bright as she added, "Think how God has brought you home from all sorts of dangers. He's given you so much!"

"You still believe, Melora? With everything coming down around our heads, you still believe that things will work out right?"

"I think God knows we're trusting Him, Clay." Then she murmured, "I love you, Clay. That's enough for me. You've been faithful to Ellen and to God. That's what's important."

They sat there in silence for a few moments; then a sound made Clay turn. He saw that Lowell had stepped out of the brush and was standing absolutely still, his rifle in his hands. His eyes were filled with hurt, and at once Clay knew that he was thinking of his mother.

"Lowell—," he said, but even as he spoke, he saw the hardness form in the boy's face, so Clay said no more.

"I came back for more ammunition," Lowell said, and walking stiff-legged, he moved to his pack, filled his pockets with shells, then gave them one look before half running out of the camp.

"I'm sorry, Clay," Melora said.

"I'll talk to him," Clay said, but he knew it would not solve anything. "Better go to bed, Melora."

"All right, Clay."

The next day Lowell got his bear, two of them just for good measure. But on the way home, there was a wall between the father and son, and nothing Clay could say could break it down.

Finally they reached the drive to the house, and Clay abruptly pulled his horse to a halt. "Lowell, you're wrong about Melora and me." He hesitated, pain on his face, then explained, "Your mother and I—don't get along. I can't explain it or defend myself. I wish it were different. But before God, I have never been unfaithful to her with any woman."

Lowell sat on his horse, his face frozen. He wanted desperately to believe what he was hearing; he had always liked and respected Melora Yancy. But the sight of his father sitting cozily with the woman by the campfire, looking at her fondly, had pulled down the younger Rocklin's defenses. He said in a tight voice, "I wish I could believe you. I'd like to. But I can't." He clenched his fists over the reins until his fingers were white. "I can't believe anything anymore, not even what you say about the war. Maybe you're just a coward! I'm joining up tomorrow, no matter what you say!"

Clay sat stiffly in the saddle, longing to find some way to convince this boy that he was telling the truth. He loved Lowell, and it seemed as though the boy was about to step off his road into a deep and dangerous chasm.

A thought came to Clay, which he rejected at first. Then it came back, so strong that he sat there considering it. Lowell, seeing his strange expression, asked, "What is it?"

"Lowell," Clay said, speaking slowly as the idea formed within him, "maybe there's a way."

"A way to what?"

"To show you you're wrong about me."

"It's too late." Lowell spurred his horse forward, leaving Clay to look after him. Time ran on, and still he sat there until finally he slapped his thigh, his mouth drawn into a tight line.

"It's the only way!" he said aloud; then he touched King

with his heels and rode toward the house, wondering if he was right in his intention. But right or wrong, he had decided that it was best to try anything to save this youngest son of his.

CHAPTER 12

THE LAST RECRUIT

$\mathcal{D}$ulcie glared with exasperation at Raimey. "You ain't going to the ball like that, I hope!"

Raimey was wearing a new dress of pale blue with a billowing hoop skirt that swept the floor. Graceful swirls of indigo velvet traced their way around the skirt, the dark blue almost an exact match for Raimey's eyes. The bodice was trimmed with fine lace interwoven with a delicate ribbon that framed the girl's graceful shoulders.

"What's wrong with this dress?" Raimey demanded. She had bought it on a shopping trip with her mother and had put it on by herself while Dulcie was helping Leona dress.

"What's wrong is that you ain't got on your corset!" Dulcie shook her head with disgust and marched over to pick up the garment stiff with whalebone stays. "Now you come out of that dress and put this on right now."

"I won't! I hate that thing, Dulcie." Raimey shoved the maid's hands away, stating flatly, "The dress fits me. I don't need to be squeezed by that stupid thing."

Dulcie had to admit that the girl was right, for the dress lay smoothly on Raimey without straining at the seams, but she was adamant. "I don't care. You've got to wear a corset. It ain't decent to go to a party without one. What will your mama say?"

"I won't tell her until we get there, and don't you tell either."

"I will, too!"

Raimey knew Dulcie very well. "If you don't tell, you can have my red dress and the petticoat that goes with it."

Greed struggled with indignation on Dulcie's face, for she had long coveted that dress. Finally she said piously, "Well, if you want to go to that party looking like a hussy and if you want to deceive your poor mama, I guess I can't stop you."

"I knew all the time you'd say that, Dulcie." A smile came to Raimey's face, and she said, "Now do my hair—and get some of that perfume that Leona uses."

Grumbling under her breath, Dulcie picked up a comb and began to coax Raimey's thick curls into order. As she worked on the lustrous hair, she talked constantly. "What about that young Rhett boy? Is he going to marry with Miss Leona? That other man, the tall captain who's been chasing after her, he's better looking, but he ain't got no money. Now I think Miss Leona better. . ."

As Dulcie rattled on, Raimey sat impatiently, anxious to be gone. It was the Presidential Ball, in honor of the Davises, and she and Leona had talked of little else for a week. After their visit with the Franklins, the two sisters had come back to Richmond and found that everyone was certain the army would be called to march into battle at any moment. The ball had been scheduled for the middle of July, but Varina Davis had persuaded her husband to set the time for the twelfth so that the officers would be sure to be in the city.

The visit with the Franklins had been, for Raimey, a splendid time. She had liked the Franklins, especially Amy, who was a cheerful woman, always happy to spend time with her young guests. She liked their daughter, Rachel, too, who was a beauty according to all she heard. The boys, Grant and Les, as expected, fell half in love with Leona—but then, all the men did.

But it was her visit to Dent's home, Gracefield, that had been the high point of the week's visit. Dent's mother, Ellen, had not been there, but his grandmother, Susanna Rocklin, had been delightful. Raimey had liked Clay Rocklin, Dent's father, very much. He had been careful to spend time with her, and even from that brief visit, Raimey could sense the goodness of the man.

Dent was there, of course, and he took the two girls all over the plantation. More often than not, however, Leona preferred to stay in the house, so Raimey went alone with Dent. He took her to the slave quarters and to the blacksmith's shop, where an elderly slave named Box made her a ring out of a nail. She had rubbed the velvet noses of the horses in the pasture, sat beside the duck pond listening to the endless gabble of the ducks, and run her hands over the glossy sides of the wild-eyed new colt.

Once she said to Dent, "I'm taking too much of your time," but he had said, "Raimey, I'm the most selfish fellow you ever met. If I'm spending a lot of time with you, it's because I want to."

They had been sitting in a sequestered nook set off by grapevines now thick with leaves, underneath a huge oak that dipped low over the pond. The afternoon sun had dropped halfway behind the distant hills, shedding golden rays that turned the pond crimson. Dent described some ducks that were making their way across the pond, saying, "They look like a small armada with feathers!" and the description had delighted Raimey.

The two young people were drinking tea and resting after

a brisk walk to the pond. Raimey turned her face to the man at her side and asked suddenly, "Why aren't you chasing after Leona, Dent? She's the most beautiful girl in the world, and the two of you surely agree about the war. I believe you could make her fall in love with you if you tried."

"Too much competition," Dent said with a smile. He sat there, sipping from his tall glass, studying Raimey. Indeed, he was puzzled at his own behavior, for he himself had thought how strange it was that he was not drawn to Leona Reed. Always he had been drawn to the most beautiful girl at hand, but he found that he merely liked Leona in a cheerful way.

"No, that's not so," Raimey said. "You're the sort of man who likes competition." Her lips were pursed in a delightful way, and he had become accustomed to the fact that the blue eyes never focused on him. "I think you're still in love with that cousin of yours, Deborah Steele."

A frown touched Dent's brow, and he demanded, "Who told you about her?" Then he shook his head, half angry at her. "This whole county's a gossip mill!"

"You were in love with her, weren't you? Everybody says so."

"I don't want to talk about it." The coldness of his tone made him ashamed, so after a moment he added, "I don't know, Raimey. Deborah's a fine girl, but she's for the Union. Why, she's a rabid abolitionist! The two of us would eat each other alive!"

Raimey, he saw, was considering his words, which made him rather nervous, for she had an uncanny ability to sift through what he said and arrive at the thoughts his words covered. Now she said slowly, "I'm sorry, Dent. It must be hard to lose someone you care for."

Dent stared at her with a mixture of exasperation and

amazement. "You know too much, Raimey," he said with a wry smile. "The man you marry won't have a secret in the world!"

"I'll never marry."

Her statement brought Dent's head up sharply. "Of course you will!"

"No." Her voice was inexorable as she added, "A blind wife would be too much to put on any man."

She had spoken quietly, and he had found no answer.

Dent never knew how to speak of Raimey's infirmity. She was matter-of-fact about it, but he could not be. It made him feel awkward.

He had gotten to his feet, saying, "I guess we'd better go in. It's getting dark."

A smile had tugged at her lips as she turned to face him and said, "That's your problem."

He admired courage greatly and knew suddenly that was why he was drawn to her. He did not fear death, but he knew deep within that he could not have handled blindness, that he would have ended his life if such a thing had ever come to him. Now as she stood there, her lips parted with humor at her own remark, he felt strangely protective, so much so that he put his hands on her shoulders. "Raimey, you're a wonder!" When she did not answer but tilted her face up to listen to his words, it seemed natural enough to lower his head and kiss her.

She did not pull away, and there was such innocence in her that instead of a light caress, he drew her closer. If she had resisted in the least, he would have released her, but she did not. When she drew away, she was in some way still with him. She was smiling, but he could not read the expression that lay on her lips, on her face.

"That was nice, Dent," she had said quietly; then they had

turned and gone to the house, not mentioning the kiss again.

❧

But now as Dulcie brushed her hair, Raimey thought of it. And not for the first time, for she had thought of it often. She was a young woman of no experience with men, having missed the usual girlhood experiences because of her blindness. When boys were around, Dulcie or someone else was there, as well. Even when she came into her teens and was taken to parties, nothing had occurred. One boy, a fat young fellow named Len Sykes, had kissed her once when she was fifteen, but it had been an awkward affair, leaving her untouched inside. Many of the books she had devoured spoke of love, but those were things in books, not life. She had tried to get Leona to tell her about such things, but Leona was embarrassed and kept herself back, saying, "It will come to you, Raimey."

But it had not come, and even as she sat feeling the comb go through her hair, hearing Leona getting ready in the next room and the clatter of hooves on the street outside, Raimey felt again the touch of Dent Rocklin's lips on hers—and was stirred.

Then it was time to leave, and she joined Leona in the carriage. Leona was excited and chattered all the way to the Masonic Hall, where the ball was to be held. All her talk was of the officers—how dull it would be when they left, but how proud they all were of them. Mr. Reed said little, and Raimey knew he was troubled. She didn't know the source of his discontent and could only think it was something to do with business. Her mother reached over to push away a curl that had fallen over her brow, saying, "You girls will probably have sore feet tomorrow. All the officers will want to dance with you."

But it wasn't like that, at least not for Raimey. The officers came to her, of course, greeting her, and were amazed that she knew them at the first word they spoke. But they did not ask her to dance. It was not their fault, for they assumed she could not dance because of her affliction. The dance went on for an hour, and Leona, of course, danced every dance. Raimey's mother was asked to help with the refreshments, which left Raimey alone, sitting in a chair, trying not to show how lonely she felt.

"I believe this is our dance, Miss Reed?"

"Oh, Mr. Rocklin!" She turned to face the voice with a smile, glad to meet Dent's father again. "How nice that you're here."

"It's good to see you, Raimey. Now how about that dance? But I'll have to warn you, I'm not much of a dancer."

Raimey rose and timidly put out her hand. "I'm no dancer at all. I never danced at a ball in my life—except with Dent at the Officers' Ball."

"Well, don't expect an old man to be as light on his feet as that young fellow, but I think we'll do all right." He took her in his arms and carefully moved out on the floor. He was, in fact, an excellent dancer, and he enjoyed watching the girl's features glow with pleasure as they moved across the floor. "You're not telling the truth, I think," he said easily. "You've danced more than once."

"Oh, we had lessons when I was fifteen, but I didn't try very hard. It didn't seem as though I'd ever need them." The tune was a fast one, but she followed him smoothly around the room and finally asked, "How's the new colt? The black one?" She listened as he spoke of the colt, then of other things she'd heard about on her visit. When the dance was over, she applauded with the others, and he took her to the refreshment table. She took the glass he handed her, and the two of them stood there talking over the sound of the music.

She wanted to say something about Dent but could not find the words. It was he who brought up the subject. "You and Dent have become good friends, haven't you, Raimey? I'm glad to see it." He hesitated, then added, "He was hit pretty hard over Deborah Steele."

"He was very much in love with her, I think."

"Well, she's a beautiful young woman—but it would have been bad if they had married. They don't agree on some important things, and they're both very stubborn. It would have been painful for both of them."

"I wonder how she feels about him now."

"My mother got a letter from her this week. It seems that Deborah is very involved with a young man. A strange sort of thing! He's from a very poor family, not really of her station. She got him to enlist; then his whole family got sick and she went to take over their care. Deborah found out her friend has a real gift for writing, and the two of them are thick. Of course, he'll be leaving any day with his unit."

"And Dent will be leaving to face him," Raimey said thoughtfully, her face suddenly losing its lightness. "Dent loved her, and she's interested in another man—and now this Northern boy and Dent may kill each other. What a terrible waste!"

"Yes, it is." Clay dropped his eyes, then lifted them. "I know you feel the war is wrong. So do I. But it's hard for a man to know what to do—" He was about to say more but broke off when he saw an officer coming across the crowded floor. "Here comes Dent, Raimey," he said quietly.

Dent had seen them and came right to where they stood.

"Hello. Have you two been having a good time?"

Something in his voice caught at Raimey. "Is something wrong, Dent?"

He glanced at her, then shrugged at his father. "Can't hide a thing from this woman! Well, not wrong—but we'll be moving out right away. Not tomorrow, but the day after."

"The Federals are on the move?" Clay asked.

"Yes, so the scouts say." Dent looked serious, but there was a light of anticipation in his eyes. "Word is that McDowell has left Washington with several divisions and is moving west. It's the real thing this time. Colonel Benton just got the word this afternoon, and he called all of us in for a staff meeting."

"I suppose this is all highly secret?" Clay said.

Dent looked around and saw his fellow officers who had been at the meeting moving about the room, talking with animation. "Supposed to be, but we've been waiting too long for this." He gave his father a calculated look, saying, "I don't think you'll enjoy the rest of the ball, Father. It'll probably be pretty much a celebration of the battle to come. I know you won't like that."

Clay said only, "Did you know your brother enlisted in the Grays this morning?"

Dent stared at him, shock pulling his mouth open. "David?" he asked incredulously.

"No, Lowell."

"But—he's only seventeen years old!"

"How many of your men are seventeen, Dent? Quite a few, and some of them even younger, I'd venture."

Dent was disturbed by the news. "He can't enlist without your permission, sir."

"I've given it."

Dent stared at his father, but no words came from his lips. Lowell had mentioned wanting to enlist, but all the young fellows wanted that. It had never come into Dent's head that his father would let him do it. It upset him, and he said angrily, "If you're so set against this war, why did you let him do it?"

Clay shook his head. "If I'd said no, he'd have run away and enlisted in another state, Dent. His mind's made up, and you know how stubborn he is. Nothing I could say made any difference." He shrugged his shoulders, then said, "Good night, Miss Reed," and left the floor.

Dent was shaken by the news. It made things different somehow, in a way that he could not quite explain. He had no fear for himself, yet the thought of his brother being killed brought a strong reaction.

The music started, and he pulled himself together. "Will you dance with me?"

Raimey said, "Yes, Dent," and the two of them joined the other couples out on the floor. She moved easily in his embrace, and when she realized that he was still thinking of the scene with his father, she said, "Are you so worried about Lowell?"

"Yes. He's too young."

"Two years younger than you and David."

He glared at her, then laughed. "You have a fiendish way of bringing a fellow down, Raimey! Yes, that's right, but he's—"

When Dent broke off, unable to find the word he sought, Raimey said, "He's young, Dent. But so are you, most of you. And so are the men who are coming to meet you."

"I know, Raimey." Dent seemed subdued, and they moved around the floor without speaking for a time. Then he said, "Blast his eyes! Why did he have to do it? Now I'll be worrying about him all the time, afraid he'll get himself shot!"

"That's exactly the way your father feels about you, Dent!" Raimey said gently. "Can't you see that?"

Dent stared at her, unable to answer. "No, he doesn't care about me."

"Don't be foolish," Raimey chided him. "If you don't sense his affection, you're a very dull man. Dent, don't you see that the things you hate about your father, they're not in him—they're in you."

Her statement hit Dent hard. "You can't know that, Raimey," he said. "You don't know what he's done to all of us, his family. He's ruined our lives!"

"Dent, being blind is pretty bad, but it has one advantage. A blind person, in some ways, is outside of things—standing off and watching, not really a part of what's happening. So he or she can be pretty objective. I've learned to get to know people better than most. What do you think about your grandmother?"

"Why, she's the best there is!"

"And does she think your father is a fool? Does she hate him?"

"Well, he's her son, Raimey."

"You know that's no answer. What about the slaves—do they hate him? No, they all respect your father. What about Rev. Irons? He's a fine man. Does he hate Clay Rocklin?" She paused, and sensing he could not answer, she grew gentle. "Is it possible that you've built up this bitterness for him and just can't let it go?"

She said no more, but her words had burned into him. When the dance was over, he took her back to her seat. "I'll be back soon. I have to talk to Major Radcliff."

He left, and the dance went on, but the officers had seen Raimey dancing and came boldly to claim her. She didn't know that several times Dent was on his way to her but stepped back when other officers came to dance with her. She sensed that she had hurt him and wished she had not spoken so bluntly.

Then, late in the evening, he came to her. Just as the music ended for one of the waltzes, he was at her side. "My dance, isn't it?" When she turned to him with a smile, he said, "I know a balcony around at the rear. Care to see it?"

"We always end up on balconies, don't we?" she said with a smile, and soon they were outside. "This is nice," she said. "The smoke gets very bad inside." Then she turned to him, her face luminous in the moonlight. "I spoke too harshly to you, Dent. I'm sorry."

He stood there studying her features. "Well, it came as quite a shock, Lowell enlisting. I wasn't ready for it."

"Do you think your brother David will enlist?"

"Not right away. David's a heavy thinker. It'll take him a year to sort the thing out. But my cousin Grant, he's in the cavalry. We grew up together. Hate to see anything happen to old Grant!" He fell silent, then said, "Up until now, it was all sort of a game, like chess. But now that it's come, I see it's not like chess at all. You can lose a pawn at chess and it's no matter. But if something happens to Lowell or Grant, it's final."

Raimey nodded. "Yes." Then she lifted her hand to his chest, wanting to touch him. "Oh, Dent, be careful!" she whispered. "Be very careful!"

He took her hand, moved by her concern, and lifted it to his lips and kissed it. "I will, Raimey."

They stood in the moonlight for a long time, saying little. He was troubled as he never had been before, and Raimey was moved by the emotions she sensed in him. Finally a cloud covered the moon, and he said heavily, "Almost time to go. We'd better get back." Impulsively he reached out and touched her face. "Remember when you touched my face—so you could remember? Well, it's my turn."

Raimey stood still as his hand moved over her cheek. It was a hard, rough hand, but it felt strong on her face. Finally he withdrew it and said with regret, "Time to go."

They left the balcony, and shortly afterward the ball broke up. In the coach on the way home, Raimey's mother said, "You'll miss the young men, won't you, girls?"

"Oh yes!" Leona said—but Raimey kept her silence, still feeling the roughness of Dent's palm on her cheek.

❧

"Sir, a recruit to see you. Says he wants to sign up."

Taylor Dewitt looked up from the map he was bending over. "Tell him to see the recruiting officer in Richmond. I don't have time for him now."

"I did tell him that, sir," Sergeant Huger insisted. He was a tall man with thick auburn hair and gray eyes. A graduate of the Virginia Military Institute, he would be an officer at some point. He had learned to read men pretty well, and he suggested, "Captain, I'd see this fellow if I were you. He looks pretty seasoned to me."

Taylor threw down his pen and made a helpless gesture toward Dent, who had been examining the map. "Well, bring him in, Sergeant."

"It's pretty late to enlist any new men, Captain," Dent commented.

"Lieutenant, I've learned to trust my sergeant. I don't know what the blazes I'm doing—but Sergeant Huger does. I feel like a child around him!"

"You'll learn. We all will," Dent said. Then he turned to face the two men who entered Captain Dewitt's tent, and shock caused his eyes to spring open.

"This is Clay Rocklin, Captain Dewitt," Sergeant Huger announced, then left the tent.

"Hello, Taylor. Good morning, Dent," Clay said. He saw that both men were staring at him in amazement. "Don't blame you for looking so shocked. I feel that way myself."

"What's this all about, Clay?" Taylor asked at once. He liked Clay, but he could not believe what Huger had said.

But Clay responded at once, "I want to enlist, Dewitt." He shrugged his heavy shoulders, adding, "I know everything you're going to say. You'll say I'm too old, that I've been against the war from the start, that I've got a bad record. Well, it's all true enough, but I'm asking you to give me a chance."

Taylor shook his head. "I don't want to do it, Clay. Blast your eyes! It's not right, somehow."

Dent asked suddenly, "Does this have anything to do with Lowell?"

Clay turned to him. "Yes, it does. I've disappointed Lowell. He thinks I've let him down. I tried to get him to stay out of the army, but he's joined up to spite me—at least that's part of it."

"Well, Clay, that's bad, but how do you think enlisting will help that situation?" Taylor asked bluntly.

"Right now, I have no idea," Clay admitted. "I guess I got the idea that if I was in his unit, I might be able to look out for him a little. Probably that's crazy. I don't know, really, but the other part is—I've got to show him that I care about him. The only way I can think of to do that is to enlist. So I'll begin the worst way in the world, Dewitt. I'll presume on our friendship. A favor. Take me into your company. Put me close to Lowell."

Taylor Dewitt stared at the man in front of him. "I thought I knew you pretty well, Clay, but I don't understand this at all."

Clay smiled without humor. "Makes two of us, Dewitt. Will you do it?"

Taylor turned to face Dent. "What do you think, Lieutenant?"

Dent realized that Captain Dewitt was leaving the decision up to him. If he said no, he knew that Taylor would turn down his father's request. And that was exactly what he wanted to do! The thought of his father serving under him seemed ridiculous. He knew it would spread throughout the regiment, and even higher, for many officers knew of his father's shameful record in the Mexican War.

And, too, he did not want to believe that his father was honest in what he was saying. If Clay Rocklin were doing this—giving up everything for a cause he didn't believe in out of love for his son—that would mean that he, Denton Rocklin, would have to admit that he was totally wrong in his bitter judgment of his father.

The silence ran on, and Clay understood what was happening. He had no idea what Dent's decision would be, but he did not beg.

Finally Dent's lips tightened. He said in a sparse tone, "Captain, you know the potential for trouble in this thing, how the men will talk. But I'm willing to let him try."

"All right, then, get him sworn in. Put him in Waco's Platoon with your brother." He turned to Clay, saying, "Another old friend of yours is the lieutenant. Bushrod Aimes. Now that's the last favor you get from me, Private Rocklin—and don't even ask one from Lieutenant Aimes!"

"Of course not, Captain Dewitt," Clay said, realizing that

the close relationship with Taylor was over, at least for a time, for there was a great gap between officers and enlisted men. "Thank you, sir."

He turned and followed Dent out of the tent. "This way to the commissary," Dent said in a clipped tone.

When they had gone past several tents, Clay said, "Sorry to put this burden on you, Dent. I know you don't like it, and I know you don't trust me. I'll do my best to make no trouble for you."

"All right, we'll leave it like that," Dent said. He was silent for six more paces, then added, "It's going to be an awkward business."

"You'll have to be harder on me than on any of the other men," Clay said flatly. "If you don't, you'll get criticized for showing favoritism. That goes for me and Lowell, as well. You know that, but I want you to pour it on, Lieutenant."

"I'll just do that, Private Rocklin!"

❧

Two days after Clay signed up with the Richmond Grays, the regiment pulled out, heading for Manassas, Virginia. Dent had been true to his word, and Clay had taken quite a bit of hazing when it was discovered that he was a wealthy aristocrat and the father of the lieutenant—and an old friend of the captain's. But the men had been convinced there would be no favoritism when Dent had assigned the worst work details in the company to his father and his younger brother.

Lowell had been almost as shocked as Dent when his father appeared in uniform. "Well, Lowell, here I am," Clay had said evenly. "Looks like we've got a war to fight."

He was a very quick young man, Lowell Rocklin. Instantly

he knew exactly why his father had enlisted. He said huskily, "You didn't have to do this, Father."

"Yes, son, I guess I did," Clay answered—and right then he knew that if he got killed with the first shot, he would at least have done one thing right with his family, with this son whom he loved so much.

The regiment marched to the train, flags flying and the band playing. When they got to the station, they were primed by refreshments and sent off with a fiery speech by the secretary of war. Then they moved to the flatcars and seated themselves, and with a blast of the whistle, the train gave a lurch and they moved out of the yard.

"There's Mother," Lowell said, waving to Ellen. "And there's Grandfather and Grandmother! Look, sir, Grandfather—he's smiling!"

So he was, Clay saw. Thomas Rocklin at last had found cause to smile at his son. Clay waved to his parents—then he saw Melora. She was alone, away from the crowd. He had seen her once before they boarded, but Ellen was there, and they had not spoken. Even now she didn't wave, but their eyes leaped the distance and something passed between them.

Lieutenant Rocklin had stood beside the Reeds for one brief moment. When the warning whistle blew, he hesitated. Mrs. Reed glanced at Raimey, aware of the agitation in this daughter's heart. She loved Raimey desperately, as a woman will love an afflicted child, and she knew—without Raimey's awareness—how the girl felt about the tall soldier standing there. At once she made a decision. "I'm sorry to inform you, Lieutenant, but you'll have to give this old woman a kiss."

Dent grinned at her, understanding at once what she was up to. He glanced at Sam Reed, who was smiling, and said, "Well,

I guess you don't get to kiss a good-looking man very often, Ellie." He kissed her soundly, then moved to Leona and gave her a kiss. Then he stepped in front of Raimey, saying, "Don't try to get away, Miss Raimey. It wouldn't be patriotic." He put his arms around her, and she lifted her face. Her lips were soft, and her hands tightened on his arms as he held her.

"Good-bye," he said abruptly and left to step aboard the train, which was moving out of the station. The men of his company had seen him kissing the women and gave him a rousing cheer, which brought a flush to his face, but he knew it was in fun.

The crowd stood cheering until the train was out of sight. Then the silence that fell was heavy and oppressive. It was similar to that moment after a graveside service when the mourners don't know what to do. Raimey felt the gloom and, as they walked away, heard one firecracker explode.

It was only a tiny popping sound, but she thought at once of the sound of cannons that would soon roar over the men who had just left. Then another firecracker made its miniature explosion, and Raimey was glad to move away from the station.

PART THREE

Bull Run

❧

CHAPTER 13

PRELUDE TO BATTLE

The appearance of a great comet in the sky on June 30, 1861, seemed to many to be a sign. The tail was in the form of a bright streamer with sides nearly straight and parallel. The *New York Herald* wrote solemnly about the "celestial visitor that has sprung upon us with such unexampled brilliancy and magnitude. . . . Many regard it with fear, looking upon it as something terrible, bringing in its train wars and desolation."

It was rumored that an elderly slave named Oola, who belonged to the Baynes family—close friends of Mary Todd Lincoln and her husband—had an evil eye and could "conjure spells." The slave woman was tall and large of frame, with eyes like gimlets and gray-black skin drawn tightly over her forehead and cheekbones. She said of the great comet, "Ye see dat great fire sword, 'blaze in de sky? Dat's a great war comin', and de handle's to'rd de Norf and de point to'rd de Souf, and de Norf's gwine take dat sword and cut de Souf's heart out. But dat Linkum man, chilluns, if he takes de sword, he's gwine perish by it!"

When Mrs. Baynes told the Lincoln boys about Oola's prophecy of war, carefully omitting the dire prediction regarding their father, Tad was greatly impressed and carried the story to his father. Mrs. Lincoln laughed, but the president seemed strangely interested.

"What was that, Tad, that she said about the comet?" he asked.

"She said," Tad answered, "that the handle was toward the North and the point toward the South and that meant the North was to cut the South's heart out. Do you think that's what it means, Pa?"

"I hope not, Tad," answered his father gravely. "I hope it won't come to that." But Mrs. Baynes reported that the president often looked intently at the comet, a forlorn look in his deep eyes.

Comet or no comet, everyone knew there would be a battle—the president, the army, the people, and certainly the press. There had to be a war! Hadn't the Rebels threatened the very substance of the nation? Horace Greeley thumped the patriotic drum daily in his newspaper with headlines that shouted, "ON TO RICHMOND!"

The young men of the North flocked to enlist by the thousands. Lincoln had called for seventy-five thousand volunteers after the fall of Sumter, but he could have trebled that number and not been disappointed. At times the whole thing looked like a big picnic. One Ohio boy wrote home about "the happy, golden days of camp life, where our only worry was that the war might end before our regiment had a chance to prove itself under fire." An Illinois soldier wrote to his people back home of "the shrill notes of the fifes and the martial beat and roll of the drums as they play in unison at early twilight." It was the sweetest of all music to him.

It did beat clerking. Boys whose recruit roster was not full rode about the country in wagons, drummer and fifer to play them along, seeking recruits. The cavalcade rode into towns with all hands, yelling, "Fourth of July every day of the year!" The training the recruits received once they reached camp was very sketchy. Almost all of them, including many of the officers, were amateurs, and it was not uncommon to see a captain on the parade ground consulting a book as he drilled his company. Most of the privates had been recruited by one of their acquaintances and, having been on a first-name basis with their officers all of their lives, could see no point whatever in military formalities. Gideon Rocklin heard one private of the Washington Blues call out after a prolonged drill to his lieutenant, "Hey, Jim, let's quit this fooling around and go over to the sutler's." These civilian-operated shops, which were located on army posts, were a favorite gathering place for the troops.

Professional soldier that he was, Rocklin had turned to rebuke the soldier, but his commanding officer, Colonel Bradford, had only laughed, saying, "You can't do anything about that, Major. These boys aren't professionals and don't intend to be. After we put the run on the Rebels, they'll take off their uniforms and go home again."

"Colonel, if we can't get the men to obey orders on a drill field, how can we expect them to obey when the bullets are flying?"

It was not a new argument, and a line of irritation creased the colonel's brow. He had raised this regiment with his own money. At first he had listened to advice from his adjutant, Major Rocklin. But as the war fever had risen in Washington, Bradford was more and more convinced that the war would be one quick battle and the Rebels would scatter. Now he turned to the major with a superior air. "Gid, you're a good soldier, but you don't know politics. The South has some great orators, and they've convinced themselves that they can pull out of the Union, but they don't have a chance!"

Gideon knew argument was hopeless, so he clamped his jaw shut. The two of them were on their way to a meeting with General Scott, and afterwards to a flag raising in front of the Capitol. There had been several of these, but this time, Rocklin realized, there would be action. He listened to Colonel Bradford speaking cheerfully as they drove to the War Department, but his mind was on the problems looming ahead—problems to which men like Bradford and some of Lincoln's cabinet seemed blind.

General Scott shared the major's concerns. He'd said to Gideon, "Blast it, Rocklin! I feel like a man on lookout up on the mast with icebergs dead ahead! And no matter how loud I shout, the politicians and the newspapers seem deaf! Do we have to rip the bottom from the ship before they'll wake up?"

When Bradford and Rocklin arrived at the large room where the president met with his cabinet, they found Scott already under fire. The old general, dropsical and infirm, a swollen and grotesque caricature of the brilliant soldier who had won the Mexican War, was flushed with anger. As the two officers entered and moved to stand along the wall, he was almost shouting, "You think the Confederates are paper men? No, sir! They are men who will fight—and we are not ready to engage the enemy at this time!"

Edwin Stanton stared across the room with hostility in his cold blue eyes. "General, we've been over this time and time again. I concede that we are not as well prepared as we would like to be, but neither are the Rebels. And I must insist that we have here more than a military problem. Surely we all realize that our people must have a victory now. If you do not know how transient and changeable men are, I do! If we do not act at once, the issue will grow stale. Already the antiwar party is shouting for peace—and many are listening. We must strike while the iron is hot!"

The argument raged back and forth for the best part of an hour, but Gideon noticed that the president was taking no part. He was sitting with his long body slumped in his chair, fatigue scoring his homely face. *He's got an impossible load to carry,* Gideon thought.

But suddenly the president stood up, his action cutting all talk short. Every man in the room was alert, waiting for his word. When it came, it was given softly, without special emphasis.

"Gentlemen, I have listened to you all—and I have prayed for wisdom. I presume that Jefferson Davis is praying for that same quality," he added with a faint glow of humor in his dark eyes, but at once he shook his head. "We have little choice. I feel that from the military point of view, General Scott is absolutely correct, but as Mr. Stanton has pointed out, there is the matter of the people. They must agree to this war, and they must have something immediately. Therefore. . .the army will move at once. General McDowell will be in command. He has his orders to march as soon as possible and engage the enemy. Some of you disagree with this decision. I can only ask you to put aside your objections—and join with me in prayer for our Union."

That ended the meeting, but General Scott grunted to Gideon, "Come along to the flag ceremony. I want some uniforms surrounding the president."

Gideon and Bradford followed the president and the cabinet to the front of the White House, where a large crowd had gathered to witness the raising of the flag. The platform was crowded, and the president took his place by his wife. Gideon looked over the brilliant groups of officers and their aides, the cabinet, and the cluster of ladies in hoop skirts and blossoming bonnets, then centered his gaze on the tall spare form of the president.

After the inevitable speeches, the moment came for the flag to be raised. The Marine Band played the national anthem, and all rose, officers at salute, civilians with their heads uncovered. Lincoln moved forward, took the cord, and gave a pull—

And the cord stuck. He pulled at it harder, and suddenly the Union flag tore, the upper corner coming off and hanging down. Those close enough to see the sinister omen gasped with surprise and horror, and when no one moved, Gideon leaped forward to where the ladies sat, extended his hands, and hissed, "Pins! Pins!"

Several were placed in his hands almost at once, women taking them out of their lace collars and dresses. Swiftly and efficiently, Gideon pinned the corner and nodded at the president.

With a look of gratitude at Gideon, Lincoln pulled the cord, and the flag rose to the top of the pole. The band had continued to play, and the people standing at attention below did not notice anything unusual except that there was a slight delay.

When the ceremony ended, the president extended his hand to Gideon, saying, "Major, you have my thanks." His hand was hard and gave the impression of tremendous physical strength. Lincoln apparently forgot that he was gripping the officer's hand. The Union's chief defender was staring at the nine stars torn from the flag by his hand. He finally released Gideon's hand, saying again, "Thank you, Major."

Gideon was not a superstitious man, but in the long days of war that followed, he often thought of that torn flag—and of the strange look in the eyes of Abraham Lincoln.

Amos Steele looked at the dress his daughter had donned for his approval. As Deborah whirled around, he noted the flush on her cheeks and the sparkle in her eyes and said, "Looks like you've succumbed to the allure of foppish attire, daughter." He added solemnly, "I saw some mission lassies on my way home. Now there are ladies who know how to wear modest attire!"

"Oh, Daddy, don't be silly!" Deborah lifted the skirt, curtsied deeply, then came to hug him. "You'd be shocked if I went to the reception wearing a dowdy old black dress." Then she laughed, adding, "Of course, I could go with a tambourine. The lasses like to shake those."

Her mother came in and caught the last of the sentence. "You young women will do anything to catch the attention of a soldier, but I forbid you to take a tambourine tonight." She was smiling, but then she frowned slightly. "A letter just came for you, Deborah. It's from Richmond."

Deborah took it at once, stared at the writing on the envelope, then said as she tore it open, "It's from Aunt Susanna." She scanned the lines and then became aware that her parents were watching her closely. They had said little about her attachment to Denton Rocklin, but she knew they were both concerned.

"She says that the world's upside down there, every man going for a soldier." She read a few more lines, then looked up with surprise. "Dent is a lieutenant now—and he's seeing a young woman quite a bit." Reading on, she seemed to stop and reread the lines; then she lowered the letter. "Her name is Raimey Reed. She's the daughter of a wealthy planter from Alabama—and she's blind."

The Steeles exchanged looks; then Amos said, "That's a strange one. Is he serious, does she say?"

"No. Just that he's seen her fairly often." Quickly she read the short letter, giving them the essence of it. "Uncle Thomas isn't well. Susanna's afraid he's going down, and the doctors can't seem to do anything." She hesitated, then added, "She gave me an invitation—more or less. But I don't think I'd want to go back, much as I'd like to see her."

Laura Steele nodded. "It might be difficult with the war hanging over us. Not very pleasant for anyone from our world to be in Richmond."

Amos pulled out his watch, squinted at it, and said, "Deborah, I'm going to see Colonel Bradford this morning. Any message for him?"

"No. He's taking me to the reception tonight. I'll see him then." There was no excitement in her face, but she brightened when she said, "I'm meeting Pat and Noel downtown at noon. We're going out to eat, and then I've got a surprise for Noel."

She turned and ran away to change, and Amos gave his wife a baffled look. "Do you think she's serious about this man Bradford?"

"I don't think so, but he's serious enough about her," Laura said. "He's taken her out three times. I don't care much for him, Amos. He's wealthy and fine looking, but a very worldly man."

"Well, he'll be gone with the regiment soon. Now I must go."

"Amos, are you sure this war is of God?"

"As sure as I've ever been of anything in my life!" He turned and left, whistling off-key as he went.

Noel Kojak stood somewhat in awe of Pat Steele. The tall brother of Deborah Steele was handsome and well educated, and at first Noel had hung back. But the two of them, being in the same platoon, soon came to be fast friends. Pat, of course, had been coaxed by Deborah to show attention to Kojak, and he did so, out of curiosity, wondering what his sister could see in a lowly workingman. He was prepared to be condescending to the young fellow but discovered to his dismay that young Kojak was a better soldier than he was.

Some of the companies got easy duty, but Lieutenant Boone Monroe of the Second Platoon, A Company, Washington Blues, had other ideas. He was a tall, raw-boned Tennessean who had come up through the ranks and was hard as nails. He worked his men hard, and Pat was soft. His first contact with Noel came when the two of them were assigned to dig a ditch. By ten o'clock Pat was gasping for breath and his palms were covered with blisters.

Noel had been watching Steele, and since they were the only two on this duty, he said, "Pat, you're going to ruin your hands. Take it easy and let me dig this old ditch."

"I can't do that!"

Noel had reached out and turned Pat's hand over. Shaking his head, he said, "You've got to toughen up. This won't hurt me, but you won't be able to hold your musket tomorrow if you keep on. Here, wrap my handkerchief around one hand and use yours for the other. Just sort of make the motions. Sergeant Gordon doesn't care who does it, as long as the ditch gets dug."

Pat had stared at his bleeding hands, then surrendered. He had wrapped his hands and watched as Noel made the dirt fly. They had talked all morning while Noel dug the ditch, and Pat discovered how mistaken he had been to assume Noel wasn't intelligent. Noel was quiet, but he had read a great deal, just as Deborah had said.

They didn't see Corporal Buck Riley, but the stocky Riley had sharp eyes. He'd seen what was going on and reported to the lieutenant. "Maybe I ought to eat them both out, Lieutenant. Can't let them get by with that."

"Let it go, Corporal," Monroe said in his twangy voice. "Anything them boys do for each other will pull 'em together. That Kojak, he ain't afraid of work, is he? And the best shot in the platoon." He thought about it, then shook his head. "I know Zale's been giving Kojak a hard time."

"Yes, sir. Mostly on account of Kojak's religion—but he's jealous, too, 'cause the boy's a better soldier than he is. I expect he'll pick a fight sooner or later." Riley shrugged, making his evaluation. "Zale's a tough one. Kojak would take a pretty stiff beating. But there's nothing we can do about that."

The trouble Corporal Riley had seen coming between Zale and Noel Kojak erupted not an hour after he had mentioned it to Lieutenant Monroe. It came when Noel and Pat returned to their tent. Most of the squad was there, having come in from drill, and Manny Zale was seething with anger over a tongue-lashing he'd taken from Sergeant Gordon for falling over his feet in drill.

When Noel and Pat came in, Zale scowled at them. He was a quarrelsome man, requiring a fight from time to time as other men require food. He had decided days earlier that he would establish his place by giving Kojak a sound thrashing. He sat there, watching as the two cleaned up, and when Kojak started outside, he made his move. Rising to his feet, Zale made for the entrance of the Sibley tent, reaching it at the same time Kojak did.

"Who you think you're shovin' around?" Zale said loudly and, with a curse, gave Noel a hard push that sent the young man sprawling in the dirt just outside the tent. Zale followed at once, and as Noel got to his feet, he yelled, "You've been bragging about what a fine Christian you are—now you go shovin' a fellow around! Well, I ain't no Christian, and you ain't either!"

Jim Freeman, a happy-go-lucky young fellow of eighteen, said, "Aw, back off, Manny!"

"Keep your trap shut, Freeman!" Zale scowled. "You're another of these imitation Christians. I'll fix you when I finish with the preacher here." He stuck his face close to Noel's, saying, "Now it says in the Bible, don't it, Preacher, that a Christian's got to turn the other cheek when somebody takes a poke at him. That right or not?"

Noel saw what was coming but could not think of any way to avoid Zale. "That's right, Manny."

Zale looked around, a grin on his wide face; then without warning his fist shot out, catching Noel high on the temple. Noel fell to the ground, the world spinning. He heard Zale say, "Well, c'mon, Preacher! Get up and turn me that other cheek!"

Noel got to his feet unsteadily, knowing that Zale would keep it up, but suddenly Pat Steele came to stand beside Noel, his eyes gleaming, and said, "Hey, Zale, I'm a Christian."

Manny Zale had no use for Pat Steele and shouted, "Well, take this, then—"

But when Zale threw a hard punch at Steele, Pat moved his head to one side, and as the burly soldier was off balance, Steele clipped him on the chin with a powerful right cross that dumped Zale on his back. A shout went up, and Zale made two tries before he got up. He was an old hand at brawls, however, and waited until his eyes cleared. Glaring at Steele, he demanded, "If you're a Christian, how come you busted me?"

Pat Steele smiled at him, then winked at Freeman and Tate Armstrong, who had come to watch. "I'm a backslider, Manny. That means that I'll beat your brains out if you don't stop throwing your weight around." Then Steele shrugged. "I'm just not as good a Christian as Noel, Manny, so come on and I'll give you the best we've got in the house."

With a snarl Manny threw himself forward, and as the two men slugged it out, a crowd gathered. Manny was tough, but so was Pat Steele. He had taken up boxing at college and had had a fine instructor. Now he stood off and with his long arms hammered at Zale's lantern-shaped jaw. Both men were bloodied when Lieutenant Monroe came strolling in. He'd been alerted but had let the two fight for a while before he came in to say, "All right, you two, break it up."

Zale and Steele stood there, gasping for breath, expecting to be punished for brawling, but Boone Monroe liked to see a tough streak in his men. "Better save some of that fer the Rebs," was all he said; then he strolled off.

Manny glared at Steele, cursed, and walked off to wash his bleeding face. Pat laughed, saying, "Come on, Noel. We've got a date with a lady. Let's see if we can get me patched up."

Noel tried to thank Steele, but the tall young man only laughed. The two of them dressed and caught a ride into town. When they got out of the wagon, Noel said, "Pat, you don't need me around. You'll want to spend the time with your sister alone."

"Nope. Deborah said to bring you along, and I always try to

mind her. She's a pest when she doesn't get her own way. Come along now. We're supposed to meet her at the Baxter House."

If he could have thought of a way, Noel would have fled, but Steele had a hold on his arm, and soon they were in front of the large white building with the imposing sign saying BAXTER HOUSE in front. Pat walked jauntily into the lobby, then took Noel's arm again. "She's probably already in the restaurant." The two of them entered the huge double doors, and when a white-coated waiter came to them, Pat inquired about his sister. The waiter said, "Yes, sir. Miss Steele is already seated. If you'll come this way, sir."

Noel followed Pat, more terrified by the elegant setting around him than he had been by anything he'd seen in the army. The enormous room was flanked with high windows admitting bars of sunlight, which caught the gleaming silverware resting on a hundred white tablecloths and glittered and refracted through the crystal chandeliers. The men and women were richly dressed: the women with jewels gleaming, the men with gold watch chains and heavy gold rings.

Then he heard Pat saying, "Well, Deborah, here we are."

Noel looked up and saw Deborah smiling at him. She said, "Come and sit down. We've been waiting for you. This is Mr. Langdon Devoe. My brother, Pat, and this is Private Noel Kojak."

Noel took the man's hand, mumbled something, and fell into his seat with relief. A waiter came, and the other three talked about food, but Noel was speechless. It came as a welcome relief when Pat said, "Noel, I've eaten here before. Would you trust me to order your dinner?" Noel nodded, never suspecting that his friend had eased the thing after getting a nod from Deborah.

The meal was fine, but Noel was so tense he could not have said later what he ate, except for the dessert, which was ice cream in a frothy crust, browned in an oven. He had relaxed a little during the meal, for the others carried the talk without demanding anything from him. Finally Pat said, getting up to leave, "Well, I've got important business. Strictly a military secret. See you back in camp, Noel."

"I'll bet that 'military secret' is a beautiful blond with blue eyes," Mr. Devoe said, smiling. He was a small man of thirty-five, with reddish hair that was receding rapidly and a full mustache that covered his lips. He wiped it now with his napkin, leaned back, and examined Noel. "Now then," he said with a gleam in his eye, "so this is your discovery, is it, Deborah?"

"Now you be nice, Mr. Devoe," Deborah said sharply. She was wearing a silk dress of green and white, and a hat covered her hair. "You can be very sharp when you want to."

"Why, I meant no harm," Devoe said in surprise. Deborah had warned him that young Kojak was terribly shy, and he saw that she had not exaggerated. He asked, "You're from Washington, Private Kojak?" and slowly he drew a response from Noel. But Devoe was a man who knew how to talk and how to make others talk, and soon he had put Noel at ease.

"Noel—if I may call you that?—I've read some of your stories. Did you ever hear of the *New Review*? No? Well, I'm the editor of the thing. Miss Steele has worked with me often, and she brought me some of your work." He put his sharp, dark eyes on Noel, saying, "I think it has potential."

"Well, it's just things I saw, Mr. Devoe. I—I don't really know much about writing."

Devoe laughed; then when Noel looked at him with alarm, he waved his hand. "Sorry. It's just that most writers have an ego bigger than the Rock of Gibraltar! Comes as quite a shock to find a young fellow who still has modesty." Then he said, "I want to print one of your stories, 'No Hope for Emily.' It's a good piece of work, though you'll need a little help in putting the finishing touches on it. I think Deborah will help you with that."

"Yes! I will, Noel—and there's more!" Deborah had gone to see Devoe with Noel's work and had practically forced him to read the stories. Now she said, "Tell him the rest, Mr. Devoe."

"Well, I'd like you to write about the war, Noel. You'll be moving out soon, I hear. You'll be very busy, but as soon as you can, write down what you've seen. It doesn't have to be about battle. Write about the marches, about the food you eat, about what the men are saying. I want to give people the real thing!"

Devoe spoke with excitement, then finally asked, "Well, will you do it? Oh yes, I forgot, you'll be paid for this, of course."

"Paid for writing?" Noel said with such amazement that the other two smiled at him. "Well, I—I don't know, Mr. Devoe—"

"Oh, Noel, you must!" Deborah cried out. "God has put this talent in you. You mustn't bury it!" Her eyes were wide, and Noel thought he'd never seen her looking so beautiful. "Please, Noel!" she begged.

Devoe looked at the two shrewdly, then rose. "You two settle it—and I hope it works out, my boy. You do have an exceptional talent, as Deborah says. I'll expect to hear from you."

After Devoe left, the two of them sat there for an hour. Noel could not believe what had transpired, and it took much persuasion on Deborah's part to bring him to agree.

Finally he said, "If you think I can do it, Deborah, I'll try."

Delighted at this, Deborah put her hand over his, smiled at him, and said, "Oh, Noel, it's going to be wonderful! You're going to be a fine writer!"

Finally she said, "Oh, pooh! It's time to go. I have to go to a reception tonight." They rose and walked out of the hotel, and she left, saying, "I'll bring your writing kit to the camp tomorrow, Noel. You can get started right away."

Noel took her hand, said good-bye, and then she was gone. He wandered the streets for several hours, then went back to camp. Pat came in later and asked, "You going to do it, Noel—be a writer?"

"I guess so."

Pat laughed. "Sure. I knew you would. Watch out for that sister of mine, Noel! She thinks she can boss every man she sees! She'll be running your life just like she does mine if you let her."

CHAPTER 14

ROAD TO MANASSAS

Captain Hiram Frost was standing outside the large tent that served both as his private quarters and as headquarters for A Company. He looked up as a soldier came on a half run from the drill field where Lieutenant Boone Monroe was putting his platoon through close-order drill.

A little earlier, Frost had been thinking about his three children and his wife, Kate, in Maine, when a message from regimental headquarters had been handed to him by one of Colonel Bradford's sergeants. He had read it and sent at once for Private Kojak. While waiting for the private to report, he resolutely put his family out of his mind and ran over the multitude of details that were his responsibility. The Blues would move out at dawn the next day, assigned to Sherman's division, and all of the details had to be complete before then. And now this message from Colonel Bradford!

Frost watched the young private approach, thinking of the sort of man he was, and it struck him that an infantry company was not too different from a large family. As the captain, he was the father, who supervised the daily routine; saw that the men were equipped, fed, clothed, and sheltered; heard their complaints;

administered punishment for minor offenses; looked after their health; provided for their general welfare; and led them into battle.

Frost knew every man by name and was fairly well acquainted with his circumstances and even individual members of his family. The lieutenants, sergeants, and corporals were his helpers, their position comparable to that of older children in a family—but the welfare of A Company lay on the shoulders of Captain Hiram Frost. As Kojak entered the room and Frost returned the private's salute, he mentally listed what he knew about him.

A workingman and a good one. Poor family and a large one. Dedicated Christian. Was having trouble over that with some of the tougher men in his platoon. A good soldier whose equipment is taken care of. Best shot in the company. Wish I had more like him.

He drew a breath, then plunged in. "Kojak, you've got a brother named Bing. Well, I've got some bad news for you." Frost paused, calculating the sudden expression on the young soldier's face, then said quickly, "He's in trouble with the law. I don't know the circumstances, but he's headed for jail."

Noel bit his lip, then said, "He's been running with a bad crowd, Captain Frost. I've been afraid something like this would happen."

"No question of his guilt, but I think it's not as serious as it might have been. The judge has given him a choice: go to jail or join the army. And he's asked to join this company."

Noel looked relieved. "That's good news, sir! Bing wouldn't be able to stand being locked up."

"I'm not sure I want him in the company, Private. He's a troublemaker, and we've got enough of those." Frost caught the disappointed look on Kojak's face, then added, "If I agree to let him join, I'll expect you to keep an eye on him. Keep him out of trouble. Be your responsibility. What about it?"

"I'll do my best, Captain. He's—pretty wild, but we've got good sergeants and a corporal who'll bear down on him. It's what he needs most and never got. One good thing is that he's fit enough, real strong."

"All right." Frost nodded. "I'll send word to have him transferred at once. And I'll advise Lieutenant Monroe to keep an eye on him. That's all, Private."

"Thank you, sir!"

Noel went through the rest of the morning automatically, worried about Bing. At noon in the chow line, Pat asked, "What's wrong with you? Your mind is someplace else, Noel." When Noel told him about Bing, revealing some of his problems, Pat shrugged and grinned. "Don't worry about it. Lieutenant Monroe will take the starch out of him!"

In fact, that was what happened. Bing arrived at camp late that afternoon, and his first interview was with First Lieutenant Boone Monroe. The camp was in a furor with men getting equipment together, ammunition being issued, and the cooks preparing rations for a three-day march. Bing Kojak stood in front of the lean officer, rebellion in his eyes, saying nothing. At first he had been relieved to escape a prison sentence, but now he was sullen and resentful.

Boone Monroe was a tough man, hardened by years in the Regular Army. He knew men, and he was an expert on the hard ones—those who fancied themselves tough. Seeing the anger burning in Kojak's eyes, he let the hammer down. "Kojak, you're no good! It ain't for me to question my commanding officer's choice, but it's me who's gotta make this platoon run. You think you're a tough pumpkin? That's fine! We'll see how tough. I reckon in a couple of days you'll be begging for a prison cell!"

Boone came to stand before Bing, his eyes hard as agates. "You're a fighter, I hear tell, a pug. Right now, you're thinking you can whup me. Go ahead, take a swing—then you can see if you're tougher than a firing squad, which is what you'll get if you ever lay your hands on me or any other officer! And I'll tell you this, you use your fists on any feller in this squad, and on every march you'll carry sixty pounds of bricks in addition to your regular pack. And you'll do it on bread and water! Any questions, Private Kojak?"

"No," Bing growled through clenched teeth.

" 'No, *sir*!' Kojak! You forget that one more time and you'll dig more latrines than you can think of. Come with me!" Boone walked out of his tent and when he found his sergeant, Jay Gordon, said, "Sergeant, this here is Bing Kojak. See that he gets equipped at once."

Gordon was a smallish man but tough. He resented big men and had just lost his two children in the epidemic. Now he stared at the tall, strong figure of Kojak and asked, "You a relation of Noel?"

"My brother."

"All right. You do as well as he does and we'll have no trouble. Get out of line one time and I'll make you miserable. We're pulling out in the morning, so I don't have time to teach you anything. You stay with your brother; do what he says."

Noel was getting his gear in shape when Bing walked in, his arms piled high with his uniform and gear. Sergeant Gordon said, "Here's your brother, Noel. Get him as ready as you can. We'll pull out at dawn, and I don't want him getting lost."

"Hello, Bing," Noel said. The other members of the squad were there, so he said nothing of the trouble that had brought Bing here. Instead he said, "This is my brother, Bing, you fellows."

"Hope you don't snore as loud as Noel," Amos Wilson quipped with a grin. He was a tall, thin young man from Illinois, a big talker who bragged about how many Rebels he would kill, but Noel felt that the talk was to cover up something.

"This is Tate Armstrong, Bing," Noel said, at the same time indicating a spot where his brother could pile his load. "He thinks he's going to be a doctor. Might as well, because he can't hit the side of a barn with his musket."

Armstrong nodded. "I'm too good a man to waste in the infantry." At twenty-two, he was short and trim and a very fast runner. He had spent much time trying to get transferred to the medical branch of the army, with no success. "Glad to see you, Bing. Hope you can shoot as good as Noel. Make up for how sorry I am."

Bing dropped his uniform and gear and turned to face the squad. "I guess I can do anything my brother can do," he said, a sour expression on his wide mouth. He was a rather formidable figure, six feet tall and powerful. His black hair was wavy and hung over his brow.

Manny Zale studied the new arrival, then asked, "You another psalm singer like your brother? If you are, I'm moving to another squad."

"Not hardly," Bing said quickly, sizing Zale up as one of his own kind. "I got no time for such stuff."

Noel said quickly, "This is Fritz Horst; that's Emmett Grant; and this is Caleb Church." Horst nodded briefly. He was German and still spoke with a strong accent. He'd joined the army because he'd been unable to find work. He was a good soldier, having served in the German army and grown accustomed to taking orders. Grant was a good-looking man of twenty-one, who was a good hand at card playing, so much so that he kept the others in the squad broke. He was terrified at the very thought of battle, though, and tried hard to cover his fear.

Caleb Church was the oldest man in the regiment. Though he was sixty, he was one of those men who had not lost any physical strength with age. He was a farmer from Ohio, and now he said, "Glad to see you, young feller. I wuz in the Mexican War, and it was the best time of my life. You come at a good time, I tell you, 'cause we're going to have some fun with those Rebels, by gum!"

Bing gave the old man a grin, for there was something comical about Church—or perhaps it was the reckless, happy-go-lucky spirit in Church that he liked. "All right, Grandpa. Maybe you're right." Then he looked at Noel, saying, "Big brother, any way I can get some grub?"

"Sure, Bing," Noel said instantly. "Let's go down to the mess hall and we'll see what we can promote."

As they left the tent and walked toward the mess hall, Bing said, "Noel, don't give me no sermons, you hear? This ain't my choice, but I'm stuck with it for three months. All I want to do is keep from getting shot, so don't try to make a soldier out of me, get it?"

"All right." Noel said no more, but he knew that sooner or later his brother would bring trouble to him. Bing always did.

At dawn the first platoon of A Company was on the way to Manassas Junction. The Washington Blues were almost lost in the host of other units headed for that small town. The first day's march allowed the men to get adjusted, and the camping out had the flavor of a boys' camp, with the men singing and playing tricks on one another. But the next two days wore them down so that there was little horseplay, and many of them had shed their heavy coats, tossing them in the supply wagons.

Watching them on the morning of July 18, Gideon said to Hiram Frost, "They look tired, Captain, but you've done a good job."

"Well, I've got some good lieutenants." Frost lifted his eyes to the distance. "Think we'll lock horns with the Rebs at Centreville, Major?"

"General McDowell thinks so," Gideon said. "He doesn't have any grandiose ideas about taking Richmond. All he wants to do is take Manassas Junction. That's a critical spot. The Manassas Gap Railroad runs through there straight to the Shenandoah Valley. As long as the Confederates hold that, they can move their troops by train to meet any attack we make. As a matter of fact, that's what I'm worried about."

"I understand General Patterson is supposed to hold the Rebel force being led by Joe Johnston in the Shenandoah. If he does, we shouldn't have any trouble whipping Beauregard at Manassas," Frost said. He had a keen grasp of military strategy and added, "We've got five divisions, which means we outnumber them greatly."

Gideon looked troubled. "If we go straight in, that's right. But if General McDowell hesitates, Joe Johnston will have time to move his army from the Shenandoah to Manassas. Then we'll be in real trouble, Hiram! I wish we had a general with more push." Then he shook his head and came up with a smile. "I'll keep my eyes open for your company. Best in the regiment, I do think!"

But there was no battle at Centreville, for the Confederates pulled back. Instead of plunging ahead against the thin ranks that had drawn up behind a small stream called Bull Run, McDowell waited. And this delay, as Gideon had predicted, gave General Joe Johnston time to move his men by train from the Shenandoah to reinforce General Beauregard—it was the first use of railroads to move masses of men to battle, and it changed the course of the battle of Bull Run.

When A Company marched across Bull Run into battle on July 21, 1861, they met not a skeleton crew, but thick ranks of tough Confederates reinforced by the likes of Thomas Jackson and his Virginians, who arrived in time to throw a blistering sheet of fire into the very face of Noel Kojak and his platoon as they advanced into their first battle.

Captain Taylor Dewitt drew a rough sketch on a sheet of paper of Manassas Junction and the small stream called Bull Run. He'd just come from a staff meeting where General Beauregard had delivered a fiery speech and given his plan of action. "Here's what we've got," Taylor said, pointing at the map with his pencil.

The officers were all tired, exhausted by the rough train ride from Shenandoah to Manassas. Captain Dewitt scratched his itchy three-day growth of whiskers, noting that his three lieutenants—Dent Rocklin, Bushrod Aimes, and Tug Ramsey—looked as rough as he did. What they needed was a good rest, but he knew there was none coming. He had gotten off the train long enough to meet with General Beauregard's staff, and now he wanted his lieutenants to know what was likely to happen in the morning.

"Our army is here along Bull Run. The Yankees are on the other side. This stream doesn't look deep, but it can only be crossed at a few fords or over the Stone Bridge. We've got those places heavily enforced. We're here on our right flank, because that's where General Beauregard thinks the attack will come. But what we're going to do is attack before the Yankees are ready. We can hit them hard and roll them up, then drive them before us all the way to Washington."

Dent stared at the map, then asked, "What if they go around our flanks?"

"We'll be in trouble, Lieutenant," Taylor said roughly, then added, "That's why we must attack. We're still outnumbered, even with Johnston's army from the Shenandoah to reinforce us. I think we'll go at that about dawn, so have your men ready. The well will run dry soon enough, so fill every canteen with water. Take fifty additional rounds of ammunition." It was already dusk as he added, "When we attack, be sure there are no stragglers. I'll be in front, but you two follow the company. Be sure your sergeants keep an eye out for men holding back."

Bushrod looked at Dewitt quizzically. "What'll we do, Captain, shoot 'em?"

"Make them think you're going to," Taylor snapped. The four officers lingered over the map, trying to convince themselves that the next day would be easy, but with no success.

Farther down the line, Waco Smith's squad was gathered around a fire where Corporal Ralph Purtle was roasting a couple of plump chickens on his bayonet. Smith sat back watching the juices drip from the birds, saying in a satisfied tone, "Purtle, if you could shoot as good as you can rustle up grub, we'd win this heah war tomorrow." Smith was a lean Texan who stood just under six feet. He had light green eyes and aquiline features and had been a buffalo hunter, a cowboy, and a Texas Ranger. He ran his squad with an iron hand, still carried a .44 in a holster tied to his thigh, and could pull and shoot the weapon in one unbelievably fast movement.

Corporal Ralph Purtle was a pudgy man of twenty-five who spent most of his waking hours either eating or thinking about eating. Waco had already decided that when the regiment outran its supply lines, Purtle was the man to do the foraging. "Hurry up with that chicken. We've got a busy day tomorrow," Waco said.

"You really think the Yankees will come at us, Sarge?" The speaker was the youngest of Waco's squad, Leo Deforest. Leo was only sixteen and had had to find a drunken recruiter in order to get accepted. He had a boyish freckled face and was eager for the fight to begin.

Private Con Ellis sat across the fire from Leo. He lifted his head, revealing battered features, the marks of his years in the ring. His eyes were hazel, almost yellow, and hard drinking had put blue veins in his nose and cheeks. "Don't be asking for that in your prayers, sonny," Con rumbled. "Army life is fine—until somebody starts shootin' at you." That summed up Ellis's philosophy. He was one of those men who was happy to let someone make his decisions for him in exchange for a few dollars a month. He had a cruel streak in him and leaned over to pick up his bayonet. He gave Homer Willis a hard rap on the soles of his boots and laughed roughly as the boy let out a yelp and drew his feet back. "That hurt, Homer? Wait till the Bluebellies put a minié ball in your guts!"

Willis bit his lip but said nothing. He was seventeen and even more immature than Deforest. He had enlisted because a girl had egged him into it, and now every night he cried into his pillow, longing to be anywhere but in this army that was marching straight into destruction.

Waco said, "Cut it out, Ellis, or I'll bat your ears down."

"Just kidding, Sarge," Ellis said. He was a rough man in a fight, but he knew that Waco was too tough a man to bluff. "What's goin' on out there?" he asked, waving toward the small stream that lay ahead of them.

"Yankees are coming, Con." Ira Sampson was a teacher of Latin and was never called anything but Professor by the men. He had fair hair and blue eyes and wore a pair of steel-rimmed spectacles. "They'll be coming for breakfast early in the morning." A wry smile came to his thin lips, and looking across the stream to where faint campfires of the Federals made flickering lights in the darkness, he said softly, *"Omni a mutantur, nos et muta murinillis."*

The strange sounds and cadence of Sampson's words caught at Lowell Rocklin, who sat back from the small fire. "What the blazes does that mean, Professor?"

"All things are changing, and we are changing with them."

"Sounds pretty confusin' to me," Buck Sergeant Holt Mattson remarked. A lean, clear-eyed man from Georgia, Mattson was Waco's right-hand man.

Clay Rocklin had been looking at the fires as they burned like small golden ingots across Bull Run. Now he turned his head swiftly toward the slight form of Sampson. "That's about right," he said softly, and his comment brought the attention of most of the squad. Clay had been the most silent member of the small group, speaking pleasantly enough but not joining in the frolic in which some of the men had engaged. He had been a rock, however, to Waco Smith, who longed to see him made a corporal. Waco had seen that the older Rocklin had whatever quality it is that commands other men. But Clay Rocklin had shown no inclination to move up, and Waco knew better than to push it.

A terrifyingly deep bass voice shattered the silence. "Well, what's that mean? I don't get it!"

Clay turned to see Jock Longley staring at him. Longley was the smallest man of the squad. He was twenty-six and had been a jockey. Now he complained constantly about having to walk, lamenting the fact that he had not joined the cavalry. "Just what it says, Jock," Clay murmured. He made a strong shape in the darkness, the high planes of his cheekbones and his deep-set eyes giving him a masklike appearance. The men around him, and men in other companies, had discussed him endlessly. They all knew he'd been a deserter or something equally rank in the Mexican War, that he was opposed to this present conflict, and that he was the owner of a huge plantation—but nothing seemed to fit. He was by far the most able man in the squad; he could outmarch the best of them, and he was a deadly shot with his musket.

Now Clay saw that they were all watching him, and he said, "Well, things are changing, aren't they, Jock? Our world's not the same."

"Yes, but it will be when we put the run on the Bluebellies, Clay." Bob Yancy sat close to Clay, for he knew the man and trusted his wisdom.

"That may not be as easy as you think, Bob," Waco interjected. "Some pretty tough boys on the other side of that creek."

"Aw, one Confederate can whip five Yankees anytime, Sarge!" Ralph Purtle said. He pushed his knife into one of the roasting birds, grinned, and said, "Suppertime!" He stripped the chickens expertly, giving each man a portion, then sat back and began to munch one of the drumsticks. "Ain't that right, Sarge?" he finally asked Waco. "What I said about us and the Bluebellies?"

"Ralph," Waco said as he chewed a chunk of white breast, "if we meet up with a bunch of Phil Kearney's division tomorrow, you'll run backwards so fast you'll lose some of that hog fat under your belt."

Lowell said quietly, "I've been wondering about that, Sarge. Will I run when the bullets start flying?"

Waco Smith said, "No man knows that until he's seen the elephant, Lowell. We can train you to drill, but when your friends start dropping around you, nobody knows if you'll keep going or not. Guess we'll find out tomorrow."

Waco's words brought a silence around the fire, and the men sat chewing on their chicken, all of them thinking of the next day. Finally Clay got to his feet, saying, "Guess I'll go listen to the chaplain."

His words stirred the group oddly. Some of the men got up at once, but Con Ellis jeered, "Got to have some religion to git you through the night, Rocklin? Not me. I'll take a good jolt of this whiskey!"

Clay made no answer, but when he arrived at the open spot where a large group of men had gathered, he was pleased to see that at least half of the squad was with him. Lowell said, "Look, there's Rev. Irons, Pa."

Large fires had been built to give light, and Jeremiah Irons had already gotten up on a small rise. He saw Clay and Lowell, nodded cheerfully, and said, "Well, I thought I could do as I pleased when I left home. But I see some of my congregation is here—so I'll have to behave myself." The men laughed, and one of them called out, "Don't worry, Preacher, we won't tell on you!"

Irons stood there smiling as the men settled down. He had volunteered for the army after a long struggle with his soul, but from his first day as chaplain of the Richmond Grays, it was obvious that he was going to be a success with the men.

He was not a hellfire-and-damnation preacher but preferred to stress the grace of God and the love of Jesus for all men. He was physically a match for most of the men, and on the long marches he often dismounted and let one of the men ride while he walked.

Now he began to speak. "We had a barber in our town who got saved last year, a man named Claude Foote. He was anxious to share his faith with people, to see someone get converted—but he found it hard to be a witness. Being a barber, he was a great talker, but he just couldn't find any way to begin telling men about God's love. Well, he came to me one day and asked me if I could help him get started. I suggested that he memorize a verse of scripture and that he simply repeat it to people."

The men were quiet, listening carefully, and Clay smiled. He knew Irons so well! The preacher was a good fisherman and knew how to lure his hearers in close so he could set the hook.

"Well, sir, Claude thought that would work. He went home that night, searched his Bible, and found a verse he thought would be effective. The next morning the first man to get into his chair was Les Burns, and a more nervous man never lived! He would jump at the sight of his own shadow. Claude put the towel around Les's neck and lathered him up good. He took his razor, stropped it until it was keen enough to cut a feather, then laid the blade right on Les's neck and said, "Les Burns—'Prepare to meet thy God'!"

The men roared, and Irons stood there smiling until they grew quiet. "Well, my verse for you men is the same as the one Claude gave to Les Burns. It's found in Amos, the fourth chapter, the twelfth verse: 'Prepare to meet thy God, O Israel.'"

Irons paused, letting the silence deepen. The sounds of men and horses stirring were on the night air, but within the grove the men felt the draw of the chaplain and strained to hear.

"Tomorrow, some of us may be in the presence of the Almighty," Irons said. "And then what will be important to you, should you be one of those who leave this earth to stand before God? Your money? What would you buy with it at God's bar of judgment throne? No, only one thing will have any importance at that awful time: Are you prepared to meet your God? And there is only one way to be prepared, men. Jesus said, 'I am the way,' and He is the only way. His blood is all that God can see. You may say, 'I was a Baptist,' but God will say, 'Where is the blood?' You may say, 'I led a good life!' But God will say, 'When I see the blood, I will pass over you and not destroy you!'"

For nearly an hour Jeremiah Irons spoke of Jesus Christ, surrounded by listening men who stood in the flickering firelight. He pointed the way to Jesus as the only hope, and when he came to an end, he said, "I feel that some of you fellows would like to prepare to meet God. But let me warn you that I am not selling fire insurance! You cannot come to God just to escape the dangers of battle, the death that may well be yours tomorrow. You must come with your life in your hands, and you must hold that life up to God, saying, 'God, I have sinned, but my hope is in the blood of Jesus. I give You my life, not just for a day—but forever!' If you're ready to follow Jesus, come and let me pray for you."

Clay watched as many men with tears on their faces, trembling in their limbs, stumbled toward the front of the clearing. Homer Willis had stood close to Clay during the sermon. Now he said, "I–I'd like to go. . .but I'm afraid."

Clay turned to the boy. "I know, Homer. We're all afraid to come to Jesus. It scared me to death. I cried like a baby!"

"Did you really?"

"Sure." Clay put his arm around the boy's thin shoulders. "Would you like for me to go with you while the chaplain prays for you?"

"Y—yes!"

Clay made his way forward, and when he got to where the chaplain stood, he met the man's eyes. "Chaplain, Homer is ready to give his life to Jesus. Will you pray for him now?"

Jeremiah Irons had left a comfortable life to join the army, giving up all security. But as he came and joined Clay Rocklin and the trembling boy, he knew it was worth it all!

CHAPTER 15

BATTLE MADNESS

Though Brigadier General Irvin McDowell, a graduate of West Point, had served with General Scott in Mexico, he had had only one battle in his military career. With a watermelon. McDowell, renowned for being a glutton of immense proportions, often became so absorbed in food that he had little time for conversation at the table. This, combined with the fact that he was short-tempered and socially inattentive, did not make him popular. Furthermore, he wore an absurd bowl-shaped straw hat, giving himself a ridiculous image that was far from what people desired for the general of the Union's first army. As for his military campaign, he once launched an attack on a watermelon, which he soundly defeated, consuming it single-handedly and giving it the epitaph of being "monstrous fine."

But on the morning of July 21, the general did not find the situation at Bull Run Creek "monstrous fine." Discovering that the Confederates were lined up across the small creek, he had determined to sweep to his left and cross with his forces at McLean's Ford, striking Brigadier General Beauregard's right flank. Then all he had to do was sweep forward, catching the Rebels from the rear.

But he soon found that Beauregard had amassed troops at that spot, including the brigade of Colonel Thomas Jackson. McDowell then thought to try the left flank of the Confederate Army, but he vacillated so long that more troops in gray had time to gather along the creek. Eventually thirty-five thousand Confederates had massed, which meant that while the Federals still had thirty-seven thousand men, the balance of power had been lost.

Finally at two o'clock in the morning, McDowell put his forces into motion. Brigadier General David Hunter, commander of the Second Division of McDowell's army, would move to the right, crossing Bull Run at Sudley's Ford. This night march proved to be dreadful, but finally the Federals came across, and at once sporadic rifle and artillery fire broke out from each side of the stream.

The battle would have been lost then and there, a glorious victory for the Union—except for Shanks Evans! Colonel Nathan G. Evans of the Confederate Army—called "Shanks" because of his lean legs—was outflanked and outnumbered, but the crusty officer had all the instincts of a rough-and-tumble brawler. He was the most accomplished braggart on the Rebel side, as well as one of its most intemperate drinkers. He even kept a special orderly with him whose chief duty was to carry a small keg of whiskey and keep it at hand at all times. But for all his faults, Shanks Evans was not a man to be tangled with!

He met Hunter's division with the fierce anger of a tiger. For an hour, with fewer than four hundred men, he held Hunter's force of ten thousand. He had saved Beauregard and Johnston from disaster, and when the Creole general and Joe Johnston became aware that the Federal attack was on their left flank, they began rushing reinforcements toward Evans—the forces of Brigadier General Barnard Bee, Colonel Francis Bartow, and Colonel Thomas Jackson.

Even as these fresh Southern troops were on their way, General Hunter fell, severely wounded with a bullet in the neck, and General Ambrose Burnside took command of the Federal forces. He threw his command forward, but just as his troops were about to overrun the Confederate line, the men of Bee and Bartow arrived and halted their advance.

Clay Rocklin and the rest of his squad had been dug in with the rest of Jackson's brigade since dawn. The Confederate troops had suffered heavy losses, including Colonel Bartow, who was killed as he led an attack; and Brigadier General Bee would be severely wounded and would die the next day. Rocklin's squad had been sure an attack was imminent, but it didn't come—and when heavy firing came from their left, Clay commented to Waco, "The fight's over there, Waco."

"I hope it stays there!" Con Ellis grunted, but the firing grew louder, and the men saw a courier come dashing up on a wild-eyed horse. The rider reined the horse in, gave some sort of message to Colonel James Benton, then rode down the line again at full speed.

"That's business," Waco murmured. "We'll get pulled out of here pretty soon." He was correct, for Major Brad Franklin came at once to speak to the captain.

"The Yankees are rolling up our left flank," he said, and there was a wild look in his eyes. "Get the company moving, Captain Dewitt, and don't waste any time!" He moved hurriedly down the line, passing the message to H Company, who were dug in behind some logs, and soon the Richmond Grays were moving toward the sound of the firing.

The double-time march took the steam out of the men, and

by the time Captain Dewitt halted them on a rise of ground, all of them were gasping for air. Clay had kept close to Lowell, and when they got to the hill, he saw that Bob Yancy was not out of breath. He grinned at the boy. "Wish I were your age, Bob!"

Then Lowell exclaimed in a shocked voice, "Look, they're running away!"

The sound was overwhelming, for Federal artillery was in action; the crackling sound of musket fire reminded Clay of corn popping over a fire or of dry wood snapping. Then they all saw the ragged line of figures in gray and butternut materializing from the smoke and coming toward them.

"They're falling back!" Clay said. "Looks like they've been cut to pieces!" The squad watched silently as the men of Bartow's command came stumbling by with ghastly faces, stunned and powder-blackened. Some of them were still firing; others had no weapons at all and were simply running.

Out of the rolling black smoke that concealed the enemy, an officer came dashing back. "That's General Bee," Dent said to Taylor Dewitt. Then he pointed, "Look, he's going to speak to Jackson." Jackson was on a slight hill next to a house called the Henry House. Dent and Taylor had moved close enough to hear Bee yell, "Jackson, they're beating us back!"

Jackson's eyes peering from under his shabby forage cap were a fierce light blue, hence his nickname "Old Blue Light."

"Well, sir," he said to Bee, "We'll give them the bayonet."

Bee nodded, turned, and rode back toward his command, yelling, "Look! There is Jackson standing like a stone wall! Rally behind the Virginians!"

C Company was in the second position of the regiment, and they crouched with their ears assaulted by the thunder of the Union guns. For two hours the battle raged as Beauregard extended his line of Confederate forces until it was fully eight miles long.

Dent moved up and down the lines, speaking to the men. "Looks like we'll get our chance pretty soon," he said, the light of battle in his dark eyes. There was no fear in him, and as the minié balls made their slipping, whining slash, he paid them no more attention than if they were butterflies. Once he came near where Lowell stood with Clay. His eyes came to rest on his younger brother, and he seemed to search for words. Finally he said, "Lowell, keep your head down when we charge."

"Sure, Dent—I mean, Lieutenant," Lowell agreed. His voice cracked, but he grinned, adding, "I'm scared spitless, to tell the truth—but I'm in good company." He glanced at his father, adding, "Lots of Rocklins here today. The Yankees can't handle us!"

Dent shifted his eyes to his father. "Watch out for him. . . and for yourself," he said.

Clay nodded. "You'll be the one up front, Lieutenant." He wanted to say something better, warmer, but knew that Dent would resent it.

"Get ready to charge!" The three men looked toward the front of the line to see the captain holding up his saber. "Come on!" Taylor Dewitt yelled over the sound of the exploding bursts of spherical shells. "Move out! Move out!"

Dent whirled and pulled his revolver from his holster, and the line moved forward. There was a house off to the left, scarred and pocked, flanked by a dense stand of timber. Nearby a Confederate artillery battery was engaged in a furious duel with the Federal gunners.

As they pressed forward, Lowell stumbled on something soft, and looking down, he saw a bleeding corpse. He didn't look down again but moved carefully to keep from stepping on any of the yielding forms that carpeted the field.

A high-pitched wailing rose above the other noises of battle, and Clay realized that he, too, was yelling with all the rest. Their cries made a weird incantation, shriller than the whining shells overhead. He lunged forward, aware that Waco Smith, a lupine expression on his long face, was moving to strike at some of the men in their platoon with the flat of his sword. Mattson was next to him, doing the same. One of the men who received a swat, Clay saw, was Leo Deforest. Leo yelped, then began to run with the rest of them.

Then Clay saw the blue forms through the smoke, undulating and weaving like dusky phantoms. The fire from the Federals rose to a crescendo, and he saw a man drop on his face down the line. Others were falling, too. Clay kept his eyes on Lowell, but there was nothing he could do—nothing any one man could do for another in that wild charge.

He felt the shock of his rifle butt against his shoulder and saw one of the blue figures driven backward. As he stopped to reload, Corporal Ralph Purtle came huffing up. The fat soldier had a scarlet face, for the charge had taken all his wind. Purtle stopped to look at Clay, his eyes white and rolling. "Clay!" he gasped. "I got to rest! I can't—"

A bullet struck Purtle in the temple, making a plunking sound, driving his head to one side. For one instant he stood there, dead on his feet; then his eyes rolled upward and he fell loosely.

"Ralph!" Homer Willis had been right behind Purtle. He fell on his face with fear, but Waco Smith yanked him up, put his revolver to the boy's ear, and said, "Willis, move out! The Bluebellies might shoot you—but I *will* shoot you here an' now if you don't get moving!"

Willis stood there, his face dissolving and his blue eyes filled with torment as he stared down at the body of Purtle. Clay had finished loading and said, "Come on, Homer. It's worse to stand here than it is to charge. Get moving." He pushed the boy forward and moved after him.

Waco panted, "Clay, these boys ain't goin' to stand much of this. You git on the other side of the line and hold 'em in place. I'll anchor this end."

"Sure, Waco!" He lifted his musket and waved his hand forward, saying, "Come on, you Richmond Grays! You volunteered to die for your country, so here's your chance!" The squad, which had been halted in the advance, looked at him. . .and something happened. The sight of Clay Rocklin's face, calm and without fear, gave them courage. Ira Sampson laughed wildly, crying out shrilly, *"Dulce et decorum est pro patria mori!"*

Holt Mattson, his lean face blackened by powder, stared at Sampson, then demanded, "What the blazes does that mean, Professor?"

Sampson grinned, his teeth white against the powder stains on his lips. "It means 'It is sweet and fitting to die for one's country.'"

Jock Longley had been listening to the exchange. Now his lips curled as he laughed harshly. "If that's whut education does for a man, I'm glad I never got any!"

Clay looked back and saw that the men would follow him. "Let's go!" he cried, and Waco's platoon swept up the hill into the blistering fire of the muskets that blinked like malevolent yellow eyes in the smoke.

❧

Major Gideon Rocklin had seen men die in action in many

ways, none of them pretty. But as he watched Laurence Bradford lose his courage as the Confederates pressed their attack, it was somehow worse than any death by bullet or cannon.

The Blues had been part of Hunter's division and so were one of the first groups to cross Bull Run. Ever since Shanks Evans's men had shattered the first line of the brigade, Colonel Bradford had been out of control. His face was drained of all color, and he was incapable of thinking. He was not the first man to discover that the skills that bring a man to prominence in the world of business or politics often are of little help when death flies thick in the air.

All along the march to Sudley's Ford, Bradford had been in an exalted mood, stopping his horse to make short speeches to the men. He had been, so it appeared, happy and excited, but Gideon had watched him carefully, for he had seen such behavior before.

Even when the first shots were fired, Bradford seemed all right. "Don't mind those bullets, boys," he'd called out gaily, riding along the front of the regiment. "We've got the Rebels where we want 'em!"

But five minutes later, a Confederate shell had exploded just in front of the line of battle. It had turned men into chunks of red meat, and a part of an arm was thrown against Colonel Bradford's chest. He had looked down at the bloody stain on his chest, then at the arm lying at his feet, and had begun to make queer sounds in his throat.

"You all right, Colonel?" Gideon had gone to him at once and had been shocked at the vacant expression in Bradford's eyes.

"Are you hit, sir?" asked one of Bradford's aides who came running up.

Gideon added urgently, "Sir, they're going to enfilade us if we don't get over to that bluff." When Bradford only stared at him, Gideon made an instant decision. "Lieutenant, take the colonel to the rear. I'll take command until he's able to return."

He didn't wait to hear the aide's answer but began shouting orders at once. "Captain Frost! Get your men in position on the top of that bluff. The Rebs will be on top of us, and they've got to come up that hill. Hold 'em back as long as you can!"

"Yes, sir!" Captain Frost ran to where Lieutenant Boone Monroe was standing. "Major Rocklin's in command, Boone—he says we've got to hold that bluff or the Rebels will break through."

"The colonel get hit?"

"No. Lost his nerve, I think. Wouldn't be good for the men to see him. Now get your platoon up!"

Frost moved quickly to the other platoons, and Boone yelled, "We'll form a line along the crest of that bluff!" Then he wheeled and shouted, "First Platoon! Let's move!"

Noel moved at once, running through the brambles that tore at his legs. Then when he got to the top of the ridge, he stopped dead still, staring through the amorphous forms of the Confederates as they appeared dimly through the smoke. As Pat came panting up to join him, Noel said, "There they come, Pat." He heard Monroe's shrill yelping command, "Shoot them down! Shoot them down!" and put his musket to his shoulder. The charging Confederates were dim figures, half hidden by the clouds of smoke. The air was filled with the shrill cries they made as they came on, and their bullets were whistling in the air around the platoon. Something clipped a branch from a sapling just to Noel's right.

Lifting his musket, Noel drew a bead on one of the gray-clad men, and for one brief moment, his finger seemed to freeze.

I'm about to kill a man! The thought flashed through his mind, and he couldn't pull the trigger. He, along with others in the company, had wondered how he would take a man's life—and fear had been in him that he would be unable to do it. But he had prayed long and, without coming to any firm theological answers, had resolved to do his duty as a soldier. He had spoken of this once to Pat, whose answer had been, "Noel, if you can't do it, get out of here. The man next to you is counting on you, just like you're counting on him. I hate it, too, but we're here, and we've got to do what we came for."

A faint cry came from Noel's left, and he shifted his glance to see Emmett Grant drop his musket and fall to the ground, clutching his stomach. His eyes were filled with terror as he looked at Noel, and he was making a mewing sound that rose above the crack of muskets.

Noel tore his glance from Emmett, took aim, and fired. His target threw up his hands in a wild helpless gesture, then fell motionless to the earth. Noel wanted to drop his musket and flee, but he clamped his lips tight, loaded his musket expertly, then fired again.

The Confederates came on, yelping like hunting dogs with their shrill, fierce cries, and Noel loaded and fired like an automaton. He was like a man building something, going through the motions of loading, then firing, then loading again.

But when the attack ran down and the Confederates melted back into the smoke, he looked around to see that men were down all along the line. He stared at Pat, who was looking across the ravine for a target, saying, "We've got some of our men down, Pat."

Pat's mouth was black from the powder of the paper cartridges, and his eyes were wide. Looking down the line, he seemed to be drugged. He drew a hand across his face, gave a ragged sigh, then said, "We made it, Noel." Then his glance shifted and he said, "Let's see about the boys."

They put their muskets down and joined Lieutenant Monroe, who was bending over Emmett Grant. Monroe's eyes were angry as he looked up. "Emmett's gone." He closed the dead soldier's eyes, and the three of them moved down the line, finding that one more of the squad had been killed—Corporal Silas Tarkington, a silent man of thirty-five from Ohio. He had taken a bullet in the throat, and the front of his uniform was drenched with scarlet.

"He was a fine fellow," Pat whispered, his throat dry from the scorching heat. "Got a wife and baby boy back home. He was proud of that boy."

"I'll have to write her a letter," Monroe said. Looking down the line, he called out, "Anybody else hurt?"

"The dirty Rebs shot me in the rump!" Manny Zale called out. "I better get to the hospital!"

Monroe walked over, said, "Pull them pants down, Zale," and discovered a slight scratch on the soldier's hip. "I've had worse than that pickin' blackberries," he snapped, dismissing the complaint with an angry gesture.

He went back to stand by Sergeant Gordon, who said, "Think they'll be back, Lieutenant?"

"You kin bet on it!"

Noel walked over to where Bing was standing. "You all right, Bing?" he asked.

Bing gave him a tight look, his mouth drawn up into a pucker. He cursed, saying, "Be better off in jail than here!" Bing Kojak did not lack physical courage—he had plenty of that—but he was a man of totally selfish impulses, and the thought of having his life cut short for nothing angered him. He had made up his mind while enduring the enemy charge that somehow he was not going to risk getting killed, but he was too crafty to say so to Noel. "You all right?" he asked finally.

"Yes. They'll be back, though." Noel hesitated, then said, "I'm glad you're all right, Bing." He got only a nod in response, then moved away. Sergeant Gordon called out, "Kojak, you and Steele take the canteens back to that creek and fill 'em up."

"Sure, Sergeant." The two men made their way to the sluggish stream, and as they were filling the canteens, Pat said, "It wasn't like I thought it would be, Noel." Holding the canteen under the surface, he thought about the action, then shook his head. "Maybe I heard too many speeches, all about how glorious the war was. But it's not, is it? It's filthy and mean."

"Always has been, Pat," Noel agreed. "Guess I'm like you. Read too many novels where the heroes went in with flags flying. But when I saw poor Emmett's eyes when he took that bullet in the stomach, I saw what it's going to be like. And it's going to get worse, Pat! I—"

He broke off, for the sound of musket fire crackled sharply. "That's our bunch, Pat!" he said, and the two scrambled back in time to join the platoon, which was under another heavy attack from the Confederates.

"Gordon's down," Corporal Buck Riley growled as the two men fell into line beside him. "And our lines are breaking. The Rebs have broke through to our left. They can come in behind us, so keep an eye out to the rear." A shell exploded down the line, scattering bodies, which flew like tattered dolls through the air. The men close to the explosion began to run for the rear but found Lieutenant Ben Finch there ready to beat them back into line.

"Can't stand too much of this, Noel!" Riley said, a bitter light in his eyes. "You two keep an eye on the boys. We gotta hold this ridge."

And hold it they did, though the battle raged on for hours. Noel lost track of the charges made by the enemy and knew that the Rebels were taking terrible losses, but so was A Company. All down the line bodies were slumped, and the survivors robbed their cartridge cases for ammunition.

Once Major Rocklin came by to encourage them. He spoke with Captain Frost, saying, "Your company has done fine work, Captain."

"What's happening, Major?"

Gideon pulled off his cap and looked around at the thin lines. "It's not good, Hiram. We waited too long, and now the enemy's got plenty of firepower." The two men spoke quietly, and finally Gideon said, "If we get hit hard one more time, I don't think the men will be able to stand it. If we have to retreat, we have to do it in an orderly fashion."

"Hate to think of retreat!" Frost snapped, shaking his head angrily. His blood was up, and he asked, "Can we charge 'em? What about the colonel?"

Gideon gave him an oblique stare, then shook his head and said bitterly, "He's at the rear. And McDowell won't give the order for a general attack. It's all that'll save us, I think." He turned and walked down the line, speaking with the men. When he got to Pat, he grinned, saying, "Well, Private Steele, you're a soldier now."

"Yes, sir, I guess so." Pat nodded, then looked at Noel. "We did the best we could. Noel here, he's the steadiest one in the platoon."

Gideon said, "I remember the day you enlisted, Kojak.

Guess you've been giving that some second thoughts? Like to be back in the factory?"

Noel flushed but said at once, "No, Major."

His brief answer pleased Gideon. "Good man! We'll come out of this. Keep your heads down." He smiled and said, "If I see Deborah, I'll tell her her recruit is doing a fine job—and her brother, as well."

Major Rocklin moved on, and Noel said, "He's a real fine man, Pat." He thought of Deborah, and as the firing began to pick up, he wondered when he'd see her again. But that seemed far off and remote, and the men rushing toward him through the smoke of battle were terribly real.

It was an hour after Rocklin left that the Confederates received fresh reinforcements. Another train had arrived at Manassas Junction, and Brigadier General E. Kirby Smith and Colonel Arnold Elzey arrived at Bull Run, throwing their forces into the battle. The turning point was a head-on cavalry charge led by Colonel Jeb Stuart. As the horses crashed into the infantry, the men in blue could not stand it. Throwing their guns down, they ran blindly, and their panic became epidemic. All up and down the line, the Federals, seeing the fleeing hordes, collapsed.

Beauregard, seeing the sudden shift, ordered a general charge of the whole line, and the gray-clad Confederates swarmed toward the thin blue line.

Captain Frost had seen other companies break and run, but he held A Company fast. "Stand still, men. We can hold 'em! Don't run!"

Noel saw the waves of Confederates sweeping across the terrain, yelling like fiends. He was aware that some of the platoon had thrown their muskets down and joined the rout— Bing among them—but he loaded his rifle, took aim, fired, then loaded again. He had no hope of survival but continued to fire until the wave broke and a lean Confederate lieutenant appeared right in front of him. His musket was not loaded, so he raised it like a club. He heard Pat yell wildly, "Noel—!" and he saw the flash of light on the revolver the Confederate officer lifted.

Then the explosion came, sending a long, cold sliver of pain through Noel's side. He tasted the dirt as his face hit the ground, and the earth seemed to swallow him as the din of battle faded into a mute silence.

CHAPTER 16

THE RESCUE

Waco's squad had fought their way halfway up the ridge, but a Federal cannon found its range, and Waco shouted, "Take cover!" He led them to a waist-deep ravine, and the men fell panting on the ground, trembling with shock. The struggle continued, making an angry clamor that drowned out everything else.

Waco's men were in the wake now, in one of those abrupt interstices of battle, and a fresh rank of butternut troops surged past them, then another, then another.

"Them's General Smith's boys," Waco said with a nod to Clay, who had plumped down near him. "Looks like we got the Yankees on the run!"

"We'd better pick up all the ammunition we can," Clay said. "And canteens, too." Waco called out an order, and soon the squad had scoured the field, bringing back all the water and cartridges they could find.

"Gives me the creeps, taking stuff from dead men," Lowell said with a shiver as he returned.

As he took a drink from a canteen, Clay looked at him quickly but said only, "They won't be needing it, Lowell, and we will."

"Think they'll come again, Clay?" Jock Longley asked, looking over the hill. "I've had plenty of what they offered us. Let them fresh boys handle it."

Waco, sitting with his head down, noticed how the men seemed to look up to Clay Rocklin. It was a thing that was in some men, he knew. If a man had it, it was there, but if he didn't, nothing could put it in him.

Clay looked at the sergeant. "I'd guess we'll do the charging from now on, don't you reckon, Waco?"

"I hope we chase the Bluebellies all the way back to Washington," Waco said. He tilted a canteen; then the sound of a beating drum rattled over the air. "Signal to form up," he said. "Let's go." He led the squad to where the regiment was being put in formation by Colonel Benton, and soon they caught up with some of the men who'd relieved them.

"What's going on, Lieutenant?" Benton demanded of one of the officers from Smith's division.

"Got a tough spot in the line up there, Colonel." The speaker was a short, red-haired lieutenant with a bristly beard. "We've hit that hill three times but can't make a dent in it. They got the whole division pinned down here."

James Benton had visions of a political future when the war was over, and he knew that a good war record would be necessary. Looking up the hill, he saw the flicker of small-arms fire, but there was no artillery. At once he said, "We'll take that piece of ground!" He wheeled his horse around and rode to where Major Brad Franklin stood waiting. "Brad, we've got to take that hill."

Franklin stared up the hill, then shook his head doubtfully. "We better wait for some artillery, Colonel. That's a long distance for the men to be under fire. They're shooting right down on us, and there's no place for a man to hide and reload."

"Have the men fix bayonets," Benton commanded. "We've got good men, and the Feds' ranks are pretty thin, I'd guess."

Franklin moved away and, passing down the line, gave the order. He stopped by C Company and spoke to Captain Taylor Dewitt and Lieutenant Dent Rocklin. "I'd just as soon wait for reinforcements, to tell the truth, but the colonel won't hear of it. Taylor, send half of your company up the hill and keep the other half in reserve."

When Franklin moved along, Dent said, "Brad's right about that hill. Why don't we go around and flank them, Captain?"

"Because that's not as glamorous as a bayonet charge," Taylor said bitterly. "Benton's got to have a headline, and I'm thinking some of us are going to pay a pretty high price for it."

Dent said abruptly, "Let me take the men up, Captain. Bushrod can stay here with the reserves."

"All right, Dent."

Half of C Company was chosen, and when Waco saw that his platoon was not going, he cursed. "We all should go up that hill," he said bitterly. But he was almost alone in his eagerness to make the charge.

Clay stood beside his son and Bob Yancy, watching the men form up, and Lowell said, "I wish Dent wasn't going up there."

"I'd guess he volunteered for it, Lowell," Clay said slowly. He didn't like the decision, believing that it was a useless charge. The Federal line was pulling back all along the stream, and the unit holding the hill would join them, given time. Benton was stubborn and proud—and he was going to put the lives of five hundred men on the line.

Benton rode out on his horse, waved his saber, and cried out, "Come on, you Richmond Grays!" As he turned and his horse moved up the hill, the company began to run.

"Benton's a fool!" Waco said, biting his words off. "He's the man on the horse. Every Yankee in that bunch will be trying to put him down!"

And he was correct, for before the men had gone fifty yards, a bullet struck Colonel Benton's horse. The animal went down, pinning Benton's leg, but he cried out to Dent Rocklin, who came running to help, "Never mind me, Rocklin! Take the men up!"

A fire was in Dent's blood, and he yelled, "Come on!" He ran up the hill shouting and was aware that the fire from the Yankees had slackened. Perhaps there were fewer of them; perhaps they were low on ammunition—whatever the reason, the lull allowed Dent and his men to push forward. Now they were halfway, then close enough to see the faces of the enemy. There were not as many as Dent had feared, but looking around, he saw that not many of his men had made it. Some were down on the ground, lying still; others were running back down the hill. Only a few men were with him, but Dent saw that if they tried to run back, they'd be shot down.

He leaped ahead, crying out, "Come on, Grays!"

His breath was ragged, and his chest felt as though it were on fire. Then, suddenly, a young Union soldier was in front of him, swinging a rifle. Dent lifted his pistol and pulled the trigger. The slug struck the soldier in the body, and he grunted, then fell to the ground. At once another soldier came at him from the right, his bayonet aimed at Dent's belly. Dent turned sideways, letting the blade go by, and shot the soldier in the chest. The man dropped his rifle, stared at Dent reproachfully as if he'd done something terribly wrong—then sat down, staring at the ground.

"Come on, men!" Dent yelled. "We can hold this spot!" It

was bad, he saw, but they had broken the line in the right place. The gray line of Confederates was convoluted, twisted and strung out to his right and to his left, but if he could get them together, they could make a stand. Men began crowding in, and he screamed, "Reload! Reload!"

Back down the hill, Captain Dewitt saw what was happening. He had watched the charge fall to pieces and knew that there was nothing he could do. Colonel Benton had scurried back to safety and stood there now, shocked and horrified by the sight of his men being cut down as though by a giant scythe.

"We've got to go help them," Taylor said.

"No!" Benton cried out. "It'll be suicide! Look at how many men we've lost!"

They were standing not ten feet away from where Clay and Waco were waiting. Clay was sickened over the slaughter. Then Lowell, who had the best eyes in the company, said, "Look! Dent's making a stand!"

"Can you see that far?" Waco demanded. "What's happening?"

"Dent's got a few men together, but they're going to get swallowed! We've got to help!"

Clay looked around and saw that some of the officers' horses had been brought up from the rear. He whirled and ran for them. When he reached them, he discovered that Waco, Lowell, and Bob Yancy had followed. Bob grinned at him, his greenish eyes alive with excitement. "I do believe we're about to join the cavalry, Clay!" he yelped. He reached out for the reins of one of the mounts, and the horse-holder, a skinny young man with a sunburned face, cried out, "Hey! You can't take these horses!"

Clay brushed him aside and swung into the saddle. Lowell and Waco had each grabbed a horse and were waiting for him.

"I'm going to get those boys!" Clay said, then drove his heels into the sides of the horse. The animal shot off like a rocket. The four of them hit the open, and Taylor Dewitt and Colonel Benton stared at them. Taylor said, "Colonel, if we don't support them, you'll never get a vote from me or my folks."

Benton glared at him, then shouted, "The devil with your votes, Taylor! Let's go, men!"

Dewitt's stubbornness and Benton's decision probably saved Clay and the others, for the brigade moved up the hill, firing as they ran, and the volley shook the defenders so badly that they dodged and were unable to hit the four horsemen.

Dent heard one of the Union soldiers scream, "Look out, you fellers! Them Rebels is coming! It's a cavalry charge!" Looking over his shoulder, Dent saw the movement of the gray line that had left the trees and was sweeping up the slope. He saw the horsemen, too, and could not understand who it could be. "Keep at 'em, boys!" he yelled and stopped to reload his revolver.

But even as he looked down, he heard one of his men scream, "Look out, Lieutenant!" A shadow fell over him, and he saw the bulk of a horse that was headed for him. He saw the uplifted saber, too, and the grim face of the Yankee captain who held it. Frantically he threw himself to one side, throwing up his pistol to fire, but he was too late. The falling saber struck his forearm, slicing into the flesh, and the gun fell from his nerveless fingers. There was no pain, just a numbness, and he stepped back, but the sun blinded his eyes. He saw the flash of the sun on the saber and tried to duck, but the blade fell inexorably, catching him on the left side of his face. He felt the blade grate against bone, and the blood spurted into his eyes, blinding him. He fell to his knees, waiting for the next blow—the one that would kill him—and was filled with a great regret.

He felt no fear—rather, he thought of all he would lose. In that one moment he thought of Gracefield, of Deborah Steele, and most clearly of all, he saw the still features of Raimey Reed. *By the Lord!* he thought in anguish. *I hate to lose it all!*

But the blow never came. Instead there was a commotion over him, and he heard a voice cry out. Then hands were on him, holding him up, and a voice was crying out, "Dent! My boy! My boy!"

Clay had driven the horse at top speed, and when he crashed into the midst of the Yankee line, he instantly saw the Yankee captain charging down on Dent. Clay's musket was empty, but the bayonet was in place, and he drove the horse forward, thrusting the bayonet into the officer's side. The man cried out and fell to the ground, and Clay, heedless of the fierce fight going on all around him, fell to his knees beside his son, lifting his head. He was weeping, thinking he was holding a dead son—then Waco's voice broke through. "Clay, we got to get that arm tied up 'fore he bleeds to death!"

The Texan shouldered Clay to one side and in a moment had taken off his neckerchief and whipped it around Dent's arm. "That's a bad cut," Waco said, "but the face looks worse! Here, let's get some of this blood away so we can see what it looks like—"

The firing had died down, and Lowell came to stand over the wounded man. As Waco wiped the blood away, Lowell grew sick, for the saber had left an awful wound. It started at the skull over Dent's left temple, and Lowell could see the whiteness of bone in the gaping crevice of flesh.

"May have got his eye," Waco said doubtfully. "Let's put a bandage on this and get him to the surgeons. That's got to be sewed up fast!"

The four men improvised a stretcher out of saplings, used the coats from dead soldiers to form a base, then made their way back to the field hospital. It was over a mile, and they were all gasping when they got there. The ground was covered with wounded men, but Dr. Carter came to them. "What is it? Put him down over here."

Clay watched numbly as the doctor examined the wounds. He was praying silently and did not know that he was crying. Lowell, pale as a sheet, came to stand beside Clay while Waco and Bob stood slightly back. "Kind of a family affair," Waco murmured to Bob Yancy. "Sure hope that young fellow makes it."

After what seemed like a long time, Carter came to stand beside Clay and Lowell. "Two bad wounds," he said abruptly. "May lose that arm and may lose his eye."

"Don't take the arm!" Clay said instantly. "I'm believing God will heal it."

Dr. Carter knew the Rocklins well. He practiced in Richmond and knew the history of the trouble between Clay and his son. He had spoken harshly of Clay when he'd heard of the stand Clay had made against the war, but now he stood there, his eyes thoughtful. Finally he said, "I'll leave it on—but he may lose it later. I think the eye is all right if the muscles aren't cut."

"Do your best, Dr. Carter," Lowell pleaded.

"Certainly, but—"

Clay saw that something else was troubling Carter. "What is it?" he asked.

"Well, I sewed up his face, but it's a terrible wound, Clay. Going to leave a frightful scar. Nothing more to be done, though." He turned away, saying, "I'll do my best on the arm."

Waco came to Clay's side, stood there for a moment, then

said, "I guess Bob and me better get back, Clay. You and Lowell stay here until you find out about the lieutenant."

"Thanks, Waco—for everything."

As Yancy and the sergeant moved away, the younger man said, "Shore hope he makes it, Waco. I've knowed the Rocklins since Hector was a pup." He chewed thoughtfully on his plug of tobacco, then added, "Mr. Dent, he was always the finest-looking feller in the county. Had his pick of all the good-looking girls. But I guess he won't be so free to pick anymore—not with a face like he's likely to wind up with."

Waco shook his head. "He's alive, Bob. That's more than some of the boys can say. I guess he'd rather be alive with his face cut up than still be handsome and dead."

Bob Yancy said only, "I dunno about that, Sarge. When a fellow's got something, he don't think about it much. But when he loses it, it can take the sap out of him. I seen that a lot, ain't you?" Waco disagreed, and the two of them argued about it as they made their way back to the company.

Clay and Lowell waited until Dr. Carter finished, then carried Dent's still form out of the tent. "I used a lot of chloroform on him," Carter said as they left. "Did the best I could with the arm. Keep it tied up tight; don't let him move it."

The day ran down, and at about eight o'clock Taylor Dewitt came to stand beside the Rocklin men. His face was gray with fatigue and strain as he asked, "How is he, Clay?" When he got the report, he nodded briefly. "We've got a lot of wounded men and plenty of prisoners. Take four men from the company and take charge of the detail."

"Ought to be Sergeant Mattson, I would think," Clay offered.

"He's dead," Taylor said briefly. Then he lifted his eyes and studied Clay. "You're a sergeant now. Need some kind of authority, and Waco says you're the man." He hesitated, then asked, "Will you do it?"

Clay nodded. "All right. I guess Lowell and Bob Yancy will do, and Leo Deforest."

"I'll send them here right away. Dr. Carter wants to get these wounded men to a hospital as quick as he can." He looked down at the still form of Dent Rocklin, then back to Clay. "That was pretty good, Clay, that ride up the hill. Colonel Benton said he was going to mention you in the report. You might even get a medal."

"I guess Dent deserves one more than I do, Captain." Clay stood there, his eyes thoughtful. "Like the men who died on that hill. . .but they won't get any medals."

"No, they won't." Taylor nodded. He saw that Clay knew the charge had been foolish, a waste of lives, but said only, "Take them to Richmond, Sergeant. Report to me when you get back."

Clay went back and sat down on the grass beside Lowell. The two of them had said little, but now Lowell began to talk. "I know you joined the army just to look out after me, sir." He broke off, unable to say what he felt. The night was dark, with few stars in the sky, but Lowell could see his brother's face swathed in white bandages and said, "I think it was for Dent's sake, too. If you hadn't led us up that hill, he'd probably be dead now. So it's a good thing we came, don't you think?"

Clay knew the boy had been scarred by the death and terror of the day, that he was looking for his father to give some kind of an answer that would put the puzzle together for him. He sat there, thinking of what had happened, and finally said, "We're sort of blind down here, Lowell. Most of the time we can't see where we are, we don't know why we've done what's in the past, and we can't even guess what's ahead. Lots of people take a look at life and give up. They just live and never ask why things are like they are. But I trust you're not one of that kind, for that's foolish."

The night air was hot, and Dent suddenly stirred, moving his legs and making a small sound. At once, Clay dipped a cloth into the pan of water beside him and bathed the fevered face. He waited silently until the wounded man lay quietly on the blanket, then sat back and looked across at his son.

"Lowell, God is in everything. We're looking at things from a pretty narrow point of view, but God knows all about us. Something happens that we think is bad, and we think God's gone to sleep or that He doesn't care. But He does care. That's why He made us, son, because He's a God of love. And even our pain, that's got something to do with God, with what He's trying to make of us." He took a sudden deep breath and added gently, "Guess you didn't ask for a sermon, but all I can say, Lowell, is that I believe that our God knows about me and you and Dent. He's working on us. And we're so blind and hard, sometimes He has to use some pretty tough means to get us straightened out. But I believe God will help us through all this. Do you believe that?"

Lowell nodded slowly, then said, "I do now. I guess I've been pretty careless with my life. But this war, it makes a man see things different—you know, what matters and what doesn't. Charging up that hill, I learned more about how good life is than I've ever learned up until then."

They sat there, speaking quietly, until Lowell finally lay back and went to sleep. Clay kept vigil all night, dozing off from time to time but coming awake instantly whenever the wounded man moaned.

Just before dawn, Dent awoke. He tried to cry out and ask for water. Clay held his head up and gave him sips of tepid water. It was hard, for Dent could not move his lips because of the stitches in his cheek.

Finally he peered at Clay through his right eye and whispered, "What—what's wrong with me?"

"You took a couple of pretty bad wounds, son," Clay said. "Don't worry. You'll be all right."

Dent was still foggy from the chloroform and lay there trying to think. Finally he asked, "Where am I hurt? In the head?"

"Yes, and don't touch the bandage. A bad cut on the cheek, another on your arm."

Dent turned his head and considered the shadowy figure beside him. "Who is this?"

"Your father, son."

Dent grew still, then asked, "Was it you who came up the hill to help us?"

Clay said, "I'll tell you about it later. Take some more water and try to rest." He gave the thirsty man another drink, and almost at once Dent dropped off to sleep. Thirty minutes later, the sun shattered the ebony darkness, lighting up the east, and Clay Rocklin got up to meet the day, knowing that the way ahead was not going to be easy.

It's just starting, he thought as he watched Dent's face in the pale light. *But we'll make it, Lord. You've got to bring us through— because no man can win out in this thing if You don't stand beside him!*

CHAPTER 17

THE PRISONERS

*W*ho are those troops? They're going the wrong way; the battle is ahead, isn't it?"

Deborah Steele turned, pulled abruptly out of her thoughts by the words of Matthew Pillow. Pillow, a congressman from her district and a friend of the family, had pulled the buggy off the road with a jolt just in time to avoid a collision with a wagonload of Federal soldiers. The driver was whipping the horses up, and soldiers were stumbling along in the wake of the wagon, trying to keep up. Many of them looked over their shoulders fearfully as they moved down the road toward Washington.

Pillow, a large man with a full beard and a foghorn voice, called out, "Here now, what's happening?"

The soldier sitting in the rear of the wagon lifted his head and called wildly, "Get back! The Rebs is coming—Black Horse Cavalry!"

Mrs. Pillow grabbed her husband's arm fearfully. "He can't be right, can he, Matthew?"

Pillow stared at the soldiers who came along the road in an ever-increasing stream, none of them carrying muskets, and shook his head. "I don't believe it! Let's go on a little and try to find an officer."

As he pulled the buggy back onto the road, Deborah sat up straighter. She'd been invited by Helen Pillow, the daughter of the congressman, to come and witness the battle. Helen, a tall, plain girl of twenty, had been excited. "You've just got to come with us, Deborah! We'll get to see a real battle—and after our men whip the Rebels, there's going to be a victory dance at Fairfax Courthouse! Isn't it exciting? You must come, Deborah. We've got the picnic lunch and plenty of room. Lots of the congressmen are going out to see the battle."

Deborah had agreed, but as they drove down the road—which was growing more and more filled with soldiers who were obviously fleeing—she knew that the easy victory the North had been expecting was not going to happen. Pillow was a stubborn man, however, and kept driving the buggy down the road, dodging to avoid wagons and even a twelve-pound Napoleon howitzer that rumbled along, pulled by heaving white-eyed horses.

An hour later Pillow pulled up, his face pale and perspiring. "I don't know about this, Helen," he gasped. "Something's gone wrong!"

At the moment he spoke, the bridge he'd just managed to get across, despite heavy traffic, was hit with a Confederate shell. It blew one side of the bridge to splinters, killing two horses that were pulling a wagon and blowing men into the creek below.

At the same time, a lone rider, an officer on a sweaty-flanked black horse, came around a bend. He pulled his mount up abruptly when he saw the confusion at the bridge.

"Captain!" Pillow shouted, waving his arms. "What's happening? Where's our army?"

The captain gave him a sour look. He was a short, muscular man with a pair of muddy brown eyes. His mouth twisted with rage as he shouted, "Our army? Probably either dead or on their way to Richmond. Get your women out of here, man! The whole Rebel army is on its way!" He drove his horse toward the creek, forded the swift stream, then rode off at full speed.

"Matthew!" Mrs. Pillow screamed, "We've got to go back!"

Pillow nodded, his face ashen. Seeing that the bridge was going to be a bottleneck, he drove his team downstream and put them across, despite their reluctance. As the wagon bucked and plunged over the rough stones of the creek bottom, the lunch basket fell out, but no one noticed. It landed upside down, and the sandwiches came out and began to float downstream. A huge loggerhead snapping turtle, as big around as a washtub, rose slowly to the surface, opened his frightful jaws, and clamped down on a cucumber sandwich. Not forty feet away, men were raging and fighting to get over the ruined bridge, but the snapping turtle paid no heed. He closed his jaws, his wise old eyes yellow in the sun, then dropped back down to the ooze of the creek bottom.

When Congressman Pillow let Deborah out at her home, she went to her mother and told her what had happened. The two of them soon found that Washington was ablaze with rumors about the battle. All day long the stragglers of the army came stumbling back to Washington, and Abraham Lincoln and General Scott made plans for a last defense of the city— they even went so far as to order the state papers to be loaded so that the capitol might be moved to another city.

For two days the tension hung on, most citizens expecting the Rebel army to come charging into the city at any moment. Deborah and her family worried about Pat, and finally Gideon came to see them. Deborah and her father sat there wordlessly as he told of the defeat. "It could have gone the other way," Gideon said bitterly. "If we'd hit them hard the first day, we'd have sent them reeling, but McDowell's no fighter. He's finished as a general, and that's a good thing!"

"Do you think the Rebels will attack?" Amos asked.

"No, they took lots of punishment," Gideon said. "But they won the battle, Amos. Now maybe people will stop that silly talk about a short war. Maybe they will finally see that the Confederates are tough—they're fighting for their homes, and they're not going to quit."

"What about Pat, Uncle Gideon?" Deborah asked. "Is he all right?"

Gideon bit his lower lip. "I hope so, Deborah. I didn't see him after the Confederates made their big push and drove us back. But one of the men in his company, a man named Jim Freeman, knew Pat was my nephew, so he came to me and told me. . .that Pat was captured."

"What exactly did he say?" Amos asked tightly.

"Pat's platoon was in a hot fight, and they got overrun by the Rebels' charge. Freeman was off to one side when they hit, so he ducked into a ditch and hid. He said that Pat took a bullet in the arm, but it wasn't a serious hit. His platoon was just overrun—and had to surrender."

"Did he mention Noel Kojak, Uncle Gideon?"

Gideon had been dreading the question. He faced Deborah, saying reluctantly, "It's bad news, Deborah. Freeman said that Kojak fought to the last, but he was shot down by one of the Confederate lieutenants. Freeman had to get away quick, so he didn't know how badly Noel was hit."

Deborah's face was pale. "It's my fault. I was the one who talked him into enlisting!"

Gideon shook his head, and his voice was kind as he answered, "You can't take the blame, Deborah. The boy was a good soldier—the best in his company, his captain said. And he may be all right. If he was wounded, he'll be taken to a hospital in Richmond. I'll find out about him and Pat as soon as I can."

"Thank you, Uncle Gideon," Deborah said evenly. She sat there quietly while the two men talked, but a heaviness such as she'd never known had come to her. She had not known until this moment how fond of Noel Kojak she'd become, and her heart broke as she pictured him dead on the field of battle, buried in a shallow grave.

Noel Kojak was not, however, in a shallow grave. Even as Gideon Rocklin was telling Deborah and her father the bad news, Noel was being jolted along in a wagon, half conscious and racked with pain. But he was alive.

He had first been taken to the same field hospital where Dent Rocklin, the man who had put the bullet in his side, was lying. A rough surgeon had looked at the wound and shaken his head, saying, "Too close to the spine. Can't do anything for him." Noel had been put on the ground with other wounded Federal soldiers and passed the night in delirium. The next morning he had awakened and found Pat beside him, his arm in a sling.

"Hey, Noel!" Pat said when he saw the young man's eyes open. "How are you?"

Noel opened his mouth to answer, but as he shifted his body, an explosion of pain blossomed in his side, and he could only gasp. He lay there until the sheets of pain ebbed, then whispered, "Where are we, Pat?"

"Prisoners," Pat said, shrugging. He looked carefully at Noel's face, not liking what he saw. "There's some soup left. I'll get you some."

"Just—water," Noel croaked, suddenly aware of a raging thirst. He gulped frantically at the tepid water Pat gave him from a dipper, then lay back, the world spinning. He tried to speak, but he was slipping back into a deep, black hole with no bottom.

Pat covered him up, knowing Noel had a fever, then sat there despondently. The doctors had worked all night and were still working. They had no time for anyone except the worst cases, so there was nothing to do but wait. All morning he sat there, giving Noel a sip of water from time to time, keeping the blanket over him.

At noon several wagons pulled up and began loading the wounded. A strong-looking Confederate in his forties came down the line of wounded. The Confederate wounded had been taken earlier. Now, as the leader of the detail came down the line, Pat struggled to his feet. He saw that many of the wounded would have to be left and said, "Please, take my friend!"

The Confederate stopped and looked down at Noel. "He hit bad? Can't take any dying men, soldier. Only those with a chance."

Pat said quickly, "He's got a bullet in him, but if he can get to a hospital, they'll take it out and he'll be all right."

"Well..." The sergeant hesitated; then something in Noel's face seemed to touch him. "All right. But we can't take you in the wagon."

"I can walk," Pat said at once. "I'll take care of him." Then he said, "God bless you, sir!"

Clay Rocklin gave him a quick look. "You're a Christian?"

"Yes. Not much of one, I guess," Pat said. He watched as the Rebels loaded Noel into the wagon with the other wounded, then waited until the train pulled out.

All afternoon Pat trudged along, several times almost ready to faint, but the pace was slow and there were frequent breaks. When they pulled into a grove of trees near a creek to camp for the night, Pat almost collapsed. He lay on the ground while the guards cut wood for a fire, then went to sleep while supper was being cooked. He came awake when a hand touched his shoulder and a voice said, "Better come and get some of this grub, son."

Pat opened his eyes with a sense of alarm, not sure where he was. Then he glanced around and saw the ground covered with the wounded—and it all came back to him. The smell of bacon and coffee hit him like a blow and was followed quickly by sharp hunger pangs. He struggled to his feet. "Your friend is over here," Clay said, and he led Pat to where Noel lay. Pat knelt down and saw that Noel's fever was high.

"He's pretty sick," Clay said gently. "That's a bad wound. Bullet ought to come out, but no way to do it here." Then he said, "Get some grub inside you. We've got a ways to go."

He led Pat to the edge of the fire and got two plates, and then they sat down. Pat ate like a starved wolf and was sleepy as soon as he'd finished. His wound had sapped his strength more than he'd realized. "Can't stay awake," he mumbled. A thought came to him, and he stared at the figure of his captor. "I guess I can't do much but thank you, sir. Are all Rebels as thoughtful as you?"

Clay chuckled. "I guess we're just like you Bluebellies. Some good, some bad." Then he saw the boy's eyelids drooping. He got up and pulled a blanket out of one of the wagons, then came back to hand it to Pat. "Get all the rest you can."

"I should stay with Noel," Pat protested.

"I'll sit with the boy," Clay assured him. "Not much I can do for him except pray, and I'll be doing that. Now go to sleep."

Pat slept like a dead man and felt better the next morning. His arm was painful, but he made the day's march in better condition. They moved slowly once again, taking many rests. Pat knew that most of the enemy would not have been so careful of their "cargo" and would have driven straight on. That night he sat with Noel after supper but again grew sleepy.

Noel was awake, though, so Pat forced himself to stay awake, too. It was well after dark when Clay came over to the two, carrying two cups of coffee. "See if you can get some of this down," he said gently, helping Noel sit up and watching as the wounded boy took the cup with trembling hands. Pat took a cup and drank slowly, leaning back against a small tree. The keening of crickets made him sleepy, and he dozed off.

The stars were out in force, a sparkling canopy spread across the velvet blackness, and Clay admired them for a while in silence. "We may be in Richmond in a couple of days," he finally said quietly to the wounded man. "They'll take care of you boys there. What's your name?"

"Noel Kojak."

"I'm Clay Rocklin."

Noel blinked and said, "I worked for a man named Rocklin. At the foundry in Washington."

Clay stared at him, then smiled. "That's my kin, Noel. My father's brother." He studied the wan face of the boy, then said, "That's a strange one. Small world, isn't it?"

Noel nodded; then a thought came to him. He looked at

Pat, trying to remember something, then licked his lips and said, "I guess Pat's some kin of yours, too. Pat—wake up!"

Clay stared at the boy as he roused, then said, "My name's Rocklin. Noel thinks we might be related. What's your name?"

"Why, I'm Pat Steele." He was confused, then said, "But my mother was a Rocklin."

Clay demanded, "Do you have a sister named Deborah?" When Pat said that he did, Clay said slowly, "It's a smaller world than I thought. I know your sister, Pat. She was at my plantation earlier in the summer. As a matter of fact, my son was quite taken with her."

Pat stared at him. This was the father of Dent Rocklin, the man Deborah had fallen for in Virginia. "She's spoken of you," Pat said, then asked, "Do you know my uncle, Major Gideon Rocklin?"

Clay sat there, stunned by the chance that had brought the three of them together. Images of Gideon and Melanie—and of all the three of them had been through—raced through his mind, but he said only, "Yes, I know him. He's my cousin, Pat."

Pat Steele suddenly remembered the fragments of family history and said, "Oh, I know you now! You're the one who—!" He broke off in confusion and stared across at Clay with embarrassment.

Clay smiled at him. "You've heard about me, I see. The wolf with the long ears and the sharp white teeth? Well, it's all true, I guess—or it was." He sat there idly, thinking of the past, then said, "I'm sorry you boys had to get shot, but I'm glad to be around to give you a hand. All in the family, isn't it?" Then he got to his feet, saying, "Better rest, boys. Long road to Richmond."

It was not, in fact, all that far to Richmond, but by the time the wagon train pulled into the city, Noel was unconscious and

Pat was exhausted. Clay found the hospital, helped get the prisoners inside, and said before he left, "Pat, I'll send a wire to your people telling them you're all right."

"Thank you, sir," Pat said, then asked, "Could you send word about Noel? To my sister, Deborah. She'll want to know about him."

"Sure, I'll do that." Clay left, then looked up the section of the hospital reserved for Confederate officers. He found Dent asleep and decided to come back later. On his way out, Clay spoke to the doctor, a thin, hard-faced man of fifty.

"The face is healing, but he's going to have a terrible scar," Dr. Amos Medlin said. He added at once, "The arm should be taken off. It's never going to be any good to him, and I'm afraid of gangrene. He fights it, though. Try to talk him into it. Better to go through life with one arm than to die with two."

Clay said, "I'll talk to him as soon as I can, Doctor." Then he asked, "You treat the Yankee prisoners, don't you?"

"Yes."

"I wish you'd go see one of them I've just brought in. Noel Kojak is his name. Got a bullet that should come out."

"What's your interest in him?"

"He works for my uncle," Clay said. "A good boy."

"All right," Medlin said with a shrug. "Talk to your son. That arm's got to come off."

Clay nodded, then left the hospital, going at once to the telegraph office. He sent a wire to Gideon and included the news of Noel Kojak, asking Gid to pass the word to Deborah. He left the telegraph office, then obtained lodging for his men. Finally he got into one of the wagons and started for Gracefield, grateful for the short leave he'd been granted upon his arrival in Richmond.

❧

The telegram reached Gideon the next day, and at once he went to the Steeles. "Just heard from Clay," he said. "Pat's all right. He'll be a prisoner, but I think we can get him exchanged."

"Thank God!" Laura Steele cried, embracing her husband.

Gideon turned to Deborah, saying, "Bad news about Noel, I'm afraid."

"Is he dead?"

"No, but he's badly wounded. Clay doesn't think he'll live."

He gave the details, and as soon as he finished, Deborah grew still, then said, "I'm going to Richmond."

The others stared at her, and her father exclaimed, "You can't do that, Deborah!"

But argument did nothing to shake her resolve. Deborah listened to them all, then said calmly, "I can see that Pat has what he needs. And I won't have Noel alone in that place."

The next morning as the train pulled out of the Washington station, Deborah was aboard. Her face was set in an expression of iron determination, and as the train raced across the countryside headed for the South, she gave no thought to the difficulties that lay ahead. She only knew one thing: She was determined to see her brother safe and out of prison—and to see Noel Kojak live.

All else seemed to fade in importance.

PART FOUR

Chimborazo

❦

CHAPTER 18

A STRANGE VOLUNTEER

The battle of Manassas was won by the Confederates, but by a perverse development, it was the North who profited most from the battle—simply by seeing the results of it.

Washington saw the worst: the sorry picnic crowd that came back bedraggled and frightened; the broken troops who came shambling in, streaked with dirt and almost out of their heads with weariness. . . . These sights quenched the "On to Richmond" fever that had forced Lincoln to send the raw troops into battle. Some of the most rabid of the warmongers made a full circle, such as Horace Greeley, who wrote Lincoln a letter full of incoherent woe.

"On every brow," he wrote despondently, "sits sullen, scorching, black despair. . . . It is best for the country and for mankind that we make peace with the Rebels at once and on their own terms!"

Abraham Lincoln, however, had steeled himself for war. "The fat's in the fire now," he wrote to his wife two days after the defeat, "and we shall have to crow small until we can retrieve the disgrace somehow. The preparations for the war will be continued with increasing vigor by the Government."

Somehow he managed to communicate some of his iron will to the people of the North, and they bowed their heads and went to work. The beaten army was placed in the hands of General George McClellan, who began to put it back together—a task McClellan would do better than any other general during the entire war. The factories began to pour forth a stream of guns, cannons, small arms, uniforms, and the thousand other items required by a huge army.

The people of the North were humiliated by the loss at Bull Run, but they did not quit. The defeat merely hardened their purpose and, in effect, forced them to become an industrial nation.

In the South, the victory at Manassas was signaled by cheering crowds, clanging church bells, and thunderous salutes of cannon fire. Stonewall Jackson, though, was not celebrating. He was one of those who saw the dangers of the victory. "It would have been better if we had lost," he said to one of his aides, "for now the people will be overconfident, thinking the worst is over." He knew that was far from the case, as did other men with a clear vision.

Manassas was but the opening note of a symphony of suffering and death that would be played by both North and South—a symphony that would crescendo for the next four years.

❧

When Deborah Steele stepped off the train at Richmond, she took a deep breath, then asked the station agent, her voice strong and determined, "How do I get to the military hospital?"

He directed her willingly enough, but she got no farther than the front gate of the hospital, where Noel Kojak lay on a bed of pain. She tried at once to see him but was stopped by a hard-eyed Confederate lieutenant named Josh Hanson. He met her with open suspicion and, upon finding out that she was from Washington, said at once, "I can't admit you to this hospital without a pass, lady."

"Where can I get a pass?"

"From the commanding officer, Colonel Prince."

But Colonel Prince was even more suspicious than Hanson. It took Deborah two days to get an audience with him, and when she stated her errand, he stared at her angrily, stating flatly, "You're in the wrong city, Miss Steele. I can't let one of the enemy have access to a Union prisoner." Donald Prince was not ordinarily a hard man, but his youngest son lay dead, shot down by a Union soldier at Bull Run. He had kept his bitterness and grief under control, but the sight of the Yankee woman caused it to spill over. "I'm giving an order that you be forbidden to enter any Confederate institution. Go back to your Yankee friends in Washington," he said bitterly and turned her out of his office harshly.

Deborah left the colonel's office and walked blindly down the street. A fine rain was falling, and she was soaked by the time she got back to her small hotel room. Stripping off her wet clothes, she dried off with the small towel provided, then wrapped up in a blanket while her dress dried. She had brought only one other dress and decided that she must save it. Going to the window, she looked down on the street below, watching it slowly turn to mud as the rain fell harder and harder. Her mind was busy, trying and rejecting plans, and finally she sat down on the bed, totally dejected.

She considered going to the Rocklins for help but rejected that idea at once. With the anti-Yankee atmosphere that was almost palpable in Richmond, she knew it would be dangerous for them to ask a favor on her behalf. Finally her mind was exhausted, and she sat there with tears running down her face. As they flowed, she began to pray. She firmly believed in prayer, but it had always been a thing of logic to her. God had made certain promises in the Bible concerning prayer, so all one had to do was memorize the promises, move forward boldly, and the thing would be done.

Well, that wasn't working. She had been praying from the time she had left Washington, yet the door was barred, and no human effort seemed likely to open it. As fatigue and frustration built up in her, Deborah did something she'd never done in her life, something that would have horrified and disgusted her if she'd seen someone else doing the same thing.

"God!" she cried aloud, coming off the bed and shaking her fists in a gesture of protest. "Don't You even care?" She was trembling, trying to hold back the tears, shocked at her own actions yet so angry that she began to walk the floor. Gripping her hands into fists, she cried out, "Where are You? I've done everything, and You haven't done a thing!"

Her angry speech grew shriller, and she suddenly dropped to the floor, pressing her face into the carpet, lying there as a paroxysm of grief shook her. She had seldom wept as a girl and never as a grown woman. Now, though, the tears flowed freely, and great tearing sobs racked her body until her chest hurt. She began gasping, "Oh God! Oh God!" and could say no more. The words had been said. Now all that was left was a terrible emptiness that frightened her more than anything she had ever known. She was like a very small child who was lost in a frightful place and who sensed terrible things lurking close, watching her.

After a time, the wrenching sobs ceased to tear through her, and she lay there with her face pressed into the wet carpet. Her spirit seemed dead, beaten flat by the storm of grief that had passed over her. And then as she lay there, something began to happen. She was never able to explain it to anyone else, but somehow a strange sense of peace began to grow in her. At first she wasn't even aware of what was happening; she only knew that she was very tired and weary. Then she suddenly realized she wasn't weeping, and she had no desire or need to grieve.

What's happening to me? she wondered, bewildered by the feeling that was sweeping over her. She lifted her tearstained face, seeing only the pale blue wallpaper of the wall, and then she rose to stand in the center of the room.

Suddenly, as she waited, she was filled with a verse of scripture. She had heard the verse many times, for it was a favorite of her father's, but now it came into her mind with a force that caused her to gasp, and she sat down on the bed, her legs having grown weak.

"My peace I give unto you."

Deborah had known about God since she had been a small child. Her life had been spent in church services, and she had godly parents who had read the Bible to her from her infancy. But for the first time, sitting on the bed in a small hotel room in Richmond, Deborah Steele met God! The sense of His presence filled the room, and she grew weak as the peace of the Almighty filled her. She sat there for a long time, her spirit open. She could never fully express to anyone what that time meant to her, but as she sat there, she finally knew what to do. And as the answer came, she lifted her hands and began to praise God.

She had sung songs of praise often, but this time it was

different. There was nothing of ritual as she prayed, no set phrases or stilted speech. Instead, joy and thanksgiving seemed to flow from her lips without effort, like a spring bubbling over. She didn't understand what had happened to her, nor did she understand the words that flowed from her lips with such ease, but when finally she rose from the bed, she knew that life for her would never be the same.

Slowly she dressed, her mind still and a smile of wonder on her face. She picked up her umbrella and left the room. She moved confidently out of the hotel, went to a store down the street, made several purchases, then returned to her room. It was growing dark—too late for her to do anything more that day—so she left her purchases, went to the dining room, ate a good supper, then sat at her table alone, thinking of the morning to come.

Finally she rose, paid her bill, and returned to her room. She undressed, put on a gown, and climbed into bed. Then as she lay there, a stab of fear came, followed by the thought, *What if I've made all this up? What if I lose this peace?*

But she rejected that thought and began to pray. It was the same as before, and as she praised the name of her God, she realized that the Comforter had come—and that He would never go away!

"But we ain't got no more beds!"

Matron Agnes Huger lifted a pair of gun-metal gray eyes to the orderly who stood in front of her desk. The matron was a woman of thirty-five and stood only five inches over five feet tall, but she held herself so erect that she seemed taller. She had come to Chimborazo Hospital with a letter from Jefferson

Davis, which had said, "Mrs. Agnes Huger will be in charge of Unit B. Medical personnel will give her full cooperation."

The physicians in charge of the overflowing hospital had resented her, and the orderlies had hated her. Since the battle, chaos had reigned in the hospital, and Mrs. Huger had done a strange thing: She had given the wounded men first priority, regardless of which uniform they wore. She started out by announcing that the distribution of all whiskey in the ward would come under her control. The surgeons and orderlies, both of whom had been imbibing freely of this commodity, raised a howl of protest. When Chief Surgeon Monroe Baskins had come raging into her office threatening to have her put out of the hospital, Mrs. Huger had listened to him rave, then asked, "Are you certain you want to offend President Davis, Dr. Baskins? Well, I'm certain he can find a place for a fine surgeon like you on the front line of battle, perhaps with General Jackson's regiment."

That had been the end of the revolt, and Matron Huger had ruled her ward firmly. Now she stared at Jesse Branch, the chief orderly, as he argued, "Ma'am, we jist ain't got no more room! Whut we ort to do is move them Bluebellies outside and let our boys have their beds!"

The hospital, a converted two-story factory, housed two hundred fifty Confederate soldiers on the first floor, while on the second floor, fifty of the wounded Federal soldiers were cared for.

"That'll be enough, Jesse," Matron Huger said sharply. "I'll have more cots brought in at once." Her eyes pinned him where he stood as she added, "The night cans in Ward B were not emptied this morning. Would you take care of that at once?"

Branch, a skinny man of thirty-five with a scraggly beard,

nodded quickly. "I'll see to it, Matron." He had been insolent to Mrs. Huger when she first came, but when she mentioned that he was the proper age for enlisting in the army, he had suddenly become quite cooperative. Now he said, "Well, we got to have some more help, ma'am, especially with the Yankees. Most of the ladies who come to help won't have nothin' to do with them."

"I'll see what can be done." The matron dismissed the orderly abruptly and rose to go to the medicine chest. She was making a list of the contents, worrying over the scarcity of drugs, when a knock sounded.

"Yes?" she called, and Jesse Branch stuck his head inside.

"Old woman out here, Matron. Says she wants to help."

"Send her in, orderly." Closing the chest door and locking it with a brass key from the small bunch that hung around her waist, Mrs. Huger moved across the room to her desk. Any volunteers were welcome, for there were few funds to pay for help. The women of Richmond had volunteered eagerly enough for a few days after the battle, but time had put a stop to that. People got excited for a time when tragedy struck, but emptying bedpans or changing the dressing on raw stumps quickly dispelled most of the "glamour" of the work in a hospital.

A woman entered, and the matron allowed a quick flash of disappointment to show in the pressure of her lips. She had been half hoping that the woman would be intelligent enough to carry some responsibility, but that did not seem to be the case. "Good morning. I'm Matron Huger," she said politely. "How may I help you?"

The woman who entered was not young, and she certainly did not look as though she had enough intelligence to do anything difficult. She was wearing a shapeless cotton dress, which was faded from countless washings and not particularly clean. A pair of rough man's brogans made a clumping on the floor as she walked, and her dirty hand held tightly to a burlap feed sack.

Lord knows how we'd ever get those nails clean enough to change a dressing, the matron thought. Brown stains spotted the front of the woman's dress—the residue of the snuff that made a pouch of the lower lip. A gum twig was stuck in the middle of the woman's mouth, and she shifted it enough to say in mushy tones, "Howdee. I come to hep with the sodjers."

"That's very good of you," Matron Huger said, nodding. "What's your name?"

A dry cackle escaped from the snuff-stained lips. "I'm Jemima," she said. Her face was difficult to see, for she wore a limp bonnet with a large hood pulled down over her eyes. She nodded vigorously, causing an iron gray lock of dirty hair to drop over her forehead. Shoving it back with a dirty forefinger, she added, "Everybody call me Jemmy."

I don't suppose she needs clean hands to empty bedpans, Matron Huger thought, and she said, "We can use help, Jemmy, but it's hard, dirty work, you understand?"

Jemmy looked around and, finding no spittoon, walked to the window and sent an amber stream onto the yellow roses outside. "Wal, missus, I ain't had nothin' but that since I wuz a younker," she said, moving back from the window in a strange sidling motion. "I reckon I better tell you, missus, I got a boy on t'other side."

"A Union soldier?"

"Aye, missus. Went off to fight with the Yankees." Jemmy nodded sadly, and her eyes seemed strangely bright to Matron Huger but were mostly hidden beneath the brim of the bonnet.

"I got to thinkin' mebbe I ort to hep some of them Yankee fellers who got here. One of 'em might have heered of my Lonnie. He's the onliest chile I got left. Cholera took the rest of 'em."

Quickly Matron Huger seized the opportunity, saying, "We need help with the cleaning. Could you come in and help with that?"

"Yes, missus. I got me a job washing dishes at a big hotel, but I can come in when I ain't workin' at that."

"That's fine, Jemmy. Now let me fill out a form for you—or can you write?"

"No, missus."

"Well, I'll do it for you, Jemmy." Quickly she filled out the basics, then wrote something on a slip of paper. "This is your pass to get into the building, Jemmy. Just give it to the guard each time you come. Don't lose it. Now when do you want to start?"

"Now as good a time as any, missus."

"Good! Come along—and you should call me Matron, Jemmy."

The two of them left the office, Jemmy following the matron with her strange gait. "Are you crippled, Jemmy?" the matron inquired.

"Oh no, Matron! Got my foot gnawed by a hog when I wuz a creeper, but it don't hurt none."

The matron led the woman through a large open room filled with beds, all occupied by wounded men. There was a fetid odor, but not as bad as it had been when Matron Huger had arrived. "These are Southern men," she explained.

When they passed out of that room, there was a hallway crossing at right angles, and a guard with a musket sat in a chair beside a stairway. "Private, this is Jemmy. She'll be coming every day to help. Her pass will be checked at the front gate, but you check it, as well."

"Yes, ma'am, I'll do that."

The old woman had some difficulty climbing the stairs, Matron Huger noted, but when they reached the top, she did not seem out of breath. Another door opened off the end of a short hall, and when the two stepped inside, Jemmy looked around at the ward. It was one large room with a sloping ceiling, the bare rafters showing and dormer windows on one side admitting light and air. The cots, most of them occupied, were arranged in rows. "We have fifty-two men in this ward," the Matron said and nodded to a short woman dressed in white. "Mrs. Keller, this is Jemmy. She's going to help with the cleaning in your ward."

Mrs. Keller was a woman of fifty, and her small black eyes lit up at Matron Huger's words. "Well, thank God! We need all the help we can get." She peered at Jemmy over her steel-rimmed spectacles and looked doubtful, but only added, "I'm glad to have you, Jemmy. These poor boys need a lot of care. When will you start?"

"Oh, I'm ready now, missus!"

In a short time Jemmy was moving down between the lines of cots, mopping with an unexpected vigor. The two women watched her from the far side of the room, and Matron Huger shook her head. "I wish I could get you more nursing help, Mrs. Keller. I'll try."

"Well, if Jemmy can mop the floor and empty bedpans, maybe take water to the men, it'll free me for other things."

Matron Huger smiled with a gentleness that usually remained hidden. "Molly, I don't know what I'd do without you! You're the only one who's been faithful to stay with these men."

Then she looked at Jemmy, who was chatting with a soldier who had lost an arm and had a bandage around his head. "She looks dreadful, doesn't she? Try to get her cleaned up. She's a country woman. I expect she's done a little primitive nursing. Maybe you can teach her to change bandages."

"I'll scrub her down myself, Matron!" Mrs. Keller exclaimed. The matron left, and Mrs. Keller kept an eye on the new volunteer for an hour. She was pleased to note that the woman did a good job on the floors, changing the water frequently, and also that she spoke to many of the men. When the job was finished, Jemmy came to ask, "Whut now, missus?"

"Call me Mrs. Keller, Jemmy. My, you did a good job on those floors!" She praised the woman carefully, then said, "Would you see that each man has fresh water? Here's the water barrel. Just fill this pitcher and fill each man's glass." She hesitated, then said carefully, "Maybe you'd like to wash your hands first. We keep a basin and soap for ourselves back in my office." She led Jemmy to the small room, which served as the supply room, as well.

Mrs. Keller watched as Jemmy washed, wanting to say something about the snuff but not daring to do so. *I'll work on it*, she thought as Jemmy took a pitcher and moved down the lines of cots. *Can't afford to offend her. She looks rough, but I don't think the boys will mind.* Mrs. Keller was a motherly woman who thought of the soldiers as boys, as in fact many of them were. She had never had children of her own, and the hospital ward had become an outlet for the very real mothering instinct that ran in her.

All morning she kept an eye on her new helper, and at noon, she said to Matron Huger, "Jemmy's going to be a great help. She's not feeble at all. These hill women are often deceptive.

Some of them work until they're ninety. I know the hospital can't afford to pay her, but I'd like to give her a little something."

"A new dress or a good used one would help. Let's see if we can make her look a little less haglike."

But though they tried, Jemmy was firm in her refusal of new clothing. "I reckon these will do," she'd said so firmly that Mrs. Keller dared not insist. She had not, however, objected to soap and water, so that afternoon she got a basic lesson in changing bandages—and had been exceptionally deft at the business.

Mrs. Keller's gratitude was boundless, and she said, "Jemmy, you're an angel!"

Jemmy cackled and wiggled the gum snuff stick wickedly. "Never knowed no angels to dip snuff," she said. "Ain't no wings sproutin', neither."

By midafternoon, the work was so far ahead of schedule that Mrs. Keller asked, "Jemmy, would you give the boys fresh water? Then you should go home. I don't want to wear you out on your first day."

"Yes, missus." Jemmy filled the pitcher and made her way around the room. One of the soldiers, who had both legs amputated at the knee, looked at her out of a pair of hopeless black eyes. Jemmy poured his water, then said, "Now looky at this! You ain't et yore chicken!"

"Not hungry."

Jemmy picked up the chicken and thrust it at the young man. "I get ferlin' mad when I see food go to waste! Now you eat that, or I'll take a switch to you!"

Several of the men who were listening laughed, and a tall fellow in the next bed said, "Better eat it, Ned! You'd be shamed forever if it got back home about how you got a switching in the hospital."

The one named Ned glared at him but grabbed the piece of chicken and began gnawing at it.

"There's a good feller!" Jemmy said with a nod. She moved along, then refilled the pitcher and moved down the line of cots directly under the windows. "Well, you done woke up, I see." She stopped to fill the glass, then asked, "Whut's yore name, sodjer?"

"Noel."

"Noel? Now that's a right purty name." Jemmy picked up the glass and said, "Kin you set up and take a drink?"

Noel looked up at the woman, confused. "Who are you? I never saw you before."

"I'm Jemmy. Come to hep you Yankee fellers git well. Now lemme hep you set up. You got a bad belly?"

"My—side!" Noel gasped, the pain shooting through him as he tried to sit up. "Had a bullet in me. . . . Doctor took it out, but—" He fell back, sweat on his forehead. "Can't do it."

"Wal, it don't matter." Jemmy moved across the room, pulled a chair beside the bed, and sat down. Picking up the water and a spoon from the table, she filled the spoon, then placed it on Noel's lips. He took the water thirstily, but after she had repeated the act several times, he said, "I'm taking too long."

"I ain't in no hurry," Jemmy said placidly.

She ladled the water carefully until he said, "That's fine. It was so good!"

"Water the best thing to drink they is." Jemmy nodded. She filled the glass again but did not rise. Her back was to the window, so all Noel could see was the outline of her face. When she didn't move, he felt uncomfortable, feeling that she was studying him. "I—I guess you must feel funny, taking care of an enemy soldier, don't you?"

"Not got much feelings about it, young feller. A sick man ain't a Yankee nor a Rebel, I don't reckon. Jus' a man." Suddenly she rose, went to the end of the room, then came back with a basin of water and a cloth. She dipped the cloth into the water, wrung it out, then began bathing Noel's face.

He lay there quietly—the cool water was the most delightful thing he'd ever felt. He'd had a fever for days, and his face seemed stretched tight. Now the coolness of the water seemed to soak into his body, and he dropped off to sleep. When he awoke, he looked around, finding Pat watching him. Pat's arm was in a sling, but he was able to sit up and even walk around. "Got yourself a nurse, didn't you?" He grinned.

Noel nodded. "I thought I dreamed it."

"She's a nice old lady." Pat nodded. "Dirty as a pig, but it'll be good to have somebody who cares in this place."

Deborah entered her room in the run-down boardinghouse, sighing wearily. She had left the hotel, taking the cheapest room she could find. She knew that if she went into a respectable hotel in her disguise, she'd become conspicuous. So she'd found a room that was just one step above staying on the streets, where nobody would notice her as she came in. All she would have to do was keep still and pay her rent.

She removed the shapeless dress and washed her mouth out, but she could not get rid of the terrible taste of snuff. *I think Jemmy's going to decide to give up snuff,* she thought, smiling grimly. She examined her hair, pleased to find that the dye had not run. Then she washed as well as she could, thinking of how her plan had gone. She had played an old crone once in a school play and now found she remembered the skill well.

Getting into bed, she pondered her plan, which was nothing less than to get Noel and Pat out of the hospital and back to the North. Ordinarily she would have been up all night worrying about it, but tonight she simply began praising God for who He was rather than for what He was going to do for her. As before, the Comforter was there, and the presence of Jesus was more real than she could ever have dreamed. The praises came to her lips freely, and she went to sleep with them in her heart.

CHAPTER 19

DEBORAH MAKES A CALL

When August came to scorch Richmond, the city was still tingling with the thrill of the victory at Manassas. For Dent Rocklin, however, as he lay on his cot in the hospital, there was nothing to cheer his spirit. His face was still puffed and swollen from the rough stitching at the field hospital; it was not healing as well as it should. Dr. Baskins had followed the customary practice of the day in keeping it bandaged. The dressing was changed, but on Thursday when he came by and examined Dent, he was not happy.

"Some infection in the face wound," he said, peering closely at Dent's cheek. "We'll keep the bandages on for another week or so." Then he unwound the bandages from Dent's arm, and when he had finished his examination, he shook his head. "Lieutenant, you've got to be reasonable. The cut destroyed too many muscles and ligaments. Even if we got this infection cured—which I don't think is possible—you'd never have the use of your hand."

"No amputation." Dent lay back, his eyes bright with fever. He had gone over this with Baskins often, and there was an adamant set to his face as he lay there. "Either I'll have two arms or I'll be dead."

Baskins stared at him helplessly. He was a heavy drinker, and the veins on his nose were inflamed. However, he was a good doctor and had talked with both Dent's father and his grandfather, urging them to convince the patient that he must have the arm amputated. Neither of them had been of any help, and now he slapped his thigh angrily. "You Rocklins are as stubborn as mules! Well, I can't force you to be sensible. But I'm washing my hands of you!"

As the doctor moved away, muttering to himself about fools, Matron Huger came to replace the bandage on Dent's arm. She bound the wrapping expertly, then stood looking down at him. "The doctor is right, Lieutenant. Your arm is lost. I wish you'd reconsider." Her gray eyes could be hard as agates, but now they were soft. She tried to be objective, to keep herself at a distance from the men—it hurt too much when they died. But for some reason, she had let her emotions get in the way of her head where Dent Rocklin was concerned.

His eyes were sunk back in his head, and his lips were cracked, the result of the fever brought on by the infection of his wounds. His eyes were bright with fever, and there was a smoky anger in them, too. "If I don't make it, you'll have an extra bed for some fellow who can be of some use."

Matron Huger started to protest, but there was such a rebellious set to his lips that she knew persuasion was fruitless. "We've got some fish today. Try to eat all you can."

He said nothing and dropped off into a restless sleep. All afternoon he tossed on his cot, the pain from his arm not allowing him to sleep soundly. Finally he heard the clatter of dishes and opened his eyes, aware that the evening meal was being served. He had a raging thirst and struggled into a sitting position, then threw the cover back and sat up on the cot. His head reeled and he swayed uncertainly, closing his eyes until the weakness passed.

Four orderlies were moving down the rows serving the men, and the room was filled with the hum of talk. The cot next to Dent was empty, the captain from Tennessee having died the previous day. The man had been in a coma since being brought in and had died without ever speaking another word. The officer on Dent's right, a cheerful second lieutenant from the tidewater, glanced at Dent but continued to speak with the man across the aisle from him. His name was Simon Alcott, and he had tried to be friendly with Dent. But after getting practically no response, he had given up.

The smell of fish came to Dent, along with the sharp tang of fresh coffee. He sat there with his head bowed, staring at his wounded arm, so lost in thought that he started slightly when a voice said, "Here now, young feller." He glanced upward and was surprised at the sight of the old woman who stood there with a tin plate and a cup of steaming coffee. "Looky here, now," she said in a nasal voice, "nice catfish today."

"Not hungry."

"Why, 'course you air hungry! Now you jist set thar, and ol' Jemmy will cut this heah fish up." She put the tray down on the table and thrust the mug toward him. "You kin sip on that whilst I fix the fish."

Dent took the cup, sipped at it cautiously, then considered the woman. "You new? Never saw you before."

"Fust time in heah." Jemmy nodded as she broke the large chunk of fish apart with a fork. "I been takin' care of them Yankee fellers upstairs." The brim of a large sunbonnet shaded her upper face, and several strands of iron gray hair slipped out from the edges. Finally she got the fish cut to her satisfaction and nodded firmly. "Now you git on the outside of this, young feller. Whut's yore name?"

"Rocklin. I don't want any fish. Just the coffee."

"Why, thet won't do! How you gonna git well if you don't eat? Now looky here, you jist hang on to that mug, and I'll shovel some o' this fish down yore gullet—there!"

Dent opened his mouth to object, but the woman pushed a morsel of the white flaky fish into it deftly, and he could only chew it. "Now thet's a good feller!" Jemmy nodded. "I fed my younguns like this, don't you see? Now you wash thet down with some cawfee, Mis' Rocker."

Dent sat there chewing slowly, finding his hunger rising, and finally he smiled at the old woman. "All right, you win. Just leave the plate. I'll promise to eat it."

"See you do!" The old woman nodded, then moved away to feed others. When she came back thirty minutes later, she looked at his plate and gave a high-pitched cackle of a laugh. "See, Colonel Rocker, you wuz plum hongry. Now you jist set...." She moved away with a curious sideways gait and soon was back with a small bowl and a fresh cup of coffee. "Got some nice cherry cobbler," she announced and then hesitated. "I better hep you with this," she announced and, holding the cobbler in one hand, took a dollop on the spoon and pushed it toward him. "Now don't argify with me! Open yer mouth!"

Dent had eaten little up until now, but his fever seemed to be down, and the sharp smell of the cherries made his mouth water. He got back onto the cot, his back against the wall, and sat there munching the succulent berries. The old woman chattered on, ladling the dessert into his mouth from time to time, and he listened as she told about the parade she'd seen the previous afternoon.

Finally she put the spoon and saucer down and stared at him. "Lemme git a rag and wipe yore face, Major Rocker." She was gone, then was back with a damp cloth. Carefully she wiped his mouth, then his unbandaged cheek. "That's a pretty bad wound, ain't it? But I reckon the good Lord will git you all healed up."

"Don't talk to me about God!" Dent's mouth drew into a sharp line, and he would say no more. When Jemmy moved away, he was aware of Simon Alcott's eyes fixed on him with displeasure.

"Wouldn't kill you to say thank you to the old woman, Rocklin," he said evenly. "You think you're some kind of special case?"

"Shut up, Alcott!"

"Yeah, I'll shut up," Alcott snapped. "You just lie there feeling sorry for yourself, Lieutenant. Never mind that some fellows have lost both arms and some both eyes. You just lie there like a big baby cryin' because you lost your dolly in the dirt." He rolled over, careful not to damage the bandage on the stump of his right leg, and began speaking to the man next to him.

Jemmy returned to the second floor, meeting Matron Huger, who was just leaving after an inspection. "Matron, thet young feller named Rocklin, he pretty bad, is he?"

Matron Huger was not surprised at the question, for Jemmy seemed to be curious about all the men. Shaking her head, she answered, "His face isn't dangerous, but if he doesn't let them take his arm off, he'll die, Jemmy. Don't say anything to him, though."

"No, ma'am." Jemmy went about her work, saying little. She stopped once to speak to Pat Steele, who was trying to shave with one hand. "You're about to cut your nose off," she observed.

"Set down and let me do that."

Steele laughed at her but surrendered the razor. "Don't cut my throat, Jemmy," he said. But she finished the job with a deft touch. "Where'd you learn to give a shave, Jemmy?"

"Used to shave my ol' man," she cackled, then whispered, "I got you and Mr. Noel a surprise. Some fresh cherry cobbler. Some lady brought a batch of it fer the fellers downstairs, but I saved enough of it fer you two. Wisht I had enough fer the hull bunch, but I couldn't make off with thet much. I'll sneak it to you at supper."

"Why, bless your heart, Jemmy!" He smiled and patted her shoulder. "Why are you so partial to Noel and me?"

"Shucks, you two air jist like my own younguns!" Jemmy looked down at Noel, who was asleep. "You take keer of the boy," she said.

Pat's face clouded. "We'll be leaving here soon. Hate to think of going to a prison camp. It'll be pretty bad."

"Better put yore trust in Jesus," Jemmy said and then left him to go down the line of cots.

"Funny old woman," Pat murmured. "Won't be any like her in the camp."

After Deborah left the hospital, she walked the streets of Richmond, thinking of Dent. She came to a park and sat down under a magnolia tree. The rich, heavy perfume of the blossoms filled the air, and pigeons came up to feed, cooing their liquid warble. Those who passed paid little heed to the old woman who seemed to be a little drunk or senile, for she was talking to herself.

There was a girl Dent was seeing—what was her name? Deborah thought, and then it came to her. *Raimey Reed, that's it! And she's a Christian girl, Aunt Susanna said.* A thought took root, growing in her, and she got up and moved down the street so quickly that it caused one man to say in surprise, "She moves fast for an old woman, don't she, now?"

❧

"There's a woman to see you, Miss Raimey. Says her name is Deborah Steele."

Raimey looked up in surprise. The name sounded vaguely familiar, but she couldn't place it. "I don't know anyone by that name, Dulcie. What does she want?"

"Don't know." Dulcie shrugged. She and Raimey had been out in the garden, where Dulcie had been reading a crazy novel called *Tristram Shandy* to her mistress. The slave was glad enough to be interrupted by the sound of the brass knocker on the front door. "She's a mighty nice-looking woman. You want to see her?"

"Why, yes," Raimey said with a nod. "Bring her out here." She listened as Dulcie's footsteps tapped across the walk, then as she spoke to someone. Raimey got to her feet as the guest was brought outside. "I'm sorry to disturb you, Miss Reed. My name is Deborah Steele. Could I speak with you a few moments— alone?"

"Get us some tea, Dulcie," Raimey said. "Won't you sit down, Miss Steele?" She heard the sound of the woman sitting down, then asked, "Have we met before?"

"No, but we have a mutual friend—Dent Rocklin." Deborah was watching the young woman closely and didn't miss a move- ment of the girl's lips. "I think he's in a bad way, Miss Reed."

"He's in the hospital, isn't he?"

"Yes, with a bad wound. Very bad." She began to speak, watching the girl's face. When she had finished, she said, "I think you should go to him, Miss Reed."

"Me? Why—I couldn't do anything!" Raimey was troubled, for she had thought of little but Dent Rocklin since the news came that he'd been wounded. Once she had mentioned going to visit him, but her mother had said, "It's not a nice place, Raimey. Wait until he's released to his parents' home; then we'll go." It had not satisfied her, and she knew that her parents were over-protective where she was concerned. Now she thought of Dent, of how they had danced, and of his kiss. Then it came to her. "I remember where I've heard of you. Dent's in love with you."

Deborah said quickly, "We were interested in each other once, but I've told him it can never go any further. And it was never as deep an attraction as Dent thought." She paused, then asked, "I know it's rude of me to ask, but—do you care for Dent?"

Raimey flinched slightly, her face coloring. "Why, he was very nice to me. But as you can see, Miss Steele, I'm blind."

Deborah said quietly, "I see that you're a very lovely girl. Being blind doesn't mean you can't love a man, does it?"

"No! It doesn't!" Raimey's voice rose with a trace of anger, and then she stopped. "But nothing can come of it. I could never ask a man to bear my affliction."

Deborah sat there, thoughts rising within, and asked for guidance from God. It was very plain that Raimey Reed was in love with Dent Rocklin, but how could she speak of it without offending the girl? Finally she decided to voice the simple truth. "May I call you Raimey? And you can call me Deborah. I've heard that you're a Christian, Raimey. Do you believe that God speaks to His people?"

"Why—certainly!" Raimey hardly knew what to make of this, but she sat there listening as Deborah told her how God had directed her to come see her.

Deborah carefully concealed any mention of Noel or Pat but said finally, "I think Dent's going to die if he doesn't get help, Raimey. There's a shadow on him. He's given up. I think he wants to die, and somehow I think that you're the one who can save him."

Raimey put her hands to her breast, shaken by what she had heard. But she felt a stirring of anger, too, which caused her to say, "It's very well for you to talk, Deborah Steele! You're beautiful, I've heard, and can have any man you want. And you can see! But it's unkind of you to come to me telling me that God wants me to do something about Dent. Why don't you save him? You're the one he loves, no matter what you say!"

Deborah sat still and, when the storm was past, said gently, "Raimey, all of us are in God's hands. I can't tell you what to do." She hesitated, then rose from her chair, noting that Raimey, catching the sound, rose at the same time. Deborah went to the girl, so innocent in the sunshine, and said, "I don't want to be unkind, but I know you love Dent, and he desperately needs someone who loves him. He won't listen to anyone in his family. But I think he may listen to you. Won't you try?"

Tears rose in Raimey's eyes, and she struggled vainly to speak. Finally she cried out, "I can't! I want to, but I don't know how to help!"

Deborah put her arm around Raimey's shoulders, saying, "I can't tell you how it will be, but I know the first thing you must do. Go to him! Go to Dent, Raimey! And then let God use you. Will you pray with me about that?"

Raimey nodded, and as Deborah prayed, she began to weep. Dulcie returned and stopped dead in her tracks with the tea tray in her hands. She had never heard anyone pray like this lady! There was something odd about it, and Dulcie was glad when

681

she heard the visitor say, "God is with you, Raimey. Trust Him!"

"Yes, Deborah. I will!"

Dulcie stepped forward, saying, "Can I show you to the door, miss?" and Deborah left at once, aware that the maid was glaring at her with disapproval in her eyes.

"Now don't you cry, Miss Raimey!" Dulcie said protectively when she came back. "She's gone now. What was she saying to make you feel so bad? I won't let her in this house again, you can bet!"

"Dulcie," Raimey said in a tone that Dulcie had never heard. "Go get Leroy to bring the carriage around. And get ready yourself."

"Where do you think we're going?" Dulcie asked in alarm. Raimey's parents were both gone for the day, and something in the expression of her mistress frightened her.

"We're going to the hospital." When Dulcie began to protest, Raimey said, "Be quiet, Dulcie. Go to the kitchen and have Evangeline make up a big basket of sweets—everything she can find."

Dulcie blinked, but she turned and left at once. As soon as she was out of hearing distance, she muttered in disgusted tones, " 'Be quiet, Dulcie!' I wish I'd never let that woman in this house!" But complaining was no good, and one hour later she was sitting beside Raimey, headed for the hospital.

CHAPTER 20

ANGEL IN THE WARD

Sometime during the night Dent flung his arm upward, striking the wall. The pain that exploded made him cry out, and he slept no more until about an hour before dawn. When he began again to stir and opened his eyes, he saw that someone was sitting in the chair beside him. He blinked and wiped his eyes with his good hand, then, seeing more clearly, said, "Hello, Mother."

Ellen Rocklin, looking totally out of place in a bright green dress and too much makeup, started guiltily, then exclaimed, "Why, you're awake! I thought I'd better let you sleep, Denton." The light of early morning fell across Dent's face, and with his ragged beard and stained bandage, he was not a pretty sight. Ellen, however, was determined to cheer him up. She said brightly, "Well, look at you! I could just kill your father! Here he's been telling me how awful you look! Why, you look just fine, Denton!"

"Sure. How've you been, Mother?"

"Oh, just terrible! I've been so worried about you! I wanted to come and see you, but your father wouldn't let me. Well, I just decided to come anyway, Denton!" The truth was that Clay had asked her to visit Dent many times, but she had resisted. Now she felt virtuous, going into her act of the Faithful Mother Visiting Her Wounded Son. Ellen always played a role; she had done so for so long that she no longer had any idea who she really was.

She babbled on, speaking of how wonderful Dent looked and how she was absolutely certain that he'd soon be home where she could take care of him properly. She stayed until breakfast was brought, insisting on waiting on him, putting sugar in his coffee (which he never took), and urging him to eat more.

After breakfast, she settled down, talking about how awful things were in Richmond—"Prices have literally gone out of sight, Denton!"; Gracefield—"Your grandfather, poor thing! I doubt if he'll live a month!"; her husband—"Clay absolutely refuses to give me what I need, Denton. You'll have to speak to him, I'm afraid. I've worn this old rag of a dress for a year or longer, and now with so many social events coming up, I simply must have some new things!"

Dent lay quietly, listening to her talk. She was a silly woman, and nothing would ever change for her. She was, he knew, an immoral woman, as well, though none of the family ever spoke of it. For years Dent had excused all of her flaws by blaming them on his father's act of desertion. Now, lying in the ward with dying men and with his arm throbbing, he suddenly understood that Ellen Rocklin had not been formed by his father's behavior. She was what she was, and the knowledge sank into him that nothing he could do—or that anyone could do—would bring sense and decency to his mother.

Ellen was talking about the party she had attended at the home of the Chesnuts when she was interrupted. "'Scuse me, missus. I need to change this feller's bandages."

Ellen turned sharply to see an old woman in a shapeless dress standing at the foot of the bed, holding a tray with bandages and medicine. "Why—of course!"

She rose and made room for the old woman, wondering why they didn't get more attractive people to take care of the men. She had a sudden vision of herself, dressed in a beautiful white uniform, moving through the hospital, bringing cheer to the boys. She saw herself saying to President Davis, "Why, it's very hard, Mr. President, but we must all do our best for our glorious cause!" The thought pleased her, but she did not watch as the woman carefully removed the bandage that covered the side of Dent's face.

When the bandage was gone, Ellen did look. The sight of her son's ravaged face shocked her so badly that she cried out, "Oh no!" and put her hands over her face. Then she turned away, putting her back to the two. She didn't see the looks of disgust on the faces of the men close by. . .nor did she see the look on her son's face.

Jemmy saw it though—and wanted to cry. Dent sat there staring at his mother; then he suddenly turned to Simon Alcott. "Give me your shaving mirror, Alcott."

Alcott said quickly, "I think I let Sim borrow it."

"It's there on the table," Dent growled. "Let me have it, blast you!"

Reluctantly Alcott picked up the small mirror and handed it to Jemmy, who just as unwillingly put it into Dent's hand. He lifted the mirror and stared into it. It was the first time he'd seen the wound—and he sat there staring at his ruined face without a word.

The saber had raked down the side of his face, narrowly

missing the eye, then had sliced through the flesh down to the cheekbone. The solid bone had turned the blade, forcing it forward so that it had narrowly missed cutting into the side of his mouth. Dr. Carter had done his best. He had pulled the flesh together as tightly as he could and put the stitches as close together as he could, but the damage was too great for his surgery to be more than a rough patch-up job.

Staring into the mirror, Dent saw a stranger, a gargoyle of a man. The eye was pulled downward at the outside edge, giving the face a sinister appearance, while the side of the mouth was pulled to the left, making it appear that a leer was fixed in place. The lips of the terrible wound were pulled together in some fashion, but the cheek was so distorted that the face staring back at him seemed to be the face of a monster.

He slowly handed the mirror back to Jemmy, saying, "Thanks for the mirror, Alcott."

A thick silence had fallen on them all, and it was Alcott who said, "Aw, it looks a little rough now, but when it heals, it'll be okay, Dent."

"It'll be worse," Dent said quietly. His voice was dead, and so were his eyes. He lay there staring at the ceiling as Jemmy finished putting on a fresh bandage, then moved away.

Ellen was trembling and tried to speak, but she could only say in a muffled tone, "I–I'll have to go now, Denton."

"Thanks for coming by, Mother."

She moved toward him as though to kiss him, then whirled and walked out of the room. Dent waited until she was gone, then looked at Alcott, saying evenly, "A mother's love is a wonderful thing, isn't it, Simon?"

"Aw, come on, Dent—!" But Alcott said no more, for Dent Rocklin had put up some sort of fence around himself, even higher and more impregnable than the one he'd already built.

❧

Raimey could sense the reluctance in Matron Agnes Huger and didn't wonder at it. She had come prepared to force her way into the hospital and had started at the beginning of the interview by saying, "You won't agree with what I want to do, Mrs. Huger, but I'm a very stubborn young woman. I want to come every day and help the men." Raimey had developed an uncanny discernment and knew at that instant that the matron was searching for a way to refuse her. "My father is Samuel Reed, Mrs. Huger. He's a very important man. In fact, he's a personal friend of President Davis."

Agnes Huger let a smile touch her lips. "So am I, Miss Reed."

Raimey stopped, thought for a brief moment, then said simply, "Then I can't threaten you with the president, can I?"

"I'm afraid not."

Raimey said quietly, "Please, Mrs. Huger, let me do this thing. I want to help so much. I'll do anything at all."

The matron was touched by the gentleness of the girl. "We need help, of course, Miss Reed, but I don't see how—"

"I thought of it before I came. The men must get lonely. Isn't that so? Well, I can talk, Mrs. Huger—my father says I talk too much!—and don't some of them need to write letters?"

"Can you do that, Miss Reed, write letters?"

"My maid Dulcie can! She's an excellent writer, so she could take the letters down, and I could talk." Raimey leaned forward and said, "There isn't much I can do. Please let me do this."

The matron made up her mind. "We'll be glad to have you, Miss Reed. When would you like to begin?"

"Now! We've brought an absolutely huge basket of cakes and pies for the men."

Her face glowed, and Matron Huger felt a pang of sorrow for the girl but said only, "They'll love that. Now let me make out passes for yourself and your servant; then I'll show you around."

Thirty minutes later Matron Huger had led the two women into the ward and was saying, "Gentlemen, this is Miss Raimey Reed and her servant Dulcie. Miss Reed wasn't certain that any of you liked cake, so you'll have to let her know if you do." She waited until the calls came from all over the room, then nodded. "If any of you need a letter written, Miss Reed's maid will be happy to write it for you. Now behave yourselves." She turned to Raimey a little uncertainly. "Would you like for me to take you around, Miss Reed?"

"Oh no," Raimey said quickly. "Dulcie and I will do very well, Matron." When the matron left, she said, "Tell me about the room, Dulcie."

The maid began describing the room, knowing exactly how to present the details. "There's five rows of beds with aisles between them—" She rattled off the details, then said, "Where you want to start?"

"At the first row of beds." She followed Dulcie as she usually did, almost by instinct, and when the maid stopped, she said, "Hello, would you like some cake?"

"Yes, miss." The soldier was smiling and added, "Sure is nice of you. . .to do this."

The break in his words had come when he had discovered she was blind, Raimey knew, but she gave no sign. "How about chocolate?"

"It's my favorite, ma'am," the soldier said.

"Let me have the basket, Dulcie. You go find somebody who wants a letter written."

Even as she spoke, a voice to her left said, "Right here, I reckon," and Dulcie moved to his side, saying, "You just tell me who it's to and what to write."

The man began dictating a letter, and Raimey opened the lid of the basket, picking out the chocolate cake. Expertly she lifted the cover, then asked, "Is there a table here?"

"Yes, miss, right here by the bed." The soldier watched, fascinated, as Raimey moved to the table, put the cake down, then sliced a piece off. As she handed it to the soldier, she asked him, "What's your name?"

"Lieutenant Hankins. I'm from Arkansas." Hankins took the cake and began to eat it. He found himself telling her about his farm—and his new bride—that he'd had to leave behind. He was lonesome and finally said, "I don't know about goin' home. I mean—well, when I left Irene I had two arms, and now I've only got one."

At once Raimey knew he was worried about how his new wife would take his injury. "Your wife will be so glad to have you back." She smiled, then began to encourage him. Finally she put her hand out, and he took it. "God bless you, Lieutenant. I'll pray that you'll soon be back on your farm with Irene."

She moved to the next bed, saying, "Hello? Do you want pie or cake?" The soldier, a tall, thin young fellow with both feet heavily bandaged, said shyly, "Pie, please." Soon Raimey had heard about his injury and knew his parents' names and promised that Dulcie would write to them for him.

After the first awkwardness, Raimey found it easy. *They're all like hurt little boys,* she thought as she moved down the line. Most of them were young and away from home for the first time, and though they would die before admitting it, they were afraid. There was an eagerness in the voices of most of them, and Raimey made slow progress. When she got to the last bed, Matron Huger approached and said, "Well, Miss Reed, you've made some of our men very happy. But you're about out of cake, I see."

"I'll bring more tomorrow," Raimey promised. She moved from the bed of the man in the last bunk, saying, "I'll bring a copy of that book tomorrow. Maybe you'll read some of it to me."

"I'll do that, Miss Reed," the soldier replied, nodding, and the matron saw his eyes follow the blind girl as she moved away.

"You did fine. Tomorrow you'll remember some of them, I'm sure."

Raimey smiled. "Give me the number of one of the beds, Matron."

"Why—number sixteen."

"That's Charlie Linkous. He's from Winchester. He's got a pretty serious wound in his thigh, but he's not going to lose the leg."

Matron Huger stopped dead still. "Can you name all the men like that, Miss Reed?"

"Yes. I have a very good memory." She changed the subject suddenly. "Mrs. Huger, is Denton Rocklin in this ward?"

"Why, yes. Are you acquainted with him?"

"Oh yes. Could I speak to him before we leave?"

"Right over here." The matron had observed that Raimey hated to be taken by the arm, so she tactfully moved closer, and the girl's hand went at once to her arm. She led the way to one end of the cots under the windows and then paused. "Here's a friend of yours, Lieutenant Rocklin."

"How are you, Dent?" Raimey asked uncertainly. He did not speak, but the matron said, "Take this chair while you visit, Miss Reed. I'll leave you now."

Raimey felt the chair, then sat down with her back stiff. Now that she was here, it all seemed crazy. Maybe he wouldn't even want to see her. She heard a slight sound, bedcovers rustling; then his voice came—"Hello, Raimey." He grunted with pain as he came to a sitting position, then added, "Nice of you to come."

His voice was different, she decided at once. He'd always had such excitement in his voice, and now that was all gone. *Deborah was right! He's lost all his hope.*

"It's very bad, the pain?"

"No worse than lots of others."

She hardly knew what to say, so heavy was the impression she got from him. "I have a little cake left, if you'd like some."

"No thanks, but you might give it to Simon. He's got a sweet tooth—" Then he realized she could not see his gesture toward Alcott. "Just leave it here, Raimey. I'll give it to him."

She put the cake down, then suddenly held out her hand on an impulse. She felt his hand close around hers and said quietly, "I'm so sorry, Dent."

He looked at her closely. Her skin was so fine it was almost translucent, and her lips were soft and vulnerable, almost maternal. He was still filled with bitterness over his mother's reaction, but now as she sat there quietly, her hand resting in his trustfully, he knew that she was grieving over him. He held her hand, marveling at the fragile bones, the softness of it, then released it. "It happens in a war, Raimey."

"I know." She sat there quietly, saying nothing. He was glad she didn't overwhelm him with assurances that he was going to be all right, glad that she just sat there. It helped, in some strange way that he couldn't understand. Finally she said, "I've thought so often of how we danced at the ball. I'll never forget it." When he didn't speak, she said, "You can't know, Dent, but you did something for me that nobody has ever done."

"A dance? That wasn't much."

"You made me feel like a woman," Raimey said, so softly that he had to lean forward. "You danced with me and then you—kissed me. It made me feel like a woman for the first time. Thank you for that, Dent."

He didn't know what to say. It had been such a small thing to him, but he saw now that it had been very important to her. "I've thought of it, too, Raimey. Just before we went in after the Yankees, I thought of that night out on the balcony with you." He let a smile come to him, thinking of it. "It was sure funny. The bullets were flying, and the shells were bursting—and there I was thinking about that night with you on the balcony. Sure was funny."

They sat there, each thinking their own thoughts; then Raimey said, "I'll be back tomorrow. Can I bring you something?"

"A new arm—and a new face," he said, and the moment was broken. "Good-bye, Raimey," he said and turned his face to the wall.

It took Raimey only four days to learn the names of every man in the ward, and the men could talk of little else. "Why, she knows who a fellow is as soon as he opens his mouth!" a short captain from Georgia said, marveling. "Never saw anything like it!"

Boredom was one of the worst aspects of confinement. There was nothing to do except talk, and that grew stale. But as Raimey came, day after day, she always had something for the men to do. On her second day, she brought four checkerboards and astounded the officers by winning a game against Simon Alcott. He was a good player and was prepared to let her win, but found himself badly beaten. He had taken a lot of ribbing about the loss but proved himself one of the best players. Raimey organized a checker tournament, and the finals had the men making so much noise that Matron had to come in to see what was happening and quiet the group down. Then she saw Raimey's small form in the center of a group of the walking wounded, and all the men cheering lustily, and she changed her mind and went back to her office, a smile on her lips.

Still, though Raimey was a success with most of the other men, Dent remained taciturn. Raimey tried everything, but nothing worked. Finally, one day she was sitting with Dent, both of them silent, when she heard the voice of Jemmy saying, "Now, Major Rocker, the doctor says you gotta be shaved."

"What for?" Dent asked roughly. "I'm not going anywhere."

Jemmy said, "Them whiskers gotta come off. Now you set there and I'll rake 'em off."

"Blasted foolishness!"

"Never mind all that fussin'," Jemmy said. "Sit up thar and lemme do something 'bout them whiskers." Dent had seen her shave Buck Libby, who had lost both hands, and Libby had testified that the old woman had good hands. He sighed and moved to the chair.

She worked up a lather, then carefully pulled the bandage away from the wounded cheek. "I'll do this hurt side fust," she announced and, moving carefully around the stitches, shaved that side of Dent's face. A thought came to her, and she said, "You ever do any barbering, missus?"

"Me?" Raimey asked in a startled tone, then smiled. "Why, no, except for cutting my sister's hair. I've done that often enough."

"Wal, you ain't too old to learn," Jemmy announced. "Come here and I'll show you how. Major Rocker, here, he'll be a good one to practice on."

Dent suddenly laughed for the first time in days. "Jemmy means, I think, if you slice my right cheek, it'll be a match for the left one." He saw that Raimey was tempted by the idea and urged her on. "Have a try, Raimey. You can't do any damage."

Raimey hesitated; then she had a thought that made her cheek flush. *If I could just touch him, maybe somehow he'd know how I feel! Maybe he wouldn't be so far away.*

"Show me, Jemmy!" she said, moving to where Dent was sitting.

"Ain't nothing to it," Jemmy said. "You jist use yore fingers 'sted of yore eyes. Here, the razor—hold it like that. Now gimme yore hand. . . ."

Dent found the sight of Raimey standing there with a straight razor in her hands amusing. He sat very still as her fingers cautiously moved across his face, tracing his cheek and jawline. Jemmy stood there instructing her, and at first Raimey was frightened. But after she moved the razor down Dent's cheek, Jemmy said, "See thar! I tole you hit wasn't nothin' to barbering. Now the hard part is the lip, so you jist hold his nose with one hand to keep from slicin' it off—"

When the job was done, Jemmy said, "Feel how smooth his cheek is, jist like a baby's bottom, ain't it now?"

Dent felt the featherlight touch of Raimey's hand and was stirred by an old memory. "You did that once before, remember?" he said, his voice soft.

"I remember."

Dent said, "The other side's changed a lot."

Jemmy said, "It's a bit harder, dodgin' all them stitches. But

I'm givin' this job to you, missus. I got plenty of Yankee boys upstairs to barber. Now looky here, gimme yore hand—"

Dent stiffened as he felt Raimey's fingers trace the scar on his cheek. He wanted to pull away, to shout angrily for her to leave him alone, but there was something in her touch that kept him still. Then the hand was gone, and Raimey said, "I'll do the best I can, Jemmy. Will you show me how to put the bandage back on? Then let me have some scissors and I'll cut his hair."

Jemmy showed the girl how to apply the bandage, then produced a pair of shears. Soon Raimey was working skillfully on Dent's shaggy hair. "I'm a little better at this," she said, smoothing his black hair and shaping it carefully. She had found that she could cut hair well. "Cutting your hair is easy," she commented. "You've got such a well-shaped head."

Finally she was satisfied. She ran her hand over his hair, saying, "How much do you usually pay to get your hair cut, Dent?"

"A quarter."

"You owe me, then," Raimey said. She stood before him, a smile on her lips, pleased and excited that she had done something for him. "I'll bring one of my father's razors tomorrow. He has one for every day, with the day of the week on the handle."

"Get the one marked Friday," Dent said. He rubbed his cheek, saying, "Feels good. I always hated not shaving."

"I'll shave you every day. You'll owe me a lot of money after a week or so."

Dent's mood shifted suddenly, and she noticed it. He said nothing, so she asked quietly, "You just thought you might not be here in a week, didn't you?"

He stared at her, shocked that she should know his thoughts. "Don't think I like you knowing me so well—but yes, it did occur to me."

"Would it be so bad, Dent? Losing your arm?"

"Raimey, I can't say how I feel to you, not about that. I mean, you've lost so much more! But somehow I can't face it. I know there are men here who'd be happy to change places with me, but it's just the way I am. I'd get by, but it's not worth it. Besides—"

He cut his words off and then laughed. "You know what I was going to say, don't you?"

"I think you were going to say something about being scarred."

He made a grimace, then said, "It's women who are supposed to be vain. But my own mother couldn't stand to look at me. I can't stand the thought of people recoiling from the sight of my face, Raimey."

He waited for her to argue, but she did no such thing. "I know, Dent. Do you think I haven't thought of ending it all?" His face registered shock, and she sensed it. "But God's given me some good things. And you have so much to give, Dent."

"It's—too hard for me, Raimey!"

She seemed to be listening to something far off. She finally whispered, "I believe God is going to give you your arm, Dent."

"I don't believe in miracles, Raimey."

She moved to the foot of his bed, her face composed. "I do," she said firmly and left the room.

Men said, "Good night," and she called each name—"Good night, Bax. Don't forget you promised to write to your cousin Donna."

After Raimey left with Dulcie, Dent struggled to his feet and moved to the window. He watched her get into the carriage, then kept his eyes on it until it passed from view. Then he turned to go back to his cot. When he sat down, he looked up to find

Simon watching him with a peculiar look in his blue eyes.

"You know, Dent," he said conversationally, "you're a pretty stupid fellow."

Dent stared at him but found no anger in the man. "Stupid? I guess so, Simon. In what specific way?"

Alcott shook his head, and there was a vague disgust in his expression. "You're too dumb to understand how you're stupid," he remarked. Then with a shake of his head, he picked up his book and continued to read.

Dent lay down, and his arm began to send daggers of pain that scraped at his nerves. *It's getting worse*, he thought as he turned over, cradling the arm. He tried to sleep but could not. It was three in the morning when he was awakened by Sanders, one of the orderlies. "What are you doing?" Dent gasped.

"You're screamin' so loud you're keeping the men awake. This is just some morphine to help you make it."

Dent tried to protest but could not. The drug took effect quickly, but he knew that he'd come to the end of something. He'd never before let them give him drugs, but now he'd stepped over some sort of line. He had hoped to die, but somehow as he drifted into sleep, he resisted that.

As sleep took Dent Rocklin over, Alcott said, "He's had it, hasn't he, Sanders?"

"Gangrene." The orderly uttered that one word, then moved away, fading into the darkness.

CHAPTER 21

DEBORAH FINDS A MAN

*Y*our father wanted to see you, Clay, but he's been feeling so weak I hated for him to make the trip."

Susanna had met Clay at the front door, kissed him, then led him into the house. "He was taken bad last week but wouldn't let me send for the doctor."

Clay said, "I'll go right up, Mother. I've got two days' leave, so we'll have lots of time to talk." He turned and mounted the large stairway that divided in the middle, took the right section, then walked quickly to the door of his parents' room. When he knocked on the door, his father's voice came at once. Entering the room, Clay found Thomas sitting in a horsehide chair, a letter in his hand.

"Come in, Clay," Thomas said. Letting the letter drop, he put his hand out, and Clay moved to take it. "Glad to see you, son."

"I'd have come earlier, but I couldn't get leave." Clay was shocked by the fragile touch of his father's hand but allowed nothing to show on his face. *Every time I see him, he's gone down,* Clay thought as he pulled a chair close and sat down. "You've been feeling a mite low, Mother says."

"Getting old, I guess."

"Not so old as all that." As a matter of fact, Thomas was only sixty-one, but he looked older. He had always been a handsome man, far better looking than his brother Stephen, but poor health had drained him of color and stripped away the flesh. There was an almost cadaverous look about him now, his eyes sunken and his lips seamed in the manner of the very old. He had the look in his eyes, Clay saw, of a sick person who is exhausted from fighting pain.

But he was glad to see Clay, and he smiled as he picked up the letter. "I got this letter from Colonel Benton three days ago," he said. "Can you guess what's in it?"

"No, not really. Is it about the regiment?"

"No, it's about you, Clay. Let me read it to you." He began reading, and Clay shifted uneasily as he went on. It was a letter of praise for Clay's action in charging up the hill in the face of intense fire. It ended with, "I think I know how proud you must be of Clay, Thomas. It will please you to know that I have mentioned the matter to General Jackson, with a recommendation for an appropriate decoration. You have a nephew who has been decorated for valor, and now I trust that you will have a son, also."

Thomas lowered the letter, and his lips trembled as he said, "I'm very much afraid I'm going to have to tell you what a good son you are to me, Clay."

Clay's face flushed, and for an instant he could think of no reply. He thought of all the grief and pain he'd brought to his parents, then shook his head. "Others did so much more, Father. And I don't know if I'd have gone up that hill if it hadn't been my own son who was in danger."

Thomas studied him carefully, thinking of how different

this man was from the younger Clay Rocklin. "I think you would. You're like your uncle Stephen, Clay. More like him than you are like me, for which I'm thankful!"

Clay said at once, "I'm a Rocklin, sir, like you and Uncle Stephen both." He changed the subject, for he saw again what he had always known, that his father felt inferior to his uncle. The two of them were very different, and Clay didn't want his father to dwell on the matter. "Lowell is doing very well," he said, and for some time he spoke of his son's accomplishments in glowing terms. "He'll be a general before he's through, I'd venture."

Thomas sat there listening carefully, then asked, "Is Dent improved at all? What about his arm?"

"No better, I'm afraid. I wish he'd let them take that arm off. It's worse every day, and it could kill him."

"Your mother thinks he's afraid to face the world with such a terrible scar on his face. He's always been such a handsome boy, Clay. Do you think he might be wanting to die so he won't have to face the world?"

"It's—possible, sir," Clay agreed. "Dent's in a deep valley now. He's always had everything, and now he's thinking he'll only be an ugly cripple. He's a man without any props, and my hope is that he'll see how helpless he is without God—and that he'll turn to Him."

"I hope so." Thomas thought about it, then asked, "What about Sam Reed's daughter? Susanna tells me she visited Dent."

"She's a fine girl," Clay said at once. "I never saw a finer. She's a good Christian, and if anyone can touch Dent, I think she's the one."

For the rest of the day, Clay moved around Gracefield, accompanied by his daughter, Rena. She was delighted to have him there, and it was a keen pleasure for him to watch her riding beside him. Clay wished that her mother was more attentive to her, though he said nothing to Rena about that.

At supper that night, Thomas felt well enough to come down, though he ate little. David, Dent's twin brother, was anxious for details about the battle. They all listened as Clay told about it, making much of the efforts of Lowell and the others and minimizing his own part.

The next morning, he mounted his horse and rode to see Buford Yancy and, in effect, was forced to tell the story again. Buford and Melora met him as he rode up, and when they all sat down to an early dinner, Melora said, "Tell us about the battle, Mister Clay." She often called him that, for it had been her first name for him when she had been a child.

"Yeah, tell us about Bob," Josh insisted. He was fourteen and frantic with excitement about the war. So Clay went over the story again, this time making Bob Yancy the hero of the piece. Finally he held up his hand. "You've done all the eating, and I've done all the talking."

"Let him eat, you chirrun," Buford said. "After you rest a bit, Clay, I'll show you whut I done about the new pens." He drove his brood outside, and Melora came over to pour fresh coffee into his cup, then got a cup for herself and sat down beside him.

"Tell me about Dent," she said. The light came through the glass window, highlighting the planes of her face. She sat there, her head turned to one side, listening to him.

"Dent's in bad shape, Melora. I'm praying for him." He laughed ruefully as a thought struck him, adding, "I'm in pretty bad shape myself, come to think of it."

"What's wrong, Clay?" she asked. "Is it the war? I know you don't believe in it."

"I don't for a fact, but that's not why I'm in bad shape." He looked at her and smiled crookedly.

She knew him so well that he didn't need to say more. She was always happy to be with him but saddened by the way things were. She knew that Clay would be faithful to his marriage and that she would never be more than a good friend to him. Many had suspected that there was more to their relationship than just friendship, but they didn't know Clay. He had emerged from his prodigal youth as a man with a sense of honor so strong that he could not even think of breaking it with a low deed.

The solemn ticking of the clock on the mantel counted out the time, and each of them thought long thoughts. Finally Clay looked at her, saying, "It's hard, Melora."

"Yes, it's hard. But we have this much."

"Not much. Seeing each other and talking once every three months. You ought to marry, Melora."

"No, that's not for me." There was no sorrow or grief in her eyes. He knew she was not a grieving woman, but he wondered at the happiness in her clear eyes. "If I reached out and tried to grab happiness with you, Clay, it wouldn't bring me anything. I think we have to take every little good thing God gives us—no matter how small—and treasure it. But if we try to grab for more than He intends, it goes bad, just like the manna the disobedient Israelites tried to hoard. God told them to gather only enough for one day, to go back for more the next day. Remember what happened to the manna some of them tried to hoard? It went rotten and was filled with worms."

Clay was always impressed with the way Melora used the scripture to live by. "Never thought of that," he said. He sat there, holding on to the moment, for he knew that one like it would not come again soon. He spoke of it finally, saying, "I'll be gone a long time, Melora. This isn't going to be an easy war. And the South is going to be in a trial of fire."

"I'll be here when you get back, Clay," she said softly, and then he rose and took her hands in his. She held to him tightly, murmuring, "We'll be faithful to God's law, Clay. This love I have for you, it's from Him, and I will never dishonor Him with it. Don't ever worry about me, and don't ever doubt about us. God is going to bless us, even if we can never be together. He always honors those that honor Him."

They stood there, knowing that the world was falling down around them but aware that somehow the fiery trial would be endured and they would not be lost in it. When Clay left that afternoon, Buford said quietly, "Might be a spell before we see Clay again, daughter."

"He'll come back, Pa," she said firmly, and he saw that there was no doubt in her as she turned to her work.

❦

Chief Surgeon Baskins studied the wound almost carelessly. He had seen so many wounds that a callousness had come over him—especially when the patient was a Yankee. He straightened up and said shortly, "Looks a little better. Keep the bandages changed, Branch," then moved on down the line.

Pat Steele watched the surgeon leave. There was a sultry anger in his eyes. "He doesn't care if we live or die!"

Jesse Branch finished slapping a bandage on Noel's side, got up, and gathered his supplies. "He's better than some, Blue-belly," he said as he left. "But you won't have to put up with him long."

Pat stared at him. "He's leaving the hospital?"

"Nope." Branch gave him a sly look. "He ain't—you are." Branch loved to gossip and lowered his voice to add, "You'll be leaving in a couple of days for a prison camp. And from what I hear, it won't be no picnic. I 'spec you'll be crying for this hospital and this good grub in a few days!"

"Noel, too?"

"Nope. You and five more, I hear."

Branch left, and Noel said, "I ought to go with you, Pat."

"No, you need to be here. I'll be all right."

But either Branch had been wrong in his information or there was a change of plans. That same day after Jemmy had helped distribute the evening meal and while she sat beside Noel, talking with the two men, a Confederate lieutenant accompanied by two privates carrying muskets came into the room. "Price, Duggins, Steele, Anderson, Lyons, and Ochner," he read from a list, then said, "Get your stuff and come with me. You're being transferred."

Pat began to gather his meager belongings. His arm was not healed completely, and Jemmy moved to help him. She caught at his arm, and in the shadow of the brim of her ever-present sunbonnet, he saw that her eyes were damp with tears. "I wisht you didn't have to go," she whispered.

"Me, too, Jemmy." Pat summoned up a smile. "You've been mighty good to all of us. Going to miss you."

Suddenly Jemmy threw her arms around him, gave him a hard squeeze, then turned and stumbled away. Pat watched her go, surprise in his eyes. "Why, that's funny!" he said. "The old lady's really got a heart for us, Noel." Then he turned and put his hand out. "So long, Noel. Hope this thing is over soon. Would you write to my people? Might not be a very good delivery service in the camp."

"Sure, Pat," Noel said. He came to his feet, grunting with the pain. "Guess I'll be seeing you pretty soon."

The two of them stood there, bound by the code that said men shouldn't show any emotion. They had grown close during the past few weeks, and finally Noel leaned forward and put his arms around Pat, whispering, "By heaven! I'm going to miss you, Pat!"

Pat Steele was suddenly choked with emotion and could only say huskily, "Me, too, Noel!"

Then the lieutenant said impatiently, "All right, you men, let's go!"

Noel moved to the window and watched as the prisoners were marched out and placed in an open wagon. Pat looked up, saw him at the window, and gave a cheerful wave. Noel returned the salute and watched until the wagon, accompanied by two armed guards on horseback, disappeared down the road. Then he moved to sit down on his cot, filled with apprehension.

Finally Noel was aware that someone had come to stand beside him, and he looked up to find Jemmy watching him. "Well, Jemmy, I'm going to miss him," he said simply.

"He's a nice young feller," Jemmy said. "I'll miss him, too."

Noel examined her more carefully. It was hard to tell her age, for the bonnet she wore concealed the upper half of her face. She had iron-gray hair, but her hands were firm and strong, not wrinkled with age, and he asked curiously, "Why did you hug him, Jemmy? Did he remind you of your son?"

She hesitated, then shrugged. "Oh, I reckon I jist got fond of the scamp."

"How old is your boy, Jemmy? You never talk about him."

"Wal, he's about yore age, I reckon." She seemed uncomfortable and shifted the subject. "Whut about you now? You got a heap of purty gals back home, ain't you now?"

Noel shook his head, smiling at her. "No, Jemmy, I guess not."

"A fine-lookin' young feller like you? Come on, now, you kin tell ol' Jemmy!" When he continued to deny that he had a string of pretty girls waiting for him, she asked curiously, "Mebbe you ain't got no bunch of gals, but I'll bet my bonnet you got *one*, ain't that so?"

Noel flushed slightly, then laughed self-consciously. "Well, in a way maybe I have, Jemmy. There is a girl back home—but it's all one-sided. I think of her all the time, but she's not for me."

"And why not?" Jemmy demanded sharply.

"Oh, she's out of my reach." Noel shrugged. "She comes from a good family. Her father's a wealthy man."

"I don't reckon she'd be marryin' yore family, would she?"

Noel said soberly, "In a way she would be. When people get married, their families are part of it. That's the way it is. And my family—"

"Well, whut about yore family?"

He hesitated but began to talk. Jemmy sat down on the chair, and after a while Noel forgot himself and told her the whole story of how he had met the young woman. Jemmy sat there silently, listening and watching him. Finally he gave a start, then smiled sheepishly. "Gosh, Jemmy, I didn't mean to tell you all that."

Jemmy's voice was usually high-pitched. As she spoke now, though, it was lower and smoother. "This heah gal, this Deb'rah? Whut you thinking 'bout her, Noel?"

Noel sat there, his face serious in the darkening room. He was not a man to say much about what he felt. His feelings were stronger than anyone had ever suspected, but he had kept them bottled up for the most part. But now he was far from home, and the wound had weakened him so that he said to Jemmy what he would not have let escape under ordinary circumstances.

"I love her, Jemmy," he said simply. "It won't ever come to anything. I sure won't ever tell her. She'd be kind enough to me because that's the way she is." His face had thinned during his illness, but there was still a stubbornness in his strong chin as he spoke. "She's a wonderful girl, Jemmy, but she's not for me."

He glanced at Jemmy, who sat so still that she seemed to have gone to sleep. Her upper face was hidden by the shadow of her bonnet, but Noel thought he saw her lips tremble. Finally she cleared her throat and said, "I reckon she's got a right to know how you feel about her." Then she rose, picked up his dishes, and left without another word.

Noel stared after her until she disappeared through the door that led to the stairway, then said slowly, "Now that's a funny one!" Then he lay down on his cot.

Jemmy left the hospital without saying good-bye to Matron Huger. Neither did she speak to the guard at the gate as was her custom. Turning to go down the road that led to her boardinghouse, she noticed a man standing beside a large oak. He was a large man and seemed to be watching the iron gate that she had just passed through. The darkness was falling fast, so she could not see his features clearly, and the slouch hat he wore was pulled down over his eyes.

Yet there was something vaguely familiar about the man, and Jemmy suddenly crossed the road. As she passed the man, he lifted his head and gave her a suspicious look. He was tall, about six feet, and had wavy dark hair that escaped the confines of the cap, and a pair of bold brown eyes. There was something about his stare, a wildness that flashed out at her, that almost frightened her. She walked by, her mind racing.

Then when she was six paces down the lane, it came to her. She stopped, turned, and moved back to the man who had been watching her. He turned his whole body to face her, alert and ready for trouble.

"What are you doing here, Bing?" Deborah asked.

Alarm leaped to Bing Kojak's eyes, and he took a step toward her, moving on his toes, ready to leap as he said, "Who the devil are you? My name's Jim!"

"The guard is watching us, Bing," Deborah said calmly. "He'll be suspicious, so come with me. Take my arm and lead me down the street."

Bing stared at her, but a glance toward the guard revealed that she was telling the truth. He took her arm in a paralyzing grip and moved away. When they were out of sight of the guard, he growled, "Now who are you?"

Deborah had been thinking rapidly and knew that Noel's brother could have only one motive in being outside the gates of Chimborazo. "I'm Deborah Steele, Bing. You've come to help Noel escape, haven't you?"

Bing was so taken aback that he could only stare at her for a long moment; then he slowly nodded. "That's it."

"Come to my room," Deborah said quickly. "We can't be seen together. I wish that guard hadn't seen us!" She led the way toward her boardinghouse but, when it was in sight, changed her mind. "No, this won't do. I don't want anyone there to see you. We'll have to talk here." She turned to face him, asking, "What brought you here, Bing? You never cared that much about your brother—or anyone else."

Bing glared at her, then suddenly nodded. "Right you are! You've got my number," he said angrily. Then he grew uncomfortable, shifting his feet and looking down at the ground. "Well, that's right enough, Miss Steele. I've been a hard one. Had to be, I guess."

"I know it's been hard on you, Bing—on all of you."

Her admission seemed to encourage the big man. Lifting his head, he said, "Well, I ain't done much to be proud of, but nobody ever accused me of being a coward. I thought—I thought I could take anything, no matter how tough it was. But then. . .when the battle started. . ." Bing gave her an anguished look and bit his lip. He had trouble speaking, then blurted out, "I run like a yellow dog, that's what I done! Noel and some of the others stayed and fought, but I run." He got control of himself, shrugged, then went on. "I didn't care at first. Just glad to be out of the thing. But it kept eatin' on me, you see? Me, Bing Kojak, runnin' away from a fight, like a spineless worm!"

"Lots of men ran away, Bing."

"Well, that's their problem! But I ain't no coward!" Bing glared at her as if challenging her to deny it, but found understanding in her eyes. "Well, I tried getting drunk, but that didn't help. Finally I knew I'd never have no rest until I showed I wasn't no coward. I could have gone back to the army, but I wanted to show Noel. I come to get him out of that hospital and back home—and I'm gonna do it, too!"

"I think that's fine, Bing," Deborah said quietly. "Do you have any ideas about how to go about it?"

"Naw, I can't figure nothing," he said, shaking his head gloomily. "Guards at all the gates and inside, too. All I know is to wait until the middle of the night, take one guard out, then go in and try to find Noel."

"He's on the second floor, Bing," Deborah said.

He stared at her, asking abruptly, "What are you doing here, all disguised?"

"The same as you, Bing," Deborah said and told him swiftly how she'd felt guilty over encouraging Noel to enlist and had come to try to do something.

"You got any ideas on how to bust him out?" Bing asked.

Deborah thought for a moment, then said, "If we get him out, Bing, it'll have to be at once. My brother Pat was with him until today. They took him to a prison camp, and I think they'll transfer Noel soon, maybe in a few days."

"We got to get him out! There must be some way!" Bing said savagely.

Deborah said, "We'll do it, Bing. If we do get him out, can we get him out of Richmond?"

"I'll handle that, right enough," he said with a nod. "There's wagons and boats and trains, and they can't watch them all. Just let me get him out of that place, and the rest will go all right!"

Deborah said at once, "Bing, you start looking for a way to get him out of Richmond. Do you have any money?"

"Not a lot," he admitted.

"I've got enough. Find a way and meet me here tomorrow about this same time."

"All right." Bing hesitated, then asked, "You got an idea how to get him out?"

Deborah said, a peculiar look in her eyes, "The Bible says that God sets the prisoners free. All I have to do is ask Him how to go about it."

Bing stared at her, then shook his head. "You talk to God, then. I'll be here tomorrow." He wheeled and disappeared into the darkness.

Deborah went to her room, but she didn't sleep that night. By the time dawn came through the grimy window of her tiny room, she still didn't have an answer.

CHAPTER 22

THE MIRACLE

"You want my advice," Chief Surgeon Baskins said, "I think we ought to put some drugs in his food, then take him down to surgery and take that arm off. When he wakes up he can rave all he wants to, but he'll still be alive." He looked across Matron Huger's office to the medicine cabinet. "Give me some whiskey."

Matron Huger frowned but didn't argue. She got the whiskey from the cabinet and put the bottle and a glass before him. Baskins sloshed the liquor into the glass and drank it down.

"We can't do that, Doctor," she said as he sat there frowning at the table. "It's his life—and besides, he has a family. If anyone makes a decision like that, it'd have to be them. And they're not going to do it."

"Blast the man!" Baskins growled, slamming the table with his fist. "Why's he making such a fuss? He ought to be thankful it's not worse."

Matron Huger didn't argue, but she thought she knew why Dent Rocklin refused surgery. She had talked with the man's grandmother, a sensible woman, and had discovered that her own guess about the man was correct.

"He's got too much pride," Susanna Rocklin had said, sorrow in her fine eyes. "He's had everything, and now he can't face up to the loss. He'll have to be broken before he'll agree to the operation—and I think he'll choose to die."

It looked as though the old woman had been correct. Matron Huger hated to lose patients, hated it with all the vigor of her soul and spirit. She rose suddenly, left the office, and went into the ward room. Raimey Reed was sitting beside Denny Gipson, a seventeen-year-old from Texas. Matron Huger waited until the boy finished telling the girl about his home along the Rio Grande, then said, "Miss Reed, may I speak with you when you're finished with Denny?"

"I think Lieutenant Gipson's told me all the tall tales about Texas that I can take for one day, Matron." She reached out, and the soldier took her hand eagerly. "I'll bring the book with me tomorrow."

Matron Huger said, "Come to my office. We'll have some tea." The two women left the room and soon were drinking tea and talking about the men in the ward. "We lost Major Glover last night," the matron said. "I've been so upset over it."

"He was a fine Christian man." Raimey nodded. "He was a widower. I don't think he's been happy since his wife died."

"I didn't know that," the older woman said in surprise. "When did she die?"

"Two years ago. He talked about her a great deal, especially the last few days." She sipped the tea, a thoughtful expression on her face. There was an inner quietness in Raimey Reed such as Matron Huger had never seen in one of Raimey's age. Usually such peace and serenity were seen only in the very old or in small children. "I was with him just before they came to get him for the surgery. He knew he was going to die, but he wasn't afraid. The last thing he said was, 'Thank God, I'll be with Doris now!'"

Tears rose to the matron's eyes, though she was not a woman who usually allowed such a thing. "Well, he's with Doris now," she murmured.

Raimey lifted her head. "Don't cry for him, Matron," she said with a fine smile. "He's happier there than he could ever have been here."

Matron Huger was taken aback. "How did you know I was crying, Raimey?" she asked.

"Your voice had tears."

Matron Huger shook her head. "You have more sensitivity than any young woman I've ever known, Raimey," she murmured. The two of them sat there drinking tea, and finally the matron said, "We're going to lose Lieutenant Rocklin, I'm afraid." She saw a break in the girl's smooth countenance, which confirmed a conviction she had formed. "Even if he agreed to the surgery, it may be too late," she went on, then leaned forward. "Why don't you talk to him, Raimey? You love him, don't you?"

Raimey nodded slightly but said, "I've begged him to have the operation."

"Have you told him you love him, that it doesn't make any difference to you that he's scarred?"

"No!" Raimey said, her lips suddenly trembling. "I—I can't do that!"

"Why can't you? Or maybe it does matter to you? Some women can't abide such things."

"You know that's not true! But. . .I can't tell him that I. . . love him!"

Matron Huger paused, then knew she had to be cruel. "Oh, I see," she said quietly. "It's your pride, then. You can't afford to risk a refusal. Well, I suppose your pride is more important than Denton Rocklin's life."

"That's not fair!" Raimey rose with an angry gesture that sent the cup in her hands to the floor. It broke into pieces, but neither woman paid any heed. "I'd do anything to save his life!"

"I think you're his last hope, Raimey," Matron Huger said, her voice insistent. "He's a strong, stubborn man, and I think he's made up his mind that there's nothing for him to live for. He's proud, too, and it comes down to this—which of you is going to have your pride broken? I think he may care for you, Raimey. I've seen him when you were with him, and he watches you with the kind of look a man has when he loves a woman. He's gotten to be good friends with Simon Alcott. Simon is a pretty sharp fellow. We talk quite a bit, and he says that Rocklin is in love with you."

"Did he say so, that he loved me?"

"Of course not! He'd never admit it to anyone. That's his pride, and it's killing him. He's been a man who could attract women with no trouble, and now his own mother flinches at the sight of him—I could murder that woman! Now he's afraid that no woman could love him, so he wants to die. But if he knew it wasn't so, he'd want to live."

Raimey stood there, trembling and clasping her hands in an effort to conceal it. Finally she whispered, "All right, I'll do it."

"Fine! Fine!" Matron Huger cried and moved to put her arms around the girl. "Do it now, Raimey. He needs you."

Raimey left the matron's office, and Dulcie was waiting for her. She began complaining at once. "I don't know how I got any fingers left on my hand! If I have to write one more letter for one of them soldiers, it'll drive me crazy, Miss Raimey!"

"You've done so much for these men, Dulcie," Raimey said gently, her thoughts elsewhere. "They all love you for it, too."

"Hmmm! I don't know about that, but they sure can eat! Susie told me she was not going to keep making a hundred pies every day!" There was a pause, and Dulcie said, "We got to get home. Your daddy said for you to be home before dark."

"I want to talk to Lieutenant Rocklin, Dulcie. Then we'll go."

Dulcie stared at her mistress, a suspicion in her bright eyes. "You talking too much to that man. He's too sick to do much talking, anyway." But she had learned that a new authority had come into her mistress, so, grumbling under her breath, she led Raimey to Dent Rocklin's cot. Then she left, saying, "We have to leave before it gets dark, you hear me?"

"All right, Dulcie." Raimey touched the chair and moved to sit down, asking, "Lieutenant Alcott?"

"Simon's down at the end playing poker." Dent's voice was ragged with exhaustion, she noted, and she thought she could smell the infected wound. He went on, "Want me to call him for you?"

"No, Dent. I'd like to talk to you."

Dent looked at her, his face hollow with the fever that had raged for several days. His eyes were dull and his speech was slow. "Guess I'm not much to talk to, Raimey." He fell silent, the pain in his arm sapping his energy. He had eaten little, and there was no hope in him.

"I don't want you to talk to me, Dent. Not now. I—I've got something to say to you."

"All right, Raimey."

He could see the pulse beating rapidly in the blue vein in

Raimey's throat and wondered what had upset her. She looked frightened—and fear was something he'd never seen on her face before. She drew a deep breath, then began speaking.

"Dent, I'm not like other girls. I've missed out on so many things that are natural with them. For a long time I was angry with God for letting me be blind. It didn't seem fair somehow. But when I was thirteen, a very wonderful thing happened to me. I was in a revival meeting with my parents, and for the first time I really heard the gospel with my heart. I guess I'd heard a thousand sermons on how people need to be saved from their sins—but I was too mad at God to believe anything. But that morning, the sermon was on the death of Jesus, and for the first time I understood what real suffering was—*His* suffering, when they nailed Him to the cross. . . ."

Dent lay there listening, half out of his head. If he had been himself, he would have refused to listen, for he had been angry at God since the battle. But his weakness kept him still, and he listened as Raimey told how she'd felt the weight of her sins and how she'd begun to grieve, finally calling on the name of Jesus.

"He saved me, Dent," she said simply, tears in her eyes. "Since that moment I've been happy."

"You're still blind," Dent said roughly. He had been touched by her story, but the bitterness in him was strong. "Why doesn't He heal your eyes?"

"I don't know why, Dent," Raimey said quietly. "But I know one thing, and that is that God loves me. And anything that comes to me—including blindness—comes through His hands. I know that, Dent, and I know that as long as I live He'll be there. There are worse things than being blind, Dent." She leaned forward, reaching out her hand, and he took it. Holding on to it as hard as she could, Raimey whispered, "Being bitter and unhappy is worse, being the way I used to be—and the way you are now!"

Dent held on to her hand, stung by her words but knowing that the ring of truth was in them. He couldn't answer, but simply lay there. As he did so, he began to feel peculiar. A strange sense of shame came to him, and myriad thoughts flowed across his mind in a montage of scenes—and in all of them he saw himself as a small man, petty and unkind. He thought of his father and how he'd spurned the advances the older man had made. These thoughts, and many more, coursed through his mind.

Finally Raimey said, "Dent?" And when he spoke, she said, "You know you're going to die if something doesn't happen?"

"Yes, I know that. Won't be much of a loss."

"It will be a great loss!" Raimey cried, clinging to his hand. Her voice wasn't loud, but it was strong. "What about your family? Your grandparents and your brothers and Rena? And your father? He loves you, Dent. They all do!"

And then when Dent made no answer, Raimey took a deep breath and went on, her voice unsteady. "What about me, Dent? Don't you know that I love you?"

Dent blinked and stared at her. His mind was working so slowly that he thought he had mistaken her words. "What did you say?"

"I—I love you, Dent," Raimey said, her head held up proudly. "I know a woman's not supposed to say things like that, and I know you don't love me—but I won't have you say that it makes no difference whether you live or die!"

Dent had been aware that Raimey Reed was a girl of powerful emotions, but he had never seen them evidenced.

Now as she sat there, her chin lifted, her lips trembling, she was beautiful. Her glossy hair gleamed faintly, and there was strength in her firm jawline and beauty in the curve of her smooth cheek. Slowly Dent reached out and put his hand on that cheek—and felt the dampness of a tear.

"Don't cry, Raimey," he whispered. "There's nothing to cry about."

"There is!" she insisted with a sob and put her hands over his. "Dent, I've never loved a man before and I'll never love another. If you die, it will be death for me!" She moved from the chair and fell on her knees, putting her face against his chest. Her hair was fragrant and soft against his face, and he held her as her slim body was wracked with sobs. "I love you, Dent, as much as any woman ever loved any man!" she sobbed. "Please live, Dent! You don't have to love me—you can marry another woman, and I'll be happy just knowing you're alive!"

Dent had known many women, but none had affected him like this one. He had been dazzled by the beauty and charm of Deborah Steele, even ready to fight for her. But now. . .now the gentleness of the woman who knelt beside him and the declaration of her love hit him hard. His mind was cloudy with fever, but he knew what it had cost her to come to him. He held her until the sobs ceased; then when she lifted her head and started to move away, he whispered, "Raimey, I'm all mixed up. I don't know what to do."

She sensed the confusion in his mind, and then something came to her. She knelt there, not moving, and the thought came back even stronger. She thought, *I can't say that! It would be cruel!* But as the doubt came to her, there was something else—a sense of the presence of God. She had felt such a thing three times in her life, and each time there had been in her spirit an absolute certainty that God was speaking to her. It was there now. Her lips parted, and she grew still as the impression became even stronger.

"What is it, Raimey?" Dent asked, noting her expression.

"Dent, will you let me pray for you?"

"Why—I guess so." The request made Dent feel uncomfortable. Others had asked the same thing, and he'd curtly refused, but now he felt strange. "I don't believe in God very much," he said finally.

"I believe that God is going to do something for you, Dent," Raimey said. She hesitated, then added, "I think He wants to heal your arm."

Dent looked down at the arm, aware that the doctors had given up, saying the infection had gone into gangrene. He was too weary now to be angry about it. So though the girl's faith seemed strange and unreal, he said, "Well, Raimey, if anyone does anything with my arm, it'll have to be God."

Raimey put her hands out, touching the ruined arm, and prayed a very simple prayer: "Oh God, my Father, in the name of Jesus Christ, I ask You to heal this infection in Dent's arm. I believe that You can do all things, that nothing is impossible for You. Give us this sign of Your power and Your love, for I ask it in the name of Jesus."

Dent lay there, then asked, "Is that all?"

"Yes." Tears flowed freely down Raimey's face, for she had been given an assurance that her prayer had been heard. "I must go." She got to her feet and called out, "Dulcie—I'm ready." Then as the maid came to get her, she turned to face Dent. Her face was luminous in the light that flowed through the window, and she whispered, "I love you, Dent!"

Dent watched her leave, then looked down at his arm. When

Simon Alcott came back from his poker game, he looked at his friend. "How's it going, Dent? Any better?"

Dent looked up at him, his face sober and his lips tight. "I don't know, Simon." He looked at his arm and then back to Alcott. "I'm going to find out pretty soon if God is real or not."

His words made Alcott blink, and he thought at once, *He's getting delirious.* But he said only, "Take it easy, Dent. You'll be all right."

It was the longest and worst night of Denton Rocklin's life. He moved from a state of half-consciousness to a coma, then came back to reality, drenched with sweat. Fragments of nightmares came, leaving him shaking with fear, and the pain in his arm grew unbearable. When morning broke, he came out of his delirium to find Mrs. Wright, a nurse, standing over him, her face filled with fear and concern.

He croaked from a dry throat, "My arm—is it well?"

Mrs. Wright saw that he was beside himself. "No, Lieutenant, it's not well. You must let them amputate!"

"No!" he said, pulling away from her. "God's going to heal it!"

Mrs. Wright glanced at Simon Alcott with frightened eyes. "I'm going to get some morphine, Simon. Don't let him get up!"

She ran to the cabinet, then came back to give Rocklin the shot. When he grew still, she asked, "What's all this about his arm being healed?"

Alcott shrugged. "Miss Reed was talking to him. She's real religious. I guess she might have got him started."

"Well, she's got to stop!" Mrs. Wright left the room and soon was giving Matron Huger her views. "You've got to speak to Miss Reed! She's got Dent Rocklin's hopes up, says that God's going to heal his arm! You know that's impossible!"

"I asked her to speak to him, but I didn't think this was

what she was going to say."

"Well, what are you going to do about it? We can't have the girl upsetting him."

Matron Huger was silent. The pressures of the job were severe, and she still was not able to accept death in a calm, logical manner. Finally she said, "He's not going to listen to anyone else, Mrs. Wright. He'll probably die, but let him die believing in God."

❦

Dent was aware that everyone thought he was crazy. *I think so, too*, he thought wryly when he saw, the morning after Raimey prayed for him, that his arm was worse than it had been. But Raimey had come to visit that day, and when he told her that he hadn't been healed, she had said, "God is never late."

Somehow her serene spirit had touched Dent, and all that day and the next he had lain in a stupor on the bed, thinking of her prayer. His father came, and his grandmother, but neither of them had urged him to have the operation.

The administration had given up, especially Dr. Baskins. The rough surgeon had said profanely, "If he's fool enough to believe in that religious nonsense, let him die! We can use his bed!"

Dent himself, by the end of the second day, was so racked with fever and pain that he was not aware of the talk. That afternoon, Raimey came and sat beside him. She said little, and Dent was beyond speech. But there was a comfort in her presence. Finally when it was time for her to go, he whispered, "I—remember what you said." He had to labor to get the words out, his lips cracked with fever. "Tell me again!"

Raimey bent over him and whispered, "I love you, Dent, and God loves you."

All night Dent lay there, hearing those words over and over: "I love you, Dent, and God loves you."

Sometime during the night, he struggled out of the black pit of unconsciousness that drew him. The moon was out and the stars glittered brightly in the sky. The room was quiet, save for the moanings and mutterings of his fellow patients. Far down the room an orderly sat at a desk, reading a book by the pale yellow light of a lamp.

And as he lay there, only half conscious, Dent became aware that there was something growing in his mind. It was like a tiny light, from somewhere far down a dark road, so dim that it could barely be seen. It grew larger and brighter. It was not, he knew, a physical light or any light at all, but his spirit seemed to glow—there was no other way he could think of it. As the sensation grew within him, he relaxed and let his body go limp. He had kept himself so tense waiting for the next jolt of pain that he ached, and now a sense of security came to him. There was nothing else, just the sense of being cared for, of being loved.

Then he knew that he was not alone, that there was someone in the room other than the two hundred fifty wounded men. Fear came to him and he drew his legs up, sending pain through his arm. But nothing happened, except that the same sense of peace washed back, driving away the fear.

There was never any sort of voice, but he kept feeling that someone was reaching out to him, that he was being loved in a way he had never known. He did something then that he'd not done for years—he began to pray. And even that was strange, for he didn't ask for anything. That was what prayer had always been to him, asking for things.

He knew he was dying, yet he did not ask to be healed.

Instead he asked that he might know peace. The longing for it was a sharp pain. Then, suddenly, he began to weep for the first time since he was a child. That was when he prayed for help, that whatever was in him, destroying him, would be taken away.

Then he prayed, "I want to know what love is, God! Take anything you see in me. I don't know what it is or how, but give me whatever I need to be the man you want me to be."

He dropped off to sleep then and didn't wake up until he heard Mrs. Wright saying, "All right, Lieutenant. Let's change this bandage and then you can have some breakfast."

Dent awoke instantly, his head clear. "All right, Mrs. Wright." He sat up, and though he was weak, there was none of the thick fogginess in his mind, and his speech was clear.

Mrs. Wright stared at him strangely, then put her hand on his forehead. "Why, your fever's gone!"

"I feel a lot better," Dent said. He looked down at his arm and slowly bent it. "Arm feels lots better, too."

Mrs. Wright removed the bandages, which were thick with dried pus and blood. She took a damp cloth and began to dab carefully at the wound, then stopped. Dent saw her staring at his arm. "What is it?" he asked.

"Your arm!" she cried out. "It's clear!" Dent looked down to see the raw edges of the wound. It was still an ugly gash, but he saw that the infection was gone, as was the swelling. All the flesh was ruddy and healthy. Mrs. Wright's hands were trembling, but she cleaned the wound, then sat there staring at it. Suddenly she put Dent's arm back across his chest. "Don't move! I'm going to get Dr. Baskins!"

She went out of the room almost at a run, and Simon Alcott woke up. He sat up on his cot, rubbed his eyes, then asked,

"What's wrong with her?"

"My arm," Dent said slowly. "It's not infected."

Alcott shut his mouth with a distinct click, then stood up to look at Dent's arm. He said nothing for a moment, then slowly straightened up and said in a strange, thick voice, "It's clean!"

He stood there, and soon the space around Dent's cot was crowded. Dr. Baskins and Matron Huger were there and two of the orderlies—not to mention several of the patients.

Baskins was staring at Dent's arm, his mouth in a thin line. "See if you can bend it," he commanded and watched as Dent obeyed. "That hurt?"

"A little," Dent answered, nodding.

The surgeon pinched the flesh around the lips of the wound, and Dent flinched. Baskins stood up and stared down, his red-rimmed eyes dark with some sort of doubt. "That flesh was dead yesterday. I pinched it then, and you didn't even know it."

"I feel it now," Dent said. He looked up at the crowd and then back at his arm. "It hurts, but it's a different kind of hurt."

Matron Huger stood there, lips trembling. "What do you think, Doctor?" she asked.

The surgeon was in some sort of struggle. He knew this man should be dying—he'd seen that type of wound with that sort of infection too many times. His reputation was on the line, for he'd proclaimed vehemently that Dent Rocklin couldn't live unless that arm came off. Now what he saw was a wound that was serious but that was healing well. Moreover, the moribund fever that had threatened Rocklin's life was gone.

Baskins stood there silently, then said, "I have no explanation. This man ought to be dead." Then he walked away with his head down, shoving his way past the patients. He went to his office and drank half a bottle of whiskey, his mind rebelling.

As soon as the doctor left, the officers began to shout and cheer, and nothing Matron Huger did could quiet them down. Finally Simon Alcott said to her, quietly so that the others could not hear, "I guess this knocks the bottom out of what I've thought of religion, Matron. What do you think?"

Matron Huger smiled at him, her eyes misty. "Simon, there are more things in heaven than you've ever dreamed of!"

When Raimey came to the hospital, she was met by the matron, who said, "He's healed, Raimey!"

Raimey stopped dead still, and her face went white. She bit hard on her lips to stop them from trembling. "I want to see him. Take me to him, Dulcie."

Dent saw her as soon as she entered. "You fellows give me a minute, will you?"

The soldiers winked at each other slyly but moved away to create some sort of privacy. Dulcie brought her mistress to him; then she, too, moved across the room away from the couple.

"Come here, Raimey," Dent said and struggled to throw his legs over the cot. She came close, and he reached up and pulled her down beside him with his good arm. "Did they tell you?"

"Yes! Oh, Dent, I'm so happy!" Her face was radiant, and she leaned against him. "Tell me everything!"

He did tell her, holding her with one arm. Finally he said, "I think I hit bottom, Raimey, and I guess that's what God was waiting for. My arm is healed, but more than that happened." He sat there, aware of her soft warmth. "I've made some kind of a new beginning, Raimey. I guess I'll fall on my face a thousand times, but last night I gave myself to God." He hesitated, then said, "I'm going to need lots of help."

"Your family will help you, Dent," Raimey answered. "They'll be so happy!"

"Sure, I know that, but I'm going to need more help than they can give. I need someone who's around all the time. It's going to be a long-term thing, Raimey. I think it's going to take a lifetime." He paused, and his arm grew tighter around her. "Tell me again, Raimey?"

"Tell you what?" she asked nervously. His arm was tight, and she was aware without seeing that every man in the room must be watching.

"Tell me that you love me," Dent said.

"Oh, I—I can't!"

"You said you did, Raimey, and I don't care if you say it again or not. I love you and I've got to have you! Will you marry me?"

Raimey could not speak, so great was the joy that welled up in her. She turned her face to him, and a smile lifted her lips. She knew that the patients were watching and listening, but she put her arms up and offered her lips. Then she drew back and said quite loudly, "Yes, I do love you, Lieutenant Rocklin—and I will marry you!" She turned to face the men gathered around them, men with missing limbs and bandages on their heads, and said sweetly, "I hope you all heard that! He's got to marry me now, with all of you as witnesses!"

A cheer such as had not been heard in Chimborazo Hospital broke out, and Dent Rocklin and his bride-to-be were swarmed by the Confederate Army of the Potomac.

CHAPTER 23

ANOTHER MIRACLE

$\mathcal{D}$ent Rocklin's recovery sent reverberations throughout the hospital, and his family came almost shouting into the ward. Clay's visit was unforgettable. When he entered the room, Dent got to his feet, saying at once, "Sir, I've been wrong. Forgive me."

Clay blinked back tears, saying, "Dent, I think you must know nothing could give me more joy than to see you well!" The two tall men hesitated, then embraced—it was the first time Clay had held his son in his arms in almost fifteen years.

Clay sat down, and they talked about the war and the future. Then Raimey came in. She was wearing a pink dress trimmed in blue, and her hair fell down her back in gleaming waves. "Here's your new daughter-in-law, sir," Dent said, rising to put his good arm around her. "I hope you approve."

"She's got a job in front of her, getting you raised," Clay said, grinning. Then he stepped to the girl. "I'll have to welcome you with a kiss, Raimey." He kissed her cheek, then stepped back. "When's the wedding?"

Dent said, "I haven't asked her father yet. He may run me off with a gun. We may have to run away!"

"He's very happy, Dent," Raimey said quickly, "and so is

Mother. I've already told him to see Rev. Irons and reserve the church. It'll be soon. You'll be going back with the Grays, won't you, Dent?"

"Yes, when I'm able."

"Take plenty of time, son," Clay said quickly. "I don't think we are going to see much action from the Federals for months. Lincoln's given the army to McClellan. He's slow, I hear. Won't move until everything suits him. Why don't you take your bride on a long honeymoon—maybe even an ocean voyage."

"Oh, that would be wonderful!" Raimey exclaimed. "Could we, Dent?"

"Well, it would be expensive—"

"Daddy's already said he'd give us whatever we wanted for a wedding present."

Clay grinned. "Well, I'm glad you're marrying into a wealthy family, son. Money comes in handy." He picked up his hat, then left, saying, "I'll leave you two alone. The doctor tells me you'll be coming home in a few days, Dent. I'll have your grandmother get your room ready."

When he left, Raimey said, "Now I'm going to give you a shave. Your face is like sandpaper!" They spent an hour together, making plans, and Dent said finally, "You know, Raimey, I can't get over how things look so different. Why, I've been thinking about that young Yankee I shot. He's here, you know, just upstairs." He rubbed his chin, saying slowly, "I've been thinking maybe I'd go visit him. Jemmy tells me he is getting better. . . but, well, I don't know, maybe he wouldn't like me to come."

"I think he might," Raimey said. "Jemmy talks about him a lot. Let me get permission from the matron, and we'll both go." It took only a few minutes, and she was back with Dulcie. "Come along," she said. "The matron said it would be fine."

Then she said, "Dulcie, Lieutenant Rocklin can go with me. You write some more letters."

Dent saw the expression on Dulcie's face, and when they were on the stairs out of hearing, he said, "Dulcie doesn't like me much."

"Oh, she's just jealous," Raimey said. "But she'll love you soon enough." She squeezed his arm possessively, adding with a smile, "After all, who wouldn't love you?"

"I can give you a long list," Dent said with a grimace. He reached up to touch the wound on his face. At Raimey's insistence he had left off the bandage, and he felt vulnerable. "I'll probably scare the poor fellow to death with this mug of mine," he said. Putting his hand over the wound, he added, "Maybe I ought to wear some kind of a cover."

"No! And don't put your hand over it," Raimey said. "It's a wound of honor, received in the service of your country."

Dent looked at her strangely. "You don't even believe in the war, Raimey."

"Neither does your father," she said at once. "But both of us love you, and we love the South. When it's all over, we'll still be here. Now don't ever try to hide your face, you hear me, Dent?"

"Yes, sir!" he said, grinning. "You sound like a tough sergeant." Then he said, "Here we are. There's Jemmy." He caught the woman's eye, and she came over to them at once. "Jemmy, do you think it would be all right if we visited with the young fellow I put in here?"

Jemmy was wearing the same shapeless dress and floppy bonnet that she wore every day. "Why, he'll be plum proud to see both of you, Major Rocker." She insisted on calling him "Rocker" and changed his rank anywhere from lieutenant to general from day to day. She turned, and the pair followed her to where a young man sat in a chair, talking with several other patients.

"This here is General Rocker, Noel," Jemmy said. "And this is his lady, Missus Reed. This here is Noel Kojak."

"Not quite a general, Private," Dent said. He was ill at ease and added, "If you don't want any company—"

"Oh no, sir!" Noel exclaimed. He got to his feet painfully and put his hand out. "I'm glad to meet you. Everyone's talking about how God healed you. Please sit down, sir—and you, Miss Reed."

When they were seated, Dent said, "A little different from our last meeting."

Noel smiled, saying, "Yes, sir. I don't remember too much about it, except that you fellows sure did make pests of yourselves, coming up that hill!"

They talked about the battle; then Raimey asked, "How are you, Noel? Jemmy says you're much better."

"Oh yes, Miss Reed," Noel said, nodding. "I expect I'll be transferred pretty soon, maybe even this week. They need the bed, you see."

Jemmy had hovered close, but when she heard this, she turned and moved away. She didn't notice when the pair left Noel, but came back just before noon to bring Noel's dinner—a plate of cabbage with a piece of pork and a slice of corn bread.

"Sure was nice of Lieutenant Rocklin to come and visit me," he said as he ate. "Did you know, Jemmy, it was Miss Reed that prayed for him to get well? Isn't that great!"

"Shore is," Jemmy said. She studied Noel, noting how his color was coming back. "Guess she's learned how to trust in the Lord."

"Yes." Noel grew thoughtful and finally said, "I wish I had that kind of faith, don't you, Jemmy? I know God is able to do anything, but somehow I can't seem to believe in asking for miracles." He suddenly lost his appetite and put the corn bread down. "I wasn't afraid of getting killed, but I'm afraid of going to a prison. Why is that, I wonder?"

Jemmy had no answer. She watched Noel's face, then said, "Don't guess you're the fust to git a mite skeered of a jail, Noel." She hesitated, then added, "Don't never let yore fears git the best of you. I been a'prayin' and I'm thinkin' the good Lord is gonna take keer of you."

She rose and left abruptly, leaving him to stare after her. She moved about mechanically, then left the hospital before long. The air was still and hot, but she didn't notice. For a time, she walked the streets, then went to a small stand of oaks that overshadowed the river. It was cooler under the trees, and all afternoon she prayed desperately. She had, in fact, prayed almost constantly since God had first spoken to her, but had felt nothing. Doggedly she kept praying, though more than once she was ready to give up. Finally it grew darker, and she moved away from the river.

❧

For the next two days she struggled, but no plan came to her. Finally on Friday, as she walked wearily toward the spot where she met Bing, bitterness swept over her.

Why did You bring me here, Lord, if I can't do anything? her heart cried out. She was tired of her masquerade, and doubt had eaten away at her. She knew that at any time Noel could be transferred—that he might even be gone now.

When she met Bing, he saw at once that she was unhappy.

"It don't look too good, does it, Deborah?" he said quietly. "I guess it's not going to work."

Deborah shook her head, saying wearily, "I don't know what to do, Bing. I've done all—"

Suddenly she broke off, and Bing asked sharply, "What is it? You think of something?"

Deborah said slowly, "Bing, I don't know if it's of God or just an idea of my own, but something just came to me." He listened as she told him, then nodded.

"It's the only shot, Deborah! Let's do it!"

"If we get caught, Bing, we could be executed for being spies."

"Can't hang us but once, can they?" Bing's eyes glowed, and he said, "How'll we work it?"

The two of them talked for half an hour; then he left, saying, "I'll meet you here at three tomorrow." He was not a man of much patience, and the waiting had worn him thin. Now with action in the making, he was excited, his eyes glittering. "If this nutty thing works, maybe I'll want to know a little more about this religion stuff." Then he was gone, and Deborah went to her room. The hard part would be the waiting, but to her surprise, after saying a short prayer, she went to bed and slept like a baby.

"Matron, Jemmy wants to see you."

Jesse Branch found Matron Huger taking a cup of tea in her office. "Well, send her in, Jesse." Then she looked up with surprise, for Branch came into the office pushing a wheelchair containing Jemmy.

"Why—what's wrong, Jemmy?" she exclaimed, getting to her feet. "Did you have an accident?"

Jemmy had a pair of crutches and several packages over her lap. Her left ankle was heavily bandaged, and disgust was in her tone as she answered, "Slipped on the dratted steps! Can't put no weight on the fool leg."

"You ought to stay in bed for a few days," Matron Huger said.

"Mebbe I will iffen it don't git no better. But I done promised that young feller with both his hands gone I'd bring him some of my plum cake. He's lookin' for'ard to it, so I brung it. Long as I'm here, I might as well set and visit with the pore child."

"That's sweet of you, Jemmy, but how can you get up the stairs?"

"Oh, that's took keer of." Jemmy nodded. "I brung my nephew to haul me around. I brung my crutches, and he kin haul me up them stairs. He a triflin' young buck. Not too bright, but he's stout. The guard, he wouldn't let him in the gate without you give him a permit."

"Well, I think you should stay off that leg, Jemmy. As a matter of fact, that's an order." The matron's face broke into a fond smile. "You can take the cake up, but I insist you stay in bed for a day or two."

"Yes'um, I reckon as how I will." She waited until Matron Huger wrote out a pass and handed it to Branch.

"Take that to the gate, Jesse," Matron said, then added, "It's just a permit for this one night, Jemmy. Now you take care of yourself. We couldn't do without you around here."

"Shore, and thank ye, Matron."

Branch took the pass to the gate and soon returned, saying as Bing took his place behind the wheelchair, "Now hang on to that pass. All the guards change at seven o'clock, and you'll need it to get out of the gates."

"Thanks."

Bing stuck the slip into his pocket, and Jemmy demanded, "Well, what are you waiting for, you big ox? Git me up them stairs!"

"Aw, don't be hollering at me, Auntie," Bing whined. But he wheeled her to the stairs, where a guard asked, "What's wrong, Jemmy?"

"Sprainged my dratted ankle, George," Jemmy said.

"Too bad. Better stay off it for a few days."

Bing pushed the chair through the door, then picked it up and walked up the stairs with no effort. "You're very strong," she said. When they got to the top of the stairs, she cautioned him, "Stay away from Noel. He might give us away if he sees you."

"Sure." He pushed her into the ward, and she got onto the crutches, then swung herself inside as Bing sat down to wait, well out of Noel's view. Most of the men she passed greeted her, asking about her leg, and she spoke to them cheerfully.

Noel got to his feet, concern on his face. She told her story, then said, "I got a plum cake for pore Andy. Come on, let's you and me try to cheer him up."

It was a long visit, and Bing sat alone, his nerves on edge, watching as Deborah moved about the ward speaking to the men. The time ran slowly, and he wished he could pull the sun down by brute force to bring on the night.

Finally the room grew dark, and most of the men started going to bed. A few of those with less serious injuries gathered to a section at one end of the room, where a card game took shape.

For another hour Deborah waited, until it was six thirty. She pushed the chair to where she could catch Bing's eye. He saw her and nodded slightly. She moved then to where Noel was sitting on his cot. He looked up at her with a smile, saying, "You're staying late tonight, Jemmy."

Deborah moved her chair as close as she could, noting that one cot next to Noel was occupied, but it was a young soldier who was in such poor condition that he seldom regained consciousness. The other bunk belonged to one of the men who was playing cards. She put out her hand, and when Noel took it in surprise, she said quietly, "Noel, you're leaving this place."

Noel's head moved sharply, and he leaned forward. "What's that you say, Jemmy?"

"Don't say anything, and don't make any sudden moves. As soon as I leave, I want you to go to the bathroom."

Noel stood absolutely still. His voice low, he asked suddenly, "Who are you?"

For one moment Deborah paused, then said, "It's Deborah, Noel. Now take this package." Deborah took the paper sack she'd kept close beside her, and he took it at once, staring at her with shock in his eyes. "Now go to the bathroom. If no one is there, put those clothes on. If someone is there, wait until they leave. When you come out, I'll be right outside."

"I'll never get down the stairs—or out the gate!"

"Noel, the clothes are like the ones I wear, a dress and a bonnet and a pair of shoes. There's a bandage, too. Put it on your ankle. Now listen. When you come out of the bathroom, take these crutches and go straight to the stairs. There's a man there. You know him, but don't say anything to him." She hesitated, then added, "It's your brother Bing." Noel's head snapped back and he opened his mouth, but Deborah said sharply, "Don't say anything! Pull the bonnet over your eyes and keep your head down. Pretend to be sick. Bing will take you past the guards and out the gate."

"But—what about you?"

"Don't worry about me! Now are you ready?"

"Yes!"

"Do it, then!"

Noel got up and walked to the bathroom, keeping the sack close to his body. He found nobody inside and did as the woman had said. It took only a few seconds, and he stepped outside to find her waiting. She handed him the crutches, whispering, "Now go to Bing!"

Noel awkwardly swung himself down the aisle. One of the men said, "Good night, Jemmy," and he nodded, saying in a muffled voice, "Good night." Then he was past the beds. When he looked up, he saw Bing standing there with the chair. He leaned the crutches against the wall and fell into the wheelchair.

Bing stepped behind the chair and shoved it through the door. He reversed the chair and began backing down the stairs. When Noel said, "Bing—!" he said in a tense voice, "No time for talk. Keep your head down. You're sick. I'll do all the talkin'!"

They reached the bottom of the stairs. Bing paused, took a deep breath, then opened the door and shoved the chair out. The guard named George looked at them, then said, "Long visit, Jemmy." Then he looked closer. "Something wrong?"

Bing said quickly, "She's poorly. I think this trip was too much for her."

The guard stood there, looking down at the form in the wheelchair. He waited so long that Bing let his hand drop to his waist, where he had a .44 beneath his coat.

"Better get her home," George finally said. "Hope you feel better tomorrow, Jemmy."

"I'll see to her," Bing said quickly and moved down the hall. There was a guard at the outside door, but he only nodded at the two and continued his argument with one of the orderlies. As they moved outside, Bing said, "Good enough. Now the gate."

The guard at the gate was perched on a chair, leaning back against the fence. He got up and took the passes that Bing handed him. It was dark, with only the pale glow of a single lantern, and he peered at them for a long time. Then he stuck one in his pocket, saying, "Have to take yours up, fellow." He looked down, then handed the other pass toward the still form. "Here you go, Jemmy. How's the leg?"

"All right," Noel mumbled.

"How's that?" The guard frowned and leaned down. "You all right?"

"She's had a bad spell," Bing said. "I've got to get her home. She shouldn't have came in the first place!"

The guard still kept his position, bending over the wheelchair. "My wife, she's had some bad spells. Lemme write you a formula for a toddy she makes up."

Bing said, "I don't think—," but the guard insisted. He fumbled in his vest pocket, found a stub of a pencil, then searched for a piece of paper. He finally used the page of a book he kept beside him, writing slowly and giving advice constantly.

Bing's nerves were screaming and he longed to dash away, but he knew he had to wait. The next shift of guards came on at seven, and the whole plan centered on that. "You'll take Noel out in the wheelchair in my place just before seven," Deborah had said. "Then the new guard will come on, and I'll walk out like I always do."

But if the new guard came along and saw what he thought was Jemmy in the wheelchair, he'd know something was wrong when Deborah came out later.

". . .so you mix all this, add a jigger of whiskey, and heat it up," the guard said and, to Bing's relief, handed over the slip of paper.

"That ort to help. Thanks a lot!" Bing nodded and had to restrain himself from going too fast as he passed through the gates. Forcing himself to walk until they were out of the guard's line of vision, he wheeled Noel behind a line of bushes, then jerked to a stop.

"Bing! What's happening?" Noel asked as he got out of the chair. He looked ridiculous in the shapeless dress and floppy bonnet, but he didn't care. He stood there as Bing explained rapidly, and when he was finished, both of them stared down the lane anxiously, waiting for a glimpse of an old woman.

As soon as Bing had disappeared through the door with Noel, Deborah walked slowly to Noel's bed and lay down on it, pulling the covers over her head. She had to stay out of sight until seven fifteen, and it was a long wait for her. Once a man came by, paused, and whispered, "Noel? You okay?" She had grunted and he had passed on. Finally she was satisfied that the time was right and lowered the edge of the blanket over her head cautiously. The card game was still going on as she slipped out of the cot. There was no way to conceal herself. If one of the men in the game spotted her, or if one of the men in the cots saw her, the game was up. She walked down the aisle, thankful that the card game was at the far end of the room. The rest of the room was dim, lit only by a single lamp that gave enough light to the orderlies and so the men could find their way to the bathroom.

Once a man snorted and gave a lurch on his cot as Deborah passed, and she stopped dead still, certain she was discovered.

But there was no alarm, and she continued. With a sigh of relief, she moved down the stairs, then got the crutches under her arms and struggled down to the main floor. The guard, a private named Lew who knew her well, exclaimed, "Why, Jemmy, I thought you was gone! George told me you left in a wheelchair!"

"I did, Lew, but I come back. Didn't he tell you? Guess he forgot—no, come to think of it, he wuz talking to Leon when I come back. Guess he didn't see me. Good night, Lew."

"Good night, Jemmy."

She passed through the next gate, receiving about the same response, then swung on the crutches to the main gate. "Hello, Pete," she said. "Lemme out, will you? I'm plum tard to death!"

Pete Riley got up and came over to her. "Thought you was sick, Jemmy. They said you left."

"Did, Pete, but had to go back. I forgot my purse. Didn't need that ol' wheelchair noways, 'cept to get up the stairs."

"Yeah? Well, lemme see your pass, Jemmy."

Deborah made a business of looking through the old purse, then said, "Oh, rats! I left the blamed thing upstairs, Pete." She turned painfully and started back, but he stopped her.

"Oh, never mind, Jemmy. I guess you ain't dangerous, are you?"

"Plum dangerous, Pete," she said and cackled as she passed on through the gate.

When he called out, "See you tomorrow, Jemmy," she made no answer. "Pore ol' thing's going batty, I reckon," Pete muttered, then leaned against the fence trying to get comfortable.

Deborah swung down the lane, and when she turned the corner, two shapes rose in the darkness. "Deborah!" She found herself being embraced. Noel grasped her so hard that he hurt his wound, as well as her. "Deborah! I don't believe it!"

Deborah stood there, a warm sensation flooding through her, but Bing said, "You two can do your lovin' later! We ain't out of this thing yet!"

Deborah drew back, nodding. "We'll find someplace to keep out of sight, Bing. We can't be out in the open until dawn. We'll be at the dock at six."

"All right. Remember, it's the *Loretta*, a steam packet. Shouldn't be no one stirring at that hour, so I'll take you to the cabin. We'll be clear of Richmond by seven o'clock. Then for home! Don't be late."

"Bing—!" Noel caught at his brother's thick arm. "Bing. . . well, thanks!"

Bing paused, gave a sheepish grin, then reached out and pulled the bonnet down over Noel's eyes. "You sure look dumb in that outfit, brother," he said. Then he looked straight at Noel. "I hope this kind of makes up for runnin' away?"

"More than makes up for it, Bing!" Noel's eyes were happy and he would have said more, but Bing whirled and ran down the lane. Noel turned to say, "Deborah—"

"What do you think about prayer now?" she interrupted him. She pulled the bonnet from her head, and then the two of them stared at one another. She faltered, remembering how she had tricked him, and she saw that he was remembering it, too.

"Deborah," he said quietly. "I learned a lot out of this."

"Did you, Noel?"

"Yes. I learned to trust God more."

"Anything else?"

He swayed toward her, and she tried to draw back. "I learned that a man's got to let a woman know how he feels. So that's what I'm doing." He pulled her forward and kissed her. She clung to him, and when he released her, he said, "When we get back home, I've got something to talk to you about."

Deborah stared at him, then flushed. "Well, I guess we'd better get away from here. If people see two old ladies kissing each other, it won't be so good, will it?" But then as they left the shelter, she paused to say, "Noel? You said you loved me."

"Yes!"

"Well, I'm expecting a little more courting than that when there's time!"

CHAPTER 24

ENCOUNTER ON THE *LORETTA*

A carriage rattled down the cobblestone street, stopping at the wharf. The darkness still enveloped the waterfront, and a fine mist threw a corona around the lantern hanging beside the gangplank. Dent got out of the carriage stiffly, walked closer to peer at the side of the ship, then came back to the carriage. "This is the *Loretta*," he said.

Raimey got out, followed by Dulcie. Dent said, "Chester, put the baggage on board; then you can go home."

"Yas, suh, Marse Dent." The slave moved from the seat, and Dent walked to the gangplank with him and Dulcie. A sailor appeared almost mystically, and Dent said, "We've got two cabins reserved under the name of Rocklin." The man gave a jerk of his head, and the two slaves followed him, all three disappearing into the misty dark.

"I still think we should have put this trip off, Dent," Raimey said as they walked up the gangplank. "There's plenty of time before our wedding, and you're not strong enough."

"Listen, woman, I may not be as bright as you are, but I never turn down anything free. If your father wants to throw his money away on all kinds of fancy dresses for our wedding,

742

that's his business. It's mine to take what he offers. Besides," he added as they stepped on deck, "it'll give us some time alone. Sort of a prehoneymoon honeymoon."

She smiled at that. *As much of a prehoneymoon as it can be with Dulcie at our side, anyway.*

Mr. Reed, Raimey's father, had insisted on sending them to Williamsburg to the best dressmaker in the South. Dent had not argued, for he wanted the time away from the family with Raimey. Mrs. Reed had wanted the two of them to get their photographs made there, as well, so he had gotten up and dressed in full uniform, including pistol and saber.

"I feel foolish in this rig," he said as the two of them stood leaning on the rail. He was still wearing a sling, but his arm was mending and the doctors were confident that he'd have full use of it—with perhaps some rheumatism when he grew older, just as a reminder.

They stood there, Dent's arm around Raimey's waist, talking quietly. He had never found anyone he could talk to as he could to this woman who had appeared so suddenly in his life. She knew him better than he knew himself, and her handicap had come to mean very little to him. Dulcie was like Raimey's eyes, and she would stay with her always.

As for Raimey, her heart was full. She had fully expected that she would never marry—and now she had a man who fit her like a glove. She loved him freely, openly, without limits, and she knew that time would only increase what she felt for him.

Dent was speaking about the plans for their stay in Williamsburg when he broke off suddenly. "What is it?" Raimey asked quickly, always sensitive to his mood.

"Somebody coming down the quay," he said. He studied the two figures who were moving slowly toward the *Loretta* and said, "Two people, but they're acting very strange. Something's wrong with them." He watched as they approached; then when they turned to climb the gangplank, he said, "Doesn't look right, Raimey. Stand back against the bulkhead. I think I'd better challenge them."

He waited until Raimey was back, then pulled his Colt free as the pair stepped on deck. He saw that one was a man, who was apparently sick, for the woman with him was holding him as though to support him. When Dent spoke, they both froze. "Hold it!" Dent said sharply. He half expected one of them to pull a gun, so careful had been their approach. "Who are you? Why are you sneaking onto this boat?"

The woman said quickly, "We have a cabin reserved."

As she spoke, Dent blinked, for she had stepped into the feeble yellow light of the lantern. "Deborah!" he said incredulously. "What are you doing here?"

Deborah and Noel had started walking much earlier, but it had proved too much for Noel. He had begun to lag, and by the time they reached the ship, he was able to do no more than stumble along with Deborah's help. Now he saw Dent standing before him, gun aimed, and he gasped, "Don't shoot! I'll go back, but let her go!"

It all was clear then, both to Dent and to Raimey. They had heard of Noel's escape, and the alarm was out to watch for a Federal soldier and an old woman. Dent looked at Deborah, and some of the old bitterness welled up in him. Deborah saw it rise in his eyes but could say nothing. She stood there, knowing that Dent had been a possessive man and was now seeing her as a woman who had been taken from him. And the man who had done the taking was in his power.

Raimey came forward and touched Dent's arm. She had

known of Dent's obsession with this girl and had even been jealous of it for a time. Now she said quietly, "Dent, what are you going to do?"

Dent stood there uncertainly. He had been haunted for so long by thoughts of Deborah Steele, and now here she stood, looking as lovely as ever. Even in the pale yellow light of the lantern, her face was beautiful.

All you have to do is turn them in.

The thought pushed at his mind, and he stood there almost ready to call for the officers of the ship.

He stood there weighing the options in his mind—and suddenly he realized that to turn them in would be to become the man he had once been! There was still something of the old Dent Rocklin in him, something that he thought had been erased, buried forever when he became a Christian. Now Dent realized that the battle for a man's soul didn't end with becoming a Christian—rather, that was when it began in earnest. If he were to give in to this base impulse to get some sort of petty revenge on Deborah because she had rejected him, he would be taking the first step back to being the man he was before God had done such wonderful miracles in his life.

Deborah was watching him, waiting for his decision—as was the soldier. Dent felt Raimey's presence, too, even more strongly than he felt the presence of the two who stood before him. He waited for his impulse to weaken, to fade—and was appalled at how it only grew fiercer! But that very fact was his salvation, for he suddenly understood that it was not Deborah and Noel who were on trial. . . . No, *he* was the one being tested!

And he knew then the power of darkness and how it could destroy a man.

He looked at Deborah and saw the honesty on her face. . .

and knew he couldn't do it. He lowered the Colt, holstered it, then said quietly, "You'd better get to your cabin. The whole city's looking for you."

At that moment steps sounded on the stones, and Bing came stumbling up the gangplank. He halted abruptly at the sight of a Confederate officer blocking the way. His face went tight and he reached under his coat, but he stopped when Deborah said, "Bing! It's all right. Let's get to the cabin."

Dent stepped back, and as Deborah passed she gave him a beautiful smile, saying, "Thank you, Lieutenant." Then the three of them disappeared into the corridor.

Raimey pulled at Dent's arm, and he turned to her. "Dent, I'm so proud of you!" She reached up and pulled his head down. Her lips were soft and gentle, yet strangely possessive. When she pulled away, she said, "Now you're really all mine, Dent. Until this moment, part of you belonged to Deborah. But no more, isn't that right?"

"No more," he whispered, and they stood there watching the sun peep over the eastern rim.

"What's going to happen to them, I wonder?" Dent mused.

"They'll be fine," Raimey said. "They're like us, Dent. They love each other, and when two people love each other, not even a war can take that away."

He held her close and said quietly, "I almost missed you, Raimey, but now I'll never let you go."

The boilers under their feet began to hiss, and the ship gave a slight shudder. An hour later the *Loretta* cleared Richmond, and as it moved down the river, there were those aboard who knew that life was good. The sun was up, bathing the ship in golden rays, and the white wake of the *Loretta* threw off golden flakes as the vessel moved toward the sea.

WHERE HONOR DWELLS

To Doug and Blanche
Our tribe is shrinking, buddy—
which makes you mean more to me than ever.
God bless you and Blanche and Mark
and the little ones!

PART ONE

The Coward

CHAPTER 1

BRAND OF A COWARD

Rachel!" Les Franklin grabbed his sister's arm and pointed toward the street. "Look, here comes Vince—and he's so drunk he can hardly sit on his horse!"

Rachel Franklin turned at once to see her half brother, Vince Franklin, dismount by almost falling off of his horse, then stagger into the arms of Bruno, a white-haired slave. She bit her lip in vexation, watching as Bruno caught Vince and kept him from falling, only to be rewarded by Vince's shoving him away roughly. Vince then turned to look across the crowd that had gathered for the wedding of Dent Rocklin and Raimey Reed. He laughed loudly and moved toward the massive steps of the Congregational church, shoving his way through the crowd.

Rachel moved quickly to where her great-uncle Mark Rocklin stood. "Uncle Mark, Vince is drunk. He'll ruin the wedding if someone doesn't stop him!"

Mark Rocklin was a tall, lean man of fifty with a pair of dark eyes that few men cared to face when they burned with anger. He had been a misfit among the children of Noah Rocklin, who was the patriarch of the Rocklin family in Virginia. Mark had never been interested in farming, as were his brother Thomas and his sister, Marianne. Mark's brothers Stephen and Mason had not cared for farming either, but they had found worthwhile occupations: Mason had been a professional soldier in the Union Army for years; Stephen owned a prosperous ironworks in Washington.

Mark, however, had been a wanderer, a gambler with no roots. He came back to visit Richmond only on rare occasions, finding little there to draw him. Little, that is, except his great-niece Rachel, for the two of them had a similar temperament and so had formed a close and warm bond. Now he smiled at her, his face lighting with an uncharacteristic tenderness.

"I'll see to him, Rachel." Mark's voice was low and even, but there was purpose in his face as he moved down the steps and halted right in front of Vincent Franklin. "Hello, Vince," he said casually.

Vince stopped abruptly, almost falling. He caught himself, looked up, blinked owlishly, then said thickly, "Oh. . .Uncle Mark. . ."

"I need some company, nephew. Come and sit with me for the wedding."

Vince reddened and an angry reply rose to his lips, but he was not too drunk to realize he had no choice. Mark Rocklin was a man of easy manners, but there was something dangerous about him. As Vince peered at his great-uncle, he suddenly remembered some of the things he'd heard about the man's past. "Why. . .sure," he muttered. He licked his lips, then said, "Maybe I'd better sit down. I don't feel so good."

"Let's sit in the balcony, Vince," Mark said, taking his arm and leading him firmly toward a side door. "We can see more from there."

As the two men disappeared inside the church, Rachel turned

to her younger brother, Les. "He'll behave now," she said, then added, "I wish he hadn't come."

"I'll get him to leave after it's over, Rachel," Les said. At seventeen he was almost an exact copy of his father, with the same fair skin and reddish hair. But as he moved away from her, Rachel knew that Les could not handle Vince. None of them could.

"Come along, now, Rachel—"

She turned to see her father and mother at the front door. She hurried up the steps, hoping her father hadn't noticed the commotion her half brother had created. But her father glanced over her shoulder and asked, "What was the trouble with Vince? I didn't know he was back." Brad Franklin was attired in the dress uniform of a major in the Confederate Army, sword and all. His rather hungry-looking face was tense, as it usually was whenever Vince was around, and he shook his head angrily. "Why did he come at all?"

Nothing brought as much humiliation to Brad Franklin as the sight of his eldest son. A product of Brad's first marriage, Vince was the image of his mother, Lila Crawford, and this alone was enough to stir painful memories. Lila had been as promiscuous and selfish as she had been pretty, but Brad had been young and in love. He had not discovered his wife's self-centered nature until after they were wed—and then it was too late.

Brad had remained firm in his convictions after their marriage. He had refused to overlook Lila's flirtations and involvements, demanding that she become the wife she had promised in her vows to be. So it was that less than a year after Vince's birth, Lila divorced her husband, took her baby, and ran away with a gambler from Natchez. All of Brad's attempts to reclaim his son had failed. He had seen Vince only a half dozen times after Lila's departure, and never for more than a few moments. Then three years after Brad's marriage to Amy Rocklin, he had received word of Lila's death. Hoping to be at last reunited with his son, he had taken five-year-old Vince into his home—but by then the boy was totally spoiled and as selfish as his mother. It hadn't been long before Vince's half brother and half sister, and his father, had little to do with the boy.

Now, staring with distaste in the direction Vince had gone, Brad shook his head again.

"Never mind, Father," Rachel said with a smile. She gave his collar a slight pull and said, "My, you look dashing! Doesn't he, Mother? And look at you, in that new dress!"

Amy Franklin, the only daughter of Thomas Rocklin, was not really a beautiful woman, but she made people think she was. She was tall and dark like her father, and her fine dark eyes were her best feature. She smiled indulgently at her daughter. "Nobody looks at old women at weddings, Rachel. Let's go take our seats before somebody else gets them."

"Not much danger of that," Brad said, holding the door open, then following the two women inside. "Sam Reed has got this wedding planned down to the last bouquet. I think you have to have a pass from him to even get in the church."

An usher met them, saying, "This way, sir," and led them to their seats. When they were situated, Rachel said, "Isn't it lovely? I've never seen so many flowers!"

"Too bad the bride can't see them, isn't it?" Brad whispered.

"She can smell them," Rachel said. "And she's gone over every one, I do think, touching them."

"A strange thing—for Dent to marry her," Rachel's father said thoughtfully. "We all thought it'd be that Yankee girl,

Deborah Steele, walking down the aisle with that boy." He gave a restless shake to his shoulders, adding, "I guess Dent thought a blind woman wouldn't mind the way he looks with all the scars."

Though he sounded cold, Major Franklin was merely voicing what many others had thought. Dent Rocklin had been one of the most handsome men in the city of Richmond, the object of many women's devotion. But a terrible saber cut on his face, which he had received at the battle of Manassas, had left him with a ghastly scar. It was, perhaps, natural that some would leap to the conclusion that he would marry someone such as Raimey Reed, who was lovely but totally blind.

Rachel shook her head firmly. "No, Daddy, it's not like that. They're really in love. I even heard Dent say that Raimey was the most wonderful gift God has ever given him. If I ever got a husband, I'd want him to love me as much as Dent loves Raimey." Then she said quickly, as if to cover up a slip, "But here I am, the spinster of Lindwood, talking about a husband, just like all the old maids."

"I wish you'd stop calling yourself that ridiculous name, Rachel!" A quick flash of anger flared in Amy Franklin's eyes, and she added, "You could have been married long ago. There are a lot of young men around."

"Lots of gophers and jackrabbits around, too."

"Oh, you drive me mad, Rachel!" her mother said, then lifted her head. "Look, it's starting!"

The organ began to whisper, then grew louder as the members of the wedding party began the old ritual. As it went on, Rachel felt tears gathering in her eyes despite herself. Angrily she blinked them away, hoping no one had seen her. She hated how easily she was moved to tears—though she seldom let them be seen. Long ago she had decided to keep a tight rein on her emotions. Usually she succeeded, but there were times when she could not stem the tide. It never ceased to shame her that she was a young woman who constantly struggled with her emotions. She had been taught from an early age that God had created her as she was, giving her gifts and characteristics that were special to her. Even so, she envied women who were always cool and stately, like her great-aunt Marianne Bristol and her own mother. *I won't cry!* she thought fiercely as the wedding proceeded, but when Dent came out accompanied by his best man—his identical twin, David—she could not ignore the pang of pity that stabbed at her.

Dent and David had always been handsome. Now as Dent stood with his scarred face turned toward the congregation and waited for his bride, everyone could see the full extent of his injury—and there stood David as a graphic reminder of what Lieutenant Denton Rocklin once had looked like.

Since Dent's injury, Rachel had instinctively avoided staring at her cousin's scarred face, not wanting to hurt him. Now that he could not see her, though, she lifted her eyes and took in the magnitude of the damage. The cut had caused Dent's left eye to droop, giving him a sinister appearance; the scar pulled the side of his mouth to the left, which only added to that impression. Rachel could not help but glance at David, noting the firm lines of his face—and then she could look no more.

Then, suddenly, the organ began to swell in volume, and Rev. Jeremiah Irons gave a signal with his hand, bringing the congregation to their feet. Rachel turned to see Raimey, her hand resting on her father's arm, coming down the aisle, a vision of loveliness all in white. A smile was on her lips and her blue eyes were clear, fixed in front of her. She moved with such confidence that it would never have occurred to someone who was seeing her for the first time that she was blind.

As she took her place in front of Irons, her father stepped back, and at once she reached out and put her hand on Dent's arm. *She knew he'd be there,* Rachel thought. *She's always sure he'll be there.* The thought pleased her, bringing a softness to her lips. *That's what love is—just knowing that the one you love will always be there! Oh, heavenly Father, that's the kind of love I want.*

Then she listened as Irons read the familiar words and as Dent and Raimey spoke their vows, pledging themselves to God and to each other. It was quiet and solemn, and their words seemed to hang in the air like the notes of an organ heard from far away.

Finally the ceremony was over, and the Franklins rose. "Well, let's go to the reception," Rachel's father said. "Reed's reserved the ballroom at the Elliot Hotel. It's going to be a dandy." Just then, Rachel glanced up toward the balcony and saw Mark Rocklin sitting there, holding Vince in place with an iron authority. Her father, following her glance, frowned. "I'm glad Mark's keeping a tight rein on him. He's done enough to humiliate this family!"

The Elliot Hotel was not the largest hotel in Richmond, but it was the most elaborate and the most expensive. The ballroom was decorated with white banners, which picked up the gleam of light thrown by the glittering chandeliers. The dresses of the women added splashes of color to the crowd, and the gray uniforms of many officers, with their gleaming black boots and gold buttons, gave a final touch of stylishness.

Long tables filled with meats, appetizers, candies, and cakes lined one wall, while other tables held crystal bowls of pink punch. The crowd was in a festive mood, and the air was filled with the sound of laughter and the hum of half a hundred conversations. A group of men had gathered in one section of the room, talking about things other than the weather— hunting, crops, horses, and especially the war. Major Brad Franklin and Colonel James Benton of the Richmond Grays were there in uniform. Clay Rocklin, Thomas's son and Amy's brother, was also in the Grays. However, as a sergeant, he had chosen to wear a brown suit, saying, "If I wore a uniform, I'd spend the whole time saluting."

Captain Taylor Dewitt, also a member of Clay's company— and one of Clay's oldest friends—was there, too. The two of them stood off to one side drinking punch while Colonel Benton spoke of the battle of Bull Run. Most of the soldiers there had been in that battle, and they had not tired of talking of the victory.

"I tell you, the Yankees are whipped!" Benton declared. He was a tall, impressive figure of a man, with white hair and a florid face. "We sent 'em scurrying back to Washington with their tails between their legs!"

It was a common view, spoken every day by many Southerners. They gleefully recounted "the sprightly running" of the Federals as they fled to Washington, and many of the young Confederate soldiers were grieved that it seemed probable that they would never have a chance to see a battle. Captain Dewitt just shook his head. "With all respects, sir, I think we'll be seeing a lot more action." Taylor was forty, one year younger than Clay Rocklin. He had a lean pale face, light blue eyes, and a clear mind that could not help analyzing things. Now he added, "You saw how they fought, Colonel. I know they broke and ran, but there were a couple of times when we were in about as bad a shape as the Yankees. It could have gone the other way if Smith and Elzey hadn't come at just the right moment."

"Oh, come now, Dewitt! I don't see that at all!" The speaker was Simon Duvall, a thin, dark-skinned man in his late thirties. His French heritage was revealed in his thin face, which he adorned with a narrow black moustache, and a pair of dark eyes that grew hot when anger took him—not a rare thing. He had fought four duels, killing one man, and his temper was a frightful thing when aroused. Now, however, he was merely arguing mildly, adding, "Why, the entire Army of the Potomac is huddled in Washington, and Lincoln fired McDowell and put McClellan in charge."

"I think President Davis was right," Clay said suddenly. He was one of the Black Rocklins, with raven hair, olive skin, and dark eyes. He was six feet two, lean and muscular, and had a temper that few men cared to challenge. His youth had been stormy, but after being away from home for many years, and after encountering the One who had loved him no matter how far he had fallen into degradation, he had returned to try to pick up his life. Sadly, he had been met with great opposition from his children, particularly from Dent, who seemed to burn with resentment toward his father. Still, Clay continued in his efforts to become the kind of man and father he believed God wanted him to be.

For his own reasons, Clay had long opposed the war, and his views had made him an unpopular man. Even so, at the last moment he had joined the Grays as a private. He had won honor by leading a charge in a crucial battle—but more important to Clay than the honor he earned was the fact that the charge had saved Dent's life. Through a course of events following, Clay and Dent had finally reconciled.

"What did the president want to do, Clay?"

The voice came from his right, and Clay turned to see that Vince Franklin, having escaped his great-uncle, had joined the group. Vince was a fine-looking man of twenty-four, with crisply curling brown hair that he wore long and a neat, full beard of the same texture. The beard covered the lower part of his face, giving him a cavalier appearance. He wore an expensive suit of light gray, and the shining boots on his feet cost as much as a good horse. He had a glass in his hand, and everyone in the group could tell by the redness in Vince's deep-set, wide-spaced brown eyes that the glass held more than the harmless punch being served by the ladies at the table.

Clay shrugged his shoulders, saying, "When the Federals ran, President Davis wanted to follow them and take Washington."

"By Harry!" Brad Franklin cried. "We ought to have listened to Davis!"

Clay said thoughtfully, "We may never have another chance like that. . .but we were about as worn down from the battle as the enemy. And they had plenty of fresh reinforcements. I don't think we would have been successful."

Vince Franklin took a drink from the glass in his hand, then grinned rashly. "Why, that would have been a tragedy! If we had taken Washington, the game would be over."

"Game?" Brad Franklin stared at his son with obvious displeasure. "This war is no game, Vince!"

"Looks like it to me! Dressing up in uniforms and playing soldier!"

Vince Franklin could not have made a more insulting remark to a more hostile audience. All of those gathered, in one way or another, were pledging their homes and their hearts in the war. Some of those present had lost family members; all of them had lost close friends at Manassas. The sudden enmity of everyone's glances would have been warning enough to most men, but Vince Franklin seemed to court the kind of encounters that others would do their best to avoid.

Clay saw Vince's father turn pale with anger, but it was Simon Duvall who answered the young man's rash words. "We fight for the honor of our country, Franklin, and I question the courage of any man who stays at home and lets other men do his fighting."

His words made many of the men blink, for it was the equivalent of a challenge. If Duvall had said such a thing to any other man in the group, there would have been a meeting at dawn with pistols. Duvall's smooth face was turned toward Vince, and Clay saw there was a pleasure in his dark eyes. *He loves this!* Clay thought, and disgust ran through him at the thought that any man could find gratification in killing another.

But Vince Franklin felt only amusement at the thought of engaging in a duel over words. He grinned at Duvall, saying, "Why, Simon, somebody has to stay at home and comfort the women while their husbands are away fighting for the Cause."

Duvall sucked in a quick breath, his dark face growing pale, and those gathered around the two waited for his response. Clay glanced at Taylor, and he could tell from the look in his friend's eyes that they shared the same thought: *Duvall already suspects that Vince has been having an affair with his wife—and he knows that every man here is aware of his suspicions.* Black anger leaped into Duvall's eyes and he stepped forward, but before he could strike Vince, the younger man wheeled and walked away, saying, "I'm not a fool, Duvall. Fight your duels with men who have no brains!"

Duvall stood there, his eyes boring into Vince's back; then he turned and stalked away without a word, his body rigid.

For a moment there was silence in the room. Then Colonel Benton said, "Vince is a fool, Brad," then turned and left. The others, finding the situation most unpleasant, moved away, leaving Clay and his brother-in-law alone.

"Benton is right, Clay," Brad said bitterly. "Why did Vince come here? His greatest delight seems to be spoiling things for others." When Clay remained silent, he added, "His mother was like that, too."

It was the most revealing thing Brad Franklin had ever said to Clay about his first marriage. It had been a bitter affair for Franklin, a stormy union that had left deep scars on the man. But his second marriage to Amy, Clay's only sister, had been happy. Their children, Grant, Rachel, and Les, were all good youngsters, taking after their mother to a large extent. With a happy and stable home, Brad had had high hopes for Vince when he brought him into his family. But the boy only seemed to grow more wild, undisciplined, and cruel, doing all he could to go his own reckless way. It had been a bitter pill for everyone involved.

Amy, who had loved the wild boy from the first time he entered her home, had prayed for him every day and had done her best to show him she cared for him. But Vince would have none of it. As the years passed, he rebuffed any advances from Amy or his half sister or half brothers and treated his father with impudence. By the time he left home, he had successfully alienated them all. To this day he made no attempt to become a part of the family, seeming instead to enjoy tormenting those who should have been the closest to him.

The reason he was able to torment them so effectively, Clay

understood, was partly because of the will that Hiram Franklin, Brad's father, had left. Brad and his father had never gotten along. In Hiram Franklin's opinion, his son was too wild and undisciplined to amount to any good. And so he had cut Brad out of his will, favoring instead his firstborn grandson, Vince. And the will provided for Brad's oldest son in a generous way—a certain amount each year until his twenty-fifth birthday, when he would receive the bulk of the inheritance—and the bulk of the control over Lindwood.

During the years since Vince had left Lindwood, he had done as he pleased, and with plenty of money, he found others to go along with him. He had an unsavory reputation as a womanizer, and since his return, his drinking and gambling habits were no secret to anyone in the county.

Clay drew a deep breath, then said, "Duvall's a dangerous man to cross, Brad. Better try to talk to Vince."

"He's not listened to me for years, Clay. Or to anyone else, for that matter."

The two men were not the only ones interested in Vince Franklin. Even as they were talking, the young Franklin was the subject of yet another conversation. Rachel had been serving punch but took a break to walk around the room with Leighton Semmes. Semmes had spoken of Vince's untimely appearance, saying, "That brother of yours seems to have little in the way of manners, Rachel." A lean man of twenty-six, with dark hair and eyes, Leighton had fine manners and wore the latest fashions, and there was an ease in him that Rachel knew had been developed by his pursuit of women. Semmes, she knew, saw the relationship between the sexes as a game. She liked the man but knew that it was not wise to encourage his interest, for he had broken the hearts of at least two other young women.

"I can't explain Vince, Leighton," she admitted, shrugging. "He's my half brother, but I have no idea what makes him act the way he does."

Semmes studied her, admiration in his dark eyes. He took in the picture she made: a tall young woman with a wealth of honey-colored hair and a pair of blue-green eyes that matched her silk emerald dress. Her eyes were strange, unique; almond-shaped and very large, with thick lashes. As he gazed at her, Semmes thought there was something almost sultry about them, though the girl herself was not aware of that. She had a squarish face, with a wide mouth and a cleft chin, which Semmes knew she hated. Still, it gave her a striking look, one that seemed to suggest that this was a young woman who kept a passionate streak under firm control, covering it with a rather pointed wit. The fact that she called herself the spinster of Lindwood was a sample of that wit, for no woman looked less like a spinster than Rachel Franklin.

Semmes had played a game with her, drawn by her beauty and wit, but sensing that if he tried to press his luck, she would mock him. Now he said, "Your father spoils him, I think. Always has."

"No," Rachel said thoughtfully, "Vince spoils himself. He has never needed Father, you know, because he has money of his own." Then she added with a quirk of a smile, "Did you know the Bible says, 'Money answereth all things'? That's in Ecclesiastes 10:19."

"I didn't know that was in the Bible," Semmes said, "but I believe it. Nothing is stronger than money."

"You're wrong about that, Leighton," Rachel said at once. "Love is stronger than anything in the world."

"You are fortunate, then, for you're made for love, Rachel."

She laughed at the eager look on his face, then shook her head, her heavy mane of hair sweeping across her back. "Never mind all that, Leighton. I know that look. You've used it on too many of my friends. They've all warned me about you!"

"It's not fair!" Semmes exclaimed. "A man smiles at a woman, and she thinks it's a proposal of marriage." He spoke quickly, wanting her to know what he believed. "Love is important, Rachel, but I've never understood the rules. I like women, and some of them have seemed to like me, but they want to draw lines that I can't fathom."

"Oh, you understand the rules well enough, Leighton," Rachel answered. "You just don't like them."

Semmes knew she was laughing at him, which pleased him in a way. Of all the women he had known, only this one could hold him at arm's length and make him almost enjoy it. "You know me too well, Rachel." He smiled. "Maybe you'll be able to reform me."

"I think that would be a difficult job, Mr. Semmes." Rachel's eyes laughed up at him, and she decided to change the subject. He was, quite simply, too attractive—and Rachel had begun to think of him far too often. This troubled her greatly, for playing at love with Leighton Semmes was like playing with live ammunition. "Let's go congratulate the bride and groom."

❧

"Has anyone heard about the newlyweds? It's been two weeks now. I hope they're still together."

Rachel smiled at Grant, knowing that her brother loved to tease her. He was wearing his uniform and looked very handsome, and as the carriage rolled along the dusty road toward Richmond, Rachel was strangely happy. "I expect Dent's worked all the foolishness out of Raimey by now," she said teasingly. "You know how they say a woman needs a strong hand now and then."

Grant laughed aloud at the idea. "I'd like to see the man who'd have the nerve to try such things with *you*, sister! You'd give him a thrashing!" He looked at her with real affection, for there was a close bond between the two. He was twenty-one, only two years older than she, and they had always shared things. While he had the fair skin and reddish-blond hair of his father, his even temper was that of his mother. Now he added, "But if you marry Semmes, he might be a handful."

"I'll never marry Leighton. He's too much in love with somebody else."

"Who is that?"

"Himself, of course." Rachel laughed at the expression on Grant's face, then sobered. "I'll just keep on being the spinster of Lindwood, Grant. It's safer that way."

"Aw, Rachel, you can't live in a cave and think small," Grant protested. "Marriage works out fine for some. Look at our folks."

"Yes, but look at Uncle Clay and Aunt Ellen." Both of them knew that their uncle's marriage to Ellen Benton had been so stormy that Clay now lived in a summerhouse on his plantation, Gracefield, to avoid contact with his wife. Ellen, on the other hand, spent most of her time in Richmond, flirting and spending money—when she had it. Rachel, who liked her uncle very much, was turned gloomy by the thought of their troubles and fell silent.

When they pulled up at the livery stable, Grant helped Rachel down, then said, "Let's go get something to eat." She agreed, and they went to French's Restaurant and had fresh veal and corn bread. While they ate, Grant spoke little of the plantation, for it was Les, the younger brother, who was a natural farmer. Grant had been at Manassas, and his whole mind was on the war. He was a second lieutenant in D Company.

Later, as they left the restaurant, Rachel said, "It'll all be over soon, I pray. I hate this war."

Grant said stubbornly, "No, sister, it won't be—"

"Grant! Hey, Grant!" The two Franklins turned to see their younger brother, Les, dash up and stand before them. His face was flushed, and hot anger lit his blue eyes. "It's Vince and Simon Duvall!" he said, speaking so fast he was hard to understand. "Come on, Grant!"

"You wait here," Grant said to Rachel, but as he and Les raced down the street, she grabbed up her skirts and flew after them. When she turned the corner, she saw a crowd of people gathered around Vince and Duvall, who were standing in an open space. There had been an argument, she saw, for Duvall's face was livid.

"Stay away from me, Duvall!" Vince was saying. His eyes, as usual, were red-rimmed from drink. As he tried to move away, Duvall reached out and caught him, whirling him around. Though Duvall was much smaller, he was wiry and strong.

"You've sullied my wife's name in public," he snarled in fury, "and now you're going to answer for it!"

Vince, Rachel saw, was pale as paper; fear had washed all the color from his face. He jerked his arm free and wheeled to move away, but Duvall stepped to a buggy tied to the rail, jerked a whip from the socket, then, in one motion, lifted it and brought it down on Vince. It curled around his neck, and when Duvall gave it a pull, Vince was stopped as if he'd run into a wall.

Rachel moved to stand beside Grant, who said, "I've got to stop this."

"Stay out of it!" Rachel took her brother's arm and held him tightly. "You know what kind of man Duvall is! He's likely to shoot anyone who interferes!"

Duvall struck Vince three times, then cried out, "Now will you fight?"

Vince, a red mark from the whip across his brow, gave a sob and broke into a run, pushing men aside. It was a disgusting thing to see, and Grant turned away, shaking his head. "He'll have to leave the country!" he said in a low voice.

Duvall shouted, "You'd better start wearing a gun, Franklin! Next time I see you, I'll kill you!" He tossed the whip down and walked stiffly down the street.

"He'll do it, too," Grant said to his brother and sister as the crowd broke into an excited jumble of voices. "Come on, let's go home."

The three of them got into the buggy, aware that people were staring at them. On the way home, Les said bitterly, "I wouldn't let a man do that to me!"

Grant shrugged. "Vince knew what Duvall was like. He should have left the man's wife alone."

"Do you think he had an affair with Rose?" Rachel asked.

"Doesn't matter much, does it? Duvall will kill him whether he did or not."

They arrived at Lindwood to find that their father was gone with his unit. Even so, they had to tell their mother what had happened. She said nothing at first, then remarked, "We need to get word to your father. Les, will you go tell him?"

"Let's both go," Grant said, and the two got their horses and left. All afternoon Rachel thought of the ugly scene, and even after she went to bed that night, it kept coming back.

Father, she prayed silently, feeling helpless, *please do something about Vince.*

Finally she got up, put on her robe, and went to the kitchen. She was drinking a cup of warm milk when suddenly Vince came through the door, a suitcase in his hand. He was obviously leaving and was shocked to see Rachel, so he stood there uncertainly.

"Well, I guess you're happy about all this," he snapped hatefully.

"No, I'm not," she answered quietly. "Are you running away?" Rachel looked at the suitcase he held in one hand and the small bag in the other.

He stared at her as if she had said something stupid. "Running away? Of course I'm running away! Did you think I'd stay around and let that fool of a duelist kill me?"

Rachel studied Vince, then asked, "Where will you go?"

"I'm taking a little ocean voyage," he said with a nod. "Been wanting to see more of the world. I'll let that hothead cool off; then I'll come back."

"Duvall won't cool off," Rachel said, quiet certainty in her voice. "You can never come home."

"Maybe he'll get killed in this war. I certainly hope so!" He moved to the door; then something prompted him to turn. He stared at Rachel, then said, "Well, good-bye. I don't guess you'll miss me much, will you?"

"Not much, Vince," she said honestly. "We haven't been close, though I've tried since you've been back. You've never thought of anyone but yourself. I can't think of a worse way to live or a quicker way to become a miserable human being." His face darkened in anger as he listened, but Rachel went on. "I will be praying for you, though. And I wish you luck. I think you'll need it."

"Just you wait until I get control of this place, dear sister," he spat at her. "Then we'll see who's miserable!" Whirling, he left the room, and soon she heard him driving his carriage, whipping his horse to a full run down the drive.

Rachel put out the lamp and left the kitchen, disturbed by the scene. She had no love for Vince—he had not opened himself to it—but he was still a part of her family. . .and as the sound of hoofbeats grew dim, a bleak sorrow came to her.

CHAPTER 2

A MIDNIGHT SWIM

The huge stern paddles of the *Memphis Queen* thrashed the muddy waters of the Mississippi into a white froth as it drove downstream under full power. Captain Daniel Harness was a bold man to thread the turns of the river at such a clip, but he knew the thousand turns and windings of the river as well as any steamboat captain afloat. In the darkness, Captain Harness stood with his feet firmly braced against the floor, seeming to feel the snags and sandbars with the soles of his feet. When he had threaded a particularly tricky maneuver that put the *Queen* around a fishhook-shaped bar, he said, "Take her, McClain."

"Yes, sir."

"Come along, Jake. Let's get a drink."

Jake Hardin followed the captain out of the pilothouse, and as the two descended to the main deck, he said, "Nice job, Captain. I think sometimes you know every snag on the Mississippi."

"I've had collisions enough to know some of 'em pretty well." Captain Harness was a short, barrel-shaped man of thirty-five, with a round head and a pair of gimlet hazel eyes. He was temperamental, as all captains were, but now he turned

769

a friendly smile on his companion. "My job is a lot safer than yours, though. You gamblers are the ones who take risks. Most of you wind up either broke or with a bullet in your head."

The two entered the salon of the *Queen*, and a waiter came rushing up. "Yes, sir, Captain. Right this way!" He led them to a table, and Harness said, "Bring us some steaks, Phil. Make mine rare."

"Well done," Hardin murmured. "And some whiskey." The two waited until the bottle and glasses came; then Hardin poured two drinks. Lifting his glass, Hardin said, "Here's luck, Dan." The two drank, and then Hardin picked up on the captain's words. "I guess you're right about my trade. I've been on the river five years, and most of the captains who were here when I started are still around. A lot of gamblers are gone, though."

He was tall, this man, and he sat loosely in his chair, running his eyes idly over the salon. He was an inch under six feet, and his 180 pounds were so solid that he looked as though he weighed less. He had sharp brown eyes and a long English nose over a wide mouth. Crisp brown hair, slightly curled, could be seen from beneath the black wide-brimmed hat he wore shoved back on his head. His fingers were long, supple, and strong.

Captain Harness took his drink slowly, studying the tanned face of his companion. He had few friends among the gamblers who traveled on the *Queen*. Indeed, he had a thinly veiled scorn for most of them. In his mind they produced nothing, and he was one who believed that a man should do or make something useful with the strength God gave him. Even so, he had grown fond of Jake Hardin, seeing in him something more than the usual greed and sloth that made up most gamblers.

The two of them had once spent some time together when

the *Queen* had hit a submerged tree just out of St. Louis and was forced to lay by while the hole was repaired. Most of the passengers had chosen to take another ship, but Hardin had stayed, and the two of them had met at dinner. Harness had spent his life studying the dangers, both obvious and hidden, of the river—and somehow he had learned to see what was hidden in men, too. As the two had lingered over meals and talked slowly about unimportant things, the captain had decided that there was none of the meanness in this man that he had come to expect from professional gamblers. Since then, Hardin had been on his boat many times, and the two of them kept up a certain brand of friendship.

"You ought to do something else, Jake." Harness squinted his eyes, peering at Hardin as if he were a difficult passage on the river. His comment made the other man shift uneasily.

"Like what? Be a captain on the river?"

"You're too old for that. How old are you, anyway?"

"Twenty-five."

"Got to start at twelve or so to do my job. You got to be responsible, too, which you ain't never been."

Hardin grinned suddenly and took a sip of his drink. "You got that right, Daniel. Got no character at all."

"Oh, you got it," Harness said. "You just ain't never *used* it." As Harness spoke, he seemed to grow somewhat angry. "Makes me mad to see a man wasting what the good Lord gave 'im. Why don't you do something worthwhile?" A thought touched him, and he demanded, "Which side you for, North or South?"

"Neither. I'm a citizen of the *Memphis Queen*, Daniel. When they start shooting at her, I'll go to war and start shooting back."

Harness glared at him. "Don't you care about slavery?"

"All men are slaves, Daniel. We just have different masters."

"Now that ain't so and you know it!"

The two men argued about the war until the food came. It amused Jake to get the captain stirred up. He liked Harness as much as any man he knew, and he knew the captain liked him—which still surprised him—but he was aware that the two of them were miles apart in their outlook on life. When they finished their steaks and were drinking cups of strong black coffee that was stiff with chicory, the gambler tried to explain to his friend how he felt. It was important to him for Harness to know that.

"Daniel, you're what you are because of a few accidents. You were born with whatever genius it is that makes a man able to memorize a river, and you happened to be born where there was a river. If you'd been born in Kansas, you'd have been a failure as a farmer because you were born to do one thing. You're for slavery and the South because you were born and raised in Tennessee, but if you'd grown up in Michigan, you'd be for the Union. You're right where you are because of a few chances, Dan. And so am I."

Harness snorted and slapped his hand hard on the table, making the bottle jump. "Jake, that's the dangedest nonsense I ever heard! I made my own decisions! And you've made yours, which is to be a lazy bum of a gambler!"

"Guess you're right. Like I say, I've got no character." He rose, stretched, then grinned down at Harness. "Got to get to the table, Captain. Fellow there named Longley is out to do me. I aim to do the same to him."

"Better stay away from Max Longley. He's a bad 'un, Jake."

"So am I, Daniel. You just said so."

"No, you're just triflin' and lazy. Longley is a real bad 'un."

"Well, he's a rich bad 'un, so I'll just relieve him of some of his cash. See you later, Daniel."

Hardin left the main salon and made his way to the section set apart for gambling. The *Memphis Queen* sported the most ornate gambling establishment on the river, complete with roulette wheels, poker tables, blackjack dealers, and a bar across the rear. Jake went at once to a table where four men sat playing poker and took a seat, saying, "Give me five hundred in chips."

The dealer, a bulky man with a catfish mouth, said, "Where you been, Hardin? I been waiting to take some of your cash."

"Had supper, Max. Had to build up some energy to carry out all that money I'm going to take from you," Hardin answered with a smile. The game went on slowly. Several times men joined the game; others left with their money mostly in front of Max Longley. Longley's brother, a dumpy man everyone called Boog, was in the game, as well. He was a sour-faced individual, in contrast to his brother, who was florid and wore a big smile.

Finally Max said, "Blast these small stakes. How about we double up?"

One man dropped out, saying, "Too rich for me," but Hardin, Boog, and two others stayed. The chips flowed across the table, again with Max the big winner. An hour later, he looked across the table, saying, "You game to double again, Jake?"

"All right with me."

It was a big game now, and people came over to watch. Many hands were worth two or three hundred dollars, and slowly the piles grew in front of Hardin and Max Longley. At midnight, only the two of them were in the game. The stakes had swelled to huge sizes.

As always in such games, the two men finally found themselves involved in one huge pot, with each of them sure he had the winning hand. The air was blue with smoke, and there was no sound except for the falling of cards on the felt or the clicking of chips as the two men continued to shove them across to the small mountain that had grown there.

Finally, Longley studied his cards and shoved most of his chips to the center. "Bet two thousand more."

Hardin watched Longley's eyes, thinking, *He expects me to fold.* He had been reading men's eyes for five years and thought he knew Longley well. But he said without emphasis, "Call you."

Longley studied his hand, then said, "I'll stand."

Every eye was on Jake Hardin, and he let the time run on. He knew that pressure could make the sand run out of a man, and he saw the confidence in Longley's eyes fade. Then he puffed his cigar, saying, "Dealer takes two."

A gasp went around the room, and Longley grinned, a savage expression on his face. "Knew you was bluffin', Jake!" He turned over his hand. "Three aces and two kings," he announced.

Hardin once again let the silence run on, then dealt himself two cards. He picked them up, studied them, then smiled and laid them down. "Royal flush," he murmured.

Several cries went up, one man saying with a curse, "He filled it! I don't believe it!"

Max Longley stared at the cards Hardin had laid down, and his wide face grew even more florid. He stared as Jake reached out and drew in his winnings. Then he said, "You dealt yourself that hand from your sleeve."

The sound of men talking was cut off as if it had been sliced with a knife, and the men sitting behind the two players hastily moved to one side. Longley got to his feet, saying, "You're not taking that pot, Hardin."

Jake sat there studying Max. There was only one thing to

do. If he backed down, he'd be marked all down the river.

"Longley, back off," he said quietly and then got to his feet. "I'm cashing in." He took a small velvet bag from his pocket and filled it with the chips, all the time keeping his eyes fixed on the man across the table. Slipping the bag into his coat pocket, he gave Longley a careful look, then turned and walked away.

He had taken only a few steps when he heard the sound of metal against leather, and at the same time a man yelled, "Look out, Jake!"

Hardin threw himself to one side, drawing his pistol from the shoulder holster. Even as he turned, the crash of Longley's gun rocked the air and he felt a tug on his right arm. He came around as he fell, bringing his gun to bear on Longley, who was drawing down on him again. The gun bucked in Jake's hand, and Longley's second shot went into the ceiling, blowing a chandelier to smithereens. Longley was propelled backward by the bullet, which drove directly into his heart, then fell to the deck and lay still.

"You all saw it," Jake said. "He didn't give me a choice." He turned and walked toward the door, forgetting that Max Longley had a brother. That lapse was a costly mistake, for Boog Longley pulled a gun and let fly one bullet. Jake felt a cold touch, heard the explosion, then was sucked into a soundless sea of black.

∿

There was sound but no meaning. From far away came the slow thudding of some sluggish machine, and with each beat, a streak of raw pain touched him like a whip of fire. The heavy darkness that enveloped him was broken at the edges by streaks of light, and something seemed to be drawing him out of the warmth and comfort and safety of the darkness. A voice came to him, muffled but insistent. When he tried to draw away, it came again.

"Jake! Come out of it!"

He knew the voice, and now the light came rolling in, but it brought such a slashing pain to his head that he lay still, gasping and waiting for it to go away.

"Wake up, Jake!"

He opened his eyes slowly and saw the dusky shadow of a man's face surrounded by a corona of yellow light. Blinking his eyes, he turned his head carefully, and the outlines of a room began to take shape. He tried to speak, but only a dry croak emerged from his throat.

"Here, have a drink of water."

He heard water being poured, then felt coolness on his lips. Thirstily he drank it down, then gasped, "More!"

"Sure, Jake." Now the man moved, and Jake saw that it was Milo Bender, a steward on the *Memphis Queen*. Bender was a good man who had become well acquainted with Jake— particularly after Jake loaned Milo two hundred dollars when one of his children was sick.

"Now sit up. Not too fast, though. That's a bad gash on the top of your head." Bender let Jake drink the water, then set the glass down. Sitting in a chair beside the bunk, he examined the gambler with a critical eye. "An inch lower and you'd be pushin' up daisies, Jake."

Carefully Hardin reached up and touched the bandage on top of his head. Just the touch brought a sharp stab of pain, and he quickly dropped his hand. He peered at the room around him. "Where is this, Milo? It's not my room."

"No, it ain't," Bender agreed. "You're under arrest for murder, Jake."

His words brought Jake's head upright, a move he instantly regretted. "For murder! Why, that's crazy, Milo! The man tried to kill me."

"Boog Longley says otherwise, and he's got two witnesses who say you pulled on his brother and killed him without giving him a chance." Bender hesitated, then said, "I sure wish you'd picked somebody else to plug, Jake. Them Longleys got lots o' money, and they just about run this county. I know you're telling the truth, but the Longleys are the he-coons. They've had men put in jail for a lot less. Old man Longley was a senator, and he's got every judge in his pocket. It don't look good."

A streak of fear threaded through Jake. "But there were witnesses who *saw* Longley shoot me first!"

"And where will they be when the trial comes? You know well as I do, Jake, that soon as we dock, everybody scatters. You can bet they won't be none of them at your trial 'cept the two Boog done bought and paid for." Milo leaned forward and whispered, "Jake, you got to get away or you'll stretch hemp for sure."

"Is there a guard outside the door?"

"Yeah, but I can get him away for a while. You can get outta this cabin, but what then?"

"Have to swim for it!"

"With that head?"

"It's the only head I've got." Jake was wide awake now and put his feet on the floor. "What about my money?"

"Boog took it. Here, I brought all I could scrape up. Only about thirty dollars."

"Milo, thanks!"

"Aw, it ain't much, Jake. Maybe I can get more against my pay, but there ain't much time."

"This will do. Where are we?"

" 'Bout an hour out of Helena. You can swim to shore easy. Cap always hugs the shoreline along here. Get to town and catch a train or another boat. I better run. Good luck, Jake. Write me a note when you get someplace. I'd like to know you made it."

"Sure. And thanks again."

"Here's a knife. You can open the door with it—just slide it along the edge. And don't lose this. It's some matches and grub all wrapped up in oilcloth. I snatched your gun off the floor and it's there, too." Bender got up and picked up the tray. "I'll tell the guard you're still out cold. He'd rather be drinkin' than guardin', so he'll be easy to convince."

Bender knocked on the door and, when it opened, slipped outside. Jake pressed his ear against the door. "He's maybe not gonna live, Charlie. Couldn't get him awake to eat. Come on, let's get some of that bonded stuff I got in my cabin," Bender said.

"Hey, Milo, I can't leave here. I'm guardin' this feller."

"Do as you please," he answered carelessly. "If you'd rather guard a stiff than drink bonded whiskey, it's your say-so."

Jake heard Milo's footsteps as he moved down the hall alone, and his heart sank. Then Charlie said, "Wait up, Milo! I reckon I got time for just one!"

Moving quickly despite the pain in his head, Hardin removed a cord from the curtains, then picked up his boots and tied them together. He checked the loads in his gun, slipped it into the shoulder holster, and stepped to the door. Using the knife he opened it easily, then moved to the stairway leading to the deck and climbed topside.

It was dark, and he could see two figures at the rail, the sound of their voices clear on the night air. Moving to the starboard rail, he peered both ways, then moved to stand beside it. The shore was a mere bulky darkness slipping by rapidly; the trees were ghostly outlines against the night sky.

Thinking of the huge paddle wheel, he moved back to the stern and stepped over the rail. Without a pause he jumped into the water, holding his boots tightly. The water was cold to his touch, sending a chill through his body, and the pounding of the massive paddle wheel throbbed into his head. Then the action of the churning wake turned him over like a doll, and he spun helplessly until he finally came to the surface, gasping in great gulps of air.

The stern lights of the *Queen* glowed like malevolent eyes in the darkness. He only glanced at the boat for an instant, then turned and began to swim for shore. It was not a long swim, but he was weak and confused by his wound, and the weight of his clothes and boots dragged him down. When his feet hit bottom he was about finished. He crawled ashore and lay on his face, gasping for breath.

The fall air was cold, and he got up as soon as he could breathe easily again, looking around. It was too dark to see clearly, so he blundered along through bamboo cane until he came to firm ground. Then, luckily, he ran into a huge tree that had been uprooted. He followed the outline of the tree to the first limb, groped around, and broke off the ends of the dead branches. It was an old tree and the wood was dry. Making a pile of the twigs, Jake dug into the oilcloth package, found the matches, and carefully struck one. It spurted with a blue flame, and when he touched it to the twigs, they caught at once. As the tiny fire grew and cast flickering beams around, he scavenged as many sticks and as much brush as he could find and soon had a large fire going.

As Jake took off his shirt and pants and dried them, he

thought of what he had said to Captain Harness. "'A man's life is made up of accidents,'" he said aloud, then asked, "Wonder if coming ashore here near this dead tree is one of those things? I could have hit a bluff and not been able to climb out." The question troubled him, but he was not a man to spend time or thought on such things.

When his clothes were dry, he put them back on, then used a sharp stick to skewer some of the bacon Milo had put in the sack. He cooked it over the fire and devoured it. He was hungry and wanted more but wrapped the rest back in the oilcloth. "Don't know how long this has to last," he said. Then he piled more sticks on the fire and lay down.

The skies were black, without even a single star. As Jake peered into the darkness, he knew that he was in big trouble. The Longleys would have the alarm out before long, and this was their country. If he stayed, they would find him. Of that he was sure. But the Mississippi River had been his home for the past five years. Where else could he go?

For a long time he lay there, but no answers came. Finally he went to sleep.

⚘

Vince Franklin looked around the saloon with distaste. *Should have known better than to come to a dump like this,* he thought. He took a drink of the raw whiskey that seemed to scratch his throat as it went down, then looked over at the woman who was drinking with him. *She looked a lot better in the dark.* He had met her on a side street in Helena, and by lantern light, she had appeared fresh and very pretty. Now he saw her rough skin and the hardened gleam in her red-rimmed eyes and knew he didn't need her.

He had gotten off the riverboat at Helena looking for an old crony, only to find that the man had joined the army. Vince was now forced to wait until the next morning to catch a packet, and so he had made a tour of the dives in the river town. There were quite a few of them, and by the time he met the woman, he was both unsteady and surly.

"You like me, honey?" the woman said with a smile, breaking into his thoughts, the gold in her teeth gleaming in the light. "I love you plenty!"

Vince suddenly came to a decision, but before he could get up, a man dressed in a checked shirt, whose face was all but hidden by a bushy, unkempt beard, came through the door. He scanned the room, and when he spotted Vince and the woman, he growled, "I got you now!"

The woman scrambled to her feet, her face filled with fear. "I was on my way home, Con! Honest I was!"

"'I was on my way home!'" The huge man stood there, filling the doorway, mocking her. Drunk as he was, Vince noticed that customers were carefully moving out of the man's range. He stood up, but the man called Con said, "Where do you think you're going, sonny?"

"I–I'm not involved in this," Vince said quickly. The sight of the man's wild eyes had sobered him up considerably, and he stepped to the side of the table.

"You stand right there!" The burly man pulled a revolver from his pocket and laid it right on Vince's chest. "I'm gonna teach you not to fool around with another man's woman!"

As bad as the moment was, Vince almost burst out laughing. He'd run all the way from Richmond to avoid getting shot by one jealous man and was now about to be killed by another.

Just then there was a movement to his right. A man wearing

a ruffled shirt and a pair of black pants stepped to stand beside him. He had on a low-crowned black hat, and his eyes were hidden in the shadow of its brim. "Back off, Con," he said in a husky voice. "My friend and I are getting out of here."

"You'll get, all right—to the cemetery!" Con cocked the revolver, but the man beside Vince had suddenly produced one of his own, and it was aimed right at the big man's forehead. Con looked at the muzzle, blinked, and considered the gun in his hand.

"This ain't yore fight!" Con muttered, trying to see the man's face more clearly.

"Anytime I see a man draw on someone who's unarmed, it's my fight," a flat, emotionless voice answered him. "Besides, I've got nothing to lose. So make up your mind. . . . What'll it be?"

Con dropped his gun and threw his hands up. "All right! All right! I ain't got no gun!"

"You about ready?" the man said to Vince. Vince grabbed his hat, nodded, and the two of them left. "We'd better move away from here in case your friend has second thoughts," the man said calmly, holstering his gun.

"Let's go to my room," Vince said. His voice was shaky, and now that the scene was over, he found that the fear made his legs weak. "Come along. I owe you a drink—or maybe more. Name's Vince Franklin, by the way."

After a noticeable silence, the man said, "Jake Hardin."

The name meant nothing to Vince, and he hurried along to the hotel. It was late, and even the night clerk was gone. Vince led the way to his room, opened the door, then went in and lit the lamp. "Have a seat, Jake," he said. "I've got a bottle here. Good stuff, too." He found the bottle, poured two drinks, then said with a nervous smile, "Here's to you, Jake Hardin. I was never so glad to see anybody in my life!"

"Glad to help, Vince." Jake downed his drink, then said, "Well, guess I'll be going."

"Here now!" Vince said quickly. "You can't run off like that. Sit down, man, and let's talk. I don't get my life saved every day!"

Vince watched the man as he sank back into his chair. "I've got nothing to lose," he'd said. Vince smiled to himself. *Anyone that desperate could prove most useful.* Soon the two men were talking easily. Vince took in the man's worn clothing, the still-raw wound on his head, and the fact that Hardin was about dead for sleep.

"You from around these parts, Jake?" he asked and sat back to listen, calculating.

Jake had not eaten for two days. He had stayed outside of town as long as he could, then had come in out of desperation. It had not taken him long to find that the Longleys had posted a reward notice for him. He had slept in an alley, sneaking into a store at the outskirts of town to buy crackers and meat, but his limited resources hadn't lasted long and his money was almost gone. He had gone to the saloon to buy a pint. From there, he didn't know what he would do.

Now the warm room and the whiskey made him sleepy— and careless—and he found himself telling Franklin about his life, revealing that he was a riverboat gambler. He broke off abruptly, saying, "I lost all my money and hit rock bottom."

Vince smiled again. The memory of Con's gun looming in front of him was still fresh in his mind, but it wasn't so much gratitude he felt toward Jake as a sense of not letting an opportunity pass by. *Who knows?* Vince thought. *Hardin might even be the answer to my problems. . . .* "I'll stake you, Jake," he said, surprising Jake. "All you need is some good clothes and a little money—plus a little luck. Tell you what, the boat's due to leave in about three hours. Go with me to New Orleans. I'll back you until you've won some money; then you can pay me back."

Jake stared at Vince but said at once, "Well, I'm in no condition to be proud. I'll just take you up on that offer."

"Fine!" Vince said. "Look, we're about the same size. Why don't you wear some of my duds? I've got too many anyhow."

When the boat bound for New Orleans left Helena, the two men got on. Jake saw a man with a sheriff's star standing by the gangplank, along with a deputy. Vince stopped and asked, "What's up, Sheriff?"

"Looking for a killer," the officer said. He looked at Vince and at Jake, noting the expensive clothes, then said, "Watch out, just in case the man gets on this boat. He'll be wearing some fine clothes that've been in the water—and he'll have a fresh bullet gash on top of his head."

Jake resisted an impulse to tug the hat Vince had given him down tighter. Instead he leaned forward, asking the sheriff, "A dangerous fellow?"

"A killer, like I said. Shot Mr. Max Longley dead. Fellow's name is Jake Hardin, but I don't guess he'd be fool enough to use it."

Vince said, "I guess not. Well, come along, Frank. Packet's about to leave."

The two of them went to stand at the rail, and as the hands cast off the lines, Vince said, "I always pay my debts, Jake."

"I figure you paid this one, Vince. Thanks."

They stood there as the paddle wheels began to churn, and soon Helena was lost as they moved down the river.

Chapter 3

Jake Gets an Offer

The trip from Helena to New Orleans should have taken only two days, but the engine developed trouble and they had to dock at a small town. By the time a part had been shipped from Memphis and installed, the *Lightning* was delayed for two more days. For Jake Hardin it was a welcome delay. It gave his nerves time to settle down and the wound in his scalp more time to heal. And, too, he found himself growing more curious about Vince Franklin. Franklin seemed amiable enough, and the two of them played cards, but only for small stakes because Jake had seen at once that Franklin was not in his class as a card player. They strolled through the small town where the ship was docked, sat on the deck during the afternoon, and ate the good food provided by the riverboat's excellent chef.

As for Vince, he felt things were going his way for once. Jake was in his debt—after all, he'd kept him from being arrested and was giving him a new start. And though Vince wasn't sure how, he knew that debt was going to work in his favor. They had just finished a fine lunch on the second day and were walking around the town when they came upon a group of men in a small field beside the blacksmith shop. "Looks like a shooting match," Vince said. The two of them stopped and listened as the men agreed on the terms. A tall man named Harrod was evidently the judge. He had a full beard, which gave him the air of a biblical prophet as he announced in a ringing voice, "Costs one dollar to enter. The three top shooters get the prizes—three jugs of the smoothest whiskey Si Edwards ever made. Now fust of all, we'll have the rifles."

The contest proceeded in a leisurely fashion, with much joking among the contestants. Jake watched the winner of the rifle shoot, saying, "That fellow is good."

Then Harrod said, "Next, pistols at the settin' target." The men lined up and took turns shooting at bottles balanced on a fence, and the winner claimed his jug with a whoop.

"Now the last prize goes to the feller who can hit a target on the fly. How many of you fellers want in?" Only four men volunteered, and Harrod snorted in disgust. "What's wrong with you fellers? Ain't you got no pride?" Then he glanced at Jake and Vince. "How about you two? You look like sportin' men to me."

Jake nudged Vince. "You want to risk a dollar?" Vince grinned and produced the cash. "I'm in," Jake stated and pulled his gun out. "Anybody got any .44 bullets?"

"I'm shootin' a .44," a short, pudgy man with bright blue eyes said. He pulled a handful of shells from his pocket, saying, "If you win, I get first go at the jug, right?"

"Sure," Jake agreed. He loaded his pistol and watched as Harrod said to the first shooter, "Ready, Mac?" When the man nodded, he tossed a glass bottle into the air as high as he could. The contestant took his shot but missed. A hoot went up. He took three more turns, hitting only one bottle.

Two of the other men hit only one in four, but the final

contestant hit three. Harrod turned to Jake, saying, "Your turn, I reckon."

Jake looked around at the men, then said, "Anybody here want to bet a little cash?"

"How much?" the one named Mac demanded.

"Much as my friend here wants to cover. But the deal is, Mr. Harrod throws all four glasses at once. If I miss even one, I lose."

"I'll just take ten dollars of that bet," Mac said and began digging in his pocket.

Vince pulled his wallet from his pocket, saying, "Step right up, gents. All bets covered."

Most of the men put a few dollars into the pot, but Harrod shook his head with a grin. "Since I'm doing the throwin' guess I better not git in on this. You ready?"

"Any time."

Harrod had to use both hands, but he tossed the four bottles high, all of them reaching their apex at about the same time. Jake lifted his gun and fired, shattering the first bottle as it paused. The next shot caught one of the bottles that had just started to fall, and the third shattered one a few feet above head level. His last shot took the final bottle just before it hit the ground.

"By gum!" Harrod exclaimed, his eyes wide. "You must be a trick shot for a circus!"

"Just had lots of practice," Jake said with a shrug. "Let's get started on that jug."

When the two men got back on board the *Lightning*, Vince handed Jake a wad of bills. "Here's your share. About thirty dollars." He considered Jake curiously. "Where'd you learn to shoot like that?" he asked.

"Like I said, lots of practice. Always been pretty fair with a handgun. Can't do as good with a rifle."

"Guess if that fellow Max Longley had seen you shoot, he wouldn't have tried to take you."

"I wish he hadn't," Jake said quietly.

"Bothers you, does it, Jake?" Vince asked curiously.

"Sure. Wouldn't it bother you?"

"Not a bit! He was trying to snuff your light, so he got what he asked for."

Jake didn't answer. Sometimes he wasn't sure that he really liked—or trusted—Vince Franklin. The two men went down to supper, and, as they ate, Vince began to talk about himself. "Got a big place outside of Richmond," he said expansively, then went on to describe Lindwood.

"Sounds like a fine place, Vince," Jake commented. "You got a family?" Jake noted with interest that the question obviously disturbed Vince.

"Well, I'm not married. My mother died when I was young. My father married again." He sipped from his wineglass, his brow knitted as he added, "My father and I don't get along too well. Matter of fact, none of the family likes me much."

"Too bad," Jake said. "Never had much of a family myself. Always envied fellows who sat around a big table with their folks. I've always wanted that."

Vince stared at him, then began to relate how little he was a part of the family. He finished by saying bitterly, "They've always shut me out, but they'll sing a different tune pretty soon! All of them!"

"How's that?"

"Why, in a few months, I'll be sitting at the head of the table!" Vince's eyes gleamed and he drank frequently of the wine as he began to speak of his future. "My grandfather Hiram made a pile of money, but my father never got along with him. So when Grandpa made his will, he left the plantation to my pa, but most of his money he put into a trust fund. Then he told my father he'd have to learn to get along with his son. And to make sure, he put it in his will that the oldest son—and that's me!—would inherit the whole fund on his twenty-fifth birthday. 'Course, it hasn't worked out quite the way Grandpa thought it would."

Jake stared at the man sitting across from him, then asked, "What went wrong, Vince?"

"My father went wrong!" Vince broke out angrily, a hardness in his eyes. "He never gave me a chance. All the time it was the others he favored—Grant and Les and Rachel! Maybe I been a little wild, but it was him that drove me to it! Well, that'll change when I get Grandpa's money."

Jake watched him silently, once again feeling uneasy about Vince's bitterness. Then, with a sigh, he shook his head. Maybe he was just overreacting. . . . Vince spoke freely of his family, dwelling on each of them and stressing how they'd have to mind their manners when he took over. It was a side of the man that Jake didn't admire, but he said nothing, as was his custom.

The *Lightning* was refitted, and as it pulled away on the last leg of the journey to New Orleans, Jake was standing at the rail watching the shore. The purser came up behind him, saying, "Mr. Franklin, your clothes are ready. Shall I put them in your cabin?"

Jake turned, and as soon as the purser saw his face, he said, "Oh, I thought you were Mr. Franklin!"

"No, I'm Mr. Franklin." Vince had come up behind the purser and was smiling.

"Why, this gentleman is enough like you to be your twin, sir!"

"He's not nearly as handsome as I am," Vince said, winking at Jake.

But the purser shook his head stubbornly. "You two are as alike as can be. Why, I thought you were brothers the first time you came on board together."

Vince looked at Hardin speculatively. "Well, maybe we do favor each other a little."

"More than that!" the purser insisted. "If you shaved your beard off, you'd look exactly like your friend!"

"Well, since my friend is a nice-looking chap, I can't take offense. Now you can put my suit in my cabin."

"Yes, sir."

As the purser left, Vince said with a smile, "How do you feel about that, Jake? Insulted, perhaps?"

"Why, no." Jake smiled. He studied Franklin's face, and as he did so, surprise came to his eyes. "He's right, you know! Your beard covers most of your face, but we've got the same features. Same brown eyes, same color hair—our noses are even shaped the same."

"I always heard that everybody has a double somewhere on earth, but I never expected to find mine," Vince said. "Strange, though, that you and I would encounter each other as we did."

"One good thing about it," Jake said, "we're the same size, so I can wear your clothes. I was looking pretty ragged in my own outfit." He looked down the river and went on, "We'll be in New Orleans tomorrow, I'd venture. Then I can go to work and quit sponging off of you, Vince."

But Vince was not listening. He was studying Hardin's face closely. "What? Oh yes, I suppose so. . .but we'll stick together for a few days, until you can put a stake together."

"No longer than I can help, Vince," Jake replied and shook his head. "Don't like to be taking from you all the time."

"Well, you saved my life, didn't you?"

"Maybe not. That fellow would probably just have roughed you up a little."

"No, I'm in your debt, Jake." He paused, about to say more, but changed his mind. "We'll have lots of time to talk when we get to New Orleans." He laughed softly, cocked his head as he studied Jake. "Funny thing, how we've gotten together. My sister, Rachel, would say God did it."

Jake raised his eyebrows. "She's religious?"

"Lord, yes! After me all the time to give up my wicked ways!"

"Well, maybe she's right, but I think it's all luck."

"That's the way a gambler would think, I suppose, but still. . .it's strange. Gives me the creeps in a way! Well, we'll talk about it later." His eyes narrowed, and he said slowly, "I've got the fragment of an idea in my head. Might be a good one."

"I owe you, Vince. If you hadn't staked me, I'd be done for. And if you hadn't covered for me with that sheriff when we got on the boat, I'd either be in prison or hung." Jake shrugged. "If I can do something for you, just name it."

"I may do that. I just may indeed!"

New Orleans had always been one of Jake's favorite cities, but caution made him say as he walked down the gangplank of the *Lightning*, "We'd better split up for a time."

"Why? I thought we were going to stay together for a while!"

"We can meet, but there's probably a wanted notice out for me. I'll have to lay low for a while."

"Hadn't thought of that," Vince said slowly, then nodded.

"I know just the place. Friend of mine owns a little place in the French Quarter. Got four or five nice rooms. He'll keep his mouth shut, too."

"Well—"

Vince waved his hand at a cab and half shoved Jake toward it. "Get in!" he ordered, then added to the driver, "French Quarter, driver. You know Tony's place on St. Charles Street?"

"Yas, sah! I does indeed!" The driver flicked his whip, and the team stepped out smartly. He drove from the wharf to the Quarter, then stopped in front of a two-story building on the narrow street. "Tony's place, sah!"

The two men got out of the cab, Vince paid the driver, and they went inside. Tony was a small Italian with a pair of sharp dark eyes, and soon he was leading the pair to the second floor. "Same room you had last time, Vince," he said. "And the one next to it's vacant. You gents make yourselves at home; then come on down and we'll see what we can find to drink."

The rooms were small but well aired and light. A balcony framed with black wrought iron gave a good view of the street below, and during their stay, Jake spent a good deal of time looking down at the crowds that thronged the street. He went out twice, but on his second time he discovered that there was indeed a warrant out for his arrest. The thought of prison frightened him; he didn't think he could keep his sanity if he were cooped up.

Vince came and went but was always cheerful, saying, "Don't give up, Jake, old boy! Something will turn up."

Finally, on the third day, the two of them stood on the balcony smoking cigars after the evening meal. For a time neither of them said anything. Finally Jake broke the silence. "I've got to get out of the country, Vince. If I stay here, I'll be caught and hanged sooner or later. Either that or prison—and I'd rather have the rope."

Vince flicked the ashes from his cigar, seemingly caught in thought. "Hard for a man to hide, Jake. Mexico is pretty tough, too, unless a fellow has lots of cash."

"I'll make out."

"Sure, you're tough, Jake, but I'd like to see you leave with some money. A fellow can live like a king down in the Caribbean if he has just a little money. Nobody will come looking for you there." He puffed three times on his cigar, then tossed it over the railing. "I'd like to help you get a good start, Jake."

"No, you've done enough for me, Vince. I can't take anything more from you."

"Well, Jake, look at it this way—I need some help from you."

Jake said at once, "That's different. What can I do, Vince?"

"You know that will I told you about, the one that lays it out that I get the money when I'm twenty-five?"

"Sure, I remember."

"Well, there's one clause in it that says I don't get the money unless I'm living at Lindwood."

Jake frowned. "I don't see the problem."

"The problem, Jake, is a man named Simon Duvall. If I go back to Richmond, he'll kill me." He looked at Jake, saw that he had his attention, and rapidly sketched the thing out, concluding by saying, "So this fellow Duvall is a dead shot. I wouldn't have a chance, Jake!"

Hardin stared at Vince, then said, "Let me guess what you have in mind. You want me to kill this Duvall."

"That's it," Vince admitted readily. "It's pretty simple. If I go back, I'm dead. If I don't go back, I don't get the money. Now here you are, dead broke and likely to stay that way. You can use a gun. It all adds up, Jake. You take Duvall out, and I put ten thousand dollars in your hand." He shook his head, adding, "Think what a life you could have down south with ten thousand in your pocket!"

Jake stood there watching the blue smoke from his cigar curl upward. He owed this man a lot, yet…there was something in the thing that went against his grain. Finally he tossed the cigar to the street, then said, "I don't like it, Vince. Sure, I've used a gun once or twice—but it was always forced on me. I'm not a hired killer."

"I thought you wanted to help me, Jake! If I'd been caught hiding you, they'd have nailed me for it. Now I'm asking you to risk a little something to get me out of a jam. How about it?"

"You're putting me on the spot, Vince—but I'll think about it."

"Sure!" Vince nodded. "You do that. We'll talk about it later."

For two days neither man mentioned the matter, and finally Vince brought it up. They were sitting in Jake's room drinking café au lait, when suddenly Vince said, "Jake, I was wrong to put you on the spot with my problem. You're not a killer. I should have seen that."

"Vince, I feel rotten—!"

"No," Vince broke in. "I know you pretty well. You're not the type to hide in a dark alley and shoot a man in the back."

Jake felt terrible, for he liked to pay his debts. "Maybe I can teach you to shoot," he offered, knowing it was no use.

"I can shoot straight enough." Vince nodded, then smiled sadly as he added, "But can you teach me to look into a gun that's aimed at me and not run? That's my problem. I'm a coward." He seemed to have no particular shame about admitting that. "Some men have courage; some don't. It's that simple. I just don't have it and you do."

"Not sure that's right."

"Well, anyway—" Vince broke off abruptly and stared blankly across the room. His brow wrinkled in thought, and he whistled softly and then laughed. "Jake, old fellow, I'm not brave, but I'm *smart*!" Reaching over, he slapped Jake on the shoulder, grinning broadly. "It's so brilliant, only I could come up with it!"

Jake gave him a curious look. "What's in your head now, Vince?"

"Why, it's like this. You couldn't kill a man in cold blood. But there's another way."

"I don't see it."

"Duvall loves to duel. He's killed more than one man. So you take my place in the duel! Don't you see it?"

"You mean I go to Richmond and pick a quarrel with Duvall, and—"

"No! No!" Excitement brightened Vince's eyes, and he leaned forward and whispered, "You don't have to do that. *You take my place!* Don't you see?" He suddenly slapped his hands together, exclaiming, "Jake, remember what that purser on the boat did? He took you for me! We look that much alike."

"Wait a minute, Vince," Jake protested. "We don't look *that* much alike. I'd be spotted in a minute!"

"No, you wouldn't. First, you grow a beard. Then we have the duel at dawn, with almost no light. You'll wear a cloak and a hat pulled down over your eyes. When it's over, I hand you the money; you shave your beard and head south. It's *perfect*, Jake!"

Jake was a quick thinker, but he sat there confused by the suddenness of Vince's plan. There was, he knew, something about the whole business he didn't like, but two things kept rising in his mind: He needed a stake, and he owed Vince a lot. If it weren't for Vince, he'd probably be in jail by now. Or dead.

Vince sat there, letting Jake search the thing out in his mind; he was calculating enough to know that the more he tried to pressure the man, the less likely Jake was to respond. Finally he saw a break in Jake's expression and said, "Of course, I'm asking you to lay your life on the line for me. And that's too much for one man to ask of another."

"No, it's not!" Suddenly the issue became very simple to Jake. "I'll do it for you, Vince. I'd do it even without the money. Matter of fact," he said thoughtfully, "I wish there were no money in it. I owe you, and the money means I'm doing it partly for that reason."

"No, that's wrong," Vince said quickly, a sense of exultation running through him. He was sure now that all his problems would be solved in one instant, and if Jake took the bullet instead of Duvall—well, that was the risk the man was taking. "You're helping me as a friend with Duvall, and I'm helping you as a friend with money. So it's settled?"

"Yes. When do you want to go to Richmond?"

"Have to let your beard grow first. That'll take a month, I guess. We can have some fun in the meantime. I'll tell you all about my family and the people you might run into." The uncertainty that had been eating at Vince since he had left his home was gone, and he laughed loudly. "Now I can sleep better!"

For a week the two of them stayed at Tony's making plans. Actually, there was little to plan, but Vince spent hours telling Jake about his family and his friends—not to mention his enemies. Once he said, "I'm telling you all this like a good

Catholic confesses to a priest, Jake. Maybe because I know it's safe. A priest can't tell anything he hears, can he? And I reckon you won't either!"

"No, I won't tell, Vince."

As Vince had talked about his life, Jake had revised his opinion of the man. At first he had thought of Vince as rather a nice scoundrel, a charming sort of reprobate—but a picture emerged from what he heard that was less pleasant. He learned of Vince's affairs with women, and while Jake was no prude, he disliked the way the man obviously thought of women as toys to be enjoyed and then cast aside. Vince's hatred for his father and his family came out also, and though he painted them with black colors, Jake realized that it would have been hard for anyone, family or otherwise, no matter how good, to put up with Vincent Franklin.

There seemed to be some sort of rotten streak in the man, and it was far worse than cowardice. Jake knew that if the two of them were together for long, they would have conflicts. Before long he began to think that it would have been better if he had left New Orleans without getting involved. More than once he toyed with the idea of running out, penniless as he was.

But he stayed. *Maybe Vince will do better when this Duvall character is taken care of,* he thought. He knew it was merely a wishful dream, though, and the idea of killing a man grew heavier and heavier, like an ominous shadow. It had all sounded logical enough when Vince had explained it, but no matter how Jake tried to think of it, the fact remained that he was going to kill a man for money. He told himself that it was not murder and that he himself could get killed, but it all seemed a feeble excuse for taking a man's life.

Slowly he came to the conclusion that he couldn't do it.

Time ran along, and as Jake tried to find a way to tell Vince what he had decided, Vince continued to talk about his past. Finally one night Jake said, "You've told me so much about your family and friends, I swear I'd recognize them if they walked through that door!"

"All right, Jake." It was late, and Vince had been happy all day. "Won't be long now, will it? I'll be master of Lindwood and you'll be living like a king down on a sunny island. Pretty soft, Jake, old boy!"

"Pretty soft, Vince," Jake answered absently. He sat there trying to find some way to put his decision to Vince, but he knew that no matter how he put it, Vince would not like it. Finally he said, "I've got something to tell you."

"What is it?"

"Well. . .I don't like to go back on my word, but it's just too raw for me, killing Duvall." Jake saw anger spark at once in Vince's eyes and added, "If it was anything else, I'd do it. But—"

"That's pretty small of you!" Vince broke his words off sharply. He pressed the point, trying to convince Jake. When that failed, he began to curse him. Finally he ran out of things to say and stood to his feet. "You'd better get out of here, Jake. I might forget myself and turn you in."

"You could do that, I guess." Jake's voice was quiet, resolved.

Vince started to turn, then paused. With a sigh he shook his head, looking at Jake with a strange, defeated light in his eyes. "No, Jake, I reckon not." He walked to the door, then stopped again. "I've waited all my life for the time when I'd be *somebody*," he said in a low voice without turning around. "Maybe I should have lived better, been more ready to listen to my father or to Rachel." Again he shook his head. "But it's too late for that now. A man's what he makes himself." He turned to look at Jake, a bitter emptiness in his eyes. "I've heard you say the same thing," he added almost sadly. "Men like you and me, we never change."

He turned, picked his coat up off Jake's bed, and put it on. He started out of the room but paused, turning and saying evenly, "I'll get somebody to put Duvall down, Jake. I'll get the money and I'll get Lindwood. But you know what? I don't really think I'll be happy when I get it. And I don't think you'll be happy on your little island or wherever you land." A sadness such as Jake had never seen in the man came to his eyes. He looked small and even a little lost as he stood there.

Then he summoned up a smile and said, "Well, we have to play what we're dealt, don't we, Jake?" Then he added so quietly that Jake almost missed it, "Somehow I think I knew all along you wouldn't do it—you're just not the type. But I've been thinking, if I'd been dealt a friend like you when I was younger, maybe I wouldn't be the rotten way I am. The one thing I wish, though. . .I sometimes wish my family thought a little better of me."

Then he was gone. Jake made a move toward the door but stopped. "I'll talk to him tomorrow," he said aloud. He moved to the bed, picked up his coat, and started to hang it up. But something fell out of the pocket, and as he picked it up he saw that it was Vince's wallet. Staring at it, he realized, *Vince must have taken my coat by mistake.* He took a step toward the door, then paused. *I'll give it to him tomorrow.*

Jake undressed slowly, thinking of how strangely Vince had behaved. The man's sad words kept echoing in his mind: *"I sometimes wish my family thought a little better of me."* Jake lay in bed, but sleep wouldn't come. Restlessly he tossed until he finally dozed off, though his sleep was fitful and he still had flashing thoughts and short dreams. One of the thoughts grew, and he suddenly awakened with the idea fully developed. Getting out of bed, he stood in the middle of the room, thinking hard.

I'll help Vince make it—and without shooting Duvall.

So firm was his resolve that he walked to the table, poured water from the pitcher into the basin, then picked up his shaving brush. Quickly he lathered his face, then shaved the two-week beard with hard, even strokes.

When he was finished, he looked at himself, feeling a satisfaction. Vince would be angry, but it set the timetable back by two weeks. Jake lay down again, looked at his watch, and saw that it was only a little after midnight. He lay there thinking. *How does one force a man to face up to his life?*

He could find no answers, but he pinned his hopes on what Vince had said: "I sometimes wish my family thought a little better of me."

Then he went to sleep, determined to stick with Vince and somehow make him see that Vince himself was the only one who could make that come to pass.

CHAPTER 4

A MIDNIGHT CALLER

Jake awoke coughing, almost strangling, and when he sat up, he gagged instantly, for the smoke that filled the room was thick.

In one terrifying moment, the thought came to him: *The hotel's on fire!*

The thought screamed silently in his mind as he rolled off the bed and lay down on the floor. The air was clearer there, but a fit of coughing grabbed him and he had to wait until it passed before he could do any more. Someone was yelling below, and Jake began to crawl toward the door. He reached up to turn the brass knob, only to jerk back when it burned his hand. The door itself was sending off heat waves, and through a crack he saw a yellow glow.

He rolled over and began crawling toward the balcony door. On the way, he stopped and grabbed his pants, which were on the chair, wiggled into them while lying flat, then pulled on his coat.

Keeping as close to the floor as possible, he moved until he got to the balcony door and opened it. As soon as it opened, a flash of light caught his eye, and he turned to see the door leading to the hall burst into flame. Quickly he stepped outside and took a deep breath of the fresh air. It was not really fresh, though, for the flames on top of the building were leaping high into the air, filling the area with thick, acrid smoke.

Time was short.

It was only ten feet to the street level, and men below were motioning to him, yelling, "Jump! Jump!"

Jake threw one leg over the rail, then suddenly paused and cast a look at the balcony outside of Vince's room. The door was shut, and he hesitated, watching the leaping flames for a moment, then pulled his leg back and ran down the balcony. The two balconies were not joined, so he climbed up on the rail and jumped as hard as he could. The heat of the fire above struck him as he fell sprawling on the other balcony. Instantly he got to his feet and tried the door. It was locked, so he stood back and began to kick at it. His foot went through and he reached inside, turning the lock and swinging the door open.

The interior of the room was filled with black smoke, and the far wall was blazing. Jake took a deep breath, went on his belly, and crawled toward the bed. It was dark in the room, and the smoke was bad, even on the floor. When Jake reached the bed, he raised himself to his knees and threw his arms across it. The smoke blinded him as he groped for Vince. Finally he found Vince's body, inert and motionless.

"Come on, Vince!" he yelled, struggling to his feet, but his mouth and eyes filled with smoke, and he was suddenly choking. Fear came then, and he knew he couldn't stand the smoke much longer. Through weeping eyes, he saw a coat thrown across a chair. Quickly he grabbed it, wrapped it around Vince's head, then reached down and picked him up. Stumbling, he made his way across the room toward the balcony, but before he got to the wall, the ceiling gave a great creaking roar, and he knew it was collapsing.

He reached the door but, blinded by the smoke, missed the opening and ran into the wall. He fell with Vince on top of him, and then the roof came down. He pulled at Vince, but at that moment something struck him a wicked blow across his right foot. The pain was almost unbearable, but he yanked his foot loose and tried again to get Vince out, crawling because he couldn't stand. Overhead the raging flames licked at the sky, and he saw that the entire room was blazing now.

With all his strength he gave a heave and the two of them rolled out onto the balcony—but the outer wall began to lean, and Jake looked up to see that it was toppling. He grabbed Vince in his arms, struggled upright, and, though he could put no weight on his right foot, lurched to the rail and simply leaned forward. He flipped over, lost his hold on Vince, and then hit the ground, landing on his back with a force that drove all the breath from his lungs.

Looking up he saw the wall of the building, blazing with yellow fire, slowly coming down on top of him. He rolled over, getting as far on his side as he could. Then something struck him, and he knew no more.

ॐ

Jake came out of unconsciousness suddenly, with no hint that he had even been in a deep coma.

One moment it was dark and quiet; the next he was awake, pain washing over him. He tried to look around, but there was something over his eyes. A man's voice was saying, "...have to keep a close watch on him. I'm afraid that he might have some internal injuries."

Jake spoke, his voice a raw croak. "What's wrong with my eyes?"

The doctor moved to his side at once. "Well, so you're awake. That's good. I need to find out some things. Just answer and tell me where you hurt and then we'll give you something for the pain."

"Right ankle," Jake whispered. "Right hand, too."

"Yes, I know about those. They'll be okay. But do you hurt inside? Chest or stomach?"

"No." Jake was hurting too bad to waste words but managed to say again, "What's wrong with my eyes?"

"You got them scorched. I want to keep the strong light off of them for a few days. No more injuries?"

"No. Yes—sore throat."

"You took in too much smoke. Now don't try to talk any more. Just relax."

Jake asked, "What about my friend?"

A pinprick touched Jake's arm as he waited for an answer, and suddenly he began sliding into a warm darkness. "What about. . . ?" His voice trailed off.

He woke again, thinking it had been only a few minutes since he drifted off, but suddenly he knew it must have been longer. He was in a dark room, but the bandages were not on his eyes. There was only a table, a chair beside the bed, and a single door. The window across the room was heavily curtained, but he could tell that it was daytime.

Looking down, he saw that his right ankle was bandaged, as were his right wrist and forearm. A raging thirst assailed him and he tried to call, but his throat was too dry. Then he saw a tiny brass bell on the table and rolled over to get it. That simple act awoke the nerves in his ankle, but he rang the bell despite the pain.

Almost at once, a man in a white coat came into the room. "Well now, you're awake! How do you feel?" He was a short man with a fat paunch and light blue eyes. He read the request in Jake's eyes and at once poured a glass of water. "Let's try to get you upright," he said, and Jake almost fainted with the pain but finally was sitting up in bed.

He drank the water greedily, then asked, "Where is this?"

"St. John's Hospital," the man said. "You've been here—let's see, oh, two days. You were hurting pretty bad when you first came."

"I'm hurting pretty bad now!" Jake whispered. His eyes burned, and he blinked them. "My eyes are better, though."

"They were scorched, but the doctor says if we keep them medicated and away from strong light for a while, they should be all right."

"What else is wrong with me?"

"No bones broken, which is a miracle!" The orderly shook his head and gave Jake an admiring look. "You're a pretty tough fellow! Not many men can have a burning building fall on them and not get killed. The leg is pretty badly strained, and the arm, as well. Got some burns, too, which must hurt like the devil. But you're alive, and that's what counts. You drink some more water, and I'll go get the doctor. He'll want to look you over."

Jake lay there, grateful, since he was left-handed, that it was his right that was hurt. Then he realized that he still didn't know about Vince. When the doctor came in a few minutes later, he asked, "How's the man I pulled out?"

The doctor, a very thin man of fifty with a pronounced Adam's apple that moved up and down when he spoke, shook his head. "I'm Dr. Sealy. Sorry to have to tell you, but he didn't make it." He pulled the chair close to the bed and sat down on it. "I think he was dead when you pulled him out. The smoke got him, I'd guess."

A sense of frustration swept over Hardin. He'd known Vince only a short time and recognized that there was something bad in him—but somehow he'd been bound to him, perhaps by the fact that Vince had gone out on a limb for him. Oh yes, he realized that Vince had actually risked little—nevertheless, he couldn't help thinking he might have been able to help him.

There'd be no way to do that now, Jake realized, and the futility of his efforts and of Vince's death came down hard on him. Dr. Sealy saw it and said briskly, "Well, well, too bad! A young man like that, but you did your best from what I hear. Now then, let's check you over."

Though the man was a good doctor, the examination was painful. Finally he said, "You ought to be dead, but really there's nothing wrong with you that rest won't repair, Mr. Franklin."

The name went off like an alarm bell in Jake's mind.

He thinks I'm Vince! That seemed impossible, but as Sealy continued to talk about his injuries, Jake suddenly remembered the mixed-up coats. *They must have found Vince's papers in the coat I was wearing. But somebody will know better—like Tony. He'll spot me right off.*

Sealy continued, speaking of the fire. "Bad thing, that fire. Not too many got out. Only three, I think. Building must have gone up like tinder."

"Did Tony make it, the owner?"

"No, he didn't. Friend of yours, I suppose."

"Yes."

Dr. Sealy stood up, his face dim in the dark room. "I sent a wire to your people as soon as I treated you. Thought it best, and there was nobody to ask." He rummaged in his pockets, came out with a slip of paper. "Got an answer this morning. It says, 'Will pick up Vincent Franklin within a week. Will travel home by steamboat.' It's signed 'Rachel Franklin.' "

"Thanks, Doctor."

"Well, you need lots of care, and the family can do it better than we can. It's a good idea, too, to go by boat. You can stay in the stateroom where it's dark during the day. I'd say you can leave as soon as she comes. Is this your mother?"

Jake took a deep breath, and feeling as though he were taking a leap into the dark, he cleared his throat. "No, Rachel is my sister."

"Well, I'll be checking on you. Don't move around too much, and don't let the light get at your eyes. I'll get you some smoked glasses to wear after you leave."

"How long will I be laid up?"

"Oh, if you mean how long till you're fully recovered, quite awhile. Say. . .two months. But you'll be able to get around with crutches within a week, maybe. Then a cane. Your eyes, though—be *very* careful of them!" He rose and went to the door, then turned and came back to the bed. "The man you pulled out of the fire, was he a good friend of yours?"

"Just a fellow I met on the boat several weeks ago. I sort of liked him."

Dr. Sealy said slowly, "His name was Jake Hardin."

"Oh?"

"He was wanted for murder. Killed a man on a gambling boat. The sheriff came and identified the body by the papers the fellow had on him, telling who he was." Sealy studied his patient carefully, then added, "A bad way to go, even for a murderer. Well, they buried him in Potter's Field. He didn't have any money, and nobody was likely to pay for his funeral."

"He had some good about him, Doctor," Jake said. "More than some I've met."

"I suppose that's so." Dr. Sealy nodded, then left the room.

Jake lay there quietly, thinking. He grieved over Vince Franklin, over the good things about him. All afternoon he lay there and finally was given a shot when the pain got bad.

The next morning he found he was able to eat a little. "Put me in a chair, Rog," he said to the orderly. "I'm sick of this bed."

"Yeah, sure," the orderly said. He helped Jake into the chair, then asked, "You want anything? I got stuff to do, Mr. Franklin."

"Go on, Rog. I'll be all right."

He sat there, relieving the muscles that had stiffened from his days in bed. Carefully he tried to move his right foot, but the stab of pain made him catch his breath. "Going to be awhile before I'll stand on that," he murmured. His wrist was not much better, but as he sat there, he was conscious of how fortunate he was. How had Rog put it? *"Not many men have a burning building fall on them and live through it!"*

Well, he was alive. Battered and burned, but alive.

The future loomed before him darkly, like a tunnel whose end he couldn't see. *Maybe there's no end to it,* he thought. *Maybe all this is just an accident.* He thought of Captain Daniel Harness with his rough-hewn theology. *Dan would never think it just happened,* Jake mused. *And Rachel wouldn't either, if what Vince said about her is so.*

He thought then of the girl who was coming to meet him, to take him home with her to a place he'd never seen, to live among people he'd never met. And he thought of the wild plan to reform Vince that had taken form in his mind on the night before the fire. Now, in the quietness of the hospital room, it seemed even more insane than he'd thought possible.

He pictured Vince as he'd seen him for the last time, standing at the door with something like grief in his eyes. *"Men like you and me, we never change."*

Something in Jake Hardin rebelled against that. He had knocked around the world quite a bit and had picked up his scars, and he'd seen many a man go down to defeat and ruin. He'd always figured that was just the way the cards had fallen to people. But now...now he was starting to wonder if a person couldn't change his hand and make life what he wanted. Maybe all a person had to do was want it badly enough.

Now the memory of the futility in Vince's words rubbed against him, making him uneasy. He didn't want to believe it.

The sun was bright outside, outlining in yellow the blanket someone had pinned over the window. The sun would never shine on Vince Franklin again, that was true enough. But if Vince had lived, he *might* have found his way. At least, Jake tried hard to believe that.

Finally he took a deep breath, put the thoughts of Vince and the futility of his death away, and forced himself to think on his own danger. "Got to get away before that girl gets here," he muttered. "She'd see in one look that I'm not Vince, and when they find that out, the next question will be 'Who *is* he?' It won't take them long to figure out that Jake Hardin isn't buried in that grave at all."

He lay awake late into the night, and though his injuries pained him, he refused to take the morphine the nurse urged on him. For hours he thought of escape, but it was hopeless. He couldn't walk or see, and he had no money. He assumed that some cash was in Vince's wallet, but he didn't think it was much.

Finally as dawn came to illuminate the cover over his window, he forced himself to hammer out a plan of sorts. *I'll get the wallet and hire someone to come and take me away the day before the girl arrives. Maybe there'll be enough to get a place to stay and someone to take care of me until I can move around. Have to be a secret place, because they'll be looking for me as soon as Rachel comes and her brother's not here.* He lay there trying to find a better way but could not. Finally he decided. *Got to try it. Not much of a chance, but like Vince said, I have to play the hand I've been dealt.*

For the next five days Jake did everything he could to put some sort of action into his plan. One of the orderlies, a man named Asa Blunt, was not a promising candidate as an accomplice, but he was the only choice. Jake took pains to be friendly toward him and quickly discovered that Blunt was open to making money and was not overly scrupulous. Jake began by mentioning that he would much rather stay in New Orleans than go back to Virginia, adding, "I've got money enough to pay for a place, but I guess my sister would find me no matter where I tried to stay out of her way."

An avaricious light had gleamed in Blunt's muddy brown eyes, and the next day he waited until after dark, then came to Jake's room. "Been thinking 'bout what you said, 'bout a place to stay." He licked his lips, glanced cautiously around, then said, "I mebbe got a place, but it'd come high."

Jake nodded, saying, "I'd pay pretty well, but it's not going to be easy. I can't check out of this place. You'd just have to roll me out to a carriage after everyone was off duty."

"Sure, that ain't no problem. Now about the money. . ."

Jake finally agreed to a larcenous figure, but after the man left, Jake was not happy. "He'd turn me over for a reward in a minute—but at least it's a way out of here."

That was on Tuesday. Jake knew he had to be out soon, so he spent every day trying to strengthen himself by eating all he could—but there was nothing he could do about his injuries. His eyes were very sensitive to light, and he could hardly bear the pain when the dressing on his ankle was changed. Still, he had no choice.

Dr. Sealy came in on Friday evening, about six o'clock, and looked him over. Standing back he said, "Well, you're better, but not much. I'll be glad when you get home and can get total care."

"You've been mighty good to me, Doc," Jake said. "Couldn't ask for better treatment."

"Thanks, but it'll be better when you get home. Well, I'll see you in the morning. Good night."

Jake closed his eyes, weary of thinking. For almost an hour he tried to think of a better way, to no avail. Finally he dropped off into a fitful sleep that was more of a twilight affair in which he was neither awake nor completely asleep. He was aware after a time that someone had come into the room and was standing beside the bed. Rousing himself, he whispered, "Blunt?"

"No, not Blunt," the man said. At the sound of his voice, Jake came fully awake with a start that jerked his body. "Easy, Jake!" the voice said, and at the same time, the man shifted around so that the feeble light from the lamp fell on his face.

A shock ran along Jake's nerves, and he lay there for one instant, thinking he was dreaming. Then he said hoarsely, "Vince!"

"It's me, Jake. Just lie still and don't call out." Vince leaned over the bed, peering at Hardin's face. "Sorry to do it this way, but I couldn't figure out any other way of getting to you without anyone knowing."

"But. . .if you're alive, who was that in your room?" Jake demanded, his mind working fast. He sat up painfully with a little assistance from Vince. "They think he was *me*."

"Just a fellow I met in the hotel lobby," Vince said, glancing around. He saw a chair and pulled it to Jake's bedside. "Listen," he whispered. "Here's what happened. When I left your room, I was pretty sick inside. Here I thought everything was all set, and then you backed out on me. I decided to get drunk, so I left and told Tony I was checking out the next day. There was a fellow standing there, and I guess he'd been trying to get a room. Tony said to me, 'Okay if this fellow has your room?' I said it was and left to get drunk."

"But you've been gone for—"

"Sure, sure, I know, but just listen," Vince insisted. "I went down to the river and boarded a paddle wheeler. Started drinking, then got in on a card game. There was a woman there, too, and she kept egging me on to drink. Anyway, I passed out, and when I woke up, the blasted ship was moving upriver! I was broke, of course, done in by the woman, I guess. I got off at the next town and got a room. Had to wire my bank for money. But it was a bank holiday so I had to wait a day for that, and then I got a copy of the paper."

"And read about the fire?"

"That was the way of it." Vince smiled. "They made me out as quite a hero, going back into a building to save a fellow. Just the dumb sort of stunt a hairpin like you would try to pull off, Jake—and one that a fellow like me would never even think of!"

Jake suddenly felt relieved. "I'm glad you're alive, Vince." He paused, then added, "I've had some bad times, thinking about you."

The words embarrassed Vince, and he laughed shortly, still

keeping his voice down. "Yeah, well—I'm glad you're alive and kicking, too, Jake."

"Listen, you've got to get me out of here. Your sister will be here any day, maybe tomorrow."

"Get you out?" Vince sounded a little surprised. "Why, I didn't come to get you out!" He saw the look of stunned amazement on Jake's face, then slapped his thigh and made a face. "Well, of course! You would think that!"

"What else is there to think?"

Vince looked over his shoulder, then said quickly, "I've got it all figured out, Jake. We go through with a little of the plan we had. You go back to Richmond—but you don't shoot Duvall."

"Go back to Richmond! You're crazy!"

"No, I'm not. Just listen and don't argue. I talked with the doctor who's been treating you. Didn't tell him who I was and kept my hat pulled low, so he thinks I'm a friend of yours. Which I am, Jake." Vince paused, then added, "You're still going to get to that island we talked about!"

Jake shook his head, saying, "Vince, it won't work!"

"Yes, it will," Vince said, and confidence showed in his eyes. "It's better than the first plan. You're a sick man, Vince Franklin, very ill. So you go back to Virginia and you stay sick until it's time to collect the big money." He saw that Jake was staring at him, then spread his hands apart. "Don't you get it? Duvall can't shoot a helpless man!" He laughed softly, adding, "He's a man of *honor*! And that's the beauty of it all."

Jake shook his head. "It won't work. Your sister will know I'm not you the first time she looks at me."

"Not a chance! Last time she saw me without a beard, I was sixteen. And you've got those burns swelling up your face.

We look a lot alike to begin with, and you don't even look like *yourself*, Jake," Vince said.

Jake shook his head stubbornly. "It's hopeless, Vince. Even if they didn't know I wasn't you by looking, they'd find out soon enough. I don't sound like you, and I don't know what you know."

"Your voice is husky from breathing in all that smoke," Vince said, "and your mind's not working very well. Dr. Sealy told me that, and that's what he'll tell Rachel. You can't remember things. Sealy hopes it'll get better, but you can see to it that it doesn't. If you don't remember the name of a cousin, well, it's just that you haven't gotten rid of the effects of your injuries."

For the next twenty minutes the two spoke, Jake arguing and Vince supplying answers. Finally Vince said, "Jake, it's our only chance. All you have to do is go to my home, stick it out for a few months, then go away for a trip after you've met the conditions of the will."

Jake thought hard, but finally a slow smile touched his lips. "Well, I guess it's like you said. We have to play the hand we're dealt!"

Vince beamed at him. "I knew you'd do it, Jake, you old son of a gun! Now you let Rachel take you home. Here's an address. You can reach me there under the name of Bill Underhill. Don't write unless you have to, and if there's trouble, try to explain without giving anything away on paper. I'll write you from time to time, and if you *have* to know something, I'll try to get it across. I don't think anyone will be reading your mail, but we'll take no chances." A thought came to him, and he smiled. "You'll have to send me money, Jake. I can't draw any out, can I?"

Jake smiled back at him. "Maybe I'll let you dangle. You'd only spend it for frivolous affairs and foppish attire anyway."

"Sure! That's what money's for, isn't it?" Then Vince sobered and said slowly, "I guess I'm in your hands, Jake. If this doesn't work, I'm a gone goose—or even worse, a penniless goose! But you won't let me down." He rose and moved away but paused to add, "Don't say any more than you have to to Rachel. She's sharp, Jake."

"Do my best for you, Vince." And then the door closed softly, and Jake lay there, his mind busy with what lay ahead.

"Guess I'll have to tell Blunt I've changed my mind," he murmured, then tried to think ahead to the next few days. Finally he thought, *No use making a lot of plans. I'll just have to take it a day at a time.* But the hopelessness that had wrapped his mind was gone. He finally believed he had a chance.

"Well, Jake, old man, I like this hand a whale of a lot better than anything I've had lately! The law's not after me anymore, and maybe, just maybe, I can do something to help Vince get his wish." He wiggled his foot, grimaced at the pain, then nodded. "Go on, hurt all you please!" Then he thought of Rachel, of what Vince had said about her, and sobered. "I hope you don't like me much, Rachel. Because the more you dislike me, the farther away from me you'll stay!" The idea pleased him, and he lay back on the bed, his fertile mind spinning one idea after another.

In it all, Jake Hardin was strangely happy.

CHAPTER 5

TRIP TO NEW ORLEANS

*R*achel was standing in the kitchen making a caramel cake when the rider came into the yard. Wiping her hands on a damp cloth, she said, "Mother, Roy Delaughter just rode in."

Her mother looked up from the table where she was peeling potatoes, concern coming into her face. Getting to her feet, she came to look out the window. "I never feel good about getting a telegram," she murmured. "I don't think good news ever comes like that."

Rachel knew what her mother was thinking, for she herself had thought instantly of her father and her brother Grant, who had been sent with their company to the Shenandoah Valley. There had been little military action since Manassas, but both women knew that it only took one small action—and one single bullet—to bring tragedy. They watched as Delaughter hitched his horse then came at once down the walk. He had been in charge of the telegraph office in Richmond since it had first been established, and he was a good friend of the Franklins.

Rachel went to the door, calling out, "Over here in the kitchen, Mr. Delaughter." He looked up sharply, then hurried down the walk and came in. Pulling off his hat, he said, "Afternoon, Amy.

How are you, Rachel?" He was a small man, neat in dress and feature. "It's not about Brad or Grant," he said, reaching into his pocket and pulling out a sheet of paper.

A wave of relief washed through both women, and Delaughter saw it in their faces. He handed the telegram to Amy Franklin. She read it aloud for Rachel: "Mr. Vincent Franklin seriously injured in hotel fire. Condition not critical. Will need extended home care. Please advise. Dr. Winford Sealy, St. John's Hospital, New Orleans."

Rachel took the telegram, scanned it, then frowned. "He's not going to die, but he must be pretty bad."

"Be a hard trip for a sick man, all the way from New Orleans," Roy Delaughter commented. "Best thing would be by ship, wouldn't it?"

Amy thought hard, then said, "Brad says that the Yankees are going to blockade the coast. It might be hard to get there—or to get back, for that matter."

"Oh, they don't have enough ships for that, Amy!" Roy said at once. "But it wouldn't be a bad idea to do it quick as possible." He pondered a moment, then said, "There's a fast ship making for New Orleans in the morning—the *Jupiter*, with Captain Maylon Stuart in command. If you want, I can get passage for you when I get back to town."

"Yes, Roy, please do that. And see if you can find out about a return passage."

"Sure, Amy. Anything else I can do, just let me know."

"Thank you, Roy. Now sit down and have something to eat before you go back." She and Rachel fixed the man a good lunch, then went to the study to talk. "I wish Brad were here," Amy said with a worried look. "I hate to send Les, though I'm sure he'd like to go. He's the only man on the place right now, and he's needed here. I'll have to go, Rachel."

"No, you can't leave, Mother," Rachel said firmly. "You're not over the flu yet. I'll go get him."

Amy gave her daughter a doubtful look; then her brow cleared. Though Rachel was only nineteen, Amy knew without a doubt that this daughter of hers was fully capable of such a mission. "Well, I think it'd be best if you did go, Rachel. We'll pack the middle-sized trunk. It's a long voyage, and you'll have to bring back with you whatever medicals Vince will need."

Rachel nodded, and the two women at once began preparing for the trip. Not knowing the exact departure time of the *Jupiter*, Rachel decided to go to Richmond at once. "I'll take a room for the night," she explained to her mother. "The ship may leave at dawn, and I don't want to miss it."

When Rachel was in the buggy with Les beside her, Amy asked, "Are you sure you have enough money? It's terribly expensive traveling so far."

"I have plenty, Mother." She leaned down, kissed her mother, and added, "Don't worry about me. Just pray for traveling safety."

"Yes, I will. Good-bye, dear!"

Les whipped up the horses; he knew only one speed of travel, and that was as fast as the horses could go. He was disappointed because he was not making the trip, but being good-natured he gave over his protests. The horses lined out at a fast gallop, and Rachel said, "For goodness' sakes, Les, slow down! You'll wear the horses out!"

"Aw, this ain't really fast," Les protested, but pulled the team down to a brisk trot. He looked at her with envy, saying, "Sure wish I could go."

"Mother needs you here, Les. You're the man of the place

now." Her words brought a flush to his fair cheeks, and she added, "I'll bring you a present from New Orleans. What'll it be?"

"A picture of some of them fancy Creole gals!"

"Not likely, you scamp!"

"Well, some fancy boots—or maybe a pistol."

"Don't know your size in either," Rachel teased him. "Better let me surprise you." They rode along talking in a lively fashion, but when they got to Richmond and were on their way to the hotel, Rachel grew serious. "I don't relish this trip, Les. You know how Vince is. He's bad enough when he's well."

"Well, if he's hurt bad, he shouldn't be able to stir up too much meanness," Les answered.

"He'll be as unpleasant as he can be, I know that!" Rachel said, frowning. Then she looked up and said, "There's the hotel. You can dump me off and get back to the house."

Les carried her trunk inside and waited until she had found out from the clerk the departure time of the *Jupiter*. Then the brother and sister walked back to the buggy.

"Be careful, sister," Les said and awkwardly leaned forward and kissed her cheek. "Don't let the Yankees get you."

"I'll shoot them with the pistol I'm going to get for your present," she said with a smile, then patted his arm. "Take care of things until I get back, Les. Don't let Mother work too hard." He grinned at her, then vaulted into the buggy. She watched as he left, then walked back into the hotel.

She knew that the *Jupiter* left at six the next morning, but feeling too restless to go to bed right away, Rachel walked around the city for an hour. At six o'clock she went to supper and was surprised to see Leighton Semmes sitting at one of the tables. He looked very handsome in his ash-gray uniform. He stood at once when she came into the room, saying, "Rachel!

I never thought to see you here! Come and bring some light into this lonely man's life."

She was glad to see him, and they had a pleasant meal. Semmes listened as she told him of her mission, as always enjoying the opportunity to watch her. He was a connoisseur of feminine beauty, and in a part of the world noted for beautiful, graceful women, Rachel Franklin held his attention. Quite honestly, this was a puzzle to him; he was a man who either got his own way from the women he pursued or else moved along to easier prey. He had done neither with Rachel.

Now he leaned back, peering at her through the aromatic smoke of his cigar, suddenly amused at himself. *Why do I put up with her rebuffs?* he wondered. *She's a good-looking woman, but there are plenty of those available.* He studied her carefully as she moved her hands from time to time in quick motions. She wore a simple blue dress with a white lace top, and her turquoise earrings reflected the blue-green of her eyes. Her lips were a little too full for true beauty, but not for drawing a man's glance. The smooth sweep of her jaw and the elegant joining of her neck into her shoulders were so strong as to be almost masculine. The deep cleft in her chin added to that impression of strength, yet there was no denying the dainty femininity of her trim figure.

Semmes moved restlessly in his seat and took a sip of his wine. An idea rose in him, and he said idly, "It's a long trip all the way to New Orleans, Rachel. Lots of pretty aggressive men on those ships. I think I can get a leave. Maybe I'd better go along to look after you."

Rachel's eyes suddenly gleamed with mirth, and her lips turned up in a smile, followed by a sudden delighted laugh. "That'd be like putting the fox to watch the chickens, Leighton!"

The thought amused her greatly, for she knew him very well indeed, but when she saw the expression on his face, she put out her hand and covered one of his. "I didn't mean to hurt your feelings, but you don't know how funny you looked, all innocent and pious!"

Leighton suddenly laughed out loud, his eyes crinkling at the corners and his mobile lips turned up. "I don't know why I keep hanging around you, Rachel!" Shaking his head, he took her hand and held it captive. "Well, you know me pretty well, I suppose. Do you think you'll ever change your opinion of me?"

Rachel considered him thoughtfully, still smiling a little. There always was a strange mixture in her of humor and seriousness, and now the two struggled. Finally she said, "You're not a tame man, Leighton. That's the one thing I couldn't stand."

Her words surprised him greatly. "That's the most revealing thing you've ever said to me, Rachel."

She gave him a half-embarrassed look, for the thought had slipped out—but now that it was spoken, she wanted to express the part of her that had given birth to it. "Many marriages seem to be so dull, don't they, Leighton? I've watched it since I was a little girl. A marriage is a woman's whole life. A man can do a hundred things. Marriage to most men is usually something they turn to when their real work is done." A look of rebellion touched her bright eyes, and her lips thinned as she shook her head. "It may sound strange, but I believe there should be more to marriage than that!"

Semmes was tremendously interested. He leaned forward, his penetrating eyes on her face. "Do you really think a marriage can be more? I've seen what you're talking about, the way many marriages fall into a habit and convenience. I'm sure they didn't start out that way. What do you think makes men and women lose that magic they feel at first?"

"Women are to blame," Rachel said instantly, then smiled at the expression of surprise that her statement drew. "They grow careless. It's as if they're saying, 'I've got him. Now I don't have to be anything except a dutiful wife.'"

"You don't think wives ought to be dutiful?"

"Wives are to obey their husbands, yes—the Bible says so. But did you know, Leighton, that the Bible *doesn't* say that wives are to love their husbands?"

"No, I didn't know that. Sounds like a mistake to me."

Rachel gave him an arch look but went on. "The Bible does say that *men* are to love their wives. Women to obey, men to love. And it's easier to obey than it is to love, did you know that?"

Semmes considered her, then shook his head. "I don't see that."

"Why, anyone can obey," Rachel said at once. "But you can't *command* love. Sometimes love doesn't even exist in a marriage, so it's no wonder that two people become more like business partners than lovers. But I will tell you this, Leighton, I will never marry—not unless I am absolutely certain of two things. One, that I love the man enough to give everything to him."

"And the second?"

"Why, that he loves me the same way." Rachel gave a short laugh, then rose to her feet. "How did I ever get to talking like this? Come walk me to my hotel, Mr. Semmes."

He paid the bill, and the two of them walked slowly along the street, speaking lightly of Rachel's upcoming journey. When they got to her hotel, he said, "Let's sit out on the balcony awhile. It's early yet."

"Just for a little while," she agreed, and the two of them

went out on the balcony of the second floor. They were alone, and for an hour they sat there talking until Rachel finally rose. "I have to be up early."

Semmes stood and came close to her. A sickle moon hung in the sky, turned butter yellow by a haze in the air. The stars were great wooly crystal masses overhead, and the large magnolia tree that rose beside them gave off a sweet savor.

Rachel stood there quietly, watching Semmes carefully. She knew that he was going to kiss her. She did not turn away, as he half expected; instead, when he put his arms around her, she lifted her face. And when his lips fell on hers, she deliberately leaned forward, meeting him halfway.

The sweetness of her lips and the feel of her as she leaned against him stirred Semmes tremendously. He pulled her closer, his desires beginning to clamor. Rachel was different from any woman he'd known; he sensed that the same emotions that moved him were in Rachel, yet she seemed strangely removed from him.

After a moment, she slid her lips away, and he released her. "Good night, Leighton," she said quietly. But she was shaken. Leighton's kiss had touched something deep within her, some part that she kept buried—and for a moment, as Semmes had held her, she had felt her control slip. That was disturbing enough.

What was even more disturbing was that Rachel was aware that Leighton knew it.

Even so, he made no effort to restrain her as she moved away, for something had come to him—a sudden knowledge that this woman could not be taken by storm. He wanted to reach out and take hold of her again, but instead he said, "Good night, Rachel. Have a good journey." Then he paused. "You've let me see something different tonight. I didn't know a woman could be so independent." Despite himself, he hungered for some modicum of commitment from her and asked again, "Do you think you could ever change your judgment of me?"

Rachel said, "You've been a woman chaser for most of your life, Leighton. But if you and I ever fell in love, I'd make sure you'd find something better at home than you could find anywhere else."

Her bluntness astonished him, and he laughed ruefully. "By heaven, I believe you would, Rachel! A man would never get tired of you as his wife."

"You and I are not placid people, Leighton," she said, looking at him with a strange smile on her lips. "No, we'd either have heaven together—or we'd explode. But we wouldn't be bored!"

Then she was gone. With a shake of his head, Semmes went to have a drink at the saloon. But he could not shake a restlessness, an awareness that she had stirred him in a way no other woman ever had.

❧

As Rachel tipped the carriage driver and followed the tiled walk toward the entrance to St. John's Hospital, she fought an impulse to turn around and run away. The trip from Richmond had been swift, and she had been thinking of Vince steadily. Now it seemed to her that there were few tasks in the world that appealed to her less than being a nurse to her half brother. But knowing that she had no choice, she squared her shoulders and entered the front door.

A small man dressed in white pants and shirt looked up from the desk that sat to the right of the large reception room. Getting to his feet, he asked, "Yes, miss?"

"My name is Rachel Franklin. I'm here to pick up one of your patients," Rachel said. "Mr. Vincent Franklin."

"Oh yes. Dr. Sealy left word that he wants to talk with you. Come along and I'll take you to his office."

"Thank you." Rachel followed the man down a long hall, and she could see, through the open doors, patients in the rooms off to each side. At the end of the hall, the orderly knocked on a door. "Dr. Sealy? Miss Franklin is here to get her brother."

The door opened, and a thin man with sparse graying hair and wearing a white suit looked out. "Thank you, Evans. Come in, Miss Franklin." He stepped aside and motioned her to a chair, the only one in the room except the one behind his desk. He waited until she was seated, then settled behind the desk. "You made a quick trip, Miss Franklin. Any trouble with the Federal navy?"

"Two days ago we were sighted by one of their ships, but the *Jupiter* was so much faster that she just ran away."

"That's good. Won't be that way for long, I'm thinking. They'll close in as soon as they build their navy. Well now, how about the voyage back?"

"The *Jupiter* is loading today and tomorrow and will leave the day after that. She'll go back to Richmond with a load of supplies. I've got a stateroom for myself and my brother."

"Good. I think he needs to be taken home right away."

Rachel asked, "How badly is he hurt, Doctor?" She listened carefully as Sealy outlined the injuries, then commented, "So it's mostly just going to take time and good nursing?"

"Exactly right, Miss Franklin," Sealy confirmed, nodding. "Now just two things. First, his physical condition. He doesn't look too good thanks to some rather serious burns on his forehead. Also, he took in so much smoke that it damaged his throat, so we haven't been able to get him to eat much. Mostly liquids and soft foods. When you first see him, don't let him see how you feel if you get a shock. He's not as bad off as he appears, though his eyes need care. Mostly you need to keep him from bright light and apply the ointment—I'll give that to you—twice a day. The burns on his right hand will heal quickly, I hope. Put the dressings on once a day and, as soon as your physician at home thinks it wise, leave the hand open to the air and light. The ankle will be painful for at least a month or more, but only time will help."

"I'll see to him, Doctor."

"Yes...well, the other thing isn't quite so easy. He had quite a shock, you understand, and he's not over it yet."

Rachel blinked, then asked directly, "Is his mind affected?"

"I don't like to put it like that," Sealy said quickly. He rubbed his chin, trying to put the thing to her well. "It's almost as if his thinking processes were slowed down. You'll notice that he doesn't respond to questions quickly. Or perhaps that's a way of his?"

"No, Vince has always been very quick with words."

"Well, I don't think it's a permanent thing, but he can't seem to remember very well. Again, I think he just needs rest, but you must be patient with him if he forgets some things."

"I'll do my best. But I assume he won't be seeing too many people at first. Just the family, and I'll tell them what you've said."

"Fine! Now I'm sure you want to see him. I'll take you to his room; then I'll leave you. I wish you'd watch the nurses change the dressings, things like that. We'll take him to the ship in our ambulance day after tomorrow." He rose and left the room, Rachel walking beside him. "This is his room. It'll be darkened, so you'll have to let your eyes get accustomed to that."

Rachel entered the room, and Dr. Sealy said, "Well, Mr. Franklin, your sister is here to take you home. Think you feel up to a sea voyage?"

"Yes, Dr. Sealy." The voice was husky and halting. Rachel would not have recognized it as Vincent's.

"I'll just leave you two alone," Sealy said. When he left, Rachel moved closer to the man in the bed. One lamp burned on a table, and some dim illumination filtered through from the covering over the window. Her eyes were not adjusted to the murky room, and she stopped when she was a few feet away.

"How do you feel?"

"Pretty well, Rachel. Better than when I first came here."

"Does your throat hurt?" she asked, squinting at him. "You sound so hoarse."

"Still hurts, but not like it did. I couldn't even croak when I first got here."

"Father would have come, or Grant, but the Grays were sent to reinforce Jackson in the Valley." She saw a chair and pulled it next to the bed and sat down. "Dr. Sealy's been telling me about your injuries. He's very hopeful."

"Good man."

Rachel leaned forward and, by the light of the lamp, got her first clear view of the injured man. She let nothing show in her face, but a shock ran through her. She would never have known Vince! She was not prepared for the sight of him without a beard; she hadn't seen him clean-shaven since she was very young. What's more, his face was hollow, much thinner than she had expected, and the raw burns on his forehead were painful just to look at. His hair, which still showed signs of having been singed, was cut short, and he was wearing a pair of smoked glasses so that she couldn't see his eyes at all.

"You look awful," she said frankly. "I hope you don't feel as bad as you look!"

That seemed to amuse him, for his lips turned up and he said in a husky tone, "Just like you to cheer a fellow up, Rachel!" Then he shook his head, adding, "It could have been worse."

"Yes, I suppose so. Well, we'll leave day after tomorrow. I'll get the nurses to teach me how to take care of you."

He said nothing, and she thought, *Just like him. I come all the way around the country to help him and he can't even grunt a thank-you!*

Rachel sat there in the dimly lit room, saying little. Sometimes he would ask a question, but not often. He dropped off to sleep, and Rachel sat there beside him wishing that she had more of a heart for Vince. She knew she should care more, that that was what the Lord would want of her—but the years had not given her the love for Vince that she had for Grant and Les.

After a moment, she squared her shoulders. If she could not love him, she would at least do her duty. *I'll get him home and do what I can to care for him. Then when he is well, he can shift for himself,* was her final thought as she rose and left the room.

She didn't like the feelings she had and wished that they were milder, gentler, more loving. But surely even God couldn't expect her to force herself to love a man who'd spent his entire life making himself despicable.

PART TWO

The Impostor

❧

CHAPTER 6

MAN WITHOUT A STAR

Rachel, holding a straight razor in one hand, had just touched the cold steel to Jake's face. He flinched, and she lifted the blade, saying firmly, "Hold still!" Reaching out, she placed her left hand on top of his head, then drew the razor through the thick foam on his right cheek, ignoring the raspy sound it made as it plowed through his whiskers.

"Be careful with that thing," Jake pleaded, then asked, "Did you ever shave anyone before?"

Rachel, biting her lower lip with concentration, did not answer until she made another clean strip appear on Jake's cheek. Wiping the blade on a towel she'd draped over his shoulder, she began work on the other cheek. Only when it was finished did she say, "No. Now put your head back."

As she gripped the crown of his head and forced his head back, Jake decided it was no time for a debate—not with the edge of the blade moving over the taut flesh of his throat. He sat up in the bed, enduring her effort, thinking that Rachel Franklin was not very feminine, at least in her manners.

She had marched into his room at dawn with a pitcher of hot water, shaving equipment, and a determined look on her face. "Sit up," she had greeted him. "I'm going to get you cleaned up." He had wrestled himself to a sitting position, and she had practically ripped the white cotton gown from him, ignoring his startled protests. He kept the sheet pulled up as high as possible, but she had washed his upper body without a flicker in her blue-green eyes.

She might as well be washing a dish for all the emotion she shows, Jake had thought, then had realized that her cold attitude was what he could expect. She had cleaned his face carefully, actually causing him much less pain than any of the orderlies who had performed the same service, then had picked up a mug and begun working up a lather with a brush. Without a word, she had lathered his face and begun shaving him.

Still, despite her brusque and cold manner, there was nothing mannish about her appearance. Her simply cut tan dress with a line of white lace at the bodice and sleeves complemented her trimly rounded figure. As she shaved him, her face was only inches away from Jake's, and he could not help admiring the clean sweep of her jaw and the silky texture of her skin. Her eyes were fixed on the progress of the razor, so he could study her without fear of being noticed, and he was somehow surprised to see that she was so pretty. He had expected less, for some reason. As she held his head firmly and ran the razor over his face, he realized that there was an element in Rachel Franklin that most women lacked—at least, most of the women he had known.

It was not, he decided, that she was pretty, even on the verge of true beauty. It was clear that she was physically attractive; it would be difficult to ignore the soft roundness of her form or the well-shaped eyes and generous mouth. But there was something more, a reserve in her eyes, and the shadow of strength, intensity, and control that intrigued him. That control was evidenced by the firm line of her lips and the deliberate light of her eyes. She was, he decided, possessed of a great degree of vitality and imagination—which he guessed were also held under careful restraint. As she moved the razor over his upper lip, he observed a hint of her will—or her pride—in the corners of her eyes and lips.

She finished the shave without speaking, carefully removed the lather with the damp cloth, then stepped back to study him. Still she didn't speak, and Jake said, "A good job, better than most barbers. Can't believe you've never shaved anyone."

"I'm going to change the bandage on your arm," she said, ignoring his remark. There was a cold efficiency in her manner, but she did a good job of removing the old bandage, which was the worst part of the job. She had a light touch yet moved firmly as she cleaned the burn, applied the ointment that Dr. Sealy had furnished, then bound the arm up in fresh bandages, saying, "In a week or two, it'll be better to leave the bandages off." She looked at his ankle, pushing at the swollen flesh, then remarked, "Going to take some time before you can get around on this."

"Not too long, I hope." He took the fresh gown she handed him, saying, "Rough on you, having to take care of a sick man."

"No worse than when one of the horses gets injured," she remarked without a change of expression. While he put on the gown, she picked up the shaving equipment and began to clean it. "We'll go down to the ship late this afternoon. The captain said he wants to leave after dark to avoid the blockade ships of the navy."

She left the room, and Jake stared after her. "Not much chance of Miss Rachel finding out I'm not who she thinks," he muttered. "She sure does despise you, Vince, old boy!" It was a relief to him, for he had envisioned having to try to carry on long talks with her, which would be dangerous.

After the noon meal, Dr. Sealy came by to check him, accompanied by Rachel. "You're looking better than I hoped when they brought you in," he said, standing over Jake. "You're a lucky man. If you'd been a few feet closer, they tell me, you'd have been crushed by that building."

"Wasn't my time to go," Jake said with a shrug.

"Well, you mind your sister," Sealy said. "Biggest problem I have with patients like you comes from their own foolishness. Don't try to get up too soon. Do what your nurse tells you."

"Guess I don't have much choice, tied to this chair." Jake put out his hand and, when Sealy took it, said, "I appreciate what you've done for me, Doctor."

"Well, good-bye, then, Vince. Take care of yourself."

As soon as the doctor left, Rachel began putting Vince's things into a small bag. There wasn't much, for the fire had destroyed all of Vince's clothing and personal things. "I got you some extra gowns—and plenty of underwear," she said. "You won't need much, and you've got all those clothes at home that you just recently bought."

"Be glad to put some pants on!"

"Well, don't get too glad, because you won't be wearing any for a while," she said calmly. "I've got to get a few things. Anything you want to take on the boat? Whiskey or some special food?"

"No. Guess not."

She was surprised. Turning to stare at him, she said, "That's the first time you ever turned down liquor as far as I can remember." She frowned and wondered for a moment what Vince was up to. Then she brushed her hair back from her forehead and left, saying only, "All right. We'll go to the *Jupiter* about four."

Jake was restless until she returned. Being bound to the care of others was galling, but he forced himself to remain calm. Blunt followed her into the room, and when it was time to get Jake into the wheelchair, he deliberately slammed him down, drawing a sharp gasp of pain from the injured man.

Rachel had been packing, but she had not missed the scene. Anger flared in her eyes, and she moved across the room to give the orderly an abrupt shove that set him back on his heels. "You clumsy ox!" she burst out. "Get out of here!" Blunt glared at her until she said, "Maybe you'd rather I take this up with Dr. Sealy." Then he scurried out of the room, his face reddened with frustrated anger.

Jake watched with interest as Rachel paused, noting that she was able to regain her composure only after a brief struggle. *She's got a hair-trigger temper—if she gets that mad over somebody she doesn't like, I'd like to see what she'd do if somebody hurt a person she really cared for.*

Something of his thought must have been visible in his face, for Rachel, giving him a sharp glance, flushed slightly. "I hate to see sloppy work," she said, then put the small case in his lap. "Time to go. Put your glasses on."

She waited until he took the smoked glasses out of the single pocket in his loose white shirt and settled them in place. "We're taking the chair with us," she said as they left the room, turning down the hall toward the front of the building. When they passed out into the light, despite the dark glasses, Jake was forced to shut his eyes against the glare of the sun. The wheels grated on the walk; then the chair was stopped, and Rachel said, "You'll have to give him some help."

"Yes, ma'am." Strong hands were placed under Jake's armpits, and he came out of the chair. Opening his eyes to slits, he got a close view of a black face; then he was suddenly lifted from the ground as easily as if he were a baby. "Jest set right down," a deep voice instructed as he was placed on a padded leather seat. "Now, miss, you get in and I'll load your gear."

"The chair goes, too," Rachel said. She stepped into the coach, and soon the driver was back in the seat. "The *Jupiter*, is it, miss?" Being assured, he sent the team down the street at an easy pace.

When they got to the dock, Jake's eyes had adjusted somewhat and he could see the outline of the ship waiting at the wharf. She was, he noted, a clipper-hulled vessel with three masts, which could be hung with canvas in a following wind. The engines sent their power through a big walking beam amidships to huge side paddles. As they pulled up, the driver leaped down, unloaded the chair, then helped Jake into it. "Thanks," Jake said. "Wish you could be on the other end to help me off."

The black man grinned but only shook his head. "You want me to wheel him on, miss?"

"No, I'll do that, but please put all our luggage aboard." Stepping behind the chair, she pushed Jake down to the gangplank, where a purser in a white coat was standing.

"*I'll* do that, miss. My name is Smythe," the purser offered, and soon Jake was in the cabin. It was plain and small—no larger than eight feet by ten feet—with two bunks, some built-in closets, and a small chair. Rachel took some money from her purse and handed it to the black driver, who grinned at her broadly then was gone. Smythe said, "Supper at six, Miss Franklin. Captain Stuart would like for you and your brother to join him. Shall I come down and help Mr. Franklin to the dining room?"

"No, thank you," Rachel said. "I can manage."

As the door closed, Jake looked around, then said, "Close quarters. This blasted chair of mine takes up all the room."

"You won't be running around much," Rachel said briefly, then began to unpack their clothes. There was nothing for Jake to do but watch. As soon as she had everything put away, she took a small package from her purse and looked around the room. A bronze lamp was fixed to the wall by a bracket attached on the outer bulkhead, exactly in the center of the wall. She took what seemed to be a hoop from the packet, but it proved to be a roll of wire. She fastened one end of it to the lamp bracket, then unwound it and, finding another bracket on the inside wall just to the left of the door, secured the free end to that. As she returned to one of the bunks where she'd placed the packet, she noticed Jake watching her.

"It's already quite dark in here. I'll cover the windows with some cloth tomorrow. That way you won't have to wear the glasses at all."

"That will be better," he commented, then asked, "What's the wire for?"

"Privacy," she answered briefly, then took some pins from the small package and began fastening them to the side of what seemed to be a piece of very lightweight canvas. When they were in place, she stood and began slipping them over the taut wire. When the last one was in place, she tested the makeshift screen by pulling at one end. The cloth slid along the wire between the two beds, which were on opposite ends of the small cabin. Satisfied, she pulled the curtain back until it bunched against the wall.

"You're resourceful," Jake conceded. "But wouldn't it be easier to have two cabins?"

Rachel looked at him coldly. "You may have money to waste, Vince. We don't. Cash is scarce now and it's going to get more so. Do you want to lie down?"

"No." He hesitated, then asked with a sarcastic tone, "Would it be too much trouble to push me around the deck?"

Rachel's face flushed for a moment; then she shook her head. "It's almost time for dinner. Let me change; then I guess we can go around the deck a few times." Pulling the curtain, she changed her dress, then emerged and pushed him out of the cabin. For the next half hour she maneuvered him around the deck. There were few passengers there—most had gone to the dining room early—but the loading of the ship was still going on, with sailors wrestling the last of the cargo into the hold. Some of their language was fairly raw, but Jake saw that Rachel was able to ignore it. She was, he considered, the sort of person who would refrain from complaining about things that she could not help. Finally she said, "Let's go to the dining room."

She pushed him into a large room of mahogany, ivory paint, and crystal lamps. Still, though the design of luxury remained and the paint was fresh and the glasswork glittered, the original elegance had quietly vanished with the ship's youth. The same purser who had taken them to their cabin saw them enter. He came across the room to say, "Let me help you, Miss Franklin."

"Thank you, Smythe," Rachel murmured and stepped back to let the man move the wheelchair to the table. Captain Stuart and the other gentlemen at the table rose gallantly. The captain was a short man and thick as a stump. He had a pair of icy blue eyes, but he said warmly, "Miss Franklin, we're waiting for you. I take it this is your brother?"

"Yes, Captain." Rachel nodded and slipped into her seat while the captain named the guests around the table for the newcomers. Afterward Jake sat silently, listening to the talk that flowed around the table, noting how Rachel drew the attention of the men. She wore a dark blue dress that fit snugly, and her neck and shoulders were coral against the shining of the lamps. The only jewelry she wore was a pair of sapphire earrings, their deep blue accenting her eyes.

The talk was of the war, or the effects of it. One of the men, a tall man named Prince with a startling crop of dundreary whiskers, wore the uniform of a Confederate major. He had been at Manassas and, at the request of Captain Stuart, gave an account of what his regiment had done there. One of the ladies at the end of the table said, "I suppose it will take another battle or two to convince the Yankees to stay where they belong, Major Prince?"

"Well—it'll be a little more difficult than that, Mrs. Lowery," Major Prince said. A thought struck him and his lips curved in a smile. "Did you hear about General Anderson? Well, after Fort Sumter fell, he became quite a hero in the North. Don't understand why, when all he did was surrender! But in any case, he had a nervous breakdown and had to be replaced." He laughed softly, adding, "His replacement was General William T. Sherman, and the joke is that Sherman's had a nervous breakdown of his own. But you know that new fellow Grant? The one who's in charge in the West? Well, he's had a drinking problem, and Sherman said, 'Grant stood by me when I was crazy, so I'll stand by him when he's drunk!'"

A laugh went around the table, and one of the men asked, "Is that who we've got coming against us, Major? Drunks and crazy men?"

Prince shook his head, seemingly reluctant to speak, but finally he said slowly, "Lincoln is listening to General Scott. He's old and too fat to ride a horse, but he's got the best military mind in the country, I do think. Scott wants to get control of the Mississippi and blockade the coast. If that happens, there will be no way we can win."

"They don't have enough ships for that, Major," Captain Stuart commented with a shrug.

"No, but they have the shipyards to build them, Captain. And they've got the ironworks, the factories, and the know-how to arm them. Do you know we have only one major ironworks in the South, the Tredgar Ironworks in Richmond?"

"We'll buy ships from England!"

"Not if the coast is blockaded," Prince replied. "If we're going to win, we'd better win in a hurry."

"I think, sir, our only hope is to be recognized by England." The speaker was a tall man with a crown of silver hair. "If we kill enough Yankees in a hurry, the North will refuse to fight. There's already a strong antiwar party there, and if we won the next two or three battles, I think Lincoln would be forced to declare a peace."

"That is indeed our only chance, sir," Major Prince said, nodding. "Without that, we will fight gallantly and to the last, but in the end we will be worn down by the North's industrial power and sheer weight of numbers."

Several men disagreed with Prince, and the talk grew lively. The food was good, but Jake was humiliated when Rachel had to cut up his meat, a fine steak. "Feel like a blasted baby!" he muttered to her, though she seemed to ignore him. He was glad when she finally said, "Captain Stuart, thank you for your invitation. I must get my brother to bed now."

The men rose, and Smythe came to take Jake out. When they were outside, Rachel said, "Thank you, Smythe. I can manage now."

"Yes, Miss Franklin. Let me know if you need anything."

The air was cool and fresh after the stale air of the dining room, and Rachel pushed the chair past the churning paddles, coming to the fantail. The night was cloudy, and after a while, Jake said, "Any stars out, Rachel? I still can't see all that clearly."

She gazed at the sky, then said, "No, I don't see any stars."

"Good thing we're not in the middle of the ocean."

Rachel looked up at the dark skies, shook her hair loose, then said, "I wish I knew more about the stars, but they weren't included in my education."

The throbbing of the engines was like the beating of a mighty heart, and as the ship drove into the darkness, Jake said finally, "I always envied sailors, knowing how to find their way by the stars." Then he looked up and added, "But you said there's no stars out now. I guess the fellow who's lost at sea could be a man without a star."

Rachel glanced down at him, saying, "That's a poetic way of putting it, Vince—a man without a star." She reached her hand up as if to touch one of the dark clouds that was racing along overhead, then withdrew it, saying, "That's a sad thought. Every man and every woman ought to have a star, something that doesn't move so they can tell where they are."

Jake listened to the sound of the wind as it whipped over the deck, then turned to see the pilothouse, which emitted only a faint pale and golden glow, and laughed shortly. "Guess that's what I am, Rachel—a man without a star."

She looked at him, a curious light in her eyes. "That's a

strange thing for you to say. You've always seemed to know exactly what you wanted."

Suddenly Jake knew he was in danger, for she was studying him carefully. He realized that he'd spoken out of his own feelings, not out of the role he was playing—and what he had said had been out of character. Vince was not a man for philosophical thought. He looked at her and smiled coldly. "Never realized you were one to be fooled by pretty talk, Rachel. If that's all it takes to change your mind about a man—"

Rachel cut him off by grabbing his chair and pushing it toward the cabin. Her voice was tight with anger as she spoke. "You're right, Vince. I should know better than to listen to anything you say." She took him to the cabin and helped him out of the chair onto the bunk. He was wearing only underwear and the long shirt, and was embarrassed as he struggled to get his leg onto the bed. Reaching down, Rachel took careful hold of it, lifted it to the bed, then pulled a sheet up over him. "Are you hurting much?" she asked, though he doubted she cared.

"Not too bad."

She studied him, then made an abrupt decision. "You'd better have something for the pain. I'll fix you a toddy." He lay there as she took the small medicine box from the drawer, poured some whiskey from a small bottle into a glass, then added some liquid from a vial. He took it and drank it down; then she said, "Call if you need something."

He grunted in response.

She moved quickly, drawing the curtain, then got undressed and put on a gown. The lamp threw off enough light for her to see, so she sat on the bunk reading a chapter of the Bible, then put it down and went to bed. She lay there listening to the man's heavy breathing as it grew slow and rhythmic.

Finally fatigue caught up with her, too.

The pounding of the engines beat steadily, and her eyelids grew heavier. In spite of herself, the last thing she thought of before she fell asleep was what Vince had said: *"Guess that's what I am, Rachel—a man without a star."*

CHAPTER 7

STORM AT SEA

The *Jupiter* darted around the Florida Keys, sighting only one Federal ship, which she easily outran. The weather was favorable, but after a quick stop at Savannah, Captain Stuart told his first mate, Alvin Sears, "We'd better skip Charleston, Sears. I don't like the feel of this weather."

Sears, a saturnine individual with a full black beard and the shoulders of a wrestler, agreed. "Be better, I think, Captain." He studied the horizon, his eyes drawn to slits, then added, "That sky reminds me of a woman. All nice and soft and pretty. But she's likely to change 'fore we can blink, and then we'll feel her claws."

"Not a great admirer of the ladies, are you?"

"Had my hide ripped too often," Sears grunted. "And I got a feeling about that sky. We'd best make the fastest run we can, or you'll see the canvas ripped to shreds."

Sears would later have reason to call Captain Stuart's attention to the accuracy of his prophecy, for as they rounded Cape Hatteras, the sun disappeared and the seas began to rise. Soon the waves were so high that the passengers staring through the portholes could see the ripped-up surface of the ocean directly in front of their eyes.

Rachel and Jake became aware of the seriousness of the matter as she pushed him around the deck toward the stern and the *Jupiter* took a trough coming around, falling into a deep gully between two waves. The ship went into the gully heavily and lay solidly there as a great ridge of water fell into her and buried her. For much too long a moment, Rachel and Jake both felt the inertness of the ship. Then the sea came aboard a second time and the well deck filled, and the port wing of the hurricane deck touched the lifting waves. Rachel grabbed a chair, bracing herself, while Jake sat there clenching the armrest of his chair with his good hand.

In the wheelhouse, Captain Stuart held the wheel of the *Jupiter* as she plunged and bucked like a half-wild horse. He waited until the ship rose and slowly swung into the seas. He peered through the misty foam and cupped his ears to catch the possible sound of surf breaking. He knew this coast too well—it was a graveyard filled with the bones of ships and men scattered on some rocky point or sucked into a remote reach of sand.

"Take in all sail, Mr. Sears," he commanded, then called down to the engine room, "Give me all you've got, Carl!"

Sears stared at the wild seas, then at the captain. "I told you she was a hussy," he muttered, then left the wheelhouse. When he got to the stern, he saw a woman pushing a man in a wheelchair and cursed under his breath. "Get below! Get below!" he bellowed, shaking his head in disgust as the woman hurriedly moved along the tilting deck and disappeared through one of the doorways. "Woman's got no sense! Acts like we're on a ferryboat!" Then he began yelling commands to the crew, who scurried aloft to take in all the canvas.

Rachel had to brace herself to keep the wheelchair from getting away from her, but finally she made it to the door of their cabin. It was a struggle to open the door while holding on to Jake's chair, but she managed it.

With a sigh she said, "Better get out of this chair and into the bunk."

Jake used his left hand and pulled himself free from the chair to stand on one leg as she moved the chair back. A sudden lurch caught him off balance, and he fell across the edge of the bunk, striking his bad leg and sending a flash of pain along his nerves. As he rolled over onto the bunk, Rachel stooped and lifted his leg. Placing it carefully down, she glanced at his face but said only, "If this gets worse, I'll have to tie you in."

"If it gets worse, the ship will go down," he answered tightly. His leg was throbbing like a sore tooth, but he ignored it. "This ship can't take much of this!"

Rachel stared at him, then asked, "Is the *Jupiter* a bad ship?"

"No, but she's made for rivers, not oceans. If this keeps up, she could break in two." Jake had been on riverboats for some time and knew their limitations. As the boat seemed to hesitate, he asked, "Feel that? The paddles came out of the water—they were beating the air. That means that the captain can't get much speed out of her. Not much hope of outrunning this thing."

Rachel was thrown forward suddenly as the ship rolled, and she saved herself only by raising her hands as they slammed against the bulkhead. She stood there, waiting for what seemed like a long time, until the ship recovered. Then she cautiously moved to sit down on her bunk. There was no sign of panic on her face, Jake noted—only an expression of heightened alertness. She said nothing, as did he. The roar of the wild water, which was kept from them only by a thin wall, was joined by the high-pitched keening of the wind. The wind was like a wild animal that prowled around the *Jupiter* seeking entrance, shrieking at times before it subsided into a low moaning sound.

For an hour the two kept to their bunks, Jake lying flat and Rachel sitting up, balancing as if she were in a small boat in tricky waters. Night came and the stygian darkness swallowed the *Jupiter*, seeming to magnify the sounds of the storm.

Rachel got up and managed to light both lamps. The yellow light flickered over the cabin, and she said, "I've never been in anything like this. It's not like a storm on land."

"No. On land you can get under something or run. Not in one of these, though. There's no place to hide."

The amber light gave her face an oriental appearance, and the shadows it cast brought her cheekbones into prominence and emphasized the greenish tint of her eyes, making her look even more Asian. Or perhaps, Hardin thought, it was her stillness, which was a characteristic of the oriental races, that brought that image to mind. But no, he decided, for he had seen Chinese coolies get frantic in a mild storm on the Mississippi.

"Are you afraid?" he asked finally.

She looked at him, wondering at his question, then nodded. "I suppose so."

"You sure don't look it!"

"No sense running and screaming, is there?"

"Well, no. But sometimes in a spot like this, it's hard not to do just that."

"We're in a dangerous storm," she said, and reaching up, she tucked a lock of honey-colored hair under a pin. It was a common enough gesture, but one that was somehow intensely feminine, or so it seemed to Jake. Most women, he reflected, wouldn't be thinking of their hair at such a time. She shrugged, then went on to say, "We may die. That's enough to make any-one afraid."

Jake lay there, wondering at her statement, for it didn't seem to go with her calmness. He thought of what Vince had told him of his sister, that she was very religious. This knowledge had not impressed him greatly, for he had seen some poor samples of Christians from time to time. It suddenly occurred to him as he lay there: *Well, I've been in a poor place to see Christians. Dealing poker in a floating saloon—it's not like I worked in a store in town.*

The thought would not leave him, and he said finally, "I guess you're so calm because you've got religion."

Something about what he had said displeased her. She gave her head a slight negative shake and clamped her lips together. "I'll go get us something to eat," she said, and she left the cabin, balancing herself like a tightrope walker.

Why did that offend her? Jake thought, a puzzled expression wrinkling his brow. *What was wrong with what I said? Maybe it wasn't the sort of thing Vince would say. Got to watch it more closely.*

Rachel came back thirty minutes later with a small sack and a pitcher. "Just sandwiches and milk," she said.

"Not sure it's a good idea to eat, anyway."

"Yes, you must eat." She pulled a sandwich from the sack, handed it to him, then picked up a cup and managed to pour it half full of milk. She sat there holding it as he ate, despite his request that she eat her own sandwich. The sandwich was dry—cold roast beef flavored with mustard. "Cow must have been a hundred years old," he complained, then took a drink from the cup she handed him. "What's it like outside?"

"I've never seen such waves," Rachel said. "Like mountains. Too dark to see much. It'd be much more frightening in the day, I suppose. Now all a person can do is guess at how high they are."

Jake suddenly gave her a thin grin. "Rather see things than think about them."

Rachel considered his statement, then said, "You don't really think that, Vince."

"Why don't I?"

She spoke evenly, without heat. "Because you've never been a man who'd look at things as they are. Even when you were a boy you'd never look trouble in the face. You'd always run away." A thought touched her, and she gave him a sharp glance. "Remember when you and Les and I rode Daddy's prize yearling?"

"Well—"

"You don't remember?" Rachel lifted her head, surprise in her eyes. "Funny you'd forget that. I was so young I shouldn't be able to remember, but I do." Then she shook her head abruptly. "The calf stepped into a hole and broke his leg. I think we were all about as scared as we'd ever been. But you said, 'Just don't say anything.' And Les said, 'No, Daddy will find out, and I'd rather get it over with.'" The ship lifted, then fell, and she waited until the paddles caught. Then with a slight look of relief on her face, she said quietly, "Les and I went to Daddy and told him. He used the strap on both of us. But you got out of it. When Daddy asked Les if you were in on it, he lied about it. Said it was just the two of us."

Jake fingered the button on his shirt, then remarked, "No one likes a whipping."

"You certainly don't," Rachel said with asperity. "You've never faced up to anything unpleasant in your life! So don't

847

tell me you'd rather watch those big waves, Vince. You know better, or—" She broke off and gave him a glimpse tinged with contempt that she made no attempt to conceal. "Or maybe you've got yourself to believing your own lies. I guess that's what all liars come to in time."

Jake had no idea how to answer but assumed that Vince would have given a bitter reply, so he said, "You're no better! All that religion is just a coat you put on. That's why you got sore when I asked you if it helped, isn't it?"

"Let's drop it." Rachel took the mug, put it down, then sat down on her bunk and ate half of a sandwich. The ship was rolling so badly that she was suddenly conscious of a certain queasiness. "Maybe you were right," she said. "Not the best time to eat."

The storm raged all night. By the next morning, both of them were half sick with the rolling. Rachel said, "We'd better skip the shave today. But I'll change your bandages." She moved about carefully and, finally, after she'd gathered the supplies, came to his bunk. It took considerable art to change his bandages as the deck tilted abruptly, but she finished, then said, "I'll go see if I can find out what's happening."

Jake waited until she left, then managed to get out of his bunk and into the wheelchair. It gave him a perverse pleasure to do something for himself instead of having Rachel do it. He put on his glasses, then rolled himself to the porthole and stood up, balancing on his good leg and bracing his left hand against the wall. The world outside was gray soup, with great dark waves appearing out of it to slap the *Jupiter* as a man would cuff a small dog, and he felt the awesome force of the blows.

He became so engrossed in watching the seas run over the deck that he didn't notice that his wheelchair had moved toward the door. And then when the ship gave an unexpected lurch and he reached back to grab the chair, his hand encountered only air. He waved his good arm wildly, then was driven backward, which was a disaster. He twisted his bad leg and cried out with the pain, then fell sideways, his head catching the steel corner of his bunk. At once he felt the hot blood trickle down over his ear as pain tore at him.

When Rachel returned ten minutes later, she found him sitting on the floor, his nightshirt drenched with blood. "What in the world—?"

Jake, angry at himself and humiliated, snapped, "I fell down."

Rachel shook her head, then bent over. "Get into the bunk," she ordered crossly. He leaned on her, and it took all her strength to help lift him. When he was in the bunk, she got her bandages out, washed the cut in his scalp, then shook her head. "Not quite bad enough for stitches." She put a fiery antiseptic on it, ignoring his involuntary grunt of pain, then bandaged it. "Just what you needed," she muttered. Then as she gathered her supplies, she asked, "How in the world did you manage to cut yourself?"

"Wanted to see out the window," Jake said defiantly. "What's the captain say?"

"I talked to one of the officers. He says if we don't sink before the storm blows itself out, we might make it. He wasn't," she added wryly, "a very optimistic soul."

"Neither am I," Jake admitted. "And it's worse lying here like a sick baby."

She moved to the porthole, looked out for a long time, then sat down on her bunk. When she picked up her Bible and started reading it, he lay there for half an hour, then said with some irritation, "Well, read some of it to me, will you?"

Rachel looked up, and the corners of her lips lifted slightly. "You want to hear some of the Bible?"

"Try to find a good part," he said morosely. "I don't need to hear all about how I'm going to hell. I know that already. Isn't there something in there about how to get out of trouble? Daniel in the lions' den, maybe?"

A thought came to Rachel, one that seemed to please her. "The twenty-seventh chapter of the book of Acts," she said, finding the place, and began to read: " 'And when it was determined that we should sail into Italy, they delivered Paul and certain other prisoners unto one named Julius, a centurion of Augustus' band....' "

Jake listened as Rachel read the story of Paul's voyage on his way to Rome. He had never read the Bible, but the story was thrilling and Rachel was a fine reader. She read how the voyage was a difficult one; then she read, " 'But not long after there arose against it a tempestuous wind, called Euroclydon—' "

"Wait a minute," Jake asked. "You mean that the storm had a name?"

"Yes. Euroclydon."

"Funny, a storm having a name, like a horse or something." He glanced out the window, then said, "If I had to name that one out there, I'd call it *Rita.*"

"*Rita?* Why *Rita?*"

"Because I had a girl once who acted about as cantankerous as that storm." He grinned, then said, "Go on—what happened to the fellows on the ship?"

Rachel read on through the chapter, and when it was finished, he said, "Well, I guess it came out all right, but the ship sank."

"But nobody died," Rachel reminded him. She ran her fingers over the page, then looked up. "I've always liked the part where in the middle of the storm—just when things looked the blackest—Paul told how an angel had come to him and promised that none of them on the ship would die."

"You think that actually happened?" Jake asked. "That there are angels and they talk to people?"

"I believe it happens sometimes, not often," Rachel said evenly. Then she smiled, "Paul said, 'I believe God, that it shall be even as it was told me.'" The ship rolled, but she smiled, seeming to forget the moaning of the wind and the cracking of the ship itself. "More than anything else, I want to say that I believe God!"

She spoke with such passion that Jake knew she had allowed part of that which she kept hidden to come out. Finally he said, "I guess you do believe it, Rachel. I hope you always do." Then he realized that such a statement from Vince would be unlikely, so he growled, "But I don't think God's going to reach down and pull us out of this storm. That's up to Captain Stuart and the crew."

"No, it's not," Rachel said calmly but then said no more.

Finally the storm lost its force, fading away like a whipped dog. It was so sudden that the silence seemed hollow somehow. When Rachel took Jake up on deck at three that afternoon, the sun was shining and the water was a sparkling blue.

"Well, it didn't get us that time, did it?" Jake said.

"No."

Her brief reply drew his attention, and he looked up at her. She was facing the bow, and the wind was pulling at her hair. Suddenly she reached up and pulled out some pins, allowing it to fall down her back. There was a smile on her broad lips and a look in her eyes that he couldn't name. Peace, maybe, but more than that.

"Look how still the sea is," she said quietly. "Just like the rolling hills back of the house at Lindwood."

"Well, I'll be glad to get there," Jake answered.

"Will you?" she asked, and it seemed his statement had driven away the lightness of her mood. "What about Duvall? He'll be there, still wanting to shoot you." When he made no reply, she said, "I don't suppose he can shoot a cripple. And that's what you're counting on, isn't it?"

He felt the pressure of her words and the obvious direction of her thoughts, but said only, "I guess so, Rachel."

The pleasure of the moment was gone, and though the weather was fine for the rest of the voyage, there was a barrier between the two of them. Rachel tended to his wounds and saw that he got his meals, but there was no warmth in her.

Going to be a rough homecoming, Jake thought as the ship dropped anchor with a loud rattle at the wharf in Richmond. *If she's this tough, what will the rest of the family be like?*

CHAPTER 8

HOMECOMING

Rachel waited until the hard, bright October sunshine began to fade, then left the *Jupiter*. She went to Harvey Simmons's livery stable to rent a wagon and, as she had expected, was questioned closely by the owner.

Simmons, a talkative man of fifty-five, chatted steadily as he hitched a horse to the buggy, giving her a running commentary on the city until he finally got down to finding out her business. "Heard you went to New Orleans to pick up Vince, Miss Rachel." His eyes were bright as a crow's as he looked up, asking innocently, "He's all right, is he?"

"He got some injuries in a hotel fire, Harvey." Her wry sense of humor came to her aid, and she rattled off the information Harvey was trying to pry out of her, including a summary of the fire itself and the hospital where Vince had stayed. Then she added, "He's got a bad right leg, a bad right hand, some burns on his face, and his eyes are sensitive to light. But with good care, he'll be fine. Just pass that along to anyone who might be interested, Harvey."

Simmons flushed, for he understood the irony in her voice, but he said only, "Well, that's fine. Folks'll be glad to hear it." He stepped back, saying, "Here you are, Miss Rachel. This here mare is real gentle. Won't give you no trouble. Lemme help you up."

Rachel accepted his hand and settled herself in the seat, saying, "Thank you, Harvey. I'll have Tad bring the rig back in the morning."

But Simmons could no more resist speaking of a juicy rumor than he could help breathing. "I heard that Simon Duvall ain't gonna let the thing drop—about Vince and his wife."

"Did he tell you that?"

"Well, no, but Leo Bates heard him say so. According to Leo, Duvall's going to open up on Vince as soon as he sees him." The man was as avid a gossip as ever drew breath, almost slavering as he probed at Rachel. "Whut you think Vince will do? I mean, he can't live in this county for long without running across Duvall, can he now?"

Rachel took the reins and spoke to the mare, and as the buggy left the stable, she called, "I'll get back to you as soon as I find out what's happening, Harvey!"

Simmons cursed under his breath, then kicked at a stall, startling the gray gelding inside. "Well, ain't she proud now! Like to take a strap to her!" Then he went inside the office and said to a long-legged man who was whittling a piece of cedar into a chain, "Leo, you know what? I think it's gonna be a shootin'—yes, sirree, I think Vince Franklin is gonna get himself perforated!" He sat down and drew out the possible scenarios for the affair, and within two or three hours he had gotten the word out that Simon Duvall and Vince Franklin were sure enough going to have a gunfight.

As she drove to the wharf, Rachel understood that putting a story of Vince's return in the paper would not get the news around Richmond nearly as fast as the long tongue of Harvey

Simmons could manage it. It was, she realized, inevitable, and she turned her thoughts from it as she pulled the buggy up in front of the gangplank of the *Jupiter*. Captain Stuart was waiting for her on deck and gave her a gallant salute. "Hoped to see you before you left," he said, smiling at her. "I sent Smythe down to get Mr. Franklin all ready, Miss Rachel."

"Why, that was thoughtful of you, Captain," Rachel said with a smile. Stuart was young enough to feel flattered and old enough to be concerned. He had picked up on some of the problems that her brother was likely to bring to her and was sorry to hear it. "It was a nice voyage, storm and all," she said.

"Well, it's going to get a little more tricky as this blockade thing keeps going. You tell your father if he wants anything shipped out or brought back, he'd better take care of it."

"I'll tell him, Captain, and you be careful. Don't let the Yankees get you." She had seen Smythe pushing the wheelchair, with two of the crew following with their luggage, and offered Stuart her hand. "Good-bye, Captain."

"I think we got everything, Miss Franklin," Smythe said. He led the way down the gangplank, then said, "Give me a hand, men." The three of them put the injured man on the seat, then loaded the chair and the rest of the luggage in the back of the buggy. "Good-bye, miss," he said, then began to protest when she held out some bills.

"You've been so good to us, Smythe," she said with a smile. "I couldn't have made it without you!"

As the buggy drove off, Smythe said, "Now there's a real lady, boys! The genuine article!" His eyes filled with admiration. He gave a bill from the cash Rachel had given him to each of the men, then added, "That brother of hers, he's not like her at all. Too bad!"

Rachel put the mare at a fast trot, and by the time they had cleared the city limits and were on the road leading to Lindwood, night had fallen. The stars were out and a silver medallion of a moon began to climb the skies, casting pale bars of light on the back of the mare.

"Good to be off the ship," Rachel said. "It was an adventure for me, but I'm not much of a sailor."

"I think you have to start in early for that," Jake agreed. He was breathing in the odors of the countryside, savoring the smell of rich earth and trees and the sharp, acrid odor of wood smoke. "I always like fall best," he remarked.

"That's not what you always said," Rachel pointed out. "How many times have I heard you curse the fall just because it meant winter was coming?"

Jake laughed quickly. "I suppose that's so. But right now it's pretty nice, especially after that little cabin—and after the hospital."

They spoke little, which was a relief to Jake. He was not on guard enough, and even a small remark such as he had made about preferring a certain season could be dangerous. *Got to keep my mouth shut*, he thought, and he did so for most of the trip.

When they turned off on a side road, Rachel said, "There's the house." When he didn't answer, she asked, "Can't you see it?"

"Well, just blurred, is all."

Rachel said no more, and soon she was pulling the buggy to a halt. As she did so, Les came running out of the house.

"Hey!" he called to Rachel with a grin. "You made it back!"

"Yes, Les," Rachel answered, smiling at him. "And now you can help us. Get that chair out of the back of the buggy, will you? And you'll have to help Vince into it."

"Sure, Rachel." Les lifted the chair and moved it beside the buggy; then, with a powerful grip, he swung Jake to the ground. Jake dropped into the chair with a grimace.

Les looked at him for a moment, then said, "You look like the devil, Vince!"

"Never mind that, Les," Rachel said. "Just bring his things in. Oh, and take the buggy back to Simmons's stable in the morning, will you? Or have Tad do it."

With that, she moved behind the chair and pushed it down the brick walkway that led to the big white house, but turned to follow a smaller walk that led around to the side. "I can't manage those front steps," she remarked. "We'll go in by the back." The ground rose slightly, and Jake saw that the back door was on ground level, or almost so. When Rachel called, "Dee! Come and open the door," a woman stepped outside. She held the door open as Rachel lifted the chair wheels up the slight step.

"We done got the downstayuhs bedroom ready," Dee said. "We even moved the furniture 'n' all from his reg'lar room, though I doan know why we done so much." She was a tall, heavy woman of sixty, no longer strong, but knowing everything about Lindwood. "We kin take bettah keer of 'im there, though."

"That's fine, Dee," Rachel said and moved down a long hall that divided the house. The door at the end was open, and she turned the chair and entered.

It was, Jake saw, a large bedroom, with heavy mahogany furniture and a large bay window opening out onto a garden. "You're probably tired," Rachel said, and she herself had lines of fatigue on her face. "I'll get you ready for bed."

"No, you go on up to yoah momma's room," Dee said. "She's done had a fall."

Rachel whirled to face the tall black woman, exclaiming, "Dee! What happened?"

"You knows that ol' porch on the little house? Miss Amy went out there three days 'go to git somethin', and she forgot about that rotten ol' porch!" Her black face was heavy as she added, "Done gone and broke one laig, and twisted t'other one, so she can't nowise git around." Dee saw the alarm on Rachel's face and moved to pat her affectionately on the shoulder. "Now, now, it ain't gonna kill her, but you go on. She's been waitin' for you."

Rachel glanced at Jake, but Dee said impatiently, "I done diapered him plenty of times, so I reckon I can still shove him into a bed! Now git on to yoah momma, chile."

She waited until Rachel hurried out of the room, then turned to Jake, and he saw her eyes harden. "Well, you want somethin' to eat?"

"Just some water, Dee."

She stared at him, asking finally, "Thas all you wants? Jes water?"

"I'm not hungry, but some cool water would be good."

"Fust time you been to bed sober since I kin remember!" She pushed the chair over to the bed and moved to help him, but he shook his head and stood on his good leg, then turned awkwardly and sat down on the bed. "I got you some fresh clothes," she said. "You want me to change you?"

"Just the water, Dee."

Jake changed into the clean nightshirt; then when Dee came back he drank thirstily from the glass she handed him. When he handed it back, he said, "I'm pretty tired. Guess I'll get some sleep."

Standing back, she cocked her head and studied him through

a pair of wise old eyes. "You looks like you been drug through a knothole," she announced. "And you sounds funny, all husky like."

"Breathed too much smoke, Dee," Jake said quickly.

She didn't move, and there was something monolithic about her. Vince had said once, *If you can fool Dee, you can fool anybody, Jake. She's as sharp as a tack! And she raised us kids, so she knows every scar on my body—least those I had before I left home.*

"You doan look like yo'self," Dee said, then shrugged. "Nevah thought shavin' off a patch of whiskahs could make so much difference in a man. You want anything, ring dat bell on the table." She moved to the lamp, turned it down until it made only a dimple of yellow light in the large room, then left, moving heavily across the floor. Jake took a deep breath, somewhat unsteadily, then closed his eyes and was asleep almost instantly.

❧

Rachel found her mother sitting up in bed reading her Bible and moved to her at once, exclaiming, "Mama—what an awful thing!"

Amy Franklin, at the age of thirty-nine, was still an attractive woman, but the accident had dimmed her natural vigor and drawn her down. "Fool thing to do!" she said, glaring bitterly at her legs under the blanket. "You'd think a woman would have enough sense to watch where she's going, wouldn't you?"

"I'll bet it hurt like fury," Rachel said, drawing up a chair. She brushed a strand of dark hair from her mother's forehead and listened as the older woman told her about the accident. But soon she said, "That's enough of that. Now tell me about Vince."

Rachel gave her the details, and her mother asked at once, "Has he changed?"

"I—don't know, Mama," Rachel said hesitantly. "It was a close call, you know. He could have died." She tried to put her thoughts together, saying slowly, "He's very quiet—not like himself at all in that way. He's not badly hurt, or not permanently, at least, but I think the whole thing must have scared him."

"What makes you think so?"

"Oh, I don't know—" She shook her head, saying, "He *looks* different. Still like Vince, but not really. There's just something that makes you look twice to be sure it's really him. You'll be shocked, I think." She went into the details—the loss of the beard, the scars on the forehead, the dark glasses. "He even *sounds* different, sort of husky. The doctor at the hospital was afraid it might be permanent, though he never told Vince that."

Amy sat there, thinking hard, then said, "We've got to have more help, Rachel."

"I can take care of the house."

"Not and take care of two invalids. Dee's getting too old to do a lot, and you know what a lot of ninnies the younger ones are. No, I want you to get a woman to come and live here until things get better."

"Who would you like?"

"I've been thinking it over, and it seems the best choice would be Melora, if she'll come."

"Why, yes, that's a good idea, Mama," Rachel said at once. "She's about the most efficient person I know—and nice, too. I'll go in the morning and talk her into coming."

"She may be glad to come," Amy said. "Can't be much of a life for her living out in the middle of the woods. The Yancys are good people, but with Lonnie and Bob gone to the army, and Royal married, it must be pretty hard out there on their place. Cora is there now—the second girl, the one who married the Day boy, and Rose is sixteen. They can take care of the two young ones." She shifted her legs, and her lips tightened at the pain. "Go early, Rachel. I think it'd be good for Melora." She smiled slightly, adding, "Rev. Irons will have to come and visit me pretty often."

Rachel shook her head. "You've been trying to marry them off for a long time, Mama." She hesitated, then asked, "What about Melora and Uncle Clay?"

Amy shook her head firmly. "Clay's married, and Ellen won't ever give him up. Melora is wasted as a single woman. She's what, almost twenty-seven now? And Brother Irons isn't getting any younger."

"He's forty-one," Rachel said, adding what they both knew. "He could have married a dozen times after his wife died— but he loves Melora." Then she laughed, her eyes bright in the lamplight. "We're getting to be worse gossips than Harvey Simmons! But I'll go talk with Melora in the morning. If she agrees, she can come back with me. I hope she'll come, though. It would be good to have her."

❧

The next morning, Jake was awakened by Dee, who came in bearing a tray of eggs, grits, ham, and biscuits. As he ate, she sat down and watched him, her eyes never swerving. Her survey made Jake nervous, and he asked, "Where's Rachel this morning?"

"Gone to git some help wif dis house." Then she said, "They wasn't no need o' dat. I speck dey's enough lazy slaves on de place to take keer of it." She sat there rocking slightly, then added, "But if we gotta have outside folks, I speck Miss Melora Yancy is de best could be had."

Jake almost asked who Melora Yancy was, then realized abruptly that he probably should know—or rather, that Vince would know. He said no more, and after breakfast, Dee insisted on cleaning him up and changing his bandages. She went at it as if he were a large doll, flopping him about and scrubbing at raw flesh without mercy. Jake hadn't realized how gentle Rachel was, but determined either to have her change the dressings or do it himself in the future.

After the ordeal, he said, "Dee, bring me the family pictures."

She looked at him with surprise, but he said, "My eyes are too sensitive to read, but I can look at pictures." He had made a guess that there would be some and was pleased when she returned with quite a collection. "Here dey is," Dee announced. "I got to go to work." She left him, and for the next hour and a half, he studied the tintypes. There were a lot of them, and he enjoyed guessing at the identity of some of the people whose names were not written under the pictures.

One group picture intrigued him—a large family portrait, obviously taken at some sort of a reunion. For a long time he studied the faces, trying to fit them with what Vince had told him. Vince's own family was the easiest, for he knew the two boys beside Rachel had to be Grant and Les and that the man and woman with them had to be her parents. He knew that the man in the uniform of a Union officer had to be either Gideon or Mason Rocklin, probably Gideon, since he looked too young to be the brother of Thomas. Clay Rocklin he was fairly certain of, for he bore a striking resemblance to his father. The others he could speculate on, but realized that in every case he'd have to listen until he heard a name given.

He heard a man's voice in the hall and looked up as the door opened and a Confederate officer came into the room. He was not much older than forty, a wiry man of medium height, with neat features and agreeable brown eyes.

"Hello, Vince," the officer said. "How are you doing?"

"Oh, very well," Jake said, his mind racing but coming up with nothing. "Sit down," he invited.

The major took a seat, saying, "Your mother is feeling better. That was a nasty break she got." He shook his head, adding, "The doctor still thinks it might give her permanent problems."

"You mean—she might be lame?"

"Well, that's what Dr. Maxwell said, but you know him, always looking on the dark side. I'm believing God will give her a perfect leg."

Suddenly it came to Jake, something that Vince had said:

"The preacher is named Jeremiah Irons. Nice enough fellow, I suppose. Falling down in love with a girl named Melora, poor white girl. Funny thing is, my uncle Clay, he's in love with her, too! A good-looking woman, dead gone on my uncle. But she won't get him. He's got a wife—or kind of a wife, I guess. So they're all three miserable!"

Jake said carefully, "Can't talk too much, Reverend. Took in too much smoke."

"Rachel told me about it," Irons said, nodding. "From what she said, you're fortunate to be alive." He gave Jake an odd look, adding, "She said you went back into the burning building to pull a man out."

Jake felt a danger here and waved his good hand in a gesture of denial. "I'd like to be a hero, Reverend, but the truth is he had some money he'd won from me, and I wanted to get it back. Sorry to disappoint you."

Irons shrugged, then began asking about how long he expected to be in the wheelchair, but in the middle of Jake's answer, the door opened and Rachel came in with a lovely dark-haired young woman. "I've brought Melora to help for a while, Vince," she said.

"Hello, Melora," Jake said slowly. "I'll try to cause you all the trouble I can. I'm a rotten patient."

"You're rotten when you're *not* a patient," Rachel said sharply, then flushed and laughed uncomfortably. "Sorry, Brother Irons. I usually try to be good when there's a minister close by."

"So do most other people, Rachel." Irons smiled at her sharp humor, then said, "I'll be moving along. Just wanted to pray with your mother and see how Vince was doing."

Jake said quickly, "You'll notice he didn't pray for me. Rev. Irons knows a hopeless case when he sees one!"

Irons shook his head, saying, "I didn't want to make you angry, like I did the last time I tried to pray for you."

Melora and Rachel exchanged smiles, and Irons added ruefully, "I thought I'd been cussed out by experts, but you made me realize there's a level in profanity far above any I'd ever suspected. But—I sneaked around and prayed for you before I came in. Not much you can do about that, is there?"

"I guess not," Jake murmured.

"Go help Melora carry her things in," Rachel commanded. "I like to see a preacher do a little work once in a while." When they were gone, she turned to Jake, asking, "Did Dee feed you and change your bandages?"

"Yes, and she won't do it again—change my bandages, I mean," Jake said adamantly. "She's got a touch like a blacksmith!"

Rachel laughed out loud, which Jake thought was a delightful sound, then said, "I guess she can feed you and I'll be the nurse. Are you going to let your whiskers grow back?"

"No, they're pretty itchy. But if you'll fix the water and strop the razor, I think I can manage it."

"With your left hand? You can't even throw a rock with your left hand," she said scornfully. She left, coming back with hot water, and as she lathered his face and picked up the razor, she talked about the farm, especially about the horses. He sat very still as she shaved him, her presence stirring him in a way that was becoming more and more familiar—which made it all that much more dangerous.

When she was finished, she carefully removed the bits of dry lather with a moist towel, saying, "I know you don't like horses much. I've bored you talking about them."

Jake loved horses, so he was glad that she'd given him a tip on how he was supposed to react. "Well, you know me and horses."

"I still think you're as much of the problem as the horses, though," she pronounced calmly. "Horses know somehow when a person is afraid of them. If you'd just get over your fear, I think you'd be a good rider."

"How do you figure that?"

"Why, you're strong and you've got good balance," she said.

Disturbed by her gaze, Jake decided to steer the conversation away from himself. He glanced at the door, saying, "The preacher, he's still mooning over Melora, I see." He saw that the remark displeased Rachel and added quickly, "What he ought to do is drag her off by the hair and make her love him. That'd bring her around."

Rachel's eyes darkened with frustration and anger at his callousness. "You're a fool, Vince," she said in a low voice.

"No, just a realist," Jake said, pushing his advantage. "She can't have Clay, so she needs to forget him and take somebody else. The preacher's a nice fellow and he wants her. I don't see what her problem is."

Rachel looked at him with thinly veiled disgust. She noted that the plaster on the cut on his forehead had not been changed and in one motion reached out, gripped it, and ripped it off with a sharp yank.

"Ow!" Jake yelled, clapping his hand to the spot. "You're worse than Dee, Rachel! Next time give a man a little warning, will you?"

Rachel gave him a withering glance. "Vince, you're probably the most unfeeling man I ever met, except, of course, when it comes to your own hide. You've been around enough to know Melora's a woman who's never done a wrong thing in her life. And then there's the good man Uncle Clay has become—and all you can say is they ought to just forget what they feel!"

"Well? What do *you* say?"

She moved away from him toward the door, pausing only long enough to say, "When you love someone, you don't toss that person away—but you'll never understand that." Then she was gone, and Jake lay there rubbing his smooth cheek, a thoughtful look on his face.

❦

Irons carried Melora's shabby suitcase to her room; then the two of them went outside. "I'm glad you're here, Melora," he said, unhitching his horse. "Amy needs you."

"I'm glad to be here, Jeremiah," Melora said, then smiled at him. "Now I can come and hear you preach to the troops in Richmond. I'd like that."

Irons brightened at once. "I'm preaching this Sunday to the whole brigade," he said. "Would you let me come and get you?"

"If I can get away—and if you really want to."

He stood there, at a loss for words, the way he usually was in her presence. She was for Irons the most desirable woman on earth, and he had not taken a wife because he longed to have her. Now he said slowly, "It's a bad time, Melora, but I'm just a simple preacher." He struggled a moment, then shrugged. "I can't think of any way to say it that I haven't already tried. I love you, Melora."

She dropped her eyes for a moment, and when she lifted them, he saw they were filled with tears. "Why—Melora!" he said, taking her hands. "I didn't mean to make you cry!"

"It's—all right, Jeremiah," she said quietly. She let her hands rest in his, then said, "You're the most loyal, persistent man in the world, Rev. Jeremiah Irons. You could have married I don't know how many fine women, but you keep on waiting around for me."

"Melora, I know you care for Clay," Irons said abruptly. "Well, so do I. He's the best friend I've ever had. But you'll never have any happiness with him, and I think you know that. He'll never leave Ellen." His grip on her hands tightened, and he urged her, "Love can come to a person, Melora. I can make you love me if you'll just give me a chance."

At that moment, Dee came out of the house calling, "Miss Melora! Miss Amy, she say come to her room soon as you kin!"

"All right, Dee."

The moment between Melora and Irons was broken, but Melora was greatly touched. She looked at the preacher and said, "Perhaps you're right. About learning to love." She paused for a moment, then smiled. "Come and get me Sunday, Jeremiah."

She turned and left, and Irons sprang into the saddle, his face glowing. It was the most encouraging thing she'd ever said to him. In a sudden burst of excitement, he kicked his horse with both heels and shot out of the driveway at a dead run.

"Dat preacher, he sho' is feelin' good," Tad said aloud as he watched the minister tear along the road. "Wonder whut got him feeling so good? He don't drink no hard likker and he ain't chasin' no gals!" The slave watched until the horse and rider disappeared, then began to whistle as he moved toward the stable.

CHAPTER 9

RACHEL'S CHALLENGE

*O*n the first day of November, Jake Hardin awoke with a grim determination. He opened his eyes, thinking at once of his resolve of the previous night. It was time to stop being an invalid. At once he threw off the blankets and struggled to a sitting position. The pain in his leg was dull now, rather than sharp as it had been when he had first arrived at Lindwood, and his hand was better—good enough so that he could flex his fingers slowly.

Carefully he swung his left leg to the floor, then used his good hand to lift his bandaged ankle and place it alongside the good one. His wheelchair was beyond his reach, but he pulled himself off the bed and, by hopping on one foot, was able to get to it. He tried to push himself around in the chair, but his right hand was too sensitive to be of much good. "Guess I could go around in a circle," he said after a futile attempt to get across the room. Finally he figured out how to move the chair by using his good left hand on both wheels—a slow method and one that irritated him, but he managed it.

He spent the next half hour shaving himself. Rachel kept his shaving gear on the dark washstand, and it was a matter of using his right hand to push things around while using his left for the careful work. Since the wheelchair wasn't high enough, he was forced to stand, using only his good leg. Stropping the blade was beyond him, but he managed to lather up in the cold water, then to scrape off his whiskers using his left hand. When he was finished, he went to sit down, his right leg aching, the left trembling with the unaccustomed exercise.

But he had done it! A sense of satisfaction ran through him as he maneuvered himself toward the large wardrobe. As he opened the door and looked through Vince's clothing, he thought of how he'd managed to survive his first week. It had been fairly simple, for he'd had no visitors and Brad and Grant were gone with the army. Jake had seen only the family and the house servants, but that had gone well.

He picked out a pair of fawn trousers that were cut rather full and decided he could get them on over his bandaged leg. He chose a white shirt with bone buttons and found fresh underwear next. Then came the monumental struggle of getting the clothes on. The trousers were the hardest, but he managed them by slipping the right trouser leg over his bandaged leg and working it up. The left leg was easy, and after he had slipped on the shirt, he stuffed the tail of it into the pants, then fastened them.

What he'd done so far had been the most exercise he'd had since the fire, but he could sense that he was on the mend. There was some pain and discomfort, but that would pass. He was a stubborn man, and now his whole mind was fixed on getting well. He would push himself hard until he was whole again.

The air was cold in the room, and he looked at the fireplace, longing to put some wood on the coals he knew were hidden under a blanket of gray ash. With a shake of his head, he decided to save that for another day.

Jake moved the chair over to the window. A group of squirrels were chattering just outside, chasing each other around a large oak tree that rose above the house itself. The day was clear, and Jake had a good view of the front yard. He looked at it in surprise—it was huge! The grass was dead and brown, of course, but in the summer he knew that it would be green and lush and clipped like a carpet. This most definitely was the home of a rich man. How different such a life was from his own. He had grown up in poverty, having to make his own way from the time he was only fifteen years old. Vince, he reflected, had had everything he had not: horses, expensive clothing, a good education. Jake had managed to have some of those things, but only because he had wrested them from the world by his wits and his muscles. He wondered what it would be like to have them come without a struggle, but could not imagine it.

Just then a flash of movement caught his eye, and he shifted his glance to see Rachel riding across a wide pasture surrounded by a white fence. She was on a sleek black horse, and as he watched, she took the fence in a perfectly executed jump. She wheeled her mount around, and Jake could see the expression of pleasure on her face as she passed. There was in her, he thought, more joy than he had found in anyone before. This was a quality he admired—perhaps because he had even less of it than most men. The hardness of his life had allowed for little except survival and had given him a cynical outlook that he could not seem to put away, even when circumstances were pleasant. He always was unconsciously getting ready for the hard things that he knew lay over the next hill.

With a sigh, he reached for the photographs, going through

them again. He had studied them for hours and, by carefully commenting on them to Dee or Melora or Rachel, had been able to learn the identity of most of the people pictured.

Dee was his best source. She didn't like him, but she was proud of the family. All Jake had to do was show her a picture and ask, "When was this one made, Dee?" and she would sit down and go over everyone, giving little incidents that helped Jake get them fixed in his mind. When Jake had showed her the first picture in this way, she glanced at it and remarked, "Now you see that scar on Mistuh Paul's face? He got dat when he fell in a horse race in Kentucky." Jake kept her talking, and before long he discovered that Paul was the oldest son of Marianne, who was Amy Franklin's aunt and the only sister of Stephen and Thomas Rocklin; that Marianne was married to Claude Bristol and that they had another son named Austin and a daughter named Marie; and that Claude was not the best husband in the world—that he had, in fact, given his wife much cause for concern through his affairs with other women.

Now Jake flipped through the pictures, including those from the part of the family in the North, and he suddenly thought, *This is a fine family. What a fool Vince is to throw it away!*

Then he became uncomfortable, for he was forced to remember his purpose for being at Lindwood. He was only going to be there long enough for Vince to be eligible for the money—at which time Vince would come back and take over as master of Lindwood. Jake frowned. Though he had not met the owner of Lindwood, he had spent some time with Amy Franklin and knew that she was a fine woman, even noble. He knew as well that when Vince took over, he would be so unbearable that the smooth flow of life at this fine home would be shattered.

Disturbed, Jake moved away from the window, making his way crabwise to the huge rolltop desk. Opening the lower drawer, he was surprised to find a stack of letters. He took them out and began reading them. They were all letters written to Vince, and he managed to piece together something of the man's life from them. Most of the letters were from friends, some of them going back to Vince's youth, and they were rather ordinary. But as Jake went through them chronologically, he discovered a pattern, a progressive loss of innocence that told him much about Vincent Franklin. The earliest letters were filled with the things that boys are interested in—hunting, fishing, a play in Richmond. But before long the tenor of the letters changed, as did the correspondents, and Jake could almost date the time that Vince began to dabble in the rougher side of life: wenching, drinking, and gambling. The most recent letters revealed a life that was completely depraved.

Some of the most revealing letters were from women, for Vince catered to women with little—or no—grace. Some of them were merely crude and vulgar; others were married women whose letters contained veiled references to secret meetings and assignations. Finally Jake had read all he could stomach. He put the letters away and was just closing the drawer when the door opened and Rachel entered.

"Well now," she said, stopping to stare at him. "I didn't know Dee had come to take care of you." She was wearing a pale rose-colored dress, and her cheeks were flushed from her ride. She looked at him more closely, saying with surprise, "You've had a shave. I'll bet Dee didn't do that!"

"No, I wouldn't risk that. I managed the job myself—and no more food trays in here. I can eat at the table."

Rachel examined him carefully, then said, "You must have

had a hard time shaving in cold water. I'll have Jupe bring you shaving water in the morning, and he can help you dress for a time. Are you ready for breakfast?"

"Sure." He put his dark glasses on, which she had picked up from his table and handed to him. As she wheeled him down the hall, he said, "If you could get me a pair of crutches, I think I'll be able to use them pretty soon. My leg's better, and the hand, too."

"Don't rush it," Rachel warned as they moved out of the hall and into the dining room. "Dee, Vince will eat in here from now on."

Dee came through the kitchen door to stare at Jake, then said, "You want eggs?"

"Eggs will be fine," Jake said, and soon he and Rachel were eating breakfast. He had trouble cutting up the large slice of ham on his plate and said ruefully, "Never knew how handy it is to have two hands."

"Let me cut it." Rachel sliced the meat into bite-sized portions, then gave him his plate back. "I forgot to tell you, if you want any letters written, I'll do it, or Melora can."

"Thanks. Guess I'll wait until I can handle the job myself."

"All right." She sat there eating and sipping her coffee, saying little, but finally she said, "I hope Father and Grant will be coming home soon."

Rachel shook her head, and there was a doubtful look on her face. "I thought when the war started that things would go so fast we couldn't keep up with it. But since Manassas back in July, nothing's happened—nothing really big. Except for most of the men being in the army, life's about the same."

"Maybe the North has had enough."

"No, I don't think so," Rachel said slowly. "Rev. Irons spends most of his time with the troops, and he's been around some of the leaders like Colonel Chesnut. They all agree that the North had its pride hurt at Manassas. But McClellan's getting an enormous army ready, and in the spring they'll come down on us like a horde of locusts."

"Things look sort of dark, I guess."

Rachel looked at him, seemingly thinking of the war, but she said evenly, "If the Yankees really whip us, we'll all be out in the cold." A smile tugged at her lips, and she added, "I know you've been looking forward to tossing us all out for a long time. Now you may be out in the streets with the rest of us."

"You're pretty sure about what I'll do, aren't you, Rachel?"

"You've been quite outspoken about it," she said, then rose and began gathering the dishes. "I'm going to town today. Can I bring you anything?"

"Some newspapers. My eyes are getting better, good enough to read a little."

"All right." She paused, then said, "Ask Melora to read to you. She's the reader around here. Makes any sort of book sound exciting."

Later on in the day, Jake did get to hear Melora read. He had said nothing to her, but she came to his room, where Jupe had built him a nice fire. He had almost dozed off when the door opened, and he looked up to see Melora enter with some books.

"I've come to read to you, Vincent," she said. Sitting down, she added, "Rachel said you might be getting bored."

"Hate to take your time, Melora."

"I'm all caught up. Now what would you like? Poetry or a novel?"

"Read something you like."

She smiled and pulled a book from the stack, saying, "You

just made a mistake. Men usually like fiction some, but most would rather read a newspaper. I like poetry."

"Well, it'll be new to me, Melora, since I've not read much."

"Here's one I like...." Melora found her place, then began reading. She had a pleasant voice, and as do most people who read aloud well, she had a lively expression.

ANNABEL LEE

"It was many and many a year ago,
In a kingdom by the sea,
That a maiden there lived whom you may know
By the name of Annabel Lee;—
And this maiden she lived with no other thought
Than to love and be loved by me.

"She was a child and I was a child,
In this kingdom by the sea,
But we loved with a love that was more than love—
I and my Annabel Lee—
With a love that the winged seraphs of Heaven
Coveted her and me.

"And this was the reason that, long ago,
In this kingdom by the sea,
A wind blew out of a cloud by night
Chilling my Annabel Lee;
So that her highborn kinsmen came
And bore her away from me,
To shut her up in a sepulchre
In this kingdom by the sea.

"The angels, not half so happy in Heaven,
Went envying her and me:—
Yes! that was the reason (as all men know,
In this kingdom by the sea)
That the wind came out of the cloud, chilling
And killing my Annabel Lee.

"But our love it was stronger by far than the love
Of those who were older than we—
Of many far wiser than we—
And neither the angels in Heaven above
Nor the demons down under the sea,
Can ever dissever my soul from the soul
Of the beautiful Annabel Lee:—

"For the moon never beams without bringing me dreams
Of the beautiful Annabel Lee;
And the stars never rise but I see the bright eyes
Of the beautiful Annabel Lee;
And so, all the night-tide, I lie down by the side
Of my darling, my darling, my life and my bride,
In her sepulchre there by the sea—
In her tomb by the side of the sea."

Jake sat still, caught by the beauty of Melora's face as much as by the words she read. "That's very nice, but it's sad. Isn't there enough real sadness in the world without reading about such things?"

Melora let the book fall, and Jake was surprised to see that the expression on her face was not sad but meditative. She had beautiful eyes, colored a deep green, and her lips were sweetly curved as she said, "There's something about it that isn't sad—at least to me."

"Not sad? But the girl dies and the lovers are parted!"

"Yes, but he still loves her. I guess that's why I like the poem. He says that nothing can take that from him. 'Neither the angels in Heaven above nor the demons down under the sea, can ever dissever my soul from the soul of the beautiful Annabel Lee.' "

Jake studied the woman before him, thinking of what Vince had told him about her love for Clay Rocklin. Finally he said, "But, Melora, if he had married another woman, he at least would have had her. Life's not very good at best, and we just have to take what we can get."

Melora looked at him, saying, "I don't like to think that we should take second best."

"Well, it sounds nice in the poem," he said finally. "Who wrote it?"

"A man named Edgar Allan Poe." She opened the book and gave him a sudden smile, saying, "He wrote some fine stories. I'll try you out on this one. It's not quite as sad as the poem. It's called 'The Purloined Letter,' and it's a detective story."

She read the story, and when she finished, Jake nodded. "Now *that's* a little more in my line, Melora! That Dupin is a sharp operator. Imagine that, hiding a letter by putting it out where everyone can see it!"

"If you ever want to hide something," Melora agreed, "now you know the way to do it. Don't hide it away, but put it right in full view of everyone." She rose and gave a short laugh. "This has been pleasant, Vince."

"I've enjoyed it, too," Jake said. "Maybe you'll even make a poetry reader out of me."

She left the room, and he wondered about her and her love for Clay Rocklin, and the preacher, Jeremiah Irons, who was totally unable to hide his love for this woman. *Looks like God could have put all that together better,* he mused. Then his face grew still as he thought, *'Course, I guess God doesn't really have a lot to do with it. We have to take whatever hand life deals us and either make it work or let it beat us. After all, look at what I've become. God sure hasn't had anything to do with me or my life!*

Leighton Semmes was delighted to meet Rachel as she came into headquarters. He rose at once, moving to greet her, saying, "Well, recruiting is picking up! You're the first volunteer we've had in two days, and the prettiest one, too."

He looked very handsome in his smart uniform, and Rachel was amused at his attention to her. "Nothing I'd like better than joining the Richmond Grays, but there's not much chance of that, Leighton." She was wearing a very pretty brown dress made of fine wool, and she saw the admiration in his dark eyes. "I came down to see if you could tell us anything about Father and Grant. Will they be home soon?"

"As a matter of fact, yes," Semmes answered. "They've been with Jackson in the Valley, but orders went out late yesterday to Colonel Benton. They'll be assigned to defend Richmond—and your father and brother will be here next week. They're being sent ahead of the rest of the regiment to take care of any advance preparations."

"Oh, Mama will be glad!" Rachel exclaimed.

"Come along," Semmes said. "It's time I took you to lunch." She began to protest, but he laughed at her. "Come now, if you try to get out of it, I'll denounce you for a Yankee spy!"

They went downtown to the Melton Hotel, and after a fine lunch, they sat there talking for a long time. Semmes was an accomplished conversationalist, and he kept her amused as he related the incidents in Richmond and at the camp. "By the way," he said, "There's to be a ball for the Grays on the fifteenth. I'm taking you to it."

"And I don't have any say in the matter?"

"Not in the least," Semmes said firmly. "Buy yourself a pretty new dress, and I'll bring my pistol along to protect you. It'll be fun, Rachel, and I'd like you to come with me."

"All right, Leighton," Rachel agreed. "I can't promise the new dress, though."

"Tell me about your trip to New Orleans—and about the patient."

Rachel gave him the details of the voyage, then spoke of Vince's recovery. "He's doing very well, but it'll be weeks before he's able to get around."

"Did you know Simon Duvall's been making his boasts about what he intends to do?"

"Yes, I've heard about it. But he's not going to shoot a cripple. That wouldn't do his reputation any good."

"With most men, I'd agree. But with a fellow like Duvall, you never can tell," Semmes said doubtfully. "He's got a fiery temper, and if he met Vince at all, he might shoot him without thinking of the consequences. If I were you, I'd talk Vince into staying out of town."

This didn't please Rachel. "He can't stay out of Richmond the rest of his life."

"I guess not, but warn him to be careful. As a matter of fact, I'll be glad to say a word to Duvall myself. I could do it right now. He's always at the Harralson House about this time of day."

Rachel knew this was an offer from Semmes to take up Vince's quarrel, and she understood that he was offering to do it for her, not because of any affection he had for her brother.

"No, Leighton, but you can take me there. I've got something to say to the big bully."

"Now wait a minute—!" Semmes protested, but despite his earnest argument, he found himself escorting Rachel to the hotel, which was only a block away. "Now just remember to keep your temper, Rachel," he said as they entered the salon. "There he is over there."

Rachel saw Duvall sitting at a table with several men, playing cards. She straightened her back and marched up to him. "Mr. Duvall, I understand you've been making threats about what you intend to do to my brother."

Her words cut off all conversation, and Duvall came out of his chair like a scalded cat. He glared at her, saying, "Miss Franklin, you shouldn't interfere. This is between your brother and myself."

"Would you shoot an injured man, Duvall?"

"I won't discuss it with a woman!"

Duvall started to turn but stopped abruptly as Rachel pulled a pistol from her purse and aimed it at him. It was the pistol she'd bought in New Orleans as a gift for Les, a finely designed .36 revolver. It had developed a flaw, and she had taken it to the gunsmith to get it repaired. It was not loaded, but Duvall didn't know that. His face washed pale, and he said nervously, "Now, now, that's no way to behave!"

"You think I'll take lessons in how to behave from a sorry bully like you, Duvall?" Rachel said, keeping the gun steadily trained on him. "You're not a man anyone would listen to."

Duvall looked at her, swallowed, then said, "Miss Franklin,

this is most unseemly!"

"No, this isn't unseemly," Rachel said. "Let me tell you what will be unseemly. If you harm my brother, I'll shoot you. Not in one of your nice little duels where you have all the advantage. I'll wait for you in a dark alley, and when you pass by, I'll shoot you in the back of the head. Now *that* would be unseemly, don't you agree?"

She looked around the room, and contempt dripped from her voice as she said, "I don't suppose any of you have much pride, if you're the friend of a creature like this. But if there's any manhood in any of you, I'd think you'd refuse to listen to this scum when he makes threats against a man who can't defend himself."

She put the pistol back in her purse, saying, "From an alley, Duvall, in the back of the head." Then she turned and walked away.

Semmes gave Duvall a hard look, saying, "I am Miss Franklin's escort. If you resent anything she's said, my man will be glad to wait on you, sir!" Then he moved to Rachel and the two of them left the salon.

"Well, that was fun," Leighton said, and a laugh bubbled up in him. "Rachel, it was wonderful!"

"My father won't think so, nor my mother." Then a giggle came from her unexpectedly. "He did look silly, though, didn't he?"

"He'll keep his mouth shut," Semmes said, nodding. "He's got no choice." Then he asked curiously, "Would you really shoot him, Rachel?"

"No, but don't tell him that."

༝

Duvall turned back to the men at the table, his face ashen.

"Well, a man can't fight a woman, can he? The hussy!"

"You'd better keep quiet about your problem with Franklin, Duvall," one of the men said. "It does look bad, threatening a cripple."

Duvall glanced around the table, saw the agreement in the faces, and quickly said, "Of course. I had no intention of fighting Franklin until he's well." But the whole affair had shaken him, and he left the salon shortly afterward. He was fuming inside, and his anger was a black thing that would not be laid to rest easily. As he was walking down the sidewalk, fighting to keep his anger back, someone spoke to him.

"Why, Mr. Duvall, how nice to see you!"

He looked up with a startled expression, nodding then as he said, "Why, good afternoon, Mrs. Rocklin." He knew Ellen Rocklin only slightly but had admired her for a long time. She was hardly young, he thought, at about forty—but she was one of those women who retained her looks and figure. She was wearing a gray dress with a scarlet cape and looked very attractive. "How have you been?"

"Just fine. I'm on my way to look at some jewelry at Mason's." She smiled archly, adding, "You seem like a man who knows what looks good on a woman."

He said instantly, "Allow me to accompany you, Mrs. Rocklin."

"Oh, we're better acquainted than that," she said, smiling. "Let's make it Ellen and Simon."

They moved away, and after they looked at the jewelry, it seemed natural enough to have dinner together. Ellen Rocklin was an enticing woman, and as she listened to Duvall's version of Rachel's actions, she put her hand over his on the table, saying sympathetically, "What a dreadful thing, Simon! Her father ought to whip her. He won't, of course. She knows how to get around him!"

Ellen knew how to get around men, too, and how to get them to do what she wanted. There was a speculative and excited light in her eyes as she spoke to Duvall. She leaned against him, and a startled look appeared in his eyes—and then he smiled. They left the restaurant and moved down the street toward the house where she kept a room. When they arrived, she led him in by a seldom-used side entrance.

CHAPTER 10

DINNER AT LINDWOOD

*D*r. Kermit Maxwell was of the old school of medicine, highly suspicious of any of the newfangled innovations coming out of medical schools. His own training had been brief, at least from an academic point of view, but his practical experience was immense. He had been setting broken bones, administering pills, and bringing babies into the world in Virginia for almost sixty years. And he looked it, too.

He had stopped by to see Amy Franklin and, at her request, had gone to give her son an examination. Jake had been taking a nap on his bed when the door burst open without the formality of a knock. That, added to a booming voice sounding almost in his ear, gave him a leaping start.

"All right, get out of them clothes and let me look you over, boy!"

Jake was pulled to a sitting position before he was completely awake, and he suddenly found himself being stripped of his shirt by a short, thickset man with a round red face and a pair of sharp blue eyes. Quickly Jake made the connection, for he'd heard Rachel tell Melora that a doctor was coming to see her mother.

But this man looked more like one of the loafers who sat outside City Hall and chewed tobacco than a physician. Still, he more or less *acted* as though he knew what he was doing. He started at the top of Jake's head, checked the gash, which was almost healed; touched the burns, which were forming pink new skin; then grabbed Jake's head and held it still while he peered into his eyes.

"Eyes bother you much?"

"Not so much now. I still wear the dark glasses in bright sunshine."

"Keep on doing it," Maxwell commanded. "Open your mouth." He peered down Jake's throat, then said, "Looks all right. Your mother says you still talk kind of husky."

"That's right, I do."

Maxwell sucked a tooth, thought about it, then shrugged. "Well, you may talk like that the rest of your life. Maybe damaged your vocal cords. But then, you don't sing in no church choirs, anyway."

Jake liked the old man. "But I might want to start, Doc."

"Not likely!" Maxwell had been doctoring the Franklins off and on for years, so he knew quite a bit about the oldest son. His practice was mostly with the hill people, so his visits were sporadic. Still, he had heard of Vince's life, so he knew the sort of man he was dealing with, even though he hadn't treated Vince personally for many years. "Whiskey voice—that's what it sounds like to me," he snapped. "You still on the bottle?"

Jake was amused. "No. I'm waiting for my doctor to tell me it's all right to start."

"You've already drunk enough to do a man for a lifetime." But Maxwell knew that his admonition would have little effect. "Let me see that arm and leg." After checking the limbs, he shrugged. "The devil looks out for his own, I guess. Leave the bandages off the arm, keep a light one on the leg, and don't do too much walking for a couple of weeks."

"Thanks, Dr. Maxwell. How's my mother?"

"Not as well as I'd like." Maxwell frowned and sucked on his tooth again, then added, "That was a bad break. As bad as I've ever seen. Don't tell your mother, but she may be lame for the rest of her life."

"Surely there must be something to do!"

"No, there's not!" Maxwell snapped with irritation. Removing a square of tobacco from his pocket, he bit off a large plug and tucked it into his jaw. "There's not a lot any of us doctors can do, which I reckon you know. People look at us like we're some kind of miracle workers, but mostly it's just common sense. You could send your mother to the finest hospital in New York, and they'd fool with her and charge you all the money you could rake up. But I'm telling you, boy, if God don't heal that break, the finest doctor in the world won't be able to do it!" He whirled and propelled himself to the door, a short, scrappy man with a busy schedule.

Jake put his shirt on, then picked out a pair of lightweight shoes made of the softest leather that could be found. He got them onto his feet, then reached out for his crutches. He had started using them four days earlier, and it had been difficult. His right hand was weak, making him drop the right crutch often so that he had to stoop awkwardly on his good leg to retrieve it, or else call for help. Still, the exercise seemed to have helped, for now he managed to hold on to the crutch with little difficulty. Swinging his right foot, he moved across the room, passed through the door, then turned and made his way to a small room that once had been a study but now had been converted to a bedroom for the mistress of Lindwood. It saved the servants and the two women the climb up to the second floor. Les had done a good job of making the room handy, moving a good bed into it, along with a few pieces of furniture.

Jake knocked on the door, waited until he heard a voice say, "Come in," then opened the door and entered.

"Why, come and sit down, Vince," Amy said quickly. She had been reading a magazine in bed, but put it down and waited until Jake was seated, then asked, "Did the doctor think you're making progress?"

"Yes. Got a clean bill of health." Jake sat there, not as uncomfortable as he had been the first time or two he'd visited. There was nothing frightening about Amy Franklin. On the contrary, she was one of the most gracious women Jake had ever met. Though the knowledge of his secret made him somewhat nervous, he had grown to like the older woman, and several times he had come to her room and sat beside her. She had sensed, he knew, that he didn't want to talk about himself, and she carefully refrained from asking anything personal. But she did talk about her family and about the things of her world—which was a great help to Jake, who soaked up the information.

Now he asked, "What did he say about you?"

Amy smiled at him with a light in her eye. "He didn't tell me what he told you. Maxwell is a blunt old fellow, but he's got some tact. What he wanted to say was that he was afraid I'd be a cripple for the rest of my life. He didn't come out with it, of course, but he's an easy man to read. That is what he told you, isn't it?"

Jake blinked and began to fumble for words, but she cut

him off. "Never mind. It was an unfair question. He's wrong, anyway."

"I hope so," Jake said quickly. "You hate being tied down, don't you?"

"Yes, I do. I've always been happy working." A thought came to her, leaving a sudden expression of interest on her face. "It might be that the Lord wanted me to be still and listen." She thought about that, then smiled slightly. "Yes, that could be it. You know, I've spent more time listening to God since I fell through that porch than I have in the last ten years!"

Jake laughed, saying, "Well, that's a pretty rough way of getting your attention. There must have been an easier way."

"No, I don't think there was. We're all about the same, I think. When things are going well, we forget to listen to God. But when the bottom falls out of our world, we start looking up for help. That's the way you were when you were a boy, Vince."

"Calling on God?"

"No, I mean when you were young. You were the most independent little boy I ever saw!" The memory softened her lips, making her look maternal. "But even when you were five years old, you didn't want any help. No, sir, not you! You'd yank your hand out of mine and go off on your own. When you'd start falling, you'd go down and scrape your knees. And *then* you'd start holding up your hands and crying out for me."

"I don't remember that."

"No, you were just a baby." A sadness came to her, and she said softly, "I guess that was about the last time you reached out and asked me for anything. It grieved me, for I loved you very much."

Jake felt his face grow warm for some reason. He had never known much of a mother's love—none, really—and now he wanted to curse Vince for turning away from this woman. "Well, Dr. Maxwell said it would have to be God who healed you."

"Yes, he's right about that. But even if I do limp, this time has been good for me. For one thing," she said, giving him a sweet smile that reminded him of Rachel, "if I hadn't been here, we wouldn't have had these talks, would we?"

"I—guess not."

She saw his embarrassment, then said, "Your father and Grant will be here for dinner tonight. They got back to Richmond yesterday from the Valley. Rachel went to town and found out that both of them have been assigned to the regiment's advance team."

"Well, that's fine," Jake said quickly. He suddenly felt a surge of panic, for meeting Brad Franklin had been something he'd thought about with apprehension. "Glad I'm on my feet for the big occasion."

"It'll just be family tonight." Amy smiled. "I'm looking forward to it. It's the longest time your father and I have ever been separated since we've been married."

Jake got to his feet awkwardly, got his crutches in place, then smiled. "Well, he'll come home to a beautiful wife," he said and was sorry at once. *Vince would never have said a thing like that!* was the thought that went off like an alarm bell.

Amy Franklin was indeed looking at him with an amazed expression. He halfway expected her to denounce him, but she suddenly smiled, then laughed. "If I'd known that having a burning building fall on you would have made such an improvement, I'd have set fire to the house a long time ago!"

Jake felt a surge of relief. "Well, it did call my attention to a few things, I guess. So if you act up, I can lead you to a rotten porch, and if I don't behave, you can push me into a fire."

After he left her room, Amy sat there thinking of the scene. She was still thinking of it when Rachel came in to bring her fresh water. Rachel looked at her mother's pensive face. "Did Vince upset you, Mama?" she asked quickly.

Amy smiled at her. "No, dear, he didn't. He actually said something quite nice."

"Vince?" Rachel said, raising her eyebrows in doubt. "Don't let him fool you, Mama. He may seem more human lately, but it's just because he's sick. Oh, he's being nice enough, but when he's well, we'll have the same old Vince."

There was a bitter tone in her voice, and Amy said, "You can't let that sort of bitterness stay in you, Rachel. You've been taught better."

Rachel looked at her mother but shook her head stubbornly. "Remember that strawberry horse I had, the one called Prince? Well, he was good, too—until he got a chance to give me a bite or kick me in the ribs! That horse would be good for three months just to get a chance to kick me once!" Her eyes flashed, and she said adamantly, "I know you pray for Vince every day of your life, but I just don't—" Then she suddenly broke off. She turned away for a few seconds, then looked at her mother with a weak smile. "Mama, you'd find something good about Judas! And I'm just an old dragon! I wish I were more like you. You never boil over like I do."

"Well, I never pulled a gun on a man," Amy agreed blandly. Rachel's hand flew to her mouth, and a dull red crept up her neck. Her mother merely pulled her daughter's hand from her embarrassed face and held it. "You have deeper feelings than I do, or maybe I should say *more* feelings."

"You could say 'crazy, wild, unsettling' feelings," Rachel offered with a wry smile. "I try to be cool and ladylike, but then

I just pop off, like a volcano. I am trying hard, though, Mama. Really I am!"

"You can't be something you're not, Rachel," Amy said quietly. "You're a woman of strong emotions, and try as you will to repress them, they'll come out eventually. God gave you those feelings and the ability to feel them intensely. So the only thing you can do is ask Him to help you. . .and to guide you when the time comes for you to share those emotions with a man."

"Oh, don't worry about me and men, Mama. The spinster of Lindwood isn't going to get carried away."

"Nonsense." She paused, then asked, "Are you serious about Leighton Semmes?"

Rachel stared at her. "How do you know about him? Have you taken up gossiping?" At the twinkle in her mother's eyes, Rachel sighed. "Well, he's handsome and rich and charming. Besides, I'm a challenge to his pride. Just about every woman he's known has practically swooned when he looked at her. Now he's got to have me, but only because he can't have me!"

"He's a worldly man, Rachel. A strong one, to be certain, but not the sort who'd make you happy, I think. He doesn't seem to me to be a man of faith."

Rachel sighed. "Well, maybe you're right, Mama. At any rate, he's taking me to the ball in Richmond. I'll tell you more about how I feel after that." A twinkle sparked in her eyes, and she added with a grin, "After I've seen him in his dress uniform." Her mother shook her head indulgently as Rachel rose and left the room, saying, "I'm going to make Vince go with us. I want him to show up in public. I want to give Simon Duvall his chance to shoot him!"

"He won't go," Amy said.

"I'll steal his pants if he doesn't! He'll have to go!"

All day Jake worried about dinner with Vince's father, but finally realized that there was no sense in that. *If he sees through me, that's that,* he finally summed it up. The thing was made easier by a short meeting he'd had with the two men earlier. He was reading in the library when he heard horses, and going to the window, he saw two men in uniform dismount and give the reins to Tad, who was grinning broadly at them.

"Might as well get the worst over," Jake said, taking his crutches and making his way down the hall. By the time he arrived, everyone seemed to be gathered in the library. He stood just beyond the doorway, listening as they talked and laughed with Rachel and Les, then swung into the room.

Brad Franklin looked up with shock in his eyes, which Jake had expected. But he said, "Well, now, I thought you'd be flat on your back, Vince."

"I'm sure you did," Jake said, a mocking tone in his voice. "But I've had good nursing."

Brad's face reddened a little at the tone in Jake's voice, but he still peered at Jake intently. Grant stared, too, and an uncomfortable silence was filling the room. Quickly Rachel said, "You can talk later, Daddy. Go now and see Mama." Jake threw her a look of gratitude, which only seemed to confuse her.

Blast! he thought. *Out of character again. I've got to be more careful.*

Drawing a breath, he said coldly, "Yes, by all means, go see Mother. That is, of course, if you've had your fill of staring at me. Though I'm sure seeing me like this brings you some pleasure, I don't appreciate being scrutinized like some deformed animal that's going to be destroyed."

"Now just a minute—!" Grant began to protest at Jake's insulting comments, but his father cut him off, placing a restraining hand on his son's arm and shaking his head. He moved to leave, saying, "I'll see you at dinner, son."

Jake said nothing in response. Grant threw him an angry look and stepped closer, then said, "You look terrible! But one thing's certain, even if I didn't recognize your face right off, your rotten personality would identify you in a second."

Jake smiled coldly. "What a shame, dear brother, that you weren't there to see me when they first pulled me out from under that building. You might have talked them into just letting me die."

With a muffled exclamation, Grant turned and left the room. Jake glanced at Rachel, noting the tightness of her expression. She merely looked at him for a moment, then shook her head and walked away. Jake sighed, relieved not to have to talk anymore. But he felt a tension growing within himself. *Grant couldn't believe I was Vince—and Mr. Franklin knows Vince better. One slip, and the whole thing's over.*

Later that night at dinner, Brad Franklin was not paying as much attention to his oldest son as he might have. He was being very attentive to his wife, who had been placed at his right hand, her leg bolstered with cushions. She was as beautiful to him as ever and had dressed for the occasion in a dress of light blue silk that set off her complexion.

The two newcomers ate hungrily, and at Les's insistence his father spoke of what had been happening. "Well, we were in the Battle of Ball's Bluff. That was on October twenty-first. General Shanks Evans—the one who held the first of the Yankee charges at Manassas—was in command at Leesburg. The old man drinks like a fish, but he's a fighter, isn't he, Grant?"

"A wildcat," Grant agreed, nodding. "I guess that Union general knows that now!"

"General Stone, that's his name." His father nodded. "He got the idea of crossing the Potomac and attacking us. Well, Stone managed to stay out of the actual fighting, so he sent Colonel Edward D. Baker to make the crossing. He did get across the river, but he ran into four whole brigades, including the Grays." He lifted his glass, took a sip of water, then shook his head. "It was a bloody massacre," he said quietly. "The poor Yankee privates were trapped, and it was like shooting fish in a barrel."

Grant continued the account. "We drove them back to the river, but there was no way for them to cross. So we had them in a crossfire." A shiver passed through Grant's shoulders, and he said, "I did my share of the shooting, but I couldn't help but think what it would be like if our fellows were pinned down like that."

"I read something about it in the paper," Les said. "There's a big public outcry, and Stone is the man they blame. And Evans is the hero around here."

Brad looked up and, seeing that the talk had disturbed Amy and Rachel, said quickly to Jake, "Well, let's hear your report, son. Tell us about the fire."

Jake was taken off guard but managed to give a brief summary of the event, then said, "It's a good thing you sent Rachel to get me, sir. I was getting pretty low in that hospital."

"Well, to tell the truth, I didn't send her," Brad said. "I was off with the company, and you know Rachel and your mother. They cooked the whole thing up."

"Dr. Maxwell says he's doing fine, Daddy," Rachel said. "I think he's right, don't you, Melora? He's not nearly so much trouble now as he was when he first got here."

Melora had listened to the major's story of the battle, and after agreeing with Rachel, she asked, "Did you see my brother, Major Franklin?"

"He didn't, but I did," Grant said. Grant was a second lieutenant of the Third Platoon of Company D. "Bushrod Aimes is your brother's lieutenant, and we were next to each other on the march and in the line. I even had mess once with the squad your brother is in."

"Is he all right?" Melora asked.

"Sure, he's fine," Grant assured her. "You don't have to worry about him." A smile came to his lips, and he added, "That's a tough platoon. Got a sergeant named Waco Smith who was a Texas gunfighter of some sort. Still carries a .44 on his hip, despite regulations. And Uncle Clay, he's in that platoon, too, and you know what a dead shot *he* is!"

A brief silence went over the room, and suddenly Grant's cheeks reddened. He had forgotten about the rumors concerning his uncle and Melora. Now he said quickly, "Clay and your brother Bobby are the best shots in the whole regiment—next to the chaplain, that is." He looked to his father for verification. "Aren't they, sir?"

"Yes, they are. I expect they'll be made sharpshooters as soon as we can get some Whitworth rifles. But Grant's right, Melora. Your brother is in a tough outfit, and they're learning how to take care of each other."

"Is Dent Rocklin back with the Grays?" Rachel asked.

"No, not yet. I think he and his bride are still too much in love for him to do much soldiering," Major Franklin said with a smile. "He'd be likely to say to a recruit who was disobeying orders, 'Now don't do that, sweetheart,' instead of bawling him out properly."

"They're back from their honeymoon," Rachel said. "I ran into Raimey a few days ago. They're staying at Gracefield. I expect Raimey will stay there with Susanna until the war's over."

"She's a fine girl," her father said. "From what I hear, she's not let her blindness spoil her life. That's a good thing, isn't it?"

"Very good," his wife said quietly. "It seems to me that God was in that meeting. There was Dent with his terrible wounds, wanting to die, and God sent what you might think would be the very *last* person to save him. But when God does things, He sometimes has to use ways that seem most strange to us."

Rachel said, "Well, if you're all finished with your stories. . . I have an announcement." Everyone looked at her, and she said soberly, "I have a gentleman friend."

"Not you, the spinster of Lindwood!" Grant exclaimed in mock horror.

"Yes, and he's got to be tested. I want to find out if he's serious. Young men can't be trusted these days, you know."

"What sort of test are you giving this young man?" her father asked.

"He's coming to take me to the ball in Richmond. I want all of you to be ready. When he comes to call for me, he'll find he's not only taking me, but my whole family!"

"Oh, come now, Rachel," her father protested with a slight smile at her proposal. "That's too hard a test for any man!"

"No, it's not," Rachel answered coolly, then added, "He's supposed to be an officer and a gentleman, and I'm going to find out if he really is."

"An officer? Which officer?" Franklin demanded.

"Captain Leighton Semmes."

"Semmes? I know him," Grant said, grinning. "He'll run

like a rabbit when he sees this crew!"

"Not if he's serious," Rachel insisted. "Now you're all to come. All except Mama."

"I'd rather stay home with your mother," Brad protested.

"I know you would, but you've got to go. You're the one who has to corner Captain Semmes and ask if his intentions are honorable."

"And I'm the one who calls him out if he says they aren't." Grant laughed. "Oh, we've got to do it, Father!"

"Yes, you can tell me all about it when you get home," Amy insisted.

"Well, he's definitely serious if he takes this whole bunch on," Brad Franklin said, smiling. "*I'd* have run like a rabbit if the whole Rocklin bunch had ganged up on me when I was courting your mother."

"No, you wouldn't," Rachel said calmly. "You'd have faced up to them, and that's what I want a man to do. I know this one can make nice speeches, but there's more to a man than that." Then she said, "All right, we all go. Agreed?" She looked around the table but paused when she saw Jake.

"You go, too, Vince. No shirkers around here."

"Why, I can't dance with this leg, and I look like the devil. Grant said so."

"You go or I'll hide your pants and saw your crutches in two," she said. "It'll do you good."

The others were looking at him, and Jake finally asked, "What about Simon Duvall? Are you going to take a pistol to him again if he threatens me?"

"What's that?" Brad asked in alarm.

"I'll tell you later, dear," Amy said quickly, then added, "You must go. I'll ask it as a favor."

Jake dropped his head in confusion, feeling their eyes on him. Finally he lifted his eyes and met Rachel's direct gaze. "Well, I guess one ball can't hurt too much."

CHAPTER 11

A FANCY BALL

The letter from Vince came on Tuesday afternoon. Jake was making his way carefully around the walk that circled the house when a buggy drove up the driveway. "Hey, Vince," the driver called out. "Got some mail for you."

Jake swung himself toward the buggy, and the driver—a short, pudgy man with a set of sweeping Burnside whiskers—reached into a box by his side and brought out a handful of letters. "Got it here somewhere," he said, cheerfully sorting through a few. "Ain't seen you since you got back. Thought maybe you might drop around and we could have a few."

"Been flat on my back most of the time," Jake said cautiously. Obviously the man was a friend. "How've you been?"

"Oh, fine. But did you hear about Grady? No? Well, he got himself in a mess with that Wadsworth girl over in Batesville." The man chattered on about the incident, finally getting a few letters separated. Shoving the bulk of them back into the box, he thrust the rest toward Jake, saying, "That's the lot. You going to the ball in Richmond tonight?"

"Guess so. Won't be doing any dancing, though."

"Well, I'll see you there," the messenger said as he grinned.

900

"Least that bum leg won't keep you from drinking. 'Sides, Mabel Richards will be glad to sit out the dances with you. See you there."

Jake waved, then turned back toward the house as the buggy pulled away. He moved slowly, managing the steps cautiously, then sat down on one of the cane-bottomed chairs. Thumbing through the letters, he found that only one was for Vince. It was addressed in strong, bold strokes—a man's handwriting. He opened it and looked at the signature, then grew still. Bill Underhill! The letter was from Vince! Jake's eyes flew to the top of the page, and he began reading.

It was innocuous enough. It began,

> Well, Vince, I've landed down in Memphis for a while. Guess I'll stay here until things get settled. Unless, of course, the Yankees come and take the city. But they'd have to take either New Orleans or Vicksburg to do that, so I'm fine for now. I am running a little low on money. Could you send me the two hundred dollars I loaned you? It would tide me over for a time.

The rest of the letter was a breezy account of Vince's activities, which Jake skimmed through. When he finished the letter, he put it back in the envelope and thought about it. He had to send the money, but it was a touchy subject, for he had no idea how Vince's financial affairs worked. He had less than fifty dollars left of the money that had been in Vince's wallet. Well, he would have to get more.

There was a busy air throughout the house, with the women scurrying around getting ready for the ball. He went to his room and began searching through the large desk, finding almost at once some canceled checks and other receipts in one of the drawers. There were several statements from the Planter's Bank of Richmond, the last one dated in September. The balance showed a figure of $540, and finding some blank checks, Jake was writing a check for $200 when a thought came to him. He then wrote a brief letter:

> *Dear Bill,*
>
> *All seems to be going well with our venture. So far I have been able to do all the things we talked about, though it has been a little touchy at times. By the way, you might let me know a little bit more about the financial end of our partnership, such as income and how to switch funds, things like that. I am enclosing a check for $200 as you requested. Let me hear from you soon, and I'll keep you posted on things here.*
>
> *Sincerely yours,*
> *Vince Franklin*
> *Richmond, Virginia*

As he put the letter and check in an envelope, he thought, *Got to get word to the bank that my signature will be different for a time.* He sealed the envelope with a stick of sealing wax he had found in the desk. But there were no stamps, so he put the envelope in his pocket and went to find Rachel.

"I don't have a stamp," he said when he found her in the kitchen. "Will you mail this for me?"

Taking the letter, she nodded, then commented, "You write better with your left hand than you do with your right." She looked at him, that curious light in her eyes again, as though something was tugging at her awareness but couldn't quite get through.

"Guess I took more care with it," Jake said, then added quickly, "I really don't think it's a good idea for me to go to that ball. Maybe I could stay home with Mother."

He saw that he had successfully distracted her from the letter. Her eyes flashed, and she retorted at once, "You need to go. It'll stop some of the talk that's going around. And while the talk may not bother you, it definitely bothers Father."

He had waited for her to tell him of her encounter with Simon Duvall, but she had never said a word. Now he asked, a mocking tone in his voice, "You going to take your pistol in case Duvall comes after me?"

Rachel showed a trace of embarrassment. "He won't come after you. All he's got is some sort of foolish pride in his dueling ability. When you get well, he may try to go on with the thing, but he can't afford to attack an injured man."

"Especially if he's likely to be shot in the back of the head from a dark alley," Jake remarked.

"Oh, I just lost my temper," Rachel said quickly, then changed the subject. "You just be ready on time tonight. Jupe will help you with your clothes."

Jake grinned at her as she turned with a flounce and walked away.

❧

When Leighton Semmes walked up the steps of the mansion at Lindwood, he felt an exhilaration such as he hadn't felt in years. His experience with women had jaded him, but the strong draw he felt to Rachel Franklin was something new. Oh, he had been with women who were more beautiful, but his attraction went beyond her looks, which actually were quite pleasing. What he found most fascinating about her was her resistance to him.

The door opened as he walked up the steps, and a black servant said, "Come in, sir. The family is just getting ready."

Semmes faltered, not knowing exactly what to think of that, but he followed the servant out of the foyer and into a large drawing room that seemed to be rather crowded.

"Ah, Captain Semmes! Just in time to turn around and go back to town!" Rachel's father came to greet him, a smile on his lean face. "Do you know everyone?"

Semmes looked around, nodding to Grant and Les, both of whom he knew slightly, but said, "All except this lady, I think."

"Melora, may I present Captain Leighton Semmes of Stuart's cavalry. Captain, this is Miss Melora Yancy."

"My pleasure, Miss Yancy," Semmes said with a bow. He had heard of her, as had most people in his circle. Now seeing her in a white dress that set off her dark beauty, he didn't wonder that the Rocklin fellow had fallen for her. Just then Rachel came into the room, and he turned to her at once.

"Well, Captain, you look very dashing," Rachel said, admiring the gray uniform set off by a scarlet sash and a gleaming saber. "You'll dazzle all the young ladies, I'm sure."

Semmes paused uncertainly, for he felt that she was laughing at him, something that had never happened before. Then her brother Les said, with a twinkle in his eye, "You won't have a chance, sister, not against those good-looking city girls!"

Semmes came up with a smile, saying, "Not at all true! You'll be the belle of the ball, Miss Franklin." His words were more than mere gallantry, too, for she was beautiful tonight. Her ball gown had delicate dove gray and rose stripes, and she had sewn clusters of pink rosebuds to gather the fullness of her billowing skirt into festoons above a silk and lace petticoat that rustled with the slightest motion. With her honey-blonde hair done up in a graceful swirl and her large blue-green eyes flashing, she was a true beauty.

"Well, we're all here except Vince," Major Franklin said, but even as he spoke, Semmes turned to see a man enter on crutches. "This is my oldest son, Vincent," the major said to Semmes. "I don't believe you two have met."

"Happy to meet you," Semmes said. He took in the light gray suit, the ruffled shirt, and the string tie that the young man was wearing, then said, "We did meet once, at a horse race in Savannah."

"I don't think I remember you, Captain," Jake said quickly.

"Well, let's get to that ball," Major Franklin said, saving Jake from any further conversation with Semmes. The major led the way to the front of the house, where a large carriage was pulled up with Tad holding the reins. "I think there's room for all of us," Franklin said.

"Oh, let's not crowd ourselves," Semmes remarked. "I'll take Miss Rachel in my buggy."

"That's a good idea," Rachel said, then added innocently, "It'll be an easier ride for you in the buggy, too, Vince. You won't have to crowd your leg into such a small space." If she saw the irritation on Semmes's face, she ignored it. "Jupe, help Mr. Vince into the buggy."

Jake was amused at the disappointment on the face of Semmes, and also at the tactics of Rachel. However, he said, "You get in first, Rachel. I think the outside would be easier on this leg. Besides, the captain didn't get all dressed up to sit beside me."

Rachel seemed to be the only one who enjoyed the ride to Richmond. The bouncing of the buggy caused Jake's injured leg to ache, and Leighton Semmes found the presence of Rachel's brother an impediment to his plans for the ride. Not that it would have mattered, for the large carriage filled with her relatives followed so closely that he could hear Les's frequent inquiries of "How's it goin' up there, Captain?"

Semmes put his horses to a fast pace, but when he pulled up in front of the hotel where the ball was to be held, he was disappointed to see that the black driver had kept up. Helping Rachel down, he whispered, "I thought you were a good girl! And here you foist your whole blasted family off on me!"

She smiled, and there was a gleam of humor in her eyes as she said, "Why, Leighton, I do believe you're put out with me!" The two of them went inside, and Les came along to give Jake a hand down.

"You three sure did make a lovely couple," he laughed, handing Jake his crutches. "Bet you ten dollars the captain sneaks off without you."

"No takers." Jake swung across the drive on his crutches and made his way awkwardly up the three steps; then he and Les went into the main ballroom, followed by the rest of the party. Jake's eyes, still sensitive to flashing lights, reacted as he walked inside, for the new, recently installed gaslights were much brighter than anything that had preceded them. He halted abruptly, half blinded, but Melora came to take his arm, saying, "Let's go sit by the wall, Vincent."

As she led him to a line of chairs and saw him seated, he thought of how sensitive she was. "Thanks, Melora. I'm blind as a bat from those lights!" She sat down beside him with an understanding smile. Before long, his eyes had adjusted, and he looked around the ballroom with curiosity.

Lighted prisms dangled below glass shades on the lofty ceiling, casting miniature rainbows upon the dancers who whirled and glided across the glistening parquet floor of the fabulous green and gold ballroom. Around the floor, green velvet draperies framed the scene. Intricately wrought Spanish ironwork decorated a broad staircase that led to the second floor and formed a balcony to accommodate the musicians. It was too late in the year for flowers, but banks of evergreen branches reached to each end of the glistening dance floor and into every available corner, filling the room with their pungent fragrance.

On the bandstand nine musicians worked at sending out the music that floated over the room. Violas and violins sang like great nightingales, a harp tinkled, and flutes and oboes added a liquid accompaniment. Jake took note that there were no vulgar instruments, such as drums, accordions, or banjos.

Shifting his gaze to the dance floor, he saw that the dominant color was the gray of the officers' uniforms, set off by the black sheen of boots and the golden flash of brass buttons. But it was the dresses of the women that caught the eye as they flashed to the strains of a waltz, some of them startlingly décolleté, glowing in flowered and looped gowns of sapphire, yellow, pink, green, and white.

Melora said, "Look, there's Dent Rocklin and his Raimey!" Jake glanced at the couple who were floating by, noting the angry scar on the man's face and remembering what had been said about the two. "I'd never believe she's blind," he murmured. "She's very beautiful, isn't she?"

"Very, and her spirit is beautiful, too." She started to say something else, but she suddenly halted. Looking quickly in the direction of her glance, Jake saw another couple moving around the floor. He identified the man at once as Clay Rocklin. *That must be his wife, Ellen,* Jake realized. *The woman Vince said was pretty loose.*

He studied the pair, saying nothing, for he remembered the rumors that Clay and Melora were in love. He saw the woman look at him, then say something to her partner, who also glanced in his direction. Then they moved across the floor toward him. Jake braced himself, knowing that they were coming to speak to him, and determined to say as little as possible.

While Ellen and Clay had been dancing, there was little pleasure in it for either of them. When Clay had come home with the Grays, he had gotten a note almost at once from regimental headquarters stating that he was to see his wife immediately, that an urgent message had come from her. When he finally had found her—not at Gracefield but at her room in Richmond—there had been no emergency except for the one in Ellen's mind.

She had demanded money, and when he had tried to explain that there was no money to be given, she had exploded in a rage. He had stood there listening to her raving and the curses that she laid on him, but had said only, "Ellen, it's all I can do to pay for your expenses here in Richmond. If you'd stay at home, you'd have more money to spend on clothes."

His words had had no effect, and finally she had released him, but not before extracting a promise that he would take her to the regimental ball. Clay had reluctantly agreed, on the condition that Rena, their fifteen-year-old daughter, would accompany them.

As Clay had expected, though, the evening was a failure. He spent most of the evening talking to Rena, dancing only when practically forced to. When Ellen had pulled him to the floor, both of them were well aware that it was for the sake of form. But then she had said, "Look, there's your nephew Vince."

Clay had glanced toward the side of the room, saying, "I

heard he was back. He must not have been hurt as badly as we heard if he's at a dance."

"Come on, let's go speak to him."

Clay was surprised, for Ellen had disliked his nephew for a long time. "All right," he agreed, but when they got to where Vince was seated, he regretted it at once—for Melora was seated beside young Franklin. He shot a glance at Ellen, who wore a cruel smile as she watched his reaction.

"Now you can see your lady friend," she hissed, but as they came to the couple, she said brightly, "Vince Franklin, I don't believe it!" She turned to Melora, saying, "Why—Miss Yancy, I didn't see you sitting here."

"How are you, Mrs. Rocklin?" Melora said calmly. She knew Ellen Rocklin had spread vile rumors about her husband and herself, calling her the "white-trash Yancy girl," but she only added, "See how well your nephew is doing, Mister Clay?"

"Yes, indeed. I'm pleased to see you on your feet, Vince, but you look quite different without your beard and moustache."

Jake risked saying, "Well, I'm lucky to be here at all." He knew that both of the Rocklins were surprised at his appearance, then added, "Look like a stray alley cat, don't I?"

"Not at all, Vincent," Ellen said at once. "I always thought you should have gotten rid of those whiskers. You look much better without them. Now I'm going to sit here and talk to Vincent, Clay, so you must ask Miss Yancy to dance with you."

It was exactly the cruel sort of thing that Ellen would think of, and she was pleased to see shock run across Clay's face. "You don't mind, do you, Miss Yancy?" she pressed.

Melora was placed in an impossible position by this request, for she was the one about whom tongues would wag for days. Even so, she rose gracefully, saying, "Of course not, Mrs. Rocklin."

Clay was left with no choice, and so he led her to the dance floor. They moved out to the sound of the music, and he said bitterly, "I'm sorry, Melora."

"Why, I think that's awful—that you're sorry to dance with me!" she said and looked up at him with a smile. "I thought you were a more gallant man than that, Mister Clay!"

He admired her tremendously at that moment for her courage and her poise. " 'Mister Clay.' " He echoed her use of his name. "That's what you called me when you were a little girl. I still like it. But I'm afraid this will be trouble for you."

"Just enjoy the dance, Mister Clay. I love the color and the music, don't you? The dance will be over in a little while, but there will be many nights that I will lie on my bed and live this moment over again! That's my treasure, you know."

"What's that, Melora?"

She was light in his arms, and he caught the faint odor of lilac, her favorite scent. The lights danced in her eyes, and her lips were curved in a faint smile as she said, "Memories. I keep them in a room in my mind, and when I get sad or lonely, I go there and look at them. Some people do that with paintings, but my treasures have sound and I can smell them and taste them. Do you remember the time we made ice cream and I put blackberries in it? I can still feel how cold the ice cream was on my teeth, making them ache, and how sharp the berries tasted—and how the juice ran down your chin!"

"You still remember that?" he asked, surprised. "Why, you were no more than twelve years old! But I remember it, too. And so many other things about you."

She blinked suddenly and dropped her head, and at once he

knew that she was sad. A heaviness came on him, and he said, "Melora, I must say something. A hard thing."

"Yes? What is it?"

Clay had trouble getting the words out, but it was a thing he had to do. It had been on his mind for a long time, and though speaking the thoughts was like a knife in his side, he said, "You've got to say good-bye to me, Melora—you must!" He spoke quickly, cutting off her attempts to speak. "Listen to me! You've got so much to offer, and it's wasted. I know you have feelings for me, and I—I have some for you, too, but we have to forget them."

"How do you do that, Mister Clay?"

Her question was spoken quietly, but it hit him hard. "I know, Melora. I know what you're saying...but I've been wrong about this thing. I should have broken it off long ago."

"What have we done that's wrong?"

"Nothing like what the gossip has put on us," he said instantly, but pain pulled his mouth into a tight shape. "But I have done a wrong thing: I have kept you from having the life you deserve, a life with a family and children. Now—right now, Melora—I'm releasing you. We've never made any promises, but the tie is there. From this night on, you're free."

"Free to do what?"

"Free to marry, to have children—to be a wife and a mother, for that's what you were born for, Melora."

She said nothing; she only finished the dance. Then as the last notes sounded, she nodded. "All right. Let it be so."

❧

As soon as Clay led Melora away, Ellen began probing Jake, asking questions about the fire and about what he'd done since he'd been home. Jake answered briefly, saying at one point, "It still hurts me to talk, thanks to all that smoke I inhaled."

"You sound so different," Ellen commented, and she studied his face carefully. There was a sharp quality in her eyes that disturbed Jake, for it was not a look of ordinary curiosity. He knew how to handle curiosity well enough, but there was some sort of predatory quality in her manner—something strange and unusual that made him tense and ill at ease. She asked so many questions that he finally said in desperation, "The fire seemed to do something to my thinking, too. For instance, I just can't seem to remember some things."

Then she deliberately put her hand on his arm in a caressing manner and leaned forward to say, "You haven't forgotten *everything*, have you?"

Suddenly Jake understood what was happening, and he recoiled from the knowledge. There was no mistaking the way that Ellen Rocklin was touching him, nor the suggestive way she leaned forward so that the full curve of her bosom pressed against him.

She and Vince Franklin must have been lovers! Jake's mind reeled. He sat there almost paralyzed, unable to think at all—but he didn't have to, for at that moment Clay and Melora appeared, and Ellen leaned back. She patted Vince's arm maternally, saying, "Look at this poor hand, dear! It was a frightful burn!"

"Oh, it's much better!" Jake said quickly and attempted to pull his hand free. But Ellen was leaning down staring at it. "It looks pretty bad," he said uncomfortably, "but the doctor said it'll be as good as new."

"Oh, that's good," Ellen said, but there was a strange gleam in her eyes as she spoke. Then she rose, saying, "You must come to see us at Gracefield. Good night, Miss Yancy."

When the two Rocklins left, Jake drew a shaky breath. He wanted to get up and run out of the ballroom but knew that he could not. "Think I'll go get some of that punch, Melora. Want to come along?"

"Yes, that would be nice."

He got to his feet, and they made their way to the long table groaning with refreshments of all kinds. They found Semmes and Rachel there, and the four of them stood together for a time, Semmes doing most of the talking.

Just when Jake was about to go back to his chair, he saw Rachel's eyes widen, then narrow. "There's Duvall," she said quietly. She looked at Jake, obviously hoping her half brother would do something, but he wanted nothing to do with Duvall. He had long ago decided that his only hope of avoiding a duel—his only chance of not having to kill the man—was to stay away from him. Now he deliberately turned and left the ballroom, turning his back on the startled Duvall. As he swung along, he was aware that he was being watched, and he saw several men curl their lips as he left the room.

Rachel, Semmes noted, had turned pale, but not with anger. "I guess that pretty much removes any doubt that Vince is a coward," she said so quietly that only he heard it.

"Well, after all, he's crippled, Rachel," Semmes offered.

"Would you do such a thing, Leighton? Run from a man like that?"

"Well, I—"

"No, you wouldn't." She looked across the room as Jake passed through the door. "I wish he'd died in that fire," she said, and there was sadness in her eyes. "Vince was never much—but he's *nothing* now!"

When Jake got outside, he found Tad, who had driven the

large carriage. "Tad, help me in."

"But the dancin' ain't ovah, Marse Vince."

"It is for me!"

Jake sat there, wishing that he were anyplace in the world but in that carriage. He longed to pick up the lines and drive the carriage as far from Richmond as possible.

But he could not. He sat there until the Franklins came and got into the carriage. No one spoke to him, and the silence was thick all the way back to Lindwood. When Tad pulled the carriage up in front of the house, they all got out and went into the house. After they were gone, Tad asked cautiously, "You want me to hep you down, Marse Vince?"

"Yes."

Jake got to the ground with the servant's help, then went to his room. He lay down on the bed, fully dressed, not even lighting the lamp. The darkness was a warm blanket that hid him from the world, and he longed for an even blacker night to cover him. But he knew that the morning would come and that he would have to face the world.

Suddenly one thought came to him, but he rejected it at once. It was the thought that he might pray to God.

"No!" he cried out between clenched teeth. "I've done without God this far! I won't whine now, like a whipped puppy!"

He put the thought away and lay there steeling himself for the sunrise, when he would have to go out and face the sneers he knew would be waiting for him.

It was a long night—but not long enough for Jake Hardin.

CHAPTER 12

AN IMPOSSIBLE TASK

*L*ike I said, boy, the devil's going to take care of his own!"

There was a hint of grudging admiration in Dr. Maxwell's tone as he stepped back and watched Jake pull down his pant leg. He had given the young man's injuries a quick inspection, and now his watchful old eyes had a speculative look as he added, "I've seen good people take twice the time to get well that you have. Don't seem fair that a wastrel like you should have such an easy time!"

Jake smiled at the elderly physician, answering, "Sorry to upset your theology, Doctor. But it'll all catch up with me in the end, I guess." He stood and picked up the light cane for which he had traded his crutches. "How's my mother?"

Maxwell scratched his thick jowl, his fingernails making a rasping sound over the stubble he hadn't bothered to shave. "Not doing as well as I'd like." He looked around the room, then asked, "You got any drinking whiskey in here?"

"There's a bottle in the library. Come along." Jake moved ahead of the doctor, favoring his leg, and soon the two men were sharing a drink of whiskey. Jake wanted more details about Amy Franklin's injuries, but there was little that Maxwell could tell him.

915

"Don't pester me, Vince," he said with a flash of irritation in his voice. "I set the bone and that's all a man can do. Like I said, it's up to God now." He sipped the whiskey, then stared at the younger man. "And you and me, we don't have much influence there, do we?"

"Can't say about you, Doctor, but I don't have any myself."

Maxwell fired a question at him suddenly. "What you going to do about Duvall? You can't run every time you see him. This world's too small for that."

It was the first reference anyone had made about the incident at the ball to Jake himself, although he knew there had been much talk. The Franklin family had not said a word, but there was a coolness toward Jake that had not been there before the ball. Rachel had not smiled at him since that night, and his father had not said more than half a dozen words to him. Amy alone had retained her warmth, and for that reason Jake had spent more time with her than with anyone else.

"They say time heals all wounds, don't they?" He answered Maxwell's question with a question, then added, "Sooner or later Duvall will either get killed in one of his duels or he'll get killed in the war—or maybe he'll just forget it."

"And so you're just going to hide in your little hole, hoping for one of those things?" Maxwell snorted in disgust, finished the whiskey, then slammed the glass down. "You're a fool, boy!" He turned angrily and stomped out of the library. Jake picked up the glasses and, as he made his way to the kitchen, heard the door slam.

"You're right about that, Doc," he murmured. Entering the kitchen, he found Melora shelling peas. She nodded at him but said nothing. She was not, he thought, angry or disappointed in him as was the rest of the household, but she did seem to have lost some of her quickness of spirit lately. He didn't understand why, but he regretted it. "Guess I'll go sit with Mother awhile," he said. "Maybe she'd like some tea."

"She's asleep right now. Wait for an hour or so."

"All right. Can I help you shell peas?"

She did smile then but shook her head. "I'm almost finished. Why don't you go down to the barn and see the new colt? You need to get out more."

"Well, maybe I will." He paused to say, "I miss having you read to me. Maybe I shouldn't have let you know that my eyes are about normal." When she only smiled and shook her head, he turned and left the room. *She's carrying some kind of load*, he thought as he put on his heavy coat and wool cap. *Wouldn't be surprised if it had something to do with Clay Rocklin. She's not been the same since the night of the ball.*

He left the house, blinking at the cold wind that bit at his face. The world seemed dead with all of the grass a dry brown color and the trees looking like skeletons with long bony fingers lifted to a colorless gray sky. Dry leaves rustled as he walked across the frozen ground, and a gust of wind gathered some of them together in a miniature whirlwind. They lurched at him and seemed to strike at his leg; then they broke apart to go tumbling across the lawn.

The barn was large, with many stalls for horses, a few for milking cows, and a huge loft stuffed with hay. Jake passed by one of the slaves, an elderly man named Delight, who was milking a cow. "Hi, Marse Vince," he said cheerfully. "You come to help me milk dis ol' cow?"

"Guess not, Delight," Jake said, smiling at the slave. "I never could get the hang of milking." He passed along to where the horses were kept and found the new colt with her dam in a walled-off section at the far end. But the leggy creature was not alone. Rachel stood there stroking his nose. She looked up as Jake entered, saying, "Hello, Vince," in a level tone.

Jake nodded, then put his weight on his good leg, saying, "Good-looking foal." He studied the long slender legs, the wide-spaced eyes, and the fine barrel of the animal, then remarked, "He might win a race or two."

Rachel was wearing her outdoor working clothes—a pair of men's overalls and a worn white shirt. A felt slouch hat was pulled down over her forehead, and she wore a pair of leather boots that were well scuffed and dirty. The old coat she wore was made of wool, but it had lost any color it might have had long ago and had only one button in front.

Even in clothes like that, she's beautiful, Jake thought with a start.

The colt stared wildly at Jake, then moved closer to Rachel, pushing at her with his silky nose. Rachel laughed. "There's your mother over there," she said, but stroked the face of the colt, allowing it to nibble at her fingers. She was, Jake thought as he watched her, more attractive in old clothes than most women were in ballroom gowns.

"What's his name?" he asked, wanting to hear her speak. Although he had not admitted it to himself, he had missed his times with Rachel more than he had thought possible. She had been hard, almost cold, but considering his role, he could understand that. Besides, he had come to know that hardness was not what Rachel was really made of; she had a fundamental sweetness that she kept concealed under a rough display of manners—and it was that hidden nature that Jake had grown to like.

"I would like to call him Precious," she said. "But he'd be

embarrassed by that when he's a big stallion. I guess he'll be Stonewall."

"After Jackson?"

"Yes. All colts are flighty, but the first time I came to see this one, he stood there stock still, and I thought of Jackson and what General Bee said about him at Manassas: 'Rally on the Virginians, men—there stands Jackson, like a stone wall!'"

"Good Southern name for a fine Southern foal," Jake said.

Rachel gave the foal a slap, which made him snort and stagger back to his dam; then she moved away toward the door. "Going back to the house?" he asked quickly, attempting to prolong their moment together.

"No, I'm going to give Crow a workout. He hasn't been ridden in a while, and you know how ornery he gets when that happens." She was at the door and waited as he followed her, hobbling a bit to keep up. When they got to a stall where a tall black horse stared at them over the bars with a pair of wicked eyes, she suddenly turned to Jake, saying, "You know, I think your fear of horses started with Crow. From the time he piled you up when you were sixteen, you've stayed away from horses. It's a shame. There are so many fine horses here, and you don't get any pleasure out of them."

Jake said carefully, "Well, maybe you're right, Rachel." He hesitated, not wanting to get too far from Vince's habits, but finally said, "I'd like to ride a little this morning—maybe not on Crow, but on a nice steady horse."

She looked at him, surprise reflected in her eyes. "Well, there's plenty of those around. If you really mean it, I'll have Lady saddled for you."

He agreed, and she called out to one of the slaves to saddle the two horses. When they were ready, Jake moved toward the mare, a smallish horse with a finely shaped head. She turned around to look at him calmly, then snorted once and waited. Tossing his cane onto a bale of hay, Jake took the reins from the slave, grabbed the saddle horn, then put his left foot into the stirrup. "Need some help?" Rachel asked. She had mounted the big stallion in one swift motion and was watching him carefully.

"No, I can make it, I think." Jake shoved off with his good leg, pulling his weight up with both hands, and managed to throw his right leg over the horse, coming to rest in the saddle with a grunt. It had brought a twinge of pain to his leg, but he was happy to know that he was able to ride. He touched Lady with his heels, and she moved obediently, stepping out of the barn into the corral, followed by the big stallion.

Rachel watched him with barely veiled amazement. "You've been on a horse before!"

Jake looked at her quickly. He had forgotten that Vince never rode, and Rachel was too much of a horsewoman for him to try to deny the obvious—that he had mounted the horse and started it out with confidence. Well, the best defense was a good offense, and if there was one thing Jake was learning to do, it was to be offensive.

He smiled mockingly. "Just because I choose not to ride doesn't mean I can't do so, dear sister. Though why that should matter to you is beyond me. Unless, of course, you're afraid that being wrong about me in one area may mean you're wrong about me in others. And that's just too much for you to take, isn't it, Rachel? Being wrong about me?"

For a brief moment, Jake thought Rachel would wheel Crow and ride away from him. Then, suddenly, her expression changed from anger to something he couldn't quite define— but it almost looked as though she was ashamed. She closed her eyes for a second, then spoke in a soft voice.

"I never thought I'd be saying this to you, Vince, but you're probably right. . .and I'm sorry."

Jake looked at her, stunned. When he didn't respond, she lifted her eyes to meet his, and the hurt and confusion he saw in her made him want to reach out and take her in his arms.

"I've had my mind made up about you for a very long time," she said. "And you've never given me any reason to change my opinion—until lately." She shook her head. "There's something different about you, Vince. I'm not sure I can trust it, but I want you to know I'm trying. And I will try to stop making judgments based on the past." She smiled wanly. "Mama says she's been praying for you for years. I guess I need to keep in mind that God just may be answering her prayers."

Jake was dumbfounded, but fortunately, Rachel didn't seem to need any response from him.

"Want to ride down to the river?" she asked, and Jake nodded. He had no idea where the river was, but he hoped it was far enough away for him to get his thoughts together. Rachel turned Crow's head toward a low-lying hill with a crop of tall timber at the crest. She kept her horse at a slow walk for Jake's benefit, but with some difficulty, for he wanted to bolt. "He's still rambunctious," Rachel commented. "I remember the day Daddy gave him to you. I cried all night," she said, smiling faintly at the old memory. "I wanted him so much!"

"Well, I guess you got him. I hear you're one of the few who can put up with his meanness," Jake commented. "He was just too much horse for me, I guess." She didn't respond, and he said, "You don't have to plod along with me, Rachel. Give him a run."

"I'll do that coming back. He needs to learn to mind." They

wound around a trail that led through a pine forest, then followed it around a small pond that was riffled with the sharp breath of wind. After crossing several fields, all forlorn-looking with their dead spikes of old cotton plants, the two riders came to the river. Actually, it was more of a creek than a river, for it was no more than twenty feet across, but it had steep banks, and Jake knew it would be a fine stream when the spring rains came.

It was a cold ride, but Jake enjoyed it. After being cooped up, he relished even the sharp bite of the wind. His face grew stiff and his hands, as well. "I like this," he said as they finally turned back. "I wish it would snow."

She looked at him curiously. "You've always hated cold weather. I remember so many times, after it had snowed, how Les and Grant and I would go out and make snowmen and have snowball fights—and you'd stay in the house huddled up to a fireplace."

"I wasn't much fun back then, was I?" he said quietly. When Rachel looked at him uncertainly, he added, "Guess I'm losing my taste for some things in my old age. People always say you do." Then he said idly, "Guess I'd be better off if I did change."

Crow suddenly lunged out, as was his habit from time to time, but Rachel gave the reins a quick jerk, bringing him to a halt. "Stop that!" she commanded and waited until Jake caught up. His remark had caught at her—if only she could believe it! After a silence, she picked up on it. "We all change, don't we? I mean, just getting older means we have to change in some ways. And that's a good thing. I'd hate to be like I was when I was twelve!"

He looked at her quickly, admiring the color the wind had brought to her smooth cheeks. "Why would you hate that?"

She laughed, seemingly embarrassed. "You don't remember what a pain in the neck I was to everyone then? Always crying or laughing—no middle ground. Every day I changed, and the world was either terrible or grand. I wonder why Daddy and Mama didn't have me put to sleep!"

Jake laughed at her outrageous conclusions, saying, "You're still a little along those lines, I think."

"Oh? I thought I was doing better. I wish I was more like Mama. She never gets flustered and bothered over things. Seems as though I cry over dead leaves!"

"Makes you more interesting." Jake grinned at her.

"That's not what you used to say," Rachel retorted. "You'd get so mad at my moods you begged Daddy to whip me."

"He didn't do much of that, did he?"

"Not enough, you'd probably say."

A question came to Jake, surprising him. He tried to put it out of his mind, but it wouldn't leave him alone. Finally he asked it carefully. "What about Leighton Semmes? You going to get emotional over him?"

"Leighton? Why, I don't know," she said, but his question disturbed her. She fell silent, and the two of them rode without speaking until they got to the crest of the hill overlooking the Big House. Pulling Crow to a stop, she said, "He's quite a fellow, isn't he? Money, looks, and all that."

Jake felt an irrational surge of annoyance at this description of the man. "You like him pretty well?" he asked, making his voice casual.

"Oh, I don't know, Vince!" she said with a trace of sudden irritation. The truth was that this question had been much on her mind, and she was upset that she had no clear answer. "Why are you so interested?"

Jake wondered at that himself but only answered, "Like to see the spinster of Lindwood get a good man. When I get old and broke, it'd be nice to have a rich brother-in-law to sponge off of."

"You're a scoundrel!" she remarked, laughing, surprised by his teasing tone. Then she grew more serious. "We're all going to change, aren't we? Nobody knows what this war will be like, not really. But I think it's going to be worse than the politicians think." She took off her slouch hat and shook her hair free, letting it fall over her shoulders. "I think we're going to lose everything."

"Father doesn't agree," Jake said. "And neither does Semmes, I'd guess. But you'd better keep thoughts like those to yourself. Anyone who speaks badly of the Cause is automatically branded a weakling—or worse."

"I know that, but I can't help what I think. Fortunately, even the war can't take everything away from me. I mean, nothing can take away what matters the most."

"Oh?" Jake looked at her curiously. Rachel returned his look, her eyes serious.

" 'Neither death, nor life, nor angels, nor principalities, nor powers, nor things present, nor things to come, nor height, nor depth, nor any other creature, shall be able to separate us from the love of God, which is in Christ Jesus our Lord,' " she quoted, her voice low and confident. "I know you don't believe in that," she said with a shrug, "but I know it's true. And I know that no matter what happens, God will be there to guide me and sustain me. *That's* what really matters."

Jake found himself strangely moved by what she said and by the confidence with which she said it. If only he could feel that way. . .

"Anyway," she said, putting on her hat, "Semmes won't be rich if we lose the war, now, will he? Maybe I'd better go North. Lots of rich Yankees, I hear." She slanted a mischievous grin at him.

"Let's both go," he said. "Bound to be some rich Yankee spinsters just waiting for a Southern gentleman to come into their lives."

Rachel giggled, saying, "We're a pair of silly fools, aren't we?"

Jake suddenly grew serious, his wide mouth growing tense. "To tell the truth, Rachel, I'd really like to cut and run. You're right about the war. The South is going to be ruined—no way she can win this war. And I don't want to see it."

Rachel glanced at him quickly. The last two weeks she'd been so ashamed of his cowardice she had avoided him. Now she was seeing something else, and for some reason it troubled her. Without thinking what she was doing, she moved Crow closer to the mare, reached out, and put her hand over his hands as they gripped the pommel. "God has given you so many gifts—and you've wasted them all."

He was acutely conscious of her firm hand on his. "Yes, I have," he said quietly, thinking of all he knew of Vince's past.

"You can change," Rachel said softly, and her voice drew his gaze. "Anybody can change—and down beneath all that anger, I believe there's a very fine man. I'd give anything to see you be that man."

He sat there, aware of her strength, her character—and of how very attractive she was to him. Suddenly he knew that under any other circumstances, he would have pulled her close and kissed her. He longed to do so with a force that startled him—and at that moment he was possessed by a most astounding realization. And that realization, with her hand, so warm and strong, on his, and the planes of her face, so soft and gentle, near his, struck him so hard that it nearly knocked the breath from him.

I love this girl!

It leaped into his mind, and he was so astonished that he could only sit still and stare at her. *Why, she's all I've ever wanted!* was his next thought, and he suddenly realized that behind all of his restless wandering had been a search for a woman like this. He had known many women, of course, but never before had he met one who stirred him as did Rachel Franklin.

Then, right on the heels of this revelation, came the cold fact of how hopeless his position was. A bleakness formed within him, and he could only say, "I'd like to be that man, Rachel—but it's not that easy."

A shadow came to her face as he said the words, and she drew her hand back. Disappointment pinched her lips together, and she said briefly, "I suppose not"; then she kicked Crow in the sides and shot off at a dead run.

Jake followed slowly. When he got to the barn and carefully dismounted, she was gone. Delight came up to say, "I'll take keer of yoah horse. You have a nice ride, Marse Vince?"

"Very nice," he said evenly and left the barn.

All during November of 1861, both North and South seemed to be caught in some sort of paralysis. After the horrible slaughter of Manassas, both nations had realized that the war was not going to be the quick affair they had expected. On November 6, in the first general election, Jefferson Davis was elected president of the Confederacy for a six-year term. On the first day of that same month, George B. McClellan officially replaced Lieutenant General Winfield Scott as general in chief of the United States Army. On November 8, two Confederate commissioners, James Mason and John Slidell, took passage aboard the British packet *Trent* out of Havana. Captain Charles Wilkes of the USS *San Jacinto* intercepted the British vessel in international waters and forced the British captain to surrender his passengers. This action came close to changing the course of the war, for it was an open act of aggression by the United States Navy against England.

There were skirmishes in the eastern sector, but the most significant military movement was the massing of Union troops in the West. An obscure officer named Ulysses S. Grant was assigned to the command of General John Charles Fremont; a red-haired, nervous general named Sherman was attached to that same army. Grant and Sherman would prove to be the most potent forces the North would bring to bear against the Confederacy. On November 13, President Lincoln paid a call on his new army chief, but McClellan kept the president waiting and finally retired for the evening without meeting his superior.

Jake Hardin heard about some of this and knew it was significant to the course of history, but it meant little to him. A much more significant event in his own life was a meeting that he had with Brad Franklin. Jake was sitting in the library reading *Ivanhoe* when Franklin came in and closed the folding doors. There was something in the man's manner that made Jake put the book down with alarm. When the major sat down in a chair and stared at him with a frown, Jake was certain that what was coming was something unpleasant.

"Vince, it's time to settle something."

"Yes, sir?"

Franklin's fair skin was windburned and rough from his

days in the field, and his rather hungry-looking face had none of the good humor to which Jake had grown accustomed. His eyes were pulled down into a squint, and his lips were tense as he said, "Maybe you can guess what I'm going to say."

"No, I don't think I can."

"All right, I'll give it to you as straight as I can. You're a failure in every way. I don't like to say that, especially since for years you've considered me to be unfair, favoring your brothers and sister over you. I'm sorry for that, but I can't change the way you feel—though it's been a grief to me."

Somewhere outside the window, some of the slaves were laughing as they raked the leaves from the oaks, and the cheerful noise of their voices sounded thin and far away, like happy crickets. The clock on the wall ticked solemnly, a ponderous and heavy brass pendulum arching in a uniform cadence from side to side.

Franklin looked down at his hands, sighed heavily, then said, "You've not been a good son. Maybe I've been a bad father— probably so—but my failures were honest ones. Yours were not. I won't lecture you, though. It's too late for that, I know."

He took some papers out of his pocket, opened them, and pressed them flat. "This is a copy of my father's will. You know what it says, or at least you know the part that pertains to you."

"Yes, sir."

"Well, my father was a difficult man, and I was a difficult son. He thought I didn't care for him, and he thought I didn't have any love in me, especially not enough to give a son if I ever had one. So he tied the bulk of the estate up in a trust and left it to my eldest son. You've been looking forward to that for a long time. As a matter of fact, it's ruined you! You never felt you had to do anything, because everything would one day be handed to you on a silver platter. You've spent your life on that trust, and I've seen it take every good thing out of you. You've become a womanizer, a drunk, and a coward—in short, Vince, you're a man without honor." He paused to ask, "Care to comment on that?"

"Well, no, sir, I guess not." Jake was wishing Vince were sitting in his chair—wishing it hard! He could not defend the life of another man, for he truly didn't know him. But he knew enough to be certain that much of what Franklin said was true.

"You've read the will carefully," Franklin said slowly, as if forcing the words from his lips, "but men have a way of seeing only what they want to see. If I could have found a way to break this will, I'd have done it in a second, but it can't be done. At least—not in the way my father might have expected."

"I don't understand you, sir."

"My father didn't respect me, but he was certain of one thing, and that was my love for the land, for Lindwood. He knew I'd do almost anything a man could do to keep the home place in the hands of Franklins. And he was right—or he was, up until now. But some things are too expensive, and I think holding on to this plantation may cost too much for us to do it."

"You're thinking about selling Lindwood?"

"No. That can't be done. Like most other planters, we live on borrowed money. What Father expected was that my oldest son, when he came into the bulk of the estate at the age of twenty-five, would save the place—pay off the mortgages, invest in new land, or buy more slaves. But you won't do those things."

"Well, it might be—"

"No, you've not shown the slightest interest in this place since you were young—at which time you apparently decided to go to the devil. Well, in a few months you'll be twenty-five, and the will says that you'll get the money." He paused, then shook his head slowly. "For years I've hoped you'd come to yourself, that you'd become a man, but you haven't changed a bit. So let me read you one little clause in the will you've probably never noticed." He lifted the copy, ran his eyes down it, then read, " 'The entire amount of the trust shall go to the eldest son of Bradford Lowell Franklin upon his twenty-fifth birthday, provided that he is at that time living at Lindwood and that my son, Bradford Lowell Franklin, certifies that he is qualified to receive the monies of the trust.' " Brad Franklin lowered the paper slowly, then shook his head. "It never occurred to Father that I'd refuse to certify you, but that's what I'm going to do."

The force of his words hit Jake a heavy blow—but not as heavy as he knew it would be to Vince! "But, sir—" he began, only to have Major Franklin cut him off.

"I won't argue this. The will states that if I don't certify that you are fit to receive the trust, it will go to charity. There are some causes that will be very happy to hear that some large sums are going to fall to them."

Jake had no idea of what to say. If only Vince were here! He finally said, "But that's foolish, isn't it? I mean, I'll be glad to see that the money goes to Lindwood—"

"Vince, you've done nothing but lie to me for years. Why would I take your word for anything?"

Jake sat there stunned, aware that Franklin was watching him with interest. *Probably expects me to start shouting and screaming*, he thought, but he knew that such behavior would have no effect. Brad Franklin was a firm man, and once he had made up his mind, no arguments would move him. Jake finally shrugged, saying, "I'm sorry it's come to this. Isn't there some way I could influence you? You may not believe me, but I'd like to see Lindwood prosper."

"Would you? You've never shown such a feeling for your home."

"Well, maybe nearly getting killed changed me some."

"I'd like to believe you. A lot of sweat and tears have gone into this place. I've put my life into it, and it was our dream—your mother's and mine—to grow old here, with our children and grandchildren around us."

"I—I'd like to see that, sir!"

When Jake said this, Franklin stared at him, letting the silence run on. He tried to see beyond the errors of his son's past and look for something that would make him feel that Vince could be honest. Finally he said, "I don't think you mean it—but if you want a chance to prove it—"

"Yes, I would like that. Very much!"

"All right, here it is—" Brad shook his head, interrupting himself long enough to say with a sour smile, "I thought you'd make some kind of offer to reform, to get the money. So if you'll do three things, I'll certify you for the trust."

"Three things?"

"All impossible, Vince, I really believe. But I'll lay them out; then you can do as you please. First, you'll ride Crow, really master him." He smiled at the expression on Jake's face. "That surprises you? Well, it's a small thing. I gave you that horse knowing that he was half outlaw. You were just starting to rebel, and I had the foolish idea that if you could learn to break a horse to your will, it would teach you something. But he won, didn't he? I saw it happen, and it's been a shame to me that my son is afraid of horses. Do you think men don't know that about you? How many times have I seen you get in a buggy like a woman, when the men were all riding horses?"

Jake had not understood that the matter of Crow was so serious, but now he saw that the horse was a symbol to Brad Franklin of his son's failure as a man. He said quietly, "You know I'm afraid of horses, and you know that Crow is a tough one. But I'll do my best with him."

"Will you? I'm thinking it's too late, but that's the easiest of the three. You can guess one of the other things, I would suspect."

Jake nodded, for it had leaped into his mind. "You want me to meet Simon Duvall."

Franklin looked grim. "I think most of this dueling business is wrong—and stupid! But a man sometimes has to choose—and you chose to be branded a coward in front of the world! I won't have it! You can take your chances with Duvall or forget about the trust. Your mother may not agree, but then again, I think she will. You may get shot, but if you do, I want to see the wounds in the front!"

Jake nodded slowly. "I agree."

Major Franklin was surprised and said so. "I don't think you'll go through with it, but you'll have to if you want the money. Now about the third thing, I had some hope that you might be willing to try a horse and a fight with Duvall. But the last thing—well, I can't see that you'll agree to it."

Jake was thinking hard, and he asked, "Does it have something to do with the war?"

"Yes, it does. You were always a quick thinker. This war, it's not what I wanted. But we didn't have the choice, most of us, so we've had to lay our lives down for our homes. You think it's foolish, this war. You've ridiculed it often enough. But if you want Lindwood, you'll have to fight for it—maybe die for it."

He leaned back, studying the face of the young man. "I'm probably asking too much, but I'm convinced that the final ruination of you would be to have great wealth put into your hands. Maybe nothing can change you, but if anything can, I think throwing yourself into a cause might. . .so I want you to join the South in their fight. The men in your regiment will know what you've stood for, and they won't make it any easier."

"No, I don't think they would." Jake felt trapped, and he said, "I'll need a little time. It's not a small thing you're asking, is it?"

"No, but there's no time for thinking. You'll either do it or you won't, Vince. If you're going to do it, I'll need to know pretty soon."

"All right." Jake got to his feet, looked around for his cane, then remembered he'd laid it aside for good the day before. "I'll make a decision as soon as I can."

As Jake left the room, Franklin was suddenly certain that his son would run. "He did before, when it was just one man after his hide," he muttered. "Why wouldn't he do the same thing when he has to face the Union Army?"

CHAPTER 13

A VERY TIGHT CORNER

For two days after Brad Franklin laid down his conditions, Jake wandered over the countryside, riding the little mare Lady for long hours. She was a fine little horse, never balking or refusing a command. Then the weather turned bad on the third day, with snow beginning to fall about ten that morning.

As the flakes came down, Jake stopped Lady and watched them with delight. He had always loved snow, but he had spent most of his life where there was little of it. Now the sight of the flakes swirling and dancing in the wind pleased him. Lifting his face, he savored the cold touch of the tiny flakes as they landed on his skin. Finally he moved toward home. By the time he arrived, the ground was white with a thin blanket.

Bob, the youngest of the grooms, unsaddled the mare, and Jake hurried into the house. Going through the front door, he was met by Melora, who said, "Vincent, there's a man to see you. He said his name was Finch."

"Finch? Did he say what he wanted?"

"No, he just said he had to see you. I put him in the library."

"Thanks, Melora." Jake turned and made his way to the library, apprehensive about the man. It had to be a friend of

Vince's—and it would be hard to fake the thing knowing no more than he did.

However, that part of it was not difficult, for the tall, rawboned man, who was sitting at the table drinking coffee, rose as he entered and asked, "Are you Vince Franklin?"

"Yes, I'm Franklin."

"Well, I got a message for you. Sort of a private message, I guess, nothing written down." He was a tough-looking man with a scar on his forehead and some teeth missing.

"Well, what is it?"

"Mrs. Rocklin—Mrs. Ellen Rocklin—she wants to see you."

Jake tried to think what she could want. His first thought was that she was trying to stir up her old romance, and he wanted no part of that. "I'll see her pretty soon. You can tell her I'll be visiting at Gracefield later on in the week."

Finch shook his head, saying, "I reckon it's pretty important. She told me to tell you that she *had* to see you—today."

"Today!"

"It's what she said. I dunno what about—" Finch hesitated, sizing up his man, then nodded. "I'd go if I was you, Mr. Franklin. Mrs. Rocklin, she was pretty stout about it. She said that if you wouldn't come, she'd have to come here—and she didn't think you'd like that."

Jake thought rapidly. He certainly didn't want Ellen coming to Lindwood, and he'd had a taste of how vindictive she could be when she'd forced Melora to dance with Clay. *Better get it over with,* he thought, then nodded. "All right. Where'll I find her?"

"She said she'd be in her room—that's in Mrs. Mulligan's boardinghouse, over by the bakery. Said she'd like to see you about one this afternoon." Then he picked up his coat, saying, "Got to get back."

Jake stood there, trying to think of a way out of the meeting but knowing that he'd have to go. He went to his room, changed to some heavier clothing, then went back to the kitchen, where Rachel was baking a cake. "I've got to go into Richmond, Rachel," he said.

"It'll be too long a trip for you," she said. "You can't ride that far."

"I'll take the buggy."

She tasted the mix, weighed the flavor of it, then put her spoon down and called out, "Melora!" When the woman appeared, she said, "Vince and I have to go to town. We'll be late getting back. Can you take care of everything?"

"Certainly, Rachel. I suppose you want me to finish that cake?"

"Yes, it's going to be a flop, I think. You can take the blame, Vince. Now go tell Tad to hitch up the sleigh while I get some heavier clothes on."

"Wait a minute!" he protested. "I don't have to have a keeper for a little trip to town."

"I need some things at the store," she said, but he saw the wink she gave to Melora. "Go on, now. I'll be quick."

In twenty minutes Jake was driving down the road with Rachel at his side, and despite the fact that he was worried about the meeting with Ellen, he enjoyed the ride. The snow was falling more gently, but it had rounded all the sharp hills to smooth cones and loaves, and the trees glistened like diamonds as the sun came out now and again to touch them.

"I've been looking for an excuse to get out and play in the snow," Rachel confessed. "I love it!"

"It is pretty," Jake agreed. "I like to see it fall like this, but it's a mess afterward."

"You'd complain if they hung you with a new rope!" Her spirits were high because she was pleased to be outside, and the trip to town was a welcome break from the monotony of work. "Everything worthwhile is trouble."

He turned to look at her, noting that the snow had fallen on her hair where it had escaped from her hat, giving it a spangled effect. "What does that mean?"

"Why, just what it says," Rachel said, surprised at his question. "Didn't you know that? I've known it for a long time. For instance, getting married is a lot of fun, so they say. What with the courtship and the wedding dress and the cake. But being married, that's work! Still, you can't just have a wedding without the marriage—so it's worth it, they say. And look at babies, Vince. All nice and cuddly and cute, but they're trouble, too—diapers and colic and Lord knows what else! So you see, everything worthwhile is trouble."

"Never thought of that." He watched the snow as it fell on the backs of the horses and was pleased with their companionable silence as they traveled. The only sound was the soft plopping of the hooves and the slight crunching of the sleigh through the snow. After a while, he asked, "Is the opposite true, then? Are things that aren't trouble worthless?"

She thought about it, holding her hand out from under the canopy and letting the flakes settle on her palm. "No, it doesn't work that way," she said. "Look at this snow. And at how nice it is to be out in it. It's no trouble, is it? But it's not worthless. I can remember a lot of times that snow has brought me joy and laughter. Even today, it has brightened my day. Nothing that does that could be worthless."

She fell silent, then said, "It's nice to have good memories, isn't it? Then when the bottom falls out of things, you've got something to think about."

Jake said evenly, "I don't think most people have as many good memories as you do, Rachel. Most of us don't have sense enough to do the little things, and we miss out on memories like this."

They talked all the way to town, and when he pulled up at the store she indicated, she turned her face to him, saying, "What a nice trip! Thanks for insisting that I come!" When he told her she'd invited herself, she stuck her tongue out, then said, "Take your time. I'll be here when you get ready to go back. Or if I'm not here, I'll be over at Grant's Café."

He left her and with some difficulty found the boardinghouse Finch had mentioned. It was a respectable enough place, Vince noticed as he tied the horses to the rail then went up on the front porch. When he knocked on the door, a tall, plain woman of fifty opened it. "I'm looking for Mrs. Rocklin," he said.

"Come in." The woman stepped back, adding, "I'm Harriet Mulligan. It's getting colder, isn't it?"

"Not too bad yet, but it could get worse."

"Mrs. Rocklin's room is right at the top of those stairs, second door to your left."

"Thank you, Mrs. Mulligan."

Jake climbed up the stairs, favoring his right leg. When he knocked on the door, it opened at once.

"Hello, Vince," Ellen said, stepping back to let him enter. "You made good time. I didn't know it was going to snow like this or I'd have waited until later." She was wearing a fashionable dress that was cut to flatter her figure, which was somewhat lush. Her hair was done up in what he supposed was the latest style.

He took the chair she offered him, on his guard. "Is something wrong, Ellen?" he asked.

"Have a drink, and we'll talk about it." She took a bottle from a cabinet and started to pour, then said, "But you like bourbon better than scotch, don't you?"

"That's right."

She put the bottle down and looked at him with excitement in her large eyes. "No, you don't like bourbon at all. You always insist on scotch."

Jake looked at her thoughtfully. Now at least he knew why he was there. What he didn't know was if he could fool Ellen. He said in a bored voice, "I'll take either one, Ellen."

Ellen admired the man's poise and poured them two glasses of the scotch. When he picked up his glass, she lifted her own and made a toast. "Here's to a profitable venture."

He stared at her, then drank the liquor. "What's on your mind, Ellen?"

She put the glass down and asked directly, "What's your real name?"

Jake shrugged. "You know my name, Ellen. And you know I don't have time for games."

He got up to go, but she said quickly, "Do you remember coming over to play with my boys when you were twelve years old? The summer that Rena broke her arm?"

"I guess I remember."

"That's odd—because Rena never had a broken arm!" Triumph was in Ellen's eyes, and she went on quickly, "But Vince Franklin did spend most of one summer at Gracefield. And *he* had a little accident. You don't remember that? No, I didn't think you would! But I remember it well enough. Vince and David were jumping off the loft into piles of hay, and Vince hit a sharp piece of wire that someone had left there. It wasn't a bad cut, but it left a small scar." She smiled and asked, "You don't remember what shape the scar was in? No, I didn't think you would. It was in the shape of a heart—a little lopsided, but a heart right between your thumb and forefinger. We joked about it quite a bit. I'm surprised that nobody else noticed it."

As he saw the triumph in the woman's eyes, Jake knew there was no hope. "You're a smart woman, Ellen. Nobody else noticed that, not even Vince's mother or Rachel. I guess they've forgotten it."

Ellen lowered her voice, even though they were alone. "What did you do to Vince?"

"I don't think I want to talk about it."

"You don't have any choice, don't you see that?" She smiled at him, then said, "Too bad I'm a Rocklin—too bad for you, that is. I've heard about the will leaving the Franklin money to the oldest son when he reached twenty-five years of age. Most people don't know that. When I saw your hand at the ball, I knew you weren't Vince. It took me a little while to figure out the rest of it."

"What have you figured, Ellen?"

"Why, it's the money, of course!" she said with surprise. "Don't take me for a fool—it has to be the money!" She looked at him carefully, then shook her head. "You look enough like him to be his twin. Did you kill him and take his place?"

"No."

Ellen began to grow angry. "Then what's it for, this masquerade?" Suddenly she had a thought, and a look of satisfaction appeared in her eyes. "Of course! That Vince! I know what he's done. . .he found you and hired you to take his place. He's got to be on the plantation to get the money, and he's afraid that Duvall will kill him." She saw his eyes widen as she spoke, then laughed. "I told you not to take me for a fool. Now where's Vince?"

Jake said slowly, "Ellen, I can't tell you anything. I'm just a hired hand."

"Well, you can tell Vince that unless I get a slice of that big pie—there won't *be* any pie!"

"Yes, I thought we'd come to that."

"Sure you did," she said swiftly. "You're a smart boy. I like smart people." She leaned forward and stroked his hand. "I'm going to enjoy doing business with you. What's your real name?"

"Jack Colt," he replied without pausing.

"Well now, Jack, I think we're at the beginning of a beautiful friendship. How long will it take you to get word to Vince that he has a new partner?"

"He's in New Orleans. I'll have to write him."

"Write today, or send a wire."

"He'll never show his face around here, Ellen."

She studied Jake's face, then nodded. "All right, get the letter off. Tell him I want half."

"You're no piker, are you?"

"Half of something is better than all of nothing, isn't it? I know Vince. He'll pay up."

"Yes, I think he will." Jake got to his feet and started for the door. There was something evil about the woman, and he wanted to have nothing to do with her. "I'll send the letter, but whatever you decide will be between you and him. I'm just a hired hand."

She came out of her chair and put her arms around his neck. "If something happened to Vince," she whispered, "you and I would have *all* the money, Jack!"

There was a heavy air of suggestiveness in the woman, and it repelled Jake. *I'd as soon kiss a cobra!* he thought as he pulled away, saying, "You'd better do your business with Vince." Then he left the room.

He climbed into the buggy and went at once to the telegraph station. If he could, he would just walk away from the whole situation. There was nothing keeping him at Lindwood, really. Nothing except the fact that he'd given Vince Franklin his word. And if there was one thing that could be counted on about Jake Hardin, it was that he didn't break his word. For whatever reason, he had always stood by the promises or deals that he made. Some men would call it an innate integrity—for Jake, it was just the way things were.

The message he sent to Vince was cryptic, one that the telegrapher could not understand enough to report to anyone. "Come at once. Deal going sour."

He paid for the wire, then left the office and went to find Rachel. She was still at the store and was surprised to see him so soon. "Let's eat before we go back," she said.

They had a good meal, though Jake ate little, and the trip home was a delight to her, if not to Jake. It was dark by the time they pulled the team into the barn, and they made their way through the snow to the house.

"Let's just stand here and enjoy it," she said. "Look, the snow is coming down in slanting lines!"

"Pretty," he said quietly as she turned to face him.

"You got some bad news in town, didn't you?" she said quietly. "I knew it as soon as you came into the store."

"You're an observant woman, Rachel."

"What is it? Anything I can help you with?" Rachel wasn't sure who was more surprised by her offer, Vince or herself.

She still wasn't sure about Vince—whether he was truly changing or if he was up to one of his schemes—but more and more she discovered that she wanted to believe in him. And as she watched him, an even more amazing realization suddenly came to her.

"No," he said slowly. "I don't think there's much anyone can do."

She stood there looking at him, still sorting through her own emotions. Finally she said, "Well, if it takes a miracle, there are precedents. I can tell you one that's happened right here at Lindwood."

"A miracle? They've been pretty rare in my life. What is it?"

She turned to watch the snow, and he could tell she was thinking, choosing her words carefully.

"What is it?" Jake asked again.

"I don't hate you anymore." She turned to face him, and shock ran through him as he saw tears in her eyes. "I have for a long time, you know. I just couldn't help it! But since you've come home, I—" She broke off, and he saw that she was trembling, not from the cold, but from sobs.

Without thought he put his arms around her, and she began to cry helplessly. He stood there waiting as an emotion ran through him such as he'd never had in his life. She was warm and desirable, but it wasn't that. It was something more than he'd ever known he could feel about a woman. She thought he was her brother and so surrendered herself to him freely. But he was painfully conscious that this woman—of all the women in the world—was the only one who would do for him!

Finally Rachel's sobs lessened, then ceased. She drew back, her tears making silver tracks on her cheeks in the moonlight.

"I'm sorry, but I warned you, didn't I? That I can only hold things in for so long and then it seems I bawl for days. But it's been so awful! I've never wanted to hate anybody—and now it's all gone." The hushed tone of amazement in her voice moved Jake deeply.

"I'm glad of that, Rachel," he said quietly.

She waited, then asked, "There's nothing that I can do to help you?"

He stood there looking down into her face, and there was nothing to guide him. He'd been like a cloud all his life, drifting where the wind sent him. Now for the first time, he wanted something, and it didn't look much as though he was likely to get it.

Finally he said, "Maybe you can help."

"What is it?"

He said slowly, "You'll hear about it soon enough, so I may as well tell you myself." He told her of the conditions her father had laid down, then said, "I've got to ride a wild horse, fight a duel, and join the Confederate Army. Almost everybody's going to think I'm a phony and a fraud. I'm going to need all the help I can get."

She suddenly grabbed his coat, her eyes enormous, and there was a great happiness in them. "You can do it, Vince! I know you can!" Then she pulled his head down and kissed him on the cheek. "I'll help you! We can do it together!"

His cheek burned like fire where she had kissed him, and he said no more. For a long time they stood there, watching the snow fall. The flakes were light as air and settled on the white crust soundlessly. She held his arm, and finally they turned and went into the house.

A red fox appeared five minutes later. He trotted up, sniffed the air in a businesslike fashion, then turned and made his way to the henhouse, where nice fat hens were sleeping without a thought of a visitor.

PART THREE
The Bravo

CHAPTER 14

ELLEN'S SECRET

When the rest of the Richmond Grays came back from the Valley to join the defensive forces that ringed Richmond, most of the men were given short leave. This was much simpler in the case of the Grays than for most units, because three-fourths of the men were from the Richmond area and could be recalled quickly in case of emergency. There was a short speech by Colonel Benton to the collected regiment, during which he applauded their service. He ended by saying, "It will be up to us to repel the enemy when they come upon us, and I am depending on you to come back determined to keep them from our homes and our land." He called on Major Jeremiah Irons to dismiss the regiment with a prayer, and when the chaplain concluded, he dismissed the men, who gave him a rousing cheer.

"Pretty soft, eh?" Lieutenant Bushrod Aimes said to Captain Taylor Dewitt. "If we were off in Tennessee with General Johnston, we'd be stuck." Aimes was a happy-go-lucky sort of man, an old crony of Dewitt's, and so he spoke freely. "Most of us will come back with massive hangovers, I expect—but it may be our last chance at relaxing for a while."

Major Brad Franklin, who had joined his regiment again for the ceremony, had been standing close enough to hear Aimes's remark and came over to say, "Better not let the chaplain hear you say that, Lieutenant. He's a pretty hard man."

Captain Dewitt grinned. "Well, I wish the rest of the regiment could shoot as well as Chaplain Irons. It's a toss-up as to whether he or Clay Rocklin is the best shot."

Bushrod said before thinking, "That's for sure, Taylor, and if those two ever got in a fight over Melora Yancy, it'd be a close thing—" Then he saw the displeasure that crossed the faces of both men and realized he'd blundered into a delicate situation. One of the disadvantages of a regiment drawn from the same area was that everybody was aware of the details of the lives of the others. Those who really knew Clay Rocklin had no doubt that his interest in Melora Yancy was free of any immorality, but there was something about the matter that caused talk nonetheless. Perhaps it was because the chaplain of the Grays was a suitor for Melora—and the fact that Melora's brother was in Clay's squad only made the matter even more involved.

Bob Yancy had heard a man from Company A make a remark about his sister and had promptly broken his jaw. It was an indication of the state of the matter that Colonel Benton had taken no action. When Aimes had given a slight rebuke to Bob Yancy, the young man had stared at him, saying, "Let another man talk about my sister and he'll get worse than a busted jaw!"

Now Lieutenant Aimes tried to extricate himself from his unfortunate remark by changing the subject and was aided by Captain Dewitt, who said quickly, "Well, let's get started on that leave." The three men separated.

Major Franklin went at once to speak to Lieutenant Dent

Rocklin, who was giving some final advice to his squad. As he waited, Franklin had a chance to study the young man. He was, the major thought, one of the finest-looking men in the army— or had been before his face had been disfigured by a Yankee saber at the battle of Manassas. He still was handsome from the right side, but the left side of his face was distorted from the wound, the eye drawn down and the mouth drooping in a sinister expression. Like others of the family, Major Franklin had feared that the young man would go sour over such a disfiguring injury, but that had not happened. Now as Dent saw him and came over to greet him, there was an ease and contentment in his expression. He smiled, saying, "Well, I get back from a honeymoon just in time to go on leave, Major."

"You're a lucky chap, Dent," Major Franklin commented with a nod. He liked the young man enormously and said, "Bring your bride over to our place tomorrow. Amy's invited the whole clan, so you may have to fight over a plate. Where's your father? I want him there with all his bunch. Well, you can tell him his sister said to be there or she'd take a stick to him."

"I'll tell him, sir," Dent assured him. "It'll be good to have the whole family together."

"I'm having one of those picture-taking fellows come over, too. Hard enough to get our tribe together under normal circumstances. Now with this war, this may be our last chance."

Though Franklin didn't say so, Dent Rocklin knew that his uncle was obliquely referring to the fact that some of them might be killed. However, he said only, "I'll give the fellow my best side."

Franklin glanced at him sharply, then smiled. "I'm glad to see you've not let your wounds make you bitter, my boy."

"I've got a lot to be thankful for," Dent said thoughtfully.

"I could be in one of those graves out there where so many of our people are. And I've got Raimey." His reference to his new bride brought a light of pride into his eyes, and he added, "She's changed the world for me. If I ever amount to anything, it'll be her doing."

"A fine woman! Well, you come prepared to stay at least two or three days." He nodded, then left saying, "See you tomorrow, Denton."

At once Dent went to locate the second platoon and found their sergeant, Waco Smith, giving them a final word of warning. "If any of you think you can get by with gettin' back late," the tall Texan stated acrimoniously, "or so drunk you can't shoot straight, get it out of your mind. The Yankees are headin' this way, and this heah squad is gonna stop 'em." He might have said more, but he glanced around to see Dent and said, "Lieutenant, you want to tie a bell to any of this bunch so's we can find 'em when we need 'em?"

"I don't guess so, Sergeant." Dent grinned, winking at the men. He waited until Smith dismissed them, then went to his father. "I've got a message for you," he said quickly. "Major Franklin said to tell you that Aunt Amy commands your presence at Lindwood tomorrow."

Clay grinned suddenly, his bronzed face looking younger. "That sister of mine always did boss me around," he said. "She summoning just me—or the whole crew?"

"It's the whole family. There's even a photographer coming to get a picture."

"Will you and Raimey be there?"

"Oh, sure," Dent said. "And the Bristols, too, I think. The whole clan of Rocklin—or the Southern branch of it, anyway." He hesitated, then spoke his thought aloud. "I think Aunt Amy has the idea that if we're ever going to get a picture of all of us, it better be now."

"She may be right about that," Clay said. "Well, we'll be there." The two men separated, Dent going hurriedly to the small house that Samuel Reed, his father-in-law, had insisted on renting for the new couple. It was a very small white house close to the Reed mansion, but it had been a haven for Dent and Raimey. When he paid the cabdriver and walked toward the house, the door opened and Raimey came flying out, throwing herself into his arms.

"Dent!" she cried out, and even as he crushed her in his arms, he marveled at her movement. *How did she know I'd catch her?* he wondered, but their short time of marriage had taught him that Raimey's loss of vision had not limited her courage or imagination.

"Hey!" he said when he had kissed her, "let's get out of this cold." Keeping his arm around her, he listened as she spoke quickly and with great animation. Dulcie, her maid from childhood, was standing inside with a smile. "Dulcie, how are you?" he said.

"Better than you gonna be if you don't get out of that cold and snow!" she said sharply. She worried him out of his coat, then hustled the two of them into the tiny dining room, where she and Raimey began feeding him at once. She practically shoved her two charges into their chairs. "Now you two set there and eat!"

The two of them ate the tender pork chops, fried squash and onions, boiled snap beans with ham hock, and a plate of thickened, greasy chicken gravy. Afterward, they topped the meal off with a dish of pickled peaches studded with cloves. Raimey ate little but told Dent what she had been doing as he ate. She ended by saying, "We're going to Lindwood tomorrow for a few days."

Dent was amused. "I thought I'd give *you* that news. Uncle Brad just told me when we left camp."

Raimey smiled slyly. "Oh, Aunt Amy and I have been planning it for a long time. It's going to be so nice, Dent!" Raimey had never had a large family, and she had claimed the Rocklins as her own family almost as soon as she and Denton were engaged. "We'll go there first thing in the morning so I can help with the work."

Dent leaned back in his chair and studied her as he sipped his coffee. It never ceased to amaze him how this girl had managed to fill his life. He knew himself well enough to realize that if she had not come along and offered her love when he was in the hospital, he would probably not have lived. Their honeymoon had been a revelation to him, for he had learned for the first time to give instead of always taking. It had been mutual, though, for Raimey had given herself so completely in every way that both of them had understood that they had that most rare possession—a marriage that was a union of both flesh and spirit.

Now he said to tease her, "Well, I guess you're tired of me, Raimey. Too bad! I thought our honeymoon would last longer."

"Why—what in the world does *that* mean?" she asked, startled.

"Just that you could have me all to yourself here in this cozy house—but you'd rather go spending time with all those people."

Raimey's quick ears picked up on the teasing note in his voice, and she said instantly, "You're spoiled, that's what you are! I declare, I'm going to have to teach you how to behave, Dent Rocklin!"

Then she came to him and bent over to kiss him. "Now that's a lesson I'd gladly be given again," he said huskily and pulled her into his lap. When Dulcie came to glance in, wondering at the sudden silence, she quickly pulled her head back and nodded with satisfaction.

The next morning they arose late, had a leisurely breakfast, then loaded into the sleigh and started for Lindwood. Dulcie, as a matter of course, was going, for she had been Raimey's eyes for years. She sat in the back, enveloped in a blanket, while Dent and Raimey sat in the front. As they made their way along, Dent found himself describing for his wife the things he saw. In the process, he noted that he was seeing things much more clearly, picking up things that he would have previously ignored. He told her of the red fox that appeared, dapper and neat, with the limp form of a rabbit in its mouth. And he described the sprightly running of a buck and two does as they seemed to float effortlessly on their way. It was a source of happiness to him to be able to bring the world to her. For she had given him so much—his faith, his joy. . .his life.

By the time they reached Lindwood, the snow was falling in tiny crystalline flakes, frozen crumbs, actually. The wind blew them so that they stung Raimey's face, and she laughed in delight. "I love snow! Maybe we'll get snowed in and have to stay a week!"

"That'd be rough on Brad and Amy," Dent said, laughing. He glanced around, seeing several sleighs, then added, "Looks like the others are here already." He stopped the team, and several of the slaves were there to take charge of them. Dent, Raimey, and Dulcie hurried inside, where they were met by

Rachel. "Hello, Rachel," Dent said, helping Raimey off with her coat. "Beginning to snow."

"Hello, Dent," Rachel said. She smiled and went to Raimey, taking her hands. "Raimey, your hands are frozen! Come along to the fire." She led the two of them through the foyer and into the large living room that faced the front. "Here's Dent and Raimey," she announced. "But Raimey's got to help me—so you get your visiting over quick."

Jake had taken a seat beside one of the large bay windows, saying as little as possible. He watched as the blind girl made herself a part of the group with ease, identifying everyone instantly by their voices. Her beauty was truly striking, and the proud look on Dent Rocklin's face as he watched his wife told him that here was a man who was very much in love.

Everyone greeted Dent and Raimey, and as the small talk ran around the room, Jake let his eyes pass over the group, making sure he knew them all. Vince had drawn a family tree when he'd first drilled Jake, and now it jumped into his mind. The founder of the family, Noah Rocklin, had died, but he'd left four boys and one daughter. Stephen owned a factory in the North, and his brother Mason was a Union officer, so Jake had not tried to fix them in his mind. Mark, Noah's youngest son, was sitting on a horsehide couch talking to his sister, Marianne. Mark had never married, so Jake had been able to remember him easily. Marianne, the only daughter, was fifty-one and still a striking woman with black hair and blue eyes. Her husband, Claude Bristol, was of French blood and reminded Jake of the things he had heard about French aristocrats—for the man was handsome, smooth, and useless. He was pleasant enough, but there was none of the toughness in him that Jake had seen in the Rocklins. From what Jake had been able to gather, Claude spent his life hunting, raising fast horses, and working as little as possible.

Their three children—Paul, Austin, and Marie—did not favor each other at all. Indeed, they were totally different in appearance. Paul, at thirty, was the oldest and looked like his mother. Austin, who was only one year younger, was short and strongly built, with light hair and brown eyes. His sister, Marie, twenty-four, had curly brown hair and hazel eyes. The two young men were not in the army, which seemed to be somewhat of a matter of embarrassment for their mother—though not for their father. Claude was saying, "Why, the whole thing will be over soon! No need for these two to interrupt their lives for such a short enlistment."

Marianne looked over at Amy and Brad, then at Clay, both of whom she knew had sons in the army. Her blue eyes were filled with what seemed to Jake to be disappointment, and he felt that she was ashamed of her husband for being a weak man. "I don't agree with that, Claude, and I suspect no one else does, either," Marianne said quietly. She glanced at her brother Thomas, who was not well enough for going out in the cold but had insisted on coming. "Did I tell you I got a letter from Gideon, Thomas?"

Thomas shook his head. "No, Marianne. What's he doing?"

"He's gone to serve with some general called Grant in the West."

"Grant?" Thomas asked with a frown. "Never heard of him. But I don't think we have to worry about that sector. President Davis has appointed Albert Sidney Johnston to serve as commander in the West—which seems to be a mistake, at least to me."

"Why is that, sir?" Clay asked. He was standing at the mantel, looking trim and fit. Jake studied him briefly and thought that at the age of forty-one, Clay Rocklin was finer looking than most of the younger men in the room.

"Oh, the war is here, in Virginia," Thomas said with a shrug. "This is where they'll hit us with everything they've got. As soon as McClellan gets the Army of the Potomac ready, they'll be knocking at our door. That's where we need to concentrate our armies, not off in the wilderness in Tennessee."

Clay shot a quick look at his brother-in-law, Major Franklin. The two of them had talked about this matter earlier, and now Clay said carefully, "Well, no doubt you're right about the Yankees hitting us here. The Northern papers are all calling for it. But they're not foolish, Lincoln and his generals—especially General McClellan. They know they'll have to divide the Southern states to win."

"How can they do that, Clay?" Thomas asked. He had been so disappointed in this tall son of his for years, and now that Clay had come back from a wild youth and had become a strong man of honor, he listened carefully to him.

"Brad thinks they'll try to get control of the rivers."

"Rivers?" Marianne asked with a puzzled frown. "Why would they do that?"

Brad Franklin was wearing his uniform, and there was a soldierly look in his thin face as he answered. "Because you can move armies and material on rivers, Marianne. The North has built up a tremendous railway system, but we have almost no major lines. The only way we can move men and munitions is either by rivers or overland. Some of the food Rachel is cooking came down the Cumberland and the Tennessee rivers—from Kentucky and Tennessee. And if the Yankees get control of those rivers, we'll be cut off here."

Grant Franklin, oldest son of Brad and Amy, said, "I've heard that we've got some forts on those rivers to keep the Yankees away."

"Well," Clay said thoughtfully, "they'd better stand, because if we lose those rivers, we'll probably lose Nashville. Then the Yankees can bring their troops all the way down the river—and they can get a foothold on the Mississippi itself."

"And if they get the Mississippi," Franklin continued, "they'll cut the Confederacy in two."

Thomas Rocklin looked at the two men, then shrugged. "Well, we'll just have to fight them off."

"And any Southern soldier can whip any six Yankee soldiers!" Lowell Rocklin said. He was, at the age of eighteen, a throwback to his great-grandfather Noah Rocklin—determined and stubborn. "Isn't that so, Dent?"

Dent Rocklin, who had gone through the fires of battle at Manassas, shook his head. "Well, Lowell, I know it's popular to say that, but I don't agree. At Bull Run, the Yankees came at us like fury. I suppose there were some who ran away—but some of our fellows ran, too. I wouldn't count on the Yankee army running away."

"But we're fighting for our homes, Dent!" Lowell argued. "That's got to make a difference."

"It does," Dent said quietly. "And I'm praying it'll make enough difference to cause the Yankees to decide that we're not worth the cost. After Manassas, I think both sides looked at the war differently—but after so many men have died, we all know this war's not a little skirmish. The Yankees have it over us in men and munitions. But it's an unpopular war in the North for many people."

"So we just have to kill enough of them to make them call

the war off? Is that it, Dent?" Thomas asked. Then he shook his head, adding, "It's a grim business. Here are the three of us"—he nodded toward his brother Mark and his sister, Marianne—"in the South, and Stephen and Mason in the North, with Mason in a Federal uniform. Now all of our sons and grandsons are headed to the battlefield, some on opposite sides."

He looked tired and ill, and Susanna Rocklin, his wife, moved to his side. "God will bring us through it, Thomas. Now let's talk about something besides the war."

"Just one more word—about the war, I mean," Brad said. "Most of you don't know, but Vince is joining the Confederate Army soon."

Jake suddenly felt very exposed, for every person there turned to stare at him. He felt like some sort of strange and exotic animal that someone had suddenly brought into the room! Nothing had shown more clearly how alienated Vince Franklin had become from his family than this moment, when Jake saw incredulity and shock in some of the faces.

Clay said quickly, "Why, that's fine! You'll be enlisting in your father's regiment, I suppose?"

Jake cleared his throat, finding it difficult to think with so many watching him. "Well, probably not. I'm not tough enough for an infantry company."

"Cavalry?" Dent asked, his eyebrows going up. He almost mentioned the fact that Vince had never been a horseman, but said instead, "Well, that's not a bad idea. Jeb Stuart's command is looking for men, or Wade Hampton's legion."

Jake knew Dent was being polite, and he also realized that they were all thinking of how he had run from Duvall. His mind worked quickly, and he plunged ahead, saying, "Well, I've got to learn to ride and shoot much better than I do now—and there's the matter of a challenge from a fellow in Richmond. If I can take care of all those things, maybe I'll make a soldier."

Clay exclaimed, "Why, you can do it. If you need any help with shooting, I'll be glad to help. And nobody knows more about horses than your brother Grant."

Jake nodded quickly. "Thanks, Uncle Clay. I'll need all the help I can get—but I've got a pretty fair teacher already where horses are concerned. Rachel's giving me some help there."

His remark brought smiles to most of the faces in the room, and Amy said, "I've tried to make a lady out of that child, but she'd rather ride a horse than dance a reel at a fancy ball!" Despite her words, it was clear she was pleased with the way things were. She added, "You two have been thick as thieves ever since you came home. If you weren't her brother, I'd think that young officer, Leighton Semmes, would have something to worry about."

Jake almost choked on that and barely managed to come up with a smile. "Well, Mother, he needn't even take note of me. Which is a good thing, because I have the matter with Duvall to concentrate on right now."

His remark pleased Vince's father, who smiled. He had given up on Vince long ago. Now, though, there was a stirring of hope within him. Of course, he could not help feeling skeptical, and the long years of disappointment over his son made him frown. Amy, his wife, saw it but held her silence. She had a confident air about her, as though she knew for a certainty that things would work out. And there was something more, too—for at times she seemed as though she held something in, some knowledge that assured her all was well. Some noticed that about her, but no one questioned it. There was a strong spirit of faith in Amy Franklin. She was still crippled by the leg that refused to heal, but she never had lost hope that one day she would be whole again. Now she applied that same hope to her husband, praying, *Lord, give him Your peace. Let him know that You will not let him down. That You are working even now to take care of all of us—even those who do not yet know You.*

Then Amy said, "Let's have some hot coffee and some of that fresh gingerbread I smell." Her eyes were steady as she watched Jake, who stood alone beside the window, looking out at the snow.

❧

The Imperial Hotel was not, in point of fact, imperial in any way. A two-story frame building squeezed in between a row of small businesses on one side and an office building on the other, it was a refuge for those who could not afford to stay in the fine hotels in the center of town, but who were too proud to stay in the shabby rooming houses inhabited by Richmond's working class. In earlier days, the Imperial had held a more exalted status, having housed in one of its rooms no less a guest than George Washington—a fact that was attested to by a large bronze plaque in the lobby.

The paint was freshened at regular intervals, and the carpets changed before the floors showed through. However, the tawdry atmosphere of Simon Duvall's rooms on the second floor kept him grimly aware of his position in Richmond society. He was putting on his second-best coat at ten o'clock in the morning, noting with displeasure that the elbow of one sleeve was noticeably worn. It was a small matter, but he cursed as he pulled it off and threw it with a violent gesture across the room.

Rose Duvall had been asleep, but the sound of his voice

awakened her. Poking her head out from under the covers on the heavy mahogany bed, she peered at her husband owlishly, then asked, "Where are you going?"

Duvall gave her an angry glance, then yanked another coat from the wardrobe. "To borrow money," he said shortly. He said no more, and there was a look on his face that brooked no further questions. He pulled the coat on, a fine blue wool model that fit him well. He remembered buying it after a big night at poker. How good it had been, that time! Going into the finest shop in Richmond, picking out the coat, and buying it without even asking the price!

But there had been no purchases like that lately, and the pinch of hard times had soured Duvall. He adjusted his tie and looked at his image in the mirror critically. He saw a lean, olive-skinned man with a fine head of black hair and a set of piercing dark eyes. He touched his moustache with a hand that was almost delicate—a hand he took pride in, for it had done no hard labor and was obviously the hand of a man of circumstance.

He picked up his hat, settled it on his head, then donned his overcoat. As he turned to the door, Rose demanded, "Simon, I've got to have some money. I don't have a penny, even to eat on."

Fishing in his pocket, he came up with a bill and tossed it to her. "Better make it last," he said. "If I don't get a loan, we'll be out of this place on our ear."

"I don't see why you don't enlist in the army," Rose reproached. She was an attractive woman with a full figure, with large brown eyes set off by a beautiful complexion. She had been a dance-hall girl in St. Louis when Simon had met her. He had been intoxicated with her beauty and was still possessive about her, but she was tiresome to him now—especially when she reminded him that he had promised her greater things than a sorry hotel room. Now she gave him a sudden suspicious glance. "You'd better not be going to see some woman!"

Duvall laughed, for he liked to torment her. "That comes ill from you, Rose, after your fling with Vince Franklin."

"I told you there was nothing between us!"

"Yes, you did—and you always tell the truth, don't you, sweetheart?" He studied her with a slight contempt, then left the room. Going down the stairs, he felt a twinge of uneasiness lest the clerk should call him and ask him to pay his bill. But the clerk was busy, and his back was turned as he put up mail. Duvall stepped quickly through the lobby, turning to his left. The air was cold, and he scowled. He hated cold weather. But he had no money for a cab, so he walked quickly until he came to his first stop. He entered the red brick building where a friend of his had an office on the third floor. As he went up the stairs, he went over the speech he planned to make, hating himself for becoming a beggar. But he had reached the end of his rope, possessing only his clothes and a few pieces of jewelry. His gambling losses had been high of late, and now he felt a tinge of fear as the thought of a future with no money rose to his mind.

Pausing before the door of his friend's business office, he straightened his back, put a confident smile on his face, and entered. But fifteen minutes later when he came out, the smile was gone and his back was no longer straight. Though it was cold, he pulled a fine silk handkerchief from his pocket, wiped his forehead with a hand that was not quite steady, then left the building quickly.

Two hours later, at noon, he was going up the stairs to the room of Ellen Rocklin. She answered his knock at once, and her eyes brightened as she saw him. Pulling him into the room, she threw her arms around him, kissing him. He responded as always, with fervor and excitement.

"Now no more of that—not for now, anyway," she said, pulling away but with a promise in her eyes. "Sit down. Can I fix you a drink?"

"Have one with me, Ellen." He took off his coat and hat, tossing them over a chair, then took a seat. He watched her as she poured two drinks, thinking of how he'd come to need her. They had become lovers weeks ago, and though she was no longer young, there was a hunger in her that he had never found in another woman.

Duvall, however, was a realist. He well knew that his relationship with Ellen was only physical. She would cast him off in a flash if she found another man who pleased her better—and he would do the same with her if circumstances required it. As he took the drink she offered him, he grasped her hand and kissed it, bringing a pleased look into her eyes. "You look beautiful, my dear," he said, glad that he could stir her with so little effort.

Ellen laughed, saying, "You must want something, Simon, coming around at noon telling me how beautiful I am." She sat down, sipping her drink and waiting for him to speak.

"I always want something when I come to you," Duvall said with a smile. He continued to flatter her, and she sat back, enjoying it. She had to have the admiration of men, and Duvall was somewhat of an aristocrat, though not much of one. Yet he knew how to say the right things, and even more important, he was discreet. No matter what else she might do, Ellen would never let her standing as Mrs. Clay Rocklin be endangered.

She did not love Clay, and she was sure that her husband

had never loved her—that he was, in fact, in love with Melora Yancy—but the life she led was easy enough. She kept her rooms in Richmond, and she was welcome in many homes due to her marriage into the Rocklin family. From time to time she would go to Gracefield, the family plantation, where she would play the role of wife and mother—fooling nobody at all but fulfilling what she saw as her role.

Finally she said, "Let's go have lunch, Simon."

Hesitating, he looked confused. Finally he gave a rueful laugh. "Nothing I'd like better, Ellen, but—I've had a bad run of cards."

"Broke? Well, this will be on me." She smiled, then got up and went over to the vanity, where she began arranging her hair carefully. "Let's go to Elliot's."

"Elliot's? That's pretty expensive."

"Just about good enough for us." She laughed. There was an excitement in her that Duvall didn't understand. He felt he knew her well by now and sensed that something was stirring in her. "You have a rich uncle die and leave you a million?" he asked, his eyes narrowing.

"Not quite, but—" She broke off, casting a look at him over her shoulder.

He waited, but she merely shrugged and turned back to the mirror. When he pressed her, she refused to say more—but when they were ready to leave, she kissed him and, stroking his hair, said, "I'm going to buy you a new suit, Simon—a fine one!"

He looked at her, then smiled. "You're *different* today, Ellen. Something's going on in that head of yours. What is it?"

She shook her head, saying, "Let's go eat. But don't let me drink too much. You might get my secret out of me!"

They left, and all through the meal and afterward at her

rooms, Duvall said nothing more about it. However, a new anticipation was rising in him.

She's up to something, he thought. *Something big! I'll have to be careful—but I'll find out what she's onto. If I play my cards right, I can get enough to turn things around.*

He stayed with her most of the day, and when he got back to his hotel, he found Rose waiting for him. "Well, did you get the loan?" she demanded.

He pulled a roll of bills out of his pocket, enjoying the surprise that came to her eyes. "Not exactly," he admitted, "but things are going to be better. I'm onto something big this time, and I have a feeling it's going to change everything!"

CHAPTER 15

RACHEL'S PUPIL

*A*ll right...hold as still as you can, please...."

A brilliant light exploded from the elongated pan the photographer held in his left hand, blinding the eyes of the house of Rocklin.

As a mutter of dismay went around, Raimey suddenly giggled, saying, "It didn't bother *me* a bit."

Dent grinned and hugged her, for he had learned that she was not at all sensitive about her handicap. "Come on, let's go see if there's anything left to eat."

The photographer, a thin man named Allen with highly nervous mannerisms, had come to take his pictures at noon, rousting them all away from the table, saying, "We have to get the best light, and with all this snow as a reflector, now is an excellent time." They had risen from the table and followed him outside, where they arranged chairs on a porch that caught the full power of the midday sun. Dent and Clay had picked up Amy's chair and carried her outside, where the older Rocklins joined her sitting in chairs. There was a shuffle when the others were grouped around them, with Amy giving instructions: "Clay, you and Ellen get closer together! And you children,

965

move in closer to them!" She watched as Dent, holding fast to Raimey, was joined by his twin, David; then Lowell and Rena moved in beside them.

"Now," Amy said, "Marianne, you and Claude sit down here with me. Paul and Austin and Marie, stand beside them—get all the Bristols together. Yes, that's nice."

Brad smiled as he came to sit down beside his wife, and she patted his arm, saying, "Now, Grant, you stand there, and, Les, you stand next to him." She waited until they pleased her, then said, "All right, Rachel, you and Vince get beside them." When the pair obeyed, she turned and faced the photographer, saying firmly, "Very well, sir, here are your subjects. Now do your job!"

Allen had fussed with his equipment briefly, then had taken several pictures. When the whole group was captured on his plates, Amy said, "Now get a picture of each family."

"Amy, I'm almost frozen!" Ellen said. She had come only that morning, unannounced and unexpected, and had complained of the weather ever since.

Amy gave her a brief glance. "You can be first," she said evenly. She sat there and watched, fascinated by the processes, pestering Allen with questions until it was time for her own family to be photographed. Then the photographer said with some asperity, "You'll have to stop talking now, Mrs. Franklin. Your lips must be absolutely still."

"I think he's telling you to shut up, my dear," Brad said with a straight face and a teasing look in his blue eyes. He winked at Allen, who at once disappeared under the black cloth that draped him and the camera, then presently surfaced crying, "Hold still, please!" The powder exploded, and then he drew a sigh of relief. "Is that *all*, Mrs. Franklin?"

"No. I want pictures of all the servants. They're waiting, as you can see." She motioned to a large group of the slaves, who were drawn up all dressed in their best, adding, "See you do a good job of them." Then she said, "Let's get inside. My nose is frozen."

The group retired, leaving the poor photographer to deal with his new subjects. When the family was inside, Dent and Clay set Amy down carefully in the dining room. Melora came in from the kitchen, asking, "All through? I took the food off so I could reheat it."

She turned to go, but Clay said quickly, "Melora, I promised your brother Bob I'd have a picture made of you. Come along and I'll have the photographer take yours before he gets started on the servants."

Melora hesitated, obviously reluctant, then said, "Let me get my coat." Clay walked from the room with her, and a small, awkward silence fell on the room.

Ellen glared after the pair, then burst out, "I thought this was a family affair. What's she doing here?"

Amy said instantly, "I asked her to come when I broke my leg, Ellen. I needed help, and you weren't here."

It was a cutting reply, a sharper one than Brad had ever heard his wife give to anyone. But he understood how close Amy had gotten to Melora, and he knew better than anyone else how she resented Ellen's treatment of Clay. He tried to think of something to say to take the sudden chill out of the air, but could not.

Ellen sat there, her face flushed with anger, well aware that she dared not lash out at Amy. She had never been close to any of the family, and though that had been her own choice, she resented the bond the others shared. She glanced at her children—Dent, David, Lowell, and Rena—and saw only embarrassment on their faces. It had been years since they had shared much with their mother, and she knew that they all were ashamed of her. She had tried to keep her affairs with men a secret, but in a society as intimate as the one in which she moved, that was impossible. Now, seeing the shame on their faces, she suddenly wished that she had lived a different sort of life. But it was too late, and she could only bite her lip, determining that if she could not strike out at these people, she certainly could do so at Clay!

And she did exactly that the first time she was alone with him. She sought him in his room, lashing out at him as she came in, "Well, did you and your lover have a good time, Clay?" Her face was stiff with anger as she stood there in the middle of the room, cursing him and watching his face. She was hoping that he would show anger, even that he would strike her, for that would show that she still had the power to stir him. But Clay said nothing as he stood there waiting, his face impassive.

When she finally ran out of words, he said, "Ellen, you know better than that. I've had nothing to do with Melora in that way—ever! She's a fine woman and would not do such a thing."

"Oh, she's a *saint*, is that it?" Ellen's words jabbed at him like knives, and she was infuriated even more because she knew that what Clay said was true. She herself had no more morality than an alley cat, but she somehow sensed that there was a goodness in Melora Yancy—a goodness she herself lacked—and this made her frantic with rage.

Clay stood there studying his wife as if she were an unusual specimen of animal. She had been a beautiful girl when he had married her, and though she had tricked him into marriage, he had tried for years to love her. Unfortunately, she had done all she could to prevent that.

Now he sighed and broke into her tirade. "Ellen, you're making a fool of yourself. Now leave it alone. Let's try to keep at least the *appearance* of a marriage, for the sake of the children."

"Clay, I'll never divorce you!"

"I know that, Ellen. It doesn't matter. Melora would never marry a divorced man." He hesitated, then added, "I can't say for certain, but I believe Melora is going to be married."

"Married?" Ellen asked, startled. "To whom?"

"That isn't for me to say, but whether she gets married or not, I want no more of your outbursts in front of my family— especially in front of the children."

"You can't tell me what to do, Clay!"

He gave her a considered glance, then said quietly, "I can cut off the money you live on, Ellen. I ought to do it anyway. Do you think I don't know the way you live? The men you run around with?" Anger began to burn in him, and he fought it down. "Do you think I don't know about you and Simon Duvall?"

"You can't prove anything!"

"Can't I? You've been seen in public with him more than once. I might just call him out. He might not find it so easy to deal with me as he did with poor Vince!"

"You wouldn't dare!" Ellen gasped. She knew that Clay was deadly with a weapon, that he could probably kill Duvall. Then she was suddenly struck with a frightening thought: *If Simon killed Clay, the Rocklins would throw me out!* It was more than a guess, for she knew that Clay's father was disgusted with her and had said that if it was his decision, he'd lock Clay's wife up at home and cut her off without a penny!

The thought of such a thing brought a stab of fear, and she

quickly lost her nerve. "Why, Clay," she said in a milder tone than she had been using. "I guess I'm just afraid of losing you."

"You lost me a long time ago, Ellen," he said quietly. "But we can at least try not to bring pain to others with the mess we've made of our own lives. Now go back to the others and try to act decently."

Ellen glared at him but left his room. Downstairs, she entered the large parlor and saw Jake standing at the window, staring out. Going to stand beside him, she whispered, "Hello, *Vince*." His expression of distaste amused her, and she added, "Thinking about all the coin we're going to get out of the real Vince?" She laughed at the anger that leaped into his eyes, saying, "Don't worry, I won't tell on you—at least, not if you're good to me."

Clay waited for half an hour after Ellen left, then left the house and walked through the snow. The sunlight striking the crystals sent off flashes that made him blink his eyes, but soon he grew accustomed to it. The scene with Ellen had depressed him, and he walked for nearly an hour, slowly letting the bitterness that she had stirred in him fade. He loved the snow, and he paused once to make a snowball, throwing it with all his force toward a rabbit that dashed frantically away. Clay grinned at the sight and said softly, "Run, you son of a gun! Wish I could run away from my problems as easily as you run away from yours!"

Finally he turned back, taking an old path that led to the brook north of the house. The field was smooth as a carpet, and he enjoyed leaving his tracks, marring the flawless surface. The brook was lined with large trees, all bare now. As he walked along the bank, a movement caught his eye. He stopped and was surprised to see Melora walking toward him. Her head was down, and she seemed unaware of his presence.

"Hello, Melora," he called out, and the sound of his voice brought her head up. She was startled, and the sight of him brought a strange expression to her face. Clay moved along the bank, coming to stand beside her. "Out for a walk?"

"Yes." She was wearing a green woolen coat but no hat, so that her hair, the blackest he'd ever seen, outlined her against the gleam of the white snow. "I love to walk in the snow."

"You always did." He settled back on his heels and thought of days gone by. "Once it snowed so deep that I had to carry you on my shoulders. You must have been about six years old."

Memory stirred her, and she stood there thinking of that time. "I remember. When we got back to our house, I made you some toasted bread and we put honey on it. Then you read to me out of one of the books you'd given me. I was more than six, though."

They walked along the bank, speaking of time past, but there was a constraint in her, something that kept her from giving him her full attention. She was a woman of warm moods, one who seldom allowed her difficulties to depress her, yet now there was none of the joy and happiness in her that Clay had come to expect.

"What's wrong, Melora?" He stopped, taking her arm, and waited for her to reply.

She said nothing for so long that he thought she would not answer at all. Then she said steadily, "Clay, I'm going to marry Jeremiah."

A sharp pain ran through him, but he allowed none of it to show in his face. He had urged her to marry for a long time...but now that it had come, a sense of loss filled him, and he knew time would not dull that feeling. He nodded, then said, "It's the best thing for you and Jeremiah, Melora."

"Is it best for you, Clay?"

"I—guess it is," he stammered. Then taking a deep breath, he summoned up a smile. "God knows I love you, Melora. But there's no way we can ever be together."

Melora's eyes began to fill, and she said in a voice that was not steady, "Clay, I've loved you ever since I was a little girl. First as a little girl loves a big brother. Then later, when I was twelve or thirteen, I had one of those crushes young girls get on older men. But when I became a woman, that changed—and now I love you as a woman."

They stood there, torn apart by the bond that drew them together and by the decision they had made together never to tarnish their love by going against what they knew was right in God's eyes. Suddenly Clay reached out to put his arms around Melora, and as he held her fiercely, she began to weep. It was not something that she did often, but she could not help it. Her body was wracked by a storm, and he could do nothing but hold her.

Finally she drew back, and in a motion as graceful and natural as anything he'd ever seen, she pulled his head down and kissed him. Then she whispered, "Good-bye, Mister Clay!"

Whirling, she ran down the path beside the small creek, leaving him standing there. He knew it was good-bye forever, and the bleakness of the years ahead without her suddenly seemed longer than eternity. When he resumed his walk, his shoulders were stooped, and there was a leaden feeling in his chest that seemed to drag him down. He wanted to run away, to get as far from Gracefield as he could, but he knew he would not. God had saved him from a dreadful life, and now he would see if he could be the kind of man who would trust God when there was nothing to hope for—nothing but the promises of God.

"Vince—Vince! Come on, get out of that bed!"

Jake suddenly came out of a sound sleep, fighting at the hands that were pulling at his shoulders. "W–what—!" he gasped, peering wildly around as if he expected to find his room filled with wild animals. He sat up and threw himself backward, cracking his head against the solid mahogany headboard. "Ow!" he yelped, and then as his eyes focused, he saw Rachel standing beside his bed. "Rachel! What the devil—!"

"Come on," Rachel said, laughing at his confusion. "It's almost six o'clock."

Jake shook his head, licked his lips, then peered at her, asking, "Six o'clock? Well, so what?"

Rachel reached out and pulled the blankets half off Jake, saying, "You're getting your riding lesson, remember? We talked about it last night. Now get out of that bed."

"Wait a minute!" Jake yelled, grabbing at the blankets and pulling them up over his waist. "I'll come—but give me a chance to get dressed first!"

"Well, get dressed, then!"

He stared at her as she stood there waiting impatiently, then said, "Do you mind stepping outside while I put my clothes on?"

Rachel lifted her eyebrows. "Aren't we *modest* this morning! Remember me? I'm the one who gave you your bath and helped you put your pants on when you couldn't do it yourself!" Then she laughed and left the room, saying, "All right, I'm leaving. But hurry up!"

Jake waited until she closed the door, then got out of the bed and dressed hurriedly. He put on his heavy wool pants and shirt, then pulled on a pair of Vince's boots—which were one size too small—and grabbed a heavy coat off a peg. When he came down the stairs, he smelled coffee and found Rachel just dumping a huge mountain of scrambled eggs into a bowl. "Pour the coffee while I dish out the food," she said. When the food was on the table, they sat down and ate hungrily.

"I'll be glad to get away," Rachel said. "I like to be around relatives, but they sure are pesky after a while!"

"You've done a good job—you and Melora—taking care of them," Jake commented. "Too bad the rest of the family can't be here, the ones from the North." He chewed a piece of toast, adding, "We haven't seen Gideon and Melissa in a long time, have we?"

Rachel gave him a quick glance. "Melissa? Do you mean Melanie?"

Jake's face flamed. Drat his memory! "Of course—Melanie! What's wrong with me?"

Rachel looked at him, concern in her eyes. "You're better physically, but you don't seem to be getting your memory back. And your voice—it's still not like it was."

Jake shrugged, thinking hard of some way to distract her from her present train of thought, but could only say, "Well, the doctor said it might take a long time for my voice to heal. And I guess my memory will take more time, too, to get better."

Rachel had finished her food and sat there considering him thoughtfully. She was a woman of action, and it made Jake nervous when she kept still, for it was out of character for her. Finally she said, "I don't understand the changes in you, Vince. I wish I knew if I could trust them. Sometimes. . .sometimes you seem to be a different man entirely."

Desperate, Jake gulped down his coffee and rose to his feet. "Oh, I guess I'll be about the same when I get all healed up,

Rachel. Come on, let's get this riding lesson over with." She rose to follow him, but he could tell she was reluctant to let the subject drop.

They left the kitchen and went directly to the barn, finding Bruno milking. He spoke to them, saying, "I ain't got them horses saddled yet, Miss Rachel. If you jes wait fo' a minute—"

"We'll do it, Bruno," Rachel replied and walked quickly down to where Crow and a bay mare were in the stalls. "First thing," she said at once, "is for you to get a saddle on Crow."

Jake had watched the big stallion being saddled many times and knew that it took two men to do the job at times—depending on how Crow happened to feel. He liked the big black horse and felt that he could probably handle him, but knew that he had a role to play.

"Rachel," he said as anxiously as he could, "it takes Tad and Bruno both to saddle Crow. And I'm still weak in the leg, and my arm isn't strong."

Rachel gave him a direct look. "It's a little too late to back out now, Vince," she said waspishly. She came to stand directly in front of him, and her brow was wrinkled with a frown. "Besides, this is the easiest thing you've got to do! I mean, the worst that can happen to you is that you'll get kicked or bitten. Crow is tough, but he's not a killer. If you can't face a horse, I don't know how you could ever expect to face a man."

"Well, I guess you're right, Rachel." Jake nodded as though thinking it over. "Duvall can put a bullet in my brain, and anyone can get killed in the army." He hesitated for a few seconds, aware that Rachel was watching him narrowly. "All right! I'll do it!" he announced firmly.

"That's the way!" Rachel said with relief. "Now just re-member, a horse knows how you feel. If you're nervous or afraid, he *knows* that, and he'll take advantage of it. So you have to ignore any sort of fear and just let that ol' horse have it! Whap him across the nose if he tries to bite you—show him who's boss!"

"Right!" Jake moved toward the stall, picked up the bridle, then climbed up on the rails of the stall. Crow whirled at once, his mouth open, and all Jake could see was a cavernous mouth and what seemed to be dozens of big teeth! It was so sudden that he reacted by jerking backward—and sprawled full-length on the floor of the stable.

"Oh, well done, brother!" Rachel laughed from where she had gone to sit down on a bale of hay and added as he picked himself up, "You sure showed him that time!"

Jake glared at her, then snatched the bridle up. He said in a grating tone, "I hope you're enjoying all this!" Then he climbed up again, but this time he was ready. He'd thrown the bridle up over the top rail, and when Crow swung around to bite him, he drove his fist right into the tender nostrils of the stallion. Crow blinked and let out a surprised neigh, then turned his head back toward the front of the stall. Slowly Jake picked up the bridle and eased it into position. Crow gave one snort and lifted his head, casting a wicked glance at Jake, who said, "Stop that!" Crow shook his head, but Jake managed to slip the bit into place and fastened the bridle before stepping down. "Now I've got him bridled, but that's not the worst of the thing."

"Maybe we'd better get Bruno to help."

"No!"

Rachel was amazed at the determined light in the man's eyes and got to her feet, ready to help. Crow came out with his head reared high, staring down at Jake. The animal was in one of his bad moods, and for the next half hour Jake struggled with him, trying to get the saddle on. He tied the bridle to the top rail, but Crow still had a large arc to swing in. The saddle was heavy, and full strength had not come back to Jake's hand, so time and time again he would heave the saddle up, only to have the big horse lurch away, sending it to the floor.

Rachel bit her lip after Crow had not only knocked the saddle to the floor, but swung around and crushed Jake against the side of the stall. "Vince, let me help!"

"Keep out of this!"

Rachel looked at him, taken aback by the fire in his voice. But Jake's blood was up now and he was not about to let any horse beat him. He didn't realize he had spoken so forcefully to Rachel. He had, in fact, forgotten about her—his mind and spirit were caught up in the duel with Crow. He stood there staring at the animal, thinking. Suddenly Rachel saw him smile, and he went to the tack room and came back with a pair of hobbles. He shortened them until they were only a foot long, then fastened them to the hooves of the horse. Then he picked up the saddle, and though Crow tried to dodge, it was not enough, and the saddle went across his back.

"Now, you black demon," Jake said, breathing hard as he tightened the girth, "we'll see who's boss!"

Rachel smiled. "Well, you've proved you're smarter than he is. But he's still bigger."

Jake stooped and removed the hobbles, then nodded. "I guess he knows that, too. Come on. Get the saddle on that mare."

Rachel saddled the mare and they led the two animals outside. Jake was a good rider, but he had seen the strength and cunning of the horse a few days earlier when Grant had tried to ride him. It had been all that Grant could do to outlast Crow's wild pitches—and Grant was probably the best horseman on the place. Rachel seemed to be the only one who knew how to handle the horse so that he didn't fight being ridden.

"I'll probably get piled up," Jake said, looking up at the high saddle.

"Are you afraid?"

He gave her a quick nod. "Can't help thinking about what he can do. I've been a cripple for a long time. Now if he falls on me or pitches me off and I break a leg, it'll be worse than the first time."

Rachel was suddenly worried, and her hand caught at his sleeve. "Vince, don't do it. Wait for a while. You've made a start. Now do that for a day or two, just until he gets used to you. Then you can ride him."

"No time for that," Jake said. "Just say a little prayer that when I hit the ground, I don't break anything." He shook her off and, with a smooth movement that surprised her, swung into the saddle. Crow stood still, caught off guard by the suddenness of Jake's mount—then he began to hunch his back in a sinister fashion.

"Look out—!" Rachel cried out, for she knew the horse well, but it was too late. Crow gave a short hop forward, then leaped high into the air, twisting into a corkscrew shape. When his hooves hit the ground, Jake—who had been thrown off balance—was flung out of the saddle and hit the ground, landing on his back. He grunted as the air was driven from his lungs and rolled to one side to escape the horse's plunging hooves. But Crow stopped at once, walked a few yards away, then turned and stared at Jake.

"Are you hurt?" Rachel was beside him, sitting in the snow and holding his head on her lap. Her eyes were wide and she was trembling. "Vince—what is it?"

Jake lay there with pain throbbing down his bad leg, unable to speak for a moment. But he wasn't sure which was causing him the most trouble—the pain of having the air knocked out of him or the feelings that raced through him at Rachel's touch. Then as some air came back into his lungs, he gasped, "I'm. . .all right." Her face was only inches from his, and he smiled feebly. "Well, it. . .looks like you're. . .back to nursing me!"

He sat up, drew a deep breath, then stared at Crow. "You ornery outfit!" he said softly, then smiled. He liked the horse's spirit and the humor he saw in the way Crow stood there staring at him, almost laughing at him. "Bring him over here, will you, Rachel?" he asked, getting to his feet painfully. "One of us has got to lose this fight—and I'll be blasted if I'll let it be me!"

An hour later, the two horses were making tracks through the snow headed toward the brook. Jake felt as though his head had been driven between his shoulders. He had been thrown four times before he learned to anticipate Crow's movement, and each time he'd gotten up more slowly. Rachel had grown afraid and had begged him to quit, but he had kept it up. Finally, when he had learned how to recognize that Crow was going to jump, he would reach out and strike the animal between the ears with a stick, shouting out, "No!" at the same time. Finally Crow could stand it no more, and all Jake had to do when he felt the huge muscles of the animal bunch was to shout, "No!"—and that took care of it.

Now they came to the brook, and Jake said, "Let's have a drink." He stepped off his horse, and they tied the lines of the horses to a low limb, then went down to the creek. He stooped and broke the ice; then, making a cup of his hands, he brought some to his lips. It was so cold it hurt his teeth, but he grinned at her. "Thirsty work, learning how to be a man, sis."

Rachel shook her head, and there was a soberness in her eyes. "I've never seen you act so determined. All your life when something didn't go right, you just walked away."

"Try some of that water," Jake said. He waited until she bent and took a drink, then glanced around. He remembered something that Vince had told him about the place and said, "There's that deep pool, the one where we used to swim."

Rachel nodded, then smiled at the memory. "I remember when I got too old to swim with you boys. I went home and cried all day." Her eyes were soft as she let the memory linger, and she added, "That was the last time you ever did anything with me. You'd hunt with the boys, but you never played with me or took me anyplace after that."

Jake had a bitter thought about Vince but could only say, "Boys are pretty mean sometimes." He hesitated, then added, "Wish I could go back and change it."

"Do you?"

"Why, sure!" Jake paused, suddenly afraid that he might say too much. She was beautiful as she stood in the snow, her cheeks reddened with the cold, and he felt a strange sense of longing run along his nerves. "If I had it to do over again, I'd—"

When he paused, she prompted him. "What would you change, Vince?"

"Well, I guess I'd take my little sister places." He smiled, then shook his head. "I was watching Dent and Raimey last night. Have you noticed how they stay close together? Oh, I know they're still newlyweds and she's blind and all that—but still, there's something in that pair I haven't seen much of."

Rachel was staring at him. She whispered, "What do you see?"

Jake gave a half-embarrassed laugh and reached out to

push a curl of her hair back from where it had fallen on her eyes. "Oh, I don't know, Rachel. It makes me feel like a fool poet talking about it." He struggled with his thoughts, then said slowly, "For a man, women are the only real beauty in this world. A mountain or a sunset—they can be beautiful—but a man can't put his arms around a sunset, can he? There's some sort of an emptiness in a man that the whole sky and sea and all the stars can't fill. Only a woman can."

Rachel was stunned. She had never dreamed such thoughts could be in Vince Franklin. She looked up at him, saying, "How long have you had thoughts like that?"

Jake saw the softness of her lips and knew that here was a woman who could fill the emptiness in him. He started to lean forward, to tell her how he felt, but stopped as though someone had dumped cold water on him. Rachel would never be his, not in the way he wanted. . .she thought he was her brother! Drawing a deep breath, he shrugged and said as casually as he could, "Why, Rachel, I don't know. I guess every man thinks about things like that."

"No, I don't think they do." Rachel bit her lower lip, then shook her head. "Why have you waited so long to—"

She broke off, and Jake said quickly, "I'm the same old Vince, Rachel. Don't let my pretty words fool you again. I'm just not strong enough to be mean yet. Come on, now, let's go back to the house."

The pair of them mounted and left the creek. Jake kept up a running conversation, but Rachel could not help thinking of what he had said about loving a woman. She knew his affairs had been shallow, physical involvements; but there seemed to be something deeper in him now. When they got back to the stables and dismounted, Jake said thoughtfully, "Well, I rode the horse—but can I shoot the man?"

"Don't do it! I'll talk to Daddy!"

Jake gave her a curious look. "I have to do it. You know I do. Only question is—*can* I do it?" He stroked the steaming sides of the black horse, then asked a question that was directed more to himself than to her, she thought.

"Can I put a bullet in Simon Duvall? What will it prove if I kill him? Or if he kills me?" Once again, Jake considered just walking away. After all, this wasn't his fight. But the thought of the hurt in Rachel's eyes when she found out that he wasn't what she believed him to be, and the thought of the disgust in Brad Franklin's eyes when he discovered that Jake was a liar and impostor. . . He shook his head. No, he was in this now and he would not back down. Only one thing would stop him, and that was if Vince came back to do these things himself.

Rachel shivered, a quick vision flashing before her eyes of a man on the ground with his life's blood draining out. Suddenly the chill she felt was much more intense than that caused by cold weather. "Why not just go on into the army? That's an honorable thing, and it will satisfy everyone." But even as she spoke, she saw the stubbornness in his jaw. Her next words were spoken in a quiet, sad voice. "You'll face Duvall, won't you? And nothing I can say will stop you."

Jake blinked at her, then suddenly took her hand and blurted out, "Rachel, if I could do anything in the world for you, I'd do it. But this job isn't of my choosing."

She slowly pulled away from him and walked into the stable. Jake thought that it was because she was angry, and he accepted that as right. But he would have been stunned by the truth. For Rachel suddenly had been invaded by strange feelings of tenderness and concern for this man who was her half brother. She knew he had been a wastrel all his life, but that no longer seemed to matter. She thought perhaps it was because she had nursed him back to life, because he had been almost like an infant in her care.

But he was no infant now! And as she left him, she discovered to her consternation that she was filled with fear over what might happen to him. If it had been Grant or Les, that would have been purely natural. But Vince! She had despised him for years, and now, suddenly, she found that impossible. Once again she heard the words he'd spoken by the river. Then the thought came to her, as strongly as anything she'd ever felt: *If I ever fall in love, I want to be for my man what Vince says a woman ought to be!*

As she walked toward the house, she tried to fit the words and the new spirit in Vince to the brother with whom she'd grown up, but it was impossible. He pretty much looked like the Vince she'd always known, as much as he could without his beard. But he certainly didn't act like him. Finally, with a shake of her head, she put away the thoughts of him as much as she could.

But his words, his smile, and his gentleness kept coming back to her, stirring in her emotions that she did not understand.

CHAPTER 16

AT THE WHITE HORSE BAR

$\mathcal{B}$y the fourth day of the family reunion, Dee was ready to run the whole bunch of Rocklins and Bristols off. She said as much to her mistress that evening as she was supervising another gargantuan meal.

"Miz Amy, this heah bunch is worse than all them locusts in Egypt!" Stirring a huge bowl filled with batter, she shook her gray head in disgust. "I ain't nevuh *seed* folks eat like they does!"

Amy sat in her wheelchair peeling potatoes. She was still weak but had grown sick of doing nothing. "Now, Dee, it may be the last time we'll have the whole family together for a long time. It's hard on you, with me not able to help, I know—but you've done *so* well!"

The praise caused Dee to sniff, but it pleased her all the same. She gave the batter a few more vigorous slaps with the wooden spoon, then poured it into a black iron skillet. Opening the door of the oven, she inserted it, then closed the door. She wiped her hands on the apron, then stood there thinking. Finally she asked, "Whut you reckon Marse Vince is up to?"

"Up to? What does that mean, Dee?"

"Why, dat young man ain't nuffin' like his ol' self, and you knows it!" Puzzlement grew on her lined black face, and she asked curiously, "Whut's Marse Franklin think dat boy gonna do? He gonna fight with dat man in Richmond? He gonna get hisself killed!"

Amy glanced at the black woman, who was more friend than slave, and shook her head. "I don't know, Dee. I've tried to talk the major out of it, but you know how stubborn he can get when he sets his mind to something. And when I try to talk to Vince—" She broke off abruptly, for the subject disturbed her. "It was fine of him to ride that horse, and I'm proud that he's decided to join the army. But that business with Duvall is terrible!"

"Miss Rachel, she got real close to him," Dee observed. "Maybe she can talk him outta it."

"She's tried, but Vince won't listen." Amy's dark eyes clouded, and there was a mixture of sorrow and anger in them. "This war—you'd think it would be enough! And now this thing with Vince—"

"Well now, don't you get all agrafretted 'bout it, you heah?" Dee came over and patted her mistress on the shoulder, then took the bowl of potatoes from her hands. "You gonna go take a nap befo' supper." She ignored Amy's protests and took her to her room and tucked her in as if she were a child. "You sleep now," she commanded, then shut the door and moved back down toward the kitchen.

When she got there, she saw Jake ride out of the stable on a big black horse. "Whar he goin' now?" she muttered, then shook her head, saying in disgust, "White folks!"

Jake had caught a glimpse of Dee in the window, but his mind was so busy that the sight of her barely registered—just the one quick thought: *I hope she didn't talk to the messenger.*

Looking up at the skies, he saw that the day was ready to fade and knew that he would not be back for supper. The skies were flat and gray with more snow in the offing, but he didn't think of that, for the message that rested in his pocket had driven all other thoughts from his mind the moment he'd received it. He'd been waiting with apprehension for Vince's reply, and when it came, it was brief: *"Meet me tonight at seven at the White Horse Bar. Underhill."*

The messenger had been a slight young man, no more than seventeen or so, and he had said, "Man who paid me to deliver this, he wants to know will you come?"

"Tell him I'll be there," Jake had said, giving him a dollar. Now as he drove Crow along at an easy gallop, he tried to find some sort of reason in the summons but failed. *If Vince gets spotted by just one person who recognizes him, it's all over,* he thought grimly. And on the heels of that thought came another: *That'd be fine with me!*

All the way to Richmond he thought about what he'd been doing and was not happy with it. No matter how he tried to rationalize it, he still had an edgy feeling. It was a lie, and though he'd done things he'd not been proud of in the past, there was something about the whole thing with Vince Franklin that made him feel dirty. Perhaps it was the way Amy Franklin had shown such love to him. More likely, he thought instantly, there was something about his relationship with Rachel that made him uneasy.

Maybe it's because I never had much of a family, he thought as he reached the outskirts of Richmond. *Always wanted to be part of a big family, and this is about as close as I've ever come. But it's all a lie, and it'll blow up in my face soon enough.*

The streetlights glowed, making yellow points in the darkness as he rode down the main thoroughfare. The snow was packed down hard, and Crow almost slipped once. "Steady, Crow!" Jake said, patting his shoulder. He asked a man standing in front of a shop, "Friend, where would the White Horse Bar be found?"

"You done passed it," the man replied. "It's back the way you come—look for the sign on yore right."

"Thanks."

When he moved back up the street, he saw the small sign and tied Crow up to the hitching rail. He entered the large room, which was filled with the acrid odor of cigarette smoke and whiskey, and looked swiftly around for Vince. It was a rough place, with a bar along one wall and a few tables and chairs covering the rest of the place. Two of the tables were occupied, but none of the men was Vince. Jake assumed that Vince would have donned some sort of disguise, so he walked to the bar. "I'm supposed to meet a fellow here."

The bartender gave him a steady glance. He was a thickset individual with misshapen ears and scar tissue around his eyes—an old fighter. He nodded toward the door at the rear of the room. "Fellow named Underhill? He's in the back room."

"Thanks."

Jake moved to the door, opened it, and stepped inside to find a single round table with a few chairs. A man was slumped in one of them, wearing a full beard and rough-looking clothes. A limp slouch hat was pulled down over his eyes. Just to make certain, Jake let him speak first.

"Sit down, Jake," Vince said, and when he lifted his head, Jake saw that his face was thin and his eyes were bloodshot. "Have a drink."

"All right." Jake sat down and took the drink Vince pushed

toward him, but didn't lift it. He was a little shocked at the man's appearance, for he knew Franklin to be a careful dresser. But perhaps that was just part of the disguise. "Nobody would know you in that rig, Vince," Jake said quietly. Then he leaned closer, peering into Vince's face. "You sick?"

"Yes." Vince nodded, then drained the glass in his hand. He braced his feet against the jolt of the liquor and at once began to cough. It was a deep, ragged cough that racked him terribly. When he finally got control of himself, he shook his head, saying, "Been sick three days. Can't seem to shake it off." He peered toward Jake, nodding as he said, "You look good. I told you we could pull it off."

"We didn't pull it off." Jake shook his head, determined to push the matter to a conclusion. "Ellen Rocklin knows I'm a fake."

"How'd she find out?"

Jake related the story, then said, "Vince, it's not going to work. And it's not just the Rocklin woman. I can't keep on forever, not knowing people. I made a stupid mistake just this morning with Rachel." He took a deep breath, then shook his head. "It was a good idea—but it's just too tricky."

"What about my father?"

Jake hesitated, then gave Vince the details—including the three tasks he had to perform.

Vince's eyes lost part of their dullness as he asked eagerly, "Well, Jake, did you ride the horse?"

"Sure, that was easy. But fighting Duvall won't be."

"You won't have to. Join up with the army. Not with a branch around here, but some outfit far away. Ride out and stay there until the time comes. If you stick it out, Father won't force the matter with Duvall."

"What if I get killed?" Jake asked curiously. "That'd put a crimp in your plan, wouldn't it?"

Vince didn't catch the irony in Jake's tone. "Well, in that case, I'd have to find some other way—" Then he saw the slight smile on Jake's lips, and he laughed. "Sorry, Jake! I'm not thinking very straight. But you can wrangle a safe spot away from the action. Maybe in the quartermaster corps."

"That still leaves Ellen."

Vince nodded. "I know, but I can handle her."

"Not without paying her off. She's a greedy woman, and she'll do just what she says if you don't give her the money."

"I can handle her, Jake," Vince insisted stubbornly. "I hope you brought the checkbook with you. I've got to have some cash."

"I brought it." He took the item out of his pocket, stared at it, then remarked, "I think I can go to jail for signing your name to these checks."

"Aw, Jake," Vince protested at once, "you know better than that. Now write a check for a thousand dollars."

Jake looked at him, startled. "Can you cash a check that large here? Won't they ask for identification?"

"I never thought of that." Vince studied the bottle, poured himself another drink, then said, "You'll have to go to the bank in the morning and get the cash. You can bunk in my room tonight."

Jake studied the man, then said, "Let's call it off. We really don't have much chance."

Vince looked startled, then began to plead, "Oh, come now, Jake, it's going to work! And we're both in a hole, and pretty bad, too. Look, let's go get something to eat and we can go over it again."

They left the bar and had a meal, then went back to the bar, where both of them drank too much. Jake was not a man who drank to excess, but he was depressed by the whole thing, and Vince kept insisting they go through with it. In the end he agreed wearily, and after a sleepless night, he went to the bank the next morning and got the cash.

"Now," Vince instructed, "you need to get away as soon as you can, Jake. Write me in care of general delivery in Savannah." He began to cough again, and this time the spasm nearly tore him in two.

"You've got to see a doctor."

"Sure, I'll do that," Vince agreed. He seemed nervous and anxious, saying, "Well, take care of yourself, Jake. Just a little while and you'll be on that island with your pocket full of money."

Jake stared at him but said only, "I'll be glad when it's over, Vince. It's not something I'm going to tell my grandchildren about."

❧

As soon as Jake left, Vince walked out of the hotel and took a cab to the house where Ellen stayed. He felt weak, but there was something he had to do before he left Richmond. The pistol he had slipped inside his belt was uncomfortable, but he ignored it.

Ellen was asleep when the knock came at her door, and it took her several minutes to come out of her slumber. Finally she threw the covers back, drew on a robe, and staggered to the door. "Who is it?"

"Open the door, Ellen!"

She hesitated, then turned the key. Opening the door a

crack, she peered outside. "I don't know you," she said to the rough-looking man who stood there. She would have closed the door, except that he put his hand out and stopped her.

"It's me, Ellen—Vince Franklin."

As he expected, her eyes opened wide, and she stepped back at once. When he entered and she had carefully shut the door, she exclaimed, "Vince! I don't believe it!"

"Ellen, I'm in a hurry," Vince said. "Let's talk business."

At once her eyes hardened, and she nodded. "I've been expecting you to pay a call. Sit down, Vince."

"No time, Ellen. Just tell me—how much?"

Ellen laughed, letting her robe fall open. "Now that's the way I like to hear you talk! Right down to brass tacks."

"How much, Ellen? Just lay it out; then we can argue over it."

"No argument." Ellen grinned. "I've got you in a box. One word from me and you'll get nothing."

Vince nodded. "I know that. But you've got to be reasonable. I won't get a huge chunk of money. I'll get control of the estate. It'll take me a little time to liquidate it."

"Of course, sweetheart!" Ellen shrugged, her eyes alive with interest. "I know about all that. What I really want is a large bonus—and then a *steady* income, you know what I mean?"

Vince knew well enough. She meant a lifetime of blackmail, but he only shrugged, saying, "I'll make you an offer. Five thousand when I come into the money, and one hundred dollars every month as long as you live."

"Oh, now, Vince, you can do better than that!" Ellen smiled. She was enjoying the thing, he saw, and now she added, "Let's say you double that, and we can do business."

"Double!" Vince exclaimed, pretending to show shock

at her proposal. But after a few minutes he caved in, saying, "Looks like you got the best of the argument, Ellen. Let's shake on it."

She took his hand, laughing at the disappointment on his face. "You and I are a lot alike." She leaned against him. "Maybe this will be more than a business deal—?"

Vince forced a smile, saying, "I'm for that—but now I've got to get out of Richmond."

"How about an advance on that first payment?" Ellen asked quickly.

"Haven't got it. I'll send you two hundred next week."

He left her then and two hours later was on the train headed for Savannah. His meeting with Ellen Rocklin had left a sour taste in his mouth, but he had already made plans for her. There was a man he knew in Savannah, a rough sort of fellow named Elvin Sloan. For five hundred dollars he would shoot his own mother.

A shock ran through Vince at the enormity of what he planned. To have a woman killed! He was truly physically sick, and the thought of doing such a thing raised his gorge.

Still, there was no other way. "She should have stayed out of it!" he muttered as the train clattered over the rails. "No-good tramp!"

He slept fitfully during the trip, but when he finally got off the train, his fever was so high that the conductor took his arm as he stumbled. "Mister, you sick?"

"No. . .all right, I'm. . .all right," he mumbled, shoving the man away. Vince straightened up and forced himself to walk carefully, but by the time he got to the cab stand, a dizziness hit him. The world seemed to reel, and he made a wild grab at the cab—only to fall headlong to the ground.

"Hey—mister—!"

He heard people speaking and felt hands pulling at him, but they could not stop him from sliding into the deep black void that seemed to be waiting for him.

CHAPTER 17

GOD IN THE CAMP

Four days before Christmas, Rev. Jeremiah Irons rode into the yard at Lindwood, determination set on his face. He stepped off his horse, quickly tied him to the hitching post, then climbed the steps and knocked on the door. He was met by House Betty, who said, "Lawsy, Rev. Irons, you look plum froze! Come on in and warm yo'self."

Irons stepped inside, took off his mittens and fur cap, then stripped off his coat. "Tell Miss Melora I want to see her, will you, Betty?"

"Yas, suh, I sho' will."

The diminutive maid bustled off quickly, saying, "You go on into the parlor, Reverend." Taking her advice, Irons went into the large, high-ceilinged room. He stood in front of the cheerful fire that blazed in the fireplace, clenching his hands nervously and glancing toward the door. Irons was not a man of a nervous temperament; quite the contrary, he was one of the calmest men imaginable under adverse circumstances. But he had slept little for several nights in a row, and now his even features were stretched tightly as he waited for Melora to appear.

Glancing across the room, he caught a glimpse of himself

in a beveled mirror and blinked in shock at his own image. *You look like a criminal appearing before a hanging judge for a sentence*, he thought grimly, then at once considered that in a sense, his condition was much the same. He had loved Melora Yancy for years and had waited for her to accept him as her husband. Now he had come to the conclusion that the thing could go on no longer. *Either she'll have me—or she won't*, he thought grimly, then turned to greet her as she entered the room.

"Hello, Jeremiah," Melora said, coming to stand before him. "Is something wrong?"

"Yes, there is," Irons said abruptly, then gave an embarrassed laugh at his greeting. "Well, no, not really."

Melora relaxed, smiling at him. "You look like someone just died. I was afraid—"

He cut her off, saying, "Melora, I've got to know what you mean to do." He reached out quickly and took her hands, his words rushing forth as if he were afraid to wait. "This isn't sudden, is it, Melora? I guess you know what I want. I've loved you for years, and I've waited for a long time—"

He broke off, and Melora stood there looking into his direct brown eyes, her hands compressed as he held to them almost desperately. A great surge of pity rose in her as she stood there, thinking of how faithful and patient he had been. No other man she knew would have done such a thing, and she understood that now she had come to a crossroad in her life. She thought of her love for Clay Rocklin—and, with one act of will, closed the door on it as firmly as one would close and seal the door of a tomb where the body of the dearest one in all the world had been placed.

Jeremiah had started speaking again, pressing his cause. She waited until he was finished, then answered evenly, "Yes,

Jeremiah, I'll marry you."

Irons stood there stock still, his face gone pale. He had expected a rejection, and now that she stood there with her hands in his, her eyes confirming her words, he could only stare at her. Finally he reached out, drew her close and kissed her lips, then held her tightly in his arms. They stood there for a long moment, the only sound the ticking of the grandfather clock in the foyer. Then he drew back, saying huskily, "You've made me a happy man, my dear!"

"I must say one thing—"

He put his hand over her lips gently. "I know. It's about Clay, but I know all about that. There is a part of you that belongs to him, and no other man can ever change that. I've always known that, Melora, but you have some feelings for me, too, I believe. And that will be enough." He smiled, adding, "Very seldom do any of us get everything we want, do we? But you and I will have children, and you need them! You were born to have children at your feet. And you'll love me more when they come. Clay is my best friend in this world, and I'll never be jealous of what you feel for him. There must not be anything hidden about this. He must come and go in our home, and he'll be a godfather to our children. Isn't that the way it will be, Melora?"

Tears gathered in Melora's eyes so that the sight of his face blurred. She whispered, "You're such a good man, Jeremiah!" Then she put her face against his chest, and he let her lie there until, finally, she drew back. She smiled, saying, "Now when will it be?"

"As soon as possible!" Irons said instantly. "I'll have to go ask your father's permission."

"You'll get no argument from him." Melora laughed. "Getting rid of an old maid daughter will suit him well enough!"

"Not so, but I must talk with Buford anyway." A thought struck him, and he said, "Come with me to the meeting at the camp. I'm preaching, and I'll announce it to the regiment."

"Yes! And I'll get up a crowd to go. You go by and talk to my father. Tell him to bring all four of the children to the meeting, and I'll try to get Rachel to bring all the Franklins who can be spared."

"I'll go by and see Clay," Jeremiah said. "I want him to hear it from me—unless you'd rather tell him yourself?"

"No, you're the proper one. I. . .don't think it will come as a great shock to him." She said no more about Clay, and Irons understood. "We'll all be there, so preach a good sermon, Chaplain."

"I probably will be so nervous I won't be able to find my text!" Then he kissed her hand and left the room. She watched from the window as he rode toward Gracefield, and a pain filled her heart as she thought of Clay—but she had made her decision and knew that she had taken a road that led her away from him.

༉

A cavalcade made up of Rocklins, Franklins, and Yancys moved toward the camp of the Richmond Grays early on the afternoon of the twenty-third of December. The roads were packed with snow, forming a hard surface, and the weather was crisp and cold. Buford Yancy led the way with his four youngest children and Melora, followed by the Franklin clan, including Jake, Rachel, Grant, and Les. Dent and Raimey drove another carriage with David, Lowell, and Rena, in addition to Irons's children, Asa and Ann, who were staying with a family from the church. Bringing up the rear was Clay, who drove a small

997

closed carriage with his parents bundled up in the rear.

Clay had said little as he drove with his parents. Susanna finally asked, "Are you all right, Clay?"

"I'm fine, Mother," he had said quickly, but a mile down the road, he said, "You'll hear an announcement tonight. Jeremiah and Melora are getting married." Then he added quickly, "I'm very happy for them. They'll have a fine life together." Thomas had opened his mouth to ask a question, but Susanna nudged him with her elbow, then shook her head firmly.

"Yes, they will," she said quickly. "A pastor needs a wife, and Melora will be a fine one for him."

Melora had told Rachel about her decision, and Rachel had gone at once to Jake, who was reading a book. She told him the news, and he had said, "That'll be hard on Uncle Clay."

"It's best for Melora, though. She needs a home and a family."

Jake had stared at her curiously, remarking, "I thought you were a romantic. All for love and things like that. This looks like a marriage of convenience."

"It'll work out. And you're going to the camp meeting tomorrow."

Jake had argued, but now as Grant drove the team along the icy road, he was glad to be going. Les sat in the front with Grant while Jake occupied the backseat with Rachel. She looked very pretty in a dark wine-colored dress, and the cold air put a sparkle in her eyes. She caught him looking at her and gave him a nudge with her elbow. "You behave yourself in the meeting, you hear me?"

Jake grinned, wondering what Vince had done to occasion such a dire warning, but only said, "You afraid I'll challenge the chaplain's theology?"

"No. But I remember how you sneaked off with that Wilcox girl at the meeting in Oak Grove."

"We were talking about the sermon," Jake said slyly.

Rachel snorted. "I know what you were up to!" Then she smiled, and the dimple in her cheek made her look younger. "One good thing about a camp meeting with the army—there won't be any pretty girls for you to run off to the bushes with!"

"I'd run off with you if you weren't my sister." He smiled at her astonished expression. "You've grown up into a handsome woman, Rachel. I don't know a woman any more attractive."

Rachel blinked at him, taken aback. "Well, that's the first compliment you ever gave me, Vince."

"It's true, though."

A flush appeared on her cheeks, and she gave a short half-laugh of embarrassment. "Well, thank you. Not that it's true—"

"Captain Semmes will think so."

Rachel protested, but when they got to the camp, it was Jeremiah Irons and Captain Semmes who were waiting to greet them. Irons went at once to Melora, saying, "You look beautiful!"

Melora looked around quickly, embarrassed at his words, but took his arm, saying, "I had a good talk with Asa and Ann before we left for the meeting. I hope they'll not think I'll be a wicked stepmother like in the fairy tales." He hastened to assure her that they were delighted with having a mother, and they moved off toward the line of tents stretched out across the open fields.

"Rachel, you're looking more beautiful than ever," Semmes said as he came forward to greet her.

Jake moved to stand beside Rachel, a sly light in his eyes. "See, Rachel? I told you the captain would be here to say that."

Semmes looked up quickly, flushing a little, but then had to laugh. "Vince, you know me too well!"

"We both have bad reputations, Semmes. I've just been doing my brotherly duty in explaining to my sister how little either of us are to be trusted." Rachel covered the smile that rose to her lips as Semmes stood there not knowing what to say. Jake merely smiled at him. "I'm sure you'd have just such a talk with your sister if I came courting her, wouldn't you?"

Semmes had planned a little scene with Rachel, hoping to get her off to one side so that he could press his case. Now the look in Jake's eyes told him that he would have difficulty achieving that. He frowned and said with as much grace as he could muster, "Perhaps so. We do have to protect the ladies."

"Well said!" Jake nodded, then turned to Rachel and gave a wink that only she could see. "Now you see that the captain agrees with me, Rachel."

"Surely I don't need protection at a gospel meeting?" Rachel smiled.

"Oh, the devil is an angel of light!" Jake nodded. "And wolves run about in sheep's clothing. I think I'd better stay at your side, sister—just in case one of them tries to destroy the solemnity of the meeting by speaking to you improperly."

And stay by Rachel's side he did, to the intense aggravation of Captain Leighton Semmes! There was a short meeting with the officers, and Jake did not move a foot away from Rachel the entire time.

An officer wearing the stars of a general came into the meeting, and Jake asked Irons, who sat beside him, "Who's that?"

"Stonewall Jackson."

Jake turned a curious gaze on the general, having heard much about him. He was wearing a plain, worn uniform and carried an equally worn forage cap in his hand. He was not a handsome man, but there was something in his features that drew attention. His men, Jake knew, called him "Old Blue Light," referring to his pale blue eyes, which were said to practically glow when Jackson led men onto the field of battle.

Colonel Benton said a few words of introduction, then quickly added, "We're privileged to have General Jackson with us this afternoon. General, it would be greatly appreciated if you would say a few words—or even more than a few."

Jackson got to his feet and turned to face the small group. He had a high-pitched voice, pleasant and very clear. "Colonel Benton, I am always made happy when the gospel of the Lord Jesus is proclaimed, and I must remark that your command is most fortunate to have a chaplain who does that as well as any minister of my acquaintance." He nodded toward Major Irons, adding, "Chaplain Irons and I have enjoyed sweet fellowship, and it is gratifying to know that the Richmond Grays have such a servant of the living God to nourish them in these difficult days."

Jackson spoke briefly. Afterward, when he was introduced to the visitors, he took Clay Rocklin's hand and paused. "I know that name—oh yes, Manassas." His blue eyes glowed, and he remarked, "It was a pleasure for me to sign the recommendation that Colonel Benton sent to me, Sergeant."

Clay flushed at the reference to his commendation for bravery, saying only, "It was a small thing that I did, General."

Jackson shook his head. "No, Sergeant, it was not." He moved on and, when introduced by Major Franklin to Rachel, bowed slightly, saying, "Your father is a good soldier, Miss Rachel. Are any other members of your family in the army?"

Rachel had never seen a pair of eyes with such power. She suddenly took Jake's arm, saying, "This is my brother, Vincent,

General. He's just recovering from a serious injury, but it's his intention to begin his service immediately."

"Indeed?" Jackson put out his hand, and when Jake took it, he held it in a strong grip. "You will be welcome, Mr. Franklin." He hesitated, then added, "Your father will have already given you wise counsel, but may I say just a word?"

Jake was startled and stammered slightly as he answered, "W—why certainly, General!"

Jackson held the young man with his eyes, and Jake felt as though the officer saw deeper than he would have liked. Finally Jackson said, "It is the duty of a soldier to put his life in jeopardy. Many of us will fall in the service of our country. That, sir, is not a tragedy as long as we are right with God. Have you put your trust in Jesus?"

A silence had fallen on those gathered there, and the blood seemed to pound in Jake's veins. He had expected advice, words encouraging him to give his all for the South or a statement of the importance of the war—anything but this! He felt Rachel's presence as she stood so close that her arm brushed his, and he could only give his head a slight shake. "I—I'm afraid not, General."

Jackson smiled then, the severity of his face broken. "There is yet time, Mr. Franklin. I will pray for you." Then he turned to greet the other visitors. Jake's legs were like rubber, for the encounter had been like nothing he had ever experienced.

Rachel was aware of his difficulty, and as they left the meeting to go to the service, she whispered, "Are you all right?"

"Well, not really." Jake swallowed and shook his head. "That fellow really knows how to shake a man up!"

"Rev. Irons says he's always like that," Rachel said quickly. "He attends all the prayer meetings and talks to a lot of the men about God. And he seems as concerned with a Sunday school he started for black children back at his home as he is with the war."

"A strange man," Jake muttered. "A blazing killer on the battlefield—and yet he's got some kind of love in him that I can feel."

Jake escorted Rachel out onto the open field where the Richmond Grays had assembled for the service. There were no chairs, but a small platform had been built for the preacher.

The service got under way when Chaplain Jeremiah Irons stood and welcomed them to the meeting. He paused, then said, "I must introduce one very special guest—the young woman who has agreed to marry me." Melora was forced to stand, blushing but smiling, and then Irons said, "Now we can begin the service."

A lieutenant with a fine singing voice mounted the platform and, after a fervent prayer, began to sing "All Hail the Power of Jesus' Name." There were no books, but the five hundred or so soldiers filled the field with their lusty singing. They sang "Rock of Ages," "O Happy Day," "On Jordan's Stormy Banks I Stand," and several others.

Rachel noticed that Jake was not singing at all, but said nothing to him. She knew her brother had stopped going to church when he was sixteen years old and had begun at that time—or even earlier—to make fun of all that was Christian. Even so, she could see that he had been troubled by Stonewall Jackson's simple question. She began to pray for him.

When the singing was over, Stonewall Jackson, having been asked by Colonel Benton to say a few words, rose and greeted the men, then asked them to pay careful attention to the message. "The power of the gospel is the greatest power there is," he declared, his high voice carrying out over the ground. "More powerful than all the guns of our armies, North and South. For guns and cannons destroy, but the gospel of Jesus Christ restores and makes whole. You will soon be facing the enemy on the field of battle, and you may be facing the great Judge of all the earth. On that day, the only question that will have any importance is this: 'Do I belong to Jesus Christ?'"

As Jackson spoke this last appeal, Rachel saw that Vince had clenched his fists so tightly that they were white. His head was bowed, and when Irons stood and began to preach, he didn't lift it at all, but stood there staring down at the ground.

When Irons stood up, he opened his Bible to the nineteenth chapter of Matthew and began to read.

"And, behold, one came and said unto him, Good Master, what good thing shall I do, that I may have eternal life?

"And he said unto him, Why callest thou me good? there is none good but one, that is, God: but if thou wilt enter into life, keep the commandments.

"He saith unto him, Which? Jesus said, Thou shalt do no murder, Thou shalt not commit adultery, Thou shalt not steal, Thou shalt not bear false witness,

"Honour thy father and thy mother: and, Thou shalt love thy neighbour as thyself.

"The young man saith unto him, All these things have I kespt from my youth up: what lack I yet?

"Jesus said unto him, If thou wilt be perfect, go and sell that thou hast, and give to the poor, and thou shalt have treasure in heaven: and come and follow me.

"But when the young man heard that saying, he

went away sorrowful: for he had great possessions."

Irons closed his Bible, looked out over the upturned faces, then said clearly, "Let me speak to you this day about disguises." A mutter ran through the ranks, and a slight smile came to the lips of the speaker. "Did you hear the story I just read? It's a story about a man who was an impostor. A man who came to Jesus under false colors, wearing a disguise. Oh, not with a false beard or dyed hair! And to speak honestly, I don't think this impostor was even aware that he *was* wearing a disguise."

Jake discovered that his hands were sweating, even in the biting cold, and he wiped them on his coat. He had the sudden impression that he was standing all alone in the vast field with Irons looking right at him! Unpleasant sensations had begun to work on him from the instant Jackson had asked, "Have you put your trust in Jesus?"

Jake Hardin was not a man of quick emotions; in fact, he had always distrusted emotional reactions. Now, however, he stood there with a weakness such as he had never known, and as Irons continued, he could only stare at the snow and try to conceal what was happening to him.

"This fine young man, the rich ruler who came to Jesus," Irons continued, "would have been a welcome addition to any church in town. I haven't heard of any church in Richmond turning down wealthy young men, have you?" A ripple of laughter went over the crowd, and Irons smiled, waiting for it to pass. "He was a *moral* young chap, much better than I was at his age. Better, in fact, than most of you! He had kept the commandments. Think of that! He had kept the commandments of God from his youth!"

He spoke of how difficult it was for a Jew to keep the multitude of laws and ordinances that made up Judaism; then his voice rose as he called out, "But I show you a greater mystery than that, and it is this: It did not matter that he had kept the rules of his religion—he was not accepted by Jesus Christ as a disciple! What does that mean? It means that not a one of us can come to Jesus because we are good. It doesn't matter that we are church members, that we have not lied or stolen as others. No! That will not do!"

Irons began to relate sections of scripture to his listeners, using illustration after illustration to show that it was not morality that God required, that there was nothing in any man that could earn him salvation.

"Now about the disguise," he said. "This rich, moral, up-standing young man had done much to appear good. He was, in fact, *disguised* by his good deeds—that is, he had put on robes of public righteousness. His fellow men saw him as a good young man, one who certainly was right with God. But Jesus saw through his disguise with one look—one look and He saw the heart of the young ruler. And what did He see? Why, He saw a man who loved money more than anything else! The young man had disguised this part of himself from men, but he couldn't hide it from God!"

The congregation was very still as Irons went on. There was an air of strain about them, and more than one soldier, Rachel noticed, was affected by the sermon. Irons said finally, "Some of you are here wearing a disguise. You know that you are not the man you appear to be. Some of you have worn many masks; some of you have played so many roles and been so many things that you no longer know *who* you are!"

Jake started, his shoulders jerking back, and suddenly he lifted his head and stared at the preacher. "But God knows who you are! Yes, He knows, and the glorious thing about it is that, knowing the worst about you—the awful, terrible things you wouldn't want your best friends to know—even knowing those things, He loves you! And here is what I've come to tell you today: Don't be afraid of God, for despite what you are, He loves you! *That's* the heart of the gospel. Not what good things you do for God, but what a grand and terrible thing He has done for you. Jesus is the friend of sinners. He came to die for sinners, just like you and me!"

A few cries began to go up, and then as Irons stopped abruptly and looked out over the crowd, he said, "I feel the Spirit of God working right now, and I invite you, no matter who you are or how you may have run from God—come and trust in Jesus! He is your friend, your hope, your salvation. And He is waiting for you to come and accept His love."

At once the song leader began to sing:

Just as I am, without one plea,
But that Thy blood was shed for me,
And that Thou bidd'st me come to Thee,
O Lamb of God, I come! I come!

The words seemed to pierce Jake Hardin like swords, and—to his amazement—he felt tears rise to his eyes! He had not wept since he was a child, and now he felt ashamed to show such weakness. He was aware that many men were making their way toward the platform—and he felt an urge to go with them. He was trembling almost violently, and a war was taking place in his spirit, a war that frightened him. He stood there, longing to go forward but filled with fear.

Rachel was aware of the struggle and finally put her hand on Jake's arm. "Why don't you go ask Brother Irons to pray for you?"

Jake could not speak, and Rachel longed to say more but was afraid to. Finally she lifted her head and caught the eye of Irons. He was looking right at her, and she motioned toward the trembling man on her left with a slight gesture of her head.

At once Irons came toward them, making his way through the crowd. He stopped in front of Jake and asked quietly, "You need God, Vince. Will you let me pray for you?"

Jake wanted to say no, but almost without volition, he found himself nodding. He felt Jeremiah's hands on his shoulders and knew that the chaplain was praying—but he could not understand the words because of the fierce battle going on in his mind. It came to this: He knew he was a liar and an impostor, and how could he come to God unless he confessed that, to God and to those he was deceiving?

Finally when Irons asked, "Will you put your trust in Jesus?" Jake shivered like a man who had been hit by a bullet. He longed to agree, to fall on his knees and let God in.

But he did not.

He lifted his head, allowing Irons to read in his eyes the tortured state of his spirit. Then he whispered huskily, "I—can't—do it!" He turned and walked away, making his way as rapidly as he could out of the crowd.

"Rachel," Irons said at once, turning to the woman whose face bore a stricken expression, "I've never seen a man more under conviction. You'll have to be patient. Pray for him, as I will." Irons slapped his hands together sharply, and pain was in his fine eyes. "He came so close!"

Rachel nodded, her own heart filled with sorrow. "Can he—will he find his way, Rev. Irons?"

"I pray he will—but for now, he's running hard. We can only pray that the Lord will catch up to him before it's too late!"

CHAPTER 18

NEW YEAR'S MIRACLE

*T*he smell of pies, cakes, baked meats, barbecue, and other spicy aromas filled the air on Christmas Day at Lindwood. Men and boys were run out of kitchens with dire warnings as the cooks prepared the succulent dishes. At three o'clock the slaves gathered in the barn, where planks had been placed across sawhorses to make tables. Lanterns were hung across the ceiling, and the food was stacked high.

Hams, chickens, ducks, turkeys, and wild game of every sort—all cooked to perfection—covered one table, and a variety of steaming vegetables in huge pots bowed another. Potatoes with thick gravy, yams that dripped syrup, mountains of biscuits, pans of fragrant corn bread, and rolls fresh from the oven added to the feast. And the children swarmed around the desserts: peach cobblers, apple pies, tarts, blackberry muffins, taffy, and candy.

Major Franklin asked a brief blessing, then lifted his head and smiled. "All right, let's get at it!"

There was a scramble, and Jake stood back, watching with a slight smile as the slaves piled their plates high with food. When the first rush was over, he moved to the tables and got some of the food, but more for appearance than because he was hungry. Since his experience at the camp meeting, he had eaten little and slept only fitfully. The shock of the emotional impact had faded, but he could not stop thinking about what had occurred.

Rachel was helping Melora bring in the gifts for the slaves, but she looked around for Jake. She had noticed how he had kept to himself since the night of the camp meeting, clear evidence of how the experience had shaken him. There was no time to go to him now, though, for the slaves were waiting with expectant smiles. Each time she handed out a gift, the recipient would cry out, "Chris'mas gift!" and there was a constant stream of giggles and shouts of pleasure as the gifts were unwrapped. Most of the gifts were clothing, but candy and other small favors were handed to the smaller children.

When the last of the gifts for the slaves was handed out, Rachel finally went to Jake. She took a small package with her and, when she reached him, said, "Christmas gift!"

Jake looked up, startled, then took the package from her, asking, "What is it?"

"It's a toecover."

Jake stared at her. "It's a *what?*"

Rachel laughed at his expression. She was wearing a red dress with white bows, and her hair gleamed as it caught the yellow rays of the lanterns overhead. "Oh, you've forgotten! A toecover is what we always called a useless sort of gift—something that's pretty but not good for anything."

He smiled and unwrapped the paper, then looked up to say, "It's not a toecover." He dropped the paper and looked closely at the heavy gold ring with the brilliant red stone. "It's a fine gift," he murmured.

GILBERT MORRIS

"Well, I didn't really buy it. It belonged to Mother's grand-father, Noah Rocklin. He left it to Mother, but she never did anything with it. I got her to let me give it to you." Her dimples flashed as she added mischievously, "I know how given you are to foppish attire—and it seemed like just the thing for a dandy."

Jake didn't respond to her teasing. He just looked at the ring, then slipped it on the third finger of his right hand. She couldn't know he was thinking, *I'll have to give this to Vince. It's part of the family.* But he was pleased with the thought that had spurred Rachel's gift and said, "That was fine of you to think of such a thing. But it's like you to do a nice thing for someone." He took her hand and, to her complete surprise, kissed it. "Thank you, Rachel."

Rachel's eyes mirrored the confusion that swept over her. She bit her lip, then shook her head, saying, "What has happened to you?"

At once Jake knew he'd made an error and covered himself quickly by saying, "I have a gift for you. It's in my room. Walk to the house with me, and I'll give it to you."

"All right." They left the barn, taking the path to the house. As they walked, Rachel wondered if she should ask him what he thought about the camp meeting. But it was a delicate subject, so she kept the conversation on other things. They entered the house, and when they got to his room, he went at once to the bureau. Opening the top drawer, he drew out a small package and came to hand it to her. "Christmas gift," he said and watched as she took away the wrapping.

"Why—these are lovely!" She ran her hand over the smooth surface of the silver brush set with mother-of-pearl, then took up the matching comb and ran it through her hair. "How in the world did you know I wanted these? I never said a word to you!"

"Mother told me," Jake said. He had discovered from Amy that Rachel had longed for this particular set, which she'd seen in the finest store in Richmond. He had bought it a week earlier, and now he stood there delighting in the sight of her obvious pleasure in the gift. He had given presents to women before but could not remember so enjoying the act. "A woman with hair like yours deserves the best in combs and brushes," he commented, then again realized that such a speech was out of character for Vince. "After all, if you're going to marry Leighton Semmes, you'll have to get used to fancy things. He's rich, isn't he?"

Rachel seemed uncomfortable with the question. She ran the comb through her hair, then turned abruptly and walked over to the window. "Oh, I don't know."

He came over to stand beside her, noting how her skin was translucent as the bright bars of brilliant sunlight bathed her. She had a few freckles across her nose, something he'd never noticed, and there was an inner well of energy about her that threatened to spill over. "What's to know? He's rich, healthy, and good looking." When she didn't respond, he pulled her around, adding, "That's better than being poor, sick, and ugly, isn't it?"

She giggled and reached up to give his hair a tug. "You fool! Let me alone about Semmes." Then she dropped her hand, asking curiously, "Why are you so anxious about my love life? You never gave a thought to it before."

He shrugged, thinking of the days that had passed since she had come to him as he lay in the hospital. "I guess being helpless and dependent changes a man. I always thought I was a pretty tough fellow, but then when I was flat on my back, not even able to wash my face—" He hesitated, and a shadow came to his eyes. "If you hadn't come to me, I think I'd have given it all up."

They stood there facing one another, and the sunlight fell across the room, filled with millions of motes swarming in the beams. Far off they heard the muted singing of the slaves, a happy sound that floated on the air like a far-off melody. He studied her face, noting that she had the prettiest blue-green eyes imaginable, admiring how the sweep of her jaw was smooth and silky, yet strong—made more so by the cleft in her chin. He was shaken again by the realization of how much she had come to mean to him, and something of his feelings came into his expression, so that she asked at once, "What is it?"

His feelings washed over him, surprising him with their intensity. He had never thought to tie himself to one woman—but that was exactly what he longed to do with Rachel Franklin. The impossibility of his situation came to him, and he forced himself to smile before she could read the pain that shot through him. "You know the cuckoo bird never builds a nest," he said, forcing his voice to be light. "She lays her eggs in the nests of other birds, leaving her chicks for the other bird to raise. Sometimes the baby cuckoo is large, so he just pushes the real chicks of the mother bird out to die."

Rachel was confused. "Why are you telling me about a cuckoo?"

"Because you've had to take care of me—and I'm just like that big overgrown cuckoo. Taking everything and giving nothing."

Her eyes grew soft, and she shook her head. "Maybe it was a little like that at first," she admitted. "I didn't like you at all, but now you're another man."

Her words seemed to strike him hard, though she didn't understand why they should. She had meant them as a compliment and added, "I'll tell you something amazing, Vince. I've decided that if I ever do get married, it'll be to somebody like you!"

Pain once again streaked through Jake, and he shook his head, a bitter light glowing dully in his eyes. "No, Rachel, you deserve better than that," he said. "I guess we better join the others." Turning, he left the room, and she followed, hurt a little by his abrupt words and by the curt dismissal in his voice. They found Amy in the parlor looking out the window at the children, who were having a snowball fight.

Looking up, she said in a strange voice, "I want to tell you two something."

"What is it, Mother?" Rachel asked. She was still thinking of Vince's strange behavior, but went to stand beside the wheelchair.

Amy said without a trace of emotion or excitement, "I'm going to get a gift from the Lord. A belated Christmas present." She smiled at the bewilderment that crossed Rachel's face and added, "I'm going to get out of this wheelchair and walk."

Rachel blinked with surprise, then said quickly, "I hope so!"

"It's not hope anymore," Amy insisted. " 'Hope deferred maketh the heart sick,' " she quoted. Then she nodded firmly, adding, "That's what I've been doing ever since the accident—hoping. But last night I had an all-night session with God. It was like Jacob wrestling with the angel at Peniel!" A rueful smile came to her lips, and she shook her head with wonder. "I behaved in a very—well, *unusual* way with the Lord. I just *demanded* that He touch my leg and heal it!"

Rachel could not resist a glance down at her mother's leg,

still propped up and looking swollen. "Oh, it's no better, Rachel," Amy said quickly. "But God gave me a promise last night. He said I'd be walking before the old year ended."

Jake was staring at Amy, disbelief on his face. Amy looked at him, then said, "I think part of my healing is for your benefit, son." When Jake looked startled, she said, "You've got a long way to go, and you need God. But you don't know if you can trust Him. Isn't that right?"

"Why—I guess most men feel like that, Mother."

"Yes, they do. But you've watched for weeks as I lay in that bed and in this chair, getting worse. And you've talked with Dr. Maxwell, and he told you I'd probably never walk again, or at best I'd be limited to using crutches, didn't he?"

"Well—"

"Of course he did! I'm not a fool, and neither are you." Amy suddenly smiled, then said, "But when you see me walk as well as I ever did, you'll know that God is able to do anything! Now go on about your business!"

Dismissed with a wave of Amy's hand, the two walked back out into the cold air. "Is she losing her mind?" Jake asked, stunned by what he had heard. "I've never heard of anything like that!"

Rachel didn't answer at once. They walked along the packed snow in silence, each considering what Amy had told them. Finally Rachel said quietly, "Vince, Mama has always been able to hear from God. You know that, too, even though you always laughed at such things. Now I think we're going to see God do something very wonderful." Then it seemed to her that the moment had come, and she said quietly, "And I believe that it's all part of what God began when General Jackson asked you if you'd ever trusted in Jesus."

She said no more and just walked on down the path, but Jake was shaken. He'd never seen God as he'd seen Him reflected in the life of Amy Franklin, and now he felt that he was being moved along a road, directed by a power he could not see or hear. Somehow, he knew, there'd come a point on that road when he'd have to make a decision about God, and the thought of it made him clench his fists. He said nothing, but he knew the clock was ticking off seconds and, sooner or later, the rendezvous with what he feared most would be at hand.

∘❦

All over the South, the threat of invasion by the Federal Army was in the air. It was in Richmond that it was strongest. Everyone knew that General George McClellan was building the largest army that had ever marched on the planet—over two hundred thousand men, it was reported. Sooner or later that force would cross the Potomac, and there was no doubt in a single mind about its objective: it would head straight for Richmond, the symbol of the Confederacy.

Perhaps because of the imminence of this threat, parties were given almost nightly in the city. There was something of the Epicurean philosophy—"Eat, drink, and be merry, for tomorrow we may die"—about the constant holiday air that prevailed. That there should be several large New Year's Eve parties, therefore, was a foregone conclusion, and Rachel had agreed to accompany Leighton to the largest of them all, which would take place at the Elliot Hotel.

She was ready when he came for her, looking quite beautiful in a pink and gold brocade gown. As they drove into town, he made all the proper gestures of gallantry, and Rachel listened to his talk, weighing it carefully. When they reached the hotel, early darkness had fallen. When he pulled the horse up, he wrapped the lines firmly around the brake and turned to her instead of getting out.

She watched him carefully, aware that he was going to kiss her. When he put his arms around her, her curiosity rose and she allowed him to pull her close. The kiss was expert, and there was, to be sure, a certain stirring in her, for Semmes was a handsome man. She had been kissed before by him, and for one moment, she let herself believe that the response she felt was love. Then she suddenly let her lips slide away and drew back.

Semmes was thrown off balance and tried to draw her into another embrace, but she smiled and shook her head. "I think we'd better go inside, Leighton."

He stared at her, then said, "You've heard that I've been a womanizer, I take it?"

"It's the common talk."

"Well, I've told other women how beautiful they are," he admitted. "I've even told some of them I loved them. I've said those things not entirely meaning them. Now I want to say them to you because I mean them—and I wish I'd never used those words before."

"At least you're honest."

"Is there a chance for me, Rachel?"

Rachel smiled quickly, then shook her head. "I don't know, Leighton. I really don't know. Now let's go inside."

He took her into the ballroom, his temper ruffled by her lack of response to him, but he was an optimistic man. *She's a woman; therefore she can be had*, was his thought, and he spent the next two hours pleasantly enough, enjoying her company and not pressing her in the least.

The room was crowded, and Rachel saw that Jake had

come along with her father. They came to speak with her, her father saying, "You look lovely, Rachel. Good thing you took after your mother and not me!"

Rachel laughed and patted him on the shoulder, then turned to Jake. "You can give that leg some practice, Vince. I've seen several young ladies waiting for you to ask them to dance, but your first one is mine."

Jake grinned at Semmes and stepped forward at once. As they moved out onto the floor, he asked as casually as he could, "Did the captain make his offer yet?"

"Oh, he made an offer, all right." Rachel laughed. "I'm not sure, though, just what kind of offer it was."

"Little girls need to beware of tall, handsome strangers with long teeth."

He seemed in better spirits than he had been for several days, and she enjoyed her dance with him. But when he took her back to where Leighton stood, he said, "Captain, be careful. This woman is dangerous!"

"Will you dance with me again?" Rachel asked him, surprising both herself and Jake. He struggled with the desire to claim all of her dances—regardless of how it might look— then sighed in surrender to common sense.

"No, my leg is growing sore again. I think I'll join the card players," he said, trying to ignore the disappointment that crossed Rachel's face. He smiled at her and Semmes. "You two look very handsome together," he said, forcing himself to play his role. But the words left a bitter taste in his mouth as he walked away.

As he left, Semmes frowned. "I can't figure that fellow out. He's not much what I expected. The word I got was that he was a pretty sorry specimen."

"He's—changed a lot since he was injured," Rachel said, watching Jake walk away, wishing she understood herself and her reactions to him. . . . Then she changed the subject.

The time went by, with everyone looking at the big clock from time to time. At eleven thirty Rachel said, "Come along, Leighton. Let's go get Vince away from that old card game."

Semmes was reluctant but had little choice. Rachel moved ahead of him, and when they entered the room used for cards, they found themselves in the middle of a drama.

There were at least fifteen men in the room, but there was almost no sound. Everyone was standing silently, gathered loosely around a table where Rachel saw her father and Jake sitting. Right across from Jake sat Simon Duvall.

He was drunk, Rachel saw at once, and seeing her brother Grant, she moved to him, whispering, "Grant—what is it?"

"Duvall came in thirty minutes ago—drunk. He forced his way into the card game, and he's been trying to get a fight out of Vince." His face was dark with anger, and he said, "If he doesn't shut his mouth, I'm going to shut it for him!"

Rachel felt a streak of fear but could only stand and watch. This was a man's world, and she knew that Vince would get no help from anyone.

Duvall threw his cards down, having lost yet another hand, and glared across the table, saying, "You been taking lessons, Franklin?"

Jake could have beaten Duvall blindfolded, for the man was a poor player. He had been taken off guard when Duvall had walked in, and alarms had gone off in his mind at once when he heard others mention Duvall's name and saw that the man was drunk and spoiling for trouble.

"Do you want to play another hand, Duvall?" he asked evenly.

Duvall cursed, saying, "Come on, you whelp! I can beat you at cards—or anything else!"

Jake dealt the cards, and the stakes rose rapidly. The other two players dropped out, and Duvall, obviously with a good hand, raised the bet again. "Now we'll see what kind of nerve you got!" he said. When Jake met his raise, he tossed his cards down with a harsh laugh. "Three aces!" he said, and he started to pull the chips in.

Jake laid his cards down, saying nothing. A full house. A mutter went around the table, and Duvall's face flared with anger. He shouted, "You cheated, Franklin."

Jake said evenly, "Careful, Duvall."

But Simon Duvall had just lost the stake he'd been waiting for for weeks, and rage washed over him. "You're a cheat and a coward! I'm taking that pot!"

He reached out, but Jake said, "Take your hands away, Duvall. Either bet or get out of the game."

Duvall stared at him; then his voice grated as he said, "I'll fight you for it."

"It's mine already," Jake said.

"You dirty little coward!" Duvall almost screamed. "I've been waiting for this. Now come on out and we'll see if you can act like a man!"

A silence fell over the room. Brad Franklin wanted to order Duvall to leave the room. In fact, he *would* have told any other man at any other time to do just that—but this time his son was on trial. One glance around showed him that every man in the room expected Vince to run. He was expecting it himself, and he steeled himself for the shame that he felt certain was coming.

Rachel closed her eyes, knowing that if Vince ran away, he

was finished. She was trembling and wanted to leave, but could not. When she opened her eyes, she saw that Jake was studying Duvall with a steady gaze.

The silence ran on, and it got to Duvall, who yelled, "Are you going to fight me or not?"

Jake said softly, "Yes, Duvall, I believe I am."

Duvall was shocked. He started to rise, a smile on his face. "Come along, then. We'll find a place—"

"This place is good as any," Jake said.

"Here?" Duvall said in a startled voice.

Jake reached into his pocket and pulled out a fine linen handkerchief. He unfolded it, then, holding one end, flipped it out, saying, "Take hold of that end, Duvall."

Duvall, acting on instinct, took the end of the handkerchief. Then he growled, "You crazy? We going to fight with handkerchiefs?"

Jake moved so smoothly that few even saw the .32 revolver that appeared in his hand. A gasp went around the room, and Duvall blinked, his sodden mind suddenly much clearer in the one instant that he saw the gun.

"You've got a gun under your coat, Duvall," Jake said. "Take it out. Then we'll hold on to the handkerchief, and on the count of three we'll start shooting."

A gasp went around the room, and Brad Franklin, fighting man that he was, could not help but grow pale. He knew it was one thing to stand twenty feet away and take a shot at a man, but to face his fire only inches away, with no chance in the world that he would miss—!

Duvall's face was a study. His lips puckered as though he had tasted something bitter, and his olive complexion grew gray as old paper. He stared at the gun that Jake had now placed on the table, but made no move to go for his own.

"This—this isn't the proper way to fight a duel!" he protested.

Jake's eyes were cold as polar ice, Rachel saw, and his voice was steady. "You've been running around calling me a coward for months, Duvall. Well, here's your chance to prove it. Now—*get your gun out!*"

Duvall flinched at the harsh command. He hunched his shoulders and squeezed his eyes together. Slowly he lifted his hand and reached inside his coat—but stopped abruptly.

"No! I won't fight you like this!" he gasped. Dropping the handkerchief, he got to his feet and would have left, but Jake's voice caught him.

"Hold it, Duvall!"

The man turned to find that Jake had picked up his gun, and he shouted, "I'm not drawing on you, Franklin!"

Jake stood up, putting his gun inside the shoulder holster. Then he said, "All right, we've both got an even chance. Pull that gun, Duvall. Let's see if you're a man or not!"

But Duvall had seen how the other had conjured the .32 out of the holster. He shook his head, saying, "I won't fight—"

Jake cut him off, moving around the table quickly despite his limp. He came to Duvall, raised his hand, and cracked him across the cheek. "Come on! Are you a man? Pull that gun!"

Duvall suddenly ducked and, shoving men to one side, ran out of the room. The sound of his short, labored breathing faded as he passed through the doors, and there was a sudden babble of voices. Men were coming to Jake and patting him on the shoulder. Rachel glanced at her father and saw tears on his cheeks.

"I want to go home, Leighton," she whispered. "But I want

to go with my father and my brother."

Later she could remember little of the ride back. Jake said almost nothing. Once her father said, "My boy, I believe I'm going to have to tell you how very proud of you I am!"

They got out of the buggy and went into the house. A light was on in the parlor, and Brad said, "I'd better turn that out. Betty must have forgotten it."

Then they all heard Amy call. "Come into the parlor, all of you."

Brad looked at the others with surprise. "Why, I guess she's waited up for us." He led the way, and as they entered, he saw Amy sitting on the couch, her wheelchair across the room. "Amy—!" he said, concerned, and started toward her, but she stopped him by crying out.

"No, stay there, Brad!" Her dark eyes picked up the reflection of the lamps, and there was a look on her face that none of them could understand.

"Amy, are you all right?" Brad asked with some confusion.

"Yes, dear, I'm all right."

She spoke quietly enough—then she suddenly gave herself a push against the arm of the horsehide sofa, coming to her feet awkwardly.

"Mother!" Rachel cried out, then pressed her fist against her lips, for her mother took two short steps, paused for one moment to gain her balance, then with a happy cry walked across the floor. Brad leaped to grab her in his arms, crying out, "Amy!"

Jake did not move but stood transfixed as Rachel ran to her mother. They were all laughing and crying at the same time, and finally Rachel asked, "Mother, did you walk before twelve o'clock?"

"It was just as God promised me," Amy said, tears gleaming in her eyes. "I waited until it was five minutes until twelve. Then I reminded the Lord of His promise. . .and then—I got up and walked!"

"It's a miracle!" Brad whispered. "Does your leg hurt?"

"Like fury!" Amy laughed. "But God didn't promise me it wouldn't hurt or that I would run around the house—just that I'd walk."

Then she turned to Jake and held out her hand. In a soft voice filled with triumph, she asked, "Now, my dear boy, do you see what God is able to do?"

Jake Hardin stood there unable to speak for a moment. Then he smiled and said, "Yes, I do see."

In a flash, the others were all talking at once—but Jake was quiet, for he knew that God had spoken to him again, this time in a manner he could neither deny nor ever forget!

CHAPTER 19

A LONG, LONG HONEYMOON!

A warm wind swept across the South, melting the snow and thawing the streams. It was exactly in the middle of January, the fifteenth, when Jake remarked to Rachel, "This weather can't last, can it? It seems too good to be true."

They had left Lindwood at noon and ridden to the foothills, stopping to water Crow and Lady at a small stream. Rachel was wearing a pair of Grant's old jeans, a worn blue blouse, and a thin sweater. Her hair crept out from beneath a wide-brimmed slouch hat, and she poked it back as she said, "I don't think so, but we can enjoy it while it lasts."

The ride had put color in her cheeks, and her clear eyes sparkled in the sunlight. "Let's race to that old pine," she said with a smile and, before he could even nod, kicked her horse into action. Jake yelled, "Hey—no fair!" then Crow shot out of the creek in pursuit of the mare. It was less than a quarter mile to the tree, and the mare was a quicker starter. But the long legs and powerful frame of the stallion began to tell, and he shot past Lady, winning the race by a length.

"You lose," Jake said, grinning. "Now pay up!"

"We didn't bet," Rachel said.

"I always get something for winning. You'll have to make me some of those fried pies."

"No. You always eat too many of them. You'll get fat."

Jake grinned wickedly; then, before Rachel could react, he brought the stallion closer, reached out to throw his arm around Rachel, and kicked Crow in the ribs, neatly picking Rachel off her horse. "Vince—!" she yelled. "You put me down!"

He kept Crow at a trot, squeezing Rachel close and ignoring her indignant cries. He came to a small depression in the ground that was filled with water. He stopped the horse and smiled down at her. "Either I get my pies or you get a bath. Which will it be?"

Rachel squirmed in his grasp, but his arm was like steel. "You wouldn't dare!" she cried, trying to hit at him.

"No? Well, let's see—"

He loosened his grip, and Rachel felt herself slipping. She screamed and grabbed at his arm. "No! Don't drop me!"

"Do I get the pies?"

"Yes!" she exclaimed breathlessly, somewhere between laughter and tears. "You beast!"

Jake laughed, tightened his grip, then moved Crow to dry earth. "Sticks and stones...," he said, amused at her anger. He abruptly reached over with his left hand and lifted her easily in front of him, holding her like a child. "Now if I was one of your gentleman callers—say, Captain Leighton Semmes—I'd get more than a fried pie out of you in a situation like this."

Rachel reached up, grabbed his hair, and gave a tremendous yank. Jake yelled, "Hey!" and shook his head to free himself. "Let me go! You're pulling my hair out!" When she persisted, he suddenly constricted his grip, holding her so tightly that she gave a gasp and released him. She looked up at him, and he thought she was angry, but then he saw she was laughing.

Rachel said saucily, "It's a good thing it's me you're hugging instead of one of those dreadful women you like to chase around with!"

As she laughed up at him, he was suddenly painfully conscious of her soft form pressed against his chest and of the gentle curve of her lips only inches away. Something in his face made her stop laughing, and then she, too, was conscious of the intimacy of his grip. For some reason she could not fathom, the touch of his iron arm around her disturbed her. She waited, trying to understand, confusion flooding her face with color. They stared at each other until she finally said, "Put me down, Vince."

At once he swung her to the ground, then dismounted and handed her Crow's reins. "I'll get Lady for you," he said and walked away, glad to have something to do. He took his time bringing the horse back, handed her the reins, then said, "Sorry for the horseplay."

"It's all right." A restless discontent had been stirring in Rachel for days, driving her to feverish activity at times, at other times bringing a desire of solitude so strong that she had gone on long rides alone. Now she was disturbed anew by the swirl of emotions struggling within her breast. Most disturbing of all was the fact that she did not understand what was making her discontented.

Suddenly she spoke. "Let's walk for a while," she said, and as they moved across the thawing ground, she struggled to put her feelings into words. "Things are so—so *fragile*!" The word didn't seem right, and she shook her head impatiently. "That doesn't make any sense, I know, but I've been so confused lately."

"I've noticed."

She looked at him with surprise, then said, "I thought I was keeping it to myself. I guess we all feel the pressure of the war. I'm afraid for Daddy and Grant—and now you'll be going to fight. I try to think that it'll be all right, but every day we get news that one of the boys we grew up with has been killed—like Bobby Felton. Remember how nice he was?"

"Fine fellow." Jake nodded.

"Now he's dead. Killed in a meaningless battle in Kentucky." Her lips drew tightly together, and she walked along silently, then said, "I saw Jenny Prescott last week. She and Bobby were engaged. Now he's dead and she's lost him. And his mother—you know how she doted on Bobby! She's a broken woman."

A cloud of blackbirds rose, filling the skies, and their raucous cries drifted back to the two people walking side by side. "I always hated blackbirds," Rachel said suddenly. "They remind me of darkness, of bad news." Then she shook her head, going back to her thoughts. "Last night I had an awful nightmare. I was all dressed in white, in a wedding gown. All the people were there, and I was coming down the aisle. I could see Rev. Irons there waiting to marry me—but I couldn't see the groom, not his face anyway." She gave a sudden shiver and fell silent.

Strangely disturbed, Jake asked, "Was that all of it?"

"No. I got to the front of the church, and the man I was marrying turned around—and he was dead!" Rachel stopped, her head lowered and her voice a whisper. "He—didn't have a face. Just a skull. And I woke up screaming. I've never done that before!"

"It was just a bad dream, Rachel."

She gave her shoulders a shake, as if to throw off the memory, then turned to him. "I know, but it's happening all around us. The best of our young men are going off, the most courageous boys, those who really love the South. What's going to happen when they die? Who'll take their place?"

Jake saw that she was terribly disturbed, and he spoke in a soothing voice. "Best not to think of those things, Rachel."

"How can you not think of them?" she demanded. "When I look at Daddy or Grant—or at you—I can't help but think you could die." She paused again, then asked, "Don't you ever think about it? About Daddy and Grant and all our friends?"

"Yes, I think of it. I think of myself, too. A man's a fool who doesn't think of that." He had not intended to speak of it, but said, "What General Jackson said was true. It hit me like a bullet, Rachel!"

"Vince—do you believe in God?"

"Yes. But that's not enough, is it? I've seen some pretty sorry specimens who claimed to be Christians. Guess that's what I've been hiding behind for a long time. But then, I've also seen the real thing. Mother and Jeremiah Irons—and you, of course."

"More than anything in the world, I want you to find peace with God. You have so much to live for!"

Jake stopped and gave her a strange look, but said only, "You really mean that, don't you? Well, I'm a hard case. Never did have much use for people who used religion as a trade with God. 'If you'll do this for me, God, then I'll do something for You.'" He shook his head, a faint sadness in his eyes. "I can't seem to do that, Rachel."

She said only, "I'm glad you can't. Any religion that worked like that wouldn't hold up. Real faith is like the sermon Brother Irons preached at the camp meeting—Jesus asks for all we are, especially whatever it is we love most."

He turned to face her, started to speak, then changed his

mind and fell silent. Finally he said, "We'd better get back."

When they arrived at the house, Rachel said, "Look, there's the gelding Brother Irons rides."

"Came to visit Mother, I guess."

✍

When they entered the house, they found Irons talking to Amy in the parlor. He rose and greeted them, and Jake would have left but was detained when Irons said, "I've been waiting to talk to you, Vince."

Amy rose, saying, "Come along, Rachel. We'll make some coffee."

When the two women had left, Irons said, "Vince, I've got to go to Fort Donelson." He seemed unhappy but shook it off, saying, "My brother is there with the army. I just got word that he's very ill, critically maybe."

"Fort Donelson? Where's that?"

"In Tennessee, way up in the northern part, almost in Kentucky. Fort Henry is on the Tennessee River, and Fort Donelson is just a few miles away on the Cumberland River." Irons shook his head, his mouth drawn up tight. "If the Federals take those two forts, they can use the rivers and pin us down."

"I've heard my father say so."

"Well, I've got to go. Baxter is my younger brother, and he may be dying. I'm leaving as soon as I can—probably tomorrow."

"I hope he makes it, Chaplain."

"I pray so, but that's not why I wanted to talk to you. You've made up your mind to join the army, and I thought this might be an opportunity for you."

Jake stared at him. "Me, Chaplain?"

Irons seemed reluctant and said, "Well, I'm probably out of line, but it occurred to me you might like to go with a troop of cavalry that's being raised to go to the defense of Donelson. Jeb Stuart's sending an officer and a few men. Everybody knows that General Johnston's spread thin, so there's an attempt to send reinforcements. Melora told me you had decided against the infantry because of your leg. All you'd have to have to join the Sixth is a horse."

Jake stood there thinking—and the more he thought of it, the better it sounded. He had come to realize that joining the war was not just something he was doing for Vince, or to fulfill Brad's requirements—he wanted to join because he felt it was the right thing for any Southern man to do. "I'd really like to go, Chaplain. But would they take me?"

"Like a shot!" Irons said with a grim smile. "They need every man they can get. The enlistment is for ninety days, so when that's over, you might want to join the Grays—or perhaps stay in Stuart's cavalry."

Jake made up his mind on the spot. "I'll do it. How do I sign up?"

"The troop will leave day after tomorrow. I'll go along, so we'll be together. Captain Wainwright will be in command of the troop. I'll tell him about you, and I know he'll be glad to have you. Bring a rifle and a sidearm. I don't think there's much in the way of arms."

Jake nodded. "I'll be ready. Where should I report?"

"Be at the camp tomorrow at eight." Irons rose to go, then paused to say, "Well, that was the easy thing. Now I've got to go tell Melora we'll have to put the wedding off until I've taken care of my brother."

"That's tough on both of you, Chaplain."

"Can't be helped." When Irons nodded and left the room, Jake went to find Amy and Rachel, who were just getting the coffee ready. "The preacher is gone," he said; then he hesitated. "I'll be leaving tomorrow."

Rachel gasped, "The army?"

"Yes. I'll be going with a troop of cavalry to Tennessee."

Amy said, "I know you think this is something you have to do, Vince—but be sure it's right. Your father and I don't agree on this thing. You've proven yourself by riding the stallion and facing Duvall down."

Jake said, "I guess I'll have to go." He wanted to explain but knew that he never would. Amy turned suddenly and left the room, and Rachel went over to stare out the window. There was a rigidity in her back, and Jake felt she was angry for some reason. "Rachel, don't be angry," he said, going to stand beside her.

She turned to face him, and he saw that tears had gathered in her eyes. The sight of her tears hit him hard, almost as if someone had struck him in the pit of the stomach. From his earliest memories, Jake Hardin could not recall anyone shedding a tear over him. Then another thought hit him even harder than the sight of her tears: Rachel was not crying for him, but for the man she thought he was. And this was a bitter thing to him.

Her voice was husky, tightly controlled, as she said, "I—wish you didn't have to go! I'm afraid!" She reached out, touching his cheek gently, her fingers tracing the line of his jaw. "I know I ought to smile and talk about how glorious it is for you to serve in the army—but I just *can't*!" Without another word, she abruptly whirled and ran blindly out of the room, leaving him standing there. She ran up to her room, threw herself on the bed, and wept. She didn't understand what was happening inside her. All she knew was that there was a dull, hollow dread in her—a void such as she had never known and that wasn't going away. After some time, she rose, washed her face, and sat down in the rocker beside her bed. For a long time she sat there, staring out the window. And then she closed her eyes and began to rock.

❧

"Melora, I'll be back soon," Irons said. "If my brother is able to be moved, I intend to bring him back with me to Richmond."

"I hope so, Jeremiah. I could help you nurse him."

The pair was standing in front of Melora's house. It was late in the afternoon, and they had just come back from a long walk down the lane. He had told her of his brother, and she had listened quietly. Finally, when he finished, she smiled at him and said, "That's like you, Jeremiah. You couldn't do anything else—being the man you are."

They had reached the house, and he had said, "I've got to go, but oh, I hate it so!"

Melora said, "I'll be here when you come back, Jeremiah."

Irons smiled and put his arms around her. "I'm the luckiest man in the world! You've made me so happy, Melora!" He kissed her then, and she responded. He drew back, smiled, and said, "You go right on planning the wedding. The day after I get back—that's the day we get married!"

"All right." She smiled, and there was a softness in her eyes as she said quickly, "We'll have a short honeymoon, I suppose, since you're in the army."

A boyish smile lifted the corner of Irons's lips, and he suddenly grabbed her around the waist, lifted her, and spun her around. When he put her down, he said, "We'll have a honeymoon for the next thirty or forty years, Melora Yancy! I promise you that." Then he kissed her again, turned, and mounted his gelding. He was still smiling, and there was a happiness in his fine brown eyes such as she'd never seen. "Good-bye, my dear! I'll be back soon—and you must get ready for that long, long honeymoon!"

He wheeled the horse, touched its sides with his spurs, and sent it galloping down the road. Melora stood and watched him, and just before he went out of sight, she saw him turn, pull his hat off, and wave it. He called out, his voice coming to her thin and clear: "A long honeymoon, Melora!"

And then he was gone, hidden by the line of straight, dead trees that reached up with lifeless fingers that seemed to be reaching to heaven.

CHAPTER 20

A LATE VISITOR

Jake had always been a light sleeper, able to awaken with all his faculties sharp, and the sound of footsteps coming toward his room woke him instantly. He lay there listening, expecting them to continue down the hallway, but when they stopped and a faint tapping came at his door, he was out of the bed at once. The room was illuminated by silver moonlight flooding in through the window as he went to the door quickly and opened it. He half expected to see Tad, for one of the mares was due to foal at any moment, and he'd told the slave to come for him when it was time.

The hallway was dark, and the figure seemed too bulky to be the slave. "Tad?" Jake asked, but then the man pushed himself forward, shoving Jake backward. Jake reacted instinctively, grabbing the coat of the intruder and swinging him around.

"Easy, Jake! It's me—Vince!"

Jake had drawn his fist back to drive a blow at the intruder, but halted abruptly. Keeping his grip on the rough coat, he leaned closer, trying to see the features of the man, but it was too dark.

"Light the lamp," Vince ordered and stood there as Jake got

a match and did so. When Jake turned around, shock widened his eyes, and Vince said, "It's me, Jake. Look like something the cat dragged in, don't I?"

Vince walked over and sat down in the rocker beside the window. Jake was shocked at his appearance, for he had lost so much weight that his clothing hung on him. Vince had always kept his beard trimmed neatly, but now it was bushy and ragged, hiding most of his face. The broad-brimmed slouch hat he wore shaded his eyes, and when he took it off, Jake saw that Vince's eyes were sunken and his cheeks had lost their fullness.

"What's going on, Vince?"

Vince looked at him carefully, then said, "I don't expect you to understand this, but here's the story."

Jake listened as Vince spoke, and his eyes narrowed as he heard how Vince had gone to Savannah to hire a man to kill Ellen. He said nothing, but his eyes were hard. Vince did not try to excuse himself but went on with the narrative.

"I got off the train at Savannah and keeled right over. Woke up in a hospital. I was so sick it was like a dream. Guess I never did really come out of it, not for a few days, anyway. When I did finally come around enough to know where I was, there was a man in the same room on a cot just across from me. He was dying, Jake, and I've never seen a more bitter man!" Vince's eyes hardened at the memory, and he waited for a moment before going on. "He cursed me, he cursed the doctors, and he cursed God! Then he told me I was going to die, too."

Jake studied Vince, then asked, "Did you believe him?"

"Yes!" Vince nodded emphatically. "And it was bad, Jake. There I was, in town to hire a killer—and dying alone in a room next to a crazy man!"

"What happened?"

"The fellow died. Went out cursing God. When they took his body out, I was alone, still sicker than I'd ever been. Then I started flickering out, Jake. My mind was gone, and all I had was crazy dreams. . . . Then something happened—I got scared!" At the memory, Vince took out his handkerchief and wiped his brow, his hands trembling slightly. When he put the handkerchief away, though, he managed a smile. It wasn't much of a smile, but it was the best he could do.

"I was there for a week, thinking every day that I was going to die. And finally all I could think of was. . .what a mess I'd made of everything! I thought I could handle anything—but I found out different."

Jake saw there was something in Vince's face that hadn't been there before and asked, "What happened?"

"I don't really know, Jake. I hit bottom—and when I did, I made myself one promise: If I lived, I'd do things differently. And then I prayed. Felt like a fool! Jake, I don't think I ever prayed in my life, but when a man's staring into his own grave, it makes him do strange things!"

"You found God?" Jake asked.

"N—no, I can't say that I did." Vince bit his lower lip, seeming to have trouble with his words. Finally he said, "It was like God was giving me some time, Jake. And I guess that's what I'm doing here. Sooner or later, I'll have to decide about God—but the time hasn't come just yet."

His words startled Jake, for they were what he had said of his own condition. He smiled grimly, shaking his head. "So you came back home?"

"Yes! I had plenty of money, but I had to stay a week in a boardinghouse to get my strength back enough to make the trip."

Jake stared at Vince, doubt in his face as plain as if it were a printed sheet. "I don't believe you. You're up to something tricky. What have you got up your sleeve now?"

Vince shook his head. "Nothing, Jake. I got all the trick shook out of me in that hospital. I walked out of there weak as a sick cat. I'm stronger now, but I'm out to win or lose." Vince's face was set, and suddenly Jake knew he was telling the truth. "I don't know how to work it out, Jake, but I'm letting you off the hook. You've done your job—more than I ever should have asked of anyone. You've faced down Crow and Duvall for me.... I wish I could have done that myself...." His voice trailed off for a moment, then a fresh determination settled on Vince's face. "At any rate, now the rest is mine. And if I make it—get the money, that is—you'll sure get your share."

Jake asked curiously, "What about the army? That's the last of the requirements your father laid down before he'd let you inherit the estate."

Vince shook his head, fatigue drawing his mouth downward. He rubbed his forehead wearily, saying, "I dunno, Jake. Guess I'll join up with the Grays."

"That won't work. In the first place, we may have looked alike once, but you've lost weight and I've gained. You show up for breakfast in the morning, and it'll be all over. In the second place, even if that didn't happen, you'd never make it with an infantry company."

Vince stared at him, but his lips drew together stubbornly. "I don't know how to do it any differently. Maybe I could leave a note saying I'm leaving to join up with an outfit someplace else."

Jake thought quickly, then said, "Listen, Vince—" and rapidly told him of the plan to send a troop of cavalry to Tennessee, including his own intention of going along. "You go away and stay hid out," he ended. "I'll put in the three months; then you'll be able to come back and I'll fade away."

Vince stared at him for a long moment, then laughed ruefully. "I really *have* changed, Jake," he said. "If I hadn't, I'd take you up on that like a shot! But I won't let you do it. I'll leave here now and catch up with that troop someplace between here and Tennessee. That way nobody here will see me. You skedaddle out of here, Jake."

The room was quiet, and the two men studied each other, a smile on Vince's lips and doubt in Jake's eyes. Finally Jake said, "I guess you mean it, which I'm glad to hear. But I'll go along with you to Tennessee." A smile touched his wide mouth, and he added, "You can join up as Jake Hardin."

"You mean it, Jake?" Vince was obviously relieved. "I'd try it on my own, but I'd feel a lot better if you were there with me until I get back to full strength."

"You get out of here," Jake said. "The troop will take the Miller Road for sure. You let us pass, then catch up with us. Tell the captain you just came in from the country." Then he added, "A man can get killed where we're going. You sure you want to do it?"

"I'm not too sure of anything, Jake," Vince said tentatively. Then he added strongly, "But I guess one thing is pretty clear—I'm not going to go back to what I was!" He got to his feet, saying, "I'd better get out of here, Jake. But I'll see you on the road. Bring along a good, well-mannered horse for me, will you? Say you want him for a spare mount." He didn't wait for a reply but moved across the room and stepped through the door, closing it after him.

Vince left as quietly as he could, but the floor squeaked

loudly. When he stepped out onto the back porch, he took a deep breath and was about to let it go with relief when a voice broke the silence.

"Stay right where you are or I'll shoot you dead!"

A violent jerk twisted Vince, but he held himself upright. Turning slowly, he saw Rachel standing in the moonlight. She was wearing a dark robe, and in her hand was a pistol aimed right at his stomach.

"Go back inside," Rachel said. "You're going to jail."

"Wait a minute—"

"Shut up and go inside! I'm going to get my brother up, and if you move, well, I'm a good shot and I can't miss at this distance. Now go inside!"

Vince said slowly, "Put the gun down, Rachel."

The sound of his voice startled her, he saw, for the gun in her hand wavered. "It's me—Vince," he said quietly. "Don't be afraid."

Rachel's lips were dry, for she was not as free from fear as she'd tried to seem. The moonlight was bright, but his back was to it, so she could not see his face clearly. "Vince? You can't be Vince!"

Taking off his hat, Vince stood before her. "It's me, all right. I know it's a shock—but just let me explain."

"You can explain to my brother and to the sheriff, whoever you are!"

Vince said, "Rachel, it's me. I've lost twenty pounds and I'm hiding behind this wild beard. I've had to hide out, but now I've come back."

It *was* Vince's voice! Rachel moved closer, looked carefully into his face, then began to tremble. She lowered the pistol, then cried, "I don't understand!"

At once Vince began to speak, explaining the ruse he had engineered. He told it all, leaving out only his intention to have Ellen killed, thinking that would have to come later. But he told her of his brush with death and how it had brought him to something new.

"I don't know how to explain it, Rachel," he said finally, "but when I thought I was going to die, I met myself for the first time—and I didn't like what I saw. Now I'm going to finish what Jake started. I'm going with that cavalry troop to Tennessee. I'll either get killed or find out if there's any good in me at all."

Rachel glanced upstairs, then back at Vince. "Who is that man?" she asked in a harsh voice.

"Like I told you, his name is Jake Hardin," Vince answered. He told her a little of how the two of them had met, then said, "He's going with me to Tennessee."

"A gambler," Rachel whispered brokenly, and there was an expression on her face that Vince didn't understand. "A fortune hunter out to make money from us!"

Vince started, then said, "Now wait, Rachel—I talked Jake into this!"

"I'll bet it wasn't hard when you promised him money, was it?"

She turned to go, but Vince caught her arm, asking, "Where are you going?"

"To tell that—that charlatan to get off the place!"

Vince held her arm, saying urgently, "Wait now, Rachel—don't do that!"

"Why shouldn't I?"

"Well, I need him, to tell the truth. I'm still pretty weak, and Jake's a pretty tough hairpin. He's going with me to the army. He'll be out of the house tomorrow." His tone assumed a pleading tone as he continued, "Rachel, you don't think much of me, and I can't blame you a bit. I know I don't deserve any breaks—especially from you—but I'm asking for one."

"What do you want?" Her voice was as cold as the winter air itself.

"Time. Just time. Don't tell anyone about this. You may not believe it, but I've got some kind of hope that I can be the kind of son my father's always wanted. But I need the chance to prove it—by going to the army. I'm asking you for that chance, Rachel." Vince's thin face was clearly outlined by the moonlight as he added, "If you call out, it's all over before I've even had a chance to try. I'll never know what sort of man I *could* be."

Rachel stood there, her lips drawn together tightly, her eyes hooded. Just when Vince had decided she would never listen to him, she started speaking so quietly that he had to lean forward to catch her words. "You're right, I don't believe it. All you've ever done was try to hurt us all. You're a coward, a liar, and a cheat. I'm ashamed to be related to you at all!"

As she spoke, her voice low with fury, Vince felt shame and remorse wash over him—but he held her angry gaze. He knew she was right and that there was no reason for her to give him any kind of consideration, but he hoped against hope that she would give him this one last chance.

She stood looking at him for a moment, then said in that same low, angry voice, "All right. Get out of here."

"Thanks, Rachel!" Vince said, relief washing over him. He would have touched her, but she drew back sharply. "Can't blame you," he said instantly. Then he turned and disappeared into the darkness.

She waited until the sound of his horse's hooves had faded,

then went back into the house. Going to her room, she put the gun in the drawer of her nightstand, then stood at the window, looking out, seeing nothing at all.

🙟

At breakfast, there was a cheerful note, for Amy determined to send Vince away with a happy memory. Rachel said little and ate almost nothing, but no one seemed to notice.

After breakfast, Jake went to his room, coming back with two rifles and two Colts in holsters. "Always carry two of everything," he said, smiling, then went outside, saying, "I'll have Tad saddle up; then I'll come back."

"Have him saddle Lady," Rachel said. "I'll ride as far as Hardee's store with you."

Jake looked at her, surprised. His mind raced for a moment, wondering how he would explain the extra horse he'd promised Vince he would bring. Then he decided they would just have to find a horse for Vince later.

"All right," he said.

He left the house but was back in a few minutes. "Guess it's time for me to go."

Amy went to him and drew his head down. "I'll pray for you—and I'm very proud of you, my son!"

Jake took her kiss, then awkwardly patted her shoulder. "Be back before you know it," he said, smiling at her. Then he asked, "Ready, Rachel?"

"Yes."

They mounted their horses, and Jake leaned down and handed some cash to Tad, saying, "Buy something real nice for everyone, Tad. Have a party on me!"

"Yas, suh!" Tad grinned. "You watch out dem Yankees doan

put nuffin' over you, Marse Vince!"

"Do my best!" Jake laughed, then pulled his horse around, and he and Rachel rode out of the yard. When they were out of sight of the house, Jake said, "Wish I didn't have to go."

Rachel made no reply. He turned to her, noting how pale her face was. Her hair was tied back, and he thought she looked very tired.

"I caught Vince going out of the house last night," she said suddenly, her voice even, as though she were remarking on the weather.

Her words seemed to explode in Jake's mind, and he stopped his horse instantly. She paused, as well, and turned to stare at him, her lips a thin line.

He looked down at his hands, squeezing the horn of his saddle. "Well, I told Vince it would never work."

She waited for him to continue but saw that he was silent. "Oh, don't worry, Mr. Hardin," she said bitterly. "I'm not going to turn you in." Still he didn't speak, and she cried out, "You must have enjoyed it a lot—making fools out of us all!"

Jake sat in the saddle, studying the ring on his hand. A thought came to him, and he took it off. He turned to face her, saying, "You can give this to Vince when he comes back—"

"Give it to him yourself!" Her eyes flared with shame, and she said, "I'll never look at that comb and brush you gave me without thinking what a fool I was! And you know what? That's good!" She threw her head back, fighting against the tears that were misting her eyes. "It'll teach me never to trust anyone again as long as I live!" She started to turn her horse's head, but he reached out and held her arm.

"Just a minute—"

She jerked her head back to look at him, fury in her eyes.

"What for? So you can have some more fun?"

His hand was clasped around her arm tightly, and his face was tense. "Rachel, you have a right to think the worst of me, but before I go, you're going to listen to me, just for a moment."

"Of course I will. You've learned how to handle women, Mr. Hardin." A bitterness hardened her lips, and she wanted to strike him. "I think you've proved that—the way you've led me around by the nose!"

Jake saw that it was no good. He released her arm, then said, "All right, Rachel, you win."

She stared at him, thinking he would speak, but he did not. There was an air of fatalism about him, and she suddenly longed to be done with the whole thing. Drawing her horse's head around, she gave Jake one last bitter look. Then as she drove her heels into Lady's flanks, she cried out, "Never come here again! Never!"

Jake watched her as she rode away, then turned Crow's head toward Richmond, as certain as he had ever been of anything that he would never see Rachel Franklin again.

And with that certainty, something inside him seemed to die.

PART FOUR

The Return

CHAPTER 21

A PERFECT TRAP

Stephen gave his wife a look of cynical humor, saying, "Ruth, don't get so excited. It's only the president of the United States." He knew, however, that it was a lost cause, for his wife had spent the last several months swimming in the huge pond that made up Washington society, and tonight the apogee of her career as a hostess had come—Abraham Lincoln and his wife were coming to her home.

True, it was not a major function, but it was a triumph, nonetheless, and Ruth Rocklin could hardly enjoy the evening for planning how she would casually drop the information to her circle of acquaintances in days to come: *What? Oh, dear me, yes, Doris! The president* did *drop by for my little reception last night. Of course, he and Stephen are rather close and went off to the library to talk about the war, so I had to spend most of my time with Mary—*"

"Come away from the window, Ruth," Stephen said, grinning at her. "It's only the president—not the Second Coming!" He looked over her shoulder to catch sight of the tall man helping a short woman out of the carriage, then said, "Let's go greet them. I don't think they'll stay long."

His remark offended Ruth, and she gave him an angry look but was too nervous to argue. "Come along, then," she said, "and don't go dragging the president off to your study to look at your old guns!"

Stephen grinned behind her back, for he well knew that the reason Lincoln had agreed to come was to get a look at his new rifle. When he had issued the invitation, he had said, "My wife wants you to come to a reception at our house, Mr. President. It'll be a bore, as all such things are, but I've got the bugs worked out of that new eight-shot musket we've talked about producing. . . ."

Now as Stephen came forward to shake hands with the president, he smiled and received an answering smile from the tall man before him. When Lincoln had agreed to come, Rocklin had said, "Now, Mr. President, we'll both have to endure some social life, but I'll kidnap you as soon as possible, and we'll go to my study."

An hour later, the two men were in the large study alone, the president holding a musket, speaking with great animation about its potential. Rocklin Ironworks had grown into one of the largest producers of muskets in the North, and Stephen had met with the president on matters of firearms several times. They were interrupted by a knock on the door, and when Rocklin answered it, an attractive young woman came in with a sheaf of papers.

"Ah yes, here they are!" Rocklin said, taking the papers eagerly. "These are the drawings of the musket." Then he said, "This is my granddaughter, Deborah Steele."

Lincoln smiled and put out his hand. "I met you at your uncle's office in the War Department, didn't I, Miss Steele?"

Deborah was amazed at the man's memory. "Yes, Mr.

President," she answered, thinking as she did so how much the president's smile added to his homely face. She noted that he had a pair of warm brown eyes and that his mobile lips smiled easily.

"General Scott appreciated Major Rocklin," Lincoln said, nodding, speaking of Gideon Rocklin, Stephen's son. "He could never find another aide to put up with his ways." His brow wrinkled, and he asked, "Didn't your uncle mention something about the young soldier who's been doing some writing?"

"Oh, that's Noel Kojak," Rocklin said, nodding. "He's a private in my son's company. Have you seen the stories that he's been writing about army life?"

"Yes, I have. They're the real article!" Lincoln nodded with approval. "Most of the stories I read about army life would be better found in a romance novel—Kojak's are so real you can almost *smell* the camps he describes."

"Private Kojak is a protégé of my granddaughter's here," Stephen said. "He was working in the mill, and she encouraged him to enlist. Then she found out he was a natural-born writer and introduced him to an editor."

"You've done the country a service, Miss Steele," Lincoln said, then frowned. "Most of the country thought this war was a nice little adventure, but they need to know the truth about it—and that's what your young man gives them, and very well."

Deborah said with some hesitation, "He's been criticized for being too realistic. Some say he takes all the glory out of war."

"Good! The sooner we get rid of that idea, the better! War is a nasty, dirty business, as your uncle or any professional soldier will tell you. That last story I read by young Kojak, about men dying of measles—it was terrible, and not in the least *romantic*! And it was exactly the way it is. Tell him to keep writing, if you would, Miss Steele—and that, if he pleases no one else, he pleases his commander in chief!"

"I'll tell him, Mr. President," Deborah said quickly. "He'll be very proud."

"I suppose you get a love letter from him now and then?" the president inquired with a smile. "In between his more intimate remarks, does he say how things are in the area he's stationed?"

Deborah flushed at his teasing but said at once, "He's very happy to be with Uncle Gideon—Major Rocklin, I mean. He says that all the men like a general called Grant because he's a fighter and the rest are not."

Lincoln's head snapped back, and a light blazed in his deep-set eyes. "Tell Kojak to put *that* in one of his stories for the country to read, Miss Steele! This man Grant, he's not one of our top men, but he *fights*! Did you read how he attacked a Confederate force in Belmont? Got into a real fight, had to cut his way out, but he *did* something!"

"My son thinks he's like a bulldog," Stephen put in. "Says he doesn't spend too much time worrying about what the enemy's going to do to him—he's too busy worrying about how to hurt the army in front of him."

Lincoln started to speak, but the door opened and Ruth Rocklin entered, a reproachful look on her face. "Now, Mr. President, I've given you and my husband plenty of time to look at guns. You *must* come out and meet my guests!"

Lincoln asked, "Did my wife send you, Mrs. Rocklin?" He grinned at her flustered expression, adding, "I knew as soon as Miss Steele came in that Mrs. Lincoln would send for me. Would you believe as homely as I am, she's still jealous of attractive young women?" He sighed and nodded to Deborah, saying, "Tell that young man of yours to keep writing, Miss

Steele—and if Grant gives your son a chance to fight, Rocklin, tell him to pour it on! I can't get McClellan to use the Army of the Potomac in Virginia."

"I heard," Stephen said with a straight face, "that you wrote him a letter saying if he didn't plan to use the army, you'd like to borrow it for a little while!"

Lincoln laughed, saying as he left the room, "It sounds like something I might say, doesn't it?"

Ruth followed the president, but Stephen detained his granddaughter, asking her, "Are you worried about Noel?"

Deborah smiled at him, saying, "Of course. You're worried about Uncle Gideon, aren't you?" Then she shook her head, adding, "I think of him a great deal—but I think of Great-Uncle Thomas's family in the Confederate Army, too. I'm sad for all of them, Grandfather!"

"It's a sad time," Rocklin agreed, his face lined with concern. "Like the hymn says, 'We're dwelling in a grand and awful time.' " Then he gave her a hug, and they left the study to join the others.

❧

Rachel and her mother had been knitting socks for the Richmond Grays when Melora came into the room. "Why, Melora," Rachel said, "I didn't expect to see you today." Melora had gone back to her home after Amy's leg had grown strong enough for her to get around, and both women had missed her. "Let me fix you something to drink."

Melora shook her head. "No, thank you, Rachel. I only have a few minutes." She seemed a little upset—which was unusual for her, Rachel thought—but when she took an envelope out of her purse, saying, "I have a letter from Jeremiah," both Rachel and her mother grew still.

"Is it bad news, Melora?" Amy asked quietly. "Is it Vince?"

"Oh no," Melora said quickly. "It's nothing like that. As a matter of fact, I came because when the messenger brought me the letter from Jeremiah, he had one for you, too. He was in a rush, so I offered to bring it to you."

Amy took the letter, opened it, and began to read. "How is Jeremiah's brother, Melora?" Rachel asked.

"Very sick, he says. I don't think Jeremiah expects him to live. He says disease is terrible at Fort Donelson. Five of the men who went with him and Vince have died, and a dozen more are down with one illness or another—mostly malaria."

"How did the letters come? We haven't heard a word from Vince."

"General Floyd sent a courier back asking President Davis for reinforcements. When Jeremiah heard about it, he asked the lieutenant to bring a letter for me; then he told Vince. From what he says, it's not likely any mail will get back here again very soon."

Amy said, "Let me read Vince's letter to you. It's not very long—:

Dear Mother and Father,

I write this in haste, for the courier is waiting right now. We made the journey to Tennessee with some difficulty. I was under the weather, but a new friend of mine named Jake Hardin nursed me along. When we arrived here, we were attached to the cavalry under General Nathan Bedford Forrest. He is a striking man indeed—a former slave trader and a wealthy man with no military training whatsoever. But he has, Jake says,

*a natural military genius. We have been on patrols
constantly, fighting skirmishes with the Yankees every day.
They are thick as fleas around Donelson! Sometimes I am
so tired when we get back to the fort it's all I can do to fall
off my horse and get to my cot. But Jake always rousts me
out and makes me eat.*

*Neither of us likes what we see here, nor do any of
the men—or the officers, either. Fort Donelson is perched
on the banks of the Cumberland River, and the Yankee
gunboats, they say, are right up the river, ready to come
and shell us. So there will be no escape by the river, and
if the Yankees close in our front, we will be caught in a
perfect trap—perfect for them, I mean.*

*Both Jake and I feel the battle will come soon, so I will
not be able to write again. If I fall, remember these last
days and try to forget and forgive the rest.*

*Rachel, thank you for your favor. I'll try not to let you
down.*

Love,
Vince

Amy looked up to see tears in Rachel's eyes. She asked
gently, "What favor does he mean, Rachel? Taking care of him
when he was injured?"

Rachel shook her head, then, dashing the tears from her
eyes, whispered, "No, Mama. It was something else."

The Tennessee River overflowed its banks, the swift current
bringing down an immense quantity of heavy driftwood,
lumber, fences, and large trees. As the serpentine line of General

Nathan Bedford Forrest's cavalry pulled up to the river's muddy banks at noon on February 6, the entire troop had a clear view of the gunboats that were headed for Fort Henry. Downstream they could see the fort, and beyond the fort itself there seemed to be troops moving.

"Dismount!" General Forrest yelled, and the men all got off to rest their horses.

"Look at that!" Jake said in awe. "They're going to squeeze those poor fellows in a vise!"

Vince was so tired he could hardly sit on his horse, but the sight of the flotilla of ships steaming toward the fort made him forget his fatigue. "Maybe the guns in Henry will do for those ships. Sure do hope so."

They watched as four large gunboats—the *Cincinnati*, *Carondolet*, *Essex*, and *St. Louis*—formed a line abreast. The wooden gunboats formed another line abreast about one-half mile astern of the ironclads and fired over them. A roaring filled the air as the *Cincinnati* opened fire. The fleet edged closer to the fort, which seemed to be a blaze of fire, and the roar of the cannons was almost deafening. Soon the guns from Henry opened fire and made hits almost at once on the gunboats. Jake saw the ship with *Essex* on the bow struck so hard that she reared out of the water, then drifted helplessly downstream. Men were wildly throwing themselves into the swollen river, trying to escape the flames and destruction. It seemed a Confederate victory was coming. But it was not to be so.

The short-lived battle turned soon after it started, for, as was later revealed, Fort Henry was built too low on the water, and most of her best guns were flooded and totally useless.

"There's the surrender," Forrest muttered to his adjutant

when a white flag was raised at the fort. "Let's get back to Donelson. They'll be coming our way pretty soon." He swung to his horse, making an imposing figure. A big man, six feet and two inches tall and strong as a blacksmith, he exuded an air of leadership. He called out, "Mount up, men!" and drove his horse on a fast trot down the winding path that led to the river. As soon as they were on the Fort Donelson road, he stepped up the pace to a fast gallop. The distance was only twelve miles, but by the time the troop arrived, Vince was hanging on by sheer nerve.

Jake pulled up, took a quick look at Vince, then dismounted and grabbed the reins of Vince's horse. "You go see about some grub," he said. "I'll take care of the horses."

Vince slid wearily out of the saddle, giving Jake a wry look. "You don't have to take care of me like you was my mama," he said. "But I guess I'll take you up on that deal."

Jake watched as Vince plodded toward the fort, then unsaddled the horses, rubbed them down, and saw that they got their fair share of the forage from the soldier in charge. As he turned toward the fort, he was thinking of Vince. *He's come a long way. Didn't think he'd make it here to Donelson, but he hung in there.* He knew that without his help, Vince probably wouldn't have made it, for he was still weak from his sickness and was not used to the hard life of a soldier. But they'd done it, Jake thought. They'd managed to join up under each other's names and to carry off the masquerade successfully. It was almost a kind of game, responding to Vince's name in public and using his own name when he and Vince were alone. It was a strain at times, but they had pulled it off. And no matter what happened now, Jake knew that Vince would never be the same. There was an element of pride in him now, and Jake could see that Vince was determined to go through whatever lay ahead of them.

He entered the fort, noting that all the guns pointed landward were in firing position. Glancing toward the side facing the Cumberland River, he saw the same condition applied there. *Guess they know what's coming*, he thought, then made his way to the long, low building where he and the rest of the troop from Virginia were quartered. As he entered, he saw Vince talking to Jeremiah Irons and went at once to where they stood.

There was a hard set to Irons's mouth, and when Jake looked at the chaplain inquiringly, he shook his head. "My brother's no better. I don't think he can make it for long."

"What about taking him to a hospital?" Jake asked. He had grown fond of Irons, and of his brother, too.

"He'd never make the trip," Irons said. "Anyway, we're pretty well ringed in by Federals, I think. General Forrest offered to send a small squad, which was fine of him. But every man is needed here, and we couldn't get through anyway."

"When we give these Yankees a thrashing," Vince said, "maybe we can rent a boat and get to the Mississippi."

"Well, we'd run right into Grant if we tried that," Jake said. "His command post is in Cairo. No Confederate ship can get past that spot."

"That's right, I'm afraid," Irons said. He seemed low in spirits, which was not strange, since he had nursed his brother almost constantly since arriving at Donelson.

"Let me sit with him, Chaplain," Jake said quickly. "I think we'll get sent out in the morning to screen the Yanks, but you need a little rest."

Irons nodded wearily. "Maybe for a couple of hours. Thank you."

He moved away, and Vince said, "You've got to be worn out yourself, Jake."

"I'm okay. Let's get a bite, then you rest. I'll grab some sleep later."

They each got a plate of beans and bacon and some coffee, then sat down to eat. "This General Forrest is a tough hairpin, isn't he, Jake?" Vince said, chewing slowly. "And those men of his are hard as nails."

"They're a tough bunch, and that's what we'll need." Jake swallowed a cup of scalding coffee, then added, "I was talking to Captain Wainwright this morning. He thinks we're in a box. Told me that General Johnston ordered a first-class fort built here, but it was never done. Johnston found out at the last minute that there was practically nothing here and had some engineers throw up this fort along with Fort Henry. But they're not much as forts go. Those big gunboats can pound them to pieces. And with the Yankees coming in Grant's army, we've got no place to retreat."

"Some of the officers say we ought to pull out now, while we can. Can't say I'd object, but I guess we came to fight."

Jake looked at Vince, a light of approval in his eyes. "If I forget to say this later, I've been proud of the way you've handled this. Your family will be proud, too."

Vince colored and drank some coffee to cover his embarrassment. "Well, I'm coming to this a little late in my life, Jake, and I couldn't have done it without you." He ate slowly, then asked, "How'd you make it with my family? You've never really said. Was it hard to fool them?"

Jake didn't like to speak of it, Vince saw, but he did say,

"God's blessed you with a fine family, Vince. I envy you."

"Well, you can come and see us after all this is over."

"Not likely." Jake hesitated, then went on. "Rachel told me never to come back again."

Something in his tone—something wistful that wasn't really like Jake—caused Vince to look up quickly. "Rachel said that? Well, she's just sore right now."

Jake rose to his feet, shaking his head. "I guess it's more than that. I deceived her. She can't ever forget that." He turned away then, saying, "Better get some sleep," and trudged off to the small room where Baxter Irons lay.

Jake's conversation with Vince had depressed him, for it reminded him of Rachel's hatred—and it was that which cut him more than anything else. He shook his head, trying to get her out of his mind, and found Irons with a higher fever than usual. He got some water and began sponging the wan face, and suddenly the sick man opened his eyes. "Jerry?" he whispered through chapped lips.

"No, it's Vince. How do you feel, Bax?"

"Can't complain."

"You never do," Jake said. He poured some water into a glass, and Irons drank a little of it.

"What's going on out there?"

"Yankees took Fort Henry this afternoon."

"That means they'll be headed for here, don't it?"

"Expect so, Bax, but we'll hold them off."

Irons shook his head weakly, his eyes sunk back into his skull. "I—tried to get Jerry to leave—but he won't do it."

"We'll be all right."

The sick man stared at him, then closed his eyes. He had an alarming habit of dropping off like this, and it was happening more often. Jake sat beside him, angered by his helplessness. Bax Irons was no more than twenty-three, and his life was over. Many others had died of sickness in this place, but Jake had taken Bax's hand more than once, and he was the only one Jake had watched slip slowly away.

An hour later, Jake awoke when Bax said, "Vince—"

"Yes—you want something, Bax?"

Bax was burning up with fever, his eyes glazed with pain. "Vince, are you a man of God?"

Jake said slowly, "No, Bax, I'm not."

"Too. . .bad! Wish you were. . . !" He labored for breath, then said with terrible effort, "I'm glad I. . .got that settled!" Then he whispered, "Vince. . .go get Jerry—"

Jake leaped up and ran full speed to where Irons slept. "Jeremiah, come quick!" he said, and Irons got to his feet at once. "I—I think he's going!"

Irons left at a run, and Jake followed. He didn't go close but let the two men have their moment together. It was dark, with only a few lanterns glowing in the long room, so he could barely see the outline of Jeremiah's body leaning over the bed.

The time ran on, and Jake closed his eyes, but he was too aware of what was going on a few feet away to sleep. Finally he heard steps and opened his eyes to see Jeremiah Irons standing there, tears running down his cheeks.

"He's gone?"

"Yes." There was pain in Irons's eyes, but his voice was even and his lips were relaxed. There was a peace about him, Jake saw with wonder, and he waited for the chaplain to speak. "He was longing to go, Vince," Irons said softly. "He gave me some messages to pass on, and then he just slipped away."

Jake blinked and bit his lips. "He was such a fine young

fellow. I'm sorry, Jeremiah."

"No, don't be. 'Precious in the sight of the Lord is the death of his saints.'" Irons hesitated, then said, "He spoke of you, Vince."

"He did?"

"Yes. He said to tell you that Jesus loves you."

Tears burned at Jake's eyes, and he couldn't speak. Finally he got control and said, "That's not easy for me to believe."

"No, you think you've got to earn God's favor. Most people do. But the New Testament denies that on almost every page. That's what grace is. We can't help God. Either the blood of Jesus is enough—or it isn't."

Jake said quietly, "Well, it was enough for Bax."

Irons said, "It's enough for you, too, my boy. It's enough for all of us!"

CHAPTER 22

ESCAPE FROM FORT DONELSON

The funeral for Baxter Irons took place at sunset, just after Jake and Vince came in from a patrol. Exhausted, they all but fell off their horses and went at once to the sector outside the fort that had been set apart for the burial ground, finding two dozen or so men there, with Jeremiah Irons standing at the head of the grave. Irons looked up as they hurried to join the group, nodded at them, then began the service.

It was a brief service, consisting mostly of readings from the scriptures. Jeremiah Irons's voice was clear on the cold air, and when he had read from the Bible, he closed it, then stood there looking down at the pine coffin. He spoke for a few moments about his brother, stressing that Baxter had put his trust in Jesus Christ, then nodded to the men beside the coffin. They picked up the ropes and lowered the coffin, then stepped aside. Irons picked up a handful of the red dirt, tossed it into the grave, then turned away. He stood there silently as the men filled the grave; then he walked away.

Jake and Vince fell into step with him, not certain of what they should say. Finally Jake said, "I guess you'll be pulling out pretty soon."

Irons shook his head. "Not for a while. We've got a lot of sick men—and lots of those who are well are pretty scared about the battle. I'll stay for a few more days."

Vince glanced in the direction of Fort Henry, saying, "You don't have a lot of time, Jeremiah. We ran into Yankee pickets today. Grant's headed this way for sure. Captain Wainwright says the generals think Commodore Foote will bring his gunboats up the river anytime."

"I guess that's right," Irons agreed. "But we've had lots of reinforcements. Heiman's troops from Fort Henry and the Second Kentucky under Bushrod Johnson. And General Buckner's division."

Jake offered, "I heard that the Yankee general Lew Wallace was on his way by river transport with his division—as many as ten thousand men. We've only got eighteen thousand men at most, so we'll be facing at least three-to-one odds, and that's not counting the fire from the ironclads."

The three men spoke of the difficulties faced by the Southern forces, and it was Vince who said, "Well, we'll just have to stand up to them, I guess. But I think you should leave now, Chaplain."

But Irons refused to go, and for the next few days he found plenty to do, working with the sick and encouraging the fainthearted. He preached every night to large groups, and more often than not Jake and Vince were there to listen. Many men professed faith in Christ, and early one morning, a large number of them braved the cold waters of the Cumberland as Chaplain Irons baptized them.

Jake stood on the bank with Vince, silently watching, wondering at the sight. There was something impressive in the way the men lined up, dressed in their oldest clothes, waiting their turn. One of the candidates, a tall soldier from Arkansas named Opie Dennis, caught everyone's attention. He stood quietly as Irons said, "Upon your profession of faith, I baptize you, my brother, in the name of the Father, the Son, and the Holy Ghost." He was so tall that Irons was forced to take a step back to lower him, and when he came up, he began to shout, "Glory to God! Glory to God!"

Vince whispered, "I guess Opie's happy enough." Then he turned to face Jake. "Kind of makes me wish I was in there, Jake. How about you?"

Jake said, "It makes a man think. I guess I hope my time will come. Your mother would be real happy if you found God—and Rachel, too."

Vince said nothing, and after the service, they were called out by Captain Wainwright for a patrol. "General Forrest wants to find out what the Yankees are up to," he said laconically. "Guess we know, but the other generals, Floyd and Pillow, are gettin' nervous."

General Forrest led a force of nearly one hundred men out on the patrol, and they rode through the bottoms for several miles. Jake saw the general suddenly throw up his hand, halting the line of troopers. Forrest was staring through the line of trees; following his glance, Jake saw the flash of the sun on metal. "There they come," he murmured to Vince, who was on his left. "The show's about to start."

He was correct, for the patrol followed the progress of the ironclads and watched them pitch into Fort Donelson at once. It was three thirty when, at a range of less than two thousand yards, the *St. Louis* opened fire. The other ironclads followed suit, and shells exploded against the thick earthworks of the fort. General Forrest passed down the line, and Jake heard him say to his aide, "Nothing but God Almighty can save that fort!"

But Foote had made a serious mistake. He had taken Fort Henry by bringing his fleet to point-blank range and blasting away—but he had either ignored, forgotten, or not known that the lower guns at Henry had been flooded, which had made his task there easy.

When the gunners at Donelson opened fire with its biggest guns—a ten-inch smoothbore Columbiad and a 32-pounder rifled gun—they practically blew the *Carondolet* out of the water, smashing the anchor and knocking the plating to pieces. All of the ships came in for a hard battering, and Foote, on board the *St. Louis*, was wounded in the foot by a shell that crashed into the pilothouse, killing the pilot and carrying away the wheel. Out of control, the ship drifted downstream after the *Louisville*. The *Pittsburg* was sinking, and all the while not a single man in the waterside batteries had been hurt.

Still, the resounding victory over the gunboats did little to lighten the gloom that had settled on Donelson's three generals. They were convinced that they could not save the fort, and that night they met and planned the breakout. Basically, they intended to slam Grant with a sudden hammer blow, then break out to the south toward a road that led to Nashville. General Gideon Pillow's men, on the Confederate left facing General McClernand's division, would attack at dawn. General Simon Buckner would leave a single regiment, the Thirteenth Tennessee Infantry, in the trenches to the right, facing General Smith's division, and move the bulk of his men to the center. Once Pillow had rolled over the Federal troops, Buckner would strike the hinge and hold the door open while Pillow's division marched out to safety. Then Buckner would follow, fighting a rear-guard action to make sure that the bulk of the army escaped intact to fight again on more opportune ground.

It was a good plan, and later on Captain Wainwright explained it to his sergeant and a few of the men, including Jake and Vince. Wainwright laid a sheet of paper on a table in the mess hall, saying, "Here's a map of the area."

"General Forrest says we'll go with General Pillow, fighting on foot. When we've rolled McClernand back, Buckner will pull his division from the right to the center and take Smith out, shoving him back. Then Pillow's men can get away through the gap in the center. We'll mount up and help Buckner fight the rear-guard action to make sure the whole army gets out. Get your muskets ready, because we'll move out to the attack at dawn."

All night long the men worked frantically, the cooks preparing three days' rations, the sergeants making certain that the men had ammunition and that their muskets were in firing order. Jake and Vince, along with the rest of the cavalrymen, saw to their horses, as well, for, as Jake said, "We'll be needing mounts if this thing works."

A winter storm spread misery that night, and a howling wind covered the noise of the Confederates as they made their preparations. By morning the ground was covered with fresh snow, and tree limbs were sheathed in ice.

As daylight brought a thin line of light in the east, the order came to leave the fort. As soon as they were outside, a line of battle was formed two lines deep. Jake and Vince were in the second line, near the left, and at once the order came to advance. The officers moved back and forth checking the lines, and the sergeants were like hunting dogs, hounding the men and shoving them into position.

The line struck the picket line of the Federals, catching them completely off guard. When two or three of the Union soldiers fell, the rest scurried away, yelling, and a cry went up from the Confederate officer, "Charge, men!" At once the entire line began to run, and Jake smelled the acrid odor of gunpowder as they rushed into the Union lines firing. The firing of the muskets reminded him of corn popping over a fire, the sound being magnified many times, and from the left came the thunder of artillery.

A shrill yelling—a yipping noise like high-pitched voices of dogs—arose from the men, and Jake found himself joining in. To his surprise, he felt no fear. He found himself eager to stay up with the line, and glancing over to his right, he saw that Vince was yelling, too. The trooper to his left, a small man named Davis, coughed suddenly then fell on his face, not moving. Jake's first impulse was to stop and help him, but Sergeant Prince yelled, "Go on! Go on!" and he picked up the pace at once.

The smoke was getting thicker, and suddenly they ran into a small camp where three of the enemy were trying to reload their muskets. They had been cooking breakfast, and as Jake watched, one of them was struck by a bullet and driven into the fire, knocking the coffeepot down. One of the other Federals threw his musket down and started to run, but a minié ball took the top of his head off before he got ten steps away.

The other soldier stood there, his empty musket in his hand, his eyes wide with shock and focused on Jake. He was no more than eighteen years old, and Jake lowered his musket, intending to tell him to surrender, but another Confederate ran at the boy and with a savage yell thrust his bayonet into his stomach. The two stood there for one moment, the Confederate grinning, the boy staring at him with a look of reproach. Then the Confederate yanked his bayonet free and, when the boy fell, lifted his musket and stabbed the helpless soldier in the chest, screeching wildly.

Jake stared at the scene, noting that Vince had stopped, as well, his face pale as paste. "Come on!" Jake yelled, and the two of them rushed to catch up with the line. As they advanced, shadowy figures were moving ahead of them, and soon they encountered a line of solid fire. Jake fired at them, then fell to the ground to reload. He saw Vince standing upright, reloading, and yelled over the crash of musketry, "Vince! Get down!" They moved forward slowly, for the Yankees had stiffened their line.

For the next three hours they were surrounded by smoke, confusion, and death. The battle was not one line against another. Instead, it was broken up into hundreds of small fights as units got separated from their brigades. But the Federals were shoved back, and a cry of victory went up from the Confederates as they gave way.

"Now's the time for General Pillow to get this army out of here," Jake panted. "The door's wide open!"

Captain Wainwright's hand had been wounded, and he was wrapping it in a handkerchief. "Yes, but it won't stay open long. Grant's going to find out pretty soon what's going on. He'll not stand to lose, not Grant!"

An hour later, the firing on the left had picked up, and Wainwright nodded. "Hear that? We've missed our chance. Some stupid general thought we could take on the whole Federal Army! Now we—"

The firing was heavy, and Jake could not hear the rest of Wainwright's words. He turned around and saw that the captain was facedown on the ground. When he rolled him over, he saw a small black hole in his temple. Jake put the officer's head down, moved down the line to Sergeant Prince, saying, "Captain Wainwright's been killed."

Prince stared at him, then said, "This thing's gone sour. No way we can get out of here."

His words were prophetic, for an hour later the Confederates were retreating. As they fell back, Vince yelled, "Look, Jake—!"

Jake turned to see Jeremiah Irons bending over a soldier. Jake glanced at the Yankee lines, which were driving toward them. "Come on!" He ran, bent over to grab Irons by the arm. "Come on! The Yanks are right behind us!"

Irons got to his feet and looked at the advancing line of Federals; then the three of them moved back. Jake fired, sending one of the enemy down; then as he was reloading, he heard Vince cry out. He whirled, expecting to see Vince down, but it was Irons who was lying on the ground and Vince running to him. Jake leaped to the wounded man's side, looking for his injury.

"It's in his chest, Jake," Vince cried. "We've got to get him out of here."

"Grab his legs," Jake said, and the two of them dropped their muskets and picked Irons up. His eyes were open, glazed with shock, and as the two men carried him across the field, he fainted. A sergeant yelled at them to leave him, but when he saw that it was an officer they were carrying, he said no more.

They got Irons back to the field hospital, where a busy surgeon came to look at him. The air was loud with the sound of muskets and artillery, but the cries of the wounded men could be heard over everything. "He's hit bad, I'm afraid," the doctor said. "If I go in for that bullet, it may kill him."

"What if you don't?" Jake demanded.

The doctor, a fat man with thick hands, gave them a hard look, then said, "He'll die, would be my guess."

"Take it out!" Jake said at once. "Any chance is better than none."

In the end, the doctor finally did just that. He was a rough man, and Jake cringed at the operation, but when it was over, the doctor said, "He may make it. Keep him warm and give him plenty to drink when he can take it." Then he turned back to the growing crowd of wounded men.

"Let's get him to bed," Vince said, and the two of them soon had Irons in a bed, wrapped with blankets. When they had done all they could, Vince asked, "Think we ought to go back to the fight, Jake?"

"No. We're penned in now. No way out." His face was grim in the dim light, and he added, "I hope the prison camp we wind up in isn't as bad as I know they can be—because that's where we're going to spend the rest of the war!"

Vince stared at him, then shook his head. He got up without a word and disappeared from the room.

❧

The three Confederate brigadiers gathered to compare notes. Buckner considered the army's position desperate. "You should have marched out as we planned, General Pillow!" he said grimly.

"We'll still get out, as soon as it gets dark," Pillow snapped. Pillow was a sharp-faced man who had earned a reputation for incompetence during the Mexican War. On one occasion, he had mistakenly ordered his men to build their breastworks on the wrong side of the trench, leaving them exposed to the enemy.

General John Floyd had fear on his face, for he had been accused of having misappropriated $870,000 as President Buchanan's secretary of war. He was certain that the Union would try him on those charges, and he had no thought except getting away.

The three men argued until one o'clock, when Nathan Bedford Forrest came to report. Forrest was shocked to discover that the generals were discussing the surrender of the army. His eyes blazed, and he exclaimed, "The Federals haven't occupied the extreme right. We can still march out. My scouts have found an old river road. It's under water—no more than three feet—but only for one hundred yards."

But Floyd said, "My medical director says our troops can't take any more punishment."

"Have you thought how much punishment they'll take in a prison camp, General?" Forrest snapped. He argued for over an hour, but finally the generals took a vote. They all agreed to surrender the men, but General Floyd spoke out and said he would not surrender himself, and Pillow at once said the same.

"I'll share the fate of the army," General Buckner said.

"If I place you in command, General Buckner," General Floyd said, "will you allow me to get out as many of my brigade as I can?"

"Yes, I will."

Floyd turned to General Pillow and said, "I turn the command over, sir."

General Pillow replied just as promptly, "I pass it on."

General Buckner said, "I assume it."

At that, Forrest snorted angrily. "I didn't come here for the purpose of surrendering my command!" he said with contempt dripping from his voice. He stomped out and in a short time had gathered his officers. He told them of the generals' decision, then said, "I'm going out. Anyone who wants to go with me is welcome. I'll get out—or die!"

❧

Vince had been wandering around the camp in despair. He'd seen one of Forrest's lieutenants, a man named Sloan, whom he knew slightly. "Lieutenant, what's General Forrest going to do?"

"Get out of this rat trap!" Sloan spat out. "We've found a way. If you want to go, be ready in half an hour. We're pulling out then."

Vince whirled and raced back to where Jake was sitting beside Irons. "Jake! We've got a way out of this place!" He quickly informed him of Forrest's plan, adding, "It's the only hope we've got. I'm going to get the rest of the troop."

"Wait a minute!" Jake indicated the motionless form of Irons. "I can't leave him here to be captured."

Vince had always been a clever enough man. His brain was working fast now, and he said, "We'll hitch our horses to a wagon. We can put him in the bed. We've got to cross some water, but I don't think it'll get as high as the bed. You get him ready while I go steal a wagon and get the horses hitched to it."

"Watch out for Crow," Jake called out as Vince left at a dead run. "It might hurt his feelings some to pull a wagon." But Vince was gone, and Jake began his own preparations. Irons was unconscious and could be left, so he took care of provisions. He made a raid on the commissary, taking as much as he could carry in two large burlap bags. By the time he got back, Vince was there with the wagon hitched up and most of the men of the troop who'd come from Virginia with him. He was telling them, "We're getting out of here. I didn't enlist to die in a prison camp! Little, you and Poteet go bring the chaplain out. He's taken a bullet, and we're taking him out with us!"

Jake was surprised to see the two men jump at Vince's command, and as they loaded the injured man onto the bed of the wagon, he said so quietly that only Vince could hear, "You make a pretty good officer, Vince. Any orders for me?"

Vince grinned at him, saying only, "Shut up, will you!" The two of them got into the wagon, and Jake took the lines. "Let's get out of this place, Jake," Vince said, and they moved out, followed by the mounted men.

They met Forrest with his command outside the fort, and by daylight the horses were belly-deep in freezing water. Many of the infantrymen had gotten word of the breakout and were wading waist-deep, but there was no complaining. At the head of the column rode General Forrest, ever alert for Federals.

"Pretty hard on a wounded man," Vince said, looking back at Irons. He got out of the seat, going back to put more blankets over the still-unconscious man. When he came back to sit beside Jake, he shook his head, saying, "He's in poor shape, Jake. I don't see how he can make it."

Jake didn't answer, but his own spirit was gloomy. Finally he shook his head, saying, "Times like this I wish I was a praying man. But all I can count on is what I can do. And I'm thinking that won't be enough."

CHAPTER 23

RETURN TO VIRGINIA

*G*rant's victory over Fort Donelson touched off celebrations all across the North. At the Union Merchants' Exchange in St. Louis, speculators stopped work to sing patriotic songs; in Cincinnati, everybody was shaking hands with everybody else, and bewhiskered men embraced each other as if they were long-lost brothers.

In the South, many believed that they had lost the war at Donelson, for the fall of the fort opened the way south and led to the fatal splitting of the Confederacy, which had been the Union plan all along.

The editor of the *Richmond Examiner* did not underrate the importance of the North's victories over Fort Henry and Fort Donelson. He saw in them the beginning of future disasters.

Rachel came into her mother's room with a copy of that paper, saying, "Mother, listen to what the *Examiner* says about Donelson:

"The fall of Fort Donelson was the heaviest blow that has yet fallen on the Confederacy. It opened up the whole of

*West Tennessee to Federal occupation, and it developed the
crisis which had long existed in the west. General Johnston
had previously ordered the evacuation of Bowling
Green, and it was executed while the battle was fought
at Donelson. Nashville was utterly indefensible; by the
sixth of April surrender of Island No. 10 had become a
military necessity. The Confederates had been compelled to
abandon what had been entitled 'The Little Gibraltar of
the Mississippi,' and experienced a loss in heavy artillery,
which was nigh irreparable.*

*"The Confederate loss was 12,000 to 15,000 prisoners,
20,000 stands of arms, 48 pieces of artillery, 17 heavy
guns, from 2,000 to 4,000 horses, and large quantities of
commissary stores. The Confederates lost more than 450
killed and 1,500 wounded, while the Union loss was 500
men killed and 2,100 wounded."*

Rachel threw the paper on the floor with an impetuous
anger, saying, "These newspapers! Can't they *ever* say anything
good about our side?"

Amy picked up the paper, read through it, then said, "Well,
it *was* a terrible loss for the Confederacy. Your father says it'll
take a miracle for us to recover."

Rachel shook her head, anger glinting in her eyes. "Fifteen
thousand of our men prisoners!" She walked around the room,
unable to curb the impatience that welled up in her. Since news
had come of the fall of Donelson, she had been on the rack,
unable to sleep for worrying about her brother. Every night
she prayed that he was a prisoner and not in an unmarked grave
outside the fort. Regret worked on her, cutting like a keen
knife at the memory of how she'd sent him away so coldly.

And she couldn't even bear to think of Jake and the last words she'd spoken to him.

Her mother had been anxious over Vince, of course, but she had noted Rachel's almost frantic activity since the news arrived. Now she said, "Rachel, you mustn't go on like this. I'm believing and praying that Vince is a prisoner. You've got to do the same."

"I know, Mother," Rachel said, forcing herself to be calm. She took a seat and began to knit a sock, her face pale and her lips tight. The two women sat there for only a few minutes, and finally Rachel said, "I'm going for a ride over to Melora's, Mother."

"Take the Yancys some of the potatoes," Amy said. "I'm sure they're getting low on food."

"I will."

Two hours later she pulled her horse up in front of the Yancy house. Buford came out, his lean form bent but his eyes bright. "Well now, Miss Rachel! Come a'callin', did you?"

"Brought you some potatoes," Rachel said. As he took the sack, she slipped to the ground and walked with him to the door, asking, "Have you heard from Bobby?"

"No. He ain't much fer writing," Buford said. Opening the door, he called out, "Melora! Company!" He tossed the potatoes on the table, saying, "Got a nice fat doe this morning. I'll go cut a quarter off for you," and left the room.

"It's so good to see you, Rachel," Melora said, coming over and kissing the younger woman. "You sit down and I'll make some tea. Have to be sassafras, I'm afraid. Unless a ship breaks through the blockade, we'll be drinking that for a time."

"That's fine, Melora." Rachel sat at the table, listening as Melora talked and made the tea. As always, she admired Melora, thinking her one of the most beautiful women she'd ever seen. She was tall with raven black hair and striking green eyes. At twenty-seven she possessed a slim figure, yet was rounded by a womanly grace. Finally she sat down, and the two women began talking.

After a short time, Rachel asked bluntly, "Melora, aren't you worried about Brother Irons?"

Melora put her slim fingers around the mug, took a sip of the tea, then nodded. "I am, a little. I wish they'd release the names of the prisoners—but they're in no hurry for that."

"I–I'm almost sick over Vince," Rachel said haltingly. She hesitated, then blurted out, "I was angry with him when he went away. I said terrible things! Oh, I could cut my tongue out!"

Melora leaned forward, put her hand on Rachel's, waiting for the girl to get control. Finally she said, "You know, Rachel, God gave each of us a spirit all our own, none of us the same. He's like an artist, wanting to make all of His creations special. That's part of the glory of God. Remember how some of the psalms talk about how varied His creation is, about all the kinds of birds and the wonderful creatures that are in the ocean?"

Rachel was caught up with the words—Melora had always spoken poetically, and wrote so, too, she suspected—but now she asked, "What does all that have to do with my being a beast to my brother?"

"Oh, I'm sure you weren't a beast, Rachel!" Melora laughed. "But you're different from other people. You've got powerful emotions that just won't be still. You're like a boiler full of steam, and you've got to let off some at times or explode."

"Full of hot air, am I?" Rachel said, amused at Melora's words.

"Full of love, full of hate, full of every kind of emotion," Melora insisted. "I wish I had more of that in me!"

Rachel stared at the older woman. "But—I've always wished I was more like *you*!" she exclaimed. "So cool and collected, you never lose your temper!"

Melora sipped her tea, then shook her head. "I'm the way God made me—and so are you. Neither of us should complain or be unhappy with the job God did on us."

Rachel put her chin in her hand, thinking about what Melora was saying. Finally she said, "Well, at least Brother Irons won't have to worry about fits of temper."

"And the man who gets you won't have to worry about being bored!" Melora giggled surprisingly. "He'll get his head skinned at times, I suppose, but he'll get something else, too."

"What will he get?"

"He'll get a woman who'll give him such love as men dream of, but few find."

Rachel's face turned scarlet, and she hid it with her hands. "Melora! You make me sound bold and wanton!"

"No, because your love will be strong in all areas: physical, emotional, and spiritual. That's just it—you have a tremendous capacity for love in all its facets." Melora came out of her chair to stand beside the girl. Putting her hands on her shoulders, she said, "You often remind me of Mary Magdalene. Not the early Mary—but the one who loved Jesus so much that she washed His feet with her tears and dried them with her hair. I don't think anyone on earth ever loved Him so much. And that's the kind of love that's in you, Rachel. All you need is a fine man to give it to."

The two women were still, and finally Melora went back to her chair, saying, "Let's pray for our men. For Vince and Jeremiah. For all of them, even the poor Northern boys who are suffering."

Rachel bowed her head, and they prayed. . .and before the final "Amen," she whispered a prayer in her heart, without really understanding why she did so, that God would watch over one reckless, deceitful gambler.

❧

A spring wind, brisk but with a hint of April warmth, brushed against Vince's face, and he lifted his head, sniffing the breeze. He turned to Jake, who was dozing beside him in the seat. He nudged him with an elbow, saying, "Jake, wake up!"

Jake woke instantly, looked around, then spotted the buildings making a smudge against the sky down the road. "Richmond?" he questioned.

"We made it, Jake!" Vince said with excitement in his voice. "By heaven, we made it!"

Jake smiled, thinking that both of them had had doubts about getting back to Virginia. First they'd had to get permission to leave the Army of Tennessee. General Forrest had listened to Vince's plea, then had given them extended leave to get back to Richmond.

He had waved off their thanks, giving Vince a pass and wishing them well. "Hope the preacher makes it," he said as they left, but there was doubt in his voice, for he'd talked to his own medical officer about Irons and had received little hope.

Getting permission to leave had been relatively easy—reaching their destination was far from that. The weather had turned even worse, so they'd had to travel between icy rainstorms and frequent snow flurries. The two of them could have forced their way through, but with Irons running a fever, they'd had to hole up in whatever shelter they could get, which meant slow progress.

Now at last, they were at Richmond, and Vince turned to look at Irons, then said, "I hope we're not too late." Jake made no answer, for he had little hope that the minister would recover. He was convinced that Irons was hanging on to life by an act of will so that he could see his children one more time. It had been a hard time for Jake, for when Irons was conscious, he'd talked about God and had repeatedly urged both men to let Christ come into their lives. It had not been a pushy thing, which would have repelled both Vince and Jake—it was simply an outgrowth of the love in Irons that was always visible. Both men knew the minister could no more help sharing his faith than he could help breathing.

As they came into the outskirts of town, Vince said, "Jake, it's time to make a switch."

Jake stared at him with a puzzled look. "A switch?"

"Right. You've been Vince Franklin too long, my friend. Today, I step back into my own shoes! But we've got some adjustments to make."

"I'd better cut out now," Jake said. "If they see the two of us together, it's all over."

"Just trust your Uncle Vince!" he said with a grin.

Jake said no more, but he decided that as soon as they got the chaplain to a hospital, he was leaving. "Think I'll go keep Jeremiah company," he said, and Vince pulled the wagon to a stop.

Jake got in the back and sat with Irons, seeing to it that he was comfortable.

"Where are we?" the sick man whispered.

"Richmond, Jerry," Jake said. "You'll be with your family real soon."

Irons looked up, his eyes glazed, but managed a smile.

"I—knew you two—would do it!"

Jake sat beside him, not talking much. He had learned that Irons liked to have someone there when he woke up from his fitful sleep. They made their way to the camp, where they were directed to the military hospital. Less than thirty minutes later, Irons was in a bed, between white sheets, and two doctors were hovering over him.

"Looks like Irons is in good hands for now," Vince said to Jake. He nodded.

"You'll want to find your father—" Jake started to say, but Vince shook his head, cutting him off.

"No, not just yet. We haven't really officially reported in, and there's something I want to take care of before we do. Come on!"

Jake started to argue, but Vince just took his arm and urged him back out to the wagon, then headed into town. Soon Vince pulled the wagon over, saying, "I'll be back in an hour, Jake. Then we can go on to the camp and report." He grinned broadly, then disappeared.

Jake went around to the back of the wagon, stretching out, weary to the bone. He wondered about Vince, what sort of scheme he was up to, but was too exhausted to care. It was over as far as he was concerned. *Just let me get rested and I'll pull out,* he thought.

He grew sleepy and was dozing when he felt the wagon give and heard Vince say, "Wake up there, Private! You look like a sloppy soldier to me!"

Glancing toward the sound of Vince's voice, Jake was shocked at what he saw. Vince stood there dressed in a spotless gray uniform, and he had been carefully barbered. His beard was neat and trim, the way it'd been when Jake had first seen him, and his hair was cut in his old fashionable style.

"What do you think, old buddy? The old Vince, eh?" He grinned. "By George, it's good to be myself again."

Jake said with an admiring glance, "You're some sight to behold! You look like a hero." He got to his feet, adding, "I'll leave you here—"

"You'll do nothing of the sort!" Vince said sharply, cutting him off. "I know you think you'll be recognized, but come along and let me show you something." Jake jumped to the ground and followed him to a store window, where Vince waved at their reflections, saying, "Take a look at yourself, Jake."

Hardin squinted into the glass and received a shock. He'd let his beard grow since leaving Richmond, and now it was a bushy mask. He'd never been able to grow a neat beard, which was one reason he'd always shaved closely. His clothes, he saw, were in tatters—not a single garment was whole. "I look like a bum," he said, studying his reflection. "But what do you need me for?"

"I don't know," Vince said honestly. "But we've gone through some rough times." He hesitated, then said quietly, "I don't have a friend in the world, Jake, except you. I need you. Isn't that enough?"

Jake looked at Vince quickly, seeing that there was none of the old cynicism in his eyes. He thought hard, then shrugged. "Okay, I'll go along, Vince."

"Fine! Now we report to the adjutant."

They drove to the camp again, and Vince went into the office at once, asking the sergeant, "Is Major Franklin here?"

"Sure is," the sergeant said, nodding. "He's over at the drill field."

Vince turned and went back to say to Jake, "He's at the drill field. Let's go find him." He got into the wagon, and when they got to the field, he said, "There he is, Jake."

Major Franklin had seen the wagon but had turned to speak with one of the sergeants. Vince had advanced to within ten feet of him before he turned back. He took one look at Vince and his face grew pale. Vince said, "Sir, I've come back to report."

Brad Franklin seemed to be frozen. He ignored Vince's salute, his arms hanging down at his sides for a moment; then he lurched forward unsteadily, crying out, "Vince—!" He grabbed the younger man, holding him with all his might, and the soldiers who were drilling watched with amazement. Until, that is, Sergeant Clay Rocklin said, "About face, ladies! On the double, march!" Then he turned to Corporal Royston. "Pete, take care of them. I'm going to welcome my nephew home!"

Major Franklin had released Vince, but his voice was unsteady. He wiped his eyes, saying, "Well, you ought to be shot for giving an old man such a shock!"

Vince's voice was husky, and he had to clear his throat before he could answer. "I—couldn't get word to you, sir." Then he handed General Forrest's pass to him, saying, "I'm on extended leave. Chaplain Irons—he's at the hospital. I'm afraid he's in bad shape."

Franklin saw Clay waiting and said, "Sergeant, come here."

Clay came at once, his face happy. "Vince, I'm happy to see you."

"Uncle Clay," Vince said abruptly, "I've brought the chaplain home. He was wounded in the battle. I—I don't see how he's lived this long."

Clay's face clouded with sadness. "I want to see him. And someone ought to go to Melora. She can tell his children.

I believe they are staying with one of the parish families."

Franklin said instantly, "Clay, you're on leave. Take care of Jeremiah. Do whatever seems best. Use my name."

"Yes, sir." Clay moved quickly to the wagon, and Major Franklin said, "Son, go at once to the house. I can't leave right now, but the family needs to know you're safe." He drew his shoulders back and said proudly, "By heaven, you're home! Thank God!"

Vince echoed his father, saying, "Thank God!" then turned and went to the wagon. Clay, he saw, was already in the wagon, waiting. As Vince approached, Jake said, "Shall I drive you to the hospital to see the chaplain?"

Vince watched with alarm as Clay looked up at the driver, but there was not a flicker of recognition in his uncle's face. "Yes, we'll go there first."

It only took a few minutes for them to reach the hospital. Vince followed Clay inside to talk with the doctors briefly and get an update on Irons's condition before talking with Melora. Then he said, "Uncle Clay, I've got to get home and tell everyone I'm all right."

"Yes, go right now. And have Rachel go with you to get Melora."

"Yes, sir, I will."

Jake was sitting on the porch but rose as Vince came out. "Come on, Jake. We've got chores to do."

Jake hesitated. "Maybe I'd better stay with the chaplain."

"No, I'll need you. Come on."

Jake followed him to the wagon, and the two of them drove off at a fast trot. Soon they were clear of town, yet Vince said nothing. He was thinking of the love he'd seen in his father's eyes when he had greeted him—something he'd wanted to see all his life!

Jake, however, was thinking of Rachel, wishing that he was anywhere in the world other than on his way back to Lindwood. But he was committed to Vince, and so, as the wagon rolled along, he sat there, dreading the moment when he'd have to face her.

All he could think of was the contempt in her voice as she'd said, "Never come here again!"

Tad came stumbling into the kitchen, where Amy was helping Dee fix potato salad. His eyes were wide and he was bawling out his words so rapidly that Dee said, "You gone crazy? Whut you yellin' about?"

"Marse Vince!" Tad finally shouted, pointing with a wavering hand. "It's Marse Vince come home!"

"Glory to God in de highest!" Dee screamed, and the two women ran out the door. Rachel was hanging clothes out on the line in the back, and when she heard the screaming, she dropped her best nightgown in the mud and ran around the house. She stopped dead still when she saw Vince leaping off of a wagon only to be engulfed by Dee and her mother.

Suddenly Rachel couldn't breathe, and the earth seemed to spin around, forcing her to stagger toward the house. She leaned against the wall until the dizziness passed, then walked unsteadily toward the three. Vince, seeing her coming, pulled away from his mother and Dee and turned to meet her. He seemed to be waiting for a sign, and Rachel saw in his eyes that he was uncertain. Remembering her anger when she'd sent him away, her heart smote her and she began to run, tears coming into her eyes. "Vince! Oh, Vince!" she cried as he caught her up in his arms.

He held her tightly, then said, "Rachel—!" His voice was choked with emotion.

She pulled back and looked at him, saying, "You're back! You're not dead!"

"Not a bit of it," he said, then turned to his mother and Dee, saying, "Could a man get a bite to eat around this place?"

This was what the women needed, something to do to take the strain off of the moment. Amy came to him, hugging him again, then said, "You come in the house right now, Vince Franklin! I'm going to feed you until you pop."

Vince stopped, then turned to the wagon and said, "Come on, Jake. I want to introduce you to my family."

Jake, feeling like a complete fool and a total fake, wrapped the lines around the seat, stepped to the ground, and advanced reluctantly a couple of steps as Vince said easily, "This is my best friend, Jake Hardin. Jake, I want you to meet my mother, Amy, and my other mother, Dee. And this is my sister, Rachel."

Amy smiled and came to offer her hand, saying, "I'm so glad you've come with Vince, Mr. Hardin!"

Jake pulled off his hat and muttered a brief thank-you, giving Amy's hand a quick shake and nodding toward the black woman. Then he looked at Rachel. She was staring at him, her face pale. He would not have been surprised if she had denounced him on the spot. But she only glanced at Vince, then said, "I'm glad to meet you, Mr. Hardin."

Vince didn't miss the awkward exchange, and he spoke quickly to relieve the strain. "I've got bad news, I'm afraid. Jeremiah Irons was wounded at Donelson. We managed to get him out—but he's in a bad way!"

Amy said at once, "We have to tell Melora!"

"That's what Father said," Vince agreed, nodding. "Rachel, he thought you might go after her, take her to get the children, then go to the hospital at the camp."

"Oh yes!" Rachel said. "I'll go right now!" She turned to Tad, who was standing ten feet away, saying, "Tad, hitch the grays to the buggy."

"Yas'um, Miss Rachel!"

"Both of you come inside," Amy insisted to the two men as Rachel ran to change clothes. "You both look so tired!" She led them into the house, and soon they were eating the best meal they'd had in weeks. Vince told the story of their escape, making little of his own part in the effort.

Jake ate very little, but when Vince was finished with his story, he said, "Mrs. Franklin, your son is the worst storyteller I've ever heard. It was his doing that got us out of Donelson. If it hadn't been for him, Chaplain Irons and I would both be in a Yankee prison right now!" He told the story again, ignoring Vince's protests.

When he finished, Amy said quietly, "Your father will be very proud, Vincent."

Vince flushed and started to protest, but Jake said, "Vince, I need to go back to camp. Could I borrow a horse?"

"Certainly you can!" Amy nodded, then had a thought and added, "But would you go with Rachel to get Miss Yancy? It'll be dark by the time she can get to Richmond, and I'd feel better if a man went along with her."

"Why—yes, Mrs. Franklin," Jake said hesitantly, seeing no way out. At just that moment, Rachel came in wearing a dark brown dress and a coat to match.

"I'll stay in town with Melora and the children, Mother. Don't worry about me."

"I'll be in tomorrow, dear," Amy said, nodding. "Mr. Hardin's going to town, too, so I asked him to go with you and Melora."

Rachel shot a strange glance at Jake but said, "That's nice of you, though I doubt we'll have any trouble."

Vince said, "I'll have Tad saddle a good horse for you, Jake. Come along." When they were clear of the house on the way to the barn, he said, "You'll have to talk to Rachel, Jake. Don't let her give us away."

"Nothing I can do about that."

"Just talk to her, and I'll talk to her tomorrow. She's hot-tempered, but she's got a good heart."

Ten minutes later, Jake drove the buggy down the road, a fine chestnut gelding tied to the rear. Rachel didn't say a word, nor did he—not for over a mile. Finally he said, "This wasn't my idea, Rachel."

"It wasn't mine, either."

Jake shifted uncomfortably on the seat, not knowing how to talk to her. Her face was stiff, and there was a rigidity in her spine as she sat beside him. Finally he said, "I can't change what you think about me, but you shouldn't be angry with your brother. He grew up while we were in Donelson." Still she said nothing, and he felt his own anger rising within him. "It's good that you've never made a mistake, Miss Franklin. Makes it real easy for you to come down hard on us poor mortals who have!"

Rachel had been sitting there, trying desperately to find a way to speak to the man beside her. She had decided that he was not the rogue she'd taken him for—and she could no longer deny that his presence, even the very sight of him, did strange things to her heart. The feelings that had so confused and troubled her when she thought Jake to be her brother now came back in a flood, and she felt her face grow warm. She longed to look at him, to drink in the sight of his face, to feel again the camaraderie they had established during their time together as "brother" and sister. . .but her pride was too great.

Then when he lashed out at her, her answering anger brought a fierce halt to any efforts she might have made to break through the walls that surrounded her. The buggy moved steadily down the road, both of them bound into silence. Rachel kept her head turned to one side, determined not to let Jake see on her face the mortification that she was sure was showing. She knew there was something mean about the way she was acting, something small and despicable. Here a man had come out of a death trap, a man who had, she sensed, brought her brother through a hard time—and all she could do was stare ahead, refusing to look at him or offer a word of thanks.

The longer it went on, the worse it got for her. She longed to turn, to ask Jake about Vince, to give him a chance to explain the strange events of the past—to tell her if everything between them had been an act. Instead, memories came to taunt her, and fear told her that he'd made a fool out of her, had probably even laughed at her. Her cheeks flamed, and finally she set her lips.

Jake Hardin might perhaps be better than she'd thought at first, she told herself, but he still was a man she'd like to see out of her life forever!

CHAPTER 24

AT ANY COST

Clay and Melora brought Irons to Lindwood three days after his being admitted to the hospital in Richmond. Both of them had stayed with him constantly, taking turns sitting up at night, and the Irons children, Asa and Ann, clung to them for assurance. Irons had rallied for two days, glad to be with his children and among friends, but then the deadly fever that had racked his frame all the way from Tennessee rose. And nothing would bring it down.

"You may as well take him home," Dr. Evans said on the third day, his long face showing regret. "He doesn't want to be here—and there's nothing I can do for him."

"We'll take him to Lindwood," Amy said at once, for the parsonage used by Irons for so many years was occupied by his successor. "We have plenty of room for everyone."

So Clay had driven the sick man home in a closed army ambulance, commandeered in the name of Major Franklin, arriving at Lindwood late in the afternoon. Irons wanted to try to walk, but Clay said, "You've been bossing me around from the pulpit for years, Brother Irons. This time *I'm* giving the orders. You can run around all you like after we get you on your feet."

Irons smiled up at him, his face so thin that the skull was plainly outlined. "I'll be running through the green pastures soon enough, my brother."

Clay blinked—he didn't miss the allusion to the psalm—but turned and called to Jake and Vince, who were standing a short distance away, "You two, make yourselves useful!"

As the two men carried the sick man inside on the stretcher, Irons said, "You two have carried me many a mile, brothers—but I guess I won't trouble you after this trip." He lay down with a sigh of relief, and his eyes closed when they put him into the bed. But he opened them to say, "I can't get to a church or a pulpit—so you two will have to be my congregation." A smile turned the corners of his lips up, and he whispered as he dropped off into a comalike sleep: "The sermon. . .will start when. . .I wake. . ."

Melora came over and arranged the covers around Irons, then sat down beside him. Clay hesitated, then asked, "Will you see that the ambulance gets back to the regiment, Vince? I don't want to leave."

"Sure, Uncle Clay." Vince left the room, followed by Jake. When they were outside the house, Vince walked slowly to the wagon, biting his lip nervously. "He's not going to make it, Jake." Shaking his head with an angry gesture, he suddenly struck the side of the wagon with the heel of his fist, saying angrily, "After all the misery we went through getting here—to lose him now—!"

Jake felt even lower than Vince, so low that he made no answer. He had not been hopeful from the time he had seen the wound, for he knew how rarely a man lived through such a thing. He had begun to respect Irons as a man long ago; now he had grown to reverence him as a man among men. Never once had Irons complained, and even when the pain must have been terrible, Irons's sole concern seemed to be for the souls of his friends.

"Guess I'll take the wagon back," Jake said heavily.

"It's too late, almost dark now. I'll take it back. I've got to go to town tomorrow morning, anyway." Vince paused, then added, "Got to go see Ellen." When he caught the sudden look Jake laid on him, he shrugged. "Got to be done, Jake. Might as well get it over with."

The next morning Vince was on his way to Richmond shortly after dawn, his horse tied to the rear of the ambulance. After dropping the ambulance off at the hospital, he rode straight to Ellen's boardinghouse. He was met by Mrs. Mulligan at the door, who said, "Mrs. Rocklin has moved." There was a tight set to her lips, and Vince was aware that she was upset.

"Is something wrong, Mrs. Mulligan?"

"Yes, there is—" She hesitated, then said firmly, "I had to ask Mrs. Rocklin to look for other quarters." Her lips drew together, and she shook her head. "Times are hard, with the war and all, and I need all the boarders I can get. But to be plain with you, sir, Mrs. Rocklin isn't a careful woman, as far as men are concerned, I mean. And I'll ask you not to come here again."

"Of course. Did she leave an address?"

"No—but you might try the Cosmopolitan Hotel. I've heard she was there."

"Thank you," Vince said. He left at once and made his way to the hotel she had mentioned. It was located in an older section of Richmond, one that was going to seed. As he dismounted and went inside, Vince noted that the Cosmopolitan had little left of pretension. The lobby smelled rank with age and odors of the years, and the clerk, a thin young man with grimy hands and hair slicked down with grease, merely nodded when Vince asked for Mrs. Rocklin.

"Number 206."

Vince ascended the stairs, took a left, and knocked on the door lightly. At first there was no answer, so he knocked louder. This time he heard a muffled voice but couldn't make out the words. Finally the door opened a crack, and Ellen peered out. Her eyes were bleary, but they opened wide when she recognized him, and she asked, "What are you doing here?"

"I have to talk to you, Ellen."

She hesitated, then opened the door. Vince entered, taking in the dilapidated condition of the room, but said only, "How have you been?"

Ellen was wearing a purple robe over her nightdress, and her hair was tangled. "I heard you were back," she said. A speculative light came into her eyes, and she asked suspiciously, "What about the money you were going to send me? I never got a dime!"

Vince said carefully, "Ellen, I think you'd better get something straight. The last time we talked, you made all kinds of crazy accusations."

Ellen stiffened and started to say something, but Vince cut her off.

"I didn't come to argue with you," he said evenly. He was disgusted with himself for ever having had anything to do with this woman. Now he wanted only to get his business done and get away from her. "I didn't think too clearly after the accident, Ellen. Maybe I was confused when we talked last time. But I'm myself now, so there'll be no money for you."

"And when I tell them about *this*—!" Ellen cried and reached out to snatch his hand with her own. "Your mother and Dee will remember the real Vince had a scar—"

"But there *is* a scar," Vince said. "Look for yourself."

Ellen stared at his hand, saw the heart-shaped scar, and the color fled from her florid face. She stood there speechless, then threw his hand away, crying, "You had it fixed! But there are other ways! You're a phony, and you know it!"

"Ellen, you've got a fine husband and fine children," Vince said quietly. "Why don't you quit all this and be a wife and a mother?"

A wildness surged into Ellen Rocklin, and lifting her hands, she clawed for his face, but Vince caught her wrists and held her easily. She struggled but could not break free. She cursed him horribly, threatening him with everything she could think of, but finally he said, "I'm going, Ellen. Don't go any further with this thing. You'll only hurt yourself and humiliate your family." Dropping her wrists, he turned and left the room.

The sound of her cursing came through the door, and he walked swiftly away, his lips set in an expression of disgust as he left the hotel.

❧

Thanks to Vince's father, Jake and Vince were granted indefinite leave. Even so, Jake would have left Lindwood despite his promise to Vince but for the fact that, twice during the next three days, Irons asked for him. He had gone at once to sit beside the dying man, and both times Irons had whispered, "Jesus loves you, my brother!" He was so weak that he could say little more, and Jake longed to give him some assurance—but had none to give.

When he wasn't with Irons, Jake kept to himself, riding

a tall roan named Dancer over the dead fields and through the evergreen timber. He had seen Rachel five times but had not spoken to her at all. Melora was friendly, but absorbed in taking care of the sick man and comforting his children. Jake longed to talk with Amy Franklin, but she seemed preoccupied. Besides, he knew they couldn't talk as they had before, when she had believed him to be her son. . . .

It was on a Friday morning that Amy surprised him by coming to join him, sitting down with him and asking about his family as he ate a piece of bread with honey. It gave him an odd feeling, talking with her, as if he were a ghost come back from oblivion—a ghost that no one even noticed.

He gave her the bare details of his history, leaving out the worst parts, and then she said, "Brother Irons is very fond of you." A frown crossed her brow, and she added quietly, "I sometimes think he's only keeping himself alive for the hope of seeing you and Vince come to God."

Jake felt a painful stab of regret. He looked down at his hands on the table, clasped them together, then said, "I—I wish it would happen, Mrs. Franklin."

She looked across the table and on impulse reached out and put her hand over his. He glanced up, startled by the gesture, and memories of the times she had talked with him came flooding back. "Vince has told me a little of how you've been such a help to him. Not many details, but he thinks you helped him find himself. And I've wanted to thank you for that." Jake shook his head, but she refused his protest. "I won't burden you with it, Jake, but if you would, Major Franklin and I would like it if you'd look on us as your family."

Jake looked up, startled—but he had no chance to respond, for just then Rachel came into the room. She stopped abruptly and stared at the two sitting there, their hands together. At once Jake rose, saying, "Thank you, Mrs. Franklin. Miss Rachel—" He nodded and left the room.

"What a fine young man!" Amy said, sadness in her tone. "What do you make of him, Rachel?"

"I don't make anything of him, Mother. After all, I really don't know him."

Amy looked up, surprised by the coldness in her daughter's voice. "Why, Rachel—what's the matter?"

Rachel bit her lip but said only, "Nothing. I'm just upset. Brother Irons is slipping away, and there's nothing we can do."

"There's one thing," Amy said at once. "We can pray for Vince and Jake Hardin. That's what is on Jeremiah's heart now. I just told Jake I believe Brother Irons is hanging on just to see the two of them saved."

Rachel shook her head. "People don't find God just because somebody wants them to," she said flatly. "If that were so, Christians wouldn't have lost relatives, would they?"

"Rachel, you sound cynical," Amy said sharply. "You were taught better!" She caught herself, then came to stand beside Rachel. "I'm sorry. I suppose all of us are upset. But I believe God answers prayers—and I've been praying for Vince for a long time. Now I'll pray for Jake Hardin. You'll join me, won't you?"

Rachel gave her an agonized look, for she was emotionally a ruin. Ever since her clash with Jake Hardin, she had been tossed by doubt and self-loathing. Now as her mother asked her to pray for Hardin, she knew that she was empty inside; she had never felt so spiritually dry since she had become a Christian. She had tried to pray, but it was no use; the heavens were brass and God seemed so far away that she even began to doubt if she herself was a believer.

"I—I *can't*, Mother!" she said, getting the words out with difficulty. "Please don't ask me to explain!" She turned and walked from the room just in time to hide the tears of frustration that sprang to her eyes.

Amy spoke to Melora about what had happened. Melora said, "Rachel's going through some sort of a crisis, Amy. She needs our prayers almost as much as Jeremiah. He's at peace—but all you have to do is look at Rachel and see that she's in misery."

The next day Jake and Vince were sitting in the library when Melora came in to say, "I think he's going. He wants to see both of you. I'm going to get the children."

Both men rose and went at once to the sickroom. Jake saw a dreadful pallor on Vince's face and felt a weakness come into his own legs. When Jeremiah held up his hand, Jake took it at once. It was cold and had no strength.

"Jake. . .Vince. . . ," Irons whispered, "want to. . .thank you both. . .for bringing me home!"

Jake suddenly could not see, and he dashed the tears away from his eyes with his free hand. His throat was thick and it ached, but he managed to say, "Wish I could do more, Jeremiah! Lord, I wish I could!"

Vince had gone to the other side of the bed. He had taken Irons's other hand, and the tears were running down his face, an expression of grief contorting his features. He kept himself from sobbing only by an effort.

Irons lay there quietly, and he seemed to be listening to something. Suddenly both Jake and Vince felt that there was a strange stillness in the room—and a *presence* somehow—that neither of them could understand.

"God is here," Irons said, and his voice was suddenly strong, not the weak whisper they had grown accustomed to. He looked up at them, his eyes clear, and as he spoke, Jake felt the cold hand tighten on his with a sudden power.

"I've wondered why God brought me back here," Irons said, speaking distinctly. "I was ready to go to Him at Donelson. All the way here, I kept asking God why He didn't call me home. Now I know! He's given me some things to say."

He lay there for a time, and Jake asked, "What is it?"

Irons looked up and tightened his hand. "It's you, Jake—and you, Vince. God is waiting for you. That's why you brought me here, not just so I could tell my family good-bye, but so you both would let God find you. That's why, boys, I've been telling you that Jesus loves you."

As Jake listened to the words, which he had heard so many times from Irons over the past days, something came to him. It was like fear, for he began to tremble—and yet it was not that exactly.

Jesus loves you!

Suddenly he knew what it was! He had heard of Jesus Christ since his boyhood. He knew the stories in the Bible about Jesus, but Jesus had always been a dim figure, a picture in a book with a halo around His head—a man like George Washington or Alexander the Great, someone about whom he had heard and in whom he had believed.

But now he was somehow aware that here, in the very room where he stood holding the hand of a dying man, someone had entered—and he knew that it was Jesus! He saw no visions, indeed, could not have seen if a physical form had been there, for his tears blinded him. But he *knew* he was not alone!

And he'd always been alone—that was what came to him as

he stood there weeping. He'd had friends, but he'd been alone in every other sense. He'd become so accustomed to it that he'd even forgotten to be sad about it. But now as Irons said, "Jesus loves you," he knew that he was being asked to give up his aloneness. It was as if someone were saying, *Let Me come into your very being. Let Me share your grief and your fears. Please, just allow Me to come in, and you'll never be alone again!*

Jake stood there trembling like a man with fever, and then Irons prayed, "Lord Jesus, these men need You. They're afraid, but take away their fear. Show them how much You love them—let them know You died for them! Let Your blood cover their sins, O Jesus!"

Jake never was able to remember exactly what happened. He knew that Irons asked him to pray, to call upon God, and he knew that he did. It was an awkward prayer, more of a cry for help than anything else—but he never forgot the peace that came into the room. . .and into his heart.

And then Irons said, "Thank you, God, for these two men!" He released Jake's hand and reached up to pull his head down, then held him there, against his chest, whispering, "My brother, love God always!"

Then he released Jake, who turned from the bed, conscious that Irons was now holding Vince in an embrace. He stumbled out of the room, made his way blindly through the house, and walked away toward the grove of trees where he would be hidden from all eyes. There he threw himself flat on the ground and began weeping with great tearing sobs, praying and calling out to God.

He never told anybody what took place during that secret meeting with God—but when he came out, Jake Hardin was a new man.

As soon as Jake and Vince left the room, Irons called for his children. He spoke with them quietly, blessing them and asking them to follow God always. Finally he appeared to grow weaker.

Melora was there, and he smiled at her.

"Clay?" he asked.

"I'll get him," she said, hurrying to the door and calling his name. Clay entered at once and came to kneel at the bedside; Melora knelt on the other side. They held his hands, and he seemed to be gone. Only the slight rise and fall of his chest told them he was still there.

Then he opened his eyes and looked first at Clay and then at Melora. His lips curved in a smile, and he said, "I have loved you, Melora." Then he turned to Clay, saying, "My brother, you have been faithful. God has told me He will reward you—"

He lay there for a moment; then his eyes closed. "God— is—faithful!" he said haltingly, then smiled and, with a sigh, expelled his breath.

Melora reached up and pushed a lock of hair from his forehead. Her eyes were brimming with tears, and when she looked at Clay, she said, "Now we know how a child of the King goes home!"

CHAPTER 25

A FINE CASE OF REVENGE

Jeremiah Irons was buried with full military honors, and one of the speakers to pay tribute was President Jefferson Davis. Melora said later, "Jeremiah would have hated all that fuss!"

After the funeral, a reporter from the *Richmond Inquirer* cornered Jake, having discovered that he had been one of the two men who'd brought Irons back all the way from Fort Donelson. Jake tried to make his escape, but when he realized that the reporter, a heavyset young man with bulging eyes and a heavy moustache, intended to make him the hero of the story, he said, "Let me give you the real story about our escape." Then he proceeded to relate how Vince Franklin had been the real leader. He told the truth, though he minimized his own efforts and expanded Vince's.

The reporter, whose name was Jarius McGonigle, scribbled madly, his eyes popping with excitement. "This is a real story, soldier! You'll read it in the paper tomorrow."

"Remember, you promised to leave me out of it."

"Sure, I'll do that," McGonigle said and scurried off, mumbling to himself.

The next day when Jake came back from a ride, Amy called

to him from the porch. He tied the horse and found the family there, with Major Franklin standing in front of them. Rachel, he saw, gave him one quick look, then dropped her eyes. She looked pale, and there was little of the vivacious quality he'd always seen in her.

"Jake, I want you to hear this, too!" Major Franklin said and unfolded a newspaper with a flourish. Holding it up, he said, "Colonel Benton brought it to me, and as soon as I read it, I got on my horse and nearly ran him into the ground getting here."

"What in the world is it, dear?" Amy asked. She had never seen Brad so excited—or rarely so—and tried to read the headline, but he was holding the paper up before his eyes as he began to read.

" 'Many brave men have taken up arms for our beloved Cause, and we honor them. It is only fitting that one of our own be mentioned here, and we pay tribute to the hero of Fort Donelson—Private Vincent Franklin.' "

A cry of astonishment ran around the group, and Vince turned pale. His father gave him a proud look, saying, "Listen to this!" He continued to read the story, and Jake smiled despite himself, for McGonigle reached the heights of oratorical splendor in describing the hair-raising escape out of the fort, led by Vince.

Brad read on, " 'No less a man than General Nathan Bedford Forrest himself said, "This young man is the epitome of our fine Southern aristocrats! With soldiers like Private Vincent Franklin under our banners, we need not fear for the future!" ' "

Vince saw the smile on Jake's face and burst out, "Blast you, Jake Hardin! You're behind all this!"

"Just told it as I saw it," Jake protested.

As her father read the account, savoring every word, Rachel

was watching Vince. By now she knew him well enough to understand that he was embarrassed over the article. She also could tell from his dour looks at Jake—and from Hardin's bland looks in return—that the truth had been stretched. But her father was so pleased that she could not be sorry. Her mother, too, she saw, was leaning forward to catch every word, as were Grant and Les.

Finally Brad finished reading, and then the paper was passed around so that each of them could read for himself. Vince refused to look at it, going to stand at the window. Jake went to him, asking slyly, "May I have your autograph?"

"You snake in the grass!" Vince snapped. "I'd like to punch your head! Why'd you tell that reporter all those lies?"

"They weren't lies, most of them. If it hadn't been for you, we'd be in a Yankee prison camp. I owe you for that, so just consider this my first payment!"

Major Franklin called for attention, saying, "Tomorrow there's going to be a special presentation ceremony. Several of the men are going to be decorated, and Colonel Benton insists on your being there, Vince. I wouldn't be surprised if you didn't come away with some kind of a decoration."

Vince protested, but his father said, "You've made it clear that you don't like such things, but it's really for the others, for those who've been at home, praying for their soldiers. Not very many good things have happened to our armies lately, and it'll be good for people to see that some fine things are taking place. You'll have to go, I'm afraid."

Vince argued but in the end agreed. Jake slipped away while the family was talking, took Dancer's reins, and led him to the barn. He stripped off the saddle and began rubbing him down, thinking with a smile of the way Vince had been taken off guard. When he was almost finished, he heard a sound and turned to see Rachel, who had walked in through the doors at the far end of the barn.

She stopped as he turned to face her, almost as if she were afraid of him. "I—came to ask you something," she said with an obvious effort.

"Sure." Jake put Dancer in the stall, filled his box with feed, then turned to say, "What is it?"

Rachel looked around to where Bruno was cleaning out a stall a few feet away. "Could we go outside?" She turned, and he followed her through the door. She glanced toward the house, then turned and walked along the path that led to a small pasture surrounded by a rail fence. Inside were five grown sheep happily nibbling at the brown grass. Rachel looked at them, and Jake came to lean on the fence a few steps away from her.

A brisk wind blew her fine hair over her face, and she reached up to tie it back with a ribbon from her pocket. Her fingers, Jake noticed, were long and tapered, and her wrists looked strong. She had fine skin, made rosy by the breeze, clear and smooth with a few freckles across her nose. As Jake studied her silently, he thought that she had always impressed him as one of the strongest women he'd ever met, determined and firm. Now, however, she seemed undecided. She picked at the top rail of the fence, stripped off a flexible splinter, held it between thumb and forefinger, then tossed it to the ground and turned to face him.

"Was that true, what the paper said about Vince?"

"Most of it. All the important parts were true."

"It was really Vince who found the way out?"

"He found General Forrest, who was leading the escape. Forrest's scouts had found the old road earlier, but it was Vince who got the men from our regiment together and persuaded them to get out while there was still time. The wagon for Jeremiah was his idea, too."

Rachel listened to him carefully, weighing his words. Her lips looked soft and vulnerable, rather than firm and almost harsh as Hardin had seen them more than once lately. She stood there, her eyes looking serious, and then some sort of embarrassment came to them and she let them fall. "I–I'm glad it was true," she said. "Daddy and Mother are so proud!"

Jake nodded but said nothing. In truth, he didn't know what to say. Just the sight of Rachel fired strong emotions within him, but he couldn't say anything. He thought, suddenly, that she seemed to be waiting for him to speak, for she lifted her eyes and her lips parted, seemingly with expectancy. His breath caught in his chest, and he struggled for control. He wanted to tell her that he loved her, that there was no other woman in the world for him, nor ever would be. He wanted to take her in his arms and kiss her, to hold her with all the strength that was in him and never let her go. He did none of these things.

Rachel saw something of the struggle going on in the tall man who stood before her, but when he remained silent, she stiffened her back and said evenly, "Thank you for telling me. I'm glad for Vince."

She moved away then, and Jake wanted to run after her. But for what? What could he say? She hated him, and with good reason. He was guilty! Even if that didn't loom before him, he was a penniless man, a gambler with no future. What could he offer any woman?

So he let her go and stood there watching her walk slowly back to the house. When she disappeared through the door, he turned and walked toward the grove of pines that crested the small hill. He found the place where he'd come to pray on the day that Jeremiah Irons had died—and discovered that it was still a good spot for meeting with the Lord.

❦

The Richmond Grays made an impressive sight as they marched onto the field, rank on rank. The president sat with his wife on the platform, along with most of the members of his cabinet, applauding the men as they went through their maneuvers smartly. After the drill exhibition, President Davis descended and met Colonel Benton, and the two of them presented decorations to several of the soldiers.

Finally when all the expected awards were made, Colonel Benton said, "We have one more award to give to a fine soldier who is not a member of the Richmond Grays. Private Vincent Franklin—front and center!"

As Vince came to stand in front of the two men, Brad Franklin rose to his feet stiffly, his face under tight control. As the president read the commendation, giving the details of Vince's exploit, Brad turned, and his eyes met those of his wife—and the two of them smiled.

The president, after reading the commendation, smiled, too. An austere man with chiseled features, he had been accused of being cold and unfeeling, but there was a warm light in his gray eyes as he said, "Your family is well represented in the army, Private Franklin. Both your father and your brother are in the Richmond Grays. I am wondering if you would like to join them in this fine regiment?"

"Yes, Mr. President!" Vince exclaimed at once.

Davis smiled more broadly, saying, "The powers of the president are strictly limited, but I think in this case there will be no protest if I use my office to make your request official. And I feel certain that Colonel Benton will welcome my request that you be appointed sergeant as of this moment!"

"Certainly, Mr. President!" Colonel Benton said instantly. "Congratulations, Sergeant Franklin!"

The ceremonies were concluded, and Vince was surrounded by many people—including some of his friends who were in the Grays, as well as by his family. He smiled and shook his head when Clay came to him, saying, "You'll have to give me lessons, Uncle Clay. I don't know a thing about being a sergeant!"

"Just yell as loud as you can," Clay said, shaking Vince's hand. "Now we're all going to the hotel for a reception, I hear."

"I guess so," Vince said. "Father insisted on it."

"He's very proud of you. We all are. God has brought you to a place of true honor."

The reception was held in the dining room of the Edwards Hotel, which was soon crowded to the walls. "We should have gotten a larger room, Amy," Brad said as he brought her a glass of lemonade after shoving his way through the crowd. "I never dreamed there'd be this many people here."

Amy took the glass, sipped the tart liquid, then looked across the room, pleased to see Vince surrounded by friends. "It's wonderful, isn't it, Brad?"

"Miraculous, I'd say," he answered. "I don't think I'll ever doubt God again, Amy. Just a short time ago Vince was going to hell as fast as he could manage it. Now it's all different!" He glanced at her, asking, "Did he tell you about what happened to him when Jeremiah died?"

"Yes! And he wants to go all the way with the Lord, Brad. He told me he wants to be baptized as soon as possible." Her eyes grew sad for a moment as she said, "I'll miss Jeremiah so much, but he died doing what he loved most—winning men to Jesus!"

"Vince says he thinks Jake Hardin was converted, too."

"We've got to help that young man, Brad! He seems so alone. You must get close to him."

"I will," Brad promised, nodding. "I'm going to try to get him transferred to the Grays so he'll be with Vince. You know, Vince told me that the worst thing about all this today is that Jake got none of the credit. He says he'd never have made it if it weren't for Jake. But we'll make it up to him!"

After an hour and a half, the crowd thinned out, and Vince saw Rachel sitting alone, looking rather forlorn. He went to her, took a seat, then said, "Well, this will be over soon. It's been fine, but I wish Jake had gotten something." He saw a shadow cross her face and asked, "What's wrong, Rachel?"

"I guess I'm just feeling a bit of a letdown," Rachel said, and then she reached over and patted his hand. "I've just got the mullygrubs."

He smiled at the word, a carryover from their childhood days that signified a case of depression. "You need a sweetheart, Rachel. What's become of Semmes? I thought there was a promising romance budding there."

Rachel smiled slightly. "Haven't you heard? He's engaged to Marianne Huger."

"Well! He caught a big one, didn't he? Her father's the biggest planter in Mississippi, I hear." He studied his sister carefully, searching for a sign that she was grieving the loss of Semmes, but could tell nothing from her face. "But how does that make you feel?"

"Leighton was never in love with me," Rachel said with a shrug. "He was just challenged. I was the only girl he'd courted who didn't fall all over herself to get him." She suddenly smiled, adding, "Now it looks as though I'm the spinster of Lindwood for good."

"Don't be ridiculous," Vince said sharply. "And don't call yourself that anymore. I don't like it."

Rachel shook her head, then changed the subject, "The talk is that McClellan is about ready to move against Richmond—" She suddenly paused, and he saw her eyes widen as she looked across the room.

He followed her gaze and saw Simon Duvall standing in the double doors leading into the dining room. "That's trouble," he said, and he got to his feet. Rachel rose and followed him, noting that Duvall's face was flushed and that he was weaving. She paused as Vince came to a halt close to Clay and Ellen. She got one glimpse of Ellen's face and saw that she was pale beneath her makeup. She was clutching at Clay's arm, trying to pull him away, but Clay stood firm, his eyes fixed on Duvall.

"What do you want, Duvall?" Vince called out, his voice carrying over the room.

Duvall blinked and with an effort focused his bloodshot eyes on Vince. He licked his lips, and when he spoke his speech was slurred. "Gonna have—it out with you...Franklin!" He was so drunk he could hardly stand, but there was a mad look in his eyes.

"You're drunk," Vince said steadily.

"Yes, I'm drunk! But I'm no coward, which is what you are!"

Major Franklin roared, "Get out of here, Duvall!"

"Whas' matter, Major? I'm not good enough for you?" Duvall sneered; then when Major Franklin took a step, he yelled out, "Stay where you are!" His hand dipped inside his coat, and when it came out, he flourished a large pistol.

"S'none of your business!"

Jake had been standing along the wall, but when Duvall had walked in, he grew alert. He had watched and listened, moving away from the wall and coming to stand a few feet away from Vince and Rachel. He wished he had a gun, but there'd been no reason to carry one. None of the other men had guns, either, he was sure. When Duvall pulled the revolver, he thought rapidly. *Too far to make a jump at him—maybe I can get around behind him.*

But there was no time, for at that moment one of the soldiers lunged at Duvall, intending to get the gun away. Duvall turned and shot the man. The bullet struck him in the shoulder and drove him back. A woman screamed, and some of the men yelled, and Duvall in his confusion simply lifted his gun and fired.

Jake saw a woman go down and, without thought, launched himself to where Rachel was standing in the line of fire. He threw his body between her and Duvall, catching a glimpse of her eyes staring at him in amazement—and something more—but before he could decipher her look, he suddenly heard the explosion of Duvall's gun and pain ripped at his head as a slug plowed along over his ear. Agony raced through him, and he began to fall.

The last thing he heard as he slipped into darkness was Rachel's voice, calling his name.

CHAPTER 26

THE WORLD IN HIS ARMS

The waiting room of Mercy Hospital was small, merely a cubicle of ten feet square, with an assortment of chairs scattered about. Cigar smoke hung in the air, making it stuffy, and after a time Clay Rocklin rose and opened the single window that looked out on Charter Street. He stood there staring out but not really seeing the traffic that passed or the pedestrians who ambled by on the walk.

The scene kept coming back to him—Duvall firing blindly, Ellen falling with a cry, and his own failure to do anything. The suddenness of it had caught him unaware, as it had all the others. He had seen Bushrod Aimes bring Duvall down by cracking him on the skull with a heavy lamp and had gone at once to Ellen, who was lying on her face, moaning softly. The back of her dress was soaked in blood, for the bullet had caught her in the small of the back as she had turned to run away.

There had been confusion then, and he had seen that Jake Hardin was lying on the floor, utterly still. His bloody head rested in Rachel's lap, while she stared at him with a pale face that was wet with tears. The lieutenant who had set Duvall's rampage off—a tall man named Smith—had gotten to his feet and walked to the carriage without help. Clay had carried Ellen to a carriage, and Vince, along with three others, had carried Jake to another.

The doctors had gone to work at once, but to those assembled in the waiting room, it seemed an eternity since they had first arrived. Once a doctor had come out to speak to the friend of Lieutenant Smith, saying, "Come along. He's all right now. Got the bullet out without much trouble."

Later another doctor, a younger man with a fresh round face, emerged, asking, "Who's waiting for the head wound?"

Rachel stood up to ask, "How is he, doctor?"

"Well, we've got the wound all sewed up, but he hasn't come to yet." A frown pulled his lips down, and he shook his head doubtfully. "Bad case of concussion, I'd say."

"But he'll be all right, won't he?" Amy asked.

Like all doctors, this one hated to be wrong. He figured it was better to put the worst face on a situation; then if something went wrong, there would be no way for the family to accuse. "I hope so—but you can never be sure with these cases. I'd say take him home and watch him. Keep him warm, and even if he wakes up, you make sure he stays put in bed."

"We'll take him with us," Major Franklin said firmly. "Vince, let's go get an ambulance. It'll be easier on him."

Amy stayed with Clay when they left, but Rachel walked out of the waiting room and caught up with the young doctor. "May I sit with him?"

"Certainly! Right this way." He led her to a room where Jake lay in a bed, his head bandaged and his eyes closed. "Your husband?"

"Oh no!" Rachel said quickly.

The doctor gave her an odd look, then decided, *Must be a*

sweetheart. He'll be a lucky fella, if he lives. That's one good-looking filly! "Just keep him warm, even if you have to use hot-water bottles," he said, then left her.

Rachel sat down beside the bed, her face on a level with Jake's, and stared at his profile steadily. As the time moved slowly, she thought of the first time she'd seen him, in another hospital. And she thought of how she'd cared for him, almost as if he were a baby. The memories of their time together came clearly, and looking back, she saw that she had been vulnerable with him while she thought of him as her brother. Now, though, she realized that all the time there had been something more to her feelings than sisterly concern. Something in her had responded to Jake's masculinity, to the tenderness and closeness he had shown her. She was sure he had known that, and yet...he had not capitalized on it as some men might have done. Instead he had treated her as a sister. And a friend.

She sat there quietly, her hands clenched tightly, watching his still face. A question kept surfacing in her, formless and wordless, but insistent. It had something to do, she understood, with her feelings for the man lying there, feelings she'd never been able to express. She was a woman born to love, but never had she found a man who stirred deep emotions in her. Until she had met Jake Hardin. But her feelings for him were complicated and confusing, particularly because she'd been convinced that all her affection had been a natural outgrowth of the fact that Jake was her half brother.

But he was not her brother, and the memory of how betrayed she'd felt when she'd suddenly discovered the masquerade came to her. Now in the still darkness of the small room, looking at Jake's face, she found herself understanding that her anger had been tied up somehow with the loss—and relief—she had felt at the discovery that this man was *not* her brother.

Slowly she reached out and laid her hand softly on his cheek. It was a caress, yet it was more than that. *Why do I feel this pain?* she cried out wordlessly. *I've never felt this way about any man!* She let her hand linger on his face, feeling the rough beard and tracing the firm line of his jaw. Then he stirred, and she quickly pulled away.

"Are you awake?" she whispered, but he kept his eyes closed, and she sat back, waiting for the ambulance.

Her life had always been full and busy, but now for some reason that wasn't clear to her, she felt a terrible emptiness—a void that needed a fulfillment that she craved but could not even pray for—because she didn't know what she really desired.

༄

Back in the waiting room, Clay and Amy sat together, saying little. There was a heaviness in Clay's expression, and when Dr. Carver came into the room, Clay got up at once and faced him. "How is she, Doctor?"

Carver, a muscular man of forty with a heavy black beard, nodded sparely. "She's alive, Sergeant Rocklin. The bullet tore through some large muscles—but I'm afraid it touched the spine."

"Will she be all right?"

Dr. Carver bit his full lower lip, then stroked his heavy beard before answering. "I'm concerned about the bullet. It's too close to the spine for me to remove."

"Can you leave it in?"

"Yes, but I must tell you, she's got no feeling in her lower body."

"She's paralyzed?" Clay asked sharply.

"I'm afraid so," Carver admitted. "It may be a temporary thing—or later we may decide to try to remove the bullet. But even if we did that, if the spine is damaged, she may be crippled permanently." He shook his head, adding, "I wish I could give you better news."

"May I see her?"

"She's still groggy from the chloroform, but you can go in." He hesitated, then said, "Let me give you one caution, Sergeant. In cases like this—I mean, if she is actually paralyzed—it's important to be very positive. She'll be frightened and confused. Try to encourage her all you can. She'll need all your support."

"Yes, Dr. Carver." Clay nodded. "Take me to her, please."

Amy watched as the two men left, depressed by the news. She thought of how Clay had been tied to a loveless marriage with Ellen for years. She thought of his love for Melora, understanding how empty his life was without her—and she thought of Melora's love for Clay. Now, if Ellen was truly paralyzed, she'd be clinging to Clay like a leech, draining him of every possible ounce of strength.

Amy closed her eyes, thinking, *And he'll stay with her! Even if she turns out to be a helpless cripple, nagging at him constantly— Clay will never leave her.*

It should have pleased her to know that there were men like Clay Rocklin who were faithful to their commitments— but she sat there heavyhearted, thinking of the long parade of empty years that her brother faced.

♫

Clay found Ellen awake and almost crazy with fear. She was crying wildly, and when she saw him, she groped for his hands, crying out, "Clay! I can't move my legs!"

"Don't be afraid, Ellen," he said quietly, taking her hands. "It'll be all right."

But she clung to him with a fierce strength, fear pouring out of her. "Clay! Help me.... I can't move—my legs won't work."

He stood there trying to comfort her, to ease the fear, but she was out of control. For years she had thrust him away, but now she clung to him, gasping, "Don't leave me! You can't leave me, Clay!"

He stood there looking down into her face, which was contorted with fear. He had long ago lost any feelings of love for her; she had given him little choice. She had gone her own way, often with other men, a fact he well knew. Now as she clung to him, all the years of abuse and cruelty from her seemed to come back. And a harsh anger that Clay had thought long buried, even forgotten, rose within him.

Then an insidious voice, thin and small, seemed to say, *If she would only die!* There was a savage pleasure in the thought, and he found himself forming a picture of how it would be: *I'd not have to put up with this intolerable thing any longer—and I could have Melora!*

Immediately on the heels of that thought came another: *Lord, forgive me!* He shook his shoulders and, in a voluntary act of will, forced himself to pray for Ellen.

And then Clay Rocklin—who had risked his life in wild, bloody action on the battlefield—did the most difficult and courageous thing he'd ever done or would ever do. He leaned down and touched Ellen on the cheek, then said quietly, "I'll never leave you, Ellen. I'll stay with you as long as I live."

&

There was nothing but an ebony sky, a total darkness without a single gleam of a star, a silent world except for thin voices that came floating over the void like the distant cries of yesterday's ghosts. And there was no time, for there was neither sun nor moon to mark it. He felt he could have been floating through the velvet blackness for centuries, all the while that the pyramids were being put together or the great canyons of the earth were being dredged, a pebble at a time.

The voices came from time to time, and with them—at times—he felt hands touching him. One of the voices he came to know, for it came more often, and the touch that accompanied it was gentler and more soothing than the rest. There was a firmness in the touch, yet at the same time he sensed a gentleness such as he had never known.

Finally the darkness began to be broken by streaks of light that hurt his eyes, and with the light came a sense of earthiness. He felt the rough texture of a blanket against his skin, and the pungent odor of alcohol made him wrinkle his nose. A fly buzzed in his ear, lit on his cheek, then made a tickling sensation as it walked across his skin.

He lifted his hand to brush the fly away and instantly heard a voice. "Jake?" The sound of his name recalled him to the world, and he opened his eyes to see a face looming over him in the dimness cloaking the room.

"Jake? Are you awake?"

His thoughts rushed through his brain, ill assorted and without order. He knew this woman who leaned over him—yet for his life could not remember her name. It bothered him, and he licked his lips, trying to speak. The face disappeared and then came back. "Here—drink this."

A coolness was at his lips, and he was aware of a raging thirst. Clumsily he gulped the water, knocking against the glass so that some of it spilled and ran down on his neck. When it was gone, he coughed and put his head back. As he lay there, some of the disorder resolved itself, and he waited until a name came to him.

"Rachel?" he whispered.

"Yes, Jake. It's Rachel." She took a cloth, dipped it into the basin of water, and bathed his face. It was cool, and her touch was soft. "How do you feel?"

There was an interval between her question and his answer, for his mind was working very slowly. "All right." He looked around the room and then back at her, trying to think about why he was here. Finally he remembered a little of it and asked, "There was a shooting—?"

"Don't try to remember," Rachel said quickly. "Just lie still. It'll all come to you soon enough."

He found that he was very sleepy but didn't want to go back into the darkness. Still, no matter how hard he tried, his lids closed, and he cried out, "Rachel—!" as the darkness closed in, like a dark ocean pulling him down into fearsome depths.

But she took his hand and put her lips close to his ear. "Go to sleep, Jake. Don't worry, I'll be right here."

Then he felt the strength of her hands and knew that he could trust her. He smiled and called her name faintly, then dropped off into a sound, normal sleep.

When he next awoke, bright sunshine was pouring in through a window, and he heard the sound of birds chirruping. He lifted his head, which brought a stab of pain, and quickly he lay back down. Lifting his hand, he touched the bandage around his temple, and then it all came rushing back to him. He remembered Duvall's twisted face and seeing a bullet striking a woman. He remembered moving in front of Rachel and the blow of the bullet.

The door opened, and Dee came in with a tray. She took one look at him and surprise came to her wrinkled black face. "Well! You done decided to cheat the debil, has you?" She moved across the room, put the tray down on a table, then bent over, peering into his eyes. What she saw pleased her, for she grunted with approval, then said, "I gotta go git Miz Amy. You lay right there, you heah me?"

She whirled and left, and Jake took time to inspect the room, realizing suddenly that it was the room he'd occupied when he had stayed at Lindwood during his masquerade. Then the door opened and Amy Franklin entered. She came to him at once, her eyes bright with expectation, exclaiming, "Praise the Lord! You're all right!"

Jake nodded, which was a mistake, for the motion sent pain streaking through his head. He blinked, waited for a moment until it passed, then asked, "How long have I been here?"

"Two days," Amy said. "You had a very bad case of concussion." She came closer and peered into his eyes. "All clear now," she announced. "We were very concerned for a time." Then she asked, "Do you want anything?"

"Something to eat!"

She laughed at his urgency, turned to Dee, and said, "Make this man some strong turkey broth and some scrambled eggs." When Dee left the room, Amy sat down beside him, a pleased look on her face. "I'll send word to Major Franklin and the boys at once. They were all called back to duty. An emergency, I believe."

The war seemed far away, having nothing to do with this pleasant room with the blue wallpaper covered with pictures of deer leaping over fences. Jake thought for a moment, then asked, "Who else got shot besides me?"

"A young lieutenant named Smith. He got hit in the shoulder but is doing fine."

She hesitated, and Jake felt a jolt of fear. "Rachel! Did Rachel get hurt?"

Amy peered at him in surprise. "What a funny thing to ask! No, she's all right. Don't you remember her at all? Her taking care of you, I mean?"

It came back to him then, how she'd been there when he'd first come out of the coma. Nodding, he said, "Why, yes, I remember now."

Amy was looking at him with a puzzled expression. "You threw yourself in front of her when Duvall started firing. Do you remember that, Jake?"

He dropped his eyes but made no answer. He did remember it, but it sounded pompous to admit doing such a thing—like something out of one of those penny romance novels! Quickly he avoided the question, asking another. "Anybody else hurt?"

Amy was curious about his refusal to admit to shielding Rachel. They had all seen him do it and had tried to reason why he would do such a thing. All but Rachel, that was. She had refused to speak of it at all. Finally Vince had gotten irritated with her, saying, "Well, Rachel, if a man risks his life for you, the least you can do is seem a little grateful!"

Now, seeing Jake's reticence to discuss his action, Amy said, "Ellen Rocklin was wounded—very seriously."

Jake glanced at her with a question in his eyes. "Is she dying?"

"She was shot in the back. The bullet lodged near her spine, too close for the doctors to operate. She'll live, but she's totally paralyzed below the waist."

He lay there for a long time, then said, "That's a tough break. I'd rather die, I think."

"Well, you almost did," Amy chided gently. "One inch to the right, the doctor said, and that bullet would have killed you." She hesitated, then said, "I must ask you, Jake—please don't get angry with me—!"

She looked agitated, and Jake was puzzled. "Go ahead. What is it?"

"When you and Vince went in to Brother Irons when he was dying, Vince gave his heart to Christ. Jake, did anything like that happen to you?"

He saw the kindness on her face and at once said, "Yes, it did." He lay there trying to find the words to express what had happened to him. "Ever since that moment, Mrs. Franklin, I've been different. Can't really explain, but for the first time in my life, I've got peace. And all the time I've got the feeling that, well, that I'm not alone." He looked at her, his eyes open with a hopeful expression. "Is that what it means—being a Christian?"

"Oh yes, Jake! That's part of it!" Amy exclaimed. Then she began to speak of the Christian life, and he lay there listening carefully. The things she said seemed impossible, but then, the peace that had come to him had seemed impossible, too! And it was far from that.

Finally Amy laughed, saying, "You're just like a baby, Jake! Oh, you're a strong man, but all of us are like babies when we first are born into the family of God!" She reached out and touched his forehead, soothing it. "I always wanted another boy to raise. Now it seems the Lord has given me one." Then she blinked her eyes and said with a short laugh, "And a *hungry* one, too! I almost forgot! I'll go help Dee with your dinner." She rose and walked to the door, but turned to say before she left, "I'll go tell Rachel that Lazarus is up and about. She's hardly left your side these past two days, Jake. She'll be mad as a wet hen that I was here when you awoke instead of her!"

But though Jake waited, Rachel didn't come. Not all that day, though he heard her voice out in the hall once or twice. Dee came, and Amy was with him often, but he caught no glimpse of Rachel—and he could not bring himself to ask about her—not until Amy came in to wish him good night.

She brought him some fresh water and smiled at him as she wished him good night, and then he asked, "Is Rachel sick or gone?"

Amy gave him an odd look, then said, "Why, no, Jake. She's here, not sick at all." She started to say more, but something kept her silent. She said, "Good night. You'll feel better tomorrow."

Then she was gone, and he lay there wondering why he had expected a woman who hated him to come and visit him.

༓

He did see Rachel again, of course, several times over the next three days. She never came to his room, but when he was able to get up and go to the table for meals, she was there.

The first time they met, she stopped dead still. Then, after an awkward silence, she said, "I'm glad to see you up and about, Jake."

"Thanks." There was something unpleasant about the meeting to him, for he felt that he was putting her into an impossible position. *She despises me, and she's forced to be polite because I protected her and I'm in her home.*

This thought grew until, five days after the accident, he got dressed, gathered his few belongings, and made his way downstairs. Amy and Rachel had gone to visit a neighbor. Dee saw him, though, and exclaimed, "Where you think you're going?"

"Time to move on, Dee," he said. He went over to her and, to her astonishment, gave her a hard hug. "Thanks for taking care of me," he said with a smile.

She sputtered and followed him, saying, "You ain't strong enough to go faunchin' around yet!"

Jake turned and smiled at her. "Tell Mrs. Franklin I'll be back to thank her properly pretty soon." He ignored her protests and walked out of the house toward the stable. He found Tad shoeing one of the horses and said, "Tad, would you hitch up the buggy for me? I need to go to town."

"Shore I will, Marse Jake," Tad agreed at once. But when he had the team hitched and Jake got up on the seat, he said, "I bettah go along, Marse Jake. You ain't got yo' strength back."

"All I have to do is sit here, Tad." Jake grinned. "Tell Mrs. Franklin I'll leave the buggy at the livery stable. Take care of yourself—"

He drove the buggy out, and Tad stood there scratching his head. Finally Tad went to the house and found Dee, who glared at him, saying, "Well? You jest *had* to hitch up dat buggy, didn't you?" When Tad began to sputter with indignation, she shook her head with exasperation, adding, "You ain't got a lick of sense!" But she knew she was really angry at herself for letting the man go, knowing that Amy would be upset.

She was exactly right, too. When the two women came in not long after Jake had left and Dee told them what had happened, Amy exclaimed, "You shouldn't have let him go, Dee!"

"Dat's right!" Dee moaned. "Everything's always *my* fault,

ain't it now? Anything goes wrong, it's Dee who done it! Well, you jest tell me dis—how I'm gonna stop him? You tell me *dat*!"

Amy, feeling remorse, for she knew that Dee could have done nothing, began to comfort her. By the time she got the indignant woman pacified, she found that Rachel had disappeared. She went upstairs, but as she passed Rachel's room on her way down the hall, she stopped abruptly—for she heard a muffled sound. She hesitated, thinking of how strangely Rachel had behaved since Jake had recovered. While Jake was unconscious, nothing could induce Rachel to leave his side. Once he had regained consciousness, however, she had refused to go near him!

Amy knocked on the door, and Rachel said in a muffled tone, "Go away!" At once Amy opened the door and saw Rachel lying across the bed, her face buried in her arms and her body jerking as she sobbed wildly.

"Rachel! What in the world is wrong?" Amy cried. Going over to the bed, she ignored Rachel's wails of protest and pulled her upright.

"Oh, Mother—leave me alone!" she gasped, but then gave a great cry and fell into Amy's arms.

Amy had long known of the depth of passion that lay in this daughter of hers, but this was the most dramatic evidence she'd seen of it. Great sobs tore through the girl, and her breath came in gasps. Amy made no attempt to speak but held the weeping girl until the sobs began to subside. Finally they stopped, and Rachel pulled away and began searching for a handkerchief. Finding one in her pocket, she wiped her eyes.

"Rachel, all of this must have something to do with Jake," Amy said quietly. "Can't you tell me about it?"

Rachel bit her lip, then threw her head back, tragedy in her blue-green eyes. "You'll think I'm crazy, Mama."

"Well, even if you're crazy, you're still my daughter."

Rachel gave her a desperate look, then began to speak. "Mama, you've got to promise me not to tell. It's not my secret!"

"Whatever it is, Rachel, I'll never tell a living soul."

Rachel knew her mother would allow herself to be torn to pieces before betraying a confidence, so she at once spilled out the story of Vince and Jake, their scheme to get hold of the inheritance. When she stopped, she looked at her mother, who had not shown one flash of emotion. "Mama—aren't you angry?"

Amy smiled, then said, "I was when I first discovered that Jake wasn't Vince, which was about twenty-four hours after you brought him home."

"You knew?" Rachel gasped, shock in her eyes.

"Of course I did," Amy said. "Am I such a ninny I can't recognize a boy who is like my own son? He looked like Vince, but he wasn't in the least *like* Vince. I can't see why the rest of you didn't see through him right off." She smiled at Rachel's confusion and said, "Why didn't I tell anyone? Because when I prayed about it, God told me to hold my peace, to sit still and see what He would do. And we have seen, haven't we? Both Vince and Jake are men of God now. What if I'd rushed in and exposed them? They both might well have been lost forever. Rachel, all of us have a time when God deals with us very directly, and this was the time for Vince and Jake."

"Mama. . .I never knew! I was so mad because he *deceived* me! He made a fool out of me!"

Amy studied the girl, then asked gently, "I think I begin to see. When you were nursing Jake, thinking he was your brother, you began to feel rather peculiarly toward him, didn't you, Rachel?"

Rachel gave a great start, her eyes flying open with shock. She had thought no one would ever find that out! "He—made me feel—"

When she broke off, unable to finish, Amy inserted, "Like a woman?"

Rachel's face flamed, and she tried to get up, to run from the room, but Amy pulled her down and asked, "Rachel, do you love Jake?"

"No! How could I love a man who—"

"Who hurt your pride?" Amy broke in. "Is that it?" Amy studied the face of her daughter, then said, "Pride's a fine thing, I suppose. But lots of Southerners have too much of it, I think. Men fight duels and kill each other because they're too proud to say 'I'm sorry.' And that's foolishness, child!"

"Mama, I can't forget the way—"

"Rachel!" Amy spoke severely. "Can pride take the place of having a man beside you? Can it keep you warm or hold you when you cry—or give you children to love?"

"Mother!"

"Rachel, I haven't known Jake very long, but I know he's been an instrument that God has used to make Vince into a man. And I know that whatever kind of man he used to be, he has changed since he first came to our home. He became a new man when he gave his heart to Jesus. Don't you believe that God can wash out the old and make us new?"

Rachel sat there staring at her mother, the words piercing her like swords. For days she had been torn by a struggle between her pride and her love, and now her own mother was calling her a fool. And she was right!

"Mother—I love him so!" she burst out, and jumping up from the bed, she began to wring her hands. "What can I do!"

"Do? Why, you absurd girl! Get on that horse of yours and ride like the wind. And when you catch up to him, tell him you've been wrong!"

"But—what if he laughs at me?"

Amy rose and, with a smile, kissed Rachel. "You're a silly child—but you're a desirable woman. Men aren't very smart sometimes. If he gives you any trouble, just let the tears well up—and fall into his arms!"

Rachel's face flushed, but she gave her mother a fierce hug. "Thank you, Mama!" she cried out, then ran out of the room. Amy went to the window and watched as Rachel ran to the barn. In a surprisingly short time, Lady came flying out of the barn with Rachel leaning low over her neck. Then with a wave at the window where she knew her mother was standing, Rachel was gone, the horse low to the ground at a dead run.

❧

Jake was slumped on the seat of the buggy, his face set doggedly, when he heard the sound of a horse approaching. It occurred to him that whoever it was was in a big hurry, so he pulled the buggy over to the edge of the road to give him plenty of room.

The sound of the hoofbeats grew louder, and then—

"Jake! Wait for me!"

Jake abruptly hauled up on the reins, nearly upsetting the team, which reared up and snorted with indignation. As he calmed them, he watched in amazement as Rachel pulled Lady to a stop, slid off, and ran toward the wagon. Taking one look at her face, Jake fell out of the wagon, ignoring the pain in his head as he struck the ground, and moved toward her. "Rachel—is somebody hurt?"

Then he saw that she was crying, and without a word she

threw herself against him. Shock ran through him, and he stood there holding her as she clung to him fiercely. Her arms were around his neck, her face was pressed against his chest, and he was intensely conscious of her warmth and softness.

Finally she drew back and looked up at him, her eyes moist. "What is it, Rachel?" he asked, his voice hoarse.

"Jake," she whispered. "I've been such a fool! I'm still a fool, because I came to tell you—"

When she faltered, he urged her, "Tell me what, Rachel?"

"To tell you. . .that no matter what happens, I love you!"

The instant she spoke the words, something inside of her relaxed and she smiled through her tears, stunning Jake with her beauty. "You may not love me, Jake Hardin, and you can laugh at me and ride away—but that won't change anything. I love you!"

Jake was completely astonished by her statement—but not so astonished that he lost all of his senses, for he drew her to him with an urgency that startled them both. She was warm and yielding in his arms, and her lips were soft and willing. He kissed her, holding her closely, drinking in the sweetness and goodness that he had known was in her, that he had long desired. He could scarcely believe that she was here, in his arms. Yet she was, giving herself to him, and he sensed the promise in her and was humbled that she had come to offer herself so courageously.

Then she drew back, and he said at once, "Rachel, I never thought I had a chance!" He took a deep breath, then let it out slowly. He began to smile. "I've got nothing to offer you—"

She put her fingers over his lips, saying firmly, "Don't ever say that! Not ever!"

He kissed her fingers, then suddenly laughed, a laugh of

pure joy such as he would never have thought he could give. "What a shock your father and mother are in for! A penniless beggar asking for their daughter's hand in marriage."

"Don't worry about that!" Rachel said instantly. "I may have chased you all over the county, but that's over. Now you can come courting me just like any other lovesick young man!"

Jake took her in his arms again and, when she protested, tightened his grasp. "A man in love will do any fool thing," he said with a gleam of humor in his eyes. "So you can expect me to come with my guitar, serenading you with love songs and offering to shoot any dandy who dares look at you. Think that'll answer?"

"Yes," she said with a twinkle in her eyes. "Yes, I believe that will do quite nicely!"

Then she kissed him, and when he drew back, he said, "Rachel, do you realize that I've got the world. . .right here in my arms?" A fierce gladness filled them both—a gladness that they were certain would not lessen, no matter what the years might bring them.

Jake held Rachel close for a moment longer, then lifted her onto the buggy seat, climbed up beside her, and turned back to Lindwood. There was a lot to be discussed, to be settled. But they had plenty of time to work it out. A lifetime, in fact.

As they drove away, Lady stood there, not understanding what had happened to her rider. Finally she snorted, gave an impatient leap, and trotted smartly after the buggy that was growing smaller in the distance as it moved down the lane.

ABOUT THE AUTHOR

Award-winning, bestselling author, Gilbert Morris is well known for penning numerous Christian novels for adults and children since 1984 with 6.5 million books in print. He is probably best known for the forty-book House of Winslow series, and his *Edge of Honor* was a 2001 Christy Award winner. He lives with his wife in Gulf Shores, Alabama.

If you enjoyed

Appomattox Saga

(Part 1)

then don't miss

Appomattox Saga

(Part 2)

Available Spring 2009